Arcania:
Beyond Where the Sidewalk Ends

Book one: If You Are a Dreamer
Book two: Twisting Trails and Wondrous Worlds
Book three: All the Colors I Am Inside
Book Four: Somewhere From Some Far-off Place

All of the text and illustrations in this book, including cover art, are the work of R.S. Royall and are human-generated. No A.I. has been used.

First edition published September 1, 2024.
© 2025 Royall, LLC. All rights reserved.
Published by Cabanga, an imprint of the Royall company
128 Race St., Grass Valley, CA 95945
+1 (808) 301-0535

This is a work of fiction. The story and illustrations are products of the author's imagination. Names, characters, places, and events are products of the author's imagination or are used fictitiously. Consistent with any literary work, indeed any creative work in any medium, there are many sources of inspiration for the work herein: life experience, wondrous creations from other artists, ideas channeled from the chimes of spirits, notions conjured from the clouds, wonderings summoned from the swamps of the ether... Regardless, no part of this story — character, person, or place — is intended to represent any person, character, or place occurring or existing, past or present, outside of, or beyond this book and the story herein. Any resemblance to actual events, locales, characters, or persons living or dead, real or imaginary, is entirely coincidental. Any opinions, thoughts, or actions expressed or implied in this book are intended to be those of the characters alone and not necessarily of the author or anyone else.

ISBN 979-8-9914547-3-5 Paperback

ISBN 979-8-9914547-1-1 Hardback

Beyond Where the Sidewalk Ends

The Arcania Story

Story and illustrations by

R.S. Royall

A Cabanga Publication
"Evolution through Imagination"

Author's Note

At the end of the day, if the doorway to reality is hinged on relative perception and fallible memory, do we ever truly know what is real and what is fantasy? The magic and fantastical adventures experienced by children may indeed be real, but as we grow up, our unadulterated creativity becomes overrun by logic; we yield to more 'reasonable' and socially-acceptable explanations of the mysterious, diminishing the magic of the world and dismissing our creative intuition. Those moments inspiring us to wonder and wander become little more than curious and quaint stories of childhood fantasy, summarily dismissed and archived in the deep places, those oft forgotten files labeled 'musings of an overactive imagination.'

This four-part series is a fictional tale about a boy who has yet to tame or outgrow his overactive imagination. In fact he nourishes it. As a result, he is rewarded with an epic adventure that prepares him for life as an artist and celebrated storyteller.

Although the Arcania series has been written primarily to be entertaining and fun, there are elements of seriousness, contemplation, introspection, and philosophy. Some passages may drift over the heads of younger readers. That's okay. This is intentional, a means of encouraging mindfulness alongside creativity and curiosity. The reader might also encounter outright nonsense and bizarre silliness seemingly out-of-place or arbitrary to the arc. This too is intentional, for life doesn't always have a clear point, or purpose, or logical flow.

I wish to express my profound gratitude to the following folks for providing valuable support, input, feedback, and/ or editing during the production of this book series: Eli Wahler, Laura Kofler, Erin McAuley, Robert Hunter, Dave Tell, Scott Young, and Jordyn Smith. Thank you!

This story is primarily inspired by, and celebrates, the work of Shel Silverstein. It also includes elements from and is inspired by my own life experiences, as well as many children's storybooks, particularly those by Dr. Seuss, Antoine de Saint-Exupéry, Joseph Jacobs, Lewis Carroll, J.M. Barrie, A.A. Milne, Maurice Sendak, and Robert Louis Stevenson, to name a few.

In my life, Silverstein's poems and stories have stood out as a rare spice in the dish of children's literature, offering a unique lens through which to view the world, see things from new perspectives.

What Shel gave me through his books, when I was a youth searching for answers in a difficult world, was both profound and priceless. I am not only compelled to give back, I am inspired to create something new.

My hope with the Arcania story is to honor Shel's memory by providing some entertainment for those seeking to trek further down the twisting trails that Shel blazed with his unique poetry, go beyond the point where his work—his sidewalk—ended.

In his book *Every Thing On It*, Silverstein requests that his readers 'writesingtelldraw' something for him after all he's writtensungtolddrawn for them. Well, Mr. Silverstein, this is my 'writesingtelldraw' for you. I hope you like it.

RS Royall

"*Imagination is more important than knowledge!*"

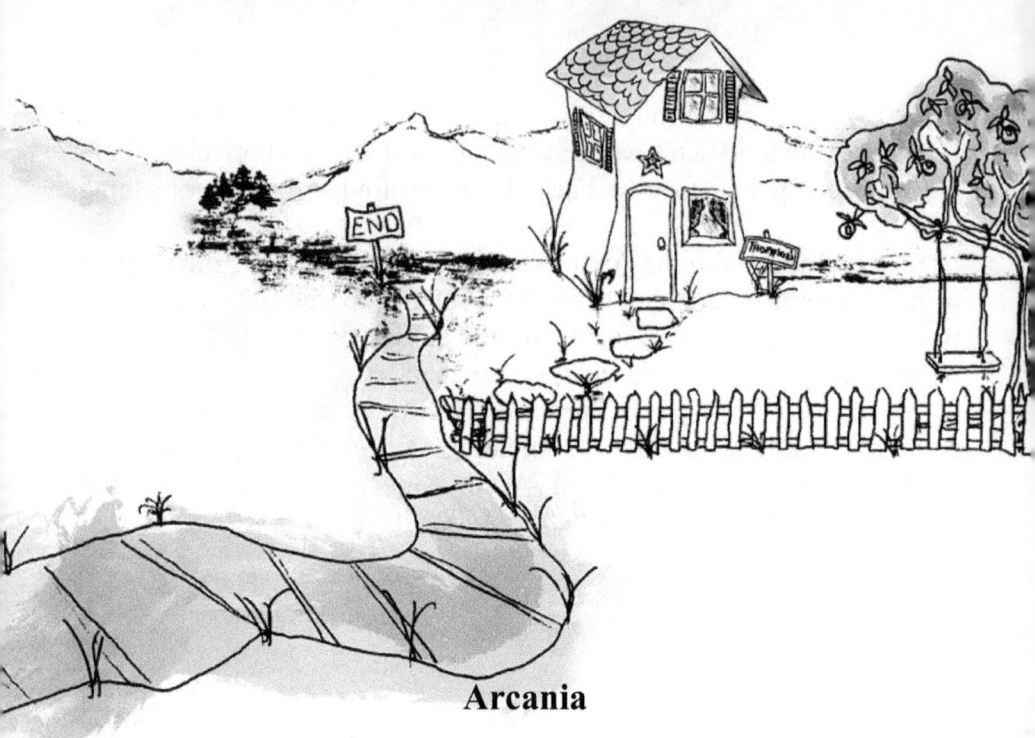

Arcania

Far out beyond where the sidewalk ends
stands a deserted house, attic light all aglow,
calling dreamers and magic bean make-believers,
to the land of flying shoes, where the giving trees grow.

Where giants roam and mermaids run free,
Where gun-toting lions frighten hunters away,
Where monsters and fat cats wax philosophically,
and witches fly vacuums and cook food-fighting fray.

Where young girls skip school to devour whole whales,
while peanut butter stick-stuck makes beggars of kings,
Where bears dance, turtles run, and crocodiles spin tales,
Where elephants climb trees and long to fly without wings.

It's a special place to let your imagination run wild,
So run with me and fall up into the blue,
to a world made for silly hearts, both grown-up and child,
The land of wonder called Arcania is waiting for you!

Book One

If You Are a Dreamer

Book One is for Lisa.
protector of childhood & encourager of dreams.

Introduction

Me and Him

Me: *Alright, listen up everybody!* Me and Him, we're gonna tell y'all a wild story.

Him: Um, excuse me. Me?

Me: Yes, Him?

Him: What if they don't want to hear a wild story? What if they don't want to hear any story at all? What if they just want to sit and play guitar and eat a blueberry muffin?

Me: A blueberry... What in tarnation are you talkin' about? Eat a muffin? Of course they want to hear a story! Who doesn't like a good story?

Him: Well who says it's good? And what if I don't want to tell it?

Me: Oh, you busselfudder! Of course it's a good story! It's about You-Know-Who, and if *you* don't want to tell it, well then you just sit back and be quiet and let *me* tell it!

Him: I-know-who? ...Hang on a sec. You must be talkin' about crazy ol' Sheldon!

Me: The one-and-only! But this story is of an earlier time, about his grand adventure as a boy.

Him: Wait! You mean the story about Sheldon's adventures in Arcania? I love that story! That's where he met—

Me: Whoa! Whoa! Don't give it away!

Him: Oh, right! Sorry. Yes indeedy, that *IS* a great tale! I especially enjoy the part where—

Me: Hey now!

Him: Oop. Sorry.

Me: All right then. Apologies, folks. So anyway, Me and Him, we're gonna tell you the tale of a young boy and how he overcame his fear of being a nobody, to find his courage, his voice, and become a somebody.

Him: Now, Me will do his best to stay out of your way and just recount the story. Isn't that right, Me?

Me: Wha? Me? You're the one who—

Him: Riiiight, Me??

Me: Ugh. Yes, Him. I'll try to keep quiet. But every once in a while, we may need to chime in here and there to—

Him: Add our own commentary!

Me: See!! You do it too! Sometimes we both get excited and carried away and we just have to—

Him: Jump in!

Me: Exactly! So, if the odd flying comment soars across the page, you'll know it's us, Me and Him.

Him: Now, we'll do our best to let the audience sort out the details for themselves. We promise! But I hope you can bear with us. You see, folks, Him and Me, we don't always agree.

Me: We don't?

Him: For instance, I like the mountains and Me prefers the sea. He wants to sleep when I want to get up and par-teee!

Me: Oh-kaaay! Thanks for sharing, Him. Maybe a bit too much? What's say we just get on with the story?

Him: Well, all right then. Who's gonna start?

Me: Oh, so now you wanna tell it too?

Him: Well, I just thought—

Me: I'm just razin' ya! Of course you can tell it with me.

Him: Oh, thanks! You know, sometimes you can be such a sweet turtle.

Me: Now pipe down while I kick this thing off!

Him: Oh... Okay. Well, I guess that's... Um, where were you, uh, planning to start?

Me: Well, I figured I'd start with the *dream*.

Him: The dream? What dream?

Me: *Theee* dream!

Him: Oh! You mean the one that sets the scene for *everything*? Yeah. That seems like a good place to start, I s'pose.

Me: Ya think?

Him: Well, yeah, because, you know, it set the scene for everything and— Ohhhh, you were doing that sarcasm thing again.

Me: Mmm hmm. Are you finished? Can I start?

Him: Sure. Go ahead. Take us back to the spring of 1943, Me!

Me: All right then. It was a dark and stormy night...

Him: Wait. What?!

Me: Just kidding.

Him: Oh! Ha ha! That was funny. At first I thought you were—

Me: Actually it *was* a dark and stormy night.

Him: Well, yeah, but not when the dream *starts*.

Me: Nope, not when it starts. So? We ready to do this thing now? This time for real?

Him: Wait, for *reeeaaal*?

Me: Well, I guess *that* remains to be seen...

Prologue

True Story

Her hair flowed wildly as she bolted through the sultry desert, beads of sweat pouring over her flexing muscles, giving her coat a brilliant sheen that glistened like wildfire in the red sunrise...

Like the rooster tail of a racing speedboat, sand and dirt flew high in her wake, while outlaw bullets cut fiercely through the crisp air, licking the ten-gallon hat and snakeskin boots of her spirited, young rider.

"I'm 'unna getcha!" warned the miniature lead missiles, flashing sinister grins as they rocketed past at a thousand miles an hour.

The boy suddenly felt a sharp stab in his side like the sting of a devil scorpion. He looked down in a panic to see a bullet slug smiling victoriously up at him.

"Gotcha!"

The boy frowned at the blood-red river discharging from his side like the Rio Grande from the Rockies. Somewhere high above in the blood-red morning sky an eagle screeched out a warning.

"You'd best find shelter, boy — and fast."

A dark cave in the distance answered the call of the eagle. "Quick, over here!"

The cowboy yanked the reins, eliciting a ferocious grunt from his horse as she deftly changed course like a swallow in flight. A mad dash for safety sent both horse and rider sailing through the entrance of the cave, and they disappeared into darkness.

Safe from the outlaws — for now — the young cowboy dismounted, grimacing as he swung his leg over the horse and slid to the ground, collapsing on the cave floor. After catching his breath, he stood slowly and examined the wound. His dread turned to relief when he realized it was a clean shot, straight through the back and out the front. A graze really. No major harm done.

"Would ya look at that!" He smiled at the liquid adventure leaking from his side. *I've survived worse!* He tore his shirt sleeves into strips for bandages and wrapped the wound. Once the worst of it was cleaned and dressed, he filled his hat with not quite ten gallons of water from the cold, dark crick that ran through the cavern. "Here y'are, ol' Sundance girl. Drink up."

The horse lapped up the refreshing water, shook her head vigorously as if to jettison the tension of the chase, then wandered off in search of anything resembling grass. Exhausted, the boy lay down and attempted to rest his head on a rock, feeling about as cozy as a catfish stranded on a cactus. The ramblin' desperado was accustomed to rough country, however, and eventually settled in. But just as the old sandman drew near — knapsack full of golden dreams atop a hunched back, wonder dust trickling through outstretched fists — a terrifying noise filled the cave, frightening the sand genie away and startling the boy awake.

The growl of a desert wildcat echoed like rolling thunder through the cave. The boy quickly jumped up and whistled for his trusty steed, nervously scanning the surroundings. *Is that a figure moving silently in the shadows or just my eyes playing tricks?* he wondered, slowly unsnapping the leather strap holding his buck knife to his belt. *Are those yellow eyes of doom staring back at me from the deep?* he wondered, carefully withdrawing the blade. *Or is my darned imagination prospecting for gold nuggets at the most inopportune time?*

Before he could discern whether he was being stalked, in a raging flash, Sundance sprang from the shadows and scooped him up, only narrowly escaping a large paw reaching out from the abyss. The cougar was taking aim at the alluring red flag that was the boy's blood-stained shirt.

Bolting toward the cave opening, Sundance lowered her head and narrowed her eyes, readying herself for another exciting chase. In the very next instant, however, her eyes widened and her head jerked back, as her rider — who couldn't seem to make up his mind — yanked hard on the reins, locking the horse's front legs. They skidded to a halt just before daylight gave them away. Rowdy calls from the gun-slinging outlaws tumbled into the cave like an avalanche of boulders roaring down a canyon. The enemy was closing in.

The boy knew he couldn't risk being out in the open, but he also didn't much care to become morning brunch for a malicious mountain lion. Out of options, he turned Sundance around to face the ferocious, glowing eyes floating there in the blackness.

"N-n-now... s-s-see here, c-c-cat! I know I p-p-probably look... m-m-mighty tasty to you, b-b-but the truth is I'm rotten to the c-c-core! Infested with p-p-parasites and scrawny all the way 'round. Nothin' but skin and b-b-bones really."

The lion emerged into the dim light, revealing her fearsome and impressive size, not less than half as big as Sundance, maybe more. "B-b-but, just outside this here c-c-cave," the boy continued in a shaky voice, "are three uh the most scrumptious and p-p-plump lunches you c-c-could ever ask for. An all-you-can-eat buffet, r-r-really."

Staring back with ravenous eyes, the cat continued to stalk the horse and rider, whispering in a confident growl, "If you want me to *not* eat you, you're going to have to *really* sell it, compadre!"

"All right. Okay. I hear ya." The cowboy nodded slowly, careful not to make any sudden moves. "Just..." he gulped, "...consider this: I think the big one out there got hold of your b-b-brother last w-w-week. Them's are hunters, they are. Mean ol' gun-lovin', animal-hatin' killers. They were comin' after me 'cause I was tryin' tuh save a helpless, little turtle. Poor guy was just out for his mornin' jog in the cool uh the desert and—"

"What do I care about turtles!" the wildcat snapped, drawing near. Her long, sharp teeth could now be seen clear as day. She wasn't buying the cowboy's story.

"You gotta believe me! Go see fer yourself. The big one's wearing cat-skin chaps right now; skin that looks a lot like yours, I reckon."

The puma grimaced and crouched low, readying to pounce. The boy closed his eyes and prepared for the end. The cat leaped! But instead of tackling the boy, she soared clean over his head, flying out of the cave with a roar that sounded a lot like, "For lunch, and vengeance!"

Both the boy and his trusty steed stood frozen, gulping sighs of relief and listening with profound satisfaction to the taunts of angry men turn to cries of scared boys as the lion chased the outlaws away into the desert sunrise.

Feeling much safer, the cowboy dismounted his horse with the pride of having outwitted his enemies; and as Sundance trotted off once more in search of food, he laid his head back down on his comfy rock, tilted his oversized hat over his eyes, and quickly fell into a deep sleep.

While the boy slept, however, another adversary was moving in the darkness. As luck would have it (bad luck), the cowboy had settled in a cave which happened to be an underground passage to the not-too-distant sea. And where there be sea, there be pirates!

With a painful jolt, the boy awoke to find himself no longer in the desert but on a beach, tied up in pirate's rope, hanging from a pirate's spit, roasting over a pirate's fire. With wide eyes he tried to call out, to scream, to whistle for Sundance, but it was no use. His mouth had been stuffed and bound with the fragments of a Jolly Roger. All he could do was rotate, and while rotating, count one, two, three ragged and dingy pirates sitting nearby, watching him spin and struggle.

As the sky spun into his view, he spotted an enormous eagle at the top of the roasting pole, looking down at him with glaring eyes.

"I showed you the cave, but you weren't supposed to stay there! You certainly weren't supposed to fall asleep in there! I'm sorry but there's nothing I can do for you now." The eagle stretched her enormous wings and lifted into the air, fanning the flames as she departed. Feeling the heat intensify, the boy became desperate for his horse. He had to get out of there! But ol' Sundance was nowhere to be found.

What could have happened to her, my trusty steed and loyal companion?

"Arrr, this be the last round up fer ye, landlubber!" A raspy, peg-leg-of-a-voice interrupted his thoughts. From behind thick smoke hanging in the air like a curtain, the boy could just make out a figure approaching. He frantically struggled to free himself but his bonds wouldn't budge. The fire crackling beneath him had helped to cauterize his bullet wound — a grace of sorts — but it was also burning him to a crisp, or so he felt.

He could sense his consciousness departing, trying to escape the pain, when suddenly a tremendous wave crashed over the rocky shore, extinguishing the fire and knocking over the pole to which the boy was tied. The heat immediately subsided as the torrent of salt water engulfed the fire pit, snapping the roasting pole and thrashing the boy against the rocky shore like laundry rags in a tub.

As the wave receded and the tumult turned to calm, the boy's spinning vision settled on the captivating figure of a woman standing on the nearby shore. He was astonished to discover that the woman was part fish! From the waist down she bore a shiny fin that flashed multi-colored as she moved gracefully in the sunlight, dancing to the tune of her triumph.

(How the she-fish was *standing,* let alone dancing, is anybody's guess. But there she was in all her glory!)

The drenched pirates scrambled to capture the rare beauty, but she was too cunning, too quick, and too slippery. Dodging the pirates' attacks, she made for the boy on the spit. Before any of the scalawags knew it, the mermaid had freed the boy and was dragging him toward the sea, no doubt with the intent of stashing her prize away in Davy Jones' Locker.

In a strange fish language that somehow the boy could understand, she spoke, "Hold onto your hat!" as she plunged into the chilly water, grasping tightly to her treasure. Down, down to the deep she swam, the boy struggling all the while in her scaly grasp, knowing full well he would drown if he could not break free. He tugged and tussled in her tangled tentacles. (Does a mermaid have tentacles?) He squirmed and shook, fidgeted and fought, pushed and pinched until finally, she'd had enough.

She stopped swimming and looked at her ungrateful captive. "Whatever is the matter, my love?" Didn't he realize she had just saved his life?

Shaking his head wildly and pointing to his mouth he signaled, "I can't breathe, you maniacal mermaid!"

The fish-lady instantly realized her mistake. This one was not fish! This one was human! And a young one at that, not unlike herself. With terrific haste, she raced the boy back to the surface.

They blasted out of the water and the boy chomped at the air, gulping for more and more as if tasting its splendor for the first time. He instantly coughed up a heap of water (probably enough to fill his long-gone ten-gallon hat) along with something that looked like a small octopus.

"Oh, you're so wild and brave and handsome," the mermaid praised. "I thought you were a mermaid like me, captured by those nasty mermaid-snatching pirates! But you're a human! With legs! How marvelous! Oh, won't you please marry me?"

"What!?" The boy was stunned. And yet, given the way things had been going, he somehow expected this sort of nonsense. "Uh, okay, look, I'll make you a deal. If you swim me to shore so I can rest a while, I'll agree to marry you."

The mermaid lit up and rushed him to the beach. Relieved and exhausted, the boy rolled in the sand, grateful to be back on dry land. "Listen," he said, standing up and brushing the sand from his clothes. "I have to go gather my things. I will be back for you on Wednesday and we can get married then. How 'bout that?"

The mermaid smiled and nodded excitedly.

Wasting no time, the boy ran off into the jungle, never to return. No sooner had he left the beach, however, than he found himself knee-deep in a swamp of quicksand.

"Why does this keep happening to me?!"

Trying not to panic, he reached for a nearby vine, which mysteriously dodged his grasp and hissed violently, "I beg your pardon!"

The vine, which had been slithering happily across the muck, minding its own business, had no intention of being man-handled by a meandering cowboy, a wannabe mermaid, or a jungle tourist; not least of all a combination of the three.

"Oh! Gosh. I'm terribly sorry! I didn't realize you were… That is, I thought you were a tree vine."

"Well, I never!" replied the snake. "As long as we're judging others by their appearance, I'd say you were a hippopotamus's buttocks." The snooty serpent began to slink away across the mire, beyond satisfied with her retort.

"No, wait! Please don't go. Help me! Help me and I'll… I'll do anything!" The boy was up to his chest and sinking fast.

"Oh, all right. Keep your pants on, if they haven't fallen off already. Grab hold of something and hang on." The snake offered the boy a middle section of her long, thick torso. Without hesitation, the boy snatched a fistful, and like a small tugboat pulling a freighter, the reluctant reptile slogged the soggy sap slowly through the slop.

The boy felt a tinge apprehensive about being dragged away from the beach, deeper into the thick, forbidding jungle, but he let it slide. When they finally reached solid ground, he looked up to see a massive silhouette towering over him. Since this figure was not a mermaid, a scurvy pirate, or a rascally outlaw cowboy, the boy was relieved… if only momentarily.

"Here you are. Dinner is served," concluded the snake, wriggling free of the boy's grip and slinking into the bushes.

"Oh, thank you, snake! I *am* starving. How did you know?" The boy's words overflowed with gratitude and anticipation of a long-overdue meal.

"I wasn't talking to you!" was the last thing the boy heard as the reptile slipped into the forest and disappeared.

"Wait. What!?" The boy froze as the snake's loaded words sank in, much like the outlaw bullet. There was no time for the snake to reply, however (not that she was going to), as a beefy, calloused hand swiftly grabbed hold of the boy's collar and yanked him from the swamp. In a blur, the boy was lifted high and hog-tied to a makeshift platform of wooden poles resting atop the shoulders of two short, stout men.

"Wait a minute! Where are you taking me? Let me go!"

The human caravan said nothing as they marched their captive through the jungle, eventually emerging into a clearing lined with mud-and-thatch huts. Dividing the clearing was a long line of people, apparently waiting for something important.

What could it be? The boy grew anxious and squirmy, strapped to his bamboo bed as the men carried him to the front of the line. Perhaps it was the line for a jungle amusement park. *How fun!* he thought, almost out loud. But before any amusement could be had, the men tore away the boy's bonds and dumped him, face down, onto the forest floor. Annoyed at being discarded like a bad poker hand, he wiped the mud from his face and looked up to see a giant beast of a man sitting atop a large throne of roots, rocks, branches, and bones, all held together by vines... or possibly snakes.

No! It can't be!

Towering over the trembling youth, wearing robes of jaguar fur adorned with what must have been a thousand pounds of brilliantly-colored parrot plumage, sat the notorious, dreaded cannibal chief of the jungle, the infamous Roast-Em-Up Roy! Everyone knew the stories of Roaster Roy, even this young cowboy from the desert.

Given the cannibal's reputation, the boy knew beyond doubt that this would be the end for sure. But just as the chief reached down to pluck his meal from the ground with an enormous fork, mouth salivating something awful, out from the crowd came a cry of protest, "MEEE FIRRRSSST!" The command rang through the forest like a war siren as an impossibly loud, impossibly impatient young girl pushed and shoved her way to the front of the line of people waiting to be seen by — or eaten by — Chief Roy.

Roy's fork paused as he glanced up with a prodigious frown, searching for the imbecile who would dare disturb his meal.

"Nobody, and I mean NOBODY makes Melinda wait in line! If there's something going on, something to do, something to see, I'll be the first. You hear me?! First to do it; first to see it; first to—"

Melinda's rant stopped abruptly as she reached the head of the line and realized with horror what awaited her and the rest of the queue. Immediately, Roy's guards seized the girl, much to her astonishment and dismay.

"Don't worry, little darling. You're next!" Roy boomed a nefarious roaring laugh as he made to resume plucking the trembling cowboy from the ground. In that very instant, however, a giant eagle swooped down, grabbed hold of the boy-who-would-be-dinner, and jetted off, soaring clean over the forest canopy.

Roy was left stunned, fork frozen in midair, as his warrior-guards sprang into action, flinging spears skyward, attempting to retrieve the airborne hors d'oeuvre. The eagle easily dodged the spears and arrows, spinning deftly in upward spirals, flying high with her captive. Once again, the boy was saved from disaster.

Overjoyed, he called to the eagle, "Oh, thank goodness! You have no idea how much I… AAAAAAHHH!!"

Without warning, the bird opened her talons, sending her catch hurtling back to Earth. The boy twisted and turned, trying to get a look at the ground, hoping to find a hot air balloon, another fluffy bird, a flying carpet... something, anything that might catch him or provide a soft landing. But there was nothing. Nothing but water. Lots and lots of water as far as the eye could see in every direction. No land in sight whatsoever.

He thought momentarily that perhaps the water might provide a soft landing, but his hopes faded as he realized there could be no mermaid, or any other creature waiting to save him this time. For the sea, he concluded with resolute terror, was rolling in a boil like a steaming-mad kettle of tea left on the stove far too long.

So, this is my destiny, he lamented. *I am to be boiled, like carrots in a stew.*

The eagle answered with a resounding screech, echoing through the sky, affirming the boy's stew-fate before disappearing into the wild blue yonder.

When the boy finally splashed down, he could feel the water only for an instant. It felt like solid concrete; unbearably hot, solid concrete. As if an egg cracked open on the scorching asphalt of Chicago in August, the boy sizzled, until the pain, lasting but an instant before everything went numb, became a distant memory. He could sense his body melting away, a pat of butter in a pan, and the last thing he felt as his eyes closed their final curtain was the sensation that his entire being was evaporating to steam, floating up to the atmosphere, forming a dense, dark cloud; the precursor to a tremendous rainstorm.

Chapter One

Illuminate

The torrent of rain that hammered the boy's roof and pelted his window throughout the long night, washing away old and preparing for new, as rainstorms do, eventually gave way to clear, calm skies filled with the faint whisper of a most unusual sunrise.

In that freshly cleansed morning, a rogue strand of sunlight appeared against the pale backdrop of the late spring dawn, like a warrior perched atop a distant hill, surveying her battlefield before war. This curious beam shone brightly from well beyond the far-away horizon, a cosmic searchlight scouring the heavens for a wayward traveler, a lost friend alone somewhere out in the world. As the playful spotlight danced and twirled across the landscape — searching, searching — a familiar thing caught her attention and she settled excitedly on a particular house, an apartment rather. There, in some modest building nestled in a nook just outside of downtown Chicago, a young boy struggled through corrupted dreams of cowboy outlaws and cannibal pirates.

On a singular window of this small apartment, the light paused, intensifying her radiance to cut a clear path through the morning fog, announcing a brand-new day, and along with it, new destiny. The focused beam, dedicated to her mission of finding her friend, eventually succeeded at penetrating the curtained window of that Chicago apartment. Into the previously darkened room she crept, silently stalking her prey. She hovered over the slumbering boy, reveling in her success at finally finding him. Then, playful as always, she smacked him right across the face.

"Take that, you loafing laggard!" she seemed to say with a laugh. The boy flinched, rolled over, and smothered his assaulted mug in his pillow, yanking his blanket over his head.

"Go away!" he complained. After all the stress and turmoil throughout the night, he felt thoroughly unprepared for a new day that was sure to bring its own challenges. But the tenacious luminescence did not go away. Undaunted, she deftly navigated the folds in the pillow and blanket. She hadn't come this far to be thwarted by feeble linens. There, at the precipice of his senses, she joined forces with the morning clamor of the house already seeping through the pillow fluff like soldiers in a snowstorm.

Wishing he could clamp his ears shut as he could his eyes, the boy growled at the intrusion. It was no use. Together, the warriors of light and sound fought a successful campaign, forcing the surrender of his slumber.

He sat up abruptly, defiantly, as the droning of his parents arguing with his aunt about some grownup nonsense came crashing into his room, a victory parade for the morning light's hard-fought battle. In the background, a radio scratched out updates about a different battle. The war overseas was escalating according to the woeful morning report, and it was dragging the economy (whatever that was), "down into the muddy trenches right along with it," reported the scratchy voice from the talking telegram.

"Ugh. Grown-ups!" the boy grumbled, rubbing the sleep from his eyes. Blinking in rapid squints, he attempted to let the intrusive dawn in only a little at a time. Upon seeing him waking, however, the full force of the morning glow crashed through the slit in his curtains like an anxious puppy, somehow looking, the boy thought, as if it were smiling.

"It's not funny! I'm tired! And what's all this racket?!" The boy shifted his squinty scowl from the window to his bedroom door, as if expecting someone to come bursting through at any moment. He frowned at the sound of his sister running around in the hall, laughing with their cousin and yelling about the bathroom or boys or bows in their braids. Oh, his spoiled kid sister, who always hogged the attention and only had one task. Only one, single, itsy-bitsy chore.

"Just take out the garbage. That's all we ask," their parents would remind her every single day. But no! She refused to do it, apparently above soiling her hands with manual labor. And she got away with it too! She got away with loads of stuff, like skipping school by feigning sick.

"I've got a sore throat; I think I swallowed a tree! ...And a headache like a house fell on me! Purple spots all over my belly. Swollen feet that make me walk all silly... No, school's just not gonna work for me today... unfortunately."

And would you believe that nonsense worked!? She could get away with anything! *But not me!* he lamented, falling back on his pillow and yanking the covers over his head, a last-ditch effort to go back to the land of dreams; even cursed ones so long as it was sleep.

Send in the reserves!

A blitzkrieg of car horns and pedestrian sounds announcing the day's commerce marched up from the streets below, joining the fight to get the kid out of bed. Noises descended over him like a storm of sewing pins, pricking his senses, making him cringe.

"Is every day National Noise Day around here?!" he barked from under his covers. He almost thought he heard a giggle in response, as if the annoying morning light were enjoying this pandemonium. "Hey, everyone, pick a noisemaker!" he scoffed, tossing the blankets off his head. "Pots and pans, clapping hands, stomping shoes, the latest news…" It was all just noise, noise, noise! What a miserable start to— *Wait! Wait just a minute!* "I'm alive!" he exclaimed aloud, quickly sitting up and taking stock of his state. "No bleeding from bullet holes or broiling over barbecues!"

The light smiled.

"No being sunk by she-fish or served up for supper!"

The light nodded.

"And no boiling alive in a giant lake, for heaven's sake!"

The light smiled and nodded.

Feeling renewed, he tossed aside his quilted blanket — along with all reservations — sending stitched cheetahs, giraffes, rhinos, and lions tumbling in all directions. Stretching a mighty stretch and yawning a mighty yawn, the boy looked around, surveying his kingdom. "Gee-whiz! Whosever room this is ought to be ashamed. What a mess!" He chuckled, and without further thought, jumped up and walked right out of his messy room… and then immediately walked back in. In a house full of people — sometimes people you don't know — it's advisable to get dressed *before* leaving your room.

The kid looked around, snatched whatever clothes were within reach, and shoved them on whichever body parts put up the least resistance, resembling a magician trying to escape a straitjacket. "What's the deal?!" It was as if his clothes belonged to someone else, as if today he were an entirely different person. Twisting and squirming and complaining — eliciting more giggles from the intruding sunbeam — the boy charged down the hall toward the bathroom, but not before closing his bedroom door with a smirk, leaving the mischievous light to find its own way.

At the small sink in the bathroom, he splashed cold water on his face and paused at the reflection in the silver-clouded mirror, making sure he was still the same person he was when he went to sleep the night before. "Hmm. Unclear." Bowing his head, he ran cool water over his scalp and pulled his hair away from his face. He slicked his mane back using its own natural, oily residue. Despite the hair which seemed to grow enthusiastically everywhere else on his body, he could swear the hair on his head was already thinning. It wasn't. In fact, after drying out, his mane liked to puff up in thick waves, curls encircling his head like a crown of smoky thoughts emanating from the fire of his imagination. This was an odd morning indeed. The mirror must've been in cahoots with the mischievous light. That, or he wasn't fully awake. For surrounding his reflection were all sorts of fanciful characters and scenes from his nightmarish dream and beyond. He glanced over his shoulder to make sure there wasn't actually a dragon looming behind him then splashed more water on his face to dissolve the illusions. After nearly drowning himself, he looked up at the face staring back at him. *Good grief.* The unruly locks, winged ears, and gap in his front teeth did little to boost his confidence. "Quite the ladies' man, aren't you?" he jested with a mournful shake of his oversized head. With one hand, he fumbled around, adjusting his uncooperative shirt and some uncooperative hairs on his head. With the other, he did his best to brush his teeth sans toothpaste. A shortage of toothpaste wasn't the worst thing he'd experienced as a result of the current economic recession, but it sure didn't help freshen up the morning routine.

Placing his toothbrush back in the cup next to the sink, he winked at his compadre in the mirror and continued into the hall. As he slunk past the adults blabbering away in the living room, he imagined gluing their mouths shut with some extra-sticky peanut butter, temporarily of course, just to get a moment's peace from all of the adult-speak jibber-jabber: those never-ending dos and don'ts, woeful criticizing and complaining.

"He mustn't!"

"She shouldn't!"

"They'll never!"

Why are adults so grumpy all the time? he wondered, shaking his head. *They're so negative and doubting of—*

"Oh, that's impossible!"

"…everything," he concluded, quietly shuffling into the kitchen, being particularly careful to avoid being seen by his father. If there ever was someone who needed his heart softened and mouth glued shut, it was his dear old, dissatisfied, disappointed, disapproving dad. If only his old man would stop complaining, stop barking orders long enough to see, to truly see, and in seeing to truly appreciate, the miracle of his children. *Maybe someday.*

The boy snatched his book bag from the hall tree and squeezed on his worn-out leather shoes, so old they looked as though they could walk (or fly) away without any feet in them. As he drifted through the kitchen, he swiped from the counter someone's toasted bread, conveniently adorned with a generous spread of peanut butter. *Probably Dad's. (Hopefully Dad's!)* His father loved peanut butter sandwiches, above all else it seemed at times. The old monarch hoarded peanut butter like pirate treasure, sneaking sandwiches when he thought no one was looking, even at suppertime when everyone else was left forcing down small trees of broccoli. *Not fair!* the boy thought, for he loved peanut butter too. *Oh, glorious peanut butter!* he reveled as he sunk his teeth into the toast, made all the more delicious by the notion of stealing it from under the nose of his pops.

"Thank you!" he whispered in the direction of his father, still grumbling away in the next room, wholly unaware that his royal coffers were being robbed. With his scrumptiously sticky treasure in hand, the boy slipped, unnoticed and unaccounted for — as usual — quietly out into the world.

Chapter Two

Everything On It

The young peanut butter thief had been walking himself to school for nearly three years now, during which time he had carved out a route that passed through some old, abandoned buildings separating Palmer Avenue and Logan Square...

On days with time to spare, he would pause and riffle through the dirt and rubble, looking for interesting treasure, typically finding naught but common items such as rusted nails, old medicine bottles, unidentifiable scraps of leather or tin…

On this particular day, however, as he kicked through mounds of dirt and detritus — the playful morning light following him around not unlike his pesky kid sister — he happened to come across an odd-looking piece of jewelry.

"Hey! Look at this!" the light seemed to say, illuminating the ground as if spotlighting an actor on stage. A shard of something beneath the surface was struggling to respond to the cue with muted reflectance. This actor was old and tired, perhaps no longer worthy of an audience. Regardless, the boy was intrigued and, bending down, pushed his stubby fingers through a combination of dirt, gravel, rubbish, and ash, helping the reluctant remnant into the limelight once more.

"Come on now," he encouraged the shard, exhuming it from its earthly tomb. "Perform for me." He spat on the piece and scrubbed away the dirt, revealing what appeared to be a large tooth from a prehistoric saber cat or a small dinosaur, perhaps a tiny tusk from a tiny elephant...

The base of the tooth was wrapped with copper wire affixing it to a thoroughly rusted necklace. He spat on it again, rubbing away more grime and examining it more closely, turning it over and over in his palm until it came clean, revealing more of its secrets. He squinted at what looked like the word, 'IF' stamped into the copper. He had never seen anything like it. And yet, something about it felt unmistakably familiar. Getting to the bottom of why that might be, however, and figuring out what this tooth thing was exactly, was going to require an expert. Luckily, he knew just the person.

Because his was the only food cart open at such an early hour for nearly four blocks in any direction, Hector's Hot Dogs was always crowded with the morning rush. Fortunately, Hector had a soft spot for our boy and always kept a warm dog ready should the youngster pass by on his way to school.

"Here you go, son, one dog dragged through the garden, just as you like it," Hector would say as he handed over a hot dog piled high with just about every topping from his cart. Although that was not 'just how he liked it,' the kid would politely smile and accept the hot mess in exchange for whatever he happened to find in the rubble that morning.

Affectionately known around the neighborhood as Hector the Collector, the hot dog man was a self-proclaimed historian of the Windy City. His food cart was adorned with all the trinkets and trifles brought to him by customers looking to trade treasure for food. Ornaments and decorations hung down from the wooden awning, giving his cart the look of a gypsy caravan — albeit a relatively small one. Although he was always more than happy to trade one of his dogs for a unique doodad or doohickey, most of the trinkets turned out to be useless junk. Every so often, however, an intriguing puzzle piece of Chicago history would be scavenged up, adding to the décor of the cart and seasoning Hector's day with excitement. Judging by what the boy was twirling in his fingers that morning, Hector suspected that it might just turn out to be one of those fortuitous days.

"It's quite remarkable, my friend," noted Hector from a distance. "I don't reckon I've seen the like... not for a very long time and not around these parts, that's for sure." Noting Hector's intrigue, the boy handed him the pendant without hesitation. The hot dog man examined the thing with great interest. "Where exactly did you find it?"

The boy just shrugged, which Hector understood to mean, "somewhere in the dirt."

Pensively stroking his beard and pursing his lips, the Collector grunted, "Hmm. Well, I'm not entirely sure what to make of this..."

o o o o o o

Hector was a short, hirsute man with a great, round belly and dark, alluring eyes that spoke volumes, telling tales of mystery and adventure even when his mouth remained shut, which was almost never. Complimenting his esoteric food cart, Hector wore extravagant outfits of cloth that looked to be hand-spun in far-away places, the fringe of the world. A curious collection of chains, chimes, and charms hung from his costume as well as from various body parts, giving him the look of a genie freshly popped from a many thousands-year-old bottle.

o o o o o o

"So you don't... know what it is?" the boy asked timidly, surprised at Hector's apparent stupefaction. It was uncommon for Hector not to be enthusiastically forthcoming with some creative and entertaining story — usually entirely made up of course — about the treasures people brought him: where the piece originated, its significance in society, purpose in life, etcetera. The kid liked to imagine that Hector, with his elaborate collection of stuff and stories, was a mystical gypsy who had only recently wandered into town from the deserts of Arabia ...or perhaps the moons of Andromeda.

"Oh, no, no. On the contrary, son. I know exactly what this is. But what a crocodile tooth of this ilk is doing in Chicago is beyond even me." The hot dog man let loose one eyebrow and like a wild animal freed from a cage, the thing shimmied up his forehead and perched atop his dome, looking menacingly down at the boy. When a peripheral flash of light caught his eye, the Collector turned and squinted at the low sun seemingly lost in the morning mist. Bits of light trickled through the streets like a search party slowly making its way through a dark forest. "Sure is a curious light over the city this morning." Hector glanced back at the boy and released the second eyebrow, which rushed to catch up with its compadre, the two caterpillar-like things scrutinizing the kid from their lofty post.

The boy looked over Hector's shoulder and scowled at the light. "Yeah, curious is one way to put it..."

Volleying, the light bounced off a window and flashed the boy square in the eyes, blinding him momentarily. "Ahh!" He jerked his head back and shielded his face, conceding defeat. Stepping back into the hot dog man's abundant shadow, the boy reached out and gingerly retrieved the pendant from Hector's sizeable hand.

"Maybe it's leftover from a colony of crocodiles that used to live in Chicago, before the city was even here." He twirled the thing in his fingers, spinning the yarn of his imagination.

"Oh?" queried Hector, his restless brows looking ferociously inquisitive.

"Yeah! They were... farmers, like the old farmers that live outside the city, and they stood up and walked on their hind legs, like us! Except, they were eight feet tall! And they liked to sing and dance!" He flung his arms around and danced about, animating his fanciful tale.

Hector laughed loudly and swiftly picked the pendant back from the boy. Bowing to the young storyteller, he stretched the chain into a wide circle and held it out as if presenting a medal for such a grand performance. "Now *that* is a good story! You have quite the imagination, Mr. Silvers." Hector placed the tooth-pendant around the neck of his creative friend and gave the boy a wide-eyed stare. Then, stealing another backward glance at the oncoming light, added with a kind, yet mysterious smile, "And likely an intriguing story unfolding around you today. I think you ought to hold onto this one, Shelby. This treasure... belongs to you!"

The boy examined the pendant with renewed curiosity, until Hector interrupted, "Now... off you go, Sheldon... before you're late!" With a wink and a nod, Hector shoved a hot dog at his friend and then shoved him off toward school.

Stumbling onward, the young Sheldon Silvers looked down at the steaming pile of rubbish Hector had placed in his hands, inspiring much more 'um...' than 'yum!' It was well-known that the hot dog man dished out the most decorative franks around, no question about that.

For Sheldon, the hot dog was of much less interest than Hector's company, his contagious laughter, and most of all, his wild stories. He and Hector shared many fanciful conversations about the history and culture of Chicago and beyond, conversations about places and happenings both real and — Sheldon's favorite — entirely made up. These fun exchanges inspired the young imaginator, he took refuge in Hector's fanciful tales, imagining worlds beyond his noisy apartment and his school. The hot dog was merely a formality of the exchange. Sheldon had never developed an affinity for meat anyway, especially those franks with everything but the kitchen sink on them. Yuck!

"Who puts jelly on a hot dog?!" Sheldon would grumble. Hector loved jams and jellies (possibly more than hot dogs! Shhh.). Why he never stuck with the food cart and opened a brick-and-mortar delicatessen — or, Sheldon mused, *a jelli-catessen* — was a mystery beyond even the boy's imagination. He figured the hot dog stand was just a side gig, a way for Hector to torture the patrons of Logan Square with his odd food combinations. He was, after all, the only street vendor known to put jelly on a hot dog, much to many-a-customer's dismay. The man did what he wanted and that's what made him interesting, especially to Sheldon, who loved to complain: "What's with all the cucumbers and onions? ...

Spinach? Really? ... Hot peppers again? ... I think it's against the law to put broccoli on a hot dog!"

Hector would just laugh his hearty laugh and watch the boy, who was raised with a good sense to appreciate whatever he was given, attempt to force down the creative franks so as to take up space in his belly that would otherwise need to be filled by the so-called 'food' served at Charles R. Darwin Elementary School.

Chapter Three, Part I

A Good Defense

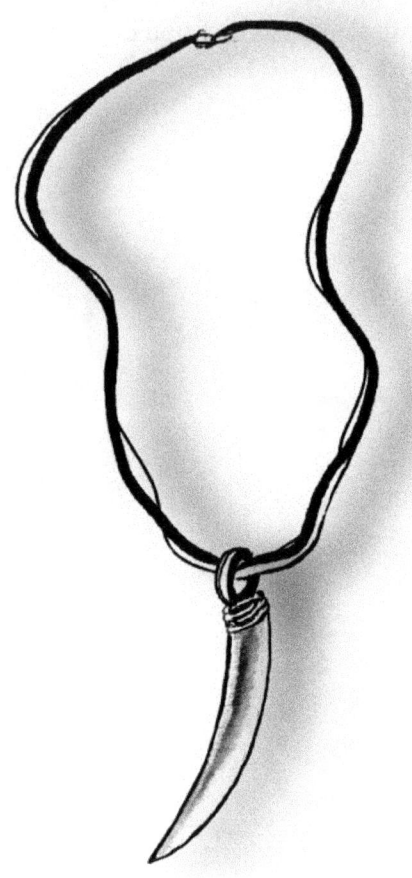

Sheldon didn't have many friends at Darwin Elementary, just two or three acquaintances who would, now and again, drone out an obligatory, "Hi, Sheldon," in passing. Most of the attention he received was earned through humiliating pranks, practical jokes, and general bullying...

He was a particularly attractive target for notes stuck to his back (or backside), shoelaces being tied together when he was daydreaming in class, or kids playing keep-away with his bookbag. That morning, despite being on campus only a few short minutes, Sheldon had already removed a note stuck to his back that read, 'Handle with care.' A postage stamp in the corner of the note indicated that someone intended to airmail him to some far-off place — which would be just fine with him.

Get me outta here! he thought, often.

On occasion, he would find some treasure on his way to school and *not* trade it for a messy hot dog (for whatever reason). On those days, upon seeing that Sheldon had found something interesting, a handful of kids would instantly become his best buddies, rubbing elbows against him from all directions, hoping he might give up his fascinating find.

Because Hector insisted that Sheldon keep the tooth pendant, and because he now wore it around his neck for all to see, sure enough, a gang of kids began to gather around, asking to see, hold, wear, even keep the treasure. As if by intention, the universe setting the scene for confrontation, a cluster of clouds gathered in the sky above, momentarily blocking out the morning sunlight, casting a shadow across the schoolyard.

"Come on, Sheldon! Don't be stingy!" came a voice from the crowd. And the mob replied in unison, "Yeah!"

The attention Sheldon got from Hector and the attention he received at school could not have been more different. On any other day he might have just given in and let the pendant go to whichever kid was the biggest or most aggressive. Out of respect for Hector and his mysterious gesture, Sheldon decided he needed to hang onto the tooth no matter the cost. He grasped the pendant in a protective fist and pushed his way through the crowd of outstretched groping hands.

"Leave me alone!" he yelled, but of course, no one listened. Most kids who Sheldon knew, those at Darwin being no exception, seemed to only speak one language: the language of action, and Sheldon was a boy of intellect, not action. (Not yet!)

As the mob grew more dense, the pushing and pulling more intense, a voice rang out like a referee's whistle, halting the rough play. "All right, you goons! You heard 'im! Back off!" Sheldon spun around to see Allison Tamaroa, a ruthless force on the Darwin playground, shoving kids aside as she made her way through the mob.

Allison wasn't a bully by any stretch. Quite the opposite, in fact. She was known as a bully-fighter, a protector of the innocent and defender of the weak, so to speak. Still, just to be safe, anyone who knew what was good for them steered clear of the Tamaroa Train (a title Allison had earned by plowing over anything in her path) unless they enjoyed knuckle sandwiches for lunch or taking naps face-down in the dirt.

Because Sheldon only encountered Allison when she came to his rescue — which was no more than once a week... twice tops... maybe three times but that's it — and because she never really acknowledged him, Sheldon was pretty sure that Allison didn't know who he was; other than just another feeble milksop regularly in need of saving. Regardless, he was awfully relieved to see her steaming her way toward him, the defense express coming to his rescue once again. With her help, eventually the two of them made it safely through the ornery crowd.

Sheldon turned to thank his knight in shining armor but before he could get any words out, the train left the station, off to her next stop, and Sheldon was left standing alone, watching his savior walk away, imagining himself inviting her to share an ice cream or soda pop. When a shove in his back from a disgruntled mobster reminded him that he'd best move along if he liked his nose in the center of his face, he did just that, carving a beeline for his classroom. Like the young cowboy to his cave, Sheldon quickly sought refuge within the dark halls of Darwin.

Most days at Darwin Elementary, Sheldon passed the entire seven-and-a-half hours in quiet solitude, drawing cartoon sketches on his homework papers without anyone, including his teacher, Miss Kelsyan, saying so much as two words to him.

Miss Kelsyan was a tall, slender woman who looked to Sheldon to be at least 150 years old. She wasn't haggard or decrepit by any means. In fact, Sheldon thought she was still rather fetching for her exceptional age, with a refined, almost royal air about her. Her manner of speech, dress, and general disposition made Sheldon suspicious, however, that she might secretly be an immortal queen from an age long past. For this mystique, Sheldon enjoyed Miss Kelsyan's presence. He made sure not to mistake his regard for her as any sort of friendship, however. She made it clear her classroom was a place of discipline, not a social club.

The morning bell called the remaining inmates back to the Kelsyan cell block and Sheldon prepared himself for another long day of confinement. That is, he took out his drawing pad and began to doodle and drift away.

The day's lectures were tuning up to the standard level of dull. So, naturally, while Miss Kelsyan droned on about the Civil War, Sheldon's note papers filled up with sketches of cartoon soldiers fighting with noodles instead of swords. He was not a fan of violence. He was, however, fascinated with the *notion* of war: how so-called civilized people, time and again, avoided prudent, reasonable negotiations in favor of the worst sort of brutalities.

Miss Kelsyan clearly was not fascinated by violence nor war and her lack of enthusiasm shone brilliantly through her soporific lectures, which were, incidentally, complimented by her drab outfits: blends of dark and light greys, like the Confederacy, or the cloudy skies hanging in perpetuity over Chicago.

While the kids at Darwin maintained the joke that she came from the black and white era, before color was invented, Sheldon was pretty sure that Miss Kelsyan — along with many, possibly most, people in Chicago — dressed to match a monochromatic existence, devoid of the brilliant colors found in the more exciting places of the world. In Chicago, with the exception of Hector's wild hot dogs, most things seemed dull and colorless, flavorless meat and potatoes. Maybe that's the reason he spent so much time at Hector's stand: it was full of colorful story and spice. Maybe that's the reason why he spent so much time drawing cartoons: he was trying to animate an otherwise woefully dreary existence.

The school day dragged on with Miss Kelsyan's lecture on U.S. history diving deep into famous naval battles. And there sat the incarcerated Sheldon, his desk an iron weight chained to his soul!

Sympathetic to his plight, his imagination threw him a lifeline. He eagerly grabbed hold and instantly felt himself pulled away to distant lands. He fantasized about being on an island, wandering through tropical jungles, being surrounded by plants and animals painted every color of the rainbow. He imagined the worldly expeditions undertaken by famous explorers like Livingstone, Hemingway, and Roosevelt. His mind trekked across a wondrous expanse of wilderness, reflected in a broad smile sweeping across his face. Danger and excitement dripped from these adventure stories like too much icing on too hot a cinnamon roll... His thoughts shifted to his father's bakery on N. Western Avenue and the exotic images evaporated under a steamy tropical sun. Hunger crept up on him like a hunter and he began salivating for rolls of dough... and for unchained freedom.

He would invariably conclude that, like his old man's famous cinnamon rolls, the hunting safari stories, specifically those taking place in Africa, were too rich for his taste. Nauseatingly so. The trophy killing of creatures like the noble rhinoceros, the regal lion, and his favorite, the majestic elephant, was utterly distasteful, to say the least. How much more sporting these epic safaris would be, he mused, if the animals could fight back with some sort of modern technology of their own? Or what if the animals were mutated in some way? He chuckled at the thought of a giraffe with two heads and six legs that could shoot flaming bananas out of its nostrils.

"Hehe!" Oops! An audible giggle! That was as likely to blip on the Kelsyan radar as a lazy LaPerm is likely to nap on a lap (which is an absolute certainty).

Sure enough, the student sitting at the desk in front of him — one of Kelsyan's informants no doubt — glanced back with a curious expression that quickly folded into a scowl when she realized Sheldon was goofing off again.

He shook his head to recall his attention to the math lesson lest he be sent to the brig. One more slip-up like that and he could expect a torpedo from the Kelsyan battleship, sinking his cruiser to the deep. Like a diving submarine, he slunk in his chair and lowered his head, trying to make himself invisible. The new posture set his eyes level with his coursework and he noticed something that surely would not please the Kelsyan commander, who always demanded tidy work. Staring back at him, holding his notes hostage, was the sketch of a lion brandishing a double-barreled shotgun, the words, "Friendly greetings from Africa," written above it. He added, "Shoot Kodachrome only, or else!" and turned the page just as Miss Kelsyan wandered by, conducting her periodic inspection of her troops.

Chapter Three, Part II

Imagination Unchained

"*Kelsyan... Kel-see-in... keel-sea-in...*"

Drop the keel in the sea! came the command from the captain... Sheldon toyed with his teacher's name as his attention wandered yet again, inspired by another messy page of lecture notes woven between random doodlings...

His thoughts drifted like a lonely boat, untethered by a careless sailor, coerced to sea by a mischievous tide. Once out in open waters, his mind sailed away, through the classroom window and up into the sky. Recalling Kelsyan's Civil War lecture, the distant clouds transformed into clipper ships with large keels stabbing deep into a tumultuous sea of vapor, swirling on cumulonimbus currents. The Navy's warships had gone airborne with the North hammering the South in a barrage of watermelon cannonballs and spaghetti grapeshot. Captains were ordering regiments of fried fish-sticks into the fray of battle with carrot bayonets on the ends of asparagus stalk rifles...

The hot dog with everything on it was wearing off.

"Is it lunchtime yet?" Sheldon's tummy rumbled. The bell for morning break answered a definitive, "Nope," startling Sheldon out of his daydream.

As he reluctantly stood up, preparing to exit the classroom, he grumbled in dismay over the daily playground puerility. According to Sheldon, recess was little more than an opportunity to flaunt one's popularity through equal measures of social intimidation and athletic prowess. Though he was coordinated enough to play most sports, he preferred instead to play at being sophisticated, avoiding playground games with the odd excuse: "It's my innate aversion to conformity which prevents me from participating." Truth was, it had more to do with his lack of self-confidence and difficulty asserting himself. Then there was his preoccupation with life beyond school, a sort of big-picture thinking not all that common for kids his age. That didn't help him fit in any easier. The only person *less* popular might have been the bear-sized dancing boy, Donald Kushvatsky. Whether he was walking to and from class in the halls or passing time on the playground, anytime he wasn't being forced to sit still at his desk, Donald was dancing.

Sheldon fancied that Donald came from a long line of Russian ballet dancers and that he was under strict orders to practice nonstop, or else! For many, Donald the dancer was infinitely amusing. For Sheldon, Donald was an invaluable asset on the playground because his dancing took the spotlight off Shel, which worked out perfectly because Donald was virtually immune to bullies. Unlike Sheldon, who required the protection of Allison, Donald was big, perhaps the biggest kid in school, a trait which had earned him the nickname, the Bear. He kept to himself mostly, and he seemed friendly enough. Still, even the toughest hooligans kept their distance from Donald, not wanting to poke the Bear and get mauled as a result.

Beyond his invincibility, Sheldon respected Donald for his devil-may-care attitude. The Bear danced whenever and wherever he wanted, pirouetting above adolescent social pressures, setting his sights instead, like Sheldon, on the bigger picture of life after Darwin.

It wasn't just the idea of life beyond school that preoccupied Sheldon. He was also obsessed with life beyond his tiny, noisy apartment; life beyond his father's bakery; life beyond Chicago. Even at the age of twelve (twelve years, eight months to be exact), he was already a self-described visionary, though most everyone else used the term 'dreamer' if they were being nice, 'space case' if not — and they were certainly not referring to the sort of dreamer who would come up with the next great invention or novelty. Instead, Sheldon was the sort of odd duck who provided odd commentary and exhibited odd mannerisms. So it went that throughout his school years, Sheldon was consistently ignored by the popular groups, and the pretty girls, and the team captains looking to pick their players. But *not* by the bullies looking to tag their targets.

After the attention he received on the playground before school that day, Sheldon was convinced there was no way he would return from recess with his pendant. Because Miss Kelsyan did not allow students to stay in the classroom during recess, Sheldon did his best to keep a low profile, circumnavigating the school yard, putting as much distance as possible between him and everyone else. Miraculously, he was able to pass the entire break without attracting any unwanted attention. The residue of Allison Tamaroa lingered in the air around him like a swarm of killer bees. *More like perfume*, Sheldon mused, convinced that he could still smell her scent, a delusion that helped calm his nerves.

Despite avoiding trouble during recess, however, Sheldon ended up in the infirmary with a bloody nose just the same. This time, it was a simple matter of bad luck, being precisely in the wrong place at the wrong time, and as a result, having been struck squarely in the face by a flying shoe! Apparently, someone's loose sneaker gleefully slid off their sweaty foot, punctuating an overly enthusiastic swing of their leg during a lively game of kick baseball — a game in which, of course, Sheldon was not invited to participate.

Obeying both the school nurses, Sheldon pinched his nose and held his head back to control the bleeding. There he sat, in the quiet, cold room of the nurses' office, listening to the school bell herald in a stampede of wound-up kids yelling and stomping their way back to class like a herd of wild animals. He sighed and loosened his grip on his nose, letting the blood flow. He'd just as soon spend the rest of the day right there in quiet solitude.

"Do I hap do go mack do glass?" he asked with his nose full of tissue and sounding as miserable as possible. "I reary don't veel well." The two nurses, who only used words when absolutely necessary, silently nodded their heads in unison like Siamese cats tracking a bouncing ball.

For whatever reason, Darwin Elementary had two nurses who filled the one role of school medic. Two dutiful twin sisters, always working together, side by side, never one without the other, as if they would perish if separated. Because Sheldon spent a good deal of time in the infirmary, he had developed — or so he imagined — a special rapport with the twins. He concluded that they were possibly the nicest people in the entire school on account of their attentive care. It was hard to tell what they were really like, however, as neither of them said much at all, which made them even more likable to Sheldon. The twins worked swiftly and effectively and let their practically-impeccable healing skills do the talking for them.

When Sheldon requested to stay in the infirmary, he expected the sweet ladies to hand him a blanket and a cup of tea, perhaps a biscuit or cookie, and conclude with some gesture for him to make himself comfortable. Instead, the nurses spoke two words. The first pointed toward the door and with a gentle smile said, "Cafeteria." The second, also behind a soft smile, concluded with, "Ice." And with that, they handed him not a cup of tea, nor a blanket, not even a cookie, but a wad of gauze and a note for his teacher, then summarily escorted him out the door.

Released back into the general population, Sheldon wandered the halls, slowly taking the scenic route to the cafeteria, which wasn't scenic at all unless one appreciated the various scratches, dents, and hues of cream on the endless rows of lockers. The windows of Darwin were few and far between, letting only a minimal amount of light in and even less imagination out. Perhaps that was best for keeping the students focused. *In other words, tame*, he concluded.

He eventually arrived at the cafeteria as the cooks were preparing their usual mystery slop for lunch. He didn't know the women who worked in the cafeteria as well as he did the nurses, but he was fascinated by them too, perhaps more so. They may have been the sweetest ladies in the world, but based on the food they prepared and the mysterious way they worked behind the counter, Sheldon had no choice but to conclude they were witches, brewing secret concoctions to suppress the energetic tendencies of the unruly masses; that is, turn the kids into mindless zombies. After all, how could so many spirited children sit still for so many hours day after day? *It's just not natural!* he thought.

These cooks appeared more mysterious to Sheldon than Miss Kelsyan, the nurses, and everyone else at the school combined. All four cooks were elderly women who wore ankle-length, dark grey dresses and large hats that concealed their long hair tied up in messy buns. They never seemed very keen to chat with any of the kids (Sheldon couldn't blame them for that). Instead, they chatted nonstop with one another in a language no one else seemed to understand.

Sheldon did not speak any language other than English, but he could recognize some foreign words from time to time. Family friends from the synagogue, patrons in his father's bakery and around Hector's stand, even some of his family members who still spoke the 'old tongues', allowed him to become accustomed to the distinct accents of Russian, German, Yiddish, Polish, French, and Italian. But these ladies spoke something altogether foreign, some language dominated by giggles and cackles.

The lunch ladies were laughing nonstop, ignoring the boy in bandages standing silently at the counter, no doubt looking terrifically pitiful. No matter. Sheldon wasn't in any hurry to get back to class. He certainly did not want to disturb the witches for fear they might turn him into a toad. So, there he stood, silently waiting at the lunch counter, long enough for the bleeding to stop in fact.

Finally, when one of the women acknowledged him and approached, he began to speak, to explain why he was there and what he needed. The woman cut him off by tossing a small bag of ice loudly onto the counter, only momentarily pausing her cackling chatter to flash a wide grin, revealing a sparse set of crooked, off-color teeth that made Sheldon cringe on the inside. How did she know exactly what he wanted?

Because she's a witch!

o o o o o o

Along the walk back to his classroom, through the desolate and dark hallways, he passed by the school's main entrance. There, he noticed that the front doors had been left slightly ajar, which was unusual for the typically locked-down Darwin.

Suddenly, a bright beam of light flashed from beyond the threshold, blinding his sight and teasing him with unattainable freedom.

"You're back!" he scoffed at the light sarcastically. "That was very rude, by the way, waking me up this morning the way you did." The light in the door stayed ruefully quiet, looking apologetic. "Oh, it's okay," offered Sheldon. "Don't sweat it."

The light perked up, dancing brightly around the room. She was calling to him, beckoning him to come and play. Sheldon shook his head. "No, I can't." *Still, I suppose a little daydream couldn't hurt.* He squinted at the lighted crack in the door and imagined a small lizard in a dark cave, slipping out through the fissure, recharging its batteries in the glorious sunshine of a wide-open desert. His mind became a wild reptile wandering free in a boundless landscape while his body adhered to the mantra of obedience recited daily within the halls of Darwin: Stand still, be quiet, keep your hands to yourself. Sit, stay, roll over. Good dog.

I wonder when things are going to evolve around here, he thought, often.

The strict discipline just seemed so old-fashioned. With a sigh, his reptilian fantasy faded, and he found himself with his hand congealed around the doorknob to Commander Kelsyan's barracks. Looking back at the school entrance, he watched as the lizard sped off into the desert without him.

"Traitor," he whispered.

The bag of ice turning his hand into a popsicle gave him a chilling thought and he took his revenge on the turncoat reptile. He imagined the warm sunshine suddenly degrading to a white-out blizzard. "Take that!" he chuckled. The freezing lizard in a blizzard was sure to get a snowflake in his gizzard. *So there!* He smiled in triumph. A moment later he felt sorry for his imaginary friend and a moment after that he moved on altogether. "Oh well. C'est la guerre!" He turned back to the classroom with a dramatic sigh.

Peering through the small window in the classroom door, he watched Miss Kelsyan going through her standard machinations. He leaned and looked to the rear of the classroom, taking stock of the typical falderal from the clowning brutes in the back row and the group of girls sitting near Charles Chesterton, the class' two-headed turtle, named after the school's eponym.

Charles was about the only thing that gave Sheldon any enjoyment in class. He liked to imagine that, at night when the school was empty, Mr. Chesterton would extend his secret legs, two yards long or more, and go running about through the dark halls. When he was feeling really frisky, Charles might even slip through a window and head out for a midnight jog around town. That sly, adventurous reptile probably even ran all the way back home sometimes, back to his old stomping grounds at the equator. Although some of the students claimed he was made of wood because he laid so still during class, Sheldon knew Mr. Chesterton's long-running secret!

Sheldon was swiftly pulled back to reality by a loud burst of laughter coming from inside the classroom, followed by a stern reprimand from Queen Kelsyan. He shook his head, lamenting how schoolboys always sparked so much trouble, throwing erasers and what-not and cracking the most unfunny jokes; while schoolgirls seemed to love nothing more than to pass notes and giggle to no end as if giggling was necessary for their survival. It was all the same nonsense day after day. There was no real stimulation, no fundamental purpose, and certainly no adventure in any of it whatsoever.

"Ugh." Another sigh of surrender preempted a reluctant turning of the door handle, ever so slowly. At the same time however, his feet, seemingly under some spell, like bloodhounds catching a scent, began turning his torso in the opposite direction, back toward the lizard in the blizzard, toward the alluring light in the doorway, and before he knew it, he was running at top speed for the exit, in pursuit of glorious, forbidden, freedom.

Chapter Three, Part III

Lion Man

"*Shel-dunnnn!*"

He thought he heard someone call his name as he flung the school doors wide and burst into the open air with explosive ferocity. The light of the world, contrasted against the dark Darwin halls, blinded the fugitive as he sprung down the steps like a pouncing wildcat, half in flight and trying not to fall on his face.

He was a rocket ship catching fire in the blazing day. Somewhere in the distance, a crowd cheered for him like they did for his hometown hero, Bruce Campbell, during the Tigers-Reds World Series a couple of years back when Campbell smashed that terrific home run. His heart pounded out of his chest as he planted his feet firmly on the sidewalk in the wide stance of a superhero. He stretched his arms out and leaned back to greet the day in all its splendor, as if to say, 'I am here! Sheldon has arrived!'

Like his desert lizard, the boy took a moment to charge his batteries, standing eyes closed to the sky in a silent gesture of gratitude for wonderful sunshine; a long-time prisoner finally breathing the free air again.

A moment later he was ready to blast off again, down the sidewalk ... out of town ... all the way to outer space! But as he readied to depart, something anchored him to that spot. Apprehension and indecision snuck up like a serpent, wrapped a firm grip around his ankle, and held him fast. He'd never ditched school before. Now that he'd broken out, he wasn't sure what to do exactly, didn't know which direction to run. Perhaps not in so many words he thought, *Where would a twelve-year-old go to play hooky from school in a bustling borough of the Windy City?* He shook his head against the urge to run home.

"Don't be a chicken!" he spoke aloud. There must be a million places he could go if he only had the gumption. But where to start? The movie theater? The ice cream shop? The toy store? ...Wait! "My billfold!" he cried, patting his pockets. His wallet had been tucked safely in his book bag back in the classroom and there was certainly no going back for that prisoner-of-war now. Not that it made any difference. *Probably empty, as usual,* he admitted. These days no one had an extra dime, let alone a dollar. He carried the leather pouch as more of an heirloom. It'd been given to him by his grandmother on behalf of his late grandfather, Sigmund, who had worked in a tannery and made the leather wallet with his own leathered hands. After Sigmund's passing, Rae, Sheldon's grandmother, handed down the wallet along with some advice: "One should always keep in one's billfold, at minimum, a one-dollar bill for good luck and prosperity." "Money attracts money, my boy," the grandfolks would say.

Sheldon's father had a different philosophy about allowing children to keep money: don't. Sheldon's dad, Patterson, did not hold much faith in the capabilities of children, especially his own it seemed. Like the school kids at Darwin, Sheldon's father deemed his son to be little more than a silly-hearted dreamer.

Patterson's folks had immigrated from Eastern Europe. Patterson was the first child in the family to be born in America. He had fought in World War I and as a result, carried a hardened heart and had very little patience for anyone who appeared discontented with a job that provided steady pay in one's pocket, a hot meal on one's plate, and a sound roof over one's head. Sheldon, unfortunately, was just such a person. He wanted more out of life than a steady job and a hot meal, and for that he was castigated and ostracized by his father. But not his mother. Sheldon's mom, Alanna, was supportive of her son's creativity and his big, beautiful dreams. She would tell Sheldon that he could accomplish whatever he set his mind to. Unfortunately, this division set Sheldon's parents at odds and their constant arguing drove Sheldon ever deeper into his imaginary world of cartoon drawings and daydreams.

o o o o o o

Out on the sidewalk in front of the school, Sheldon reached into all four pockets, one by one, searching for a nickel or even a penny but finding nothing but lint and holes. Money always seemed to burn right through Sheldon's pockets. There was always some piece of candy or bubble gum with baseball cards, a comic book, or literary novel that would catch his eye. In that respect, and that alone, Sheldon was just like every other boy his age.

As he stood at the base of the steps, he balanced the weight of his own willing incarceration on one scale and a life daring him to live on the other. It then occurred to him that it didn't matter in which direction he ran, so long as he ran. It was either that or go back inside, and that was most certainly not an option.

Run Shelby! Quick! Before they catch you!

He blasted off. The further he got from school, the more he became suited to the notion that he did not need any destination. He just needed to keep running. He paused for a moment in Logan Square Park to marvel at the Centennial Monument before continuing toward one of his favorite haunts. As he rounded the alley heading to his beloved Logan Theater, however, running as fast as his appetite for freedom would carry him, he plowed into two street cops who were casually searching a potential perpetrator for purloined paraphernalia.

Exhausted from running and surprised by the police, Sheldon gasped for air and immediately choked on the thick irony hanging over him like fog. His would-be (could-be, should-be) free life seemed bent on oppression, as if his very spirit had become institutionalized to well-defined boundaries and controls and discipline... *What was I thinking? I just left school? I never do that! I shouldn't have left. I knew it!*

One of the policemen reacted swiftly, grabbing the wayward boy by the collar. "Oh, hello there! May I ask why we're running today?" Sheldon, terribly out of breath, was taken aback by the policeman's politeness. "Now just calm yourself, son. It's okay. Why don't you tell me where you're headed in such a rush."

Sheldon's instinct was to make up some story, some wild excuse to avoid culpability. Oddly, all he could think of was claiming that a thief had stolen his knees and he knee-ded to get them back. This of course made no sense.

"Please, son. Where might your parents be? And why are you not in school at this hour, may I ask?"

Sheldon's mind was flipping through his encyclopedia of excuses but nothing stayed still long enough to grasp it. He wished desperately that he could hitch a ride along with his runaway thoughts to anywhere but there.

"I'm terribly sorry to have to do this son, but you're going to have to come with me if you don't mind, back to the station. That is if you're not going to answer any of my questions."

Is this cop trying to be funny with his manners? Confused, Sheldon grew even more tongue-tied, and like a deflating balloon, surrendered to his capture. His adrenaline meanwhile still flowed like fire, burning him up on the inside. The more his mind whirled and twisted, trying to sort out what to do, the more he could feel himself slipping away as if turning to ash. The cop's voice faded, along with all the other street noise, to an overwhelming buzz. Sheldon dropped his head uncontrollably, as if an invisible spirit had placed a lead crown of shame upon his head. His eyesight blurred to a tunnel of black and white static as he stared fixedly at his ratted shoes, the only thing remaining in his field of vision. *Why did you fly me away like that?* he blamed the sneakers.

As he stared at his feet, the concrete beneath him liquified to quicksand and he could feel his body sink under the weight of self-pity. Guilt hung from him like sandbags on a dirigible, pulling him ever farther down into the mortal mire. This was it, his nightmare coming true! Would he next be dragged off to become dinner for some sinister cannibal of the concrete jungle? It wasn't long before he found himself sunk up to his ears, the sounds of the world now a distant hum, his head vibrating, his body numb. He closed his eyes, tilted his head back to face the sky, and stretched his neck as far as he could to catch one… last… breath, before sinking into oblivion. But just before going under, he heard a faint voice.

"Open your eyes, you fuddle-dupper! Don't be so dramatic."

Obeying the pragmatic advice, more on instinct than anything, he reluctantly pried one eyelid open just a slit, just enough to catch a flash from that playful beam of light. It was his luminous guide calling to him again. His eyes shot open in excitement, and he immediately squinted from the intense brightness. He was alive, not sinking into quicksand, not fading away... But still captured. This time the light was coming from some distant alley, perhaps reflecting off a building. Who knew? Just as before, back in the school hallway, his feet suddenly became animated under their own ascendancy. His body spasmed and he spun in a wobbly circle before starting in the direction of the mysterious glare. He didn't get far, however. The polite cop was still holding tight to his jacket collar, and he was jerked backward as if hooked to a rubber band.

"Excuse me, son. Would you mind holding still please?"

Sheldon instinctively shook his torso, invoking the old, 'severed-lizard's-tail' trick. It was just enough. The cop tightened his grip on the boy's jacket, but the contents slipped away like ice cream left out on the porch in July. As the little devil sped off, the second policeman took chase. Obviously this kid must have stolen or vandalized something, and this cop was going to nab someone before the day was out, so help him. Even if it was just a young boy.

Darting through sidewalk traffic, Sheldon was half crying and half laughing. This was certainly the most trouble he'd ever incited, and although he was terrified of what consequences awaited him upon capture, the excitement was too alluring. Still confounded as to a destination, especially now with the pressure of the police bearing down, Sheldon ran in all directions at once, jogging left, darting right, running in circles then doubling back in the opposite direction. He ran out into busy streets, dodging cars and fast-moving trollies, the passengers on which yelled and barked at him when they saw the policeman in pursuit. He ran past street vendors and accidentally bumped into a delivery man who fumbled and then dropped his crates of milk, spilling the white gold over the sidewalk, much to the delight of some stray dogs. For a moment, Sheldon felt a jolt of remorse about his recklessness, but a second later his remorse was chomped on, chewed up, and spit out by the monster called mischievous thrill.

As he leaped over a pile of boxes — possibly a house for some poor, unfortunate guttersnipe — he looked back to see if the policeman had successfully surmounted the hobo hotel and ran smack into a large, broad man, bringing the shenanigans to immediate arrest. The human wall grabbed hold of the boy firmly, his herculean hands wrapping almost twice around the kid's biceps. Frightened, Sheldon looked up to see a deeply tanned, bucolic face framing sympathetic eyes asking, 'Why are you running?'

The man wore a thick head of blonde hair that flowed like a river into an unkempt, golden beard. Together, the tangled mop gave the impression of a lion's mane. But this lion bore no long, sharp teeth, Sheldon noted as the man's welcoming smile reassured that all was well and he was friendly. This cat was wearing an army uniform, looking as though he were either off to the war overseas or had just returned. He released Sheldon's left arm but held firmly, yet gently, onto his right. "Slow down there, fella. Where's the fire?"

Sheldon opened his mouth, but as before, failed to push any words out. "You okay?" the man prodded, tilting his head to one side. Sheldon just stared silently with his mouth agape, so the soldier slowed his speech. "Where … are … your ... folks?" Still breathing hard, Sheldon shifted his eyes away from the soldier, back in the direction he'd been running. Noting the boy's preoccupation, the soldier glanced down the sidewalk. "Is someone chasin' ya?"

Just then, the tenacious policeman rounded the far corner of the block, out of both breath and patience. Upon seeing the soldier with the apprehended youth, the cop began shoving his way through the crowd, pointing, blowing his whistle, and crying out, "Stop that boy!"

Put off by the gruff manner of the policeman, the soldier turned his attention back to his captive. As he did, he noted the unusual tooth pendant hanging around Sheldon's neck. With his free hand, the man reached down and gently took the pendant in his massive palm for closer inspection.

"Now this is a curious trinket." The man looked Sheldon in the eyes and was met with desperation mixed with a hint of what the lion recognized from years of combat as innocent fear. Taking pity on the boy, the soldier suspended judgment and allowed himself a moment of nostalgia for his own rascally childhood. Then, without realizing, caught in distant recapitulation, the lion-man loosened his grip on the boy's arm. Immediately, Sheldon shook off the giant hand and darted away, but not before turning back with a smile and a wave of gratitude.

That was Sheldon's first encounter with a real soldier, and it was not one he would soon forget — especially since he miscalculated his escape and ran off with his pendant still sitting squarely in the palm of the lion-man's hand

"Wait! Hey, kid!" the soldier called out, surprised by the boy's sudden departure. But it was too late. Sheldon wasn't about to stop running so the police could catch him. Unfortunately, the pendant had become entangled in the soldier's large fingers as Sheldon wriggled free, and he was too full of adrenaline to feel the rusty chain snap from around his neck as he jerked away.

As the policeman bolted by, he scowled at the soldier for letting the fugitive go. In defiant response, the lion raised his pendant-adorned fist at Sheldon and cheered, "Give 'em hell, kid!"

Chapter Four

A Long Walk

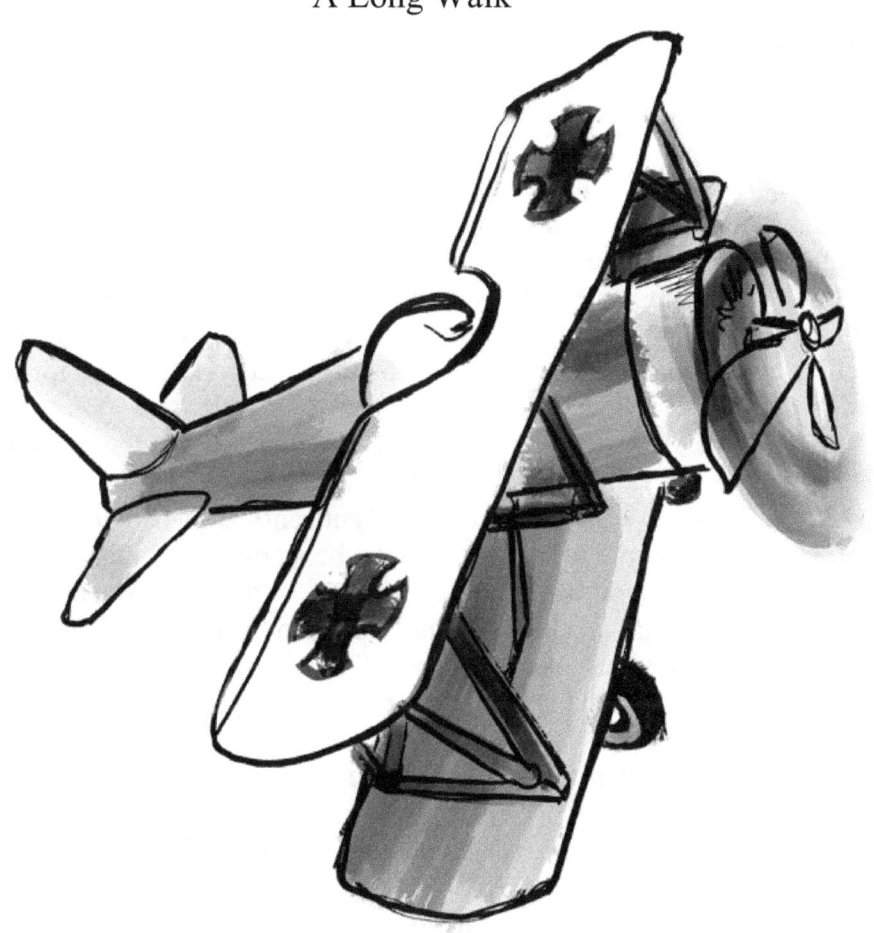

The young outlaw ran until his lungs burned and his legs felt like noodles. Eventually, he came to rest in front of a large department store with glass walls and fancy gold lettering that glowed in the incident light of the late morning...

A steady stream of patrons flowed in and out of the entryway, busying themselves with grown-up tasks, ignoring the goings-on of the natural world persisting all around them despite the sterile concrete and steel. Wonderfully crisp, spring air sang sweetly into deaf ears. Brilliant sunlight danced playfully in front of blind eyes. Insects and birds and rodents scuttled about in anonymity, busy building bridges connecting miniature islands of stubborn life refusing to submit: A tuft of weeds pushing through eventual cracks in a sidewalk too old and tired to resist; a makeshift life-raft-of-a-bird's-nest sheltering in the crook of a rusted lamp post. Catching his breath, Sheldon paused to admire the miracle of this otherwise invisible world. The more he looked and listened, the more of it he saw and heard. Even here in the city drab — man's monumental effort to keep the wild spaces out — nature could yet be found for those with eyes to see it and ears to hear it.

There he stood on the busy sidewalk, considering the freedom of the open streets versus the potential for losing his pursuers amongst the chaos of commerce. A nudge from his gut sent his glance upwards and he felt a sudden urge to move on lest he be smushed by a falling piano, iron safe, or air conditioner set loose from an overhead apartment window like a guard dog off its chain. Placing a hand to his forehead in a military salute, he shielded his eyes from the sunlight and surveyed the windows upon windows stacked like a vertical glass highway stretching all the way to heaven. There were no flying pianos... unless they were invisible flying pianos — those being the most dangerous sort, of course. Still, he felt it was best to not stand in one spot, just in case. He calmed his nerves with a deep breath through expanded nostrils, calmed his disheveled hair with a pass of a licked-wet hand over his head, then slipped — a lost minnow joining a school of fish — into the busy store.

He wandered around for a good amount of time, marveling at all the bright and clean and novel items available to those who could afford such things, which was not his family. Gold and silver necklaces sparkled viciously at him. 'Keep dreaming, kid,' they scoffed as they came to rest on necks wreathed in the fur of dead animals. Sheldon shook his head, not in envy but in pity, and walked on.

He passed displays of modern conveniences for kitchens and bathrooms; displays of more shoes than were feet in the world to fill them, more hats than heads to hold them; displays advertising luggage and gelato. *That's an odd combination*, he thought. He wandered into a music shop with ten or more pianos on the showroom floor and began lightly tapping a haunting tune, until some official-looking lad who was playing at being a plumber shooed him away with a dripping wet plunger. He stopped in front of a window to marvel at an array of television sets, each playing the same show about three bumbling men with silly-looking haircuts, poking fun at one another while getting into all sorts of mischief. When he noticed the reflection in the television screens of people behind him beginning to stare, no doubt curious about a lone child in the city during school hours, he lowered his head and quickly moseyed off in the general flow of traffic. Realizing that he was likely to catch the attention of a security guard eventually, he diverged from the school of nosey fish and slipped through the nearest exit — which did not spit him out onto the same street from which he entered.

Here the buildings were entirely unfamiliar and much larger than the ones in his Palmer Square neighborhood. The streets here were darkened by buildings scraping the underbelly of the cosmos, like giants, blocking out the morning sun climbing ever higher on its slow-moving, invisible escalator. The boy's emotions volleyed between apprehension and amazement at the looming titans, replacing his thoughts about pursuing policemen with a daydream wherein he was the adventurous Jack Spriggins, coursing through the clouds amongst man-eating giants, golden-egg-laying hens, and magical singing harps. Unlike the unfriendly necklaces in the store, the golden harps of *his* castle in the sky — rays of magnificent sun — shined on him like a spotlight of fortune, giving him a fleeting sense of importance, dare he say *royalty*. But it was not to last. The golden glow became so bright it jolted him out of his dream like an electric shock.

He immediately recognized the familiar flash as his aberrant luminous guide. She was back, and so he resumed his pursuit of her. He had to. What choice did he have but to seek out her source, her purpose in contacting him, the reason why she kept calling to him? Beyond this mission he hadn't any plan. He was simply responding to the whispers of the world, the will of nature, the whims of this strange and wonderful guiding glow. The lack of a master plan in his meanderings didn't bother him so much. In fact, he rather enjoyed this little bit of 'living by the seat of one's pants,' going as the wind blows — or in this case, as the sun shines. Normal life for Sheldon wasn't like this. Most days he felt powerless, like the world moved on around him, despite him, regardless, and well beyond his control. Such was the catalyst for his incessant daydreaming, because at least with daydreaming one can control what happens... mostly. This adventure felt different, however. He still felt small and powerless below such impressive buildings, amidst all this street traffic, all these busy people coming and going, with important places to be and things to do. But, small and powerless or not, there he was, entirely by his own free will. He had created his current situation and that was a sort of power, he figured. This time, even if it was by accident, he was pursuing a largely aimless pursuit, following these strange flashes from some invisible, heavenly lighthouse spinning in long, slow circles over the earth. In this way, the adventure itself had become its own destination. All he knew was that each time he saw the flash he felt compelled to move, as if a friend were prodding him gently. "Time to go, Sheldon." So, without a real destination but with plenty of energy, he ran on, fueled by the confluence of instinct, light, and this sturdy sidewalk under his feet.

He ran until the giants of glass and steel yielded to shorter and longer stone buildings with smaller windows or no windows at all. In places where windows might have been there were large signs or murals painted over brick, identifying manufacturing and processing plants, textile factories, mills, canneries, tanneries, utility stations... The industrial sector, even though it felt more familiar, also felt more deserted, less inviting.

Sheldon's run settled to a walk as he scrutinized one building after another, becoming ever more familiar with his city so obviously full of fascinating history. How ingenious were the original architects of industry? How skilled were the masons of civilization's foundations? What spirits still haunted these age-old buildings, these serpentine streets? He shivered. The chill of this dark part of town was palpable. He began to miss his jacket, *Which the cops now have*! He frowned, rubbing his arms and hugging himself. Where was his warm, luminous friend now? His head swiveled like a weathervane in a storm, looking for the spotlight, and for signs that people might be following him. Surely curious eyes must be watching him from within the old warehouses. As usual, no one seemed the least bit interested in him. Alone and anonymous he walked on, quietly observing the slow transition of Chicago's industrial sector shrinking into quaint, suburban neighborhoods, as this strange and wonderful day stretched out, reaching ever farther for new hours on which to feed.

The sun was well past its zenith when Sheldon paused to rehydrate at a park fountain. The large city buildings had become a thing of the past, replaced by small mom-and-pop shops, modest houses, and well-groomed green spaces. A group of kids were enjoying a game of basketball. Sheldon wondered if perhaps they too were playing hooky from school, a thought which made him feel less alone. Only slightly, however, for unlike his kind, these kids were suburbanites. There were many things separating him from his peers at Darwin, but in this one thing they were aligned: they loathed the kids from the suburbs, and the suburban kids loathed the inner-city kids right back. It was a mutually agreeable rivalry. He had to admit, however, that he was rather enjoying his walk through suburbia. It was quite nice actually, calm and bright and inviting, like coming home and falling on the couch after a long day. But this place was more comfortable than even the davenport in his living room. Out here there wasn't the constant harangue of the apartment. Here, there were no parents arguing or yelling at one another, or at him. Here his dad wasn't berating and belittling him. Out here, he could breathe.

This perspective yielded a new appreciation for the outer bands of the atom in which he existed. Somewhere a slight *creak* could be heard as his mind opened and expanded. His judgment against suburban Chicagoans, which had felt as normal as putting on the same pair of shoes every day, now felt uncomfortable, antiquated, constraining for his maturing soul. He stretched his torso to match his broadening mind. Standing up straight and tall he looked over his shoulder and immediately his eyes widened to compliment a silly grin instantly sweeping across his face as if by brushstroke. An old-fashioned soda fountain shop was calling his name. He stopped in his tracks and drooled at the thought of a sundae or root beer float; until his eyes yanked his attention away from the sugary treats to something even sweeter: motorcycles!

Keeping good company with the soda parlor was a repair garage where several shiny, newer-looking bikes sat on display. The fugitive began toying with the notion of jumping on one of them and speeding off into the sunset. There was only one problem with his plan… Actually, there were at least a dozen problems with this plan, one being that the sun wouldn't be setting for another five or six hours.

"Okay, so maybe putter off into the *eventual* sunset," he chuckled.

The bigger problem was that Sheldon didn't know *how* to drive a motorcycle. *But I could learn! Yes! I could get a job in the repair shop right here and now! Never go back to school!* He figured he could become a master mechanic and restore old Indians, Husqvarnas, and Harley-Davidsons to their full glory. He could build himself a safari-ready enduro and ride across the African continent on the ultimate two-wheeled adventure. *Yes! That's it!* he mused. He would seek out the great Zulu king and teach him to ride a wheelie. He would race a cheetah for top land speed record. He would ride to the top of Mount Kilimanjaro and proclaim from the roof of Africa for all to see and hear, that the great Sheldon Silvers was the first motorcyclist in history to triumph over the wild continent!

"Well, that settles it," he wagged a finger at destiny. "The bike will have to be a Triumph!" And when his great escapade was utterly spent, having conquered the most incredible features and elements, zebras and elephants, the world's wildest continent could throw at him, he would sell his trophy bike and buy himself an airplane, fly off over the savannah, across the Rift Valley and the dark Congo, out over the vast Atlantic, to his next grand adventure in the uncharted Amazon! Or perchance he might go east to the Himalayas! Just one problem: (just one?) he didn't know how to fly a plane.

Onward, Sheldon noticed other boys about his age hard at work baling hay or delivering newspapers on bicycles or scrubbing car tires at fueling stations. He felt slightly jealous and wondered why he couldn't just drop out of school and take up the occupation of drawing and writing stories. His father wouldn't object to him dropping out so long as he went to work at the bakery full-time... *Yeah, never mind. I think I'll stay in school, thanks.* As he strolled, he entertained himself, humming a tune to narrate his journey.

Wandering by a pungent delicatessen,
Cuts of pork and poultry on display,
I shake my head and lament with bitter sorrow,
How innocent animals are treated in this way.
I pass a barbershop and watch with glee,
As a man with a double nose and double chin,
Sips a glass of golden grown-up tea,
While taking in a shave and mustache trim.
A general store painfully reminds me,
I've had no lunch and now am starving hungry.
Oh, how I wish I had a nickel or a penny,
To buy myself a chocolate or some candy.

A shoe sales and cobbler shop followed the general store and Sheldon, soles feeling worn thin from so much walking, smirked at the thought of popping in to get his feet repaired. A large mercantile hobby shop rounded out commercial row, queuing up several dozen homes scattered here and there, each with nice big yards, most with laundry hung out to dry, some with small play sets for children.

The quaint town shops and cookie-cutter houses became less and less frequent until, eventually, the surroundings opened to vast stretches of farmland with the occasional ranch house stuck in the far corner of a windrow-lined plot. The serenity of the countryside soothed any remaining anxiety Sheldon felt as a result of running away from school and the subsequent police chase. Though he had never lived anywhere but the city, he felt right at home there in farm country. He even found himself chatting with the odd cow or flock of sheep. Upon seeing some horses running and playing in a nearby field, he traded in his African motorcycle fantasy for an Arabian horseback fantasy.

Long robes of silk flowing wildly in his wake as he races along sandy peaks in an endless sea of scorching dunes. A merciless sun works overtime, extracting every last bead of moisture from both rider and stallion. They're a raging haboob, moving as one, like a cobra on the hunt, driven by mad thirst, carving a disappearing trail atop drifting sand in relentless pursuit of the bazaar at the oasis. Giant palm trees sway in the distance, calling to them like sirens at sea signaling safe harbor. And yet, the distant sanctuary, shimmering in the sweltering heat, tenaciously holds fast to an ever-elusive horizon. Could it be… a mirage???

"Nooooo!" Sheldon bellowed in a dramatic whisper, arms flapping in the air. He broke into a laugh, quite satisfied with his *Arabian Nights* detour, and walked on. After some time, the endless farmland became rather monotonous and his gaze drifted lazily southward, fixating on his shuffling shoes.

'Swoosh, swoosh, swoosh,' went his sneakers, back and forth, back and forth. His mind became lost in the rhythmic pendulum of his feet swinging in step with the cracks in this persistent pavement, this walkway of wonders that had carried him from the city, through suburbia, beyond rural Chicago, and out past the Illinois farm fields.

"Careful now," he mused. "Mustn't step on the crack or we'll break mamma's... Oops! Sorry ma!" He laughed, enjoying this late afternoon stroll, a nowhere man all alone in nowhere land.

'Swish, swish,' sounded his pants as they shuffled. 'Swoosh, swoosh,' replied his sneakers. It was a textile discourse about the simple meaning of— *What's this?*

He stopped and bent down to pick up what appeared to be a wooden jigsaw puzzle piece lying lonely on the sidewalk. As he did, he suddenly became aware of the missing pendant no longer hanging around his neck, which otherwise might have brushed across his face when he bent down.

"Wha?! NO!"

He stood bolt upright, grasping his shirt collar, patting himself all over, desperately searching in case the pendant had become entangled in his clothes somewhere. *It must've fallen off when I was running*, he told himself, lamenting the loss of his unique treasure. He turned and for half a second considered going back for it but quickly conceded there would be no point. It was gone.

Feeling sad and angry, he bent down and picked up the lonely puzzle piece — a consolation prize to replace his pendant — along with some stones. He took to chucking rocks at an old tin can by the side of the road and that made him feel a little better.

Examining the puzzle piece, half covered in dirt that didn't seem to want to come off no matter how much spit he dripped on it, he could see that it was mostly blue with some red speckled here and there. The word 'image' was stamped on it in faded white lettering with the 'e' at the end smudged such that it looked more like an 'i'.

"Image... Well, duh," he scoffed, turning the piece over. The back side was blank and covered in more dirt than the front. It was impossible to tell into what larger picture this piece might fit. There were so many possibilities. Sheldon instantly empathized with this lonely fragment, seemingly minuscule and insignificant and already labeled in the most obvious way. Yet, certainly there was more to the story. Certainly this individual piece contributed in a unique way to a bigger picture. Certainly without this particular piece the whole story would forever be incomplete.

Interesting, he thought as he placed the piece in his pocket and stood up. He looked out over the fields and considered the bigger picture into which he fit. He faced the low sun in the west, whose diminished light now gave the wheat fields a warm, golden glow, and he thought about his life in that moment. This boy, this unique puzzle piece, despite still not having a defined purpose for leaving school and walking so far away, was overcome with the sense that things were slowly coming together, not falling apart.

That was the moment he became aware of the missing road. The tarmac had apparently quit some time back, and this concrete walkway on which he stood was now chaperoned only by rough gravel. He contemplated the absence of asphalt and the absence of traffic, the absence of houses and towns and people.

Wrapped in an eerie sense of aloneness, his gaze drifted upwards. The sun had only another hour or so before it would head off to shine on some other, distant land.

The thought of impending darkness startled him and he began running again — slowly at first, hesitation providing resistance as though he were moving through water. Overcoming doubt with a renewed sense of adventure, he was soon running as fast as he could, trying to race the sunlight, to keep the night at bay. Eventually, he conceded that he was only racing further into darkness. His run slowed to a jog before he stopped altogether.

Struggling to catch his runaway breath, he glanced back in the direction he'd come. Instantly a fog of sadness fell over him, the weight of which sent him to his knees. There he knelt, wondering about his predicament. There would likely come a time when he would miss the attention of his troubled family, the comfort and safety of his noisy home, the warm yet small meals, even the militarized routine of Darwin. But not yet.

As unappealing as the thought of returning home was, even more compelling was the feeling that he would be giving up on something were he to turn back. What exactly, he did not know, but he could feel it, deep in his gut. He had to keep going despite the darkness creeping toward him from the far end of the sidewalk like ruffians on a playground stalking their prey. He could feel his courage draining. That's when he saw it again: his luminous friend flashing a timely ray of hope. It was so obviously the same beam of light that had awakened him to this fateful day, had called him out and away from school, had guided him safely away from the police, then compelled him all this way out into the world, so very far from home.

"What are you?" he whispered. The light twinkled secretively, excitedly, as if it had a present hiding behind its back and couldn't wait for him to open it.

To the west, emerging from a low-hanging cloud, the setting sun flashed a complimentary glow, signaling its retirement and passing of the torch to the mysterious guiding light. In response, like an eager youth entrusted with an important task, the easterly illumination shined brighter than ever, brandishing a steady glow, no longer intermittent and fleeting, no longer obscured by dropped curtains, closed doors, or giant buildings. Sheldon stood up to witness his brilliant friend, and as he did, he caught sight of the bigger picture. His gaze lazily drifted out over the remarkably vast and wild landscape, no roads to define it or fences to corral it. This was the first time he could recall being able to see all the way to the natural horizon in all directions. All around him was open land and endless sky as far as the eye could see. He felt his soul take a long, deep breath in a way entirely new. Inside, a voice comforted him with inaudible words, like a friend placing a gentle hand around his shoulder. Reassured, he turned away from the sorrowful walk home and embraced the exciting walk to...

...wherever this rogue sidewalk would lead.

Chapter Five

A Light in the Attic

Sheldon was starving, exhausted, and terribly thirsty, but he also felt renewed by this new experience of soul freedom, the excitement of untold adventures propelling him toward this mysterious spotlight still shining on him as if he were the main event. He was too excited to walk, and so he ran (mostly skipped actually, but that's our secret), until the source of the light suddenly came into view, stopping him instantly in his tracks. The gravel road from town, which had now devolved into a narrow, red dirt two-track, led right to the only house he'd seen for what must have been hours.

There it is!

Just up ahead stood a magnificent old farmhouse, painted all white save for a faded red roof, from the top of which protruded a tall, narrow attic, brilliantly lit from the inside, giving it the look of a lighthouse on a cliff. The tall grass surrounding the house bent and swayed in the wind like waves on the ocean. Despite being nowhere near the sea, sounds of gulls and crashing waves could be heard in the distance. Sheldon's imagination was winding up again. He spotted a clipper ship coursing the turbulent farmland waters, bowing to one side then the other in respect to the wind and waves.

Hmmm. Pirates!

Beyond the house he could see the sidewalk stretching onward, disappearing into a dark forest, beckoning him to deeper adventure. He looked back from where he had come. There appeared to be nothing in either direction, nothing but the farmhouse. Knocking at the front door now while he still had a sliver of light by which to escape if necessary, seemed his only option if he didn't want to sleep outside, alone in the cold. Besides, he was eager to finally pin down the source of this perplexing light.

The setting sun cast a warm flush over the house, putting the boy's mind at ease with a hunch that the nicest family lived there. He imagined a father, with a gentle smile and kind eyes, washing up for supper after a long and tiring but rewarding day in the fields. The man's dear wife was brushing an egg-white glaze atop an apple pie before setting it in the oven to crisp, their two children already seated quietly at the table. She was the sweetest mom, always attentive and never cross. The kids were obedient and well-mannered. The wayward youth wouldn't be an intrusion at all. He would be welcomed graciously and would be well-looked-after until his parents could come collect him. Surely these good folks would have a telephone he could use. If not, of course Mr. Thompson (Sheldon had already named the family) would drive him home first thing after supper.

Sheldon was convinced. He pushed the white picket gate open and began walking confidently to the front door. The sound of steel clicking behind him made him jump and he froze at the thought that he had made a terrible mistake and now stood at the dangerous end of a cocked rifle. He slowly glanced back.

"Just the gate," he reassured himself with a slight grin, admitting that perhaps he'd been too liberal with his imagination as of late. Continuing towards the house, he licked his lips in anticipation of a glorious meal. As he climbed the porch steps — careful not to trip on the old, twisting wood treads, curling upward at the ends, trying to break free — he noticed a peculiar wooden sign hanging high on the door.

'Jays dwell here and sunbeams too.'

"Wonder what that means," he queried aloud to the evening. In the distance, a jaybird screeched. He might have been frightened by the ominous reply were it not for his stomach growling out closing arguments, convincing him that he could already smell the apple pie baking in the oven. "My goodness!" he delighted quietly as he gave the Marley knocker a few good raps before stepping back and straightening his posture for presentation to the Thompson family.

But no one answered.

They must be busy laughing and sharing stories of the day. His stomach grumbled, complaining about the delay, teased by imaginings of roast chicken with perfectly crisped, golden-brown skin the color of the countryside; mounds of creamed potatoes complimented with pats of melting butter slipping down like sleds on a hill of snow; tugboat mushrooms floating in meandering rivers of gravy; freshly-felled trees of broccoli waiting to be milled, lain alongside whole logs of red and white carrots...

The carrots he could stomach, but he'd never been fond of broccoli. "And yet, given our famished state..." his imagination argued, "...of course we wouldn't want to be rude..." It was settled: he would even be enjoying his vegetables tonight.

You're daydreaming again. He shook himself back to reality, realizing he'd probably been standing on the porch for several long minutes, gorging on naught but illusion. *What's taking them? The pie should be out of the oven by now!*

He wiped the drool from his chin and hammered the brass knocker, this time much harder. Taking a step back, he held his breath. Behind him, the last slivers of sunlight whispered, "Farewell and good luck!" from below the distant tree line. Darkness charged over the eastern hills like the migration of ten thousand crows, and as the lighting over the landscape changed, so did the boy's perception of the farmhouse. The warm light that made him feel safe had turned stale and cold while he waited on the porch. Sheldon's brilliant and beautiful lighthouse had suddenly gone lifeless as if turned to stone by the terrible Medusa. Forgetting the food momentarily, he jumped from the porch and peered up at the attic window from where the beacon light had originated, hopeful that the friendly beam would reassure his fading spirit. But the window had also gone dark. It now looked like the surface of a northern lake in winter, not frozen, but completely still and silvery, almost mirror-like.

Had it all been an illusion?

He had to concede the illogic of a single light from the attic of a rural farmhouse being seen from miles away, deep in the urban labyrinth, unobstructed by trees or buildings or telephone poles or chimneys...

This makes no sense. A whisper of a thought sailed through his mind like a ghost ship. Thoroughly confused, he jumped up on the porch again and, in a fit of frustration and desperation, pounded on the door, nearly breaking through the aged wood planks. Immediately he regretted his outburst, as this would certainly upset the otherwise mild-mannered Mr. Thompson.

In a panic, he turned and bolted from the house, running as fast as he could back down the walkway. He didn't bother with the gate, choosing instead to launch himself over the fence. But as he pushed off the top of the pickets with both hands, flinging his legs high in the air uncontrollably, one of his pantlegs became ensnared in a bush of climbing roses also trying to escape, and he tumbled to the ground, hitting the back of his head hard on the concrete before coming to rest, face down on the sidewalk.

For several minutes he lay motionless from pain, dizziness, and fear, hoping that he was below the sightline of Mr. Thompson's rifle irons. Surely the man of the house must now be standing guard with his firearm trained on the commotion in the twilight, ready to defend his beloved family... and his dinner, which was now getting cold thanks to this interruption!

Sheldon felt emotion swelling in his eyes with the realization that he would never get to enjoy the delicious roast chicken and the company of this sweet family. Succumbing to exhaustion, frustration, and hunger, tears began to flow uncontrollably and he slammed his fists on the concrete, feeling thoroughly betrayed by his closest friend: this cruel, overactive imagination.

Chapter Six

Where the Sidewalk Ends

As he lay on the sidewalk, too angry and afraid to move, Sheldon felt a soothing warmth seep up through his clothes, calming his nerves. The sunlight that had been absorbed by the concrete throughout that hard but rewarding day was now radiating back out like memory...

Closing his eyes, he calmed his breath and recalled the events of the day: the repellent babble inside his house, the droning nonsense of school, the exciting police chase, the discovery of new places and new freedoms, and now this wide-open space with room for his spirit to roam. But did he roam too far?

With a sigh, he whisper-sang...

> *Here lies Sheldon. What a life he almost had!*
> *Born a playful pup, warned never to grow up.*
> *But he grow'd up just the same,*
> *And departed without a name.*
> *...And that's all that ever happened to the lad!*

With another sigh and a shift in his posture to align his body with the uneven sidewalk, he carefully placed an arm behind his throbbing head and looked up at the billowing clouds of dusk. The first stars of the evening were clocking in for the night shift, countless shades of blue blending ever darker as this most peculiar day yielded to untold adventures of night.

The sidewalk felt so warm and comforting that he thought he might just sleep right there were it not for his restless mind attempting to reel in the bizarre circumstance of the light in the attic. Finding that task nothing short of impossible, Sheldon surrendered his thoughts, deciding instead to admire the appearance of ever more stars in the sky, gathering like a reunion of old friends.

Looking up at the heavens he was reminded of a curious story his mother read to him and his kid sister. He imagined himself as the boy prince who lived on the small star with his only friend, a delicate rose. He recalled the images of the prince traveling from planet to planet in search of a cure for his ailing friend, his soulmate, his—

WHAT IN THE COSMOS WAS THAT?!

With a jolt, he sat up and watched as something rocketed by just overhead, flying low and fast across the sky.

"Smokes!" he gasped, tracing the object as it sailed off in the direction where the sidewalk led, to the now-very-dark forest. The thing was soaring too low and looked too small to be an airplane, but it was much too large to be a bird — any bird that he knew of anyway. Forgetting the pain in his head he jumped to his feet and took a step towards the trees, then paused, unsure what to do. Thinking he heard a faint cry for help, he sputtered forward, little by little, listening as the distress call trailed off in the wake of the puzzling flying thing, over the trees and out of sight.

Unable to resist his lust for adventure, his walk turned to a full sprint until the grip of fear squeezed the courage from him like juice from a lemon. His run slowed to a putter, sneakers dragging on the sidewalk for brakes, before he eventually stopped still. But not from fear as it turned out. Instead, he was halted by a sudden realization that ensnared his curiosity.

He glanced down at his feet. He looked to his left and then to his right. He looked behind him and then spun around in a circle. The farmhouse was no longer within view. There were no buildings or even building lights to be seen anywhere. Even the dirt road was gone. He was surrounded by tall, dry weeds so blonde they appeared to glow in the moonlight. He found himself smack in the middle of an open field, guarded in the distance by primeval forest. Yet, despite nothing but fields and forest and wildland, the sidewalk remained.

There he stood, a small boy on a lonely sidewalk in the middle of nowhere, his only company a handful of stars in a fledgling night sky and the chirping of a solitary bird bathing contentedly in the crescent moonlight. The setting felt magical and welcoming in a way that helped assuage his fear, and he was suddenly compelled to seek out the ultimate destination of this persistent pathway.

He took a few steps, testing his resolve. Feeling brave, the intrepid explorer trudged on, marveling at his surroundings and imagining what wonders awaited at the terminus of this walkway.

Surely it must lead to something important, he reasoned with an excitement that catalyzed an increasingly brisk pace. *After all, who would put all this work into such a nice sidewalk for nothing?* He wondered if it might pass all the way through the dark forest. *Perhaps it goes all the way to Lake Michigan or the Mississippi River. I know! I'll bet it goes to—*

SPLISH!

He stopped, his back foot still on solid sidewalk, but his front now bathing in the shallow end of a boggy marsh.

"Ugh!" He tossed his head back and rolled his eyes. Eventually, his gaze settled on a peculiar wooden sign just there to his right. On the sign was painted the obvious 'Sidewalk Ends' in clear, bold lettering. He stood for a moment staring at the pithy guidepost, one foot soaking in a swamp, the other still connected — albeit by many miles — to the city, to home.

Home, he thought, *where mother makes me wash my hands and father makes constant demands; where sister yells and sister cries, and inspiration withers and dies.*

He looked at the sign, looked at the forest, looked at his foot in the puddle, then back toward home. "Can't go back. Notchet. ... I wanna see what's out there. I want to explore. There must be something in the world for me. There must be something more!"

He looked down again at the puddle.

"Oh, hello."

Staring back at him was an upside-down reflection of his youthful face dancing in the ripples and illuminated by the rising moon.

"Maybe *I* am the reflection and *you* are right-side up? Perhaps in another world, you are *liked* for being weird, or maybe you're not weird at all. Maybe in another world, you're normal and it's weird *not* to be weird, to *not* imagine and daydream and make-believe and..." His words trailed off. He withdrew his foot from the water and planted it firmly back on what remained of civilization.

Standing there at the threshold to the wilderness, the edge of the unknown, swamp water draining from his left shoe, he might have been scared out of his wits were it not for a decent moonlight penetrating the canopy, inspiring a calming chirp-song from the persistent midnight bird. A grove of fascinatingly twisted oaks appeared as moonbeam dripped over the landscape like bright acrylic on black canvas. The forest now seemed more familiar than frightening, and there was an odd smell of peppermint in the air (which is always reassuring, wouldn't you agree?).

"So, this is where the sidewalk ends," he spoke out loud to the forest. "Now what?"

As if in response to his query, he suddenly heard again the cry for help and was jolted from his peppermint chill. Had he any notion of what was to transpire, he might've paused to reconsider. He might've turned and gone home. But how was he to know?

He peered up at the sign that called out a clear and final transition between the known world and the mysteries of the beyond, as if to look civilization square in the eye to say goodbye, and then deliberately and confidently stepped off the sidewalk into the unknown,

...being careful not to step in the soggy marsh again.

Chapter Seven, Part I

Falling Up

Once free from the predetermined pathway, Sheldon stood motionless, holding his breath to see if he would implode or maybe get hauled off by some wild thing. But nothing happened. It turned out that the dark, scary woods, like most people he encountered, couldn't have cared less about him. He exhaled deeply at the anticlimax of what he considered to be a symbolic and monumental achievement, and couldn't help but feel disappointed that there wasn't some great, universal celebration at his triumph of shedding the constructs of authority, breaking the bonds of discipline, cutting the cords of—

Wait. What's happening?

He suddenly felt himself shedding something much more tangible than authority: gravity!

As if under some spell, his feet began lifting off the ground. He scrambled wildly, grasping for any tree branch within reach, finding naught but air.

"Hey! Whoa! Aaaaah! Wait... WAAAIIIT! HELLLP!" Now *he* was the one calling for help as he realized he was floating up like a helium balloon cut loose at a birthday party. Gravity — or some force like it — was pulling on him but entirely in the wrong direction! At some good distance off the ground, he was finally able to grab hold of a small branch. That only served to slow him down momentarily, however, before the branch gave way, snapping off the tree and smacking him on the head in a bon voyage love tap of, "Good luck out there, kid!"

There was no resisting the force pulling him away from the Earth. Thus, he sped faster and faster outward, onward, upward, falling freely up, up, up at near-terminal-velocity when suddenly—

CRASH!

He landed hard on something — or rather *in* something; something that was moving; something that was flying; something that smelled of burnt coffee and old socks.

Chapter Seven, Part II

The Festoon Brigade

"*What was that?*"
"Uhhh… I think we just caught a bird!"
"Well, give it 'a me so's I can add 'er to the stew!"

Sheldon landed in what felt like (and smelled like) a pile of laundry. He tried to stand up but immediately stumbled in response to the zigzagging of the flying object in which he found himself. Tripping over something hard, he fell back into the pile of fabric and sundries: shirts, pants, linens, socks... *Is that... underwear?*

With the constant jolting and fumbling about, he became entangled in the laundry, unable to see where he was or what was going on. The more he struggled, the more the laundry clung to him, like the burrs and foxtails on his pantlegs after running through empty lots on his way to and from school. But there were more than just clingy clothes in this pile. Items that felt like books, blocks, pots, and pans kept tramping on his toes, knocking against his knees, and whacking him upside the head. He yelled out in frustration, "AAARGH!"

"Whoa, now! That ain't no bird!" said an anxious voice.

"Well don't just stand there, grab holda it!" said another, more bossy voice.

From within the laundry pile, Sheldon felt a hand grab his ankle and give a tug before quickly letting go.

"Hey!" he protested.

"It's massive. I ain't gettin' near it!"

"Well, what is it?!" asked the bossy voice.

"Here, hit it with this," said another, holding out a large wooden spoon.

Sheldon felt a rapping on his shoulder, a poke around his midsection, and a prod to his legs. "Quit it!" he demanded, grunting and thrashing about, trying to fight off both the laundry and the incessant poking.

"Ahhh! It's a monster!" shrieked one of them.

"Abandon ship!" yelled another.

"The Festoon's been compromised! Every flyer for himself!" cried a third.

"HELP!" All three called out in unison amongst a great deal of commotion and running about. Three thumps, followed by a loud crash, rocked the vessel enough to knock Sheldon over again. Upon landing, his eyes found a hole in the clothes pile and he got his first glimpse of his surroundings. Reaching out, he grabbed hold of something solid and pulled himself up to get a look at the scene, astonished to discover that he appeared to be flying in some sort of open-topped airplane, shaped oddly like... a shoe!

A flash of light in the distance ensnared his attention. It was the same farmhouse about fifty feet or so below them, fading into the darkness, and the light in the attic was on, once again shining brightly, a cheerful beacon in an otherwise utterly cantankerous night.

"What?!" He grabbed his head to keep it from spinning off, then stole a second glance to make sure he wasn't seeing things. Sure enough! The light in the house attic was inexplicably glowing once more. And then, as if winking at him, the light flashed off and back on again in one last goodbye before passing beyond view.

Confusion and disorientation allowed him to forget for a moment that he was in a flying shoe-thing with three unknown creatures, and Sheldon's attention drifted to the dark expanse of the night sky, settling uneasily on the great mass of lights well beyond the farm.

Must be Chicago...

He locked his thoughts on the fading skyline and watched the lights slip beyond view as the vessel sailed ever higher, up through the low clouds of this impossible spring evening. A cloud of loneliness descended over him until a gentle nudge from a curious breeze — more peppermint — reminded him that there were others on board this shoe-ship-thing.

Or were there? Where did they go? He looked around nervously but saw no one.

"They're gone," he whispered cautiously, mind racing. *I frightened them away. They all jumped overboard!* "Ha! Triumph!" he exclaimed to the night, before pausing to scratch his head. "Now what?" His eyes shifted, taking stock of the situation.

(We already established that he didn't know how to fly a plane. He *certainly* didn't know how to fly a shoe!)

Hang on! What's this?

Three lumps lay on the floor of the ship, all about his size, perhaps a smidge smaller, each with a long beard and different style of hat, and all sleeping, apparently. That, or dead.

They're like Cinderella's dwarves, he thought. *No, that's Sleeping Beauty... Whatever...*

He glanced about the ship, wondering how in the world the thing was flying, especially given that the crew appeared to be unconscious on the floor.

"Hey!" he yelled at the three dwarf-looking lumps. His hands jerked to his mouth to keep any more nonsense from spilling out, realizing there could be more of them hiding and that he should probably exercise a tad more stealth.

Doncha think you oughta maybe tie 'em up first and THEN wake 'em up? he argued to himself.

"Well, where might I find some rope?" he replied aloud.

"How about a shoelace?" himself answered.

Through small portholes at the ship's sides, a thick rope weaved in and out like laces in a shoe, one end dangling conveniently at Sheldon's feet. He grabbed the rope and began dragging it to where the sleeping lumps lay. But as he did, the lace became taut and — *WHOOSH!* — the entire ship pitched steeply to one side. The unexpected shift threw Sheldon off balance and he stumbled across the deck, arms waving, searching for something to hold onto. All he could find was the rope already in his hands, so he tugged on that for support. Unfortunately, the rope turned out to be a control line for the ship, and the more he pulled, the more the ship pitched to one side. The pitching caused him to stumble further and pull harder on the rope, and so on in a catastrophic cascade.

As the ship listed further and further, threatening to tip completely over, everything onboard tumbled chaotically across the ship's deck, including the three bearded lumps, who rolled around like logs on a river barge. Their charade — opossums feigning lifelessness to avoid being eaten by the fox — was now very much over. One by one they sounded expressions of alarm as they tried not to fall out of their ship.

Sheldon, being much less accustomed to flying, or sailing, or whatever this was, lost his footing and careened overboard. By sheer dumb luck, the shoelace rope became wrapped around his leg. So instead of falling to his doom, he simply dangled below the ship like an anchor — though he was screaming much louder than a typical anchor might. The one advantage Sheldon had, hanging in mid-air like that, was he no longer had to worry about staying on board, for the flying thing was nearly upside down and the other crew members were having a heck of a time staying in.

"Hang on!" one of them cried.

"Stay in!" another added.

"I think I'm going to be sick!" the third yelled.

From his vantage point, suspended in mid-air, Sheldon marveled as one of the crew members popped up and began deftly maneuvering about the inverted ship like a spider in a web. The small figure swiftly retrieved the port-side control rope and began heaving and wrenching on it methodically. His efforts countered the erratic tugging on the starboard line by a dangling Sheldon, bobbing around like a yo-yo in space. Almost instantaneously, the ship began to right itself. As it spun back to right-side-up, the rope tied to Sheldon's leg became taut, flinging him back on board with a whip-like crash. The little man quickly grabbed Sheldon's rope and, together with the rope already in his grasp, yanked both lines as if bringing a runaway horse to a halt, smoothing the turbulence and correcting the ship's attitude. The attitude of her crew, however, was not so easily fixed.

As everyone got settled, dusting off the chaos and taking stock of their limbs, one of the long beards spoke up. "Right then! Who's hungry? Mulligan stew anyone?"

"Aaarrrgh!" another one yelled, lunging at the boy intruder. Sheldon looked up to see the small person who had just saved them, flying through the air at him.

"Humpf!" Sheldon gasped as the stout brute landed on top of him with the weight of several wet sandbags. Instantly, a riotous rasslin' match ensued.

Despite Sheldon's young age, he was pretty scrappy, having had plenty of practice defending himself on the schoolyard. The little squab attacking him was also a skilled tumbler but was on the small side. Although clearly having the weight advantage, the attacker must've been at least a full head shorter than Sheldon.

"Wallop 'im!" cried one of the onlookers.

"Gragurflumpum!" shouted another with a mouth full of stew.

"Wait, who you rootin' fer?" said the first.

"The big one!" said the second, swallowing the soup in one gulp.

"Yeah, me too! ...Wait, which one's the big one?"

There was a pause in heckling as the two cheerleaders pondered for whom they should be cheering. Meanwhile, as the wrestlers continued their epic battle, they became entangled once more in the mess of sundries strewn about the vessel, including Sheldon's nemesis: the dubious laundry pile!

"Well, I s'pose we ought to root fer the one that wins. That would make the most sense, I think," said the soup-eater, taking his now empty bowl and placing it atop his head like a helmet.

"Right. Uh, which one's that?" said the other.

The two rasslers were having a tough time unrav'lin' themselves from one another, and from the clingy clothes. Eventually one of them stood up, tossed a nightshirt off his head, and pointed a large wooden spoon like a sword at the lump still lying on the floor, buried under the laundry.

With his mighty spoon in hand, after taking a moment to catch his breath, the stout man bellowed, "As captain of this here shoe, and commander of the Flying Festoon Brigade, I insist that you, oh mighty trespasser, show yerself and state yer purpose at once, or face the consequences!"

Frustrated and humiliated, Sheldon weighed the option of having another go at the furry, wee captain, muttering under his breath from under the laundry pile, "Captain, my eye! Shoe captain, is it?"

"Yeah, that's right!" replied the man, straightening himself as tall as he could and jabbing the spoon at the air triumphantly.

"Who flies a shoe? That's absurd!" Sheldon angrily discharged the clothes and jumped up, revealing his full size. "My name's Sheldon Silvers and I am NOT a trespasser!" The onlookers reeled backward and gasped. They'd seen the trespasser only in fleeting glimpses, bouncing around the ship and wrestling with the captain. This was their first good look at the intruder. They half expected to see a grotesque monster with claws and fangs and spikes on its back. (Like Sheldon, they too had overactive imaginations.) Instead, there stood a rather plain-looking kid.

"My word!" exclaimed the soup-muncher, now stirring a large pot with agitated vigor and wearing an expression of amazement. "Uh, would you like some soup, young man?"

"Zip it, Pots!" retorted the captain, whipping the wooden spoon around and pointing it menacingly at his compadre standing over the cauldron, who immediately ducked down behind the steaming pot. The captain then swung the spoon back to the boy. "What do you want with my ship?" he demanded.

Sheldon cocked his head sideways and squinted. After a momentary staring contest, he shifted his defiant stare to the person standing to the captain's left, taking stock of the three adversaries (four if you counted the laundry).

"Careful, Tick, he's eyeballin' ya!" said the stew chef, still crouching behind the rampart cauldron. At that nonsense, Sheldon shot a razor-sharp glare over to the chef. They locked eyes for a brief second before the cook retreated further behind his pot, not wanting to incur the wrath of this unpredictable, wayward drifter, this wild-eyed, celestial gypsy.

"Ha! Pots, yuh look like when ya accident'ly woke that sleeping dragon, throwing stones into his cave. Where was that again? Oh yeah! Berfelda—"

"Enough, Tick!" scolded the captain.

Sheldon noted the captain's gruff manner, along with the fear in the soup chef's eyes. Wanting to put an end to all the puffed-up posturing, he decided to soften his defenses and extend an olive branch. "You know, I think I *would* like some of your soup, Mr. Soup Man." He then shot the captain a look that said, 'Take that, you bully!'

Chef Picklepots transformed his look of terror into an ear-to-ear grin as he stood up tall with pride and delighted, "Ha, d'ja hear that, Tick? He called me 'Mr. Soup Man'!"

"Yeah. Almost sounds like Superman!" Together, the crew member called Tick — short for Tickletoes — and the soup chef, Pick — short for Picklepots — broke out in laughter, a common occurrence with those two.

"Enough! Both of you!" interjected the bossy captain. The two chucklers instantly snapped quiet, but that didn't last long. Their unsinkable, jovial nature being what it was, they couldn't help but regrow silent smiles after their grumpy captain looked away, turning his attention back to the intruder. "I am captain of this crew, and there'll be no soup... or anything else... until we get to the bottom of this... this... this stowaway-ness!"

Picklepots whispered, "I'd rather get to the bottom of this stewpot." Tickletoes giggled while Captain Fickleface missed the remark.

Sheldon, who also didn't catch the tension-cutting comment, wasted no time defending himself. "I told you already, I am not a trespasser! And I am not a stowaway! I don't want your ship. I don't want anything to *do* with your ship. I'm here by accident. I simply fell into it as I was—"

The captain hoisted a skeptical eyebrow like a pirate raising the Jolly Roger, a clear warning. Pointing the wooden spoon at the boy, who had trailed off, the captain pressed slowly, "As you were *what*?"

"As I was... um... falling?" Sheldon shrugged.

"You were falling? From where? Ain't no treetops or mountains up that high 'round them's parts... buildings neither. Did you happen to drop out of a hot air balloon then?"

"No." Sheldon hesitated a moment before proceeding. "I was falling... um... up." The boy smiled sheepishly at the captain.

"Falling... up?"

"Yup. That's right."

"You're a tootin' liar!" the captain wagged his spoon wildly in front of the boy's face, trying to look as threatening as possible given his small stature and ridiculous weapon.

Sheldon threw up his hands to protect himself from the wagging spoon and inadvertently swatted the thing right out of the captain's hand, sending it zipping across the ship with destructive velocity, striking the soup man square in the mouth, knocking the smile right off of *his* face and sending it over to his friend, Tick's face, who thought the whole incident was hilarious.

"OWWW! My TOOF!" Picklepots wailed as he covered his mouth with one hand and held out the other, palm up, displaying a large tooth, tears streaming down his chubby cheeks.

"Oops!" Sheldon covered his mouth sympathetically.

Immediately, the captain ran over to console his friend. As he comforted the soup chef, he glared at the assailant with beady, hate-filled eyes. The incident had confirmed his suspicions that this nefarious mister Sheldon character was out for blood.

"Tickletoes!" yelled the captain. "Grab them reins and set Delilah on course fer Champion Ridge. We're goin' tuh see Manny!"

Chapter Eight

World Traveler

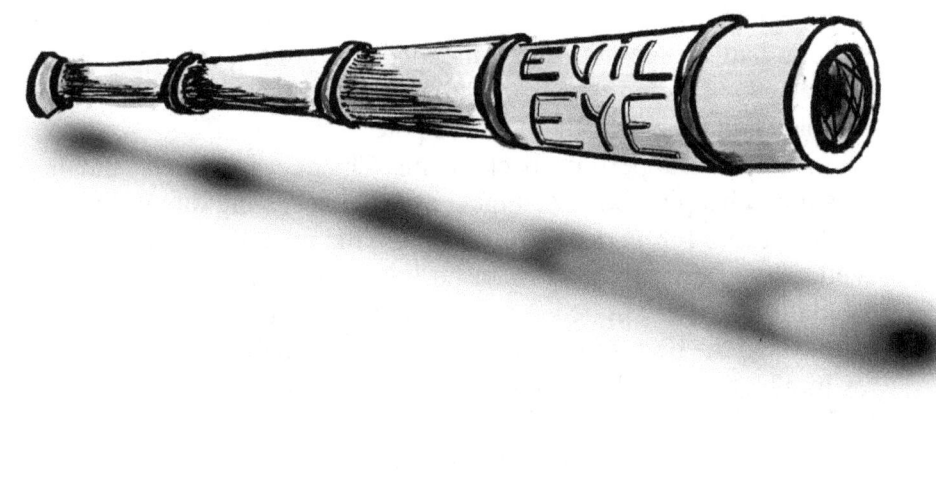

The ship flew on for what seemed like hours, with her crew sitting on one side of the deck, Sheldon on the opposite side, each giving the other a wide berth in order to avoid further conflict. Sheldon did not like conflict. He liked peace. As did the three shipmates. But neither knew that about the other and so tensions lingered like the stink of the laundry pile in which Sheldon sat, that being the farthest spot from the others.

Overcome by exhaustion, Sheldon couldn't resist sleep descending, the silence of the night weighing heavy on his eyes. The sandman's undeniable charm left him little choice but to put his life in the hands of fate as he drifted off, finally bringing a close to this utterly unbelievable day.

Amid countless hours of deep sleep, Sheldon experienced a fleeting, yet undeniably real, dream about waking up in a strange bed in a strange house. Faint music played in the background, familiar but impossible to place. The dream faded just as an unknown man — a very large man with oversized eyes, even larger nose, and ears larger still, dressed in a grey-blue shirt and aged overalls — came into the room where Sheldon lay. The man was carrying something, a tray or board. Sheldon had the feeling it was intended for him but couldn't see what it was exactly. The more he concentrated on the man, the faster the dream dissipated and soon another took its place.

It was suppertime back in his Chicago apartment and he was finishing a heaping bowl of junket after a nauseating dinner of broccoli. He didn't care for broccoli at all. But, oh, the junket! And Mom and Dad! Well, Mom, anyway. Of course he loved his dad, even through all the tribulations. After all, he knew — or at least he reasoned — that his dad just wanted the best for him. But did his dad actually know what *was* best for him? Taking over the family business was *not* Sheldon's idea of a fulfilling life.

I'm not meant to be a baker. I'm not meant to be a businessman. I want to create, to draw, and write. I want to see the world! Sheldon told himself in his dream. *Yes, I know*, himself answered. He slowly awoke with the words, "So do it!" echoing in his head. Recalling something about being back home, something about his father, Sheldon's thoughts lingered on being a regular disappointment to his old man. Despite that, he still felt homesick as never before. Or was it motion sickness?

Groggily, Sheldon peeled his eyes open and looked around. It was still dark, and... *Wait a minute!* Utter disbelief charged through him like an electric chill. *There's no way all of that wasn't a dream! There's no way this is real. The flying shoe thing. The three Disney dwarves...*

Walking backward through his memory, he attempted to piece together all the recent, bizarre events. *Am I actually on board a flying boot?* He shook his head and fought the urge to close his eyes and whimper, 'There's no place like home, there's no place like home!' *Darn it! I forgot to pack my ruby slippers!* he mused with a chuckle, trying to lighten his mood and make the best of his predicament. "What a world!" he mumbled, and with an, "Oh well," sat upright, yawned, stretched, resigned himself to a reality of sheer nonsense, and decided that he might just as well prepare for more adventure.

"So, what's for supper?" he barked aloud. Still nursing his friend's injury, the wee captain scowled at the boy and his misplaced can-do attitude. Sheldon ignored the gloomy captain and tossed his attention overboard to the scene below. The Chicago skyline was long gone. There were no lights to be seen anywhere, but the midnight moon lit up a decent portion of an entirely unfamiliar landscape. Feeling very much like a stranger in a strange land, he slunk down to contemplate his next move and caught sight of the large soup caldron stationed at the rear of the ship. He stole a glance at the three shipmates, assessing his odds at successfully making himself at home — as much as was possible given the circumstances — by helping himself to some food.

Feeling that the coast was more or less clear, he stood up, mustered his confidence, and walked over to the fine-smelling 'kitchen,' retrieved a small wooden bowl from inside one of the slanted cupboards containing disheveled mounds of cookware, and began dishing himself some soup.

The three crewmates looked on, each harboring different opinions about the boy and his gumption. The captain was wondering if the kid would try some sneaky attack, of course, while Chef Picklepots was wondering how the boy would rate his stew. The third, the one called Tickletoes, was wondering if this kid might know how to play an instrument that could complement bagpipes. The shoe sailors were in need of a new rhythm accompaniment ever since their previous bandmate — a Baroque bassist from Barcelona — had run off with a young matador during a Running of the Bulls ceremony in Pamplona. (*That* story is for another time.)

With defensive intent, the captain made ready to stand and confront the brazen boy, but the soup man put a gentle hand on his shoulder and gave him a look that said, 'I'll handle this.' Reluctantly, the captain at-eased and sat down, much to Sheldon's relief.

Straightening himself as tall as he could, which was only about as high as Sheldon's chin, Picklepots the soup man, still holding a cloth rag to his wounded face, walked cautiously towards the boy. Through cotton fabric and grimaces of pain, the chef eked out the words. "It's Mulligan stew, an old recipe that's been in my family for generations."

"Smells delicious," Sheldon remarked without looking up. Picklepots glanced back at his mates, who were observing the exchange with great interest, and shrugged. The captain opened his mouth to protest when Sheldon offered, "I'm really sorry about your tooth." He glanced up and locked eyes with the soup man. "I certainly didn't mean to do that. Are you okay?"

The chef paused and then nodded, surprised at the boy's unexpected but much-welcomed kindness. Again, he glanced back at his friends and shrugged before returning almost entirely to his normal easy-going self.

"Ah, heck, don't worry about it none." He swung a hand at the boy as if casually tossing a baseball. "It's nuthin'. Happens all the time."

"Pshhhh," came an objection from one of the crew. The less grumpy one gave an approving chuckle.

"This really is some delicious supper," Sheldon gurgled, as he wolfed down the glop. He had forgotten how hungry he was, given all the distractions. Slurping up the last morsels, then holding out the empty dish, he asked, "May I have seconds, please?"

"Hey! Whadduya know? He likes me stew! Sure thing, kid. Here, allow me." The chef neglected his injury and took the ladle, plunged it into the stew, and began scraping the bottom of the pot. "The best stuff settles down in the deep. Here, give that a go." He filled the kid's bowl. "But just so's ya know, this ain't supper. It's more like early breakfast. Dawn'll be here 'fore ya know it."

The hungry boy didn't much care what time it was. He closed his eyes to enjoy the full flavor better and shoveled in a large spoonful of the lumpy gravy, filling both his stomach and his heart, not bothering to wait until his mouth was empty before spitting out the words — along with a bit of soup — "So ... delicious!"

"Check out Mr. Dupree here," Tickletoes teased. "Says your soup isn't half bad! Doesn't even bother swallowin' 'fore cheerin' yer praise, Pots!"

"Dupree?" Sheldon inquired in between another bite.

"Oh, it's nothin'. Dupree is a friend uh ours, is all. Always talking with his mouth full uh food's'all."

Sheldon stopped chewing and swallowed with pronounced effort. "Oh. I'm sorry. I'm just really hungry. I don't know anyone by the name of Dupree. My name is—"

"Sheldon. Yes, we heard you the first time," the captain grumbled.

Tickletoes, who was sitting next to the captain, came to Sheldon's defense. "That there's Captain Fickleface. Don't mind 'im. He's just an ol' scruffle-grumps is all. He doesn't mean anything by it. He's just hungry is all. Hungry and angry. All the time hangry he is!"

The one called Tickletoes seemed friendly enough to Sheldon. He couldn't help but notice that this crew mate spoke in a higher, softer pitch than the others, and had bright blue eyes that sparkled under long eyelashes, making Sheldon wonder if, despite the beard, this one might actually be a she.

Tickletoes turned to the captain. "Go on! Go get ya some glop, ya old rubber-knuckle." Then, turning back to the boy, added, "My name's Tickletoes. You can call me Tickles or Tick fer short, or Toesies if yer feelin' sweet." A loud giggle came from the soup chef and Tickles' smile broadened. "I'm the first mate of this here ship and honorary bagpiper of the Flying Festoon Brigade band."

Sheldon nodded. "It's nice to meet you all. I'm sorry about crash-landing on your… flying boat-thing."

"Her name's Delilah. And she ain't a boat. She's a boot! Take notes, boy," scolded Captain Fickleface.

Sheldon smirked. "Boy? No thanks. You can just call me Shel." Two out of the three smiled. "So, a flying... shoe?" Shel wasn't sure he believed the words that had just come out of his mouth. He *must* still be dreaming.

"That's right! Delilah's the best flyin' shoe ever made. Ain't that right gents?" Tickles didn't wait for an answer from her mates. "Well, Mr. Shel, it's nice to make your acquaintance, I'm sure. Seein's how introductories be in order... Your master soup man over there, his name is Picklepots. We's call 'im Pots, but he also goes by Pickles if ya like, or just Pick when yer short on time."

Pickles piped up on cue, "Here ya go! Heard ya say you was hungry. So, why not have another bowl?" He handed the boy more soup. "My name's Picklepah— Oh, Tick just said that, didn't she?" (That confirmed it!) "Anyhoo, I'm the one n' only cook uh the Festoon. And if ya git thirsty, I'll also be serving coffee, once the captain tells us it's safe tuh move about the cabin, that is." Pickles laughed at Fickleface. The captain just squinted and scowled.

"Um, I don't know about coffee, but this soup is about the best I've ever had," replied Shel. He didn't care if he was still dreaming. He was starving and this thick soup-stew-gumbo-gravy-glop — whatever it was — was hitting the spot.

"You see? You see?! I've been tryin' to tell these ingrates fer years!" exclaimed Pickles. "Me stew is the best-tastin' burgoo this side uh the Qallapeck River! Y'all take it for granted, but yuh been eatin' like spoiled kings fer years!"

At that, they all shared a laugh as Pickles passed around a loaf of homemade sourdough bread. Even ol' Captain Fickleface let out a little chuckle. Sheldon took the liberty of continuing the chit-chat, considering that the captain appeared to be warming up a tad.

"So, let me see if I have this right. The Festoon is a flying shoe named Delilah."

They nodded.

"And how long have you all been flying her?"

"Oh, I'd wager we been flyin' ol' Delilah now, what, prolly as many years as you been alive, kid. If not more," Tickletoes answered.

"Oh, way more'n that!" corrected the captain. He turned to Shel. "What are ya anyway? Eight? Nine?"

"Wha? No! I'm twelve! I'll be thirteen in a few months."

"Ah, a teenager!" scoffed Pickles.

"Uh, correction!" jousted the captain. "Pre-teen. Not a teenager yet. There's a difference, Pick."

"True," Pickles replied. "But preteen can be just as moody. It's no wonder yer so rowdy! Got all that angst and restlessness broilin' aroun' inside. Is that why yer out here travelin' the world all alone and all? Longin' for adventure, are ya? Things a bit too quiet back home, are they?"

Shel admired himself through the eyes of his shipmates for a moment. *A world traveler. An adventurer. Yes! That's me! Except...* "Quiet? No, definitely not," he replied to the chef. "Home is definitely not quiet. But is that why I'm here now?" He shrugged. "I'm not sure what's going on."

Feeling a wild hair fly up his nose, the captain got all uppity. "Well, what's goin' on is we're headed back home to Champion Ridge to see Manny because you knocked Pick's tooth clean out. That's what's goin' on!"

Shel frowned but didn't respond to Fickles' invitation to another argument. "Your home. I see. Aaand which state is that in? Are we still in Illinois?" Shel asked, trying to put the pieces together, make sense of the nonsense, which felt a bit like trying to unscramble an omelet.

Captain Fickleface rounded on Shel, trying to sound authoritative. "What state's that in? How in the blazes should I know?! The state of Now, I suppose."

Shel was taken aback. He thought they were past all the aggressive bravado bologna. "You know I didn't do it on purpose. And I said I was sorry. Besides, I wouldn't have had to defend myself if you weren't shoving that spoon in my face."

Feeling challenged, the captain jumped to his feet.

"Oh, sit down Captain Ego Pants," Pickles jested. "I'm fine. I don't need defendin'. No more'n you do, and you don't. This here kid ain't no threat. He said he was sorry, so leave 'im be. Besides, I've had worse." He looked at Shel with a wink and a grin. "Don't mind the cappy, he's just tired s'all."

The captain exploded. "WELL, WHICH IS IT?! Am I grumpy 'cause I'm old or 'cause I'm hungry? Or is it 'cause I'm tired? Huh? Which one?"

Tickle's hand shot up. "Oh, oh, pick me! Pick me!"

Pickles giggled and pointed at the bagpiper, "Yes, Tick? What's the correct answer?"

Tickles sat up straight and cleared her throat like she was going to give a speech. "Ahem. Yes. The answer to Cappy's question is, 'D', all of the above."

"Ding, ding, ding," rang Pickles. "Correct-a-mundo! We have a winner. Tell the lady what she's won, Shel." Shel just sat there while Pick and Tick laughed their heads off at his confused expression. "What's-a-matta, kid? You didn't bring any prizes with ya? Let's see whatcha got. Empty them pockets," jested Picklepots.

Shel cracked a smile and redirected the subject by looking directly at Tickletoes and inquiring, "Um, not to be rude, but I have to ask..." Pickles and Tickles continued to chuckle but looked at Shel with an invitation to ask away. "Well, it's just that I've never seen a woman who looked like you before, Miss Tickletoes."

"Oh, you mean as beautiful?" Tickles replied, fanning out her beard. "Yes, I know. I get that a lot. Thank you."

"You're welcome?"

"He means the beard, sweetheart," piped the captain.

"Tosies is one of a kind, she is," said Pickles. "The three of us are brothers, or at least we were gunna be. But then a sister came along instead, and we love her all the more for it. Don't we?" Pickles grabbed his two siblings' beards and tugged on them affectionately.

"Ouch! Knock it off, Picks," grumbled the captain. "What Picklepots is tryin' tuh say is that we three are twins. All born on the same day, at the same time, in the same place."

"Yeah," added Picklepots, "And we all have the same ma and pa too, if you can believe it!" Tickletoes barked with laughter.

"Triplets. I see. Okay. Well..." Shel was at a loss for words. He'd never met such interesting people before. He'd never been on a flying shoe ride before. He'd never been so far away from home. It was all a bit overwhelming, and the Flying Boot Brigade could tell.

"It'll be all right, kid," offered Pickles with a kind smile that showed off his missing tooth. "The universe, She challenges us with just what we need. Musta been a part of ya that needed tuh get away and seek out adventure, else ya wouldn't uh landed smack in our laps." The others nodded, mumbling various agreements as they got back to their soup.

Sheldon grinned. "I suppose you're right." More mumble nods accompanied a good scraping of the last bits of soup from their bowls. "Socrates," Shel concluded.

Picklepots looked up. "What's that?"

"Oh, nothing. You just sounded like a philosopher. That's all."

Pickles chuckled. "Well, sorta comes with the territory I s'pose, flyin' 'round the cosmos 'n all in an old boot." At that, they all had a bit of a laugh and got to wiping their dishes clean with Pickles' tasty bread. A quiet moment followed, allowing the strangers to consider one another.

"So, why were you all yelling for help?" Sheldon was the first to break the silence. The three beards looked up from their bowls, mouths stuffed with dough, eyebrows floating over their heads, all blinking in unison. "When I saw you fly over me back in Chicago."

Blank stares were had by all. The crew turned and whispered to one another. Then the captain looked sideways at Shel. "Is that where we were? Chicago?"

Shel nodded with his own mouth full of bread and the twins whispered amongst themselves. Somewhat agitated by the secrecy, Shel repeated his question, "So... why were you calling for help? Back at that farmhouse? Was something wrong with Delilah?"

"Wellll," answered Captain Fickleface, slowly, "I'm not certain to what farmhouse you're referrin', kid, but I 'magine that's precisely *why* we were callin' fer help. We had no idea where we were nor how we got there. It was like the Festoon was just goin' wherever she wanted."

"Which is actually quite normal for Delilah," interjected Picklepots.

"Well, okay... maybe," replied Fickles. "Sometimes she does what she wants sure 'nough. But this time she was flyin' all catawampus like; like she had a mind uh her own, and she was entirely out of it!"

"Her mind?" asked Shel.

"Yeah! It was like she had her own agenda and we weren't regarded for it one bit!" As Fickles gesticulated the details, his audience sat with eyes wide and mouths agape, like little kids being read a ghost story. Even Pickles and Tickles who had experienced the whole thing looked enthralled. "We couldn't stop 'er. She was goin' madder'n'a wet hen, she was!"

"Ain't that a typical Jezebel!" chimed Pickles.

"Careful now! She'll hear ya!" warned the captain.

"Yeah, whadduya mean by that, Pick?" asked Tickletoes.

An animated discussion ensued, which Sheldon couldn't really follow. It sounded a lot like the sort of grown-up speak he tried to avoid back home. So, taking advantage of being temporarily invisible, he helped himself to the captain's spyglass.

Mounted through one of the ship's shoelace holes was a weathered, wood-and-brass telescope with the words 'Evil Eye' engraved on it. Shel peered over the side of Delilah to examine the surroundings now that the flower of sunlight was beginning to bloom again, illuminating the strange, new world below. As he suspected, not a thing was recognizable. Trees were odd shapes, hillsides curled up like ocean waves or appeared to float in the air like hanging house plants. Various things moved across the surface of the land but he couldn't make out what they were: two-story tractors plowing two-story fields of corn; dinosaur-sized blackberries rolling around on dinosaur-sized thorns; giant rhinoceroses with giant lampshades on their giant horns... One thing was certain, he was no longer in Illinois.

Must be Iowa.

Chapter Nine

Delilah

"So, what makes this thingy fly, anyway? How does Delilah, um, work?"

Shel fished for answers from the boot crew, still unable to shake the feeling that this was all just a dream. He felt as though he were balancing precariously atop a wall that separated Crazytown from its neighbors, Fantasyland and Cuckoosville. "I just mean that I don't see any wings, like on an airplane." The three bootaneers paused their discussion and looked around at one another as if they'd never been asked such an obvious question before.

"Well," said Picklepots, "I s'pose it's like this empty bowl here." He picked up a bowl and placed it inside of the wash bin filled with soapy water, ready for soiled dishes. "If I set 'er in the water, she floats. Right?"

Shel shrugged. "Mmm-kay."

"But if I fill the bowl up with water," Pickles ladled a large scoop into the bowl, "she's gonna sink. So, all we need to do is make sure we don't fill Delilah with too much stuff and she stays afloat just fine."

Shel considered the analogy. "So, Delilah is like a dirigible then? She's filled with hot air?"

The twins broke out in raucous laughter. "Yeah! That she is!" replied Tickles with a chuckle.

"Yup, she's definitely filled with hot air, ain't that right, Delilah?!" added Pickles.

Shel felt the ship rock back and forth in response, making him uneasy and reminding him of something. "Wait a minute! Back there, when I fell on board, the whole ship flipped upside-down, I'm pretty sure."

"I believe she did indeed, prit' near anyway," replied Tickletoes. "Thanks for givin' us all a good shake-up!"

Pots and Tosies laughed. Fickleface did not.

"Then how in the world did everything not fall out? Especially the soup?" challenged Shel.

"Ha ha!" Pickles roared. "Kid, this ain't our first rodeo. My stew pot has a lid what stays latched when I'm not servin'. Mostly so's ol' Fickleface here doesn't eat all of it when we're not lookin'. Ain't that right, Cappy?"

Fickles squinted at the chef. "Mmm. We keep most everything strapped down for just such occasions."

"Really? Strapped down? Like that loose laundry over there?" Shel cross-examined. "Please tell me those clothes are clean." The three of them looked in the direction of the laundry pile and the laundry pile seemed to stare right back at all of them.

"Well they *were* clean," replied Tickles.

"Yeah. We had everythin' folded nice and neat 'til you rocked the boat!" added the captain, wild hair a-flyin' once more.

"Yup, now it's all jumbled together: clean clothes, dirty clothes, kitchen utensils, books, walking sticks, my lucky bowling ball…"

Shel rubbed his head, "Is that what that was?"

"Nope. That was Tickletoes rappin' ya on the head with this here wooden spoon." Pickles held out a large ladle.

"Op, yeah. Sorry 'bout that," said Tickles.

Shel sat for a moment rubbing his head, more from confusion than pain. He was still perplexed and concerned as to how exactly he got to where he was and what exactly was going on. Then he sunk his teeth into something the captain had just mentioned.

"You said you prepare for just such occasions? That's what you just said, 'just such occasions', right? So, I must not be the first kid that you've sucked up into your spaceship!" Fickles stared back at Shel, speechless. Before he had a chance to answer, Shel came to his own conclusion. "I knew it! How'd you do it? A giant vacuum?" The boot crew stared at Shel, utterly perplexed. Shel looked at each of them, one at a time. "What planet are you guys from? You look… pretty normal… mostly." All of the tales from Shel's comic books began flooding his imagination and his eyes widened as he suddenly recalled the recent radio broadcast of H.G. Wells's The War of the Worlds. "I knew it! I knew it was real!" he repeated excitedly.

"Calm down, kid," the shoe captain held up his hand to steady the exuberant youth. "We're not aliens from another planet. And Delilah ain't no outer-space-mobile. She's just an old shoe what likes flyin' 'stead uh walkin'. Now, as to how you came aboard the Festoon… well, I'd hoped you'd tell us. I don't see no wings on your back, so ain't no angel nor fairy o' any kind I ever seen."

"You've seen fairies and angels?" Shel rallied.

"None like you, that's fer sure!" Pickles waved a finger at the boy and laughed.

It was becoming evident that Shel and the bearded folk were from entirely different parts of the world. Shel figured the boot crew were from someplace not unlike the worlds described in his fantasy books. He glanced at the sky to see if their heading might happen to be the second star to the right.

"Say, what were you doin' flyin' through the air at such a late hour anyway?" asked Fickles, changing the subject to something he felt to be more relevant.

Shel wasn't sure what to make of that question though. Usually people just asked about his parents, as if he were nothing more than a lost piece of property. But these guys hadn't asked about his parents once. It was almost as if they accepted him as a stand-alone individual. For that he was grateful, perhaps more than he yet realized. But instead of discussing that, or the fact that he hadn't actually been flying through the air, for some reason he settled on, "It wasn't that late."

"Oh, I'd say it was pretty late for a young lad like you to be flyin' around in the dark and all. Never know what might be out there in the cold night sky ready to swoop you right up!" The captain grinned a mischievous grin and lobbed a mischievous brow, startling the youth.

"Wait. What?!? What do you—" Sheldon stopped short, suddenly becoming dizzy. His train of thought jumped right off the tracks and careened down a deep, dark ravine. Despite only having just woken up from a nap not long ago, he suddenly felt the need to lie down again; his head drooping as if it were filled with viscous honey, eyelids weighed down by tremendous ballasts forged from a day packed with excitement, doubt, and triumph. His triumph over doubt during his long trek on the 'sidewalk-of-fate' had been rewarded with a new sense of self-confidence, and unimaginable adventure. But his triumph in the trials aboard the flying shoe — especially since triumph was an unheard-of outcome in his deliberations with adversaries (fathers included) — had rewarded him with the best gift of all: new friendships.

The last thing Shel saw as he drifted off to sleep was a smile from none other than the boot captain himself, laying a heavy wool blanket over him. Meanwhile, off in the farthest corner of the early morning sky, some invisible giant reached up with her empyrean paintbrush and merrily splashed a thin blue glaze above the horizon, marking the starting line for the coming dawn.

Chapter Ten

Watch Your Step, the Game Is Afoot

The Festoon landed at Champion Ridge near midday with the sun king sitting comfortably atop his zenith throne, smiling down upon Delilah, her passengers, and all the other wondrous life in the Valley...

Sheldon was just waking from his extended slumber, feeling not disoriented or groggy, but completely renewed and excited to take on the day.

"Wow! I feel terrific," he exclaimed as he jumped up, stretched, and looked about. "Where in the world are we?!"

Tickles sat packing a hiking satchel. "You *oughta* feel terrific, yuh slept most of the way here! Knocked out good and proper by Pick's gumbo I'd wager."

Grinning a gap-toothed grin, Pickles agreed. "Does the trick every time. Sneaks up on ya like a ton o' bricks, dunnit? Anyway," he stretched his arms out to present the surroundings, "*this* is Champion Valley. This is where Manny lives. I git tuh git ma tooth fixed tuday!"

Fickles smiled and nodded at his friend before putting his captain hat back on. "All right crew, Jimmy-Jack-John has called the dawn by more hours than I had hoped. So let's get crackin' 'fore it gets too darned hot."

"Yes sir!" replied Tickles, finishing up her packing.

"Hey, Tick, toss a few o' them apples in my satchel, would ya? We're gunna need scrubbed teeth and fresh breath for Manny," Fickles said with a laugh. It was clear the captain was in high spirits that morning.

They finished loading up and hit the trail, each with their own ornately carved walking stick. Shel borrowed a pole from Pickles, which was actually an oversized soup spoon. The triplets whistled a spritely tune as the gang marched down a path through a wide-open valley surrounded by flowing hills covered in bright green clumps of billowing foliage.

"These are odd-looking bushes," observed Shel, brushing some over with his shoe.

"Whoa! Careful there," warned Fickles in hushed alarm, looking around as if someone might be watching.

Tickles chuckled. "Hey, tire-kicker, them's ain't no bushes. This here's broccoli, and uh the highest variety!"

Shel's brow furrowed. "Broccoli? Yuck! I don't like broccoli."

The three shoe pirates cracked up. "Don't like broccoli, huh?" Tickles chirped between fits of laughter, "Sure didn't seem to mind it last night!"

"What are you talking about?" Shel challenged.

"Broccoli, my boy, and Champion Valley broccoli no less, is the main ingredient in me world-famous stew," answered Picklepots. "The stew you couldn't get enough of last night, recollect?" Shel looked shocked. Pots laughed. "Sure 'nough! We'll be back here in a few weeks to join the rest of the province for the harvest. And it looks like it's gonna be a banner season!"

At Pickles' nod to the landscape, they continued in silence, admiring the great expanse of the magnificent crop blanketing the hills and valleys as far as the eye could see. The trail on which they were walking, connecting Champion Ridge to Fallshugger Ridge, cut through hillsides crowded with budding plants so bright it looked as if the entire valley were glowing. This was certainly a variety of vegetable the likes of which Shel had never seen.

"There's so much of it!" Shel broke the silence after a while, thinking of the recession-fueled food shortage back home.

"Indeed!" replied Pickles. "It's a shame so much of it'll go to waste." He then added with a snobbish accent, "That is, not consumed by true connoisseurs." This comment made the others giggle. "Only a handful uh folks know the proper preparation what brings about the full flavor uh the unique Gambrine variety uh broccoli."

"Yup," added Tickletoes, "and it's a good thing, too. This place'd be right overrun and ruined if word got out of its speh-shee-ality. That's why the Gambrine protect it so fiercely." Then she turned to Shel. "And why YOU need to watch where yer swipin' them shoes."

Shel smirked, looked down at his feet in silent shame, then, curiosity always on standby, asked, "Gambrine?"

"Mmmm," nodded Fickles. "The Gambrine are the keepers of the valley. They tend tuh this crop and ensure any and all who pass here are respectful uh the plants. Very respectful."

"Ain't that the truth?! Goodness are they excellent farmers and plant 'tendants, being so low to the ground and all..." Tickle's enthusiasm dwindled and her smile faded. "But just as low is their tolerance for any behavior what might disturb or, heaven forbid, threaten their crop." She looked at Shel with high brows that dared him to doubt her. "And they have really big mouths and an awful lot of really sharp teeth." The others nodded in somber agreement. "Best to stick to the path and leave the crops alone."

"Best to stick to the path," agreed Pickles.

"Stick to the path," repeated the triplets in hushed unison, as if under a spell.

There was a moment of silent reverence before Fickles sliced through the tension. "So, kid, tell us more 'bout Chicago. What's the thing tuh do back home? Go to the circus?"

"The circus? No, I don't really do the circus."

"Well, why not?!" squelched Pickles, swatting a mob of flies from his face.

"If I want to see animals I visit the zoo and that's bad enough, all caged up. I don't like them being forced to do tricks."

"Oh, I dunno," Fickles countered. "I 'magine some uh them enjoy bein' in the limelight of the circus … n'joy performin' an' doin' tricks, makin' kids smile..."

Shel shrugged. "Maybe." Then his face lit up. "I like going to baseball games!"

Tickletoes looked sideways at Shel. "Baseball? What's that?"

Shel stopped walking. "Are you serious?! You don't know what baseball is?" The three beards looked at Shel, shaking heads and shrugging shoulders. Excited, Sheldon proceeded to explain the great American pastime to the Boot Brigade as they bounced along the trail, regaling them with stories of greats like Lou Gehrig, Mel Ott, and Joe DiMaggio. Not to mention the heart-stopping moment when the Great Bambino called his shot in the '32 World Series. Sheldon was just a little bambino himself at the time, but the moment lived on for years in the streets of Chicago, especially since the Yankees trounced the Cubs that year.

"I don't normally go in for the Yanks, but my team didn't make the Series. And the Cubs are our biggest rivals, see. So we all cheered for New York that year. Plus, my dad likes 'em." Shel's shoulders bounced. "I guess they're an alright team." His favorite stories, and thus the most enthralling for his audience, were the tales of Shoeless Joe Jackson, Sheldon's all-time favorite player on his home team, the White Sox. "Poor Shoeless Joe was thrown out of baseball in 1921. A real shame. He really was the greatest."

"What's 'thrown out'?" they asked.

"It means he was kicked out, as in they no longer let him play... in the major leagues anyway."

"But why? Who no longer let him play? What happened to him?"

"Well, nothing happened *to* him. He was kicked out for throwing the World Series to the Reds. But Joe played great during that whole series. There's no way he was on the take!"

The Boot Brigade had no idea what a World Series was, nor who the Reds were, nor what the words 'throw' and 'take' meant in that context. So, the questions continued and Shel's stories flowed like the Ohio River in springtime. And despite the shoe sailors not being able to follow all the details, one thing was clear: this young Mr. Shel Silvers was a fascinating storyteller — no doubt a result of his time in the company of his master storyteller friend, Hector. Shel also told them a bit about his school, his neighborhood, and his family, reigniting the fire of nostalgia within his heart. His dismay quickly became apparent to his new friends, who were attentive listeners, very well tuned in.

"Tell ya what kid, as soon as we're done fixing Pick's tooth here," promised the captain, "we'll fly you right on back to Chicago and get you home safe to your parents. Deal?"

"It's a deal!" agreed Shel emphatically.

o o o o o o

The gang walked on, following a jade-green brook that ran through spring meadows and small groves of tanglewood forest. They clambered up mossy boulders, down grassy hills, and traversed a few precarious bridges made from rope so old and overgrown that it was impossible to tell where the rope stopped and forest vines took over. Eventually, they emerged into a small glen of tall, beautiful, wonderfully soft grass bordered by odd-looking, towering trees that appeared to be a crossbreed of mighty oak and dainty rose. A modest waterfall at the far end of the glen fed a crystal-clear creek running underneath a charming, thatch-roofed, stone house. The cold water kept the glen in cool climate, which was wonderfully refreshing after being out in the valley heat all day.

The scene was utterly magical, as if it had been plucked straight from one of Shel's Joseph Jacobs' fairy tale books. On the opposite side of the glen from where the group stood, the groomed landscape returned to wild, a transition demarcated by unkempt broccoli weeds growing everywhere, some as tall as trees.

"Ah, here we be!" announced Fickleface, as they approached a wooden door at the front of the house.

"This… is a dentist's office?" Shel asked skeptically. "Here? In the middle of nowhere?"

"What do you mean, *nowhere*? *We're* here aren't we? So must be somewhere," retorted Tickletoes.

"Nope, Shel," chimed Fickles. "This ain't no office. This is Manny's home." He looked back at the boy. "We shan't go to his office on Friendsday." The captain opened the door and stepped inside. "He'd be closed up right tight, and this be an emergency."

With that, the three beards slipped inside the dark house and disappeared, leaving Shel standing outside alone. "You just barge right in without knocking?"

"Knocking what?" asked Tickles, sticking her head back through the doorway into the light.

Another head popped out of an adjacent window. "Come on, kid. Quit messin' 'round. Let's git to it," huffed toothless Picklepots.

Shel shrugged and slipped in through the small doorway, eyes struggling to adjust to the darkness in time to see the triplets scatter, leaving him standing at the entrance wondering what to do next.

"Hellooo?" hollered Pickles. "Anyone hooome?"

"Hello?" answered a distant voice from a dark hallway.

"Manny? 'S'thachoo?" asked Tickles.

"Who's there?" called the voice from the hall.

"It's us!" replied Fickles. "Got a tooth here needs fixin'."

"Who's us?! I'm not working today. Don'cha know what day it is?" The voice was growing louder. "It's Friendsday!"

A little scruffy man with thinning hair emerged from the dark hallway. Other than a missing beard, he was not unlike the Boot Brigade in stature and appearance, and was most definitely a dentist if his outfit had anything to say about it.

"A day for spendin' with friends, don'cha know? And I intend to spend it with my... Fickleface? Is that you? And ol' Pots and Tosies too? Hey, hey! The gang's all here!" The dentist shouted excitedly and rocked back and forth as if he were a bottom-weighted punching bag. He was a bundle of energy, make no mistake.

At his invitation of waving his arms about, the group huddled together like a football team, with Shel left out on the sidelines as usual.

"Well, well! Why didn't you say it was *us*?!" The dentist slapped the backs of his pals.

"We did! I said, 'it's us!' Didn't ya hear me?" replied Fickles, mostly to himself, knowing Manny would likely ignore him, which he did. The dentist poked his head out of the huddle and examined Shel head-to-toe.

"Say, who's this funny-lookin' fella ya got with ya?"

Shel started, "My name's—"

"Say you guys," the dentist interrupted. "I'm kinda in the middle of somethin' right now."

Shel scrunched his lips at being cut off, but Manny ignored that too.

"I'm actually with an important patient, back in the back. Kind of an emergency actually." He leaned toward Fickles and whispered something. Then his eyes grew large to compliment a suspiciously wide grin. Leaning back upright, he addressed the group. "Got a pretty bad toothache actually. Goin' tuh need some 'stractions I figure. Won't take but a jiff, really." At that, Manny turned and walked briskly back down the dark hallway, abandoning his audience to stunned silence, a hurricane leaving a flattened town in its wake.

A door creaked open and some faint words were exchanged. Then the door slammed shut and all went quiet. The visitors stood and stared at each other, speechless. Suddenly, the entire house became filled with the wailing sounds of someone in great pain. Frightened, the beards grabbed hold of one another.

"Wuh… Whudid he suh… say it was?" Pickles stuttered.

Fickles paused in disbelief at the words that were about to come out. "A brocosmile," he spoke slowly. They all gasped; all but Shel, oblivious as to what that meant.

"A broco-what?" asked Shel casually. The beards did not respond or even look at the boy. They were all wearing expressions of astonishment and staring fixedly down the hallway in the direction of the cries. "What's a broco… smell? Sail? Snail? Whatever."

"A broco-*smile*," corrected Pickles. "S'what the locals call the Gambrine, on account uh their large mouths an' typically very healthy teeth. Yuh know... from eatin' so much broccoli."

Shel gagged at the word 'broccoli'.

Pickles chuckled a smidge and continued. "Yeah, well... Wouldn't think it, because uh their ferocious look an' long, sharp teeth, but Gambrine rarely eat anything but brocco—"

BANG!

A thunderous clap echoed through the house. Not knowing what the noise was, Shel and the beards all scattered in different directions, running away from what they figured was either an intruder or a part of the house falling down.

After the ceiling stayed put, no invading army came bursting through the door, and everything returned to quiet, the guests all reunited in the main room of the house, just in time to see the tail of a brocosmile slink out the front door. As the door closed, it latched with a loud *click* that made everyone jump.

The triplets froze in terror. Shel, on the other hand, still unaware of the grievous situation underfoot and curious about this terrifying creature of legend, peered out of the living room window to catch a glimpse of what looked to be an oversized crocodile walking upright on its two hind legs.

Could it be?! Shel instinctively put his hand to his chest where the tooth pendant would have hung. He squinted in confusion and disbelief, and without looking away, noted, "That looks like a croco—" he paused when he looked behind him to find the shoe crew had gone. Turning back to the window, he watched the crocodile thing crouch down on all fours and disappear into the broccoli bushes like smoke in a dream.

The beards slowly wandered down the dark hallway in search of their friend who should have come out of his operating room by now. Since he had not appeared, they expected they might find him napping or maybe on the toilet… or both.

But they didn't.

They thought perhaps he might be delayed on a long-distance call or busy balancing his ledger.

But he wasn't.

They wondered if maybe he'd snuck out the back for a post-op puff on a pipe.

But he hadn't.

Perhaps he left a note or a forwarding address?

Nope.

Perhaps his favorite holiday shirt was missing from the closet along with his tweed suitcase and passport?

Nuh-uh.

Perhaps he had—

No!

There was no other possible explanation! The evidence pointed to one clear conclusion:

The brocosmile had *eaten* Manny the dentist!

As one might expect, the boot crew refused to believe that their friend was gone just like that, wiped clean off the map. So, the infallible, courageous (and oft reckless) Flying Festoon Brigade — this triumphant trio who had tickled the maleficent dragon of Grundly Grisp and somehow avoided being fried to a crisp; the three stout-hearted shoe sailors who belonged to an elite minority to have actually bumped a Glump-on-a-Rail and lived to tell the tale — those three brave and bold bootaneers decided, in the name of honor and friendship, they had no other choice but to track down that recreant reptile and get to the bottom of...

...the mystery of the missing dentist!

o o o o o o

Eventually Shel made his way to the office at the end of the hall. "Where's Manny?" he asked innocently.

Pickles and Tickles shrugged. Captain Fickleface turned to face the young man, placed a hand on his shoulder and advised him, "Hang tight here, kid. We need tuh go check on a few things." He spoke in a serious tone but with a kind smile that reassured the boy. "Not to worry. We'll be back in no time!"

Shel squinted at the captain, not sure he understood exactly what was going on nor that he really wanted to be left behind. But as squinty as he was, the shoe crew left just the same. Before he knew it, Sheldon was alone in an empty house, watching from the window as the three stout beards scuttled into the broccoli weeds in hot pursuit of the mysterious croco-broco-thingy.

Chapter Eléphen

Imagining

Shel woke with a jolt, startled by some loud noise. Whether a crash of something breaking, bang of something falling, or boom of something exploding, he wasn't sure. Perhaps it was something in his dream that startled him. He tried to recall what he was dreaming about but the abrupt awakening frazzled his memory. In fact, he hadn't even realized that he'd fallen asleep in the first place... *in a dentist's chair?! What am I doing in a— Oh, that's right.* Again he had to remind himself of this strange reality, that he hadn't simply been dreaming of flying shoes, dwarves, and upright-walking crocodiles. There wasn't a doubt in his mind that he should be waking up in his own bed, in his own house. Instead, he was waking up in a strange dentist's office, in an even stranger cottage, in the strangest of lands. The disorientation was so profound that for a moment he thought he might be waking up from anesthesia after having a tooth pulled. *That's it! I'm actually at the dentist's in Chicago! And this has all been a dream!*

He yawned and stretched and looked around, reorienting himself with his surroundings and recalling recent events. *Nope, not a dream.*

"Those darned boot folk!" he grumbled aloud to an empty room. It felt like hours had passed since Fickleface and crew had left, and Shel was beginning to feel hungry. Ah, ha! Now he remembered everything. He had climbed into the dentist's chair after exploring the house in search of Manny — sort of. Mostly he was searching for something to snack on. Truth was, Manny's disappearance just didn't seem all that significant to him. He wasn't accustomed to life and death situations and therefore couldn't possibly believe Manny had been eaten. *I mean, come on! Eaten?! Really?!?*

He had a hunch the dentist had simply slipped out the back door, not wishing to entertain his unannounced visitors and not wishing to explain that he did not wish to entertain them. Hiding from uninvited, unwanted visitors was not uncommon in Shel's world. He wouldn't have blamed anyone for trying to hide from that ornery boot captain, that's for sure.

He didn't find Manny hiding in any cupboards or cabinets or closets, however. Unfortunately, he didn't find any tasty treats either. All he found were jars of canned broccoli soaking in some sort of gelatinous brine. "No thanks!"

Shel sat, reclining in the red leather dentist chair, pondering what to do next, when all of a sudden he heard again the same jolting sound that woke him up — previously dismissed as an echo of anesthesia dreams.

Wiping the remains of sleep from his eyes, he rushed to the window just in time to see an enormous lumbering shadow round the corner of the house and disappear. As he leaned forward to see where the shadow went, he smacked his face against the closed window. "Ouch!" He rubbed his forehead, annoyed. Now he was definitely awake. Holding a hand over his throbbing brow, Shel attacked the locks on the back door: a knob and latch, two deadbolts, and a chain secured the door against pretty much everything by the looks (and locks) of it. After opening the door cautiously and seeing that the coast was clear, he jumped down the steps onto the stone walkway that encircled Manny's house like a moat.

At the base of the steps he froze, listening to the not-too-distant sounds of rocks crunching and tree branches snapping, sending chills up his spine. The ground vibrated under his feet while his heart vibrated in his chest. He jumped when he heard it again: the unmistakable trumpeting of an elephant!

Oh, how Shel adored elephants, though he'd never seen one in the wild. Back home, whenever he had the opportunity, he would go to visit Ziggy, a massive Asian elephant at the Brookfield Zoo. More often, however, he would endure a longer walk to enjoy lunch at the Lincoln Park Zoo, where he would spend hours watching and talking with Duchess, another Asian elephant. Duchess was smaller than Ziggy but, in Shel's opinion, considerably sweeter. When he imagined the elephants talking, he would give Ziggy a sarcastic tone on account of the elephant's obstinate behavior; behavior that was perfectly justified, Shel figured. Any animal who had to endure the confinement of a zoological institution — or any institution for that matter — would certainly feel some resentment. He felt sorry for Ziggy and Duchess. Still, he loved visiting them and imagining himself in the jungles of Asia or the plains of Africa.

But, Shel was not in Asia or Africa. This place was Weirdosville, capital of Bizzaroworld. He figured he was likely to round the house to encounter an ostrich with the trunk of an elephant and legs of an armadillo. Instead, when he came around the corner in pursuit of the shadow and the noise, he did not find an elephant, nor an ostrich. There wasn't even a wee, little armadillo. Like his encounter with the phantom light in the window of the old farmhouse, Shel found himself standing alone with nothing but his healthy imagination once again playing its tricks. He sighed and kicked stones from the walkway into the broccoli weeds. "Oops!"

His thoughts volleyed back and forth between the nonsensical crocodile on two legs and the elephant shadow ghost. *Maybe I'm still feeling the side effects from the anesthesia?*

He closed his eyes, put both hands to his forehead, and slowly pushed his fingernails into his scalp, dragging his fingers across his head and gritting his teeth at the absurdity of it all. "Aaaaargh!" he complained.

"PWEEEESH!" replied a tremendous trumpeting from a terrific trunk.

"Aaaahhh!" Shel screamed and jumped into the bushes to avoid what sounded like an elephant about to pounce on him.

Sure enough! He whipped his head up to see a massive, full-grown elephant looking down at him with disturbingly large eyes, clinging unsteadily to a disturbingly small branch of an oaken-rose tree. The poor branch couldn't have been much larger in diameter than the elephant's trunk, possibly even its tail, and it was bobbing up and down, nodding like a crazy person. "Yup, yup, YUP! I'm about to crack, crack, CRACK! Better watch out, out, OUT!"

Shel scrambled to get out from under the tree, diving into a patch of broccoli bushes. From his hiding place, he risked another peek at the precariously perched pachyderm.

No! Impossible! Couldn't be! I must be imagining a giant elephant in a tree. It must be an oversized bear or some strange bird that looks like an elephant! Whatever it was, it was staring right at him with the most intense eyes Shel had ever seen.

Now would be a great time to run... away! Fast! Shel's thoughts prodded him but he was stuck. He couldn't move. *Any time now, Sheldon!* But try as he might, he was unable to pull himself from the elephant's hypnotic stare. It was mesmerizing. It was piercing. It was oh, so creepy!

The preposterous pachyderm was sitting almost completely motionless, having achieved a sort of otherworldly zen with the tree and the unlucky twig on which he perched, when a soft voice whispered, "Heyyyyy there," and Shel whipped his head side-to-side, looking around nervously to see who else was there with him watching this ridiculous performance. "Up here," the whisperer continued, calling the boy's attention to the tree.

Sheldon's mind raced. *Is there someone trapped up in the tree with that massive beast? OH, NO! The elephant is sitting on a nest like that ridiculous Horton character!* He scanned the tree for other signs of life but saw no movement, just a giant tusker who shouldn't be two inches off the ground let alone ten feet.

"Psssst. Up here! In the tree," came the voice again.

"Uh," Shel stammered. "Is there someone... up... in that... tree?" He pointed with a cautious finger. "Perhaps behind, or maybe underneath, that... very large... animal?"

"Can you see me?"

"I don't know. Can I?" Shel was worried the whispering might actually be coming from the elephant itself.

"Nope. Ya can't. 'Cause I'm hiding."

When Shel saw the elephant's mouth move, his fear was confirmed. Not only was he now seeing elephants in trees, he was seeing *talking* elephants in trees. He felt on the verge of a total mental breakdown. "Uhhhh—," he hesitated, unsure of what was coming next.

"Heyyyy!" it whispered again. "I'm up in the—"

"TREE!" Shel blurted uncontrollably. "I know!" Suddenly released from the elephant's spell, he stood up and shoved his arms out in front of him, presenting this crazy elephant in a tree *to* the crazy elephant in the tree. "You're a huge... MASSIVE... ELEPHANT... IN A TREE! Of course I can see you!" With eyes and mouth open wide, he shoved his arms out a second time and shook his head.

Feeling rather deflated, the oversized temporary tree-dweller replied, "Oh. Well, okay then," and relaxed his statuesque posture, but not before taking one last scrutinizing look at the boy. With squinted eyes and cocked head, he gruffed, "So, you're sure you can see me then?"

Exasperated, Shel shoved his arms out a third time, feeling ready to snap like the branches which looked as if they too had just about enough of this elephant-in-a-tree business. "I have no idea how you got up there, but you'd better get down before that tree spits you out." Shel turned to go back inside Manny's house when a disturbing noise stopped him and spun him around. What a sight! A full-grown elephant 'climbing' down out of a tree just like a monkey (actually nothing at all like a monkey). The astonishing descent was the most awkward-looking effort Shel had ever witnessed. There was scrambling, slipping, stretching, shimmying, slumping, snorting, squealing, and even some swapping of heads for tails when the elephant flipped upside-down and it seemed he'd never get out of the woods. At one point the pachyderm made it to the lowest branch, nearly touching the ground. Just a few… more… inches… He stretched his leg as far as it would go but couldn't… quite… reach. So he gave up, climbed back to the top to start over, aaannnd… *SNAP!* The branches gave way, dropping the elephant to the ground with an earth-shattering *THUD!*

Shel stood dumbfounded, mouth agape and eyes wide, as the big, bumbling beast got up, brushed himself off, stretched out his sore limbs, and with one last 'so there' stare, lumbered off through the bushes. With the frightening and absurd incident over with, Shel had a moment to consider what had just taken place. This was his first encounter with a real elephant in the wild and this particular specimen happened to be able to climb trees (sort of) and talk! Without thinking and letting curiosity get the better of him, Shel gave chase. He called out but the elephant ignored him in favor of nursing his injured pride, which hurt worse than his back, and that hurt pretty badly. Shel picked up the pace, caught up, and began jogging alongside. "Why were you—"

"PWEEEEESH!" The elephant interrupted with a blustering blast from his prodigious proboscis. Shel crouched, covered his ears, and closed his eyes tight, trying to block out the noise. When the trumpeting stopped, he squinted at the elephant, expecting to see a raging bull ready for battle. Instead, all he saw was a large swaying elephant butt trailing through an increasingly dense patch of wild broccoli, tail-a-swooshing back and forth like a finger wagging, "Nope, nope, nope, nope…"

Unable to let it go, Shel caught up once more and resumed his interrogation. "How did you get up in that tree?"

The elephant conjured an impressively melodramatic 'what-a-ridiculous-question' sigh and executed his best 'so-glad-you're-back' eye roll. His theatrical expressions were so exaggerated it made Shel chuckle and he wished Tick and Pick were there to share a good laugh. He quickly squashed the giggling, however, when he saw the look of irritation on the elephant's face.

"Okaaay. So you climbed."

"Well I didn't jump," retorted the elephant in a voice that matched his intimidating size.

Shel leaped back. He was already tuned in to the fact that this was a talking elephant but to hear that voice so loud and clear, and in the context of a 'conversation' was quite a shocker. "And you talk!"

The elephant stopped walking, irked by two obvious questions in a row. More than that, he was admittedly curious about Shel's apparent lack of awareness of things in general. He looked the boy up and down skeptically, not sure if the kid was pulling his leg or... No, the boy definitely was not pulling *his* leg. Oh, he'd know if someone was pulling *HIS* leg. He'd never put up with that nonsense! The elephant started walking again, gurgling something under his breath. "I'd stomp anyone who tried to pull on MY legs! I'd ram 'em with my thick head, take my tusks and—"

"What's that?" Sheldon cut in, unable to discern what the elephant was mumbling about.

"No, you're probably right. That *is* a bit harsh I suppose," the elephant huffed, still grumbling to himself.

"Sorry? Um, I'm not following—"

"Oh, but you are, aren't you!" the elephant halted. "You've been following me all the way from Manny's house... and a bit too closely I might add. Ever heard of personal space? Sheesh!"

"Oh. I uh... I'm sorry. I'll just—" Sheldon slowed down to put some distance between them. As he did, he accidentally trampled some broccoli bushes.

"Woah! What do you think you're doing? Are you *trying* to get us both killed?! Hasn't anyone ever told you to stick to the path?"

Shel stopped walking and stared at the elephant, wondering what he did to get so far under the pachyderm's thick skin in such a short time. The elephant glared back at the odd kid, wondering why he seemed to be unaware of some basic rules of life, like don't mess with the broccoli and elephants talk. Duh. The elephant reached his enormous trunk, wrapped it around the boy, and lifted him off the ground. Once again Shel found himself staring into those mesmerizing, basketball-sized peepers, now only inches away. "Yeahuuuup! I talk," he said matter-of-factly, then pushed Sheldon away, holding him in the air so as to get a good look at him. "You're not from around here, are you?"

Shel squirmed in the grip of the trunk, pushing out syllables between breaths, "No. I'm… from… Chi… ca… go."

The elephant's eyes remained squinty while his brows arched in surprise. "Shihhh-caaaww-goohhh, eh? You don't say." He examined Shel with curiosity. "Well, what are you doing *here*, so far from home?" Shel hesitated long enough for the elephant to come to his own conclusion. "Oh no. You're not one of Romanov's guys, are you? Did the Falcon send you?" He scrunched his face in suspicion.

"What?" Shel replied. "Who's the Falcon? Why does everyone keep assuming I want something? Why is everyone here so paranoid?"

The elephant brought his captive up close again, right up to his eyes. "Paranoid?! Should I be paranoid about something?" His stare intensified as his grip tightened around the boy.

Shel struggled in the snake-like trunk. "Look, I don't know *who* you are, and I don't know who this Falcon fella is. I was sitting back at Manny's house, heard you romping around outside, so I went to check it out. That's all."

The elephant stared at Shel as if trying to see through him. "Hmmm." He set the youngster back on solid ground, not entirely gently. "Well, Chi-ca-go, I don't know what you're doing here but you'd best get back to Manny's place. Going to be getting dark soon and you don't want to be caught wandering through the bushes after dark." He turned and began walking away. Uneasy, Shel looked around then followed after.

"Why? Are there Gambrine around here?"

"Gambrine? Ha! No. ...I mean yes. There are Gambrine. There are Gambrine everywhere around these parts. But they won't bother you…"

"Unless you bother their crop," both spoke in unison.

The elephant stopped and looked sideways at the boy. "So you *do* know something after all." He continued walking. "No, Champion Valley is home to worse creatures than— Wait." He stopped again. "What were you doing at Manny's house anyway? I don't suppose you came all the way from Chicago because you need a dentist, even if he is the best."

"Was," he replied under his breath, but the big-eared beast had no trouble hearing.

"Was?"

"Yeah, I don't think that dentist will be fixing any more teeth anytime soon."

"Excuse me?!"

"He disappeared while working on a broco… smear." (Sheldon knew the name but decided to have some fun with the pachyderm.)

The elephant frowned, as much as an elephant *can* frown. "Smile. Broco-*smile*. Sheesh. What do you mean he disappeared? And his *naaame* is Manny."

"Well, *Manny* went into his office with one of those Gambrine creatures, and a little while later only the Gambrine came out."

"Well where did he go? …Manny, not the Gambrine."

"Ummm, I don't know. Maybe the broco smelly—"

"Smile!"

Shel smiled wide, which made the elephant frown wider. "Maybe the brocosmile ate him?" he shrugged.

"Whoa! *Ate* him?!?" The elephant put his face up to Shel's. "Are you nuts?! Brocosmiles don't eat dentists! They eat broccoli! And they like it. That's why they call 'em broco-SMILES!" The elephant shook his head. "Hang on a second. Back up." Shel took a step backward. "You're telling me that Manny disappeared into thin air and you were the last person to see him alive?" Shel couldn't manage more than an 'uhhh' before the tusker continued, all the while advancing on the boy. "You came aaalll this way from Shih-cah-gohhh, a complete stranger to the Valley…" He stopped suddenly, switching gears and prodding the boy in the chest with his trunk. "Who are you anyway?" Shel stumbled backward and tried to answer but the elephant cut him off again with more prodding. "Why're you here?" Again, Shel tried to reply while tripping over rocks and catching himself in the weeds. Again, the elephant interrupted. "How do you even know Manny?" Fed up over being pushed around, Shel straightened himself up and stood his ground, staring perilously back at his pursuer. He didn't bother to attempt an answer though, knowing full well what was about to— "Where are your parents, kid??" And there it was, the standard inquiry. Without thinking, Shel reached into his pocket and began fumbling with the puzzle piece he'd picked up off the sidewalk, reminding himself that he was more than just his parents' baggage. *Parents.* It was the first time he had thought about his folks in a while. Noticing the boy's preoccupation, the elephant grew impatient. His eyes shifted wildly, head bobbing, running through all the answers the boy wasn't giving him. "Oh, forget it!" The pachyderm turned away, heading back in the direction they'd come. Sheldon shook off the nostalgia that had begun to invade him like ants on a drip of honey and sprang into action.

Chapter Twelve

Emmentaler

"*Hey, wait up!* Where you goin'?"

"I'm going to find Manny, not that it's any of your business," the elephant hollered, adding quietly to himself, "I should've known something wasn't right when he didn't come out to greet me with his usual song and dance on that funky, old guitar."

"Manny plays guitar?" Shel intruded on the elephant's private conversation. "I like to play—"

"Whoaaa!" the tusker gasped and turned back with a look of utter surprise. "Can you... hear my thoughts?"

Shel paused. "What?"

The elephant stared with wide eyes, waiting for a better answer.

"Uhhh... noooo," Shel continued slowly. "But I can hear you when you speak."

"Oh." The pachyderm looked only slightly relieved. "Shoot! Was I talking in my sleep again?"

"What?? You're wide-a—" Shel paused and squinted at the elephant, thoroughly confused. "Nope, you were talking in your awake."

"Oh, cacahuates!" the elephant snapped, and with his brow resuming its standard level of furrowness, trekked on.

"Cock-a-what... ace?"

"Huh?" the elephant grunted. There was a short pause while they both tried to sort out what the other was saying. "Lemme guess, you don't speak Español?"

Shel squinted, no.

The elephant sighed and mumbled to himself. "Figures. I saaaiiid cacahuates. It means peanuts. I said, 'Oh, peanuts.' You know, like 'oh, nuts,' or 'oh, fiddle-farts'..." the elephant faded out, continuing to march, pretending everything was normal.

"Fiddle... farts? I get the peanuts thing. Everyone knows that elephants love peanuts but—"

"No! No, they don't. That's exactly the point. Ugh." The elephant turned and faced the tag-along. "That's a myth my friend, like the Oracle at Delphi... or the White Sox ever winning another World Series."

Shel cocked his head. "How do you know about the White Sox?!"

The animal bypassed the baseball question. "Elephants do not like peanuts. They're terrible. Hence the use of the phrase, 'Oh, peanuts!' to describe something that's gone wrong or is just no good."

They both stared at one another for a moment, guessing at what could possibly come next. "I love peanuts," Shel said quietly. Then he piped up, "And the White Sox are the best!" unable to think of anything else to say.

"Oh, come off it! They haven't won a series in over twenty years! Time to hang it up, don't ya think?"

"No, I don't think!"

"Clearly," smirked the elephant.

"Hey! Oh yeah? Well, you're..." The elephant waited for it. "You're just cacahuates!"

"Okay." The elephant rolled his eyes. "You can't use my phrases, kid. We don't know each other well enough yet."

"Oh, I think I know you well enough already," Shel grumbled.

"What was that?" The elephant swung a jumbo-sized ear in Shel's direction.

"Uh, I said... What do you know about the White Sox anyway? What do you know about Chicago??"

"Well, I know that the White Sox have been cursed since they turned into the 'Black Sox' during the 1919 World Series thanks to Shoeless Joe and his hooligan buddies."

"You take that back!" Shel's face reddened and he tightened his fists, ready to box something.

"Calm down, Joe Lewis. I'm not gonna fight you." The elephant set aside baseball to get back to the issue at hand. He prodded at the kid's stomach with his trunk. "But I *do* want to know just who in the world *you* are, boy."

"Boy?" Shel squawked.

"Oh, forget it!" The elephant turned and walked away. "I don't have time for ego trippin', kid. I have to find my friend — whom YOU lost! Whoever *you* are."

"Well my name is—"

"No!" The elephant interjected. "What I want to know is who you *are*, not what you're called."

"But that's my... Wait, what do you mean?"

"What do I meeeaaan? What do I mean? What I mean is how might you identify yourself if you were, I dunno, say, an explorer landing your ship on a strange island for the first time? You'd have to use more than just your name to let the locals know who you are and what you're doing there. Like, 'I'm the Prince of Party Pants and I have come to eat all your coconuts."

"What in the world are you talking about? Party pants?" Shel whined.

The elephant looked affronted. "Good grief." He took a deep breath. "Look, what is it that you do that makes you unique, makes you special, like no one else? Maybe you can identify yourself by who you're not." Shel fidgeted with the puzzle piece in his pocket and shrugged. "Okaaay, well how would I tell you apart from a dog or a horse or... or a tree... or all the other crazy things in this world, say, if I couldn't see you, if we were pen pals across the ocean or something?"

Shel stared at the elephant, growing tired of the inquisition. "I'm not sure you and I would be pen pals..."

"Oh, whatever. Look, what about... I don't know, what have you done that's worthy of honorable mention? Maybe that's the important question."

Shel's head dropped and he looked to the ground. "Nothing," he said, and the two of them fell silent.

Shel was now feeling sorry for his lack of accomplishments, his lack of identity. To top it off, he was admittedly overwhelmed by the philosophical, three-course meal the elephant had placed in front of him. The elephant, meanwhile, was realizing that perhaps he'd been a tad rough with this kid who seemed a bit on the slow side. He began to think maybe he should extend a morsel of pity to the dim-witted pipsqueak. So it was that the two strangers walked on in silence for the rest of the trip back to Manny's house, giving Shel ample time to digest the rhetorical entrée. By the time they reached their destination, Shel had decided that he was ready to assert himself and order up some dessert. "I am—"

"Shhhh!" The elephant smothered Shel's face in a thick, moist trunk — not the dessert the boy had in mind. The animal's eyes shifted back and forth, looking to see if anyone was around before attempting to squeeze through an open window at the back of the house.

This elephant has absolutely no concept of just how huge he is! Shel thought.

"Um, you do realize you're an elephant, right? And not a cat?"

The elephant looked back with a hardy-har-har.

"Or a bird?" Shel pitched an underhanded fastball.

The tusker mumbled something about tree-climbing-expert-somethin'-or-other and made more shushing sounds. Shel ignored him, walked around the corner of the house, and proceeded through the side door just as the elephant came crashing through the window. Shel gasped as the beast tumbled to the ground, bringing most of the wall with him.

Utterly shocked, Shel stood and stared at this unbelievable creature. "Wow! That was... insane. You okay?!"

"Shhhh!" the elephant continued his charade as he stood up and brushed himself off. He put his trunk up to his own face this time, like a finger, stiffened himself against the wall, and sucked in his ginormous gut.

"Uh, yeeaahh," Shel growled. "I think we've pretty much lost the element of surprise."

"Hey! That's it!" Suddenly, with the voice of a boxing match announcer, the elephant exclaimed, "Here comes... THE *ELEPHANT* OF SURPRISE!"

Shel rolled his eyes and clapped his hands to his ears as the pachyderm leaped into the hallway and charged toward the living room, trumpet on full volume. "I said ele-MENT, not elef—oh, never mind." He watched in horror as Manny's walls became Swiss cheese, pieces of ceiling fell to the floor, and floorboards became splintered toothpicks for giants. As his rampage sputtered out, Shel slowly approached the elephant. "Well, if Manny *was* still here, he's certainly dead now."

The sarcastic comment slapped the elephant cold and he froze like a statue. Paralyzed with astonishment, Shel also stayed motionless, watching the elephant panting and steaming, trying to catch his breath, as remnants of the house continued to crash to the ground like drops of water from a leaky faucet.

Exhausted, the pachyderm sat down on what remained of Manny's couch, which held for about two seconds before collapsing through what remained of Manny's floor. A final, loud crash resounded through the skeletal remains of the house. Then all went quiet, save for the ringing in their ears.

Chapter Thirteen

Nine Lives

$\mathcal{Shel}$ $\mathit{muttered}$ $\mathit{something}$ about the senseless destruction of such a nice cottage but the behemoth tusker wasn't paying attention. His head was bowed in sadness and surrender. As it hung, something curious on the ground caught his eye. He reached out his tired trunk and grabbed hold of a gleaming white object sticking out from the rubble a few feet in front of him.

"Hey!" exclaimed Shel. "I know what that is! That's a crocodile tooth!"

"Yup! Well, a brocosmile actually, and freshly pulled by the look of it. Note the root, and these markings here…" The elephant detective pointed out the impressions made by dental pliers. "See that? Brocosmiles are polyphyodonts, just like sharks, and ele-phonts," he smiled cleverly.

Shel noted the pachyderm's play on words but also noted that it wasn't worth noting. "Poly-fi-oh-what?" he asked.

"Polyphyodont. It means we lose and re-grow our teeth over and over throughout our life. So, finding an intact incisor lying around isn't all that unusual, especially here in Gambrine country. But this one didn't fall out, and it wasn't discarded naturally. This one was pulled." Quietly, the elephant continued to himself, rapping the tip of his trunk like a finger to his forehead as if trying to wake up his brain. "But why pull a perfectly good cuspid? Especially since Manny stopped working on brocosmiles years ago…," Shel looked up at him curiously and he looked the boy in the eye, "…when one of them… ate his cat," he concluded with an intense stare.

"Ate his cat?!" Shel blurted disapprovingly.

The elephont (noted) stared off into the distance and added dramatically as if narrating on stage, "Old Buddha Baggs."

"Buddha… bags?" Shel repeated.

"Yeah, that was his name. Good old Baggy Bones. That cat was so big," he turned to look at Shel "and so, so fat!" he chuckled. "So big that he looked like a small bear. But, oh, was he the most jolly and cuddly of creatures! Never rude or clawsome..." Shel sat, attentively listening to the ramble like a good friend would, even though he wasn't a good friend (yet). "Manny always talked about how he found Baggs wandering around in the snowy range of the Himalayas, on one of his many adventures abroad. Said that Baggs just climbed aboard his hot air balloon and curled up on his lap, nearly smothering him to death." The elephant chuckled softly at the vision of Manny and big, ol' Buddha together. "So, naturally, Manny brought Buddha back to the more temperate and lush climate of the Valley; much more suitable for a jolly, fat bugger like Baggs. What a place we have here!" The elephant looked out at the fields. Shel followed the storyteller's gaze out of the room and over the landscape. The two sat for a moment admiring the surrounding greenery, the beauty of which one would typically need a window in order to enjoy. But now, what with all the holes in the walls — some walls missing entirely — the beauty of Champion Valley could come and go with the breeze.

A shiver from the youngster caught the elephant's attention and he glanced down at the boy, wondering if he might get approval of his ramblings, and in that approval, perchance a smidge of forgiveness for his destructive tantrum. "You cold?" the elephant asked. Shel looked up and shrugged. He might have been shivering from any number of shocking experiences he'd had as of late. Not finding the forgiveness he was seeking, the elephant continued with his story, albeit a little less enthusiastically. "With places like the Valley, who would ever want to live on a frozen mountain range? Am I right, kid?" he asked facetiously with a nudge of his trunk. "And if you ever asked him why he had chosen to live in the Himalayas in the first place, way up there at the top of the world, ol' Baggy Claws would deny it and reply, 'Now what would a cat like me be doing in a place like that?' Ha!" The elephant laughed heartily at his impression of a cat. Shel grinned, playing the attentive companion. "And then," the elephant added, pushing out words between hiccups of giggles — he was beginning to laugh so hard that tears were pooling in his eyes — "then, Baggs would drone on and on with some philosophical diatribe about finding peace from within no matter where life takes you. ''Tis the Buddhist way,' he would say." And with that, the elephant burst into a roaring fit. "He was — *Ha Ha* — the strangest cat — *Heh Heh* — I ever met — *Oh, Ho Ho Ho!*" His contagious laughing ensnared Shel, and before they knew it, they were hugging and swaying together in a hammock of hysteria. It was a precious moment… which didn't last long.

The pachyderm's hysterical laughing turned to hysterical crying as he navigated the labyrinth of grief, suddenly flipping from a jolly, happy elephant, rambling nonsensically about some old cat, to a somber and suspicious bull. Sniffling and smearing away his tears, the elephant looked sideways at his cuddle mate with the wide-eyed, sober expression of a comedian on stage suddenly run out of jokes. A moment later, he was squinting and smirking, furrowing and frowning at the kid, maliciously flexing his talent of facial expression acrobatics and prodding the kid with a blunt yet effective tusk. "You know what? I don't trust you, newcomer!" Shel flinched, backing away from the intruding tusk and gulping down a heaping dish of bitter, cold surprise. "I don't trust you any farther than I can throw you," the looming tusker boomed with a few more prods to the boy's ribs.

The poking was not appreciated. Shel sat upright and scowled. His emotional ramparts would not go undefended. "Well, that seems pretty reasonable to me," the boy volleyed, shoving the intrusive tusk away. "You could probably chuck me halfway across the valley. Which would be entirely appropriate, I'll have you know, because I happen to be a pretty trustworthy guy."

The elephant hung his ear on the snide remark and began backpedaling. "Er, what I meant was, I only trust you as far as YOU can throw ME!" Shel stared at him, one eyebrow cocked back as if threatening to fling it. "How about that?" the pachyderm poked, daring the boy to let it fly. Shel raised the second brow, increasing the threat. Undeterred, the elephant proceeded. "Which is not at all," he clarified. "You couldn't lift me one scaly fish fin off the ground, let alone give me a toss anywheres."

"Is that all? Are you finished?"

"Means I don't trust you."

"Yeah, I get it."

"At all."

"Okay, yeah, I get it." Shel stood up and walked away.

The elephant sent a few words following after like hitmen. "You were the last person to see Manny alive—"

"I wasn't alone!" The kid turned sharply with a timely interruption, cutting the hitmen down.

A brief moment of silence for the fallen allowed the elephant digested the surprise retort. Slowly, he stood up and walked towards the boy, bending his ear over him like a soggy umbrella. "Ex-kewwwz-meee?

"I said—"

"Oh, I heard what you said! What in the rippled raven's beak are you talking about?"

Shel gulped. The sight of the towering elephant reminded him of getting caught in a terrifying hailstorm while walking home from Darwin the previous year. The darkness that surrounded him, the cold that bit into him, the deafening sound of pelting hail drowning out all the other sounds of the city. The chilling memory expanded in Shel's mind like ink in water, and he could see himself there again, standing alone on the sidewalk soaking in the storm. Then something in the vision changed. His fallible memory had diluted the truth about that day, the fact that he'd actually not been alone. His little sister, Meg, had been standing next to him, soaking and freezing too, trying not to panic. She was looking up at him expectantly, waiting for her big brother to lead her safely home.

Facing the looming elephant, Shel's perception of that memory shifted. He came to understand that the rain and hail had not fallen to punish him, nor was the storm sympathetic to his woes as he'd previously thought. The storm was indifferent. Yet, it meant something to each person it touched. Thinking of his kid sister, he suddenly realized he was meant to be something more than just afraid, meant to do something more than just stand there feeling sorry for himself. He took a deep breath and recalled how the piercing ice storm had filled his lungs. But this time he embraced the punch, the stabbing cold, and boldly ventured back out of the memory to face the elephant in the room.

"I came here with three others who were looking for Manny to help with a tooth problem."

The elephant loomed larger than ever, slowly spitting out the words, "What … three … others?"

Shel had a feeling he shouldn't say their names but proceeded nonetheless. "Um, Fickleface, Tickletoes, and—"

"Whaaaat?!" The elephant bounced backward as if on springs. "You're friends with the Flying Shoe Crew?"

"Well, no, not really. Kind of. I mean, I just met them..."

"Admit it! You're buddied up with the Buoyant Boot Brigade."

"What?! No, I—"

"You're aligned with the Airborne Apostles of Ambulatory Accessories."

"Muuh... huh? What's ambew lat—?"

"You're in cahoots with the Carefree Club of—"

"Okay, enough already! No, I am not teamed up with the terrible troubadours of tittely-too. Nor have I joined forces with the jolly jamboree of jintery-joo." Shel was turning dark red.

The elephant stopped. "What are you...? No, no. That's all wrong! You can't just make up words. You have to rhyme *real* words."

"Since when? Since when are we rhyming? Who do you think you are? Dr. Seuss?!" snapped Shel.

The elephant softened his tone. "Well, I thought I was being rather clever. Who's Doctor Suits?"

"It's Doctor Soooos! And no, you weren't being clever. That's the thing with you, isn't it? You think you're so clever, that you're the big boss man. Don't you? But you're not the big boss. You're just big."

Despite being lost in some strange Neverland sort of world, like one of Peter Pan's Lost Boys (Shel loved the story of The Boy Who Wouldn't Grow Up), he was definitely beginning to find his voice, and in his voice, his identity. "You don't trust me, huh? Well, I don't entirely trust you either, come to think of it. For all I know, *you* could be the one behind Manny's disappearance. After all, you did show up just after the whole incident." The elephant thought about this for a moment. The boy's logic was sound, his argument not without merit. Maybe this kid wasn't as dim-witted as he'd thought. He looked down at the brocosmile tooth still wrapped in his trunk, propelling him further along the labyrinth of grief to his next stop: vengeance! "And another thing—" Shel attempted more lecturing but the elephant cut him off, raising the tooth in the air.

"You're absolutely right, young man! This... this right here is the clue to Manny's disappearance." He pushed the tooth at Shel. "We shouldn't be fighting with each other. We should be working together, all buddy, buddy! I'm talkin' salt and lime time, man! Not this orange juice and toothpaste nonsense."

"Salt and lime? Orange juice and toothpaste?"

"Yeah. You know. Orange juice and toothpaste don't mix. Yuck! You and I, we need to be like salt and lime. We need to mob up! Find out just what in the hopscotch happened here! We need to get our friend back!"

Shel quietly interjected, "Well... he wasn't really my friend. I mean, I just met him..."

"And I know just where to start." The elephant was clearly not listening. "Come on! You and I are going to need help tracking down that caitiffrous Gambrine, and I have the perfect man for the job!"

"Kai-tifferrrr—?"

"Caitiffrous. Means cowardly... more or less. I may have just made that one up. Don't worry about it! Come on!"

"Oh-kaayyy... Hey look, I can tell you're all gung-ho about this salt and lime whatever, but I should probably just stay here and wait for the boot crew to return. I'm sure they'll be wondering what happened—"

"Hey, I get it. That's groovy. No sweat! You can tell me all about it on the way. I'll even let you be the lime. I'm kind of an old, salty dog anyway..."

So now the elephant's a dog? Shel's eyes rolled. It was clear the big guy was going to dismiss any attempt to dissolve his new crime-fighting club. He shoved the tooth at Shel, "Here, hold onto this," and in one swift motion, plucked the surprised boy from the ground and tossed him up onto his back. As he did, a screech rang out across the sky. It was the call of an eagle from somewhere beyond the clouds. The elephant looked up, startled, expecting to see a giant bird swooping down to snatch the boy who was also looking up, squinting with a tinge of apprehension.

Struck with a sense of déjà vu, Sheldon risked the question, "There don't happen to be any boiling lakes in Champion Valley by chance?"

Seeing no threat from the eagle, the elephant started down a path that led away from Manny's house (what was left of it), in the opposite direction of where the Festoon Brigade landed ol' Delilah. Apparently their mission to find Manny was taking them deeper into this strange land.

"What's that? Boiling lakes?! Heavens no! Why? You feel like going for a dip in some hot, hot, hot springs?" The elephant chuckled. "Is that like some sort of new-age shock therapy or something? Ha. Kids these days."

Shel laughed uneasily. "No. Just making sure." He sighed and slowly relaxed his defenses. Leaning back, he put his arms behind his head, making himself as comfortable as possible atop the elephant's leathery back. "I'm still trying to sort out where Champion Valley is exactly." Shel changed the subject. "Like, what state are we in?"

"What state? What state? The state of *Now*, little buddy, that's what." The elephant laughed.

"Noooo. I mean, where *are* we? Like what country is this? ...Or what planet more like."

"Planet?" the elephant snort-laughed. "Thought you said you were from Chicago. Last time I checked Chicago was in Illinois. No? Arcania's not *that* far away! ...Least I don't think it is."

"Arcania?"

"Yeah. That's what this place is called."

"Wait. Arcania? Really?" Shel asked skeptically. "I thought it was called Champion Valley?"

"It is. Champion Valley, Fallshugger Province, Gambrinstown, Kantcomplainistan — are all places in Arcania."

"Huh... I've never heard of any of those places." Shel shrugged. He was still feeling wholly uneasy about being in a strange land, in strange company, so far from home. But putting a name to the place gave him a sense of normalcy, dare he say, an inkling of familiarity. He settled into his high post on the elephant's back and quietly absorbed this new feeling as the elephant lumbered down the trail, chattering away, rattling off interesting factoids about Arcania. Catching only a smidge of the elephant's ramblings, Shel looked skyward, marveling at the puffy, white clouds swelling in the warm, spring afternoon skies. He couldn't decide if the shapes he saw forming were visions of good times to come, or if a considerable storm was brewing. Either way, he concluded that he was ready for more adventure, surprised to discover that he was actually looking forward to this Manny-finding mission with his new elephant friend — whom, he just realized, had yet to formally introduce himself.

"Say, what's your name anyway?" he interrupted his tour guide.

"Nope! No time for that now!" bellowed the elephant with renewed vigor and a quickening pace. "Best hang on up there, little buddy! 'Cause I have a feeling that this, my friend, is going to be one wild ride!"

Twisting Trails and Wondrous Worlds

Book Two is for Lily, Ella, and Saige.
Stay curious!

Introduction

Me and Him, Again

Me: Hey! Nice to see y'all back for more adventures in Arcania!

Him: Yeah! D'jou miss us?

Me: I think what Him is trying to say is that we hope you enjoyed the first part of the story and we're glad you're back for more. We think you'll find that in act two—

Him: Act two? How many acts are in this story? I mean, what did I commit to here? I can't hang out forever. I've got things to do, people to—

Me: Oh really? You've got what things to do? You've got exactly nothing going on, Him, 'cept hangin' out here with me, tellin' this story for all these good folks. This right here is the best thing that's ever happened to us. So, just relax and settle in whydoncha. After all, this is when the action really picks up.

Him: Oh, yeah? That doesn't sound too bad. What kind of action are we talking about here?

Me: Well, in the first book we followed our hero as he broke down the walls that grown-ups had built — and were continuing to build — around him, and he cut loose the bonds that kept him tied to his small world in Chicago. We watched as he discovered a new world, and found that he had his own individuality, his own voice.

Him: That's right! Oh, it was so exciting to see him finally get out on his own.

Me: Indeed. And in *this* book, we get to see Shel's exploration of his individuality really blossom.

Him: Like a flower!

Me: Um, okay. Like a flower. But I have to warn you, in order for Shel to *really* become his own man and break free from the cocoon of childhood—

Him: Like a butterfly!

Me: Sure Him, like a butterfly. Anyway, Shel will have to endure some hardships and overcome a few difficult trials. Such is the passage for any child becoming their own person.

Him: That sounds intense. Will it be scary?

Me: Well, I don't want to give away the story, but I will say that there are monsters in this book. Some are good, others not so much. But don't worry, Shel has many friends to help him along the way.

Him: Like the Boot Brigade! And that crazy tree-climbing elephant!

Me: Exactly. And in this book, Sheldon makes a few new friends, too.

Him: Sweet! ...Like who?

Me: Well, why don't we start the story and find out, shall we?

Him: Yes, great idea. Let's get to it!

Me: All righty then. You wanna kick it off, or shall I?

Him: Whydoncha go ahead, Me. I like how you tell it.

Me: And I like the way *you* tell it! How about you start this one?

Him: Well, groovy. Ok then, hold onto your shell... ha, get it? Your Shellll?

Me: Yeah. Good one, Him. Ok. I think they're ready.

Him: Ok. Ok. Let's do this!

Prologue

Folks

Oh, the innocence and carefree whims of childhood! When one is a child, it is rather impossible to comprehend just how much one's parents care about one's safety, well-being, happiness... willingness to do the dishes and take out the trash, potential to earn a good living so that one might take care of one's parents in their twilight years, and so on. Sometimes there's so much caring and affection that a parent's love can feel like a wet blanket on the passionate fire of youth.

Some kids will grow up and have kids of their own. In that case, they may come to understand the profound concern of a parent. But for young Sheldon Silvers, sitting atop the back of a most extraordinary elephant, traveling through a most mysterious land, having the most incredible adventure, his profound concern was not for his own safety and well-being, and it certainly was not for the anxiety he was causing his parents. His concern was for adventure and adventure alone. He was too preoccupied with the fantasy in which he now floundered — and flourished — to consider the grief he might be stirring up back home.

Meanwhile, back at the small Chicago apartment, Shel's parents were tearing their hair out over their lost boy. They had called the police multiple times, which proved to be nothing but frustrating when the police advised to simply, "wait it out." The cops figured that Sheldon was probably just another hooligan, that he would return home in his own good time, which, according to Johnny Law, would likely be in a few short hours.

"Please, Sir, Ma'am, try to relax and keep calm," repeated the police, several times.

Shel's folks also called the local paper to place an advertisement. This only added to their frustration, however, as the periodical refused to publish anything without an official police report. They drove to the school and scoured the campus but none of the faculty had seen the boy since he left the nurse's office following the incident with the bloody nose. "Bloody nose?! What bloody nose?!" Now his folks had even more reason to be on tenterhooks.

They called every family member and friend they could think of but no one had seen him or heard from him.

For some families in the boroughs, not seeing their children for hours on end was normal. Sheldon, however, never left school early and his parents almost always knew exactly where he was, what with his father being so strict and Sheldon having very few friends. Without any real friends to speak of, his parents could rule out the possibility that he was coerced into cutting class by some peer of ill repute. Mr. and Mrs. Silvers were completely at a loss and so they reverted, as adults sometimes do, to drowning their sorrows in drink — an unconventional activity for Sheldon's parents, make no mistake.

For the most part, his parents were garden-variety folks, mostly kind and caring, not overly affectionate. Indeed they largely ignored their children, apart from standard parental obligations such as bathing, feeding, bandaging, putting to bed, etcetera.

On account of their lack of affection, Sheldon didn't feel very close to either of his parents. From time to time, people would point out that he had his mother's hair or his father's nose. Other than that, Shel wasn't entirely sure that he hadn't come from a different set of parents entirely — a fantasy that would often have him wondering why he couldn't've been adopted by the charismatic, well-to-do Chicagoan, J. D. MacArthur.

Shel's family didn't consider themselves poor but they were much nearer to poverty than financial security, and daily life for Shel mirrored the difficulties felt by many families during the Great Depression. That is, lights were not left on in rooms unattended (actually, the lights often went out when too many apartment dwellers plugged in too many appliances at the same time); warm clothes were always a prerequisite to the furnace; and plates were never returned to the kitchen with food still on them (with the exception of inedible scraps… sometimes).

A regular complaint from Sheldon was that the landlord didn't allow pets in the apartment complex. No fun pets anyway. Sure, one could have a fish. But who wants a tiny, boring, silent fish? Why couldn't he have, say, a monkey or a kangaroo? He couldn't even have a dog! What sort of boy grows up without a dog?! A sad, lonely one, that's what.

But why settle on a dog when I could have a rhinoceros? he would muse. *Or a dinosaur?! Yeah! Now we're talkin'! A brontosaurus named Morace... who could lift you up to a secret treehouse in the forest... and guard against nosey, uninvited tourists! How great would that be? A dinosaur for a pet in a treehouse free of rent? But NO! We have to live in an anti-pet apart-a-ment.*

What about Zelda? (Zelda was the lady in 2B who had about a zillion cats on account of her inability to turn away any old stray on any given day). *It just isn't fair!*

Not having much choice where he lived — being only twelve years old (going on thirteen!) — at least Sheldon could go places in his mind and dream up any sort of pet he wanted. And so he did.

Skilled at imagining though he was, his daydreaming was rarely enough to silence the discouraging voice of his father ever echoing through his head. Sheldon's dad was constantly reminding him to appreciate what he had, telling him that daydreaming was a waste of time, even blasphemous if it involved coveting impossible possessions, unreachable riches, an unlivable life...

Did Sheldon wish for another life? A *better* one? In truth, not really. Just a few changes to the one he had. A life in which his friends outnumbered his adversaries could be nice. A life in which his father supported his passions didn't sound so bad.

Oftentimes, Shel's father's advice sounded like rhetoric straight out of the Torah. His parents levied their faith to impress manners and an appreciation for the simple things in life like regular meals and a roof over one's head. Their religion helped the family cultivate humility and gratitude. It guided not only their behavior but their life choices as well.

A few years back, when a growing threat overseas began impacting life for Jewish Americans, practicing and non-practicing Jews all over Chicago took to meeting privately to discuss the war and its potential outcomes. Conversations at the synagogue began focusing on contingency preparedness and the importance of community. Shel had even begun to see new, unfamiliar faces at service, noting that some of the newcomers did not speak English. These 'visitors' were said to be, "brethren in need of safe haven."

At one point, Sheldon's family invited a young couple, who spoke very little English, to stay with them in their home. Despite limited communication, Shel found the husband, whom they called "Len", to be quite entertaining. Len would often spend hours with Shel after school, teaching the boy how to play the mandolin. Shel had exhibited aptitude for the instrument and about five months into his lessons, his dad came home with a proper guitar. His old man made it clear that the instrument was on loan from a friend and that Sheldon had better look after it as if it were a newborn baby, or else! Despite the manner in which the guitar was presented, the gift was perhaps the nicest thing his dad had ever done for him.

Sheldon understood the warning to, "look after it like a newborn baby," as a reference to when Sheldon's little sister had come home from the hospital and Sheldon was instructed to, "treat her like a porcelain teacup" — a subsequent reference to the old tea set which glared down at Sheldon from the top shelf of his great-great-grandmother's cabinet. The Silvers kids were forbidden to go anywhere near *that* old block of wood.

The cabinet, which contained *all* the family treasures in one place, was treated with more care and reverence than anything (or anyone) in the house because it was one of the few possessions — along with the tea set — that had migrated with the family from the 'old country'.

Having been chopped into pieces so as to fit into various-sized suitcases for transport across the ocean, the cabinet was reassembled upon arrival by Sheldon's grandfather, and not entirely in the correct order. The dim lighting of the far dining room corner where the cabinet lived gave the fragmented furniture an eerie, beast-like profile. Sheldon often imagined the towering heirloom, with its random pieces of wood sticking out here and there, to be a grotesque monster waiting to devour anything that got too close. This was, incidentally, the exact deterring effect his parents and grandparents were hoping for. "Steer clear of the cabinet," could have been inscribed on the family crest.

Sheldon's little sister, Megan, now a budding eight-year-old, was still a handful for their parents. Often left in the care of her big brother after school and on weekends, Shel and Meg would frequent their father's bakery, occasionally collecting packs of old bagels that were no longer suitable for the public. Some nights at home, days-old stale bread would be all the family could scrape together for dinner. (Thank God for peanut butter!)

One particular winter morning, after a difficult night at home with naught but stale grains for supper, Shel and Meg decided to escape the doldrums of the apartment and brave the bitter chill of Chicago. The two of them ventured out to nearby Humboldt Park to test the sturdiness of the resident pond — glazed over in dark blue and green ice — using a pair of old skates they'd found abandoned in the basement of their apartment building. It was one of those days, ominous skies above and the griping of grown-ups ringing in their ears, unsettling their hearts, which foretold of disaster in every direction, beginning no doubt with the ice.

Trouble was, the skates they brought were of the roller variety. That would have to do, however, as it was all they had. To make matters worse, the roller shoes had turned out to be too big for Meg and too small for Shel. The kids took turns wearing them out nonetheless, and wearing out their toes in the process. Their feet, knees, and backsides didn't fare any better as they careened and crashed over and over on the frozen surface.

Most days, Shel wanted to put his kid sister up for sale, auction her off to the highest bidder... or lowest, whichever came first. That day, despite the skates being a complete disaster — wheels on ice being nigh-uncontrollable — the siblings had more fun than could be recalled in a very long time. Shel even took Meg to his special hot dog stand on the way home and treated her to a Hector's garden special. He knew that she too would be starving after the previous night's poor excuse for a meal.

The memories of Shel's home life could be bitter and cold, like the weather on that dark, winter day. But the ice-skating memory was so sweet that Shel, who had been riding atop an elephant for hours, mind wandering freely over an exotic landscape, was really starting to miss home, and wondering when, if ever, he might go back.

Chapter One: The Philosophers

Part One: Water on Rock

With the sun descending over Champion Ridge, the fields of broccoli had become painted in a hue of emerald green, giving the valley a breathtakingly magical luminescence...

That time of day, known the world over as the witching hour, when mysterious things abound and curious creatures come out to play, found one creature in particular wandering the wild: an enormous elephant with an unusual bump on its back, looking suspiciously like the elusive camelphant — part camel, part elephant — believed to have gone extinct ages ago...

"So, where are we headed, Mr. Elephant?"

"What's that?" the animal replied, swinging a large ear at Shel, almost knocking the boy to the ground.

"I said, where are we headed?"

"No, no. The second part."

"Oh. Well I don't know your actual name, do I?"

"Yeah, well, Mr. Elephant isn't very creative, is it?"

"Ok. Sorry. I—"

"I mean, I don't go around calling you Mr. Boy, do I?"

"Well, I—"

"Say, Mr. Boy, what's your name anyway?" the elephant snorted sarcastically through his trunk.

"Sorry. I just—"

"No, really..." The pachyderm cut Sheldon short, shifting to a sincere tone. "Um, I actually don't... *ahem*... know *your* name either."

"Oh…" Shel paused, unsure if the elephant would make fun or—

"How 'bout I start?"

...interrupt him.

The tusker cleared his throat loudly, "My name..." he paused for effect, "is Israel Tuskinsky. Izzy the Elephant, as they say. Named after the famous juggler, the story-telling wild-man from the next valley over, Valley of Pen or Pencil or some such writing device." He trailed off in a mutter, "Must be full of writers... and poets... and Banzas..."

"'S'cuse me?" Shel nudged. "What's that?"

"Eh? Oh, nothing. Anyway, I'm pleased to meet you, Misterrr…?" The elephant teed up the boy for an introduction but Shel missed the cue, too busy thinking about what 'story-telling wild-man' and 'Banzas' meant. The elephant gave a little buck to remind the kid that he was up to bat. "Misterrr?"

"Oh, sorry! Sheldon. My name's Sheldon. Or Shelby I guess. Just Shel, actually."

"Wellll, Mr. Boy Sheldon Shelby Just Shel Actually, it's nice to make your acquaintance."

"You can just call me Shel."

"Okay! Great! Well, Shelllll," the elephant dragged his name through the air like a banner from a biplane advertising something. An impending favor perhaps? "You can just call me Izzy. And... would you be so kind as to scratchy my backy?" There it was. "I'd be ever so grateful. Right between my shoulder blades, if you please. It's a rather impossible spot for an elephant to reach. And since I've been nice enough to let you ride on my back all this way, perchance you could work some magic with your human claws while you're in the neighborhood?"

Shel hesitated. "Uh…"

"Pleeease? Look, I'll give you two bucks. How's that?"

"Really? Okay, yeah, sure!"

As the boy got to scratchin', the elephant got to rejoicin'.

"Oh, yeah! That's the ticket! That's good stuff right there. Oooh, a little to the left… higher… higher… lower… to the right… the other right… oh, Nelly, that's the spot!" Izzy kept the boy busy for a good while until Shel's arms couldn't take anymore.

"I'm tired, Izzy. Can I stop scratching now?"

"Ahhh," the elephant sighed with relief. "If you must."

"And?"

"And what?"

"Where's my two bucks?"

"What's that?" Izzy was off in la-la land, still tingling from the bristly massage.

"You said you'd give me two bucks for scratching your back."

"Why would I do that? My back doesn't itch anymore," declared the elephant, pleased with his salesmanship.

"Oh, come on!"

"Fine!" scoffed Izzy. "Here, how 'bout this!" He launched his hindquarters into the air twice, twice nearly sending Sheldon flying into the bushes.

"Hey!"

"Hold on! It's a crazy, wild ride, just like I said it would be."

"Izzy!"

"Little known fact: I was raised by buckin' broncos in the Wild West!" The elephant continued to bump and twitch like an old-time wagon on a dusty trail of the frontier. Sheldon was having a heck of a time staying put. He reached for the animal's ears for something to hold on to and grabbed hold tightly.

"Will… you… knock… it… off?!"

Izzy calmed down and sauntered on, catching his breath and chuckling to himself, "No charge for the extra bucks."

"Please don't do that again," whined Shel.

"Why not? Seems your life could use a good shake-up." Izzy twitched his hips a bit more.

"Stop it! I think my life's already been shaken up quite enough, thank you. I mean, look at me, riding on a talking elephant, going who knows where... Could you at least tell me where you're taking me?"

"Of course! We, my young friend, are headed to see the famous hunter and tracker from the famous Falconovich Circus, in the famous Land of Happy, which is a bit of a misnomer actually," he added under his breath, then fell quiet.

"The Land of Happy?"

"Yessir. At least it used to be. Who knows what it's like these days? Could be happy. Could be sad. Could be like moldy cheese and smell terribly bad..." Izzy was rambling.

"What in the world are you talking about?"

"The place was once a land where everyone was welcome and the king's only rule was that you had to be happy. But, the king has grown old. Times change, as we all know. He's had a bit of a rough life and is no longer so welcoming. And sadly, not so happy these days."

"What happened? Why not?" asked Shel, thinking peripherally about his father.

"No one knows for sure. Probably a lot of little things just wore him down over time, like drops of water on rock."

"I don't get it."

"Well, rock is solid and strong and seems impenetrable, right? Shel nodded.

"...While water, on the other hand, is fluid and soft and can therefore appear weak, relatively speaking. But eventually, given enough time, rock always gives way to water; the strong and rigid things yield to the soft, persistent things, given enough time."

"Are you sure about that?" Shel challenged. "Some rocks are huge, like boulders. Little drops of water can't break them apart, can they?"

Shel was imagining the large mountains of rock he had seen in photographs displayed at the Art Institute of Chicago during a school field trip. The trip was the highlight of the semester and inspired in him a desire to be the next Ansel Adams, the prominent photographer of the exhibit.

Though recalling images of the great Rocky Mountains and King's Canyon, Shel was actually thinking of his dad, how immovable his father appeared, how impenetrable his emotions seemed. He wondered if, despite being so feeble compared to his war-veteran father, if he could be like a subtle yet persistent drop of water and eventually break through his dad's tough, practically invulnerable armor.

"You know anything about the Grand Canyon?" replied Izzy.

Shel looked down at the elephant, squinting with curiosity. It was as if he were reading Shel's thoughts — images of the Grand Canyon had been a centerpiece of the photography exhibition. Shel couldn't see Izzy's face, but if he could've, he would have seen a sly, knowing smirk.

"That's exactly how the canyon was formed, water flowing over rock for millions of years. All it takes is enough time, my young friend, and the littlest of things can change even the biggest of things."

Chapter One: The Philosophers

Part Two: Cloud Heads

They walked in silence for a while, each mulling on their own thoughts and enjoying the serene surroundings, until the elephant finally let the proverbial cat out of the rucksack so it could breathe a little.

"You know, you and I have something in common..."

Shel replied in a distant voice, his gaze carried off by the fading sun over distant hills, "Oh yeah? What's that? We both like peanut butter?"

"What? Ew! Gross. No! I'm talking about our dads. Mine was difficult too, hardly ever around, always busy with work, über proficient at ignoring kids, especially his own. He was a tough nut to crack, that's for sure."

"A tough *peanut* to crack?"

"Would you stop it already?! Sheesh. You ought to get along great with the king, both peanut butter-loving nut heads."

Shel giggled, his mood lifted. (Nothing like bugging someone else to make one feel better!) "That right? Is he a peanut butter fan too?"

"A fan?! That's putting it mildly. He's the biggest peanut butter fanatic you ever met! There's no one in this wide world who loves peanut butter more than ol' Skippy."

"Skippy?" Shel laughed. "Is that his name?"

"King Solomon Skippingston Longsmiles the Third, actually. But everyone just calls him Skippy. But don't call him that to his face. He'd probably have you beheaded."

Shel winced. "Geez. Sounds like a real sweetheart. Just like my old man."

"Oh, I doubt that. Surely your dad loves you. Under that hard exterior, I'll bet he's a real softy. Like a crusty, old peanut butter sandwich left out on the countertop too long. You just need to get past the stale bread on the outside, get to the sweet, gooey stuff on the inside."

"That's a nice analogy, Izzy, but I don't think my dad has any sweet gooiness in him. I think he's crust and mold all the way through."

Izzy chuckled, then let a bit of silence reign over them, like a gentle drizzle washing away a layer of dirt. "Yeah... my dad was pretty crusty too, never really accepted me either. At least not for who I wanted to be. He wanted me to be a performer, a circus trick. Sure, there were fun times, don't get me wrong. A kid growing up in the circus? Who wouldn't like that, right? You would think."

Like any friend should, Shel turned his attention to the elephant, who was clearly sharing some deeper, more sensitive sentiments.

"I don't know," Izzy continued his ramble. "I was different though. My dream has always been to fly."

"You want... to fly?" Shel asked.

"Well, yeah. I mean, I always wanted to be a pilot, to fly planes, you know. But they don't let elephants fly planes, do they?"

"Um..." Shel wasn't sure that was an actual question. He was pretty sure that somewhere in Arcania there were likely to be all sorts of odd flying things piloted by all kinds of odd creatures.

"Nope! They don't," Izzy slammed the door on that one. "But, we shan't give up on our dreams, now shan't we?"

"Uh, yeah... I mean, no. People shouldn't... shan't. They shan't give up. Shan't... do that, now shan'tn't we? Nope, we shan't-n't-ingle jingle, jangle, jingle..." Shel transitioned to singing one of his favorite songs — "I got spurs that jingle, jangle, jingle..." — until Izzy cut in.

"Ok. Ok. Don't hurt yourself," Izzy chuckled. "By the way, spurs on any animal are an immediate no-go. You know that, right?"

"Of course! I don't agree with the lyrics, necessarily. I just like the tune. It's catchy." Shel began to sing once more, much to Izzy's delight. "Oh Lily Bell, Oh Lily Bell... though I may have done somethin', this is why I'm never full..."

The elephant wiggled, dancing on down the trail. "Quite a voice you got there. Awfully unique, innit? Those aren't exactly the right words, buuut..."

"Yeah, I know."

"But, you're hitting all the right notes... and you sure got the rhythm! That's what really matters. Sing it, boy!"

Shel sang until his enthusiasm sputtered out. He took a moment to catch his breath and then caught up with the previous conversation. "So, you didn't give up on your dream, did you? You're still trying to become a pilot?"

"Pilot? No, not really. Pops kinda put the kibosh on that dream. But I've—"

"What'd he do?"

"Uh, well, nothing really. He just told me it was an impossible dream, told me to get my head out of the clouds."

"Oh, yeah. That old phrase. That's one of my dad's favorites."

"Yeah. Dads love that one, don't they? But, it's okay, I discovered other possibilities."

"Of flying?"

"Of trying, sure. Anyway, you see what I'm saying? I told you we had stuff in common."

"Yeah, I guess we do." Shel thought about something for a moment. "Sorry, Izzy."

"'Bout what?"

"That you had to deal with a dad like that."

"Oh, it's all right. That was a long time ago. Besides, he wasn't my *real* dad anyway."

"Not your... what do you mean? Who was your real dad?"

Izzy mumbled something.

"Izzy?"

"Never mind kid. I'll tell you about that some other time. Just don't give up on your dreams, whatever they are. You're a good kid, even if your dad can't see it yet. He will someday, I can promise you that."

"Thanks Izzy." A solemn moment passed before Shel lightened the mood. "I don't know about being a pilot when I grow up, but I'd sure like to fly someday. Let me know when you figure out the trick and you can take me with you, up to the sky, right here on your back where I belong."

"Ha. Yeah. You betcha!" replied Izzy with a chuckle. "We'll fly on up to the great, blue yonder and both stick our heads in the clouds. How 'bout that? That'll show 'em!"

They had a good laugh and then both quieted down to listen to night approaching.

Chapter One: The Philosophers

Part Three: Poets

Izzy was deep in thought, trying to stay afloat in the swamp of wonderings about the dentist and his untimely disappearance, trying to come up with an ingenious plan to recover his friend when Shel butted in, also thinking of Manny...

"Izzy, what do you plan to tell Manny about his house?"

"What's the thing? Who's house? Where'd it what?" The elephant was jolted out of his head space.

"Manny's house. If you find Manny—"

"*WE*, Sheldon. WEEEE. And not *IF*, *WHEN*. *WHEN* WEEE find Manny."

"Right. Of course. When *weee* find Manny, he's not going to have a house to come home to."

"Yeah, yeah. Don't worry, kid. I have the whole thing figured out. I'll just tell him there was a great, big furniture bash at his place and that we—"

"Furniture... bash?"

"Exactly. You know, where the couch turns on the dresser, and the desk finally gets fed up with the chairs... A brawl is bound to break out eventually, with a fight to the finish. Happens all the time around here. He'll never suspect a thing."

Shel mumbled, "I doubt that sort of thing happens all the time..." He then spoke up. "Izzy, don't you think you'd better just tell him the truth?"

Izzy seemed preoccupied by the evening creeping up on them from all sides. "The truth? Nah. The truth is so… relative."

"Is it?" Shel asked rhetorically. "I thought the truth was the truth and that's that."

"Ha! One would think. Seems logical enough. But, the truth of reality is that each person's truth is determined by their reality, and reality is governed by perception. And perception is most certainly relative — eye of the beholder and all that."

"But a chair is a chair, no matter how much we call it a table. And tables and chairs don't come to life and fight. That's reality."

"Hmmm. Maybe that's been *your* reality, Shel, because that's what you've been taught. But weren't you also taught that elephants can't talk?" Shel opened his mouth but then shut it again, eyes asquint. Izzy continued. "Once upon a time, people's reality told them that the sun revolved around the Earth, pulled on a cart by a team of horses or some such silliness. People also used to subscribe to the reality that the world was flat, and that the ocean just fell off a cliff, a waterfall of infinity. History is filled with this cycle, people adamantly believing one thing and then discovering that they were wrong when a new reality presents itself. And yet, they cling to their convictions time and again, sink their soul into their opinions on reality, fighting wars and destroying one another, motivated by ephemeral beliefs." Shel's head was aching, but Izzy didn't let up. "Reality is a byproduct of perception, Shelby, and oftentimes our reality is limited only by our ability to imagine possibilities."

Shel squinted harder as if trying to see something far away, Izzy's words making his brain feel like Sisyphus pushing the boulder up that impossible mountain. Eventually, Shel relaxed his scrunched face as he realized Izzy was actually speaking his language: the language of philosophers, the language of *dreamers*!

"You know what I think? I think you've got more imagination in you than you know, Shelby. Seems to be overflowing in fact, spilling over the dams which have been built up to keep in a certain reality. I think it's ready to come out and play. Maybe it's high time you opened up and let it flow instead of trying to contain it, trying to live within the boundaries of what you've been taught."

Shel grinned as a warmth in his chest spread with Izzy's words of encouragement. "I'll try," he said, his Sisyphus boulder reduced to a mere pebble, gliding easily up wisdom hill.

"Splendid!" Izzy replied before suddenly becoming anxious over the fading light of day. "So, uh, listen, Mr. Boy Shelby Just Shel..." Izzy smiled, Shel frowned. "All this chatting is nice and all, but I'm thinking we'd better find a safe place to hide... SLEEP! I meant sleep. We'd better find a nice place to sleep for the night. Not to worry, no need to hide. Champion Valley is quite safe. I just meant that an inexperienced kid like you... not that you're a little kid..." Izzy was really stumbling over his words. "Just that someone not accustomed to this place might... um, inadvertently attract some unwanted attention, you know?"

"Not really." Shel wasn't following Izzy's ramblings. The elephant was obviously uneasy about something — a disposition punctuated by gurgling noises coming from his stomach. Little did Shel know, the sounds were *not* coming from Izzy at all, but from somewhere in the distance. "Izzy, you okay? You hungry?"

"Huh? No, not especially. Why? Do you have some food? Perhaps some cantaloupe?" He perked up.

"Cantaloupe? Eww. No. It's just... your stomach seems to be making a lot of noise."

"Oh, really? I hadn't noticed. Is my tummy saying, 'No more ice cream and sauerkraut'? Because I've been binging a little lately." Izzy stopped walking to get a listen. But when he stopped — giant elephant feet no longer crunching the underbrush — all went quiet. Having become considerably overgrown from lack of use, the trail they were following was certainly the path less traveled (Frost would have been pleased). As they climbed upward through the high country of Champion

Ridge, overlooking the expanse of broccoli below, a sweet breeze pushed up from the valley and the they paused, tuning into the susurrant wind caressing the grass and tree leaves. The large elephant with the small boy on top, silhouetted against a darkening sky like a disfigured snowman, trudged on, watching the last splashes of light paint — across an expanding twilight canvas — the conclusion to another remarkable day. The evening birds, frogs, and crickets serenaded a nocturnal cast of actors to the stage while lulling the diurnal players to dreams.

"I wonder what they're saying," Shel sighed.

Izzy twisted his neck, attempting to glare at the boy. "Don't tell me you don't speak Spanish *OR* Artilan?"

"Artilan?"

"Artilan. Flower Speak," clarified Izzy. Shel delivered a puzzled look. "Why am I not surprised?" Izzy mumbled, then began an animated speech in another one of his unplaceable accents, a fanciful player on the world stage. "Flower Speak, ma boy, is what we call the sacred tongue of nature. It is the sound and the fury — to quote a great poet — of all creatures great and small — to quote another grand poet. It is not for trivial conversation and chit-chat, not for talk of money or possessions or social status, but for the discussion of beauty, the elucidation of wonder, the explication of the grand design, and for construing proper order within the chaos that is all of creation."

Shel stared down at his elephant chariot in wide-eyed wonder, unsure what to say. His mind felt like a trout-sized fishing pole trying to reel in a whale. The elephant closed his eyes, listening to the surroundings. Shel followed suit, trying to concentrate, but all he heard was the crunching of Izzy's feet on the path and the echo of the elephant's speech in his head. He ignored the background noise of Izzy's growling tummy (which was not Izzy's tummy).

"That sounded very poetic, Izzy. Are you a poet?"

"Nah. But I do like poetry," Izzy replied cheerfully, then quickly ducked his head and looked around nervously as if afraid someone might be listening. He turned to look toward the shadowed bushes and spoke loudly, making sure the bushes could hear him. "But I'm not one of them crazy, lazy, whimsical, flimsical poet types. That's for sure!"

Shel looked around. "Who ya talkin' to there, big guy?"

"Shhhh. There might be a Banzakoot nearby."

Shel looked confused then frightened. "A banza... cute?"

"Koot, not cute. They're definitely not cute. The Banza's like an oversized buffalo, or better yet, a Gruffalo! Massive upward-curved tusks and gnarled-up nose... Lives in the underbrush and feeds on poets and pomegranate tea."

"Poets... and... pomegranate tea? That doesn't make any sense. Are you feelin' okay?"

"What? Yes! I'm fine. The Banzakoot doesn't like poetry, Shel. So it eats it up, trying to rid the world of it."

"Huh?! Why? What's wrong with poetry?"

"Nothing! Poetry is great! I mean, if you like that sort of thing." Izzy got back to hushed tones and shifty eyes. "But the Banza considers poetry to be a vocation of convenience, how some people view art in general. You know?"

"What? No, I don't know."

"The Banzakoot is hyper-focused on productivity. For the Banza, there's no time for pastimes, especially art, and most especially poetry. A real philistine, the Banza is."

"Phila-huh?"

"Philistine. An art antagonist. A culture crusher."

"But... art is important! Art is inspiration! What fun would the world be without art? Without culture?! Come on! ...No creativity? What about people whose job is *making* art, like singers and writers and painters? Some artists go crazy for their art, like Van Gogh or Michelangelo." Izzy raised his brows at Shel. "We studied them in school," Shel smiled. "I doubt people like them would say art is convenient. Right?"

"No, likely not," agreed Izzy.

Shel thought about his own creative tendencies, how they'd done little to help his relationship with his father or friends, nor his performance in school. "I think, for some people, the need to make art can be a real burden, a ball and chain."

"I suppose that's true enough," Izzy replied, reaching his trunk back toward Shel's leg. "Have your shoes been bothering you? Because I think there may be a philosopher somewhere in your soul. Take 'em off, let me see." Izzy grabbed Shel by the ankle and lifted the boy into the air, flipping him upside down.

"Hey! Put me down!" Shel yelled, laughing all the while.

"Or maybe a politician? Have you considered running for office?" Izzy set the complainy kid on the ground and they both laughed.

Shel dusted himself off after being dropped in the dirt. "Run for office? I don't know what that is. I only run for gym class. But I think I'll walk for a bit if you don't mind."

"Suit yourself." Izzy smiled, and the two continued walking side-by-side in the twilight. "I would agree," continued Izzy, "that for some artists their passion is not convenient but more of a burden, as you point out, if it compels them regardless of circumstance or time or money or relationships, and so on. *Any* obsession can get in the way of living if you let it." Shel nodded. "But the Banzakoot doesn't recognize art as a burden. To it, art is evidence of having too much time on one's hands, not being sufficiently burdened by, 'real' (Izzy used his trunk to gesture quotation marks) tasks that need doing, things like building shelter, gathering food, preparing for winter... Stuff like that. To the Banza, hard work is the grease that keeps the cogs of civilization spinning."

"Hmm. I think that for some people the cogs spin from hard work. But the grease, that's art for sure. Art makes life enjoyable. Without art, life would be dull and boring, colorless. ...Flavorless meat and potatoes! Maybe the cogs would still spin but it would be gritty and rough, probably not much fun at all... Probably wouldn't last long either, everything torn apart by friction. ...Kaboom!" He threw his hands in the air.

Izzy chuckled at Shel's histrionics then nodded slowly. He was really impressed by this kid, not yet thirteen but already able to hold his own in the ring of philosophical discourse. To Izzy, being who he was (with such a large head and such large feet), this was no small feat.

"Plus, art requires imagination, and imagination is how we evolve," Shel added, a punctuation mark to Izzy's admiration.

The elephant raised his brow. "Evolve? Pretty deep there, kid. You need to come up for some air?" Shel smirked. Izzy laughed and continued. "No, I agree. You're right. The boring old Banza is going extinct. That's for sure."

They both chuckled. Then Shel dropped his head. "I think my dad has a Banzakoot in *his* soul. Maybe someone should check *his* shoes."

Izzy smiled. "Maybe. But maybe it's not his fault."

Shel looked up. "What do you mean?"

"Floccinaucinihilipilification," answered Izzy.

"Flocks-a-nox-a-what in the world did you just say?"

"Floccinaucinihilipilification. It's a state of mind, a way of regarding things as if they have no intrinsic value. It's this myopic ailment that affects the Banzakoot. People too sometimes. It's a disease that restricts vision, like blinders on a racehorse. Maybe your dad's just suffering from tunnel vision. Many in the world think art is superfluous."

"Soup-er-floo-us?"

"Unnecessary. A distraction."

Shel smirked. "You're like a walking dictionary."

"More like an encyclopedia!" Izzy laughed triumphantly. "Elephants are famous for our ability to remember things, retain information. We remember a lot of things by singing, actually."

"Singing? Really? You sing?"

"Of course! Like I said, you and I have a lot in common." They smiled at one another. "Where I come from there's even a song about art, for guys just like you, Shelby." Izzy stopped walking and began to sing in a low, gruff voice.

> *Oh, nobody's sculpting statues of David*
> *from the red, earthen clay.*
> *Though it be soft and though it be fine,*
> *nobody's sculpting statues today.*
> *So put down your chisel and pick up your spade.*
> *In the copper mines we slave away.*
> *Down in the mud, down in the mire,*
> *art shall be buried by work today.*

"Wow, Izzy. You have a pretty good voice."

"Thanks. It sounds better in my native tongue."

"So, Nobody's a skilled sculptor then, eh?" Shel said, sounding facetious.

"Not if they're miners. No time to sculpt when you're busy digging in the dirt for shiny rocks all the time."

Shel nodded then smirked. "You know, Nobody was my friend when I was a kid."

"Is that right?" Izzy replied, not sure he was catching what the kid was throwing at him. "Sounds sad."

"Not really. Nobody was a pretty good friend, actually. Nobody would laugh at all my jokes. Nobody helped me with my homework. Nobody would walk with me to school—"

"Ah, yeah. Okay. I get it. Very funny." Izzy sat down in the cool grass to admire the moonrise over the valley, affectionately lifting the boy up to his shoulders the way a dad might for his kid at a carnival. All that was missing was the cotton candy.

Shel squirmed to get comfortable, then laid his head down on the elephant's dome, a hard and scratchy pillow. It was clear the unlikely pair were growing fond of one another.

"So, your native tongue? Is that Artil…uh… What was it?"

"Artilan? No, that's everyone's native tongue. Everyone is born being able to understand Artilan."

"Everyone? Even Nobody?" Shel tried to be funny. Izzy just scoffed, humoring him. "So, you're telling me that everyone at one point could understand what the crickets and the wind are saying?"

"Oh, absolutely. Most just forget it as they grow up, as they become more entangled in the artificialities of life, as they move farther away from nature in pursuit of professions, possessions, and power!" Izzy flexed his trunk like a bicep for effect. "Even you could, once upon a time."

Shel considered this very curious elephant who could not only speak but could speak intelligently, profoundly, with a rare and remarkable awareness of the world — many worlds it seemed. Then he thought about his childhood and about his dad, always so focused on productivity, like a crotchety old Banzakoot. Intentional or not, his dad was such an antagonist to creative whimsy, it was nearly impossible to imagine his old man ever being able to understand the language of nature. Shel leaned on Izzy's head and looked up at the stars trickling into the dark stadium, packing the house for an all-night performance. "You said that song is sung back where you're from. You're not from here?" asked Shel.

"Arcania? No. I'm from a land far away from here actually."

"Oh? Where's that? Are you from Africa?" asked Shel excitedly.

Izzy sighed. "Kid, that story is for another time."

The two of them sat silently, staring out at the valley, which seemed to glow in the moonlight. Above them, a million stars slowly appeared like a photograph developing in a darkroom, filling the brilliant sky with magic, while soft sounds of the evening filled their hearts.

Chapter Two

The Worst

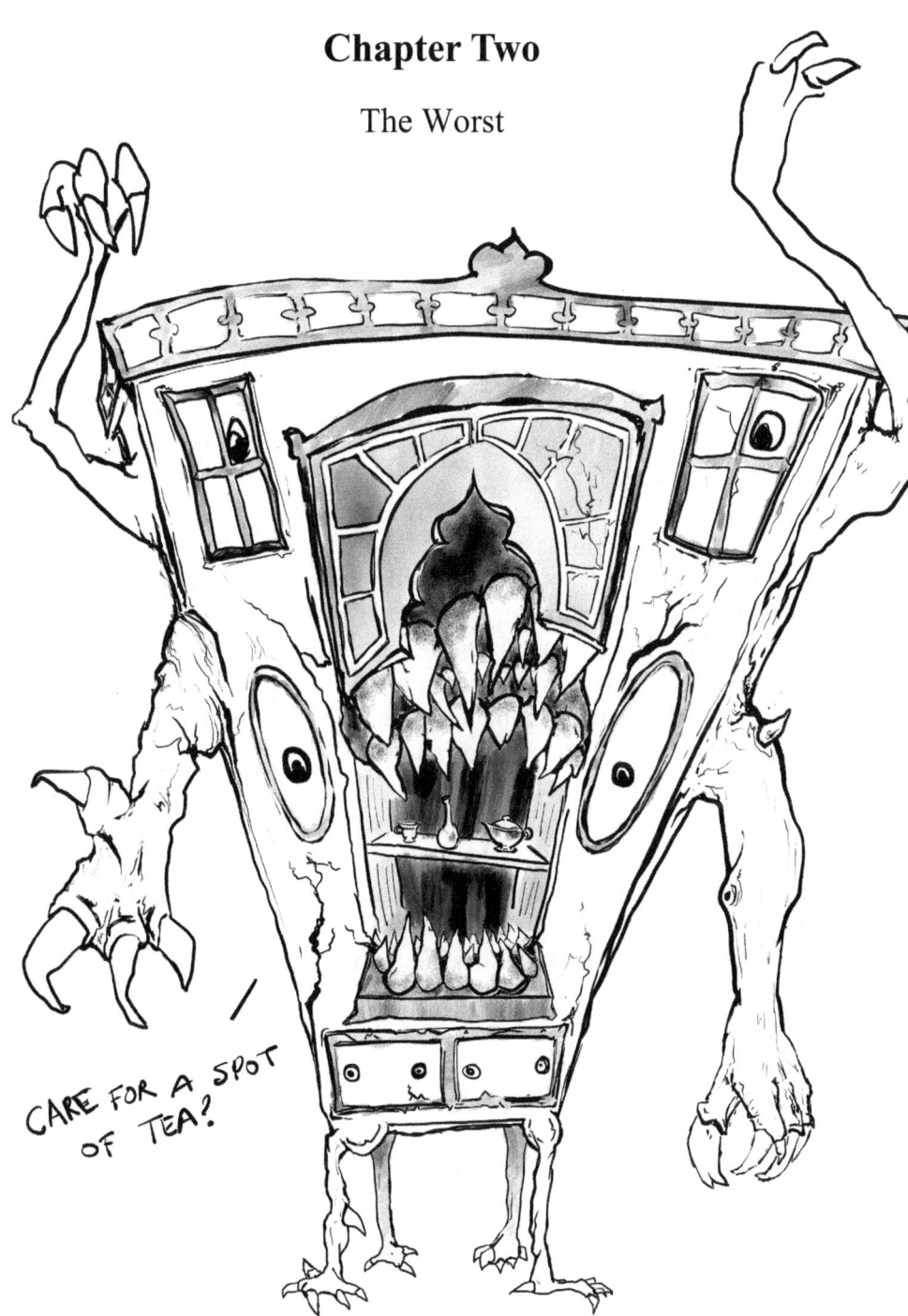

CARE FOR A SPOT OF TEA?

The musical score of twilight was so comforting that both Shel and Izzy could have fallen asleep right there in the weeds were it not for a gang of storm clouds gathering in the distance, conspiring to spoil their party.

Eventually, the fog smothered the diffident moon, a warning that the travelers would do well to find shelter if they wished to stay dry. That, combined with Izzy's supposed grumbling tummy — which had gone silent for a time but was now back with a vengeance, growing louder by the minute — made the elephant jerk such that Shel had to quickly grab hold of Izzy's ears lest he tumble off the elephant's broad shoulders.

The elephant turned to face the darkness surrounding them on all sides. "Did you hear that, Shel?"

"Sure did. You need a sandwich, big guy?"

"No! I'm not hungry. I mean, I kind of am actually. ...Why? Do you have a sandwich? Actually, I could really go for a bowl of dim sum 'bout now... or a cantaloupe. Now that I think of it, there's actually a pretty decent restaurant just over the next ridge there. Wait! What am I saying?! *I'm* not starving, but something out there definitely is!" He jerked toward the bushes on the opposite side but found nothing except a slight drizzle of rain beginning to fall.

"It's raining," complained Shel. Then he encountered something worse. "Ugh! Izzy, what's that awful smell? Is that you?"

Izzy began spinning slowly in a circle. "That's not me, you nincompoop! I'm thinking that... I need to... I think we should probably... it might be best if we... RUUUUUUUUN!"

Izzy quickly wrapped Shel in his trunk with a, "Hold on tight!" as he bolted down the path at full stampede, very much with the intent of knocking down or otherwise smashing to bits anything that stood in their way.

"IZZEEEE! What's happening?!" Shel shot looks of fright in all directions but saw nothing, the cloak of drizzle and darkness keeping hidden whatever madness spurred the elephant's flight. His ears weren't much use either in determining why they were running, both drums filled to capacity by the crashing and pounding of Izzy steamrolling the underbrush, kicking up rocks, snapping branches, smashing bushes — including any and all broccoli plants that lay in his path.

That's it! We're being chased by Gambrine, fed up with this elephant romping through their crops! Shel reasoned. ...Until he saw it!

Bursting out from a thick of trees came a terrifying beast with gnashing teeth and outstretched arms, thrashing wildly out of control like a rag doll dragged by a rope behind a bully's bicycle. The monster, which looked like a twelve-foot wall of naught but claws and jaws — only splotches of fur here and there for effect — was gaining on them, tearing through the forest understory as if it were tissue paper, growling as if the thing hadn't eaten in a decade.

Shel let out a blood-curdling scream that made Izzy think maybe he'd been snatched up. "SHEL!"

"Run FASTER!" replied a still-alive-but-scared-out-of-his-wits boy. Never in his wildest dreams did he envision riding atop an elephant, running from a creature that looked as if a six-year-old had haphazardly glued together the remnants of a half-eaten tyrannosaurus rex... along with whatever the kid found lying around the yard: sticks, stones, old dog bones; cotton lint, fire flint; macaroni, bubble gum, scrap tin aluminum; rotten dried banana peels, busted-up wagon wheels; toothpicks, paperclips... and a hundred-foot spool of old, rusted barbed wire...

Something in the back of Shel's mind recalled his family's cabinet with its mismatched boards sticking out at odd angles. "Izzy! DO SOMETHING!" he wailed.

"We have to get to high ground," Izzy hollered back. "We have to climb a tree! Worsts can't climb trees!"

"Worsts?" Shel hollered. "No, no, no, Izzy! I've seen you climb a tree. That's a baaad idea!"

The elephant veered toward a stretch of land that looked as if it might lead to a grove of large sycamores, good for climbing. But it didn't. Instead, the path funneled them onto a narrow ridge rising high above the forest canopy and they soon found themselves flanked on the right by a rocky cliff, on their left by a steep hill covered in tall grass — likely filled with brocosmiles and Banzakoots, or so Shel imagined.

"Yeeeeeooowwww!" Izzy howled.

Shel turned quickly to see the Worst monster not ten feet away. The ogre-like savage had swiped the elephant's backside in a not-so-gentle reminder that death was knocking at his oversized back door.

Izzy desperately scanned the surroundings for any place where they might find refuge but saw nothing save for the misty wetness floating in the air all around. Knowing he had to do something immediately, the elephant closed his eyes and yelled, "HAAANG ON!" as he whipped sharply to the left, leaping off the ridge into the abyss. Izzy's massive body took flight just as the Worst reached out to snatch young Sheldon off the elephant's back like a gorilla plucking a flea.

At the mercy of unbridled savagery, the Worst flung its oversized arms desperately toward the escaping dinner. As a result, the monster was thrown completely off balance.

Tumbling uncontrollably, the creature flew clean over the rocky cliff, down the steep escarpment on the opposite side of the ridge from where Izzy jumped. Thunderous wails and a deafening crash shook the valley from the forest floor to the tops of the trees, the resounding echo of which left scarred the once-peaceful night.

Izzy couldn't stop to see what had happened even if he'd wanted, for he too was careening uncontrollably, but down an entirely different slope.

His hillside wasn't so steep, and it was, mercifully, covered in thick, soft grass, being on the windward side of the mountain. The rain of the evening made the foliage slick such that the elephant went sliding and spinning on his belly like a waxed saucer in snow.

As the slope leveled out, he gradually slowed, eventually slipping backside-first through the mouth of a shallow cave, finally coming to an abrupt stop when he crashed into the rock wall at the rear of the cave, which was thankfully skirted in thick sagebrush.

The elephant lay battered and bruised but relieved to find that the worst was behind him, that the monster had not followed them into the cave. For this was a hollow just large enough to swallow the elephant and the boy and nothing else.

Chapter Three

The End

Izzy sat. catching his breath and dusting himself off. "Holy handshakes of Hades! My word! That... was... a... kuhh-lose one!" ...

"I mean, shoooo-weeee! I've seen Worst footprints, and even some Worst scat before, if you can imagine that... Worst scat. It's truly... the *worst*! Haha."

He laughed uneasily, trying to rinse off the residue of fear with a splash of humor, but the overwhelming adrenaline sent him into a fit of uncontrollable blabbering.

"They say it's hard to tell them apart sometimes: the real deal from the digested meal. Apparently, they even smell alike! 'Be careful of that dung heap,' they say, 'it could be a baby Worst!' Because, actually, the babies are quite dangerous, like diamondback rattlesnakes, no restraint. The rule of thumb is that if it doesn't move when you poke it, it's probably just a pile of poo. Still, best to steer clear just the same. My friends don't believe me, but once when I was waaay out in the mountains — I'm talkin' way out — I swear I saw a full-grown Worst bull romping through the bushes. The thing was pretty far away, I'll admit, so I can't be certain, I s'pose, but I heard what sounded most definitely like a Worst growl, and I smelled something awfully foul... I've never actually encountered one face-to-face though... before tonight that is. Not that this was exactly face-to-face. Know what I mean? Like, I didn't even get a good look at it really. But you! You were right there! Was all breathin' down your neck and... my goodness! I can't imagine... can't imagine what you must've been thinkin', man. I mean, braid my tail and call me Travis! Because I'm... I'm... I don't even *know* what I'm saying right now. I'm just so happy we're safe. You know? That was *way* too close... way, way, WAAAY too close for comfort. M'y right? Right?? Shel? You get a good look at it?" Izzy realized he had been yammering nonstop without any interjection or reply.

"Shel?"

No response.

"Shelby?"

Nothing.

He glanced upward, trying to get a look at his back, but it's not easy for an overgrown elephant to see what's directly behind that big head.

"Hey! You asleep up there?" he bucked his shoulders to give the boy a jolt. When there was still no reply, he began turning in circles, chasing his tail, trying to see what Sheldon was up to, figuring he'd find the kid smiling down in a playful, cruel trick. "This ain't funny, Shel!" He couldn't feel anything on his back but that didn't mean the boy wasn't there. His whole backside had gone numb after the Worst's vicious clawing, and then sliding into the cave wall.

"Shel! Answer me!"

Fearing the worst, the elephant bucked wildly and spun in such a circle that no boy would be able to hold on. And yet, no boy came flying off. "Oh, dear lord! Oh, no!" He stopped spinning and stared out at the night from inside of the cave, terrified of the obvious conclusion. "No, no, no no no! No, Shel, nooooo!" He was petrified by the thought of what awaited him in the dark of night. But it didn't matter. It didn't matter if he had to face a hundred Worsts. Little Sheldon was his friend, his compadre, and he wasn't about to abandon his companion and leave him to be chomped on by some big, nasty, stinky, claw-filled, jaw-filled... terribly... terrifying... Oh lord. *Are you sure about this??* Izzy cried to himself.

He closed his eyes, took a deep breath, and, mustering every ounce of bravery he had left, charged out of the cave with a booming, "Hold on Shelby, Izzy's coming for youuuu!"

Sadly, our young hero couldn't hear the elephant's war cry from the other side of the ridge. To this day it's still unclear exactly what happened to Sheldon after Izzy made that tight, left-hand turn. Did he take a tumble down the ravine alongside the Worst and ultimately end up as dinner? Did he get batted off Izzy's back by the monster and end up flying through the air only to become stuck in a treetop somewhere? Did he get snatched up by a giant eagle again? Sadly, we'll never know.

The End.

Roll credits.

o o o o o o

Just kidding.

It's just that Shel doesn't recall what happened to him, how he got from the elephant's back one instant to the bottom of the ravine the next. So there's a bit of a blank space in the story. Apologies for that. But, all's well that ends well, so they say. Sheldon ended up landing safely in a rather soft, thornless blackberry bush. There he slept the night, having blacked out from the fall, or perhaps fear, or fatigue... or most likely all of the above.

Chapter Four

More Monsters

$\mathscr{S}hel$ $woke$ up drenched from the rain of the evening, shivering from the cold, and scared out of his wits, wondering where Izzy was and if the Worst beast was still out there somewhere. This time, he did not have to review recent events to reorient himself with his new reality. This time, the reality of being alone, cold, wet, and afraid in a strange land was bearing down on him like an Annapurna avalanche.

Not knowing what else to do, and being awfully hungry, Sheldon commenced eating his fill of the berries from the bush in which he'd spent the night. After gorging on berries then untangling himself from the bramble, he wandered off in whatever direction seemed most interesting, having no other metric for deciding where to go. He only knew he had to find his elephant friend. Luckily for Shel, he didn't have to wander far, for after a few short minutes of crying out for Izzy, he was discovered by an odd pair of strangers.

"Well, what do we have here?" said a voice.

Shel stopped dead in his tracks as he rounded a bend and came face-to-face with another hideous monster, two in fact. These two, however, were much smaller and a fair bit less scary-looking than the Worst beast — though still frightening, make no mistake. Thus, fear snatched the voice from Shel's throat and the stride from his legs. He was cemented on the spot. He'd only heard of such creatures in storybooks, and not the sort of storybooks one reads alone in the dark.

"Looks to be but a young lad," said the second monster to the first, "soaked to the core and covered in… is that blood? Good heavens!"

"Oh, no!" replied the first. "Best not let Drac see that. He'll go all counterclockwise and lose it for sure."

Shel strained to look down at his shirt and pants. Sure enough, he appeared to be dressed to attract the wrong sort of attention, clothes stained blood-red from a hundred and twelve blackberries.

"You look worried, young friend," said the first monster.

"And cold," added the second. "We've got a fire going back at camp. What say you come with us and get warmed up?" The monster licked his lips. "I believe we can find something to roast over the fire if you fancy a bite. I know I do."

I'm sure you do, thought Shel in his trembling brain. *Something to roast over the fire, my eye! …Which is probably exactly what you'd like to roast!*

The blackberries had served to trick his belly temporarily, but the sugary filler left Shel feeling famished deep down. He hadn't had a decent meal since the stew on the flying shoe... and he was cold and wet and tired to boot.

He wanted desperately to follow these two creatures back to their campfire and enjoy a solid meal, but this was so obviously a trap. There was no doubt in his mind that they were going to cook him and eat him, possibly not in that order. After all, what sort of monsters wouldn't want to eat a lost boy all alone in the woods?

With an audible fright, Shel spoke the first words that came to him. "Y-y-you... d-d-don't want to eat m-m-me. I'm all r-r-rotten inside." He instantly recalled the dream of the wildcat in the cave. While that excuse may have worked with the lion, he realized how ridiculous it must have sounded to these monsters. They probably *preferred* their food to be rotten. He probably just whet their appetite for roast kid-on-a-stick... Chicago-style! Here he was, a lost boy all covered in 'blood,' practically begging to be devoured!

On the contrary, the monsters didn't take the bait. They just stared at Shel with inquisitive expressions. And then, as if on cue, burst into laughter.

"Haha, ha! We're not going to eat you!" exclaimed one.

"Yeah, gross! You're not exactly *kosher* for me and my friend here," added the other. "Besides, it looks like you've hardly any meat on you."

Shel wasn't sure if they were just messing with him. "You're... you're not going to eat me?" he sputtered.

"You sound disappointed," replied the first. "Got self-confidence issues, do we?"

A momentary pause allowed the three of them to admire a lone bird chirping somewhere in the distance. Shel thought it might be calling out a warning.

"You know what I think?" began the second monster, "I think it's more likely that *you* might try to eat one of *us*! That's what I'd say. Don't ya think, Karl?"

"Oh, yeah, definitely, Walter! We'd better keep an eye on this one. He looks rascally."

Shel took a second look at his tattered clothes. "Me? I look dangerous to YOU? But you're... you're a werewolf!" he pointed at one of the monsters. "And you're... you're a... I don't even know *what* you are. What *are* you?"

"Well, how about that!? Dangerous *and* rude," laughed the monster called Karl.

A look of surprise washed over Sheldon's face.

"Oh, relax. I'm only joking. I'm a phantom. A ghost. A ghoulie-ghoul. You couldn't figure that out, you bonehead? Get it? Bone... head. Because you have a skull... and I don't. Oh, never mind."

Shel squinted.

"I don't think he likes your jokes, Karl," noted the other monster, Walter.

"Hmmm." Karl scrunched his 'face.'

"That's Karl, the comedian," Walter stretched out his arm to introduce the ghoul. "My name is Walter, and you've already figured out that I'm a werewolf, you sharp-witted detective, you. Buuuut... did you know that in some parts of the world I'm also called a devil? So is Karl. Aaand Drac too. Bet you didn't know that!" Walter smirked, "We're all stigmatized, no matter where we go. Devils the lot!"

"Yeah, which is why we *stick-matize* together," commented Karl, trying to be funny again. "Safety in numbers!"

"Karl the comedian strikes again," jested Walter.

"Safety? In... numbers?" replied Shel, still stuttery. "You're worried... about safety? Isn't that backwards? Aren't *people* supposed to be afraid of *monsters*?"

Both monsters nodded their heads in unison, as if rehearsed.

"That's how the story goes," replied Walter the werewolf. "We're portrayed as the bad guys because we're 'hideously ugly' and all that... by human standards."

"Walter's right, wee-man. Humans like to judge things according to their own values, in case you hadn't noticed. You humans are very egotistical and self-centered creatures." Karl was pointing with a determined 'finger'. "We monsters are a mystery only because we're different and people don't want to bother taking the time to get to know us. Y'all like to shoot first and ask questions later, assuming we're out to eat you. Just like you did."

"Did I?" asked Shel, half shaking in his shoes.

Walter leaned toward Shel and growled lightly. Shel cowered in response.

"See?"

Shel stood back up when he realized Walter wasn't actually threatening him. "What do you mean, 'See'? You're scary! That was scary!"

"And why am I scary?"

"Because! Look at you!" Shel exclaimed.

"So you're judging me by my looks?"

"Well… yeah, I guess. But you growled too."

"Barely. You want to hear a real growl?" Walter smiled.

"No! Thank you, no. I just always thought… I mean, in all the stories and shows and books, monsters are always evil and mean and scary… and trying to get people… and stuff…" Shel trailed off.

"You done?" asked Karl.

Shel shrugged and mumbled something.

"May I ask, have you ever heard the story of La Belle et la Bête?" Walter asked.

Shel shook his head no.

"Beauty and the Beast," clarified Karl.

Shel shrugged again. If he'd heard the story he wasn't recalling it.

"Well that story, like many others, describes a monster who is misunderstood," began Walter. "The townsfolk, instead of seeking a conference with mean ol' Mr. Beast or, lord-forbid, invite the guy to dinner, they hastily grab their pitchforks and torches and invade the monster's castle with the intent of destroying him, just because they heard he was a big scary-looking thing with hair all over his body, fangs, and claws. I think they were just jealous of the guy really; that big, beautiful brute in his big, beautiful castle." Walter laughed. "In my experience, humans just want to dominate things, especially things they don't understand."

Shel squinted at the werewolf skeptically.

"You want more proof?" Walter rallied. "Just look at how they try to dominate the Earth and all other animals. Think about the great white shark, a sharp-fanged tiger, or a black-winged, blood-sucking bat. All very scary things to people, right?" Shel nodded slightly. "But none of those animals pollute the planet like humans do. If humans took the time to understand the relationship between all living things, the essential functions provided by even the most frightening of creatures, they'd appreciate animals a whole lot more; they'd be much less concerned with industry and their precious economy, and much more concerned with ecology."

"Yeah! And they wouldn't hunt animals for sport!" added Karl.

"I know!" blurted Shel without meaning to. Walter's rant was a bit much to digest but Karl's comment struck a chord. "That's what I say too but people just think I'm a sissy, sticking up for animals."

"No kidding? So, you're a wildlife defender, eh? Well then you, my young friend, are no sissy!" replied Karl.

"Yup. You're calling it as it is, buddy," said Walter. "Man is the most dangerous creature in the history of the planet, and that includes the great Tyrannosaurus Rex and his distant cousin, the Worst."

"You know about the Worst?!" cried Shel.

"Of course! That thing's the worst! But even the Worst isn't as judgy as humans. People want to judge us monsters as terrible and evil simply because we're not winning any beauty contests. Well, I say that's a pile of stinky mummy rags! They ought to look in a mirror if they want to see a real monster!"

Karl chuckled at his compadre's rant while Shel nodded or shrugged or smiled, whichever seemed most appropriate and least offensive.

"Look, kid," continued Walter, "we all know the stories and how monsters are portrayed. But have you asked yourself, who writes those stories? Who prints the books? Who creates the shows?"

Shel shrugged.

"People do! That's who!"

"Okay, Walter. I think we get your point," suggested Karl. But Walter wasn't finished.

"The only time we're actually celebrated is on Halloween, and for most people that's nothing more than an excuse to gorge on sweets! But watch out, 'trick or treating' was invented by the union of dentists, those crafty little tooth plumbers!"

Behind Walter, Karl whispered bitterly, "Manfred!"

Shel thought of Manny the dentist, but colorful images of trick-or-treating quickly shoved Manny aside. "Mmm. I love Halloween," admitted Shel aloud.

"Of course you do! What's not to love? Candy celebration, spooks, fun... the chance to let your freaky side run wild! But the day after Halloween, I tell ya, all those glorious costumes — all the skeletons, spirits, and haunts — they all go on sale for a nickel a pail! That's because *people* are runin' the show. It's people who tell the story of Halloween, not the werewolf, the ghoul, or the vampire. Heck, even animals don't get to tell their own tale. People tell the story of the ape, the shark, the elephant—"

"Izzy!" Shel exclaimed.

Walter stopped. "Is that your name? Izzy? Did you just remember it? Amnesia is a terrible thing. I once had a dead aunt who suffered from amnesia. She couldn't remember that she was supposed to be dead, so she kept getting up and walking around. Incidentally, that's how zombies were invented."

"Oh, come on Walter," Karl laughed. "Your aunt *invented* zombies?!"

"That's right, Karl! You got a problem with that?" Walter tried to give Karl a shove, all in good humor, but his arm passed right through his friend.

"Ghoul, remember! You bonehead!" Karl stuck his 'tongue' out at Walter.

In response, Walter's eyes did a summersault — "You really need to come up with a new insult, Karl" — and they both lit up in laughter.

"Guys, I don't have amnesia!" Shel interjected. "My name's not Izzy. I'm Shel. Izzy is a friend of mine. He's an elephant."

"Hey! Izzy the elephant! We know Izzy. Isn't that right, Karl?"

Karl let out a few residual chuckles. "Indeed we do! Indeeeeed we dooo!"

"And your name's Shel, you say?" Walter continued. "Hmmm. Don't know any Shel. Where did you say you're from?"

"Well, I didn't say. But I'm from Chicago."

"Iowa?" asked Karl.

Shel squinted. "No. Illinois. But, close."

"Ah, right. Sorry. I'm terrible with directions. Say, you couldn't tell me how to get to Denver, could you? I always wanted to go rafting on the Colorado, down through the Grand Canyon."

"Denver? I don't think so," replied Shel. "I mean, I don't even know where I am right now."

"Oh? Well, you're in Arcania, southeastern Champion Valley, on the eastern slope of Champion Ridge to be precise." Walter pointed up at the nearby cliffs towering over them. "That much I *do* know."

Shel experienced a fleeting recollection of tumbling down the cliff, but the memory quickly escaped as soon as he tried to pin it down. *Where is Izzy?* he thought. *Oh, my goodness! I wonder if... no! The Worst!* "I have to find him!" he howled in a panic.

"Find who?" asked Walter.

"Izzy! I think he's in trouble."

"Trouble? What sort of trouble? What happened?"

Shel told Karl and Walter the story of the Worst encounter. By the end of it, his new monster friends agreed to help him look for the missing elephant.

"But first we need to catch up with the count," Karl insisted. "We said we'd only be gone for a smidge, just to grab some firewood and maybe collect some berries."

Walter nodded but had become distracted by something red and shiny sticking out of the nearby bushes.

"The count?" asked Shel.

"Yes. Count Dracula. He's—"

"A vampire!" Shel squirmed.

"Of course you know him," replied Karl, unsurprised. "Everyone knows Drac. That guy can't walk ten feet without someone either fleeing in fear or fiending for an autograph. Anyway, he's probably wondering what's keeping us. So, why don't we head back to camp, get you dried off and fed, and then we'll all have a party? How does that sound?"

"A party?" Shel scowled.

"Yeah! A *search* party!" Karl replied. This time Walter's eyes did a backflip.

Shel was hesitant to agree to anything but the search party as he was anxious to find Izzy. Plus, he still wasn't entirely sure they weren't going to fry him up for supper. He knew he had little choice but to trust them, however, if he wanted their help.

"Yeah, okay, fine. Let's go," he said, and began walking.

"Wait!" chimed Walter. Shel and Karl stopped and turned.

"What is it this time, Wally?" asked Karl.

"Um, I was wondering if perhaps I could borrow... your bicycle?" Walter looked at Shel with pleading eyes.

"My what?" asked Shel.

"Your bike. There, in the bushes."

Shel looked over to where the wolfman was pointing.

"Huh." He suddenly felt very confused. "That's not my... bike. It can't be. Can it?" He had to admit the red bicycle did look awfully familiar. In fact, it looked exactly like the bicycle he had back home in Chicago. He walked over and yanked it from the bushes. Sure enough, it had the same familiar scratches in the paint, including the initials J.T. —

likely from the former owner. And there stuck in the spokes was his 1936 George Haas baseball card!

George Haas was not an all-star player by any stretch. He was certainly no John 'Zeke' Bonura or Raymond 'Rip' Radcliff. Still, Haas was solid and dependable, which is why they called him the 'Mule'. But Shel didn't keep the card because he particularly liked the Mule. Shel had simply acquired it one memorable day when he was about eight years old.

As far as Sheldon could tell, there was nothing particularly exciting about that summer day to have put his father in such a good mood. But for some reason, his dad — who his friends called Patty as opposed to Patterson, his given name after passing through Ellis Island in the early nineteen hundreds — seemed to be in high spirits, as if nothing could bring him down. Patty had decided that day was just right for taking his son out for a walk through the neighborhood, apparently for no other reason than to get out of the stuffy apartment and enjoy the fresh air and sunshine, which seemed brighter and warmer than usual, as if the day itself were celebrating something.

At one point during their walk, Patty stopped in the local market to buy a newspaper and a soda pop. He stepped out of character to splurge, springing for a pack of Goudey chewing gum that came with some baseball cards. Popping stick after stick of gum into their mouths, father and son sat on the steps of the market, thumbing through the roster of paper players. As they did, Patterson indulged in some creative storytelling about the athletes they came across.

He had followed the game of baseball enthusiastically ever since immigrating from his home country of Poland. His family had settled in New York when they first arrived, so he was first a Yankees fan. On the other hand, Sheldon, having been born in Chicago, had always loved the White Sox. This baseball rivalry was another source of discord between father and son. But on that day, the two of them set aside their differences and united around their love for the great American pastime.

For some reason, the story of the Mule seemed to strike a chord with Sheldon, so his father let him hang onto that one card. Perhaps it was the fact that Hass was so unremarkable, yet he still made it to the big leagues. In that way, to young Sheldon, the Mule was an everyday hero, not unlike Shel's all-time favorite player, Shoeless Joe Jackson. And despite his shortcomings and his love of the Yankees, not unlike Shel's own dad.

As was the Mule, so too was that day: modestly plain and simply good. Just the two of them sitting there in the warm sunshine on the steps of the Avondale Market. That day was, hands down, Shel's fondest memory of his father. And now, right there in front of him, in that strange land so far from home, was the souvenir from that day. But just how in the world did that baseball card — and his bike — get to Arcania?

As Shel stood there marveling at the impossible bicycle, he failed to notice the werewolf sneaking up behind him, stalking, readying to pounce. Without warning, Walter reached out his sharp claws and... snatched that bike right out of Shel's hands.

"Thanks, my man! Back in a jiff!" called the werewolf as he rode away, down a sandy trail, the kidnapped Mule Haas clicking and flapping in the spokes, crying out for help.

"Walter! Come back here you devil!" yelled Karl. But the dirty dog just waved and disappeared in a triumphant cloud of dust. Karl shrugged. "Oh well. He'll be back soon, I'm sure. He's just excited, loves riding bikes for some reason. Always has. Anyway, guess it's just you and me now, kid. Come on. Let's get back to camp. Drac is going to looove you!" They turned to go then Karl stopped. "Hang on. That isn't blood on your clothes, right?"

Shel held out his shirt and looked down once more. "No, it's definitely berry juice. I slept in a berry patch last night."

Karl's brow — the place where a brow might have been anyway — furrowed. "You're a strange one, aren't you?" Then, smiling, he added, "Come on, you'll fit right in."

Chapter Five

A Reunion

It took Izzy a day and a half plus two whole nights to locate his friend. Eventually he found the poor soul wandering alone in the bushes, dazed and confused but not much the worse for wear...

"SHEL!! Bless my canoes! YOU'RE ALIVE!!"

"Huh?"

"Thank the cherubs of cherries, I found you! I can't believe it!"

"Izzy? Is that you?"

"Oh, saint sisters on Sunday! I thought you were a goner. I've been looking all over for you. Where were you? What happened? I thought you got eaten by that terrible beast!"

"Izzy!" Shel grabbed hold of the elephant's thick leg and hugged it tight.

"Don't worry, kid. I'm here." Izzy wrapped his trunk around the boy.

"I'm so happy to see you! I thought YOU were a goner! I thought I'd never see *you* again," cried Shel.

"Me too, kid! Me too! Hey, listen, I've been wandering around out here for almost two days looking for you and I'm pretty beat. Plus, it's really not entirely safe out here in the bush. I've been hearing some strange noises. Rumor has it that werewolves and vampires and such hang out in these parts. How about you fill me in on what happened while we head back to the cave."

"Cave?"

"Yeah." Izzy picked up the boy and set him on his back. "It's where I ended up after the chase. It's likely the safest place for us to spend the night, seeing as how it's already getting late in the day and my feet are killing me."

"Oh, Izzy, I'm sorry you had to—"

"No! No. None of that! I'm just glad you're safe! So, you had an adventure, eh? What happened?"

"Yeah, well, I don't exactly recall how I got there, but I woke up in a patch of blackberries."

"Ouch!" Izzy winced. "Yeah, you look like you've been rolling around in a berry patch."

"Yeah, I know. Normally 'ouch' would be right but this bush didn't seem to have any thorns."

"Ohhh?" Izzy replied with pronounced curiosity.

"Nope. But the berries were super juicy, and they were twice the size of the berries we have back home!"

Izzy stopped walking. "Uh, you didn't eat them, did you?!"

"Well, yeah, of course I did. I was starving. Why?"

The elephant shook his head and walked on. "I can't believe you survived out here for two days on your own. Those aren't blackberries, you B'jundi! Those are Champion berries. They're quite rare, actually. People will spend weeks out in the bush searching for them."

"Huh? Why? What's a Buh-jundy?"

"A B'jundi... well, it's just another thing here in the Valley that eats kids, like a ghoul more or less. Don't worry about it, you're with me now. Safe and sound. But those berries, they're not for eating, my friend. Let's just say they have certain *medicinal* properties. According to local folklore, if you boil them, along with a few other rare herbs, and then drink the tea, you might experience certain visions, like of the future, or maybe of other worlds. Or maybe you might visit the spirits of your ancestors... some such voodoo witchcraft. Who knows?"

"Well, I don't know about that," replied Shel.

"Anyway, what happened after you ate the berries?"

"Nothing. The berries tasted amazing, and they filled me up. That's about it."

"Nothing? You mean you just walked around in the bushes for two days doing nothing?"

"Well, no, not exactly. I mean, I did stumble across a vampire. Does that count?"

Izzy laughed. "Vampire. Count. Very funny." He stopped laughing when he saw Shel's straight face. "Oh, come on. You saw a vampire? Right. And my name's Frankenstein."

Shel smirked. "Well, it's nice to meet you, Frankenstein, because I really did meet a vampire, ...and a ghost... or ghoul, or B'jundi, or whatever you call it. And a werewolf too."

"Yeaaah, uh, I hate to break it to you but that all sounds a bit suspicious. I mean, you're telling me you ran across a B'jundi, which is dangerous enough all by itself, and a vampire, AND a werewolf? There's not a scratch on you!"

"Izzy, I'm sorry, but are you assuming that just because they're monsters, they're dangerous, and that I'm lucky to be alive?"

"What are you—? Of course they're dangerous! They're monsters for Pete's sake! And look at you! Just a helpless, lost kid out in the wilderness. If you really encountered such demons you would've most certainly been eaten, ragged old boots and all!"

Shel looked down at his old shoes and frowned. Izzy's insinuation that he was making it all up, that he had imagined the whole thing made him feel uneasy.

Izzy watched the color fade from Shel's face. "Buuut, I suppose it *is* possible that you weren't, um… seeing things."

Remaining silent, Shel recalled his time with the monsters. *I didn't just dream all of that. I'm sure of it!* Still, he had to admit, the way Walter and Karl and Drac just sort of wandered away and disappeared into the bush when they were all supposed to be looking for Izzy, that was pretty strange. And the thing with Shel's old bike, that was really weird. He couldn't explain any of it.

Izzy intruded on Shel's moment of reflection, attempting to bring comfort back to his friend. "Sooo! Were they trying to attack you? Suck your blood and all that jazz?"

"What? Suck my blood? The monsters? So you believe me now?" Izzy looked apologetic and Shel silently forgave him. "You know, you really need to work on your stereotyping," Shel chided. The elephant looked sheepish and blushed. Shel smiled. "No, they were pretty nice actually. One of them wanted directions to… Where was it? Oh, yeah! The Grand Canyon! Water on rock!"

"Water on rock," Izzy nodded. "Who wanted directions to the Grand Canyon, the vampire?"

"No, the B'jundi, ghost thing."

"Huh. Okaaay. Well, you know, he was probably trying to find his way to the Pearly Gates." Izzy chuckled at his own joke. "And the others?"

"Well, the vampire was looking for change and—"

"Change? Ha! That's ridiculous! Surely a vampire knows that once a monster, always a monster. There's no changing that!"

"No, Iz. I meant that he asked me for some spare change, as in money."

"I see. He needed some cash. Yeah. Makes sense. I suppose it's not easy finding honest work these days for vampires." Izzy's eyes rolled. "And the werewolf?"

"Um, he just wanted to borrow my bike."

"What?! That's weird. What did you tell him?"

"Well, I gave it to him."

"Gave him what?"

"My bike."

"Oh. Well, I guess that makes sense too, him being a werewolf and all. Wouldn't want to refuse. Could be the last thing you do," Izzy chuckled under his breath.

"Yeah, I suppose not," replied Shel.

"Yeah. Except there's one problem, Shel."

"What's that?"

"You don't have a bike!" barked the elephant.

Shel picked up a stick and slapped a nearby bush. "Dang it! I did imagine the whole thing!"

Izzy put his trunk around the boy's shoulders. "Look, I've never been one to judge or persecute. I mean, who am I to say what may or may not have happened? After all, Arcania is filled to the brim with magic and nonsense. Weird stuff happens all the time around here. So, who knows, you know? I don't know."

"I don't know either, Izzy. I'm so darned confused by everything that's happened since I left Chicago."

Izzy pulled the boy close for a hug. "Well, I'm real. At least I think so." He patted himself with his trunk in various places, which made the boy smile.

"Haha, yeah, I know. Oh! And they said they know you too!"

"Really?! Wait, the monsters said they know *me*?"

"Yup! We talked about you a bunch while sitting around the campfire, swapping stories."

"Oh yeah?"

"Yeah. They were supposed to be helping me look for you, too. But I guess we got separated. I don't know where they went."

"Okaaay. Do these monsters have names?"

"Of course! Their names are… um… uh… You know, I can't seem to recall their names," Shel confessed, his uneasiness returning in spades.

"Well, what did you talk about, other than crazy ol' Izzy?"

"We talked about loads of stuff. Oh, and we played some games!"

"You played games? Like what, pin the tail on the mummy?"

"No. Mummies don't have tails, smart-aleck. We had a contest to see who could make the ugliest, scariest face!"

"Oh yeah?" laughed Izzy.

"Yeah! And I won!" Shel reached into his shirt and pulled out a medal hanging around his neck.

"What in the Glowing Gryo?! Okay. Uh, first of all, you realize that winning an ugly contest with a ghoul, a vampire, and a werewolf isn't necessarily a good thing, right?"

"Oh, I don't know, the werewolf said that winning an ugly contest is better than losing a beauty contest, which apparently he did once or twice. He said that one time he came in fifth place out of only three participants."

"That's funny," Izzy laughed. "But, Shel, do you know what else this medal means?!"

"Other than I'm awesome?" Shel giggled.

"Very funny. It means you weren't hallucinating."

"Oh, my gosh!" cried Shel. "You're right!"

Izzy gave his conclusion a second thought, realizing Shel could have just found the medal lying on the ground. "Hang on a sec," he said, "let me see that. He reached out and gave the medallion a sniff with his trunk. "Why does the medal say, 'Best Mask' on it?"

"Oh, well the vampire said he won it in a scary mask contest when he was a kid, even though he wasn't wearing a mask. Poor guy. He didn't seem to mind though. He said that his face is like a permanent mask, that underneath his scary face is his real face that no one can see or judge."

Izzy raised an eyebrow. "Your vampire friend sounds rather intelligent." Then he squinted at Shel, thinking deeper about where all of this might be coming from. "Is that maybe how you feel, Shel, with your friends back home in Chicago? That you sometimes hide your true face?"

Shel shrugged. "I don't know. Maybe. I guess I never thought about it like that. But, when I won the contest, the vampire gave his medal to me. How great is that?"

"Well, real or not, they seem like they were good to you, those monsters."

"Yeah, they were pretty great." Shel looked down at the medallion and twirled it over in his hand like he was winding a watch. Then he looked up suddenly. "Oh! Walter... and Karl! Those were their names. And Dracula, of course."

"Ha. How about that!? Walter and Karl and Dracula, of course. Can't say any of those names ring a bell but I don't have any songs about werewolves and vampires. So I may have forgotten. Anyway, what else did you do with your monster buddies around the campfire?"

Happy that the elephant was taking him seriously, Shel exclaimed, "Well, we told creepy, spooky, grizzly, gory, blood-curdling ghost stories!"

Izzy eyes went over the rainbow. "Naturally!"

Chapter Six

The Nuthouse

After a night in Izzy's den, catching up on tales of monsters and mishaps, along with a good bit of rest, the two adventurers were greeted by a bright, late morning sun shining deep into the cave, heralding life anew and the most profound gratitude for it.

One can be excited to be alive and still be very sleepy at the same time, however, and that was our Sheldon. Izzy nudged his snoozing companion — "Up and at 'em, sunshine! Time to get a move on!" — and grumbled about their being, "a lot of ground to cover and not a lot of time to cover it."

"Ugh! I can't get a move on. My legs are asleep."

"I see." Izzy picked up a good-sized stick. "Hold still, I'll smack 'em with this here log. That oughta wake 'em up!"

"Aaaa. Nooo!" Shel jumped up and quickly stumbled to the cave wall to steady himself.

Laughing, Izzy tossed the branch aside, grabbed Shel, and hoisted him onto his back with a flick of his trunk before setting off at an elephant's pace. "Come on, buddy. The early bird has long flown. We slept in right proper, too much in fact, and now we have a couple goodfew, somany miles to put behind us before nightfall."

Shel cringed. "But we're worms today."

"Worms?"

"Yeah, the early bird catches the worm, right? So, if you're a bird, get up early. But, if you're a worm, better to sleep late."

Izzy laughed, Shel giggled, and the pair walked on for a time, each contemplating the exciting events of the past few days and wondering what adventures were yet to come. As the sun climbed high, Shel bumping up and down on Izzy's back, the boy's thoughts drifted to Chicago, back toward relative normalcy. For a moment he was sitting comfortably in his living room, listening to some Ernest Tubbs on the radio and munching on a delicious apple. How nice it was to be home, if only for a moment in a daydream. He smirked, thinking on the irony of daydreaming about the mediocrity of home while riding atop an elephant in wild Arcania, when suddenly he was interrupted by something smacking his belly, landing in his lap. An apple!

"Figured you might be hungry. The juiciest ones are up at the tops of the trees, where only us elephants can reach. You're welcome."

Izzy couldn't see it, but Shel looked skeptical. "Huh. Yeah. Elephants... and birds."

"What's that? Oh, yes, well of course, birds too. Just us elephants and the birds."

"And monkeys," continued the smart aleck. "Or anything that can climb, really."

"Yeah. Yeah. Okay."

"Giraffes, ants, snakes…"

"Snakes? Snakes don't eat apples!" contended Izzy.

"Well, maybe not snakes. But what about horses?" Shel asked facetiously, mouth full of apple.

"You bet! Horses love apples! But they don't climb trees."

"Exactly! And neither do elephants."

Izzy abruptly stopped walking, nearly throwing Shel over his head. "Now just what do you mean by that?!"

Seeing that he had poked a sore spot on his friend, Shel let up a little. "It's just that I've never seen an elephant climb a tree before. That's all."

Izzy reached up, grabbed hold of the boy, and lowered him down so they could look at one another. "How many elephants have you known in your long life, kid?"

"I'm actually friends with a *few* elephants back home, thank you very much," replied Shel, squirming his way to solid ground. The pair walk onward.

"Is that so?" Izzy laughed. "What are their names? Maybe I know 'em."

"I doubt that Izzy. You know all the elephants in the world?"

"Maybe I do. Maybe I don't. What're their names and I'll tell you if I know 'em."

"Ok. Well, one's named Duchess and the other is Ziggy."

"Ah, Duchess and Ziggy. Mmm hmm," Izzy nodded. "And the others?"

"That's it."

"That's it? So, you know exactly two elephants?" Shel nodded reluctantly. "And I suppose you've had some deeply insightful conversations with Duchess and Ziggy, yeah?"

"Well, I, uh…"

"Wherein they've divulged all our juicy elephant secrets?"

"I don't know about *secrets*…"

"And now you're the premier pachyderm pundit, s'that right?" Izzy laughed. Shel smirked. "You know… when I was your age, in human years — what are you, about ten? Aaaanyway! Not only did I walk to school seven miles — barefoot no less! But I knew at least forty-three elephants. And only thirty-two of 'em were relatives. Plus, *I* actually speak elephant, if you can believe it. So out of the two of us, I'd say *I* am the elephant expert. Wouldn't you agree?" Izzy was on a roll and wasn't about to wait for a response. "Why do you think elephants' feet are flat anyway?"

"Uh…" Shel shrugged, feeling rather flat himself.

"From jumping out of trees, you bobble!"

Shel laughed loudly. "What?! You're insane." Izzy laughed even louder than Shel and they both had a good romp for a spell.

"Isn't this great?" Izzy sighed.

"What's that?" replied Shel, back in his pachyderm perch.

"Shelby and Izzy, together on another grand adventure!" Shel smiled and reclined, folded arms for a pillow, feet kicked up and crossed on the back of Izzy's head. "Make yourself comfortable up there, why doncha?" Izzy scoffed. Shel snorted. "So, tell me, my elephant expert friend, where in Chicago do you typically go to socialize with your friends Zuchess and Diggy? By any chance, would it happen be… the zoo?" Izzy already knew the answer and proceeded accordingly. "I wonder, have you ever considered—"

"It's Duchess and Ziggy," interrupted Shel coolly. He felt a nerve struck. "And have I ever considered what it would be like if *I* were the one in the cage instead of them? If it were *me* behind bars who all the animals came to gawk at? Maybe some would even throw things or spit at me? Young animals would come yell at me to do a trick, or mock me with dumb noises, trying to communicate in my language? …No, Izzy, I've never thought about any of that."

Izzy paused to let the steam dissipate from Shel's ears. "Welllll, I was *going* to ask if you've ever considered that your elephant friends might climb trees if they were in their natural habitat instead of trapped in a zoo, buuut…" Shel didn't respond. He just looked up at the empty sky, thinking of the freedom his two friends back home would never know. The boy's down-hearted disposition made him weigh heavy on Izzy's back as if he'd channeled the spirit of overstuffed luggage. The elephant tried to lighten the baggage with some humor. "Look, you say you've never seen elephants climb trees. But have you ever thought maybe that's because you can't see them?"

"What? We're talking about elephants, not ants."

"I mean camouflage. You know, disguises."

"Elephant disguises? Are you kidding me?"

"We're pretty good at hiding when we don't want to be seen. Never underestimate the effectiveness of a good toenail painting... or facemask for that matter."

"Toenail painting? What in the world are you talking about, Izzy?"

"I know, right? You'd never know it, but elephants paint their toenails for camouflage. Maybe that's why you've never seen one in a tree." Sheldon squinted. He wasn't buying it. Izzy chuckled and decided to simply change the subject. "Listen, are you hungry? I'll bet you're starving."

"Yeah! I am!"

"Great! You remember that restaurant I told you about, back there before the... the..." Izzy couldn't bring himself to talk about the Worst encounter. "Well, you know, the incident back there?" Shel nodded, his own fear bubbling up from his gut, making him nauseous. "Well, some of the best food around is just beyond that grove of trees over the next ridge." Izzy pointed his trunk. "It's a bit of a hike but shouldn't be more than an hour or so. What say we pop in, enjoy a nice supper? My treat!"

Shel's half smile was confirmation enough.

Tired and hungry, the travelers arrived at an odd-looking house that began underground and wound its way up into the branches of a giant oak tree. There was no sign out front but the sounds and smells coming from inside gave the treehouse away as a bustling eatery. The boy and elephant stepped through a partially hidden door at the base of the tree and immediately Shel noticed that the restaurant was considerably more spacious on the inside than it appeared on the out, with plenty of room for the plus-sized pair. Izzy was far from the only animal in the place, too, large or small. There were chickens and ducks and cows and dogs, fish and sheep and horses and hogs... many of them dressed as if they worked there, many dressed as if they hadn't a care. Under normal circumstances, Sheldon would have been dumbfounded to see chicken and cow waiters and waitresses, but he was beginning to accept this sort of silliness as the new normal.

The first thing the two travelers heard as they passed through the entry hall was the jolting sounds of plates, platters, pots, and pans being dropped, shattering on the floor.

"Well, that's one way to avoid having to wash the dishes," Shel jested, eliciting a good chuckle from Izzy.

"Welcome to the Nuthouse, Champion Valley's oldest treehouse diner." A monotone and melancholy maître d'hôtel met them in the entryway. "Two for dinner?"

Shel stood in stunned silence while Izzy nodded at the sharply dressed fox standing upright and proper on her two hind legs.

"It's a walking, talking... dressed up fox!" whispered Shel.

Izzy coughed in embarrassment. "Uh, don't mind him. He was just born... only yesterday I believe." He grinned innocently at the unamused maître d'. "Isn't that right, Shelby?"

Shel frowned and the fox frowned.

"If you have a hat or an overcoat or some such accoutrement, you may hang it here," said the host in a French accent, gesturing to a large moose, standing as still as possible in the entryway, various coats and hats hanging off its antlers. "Do be advised, however, that if Zebo decides to run off, you might lose your items. We cannot be responsible for lost items. Hang them on Zebo's antlers at your own risk."

"It's okay, we don't have anything," Izzy replied, smiling wide at Zebo the moose, who smiled wide back.

"Fine. Now, if you'll please follow me." The fox showed them to their seats. With a "Bon appétit," and a bow, she placed two menus on the table and summarily dismissed herself to attend her next task.

The pair took their seats at a semi-circular booth with merlot-colored fabric and a table cut from a thick slab of oak. They both giggled at the other turning myriad hues from the rainbow light cast by a large stained-glass window nestled in the corner.

"Oh boy!" exclaimed Izzy. "I'm starving! Are you hungry? I recommend the cantaloupe. But really you can't go wrong in this place. Every dish here is delish!"

"What's with you and cantaloupe?" Shel asked as he took a sip of water from the glass set in front of him by a passing server.

"You don't like cantaloupe?" asked Izzy.

"Nope. Used to. Not anymore."

"Why not?!"

"Well, this one day at school we looked at all these different foods under a microscope, for science 'n stuff, and I'll never forget what I saw: lots of weird things growing all over the cantaloupes especially. It was like a whole city of germs on there."

Izzy's face crumpled. "Oh. Well, you know some germs are good for you? Did you know that?"

"You just made that up," challenged Shel.

"No, I didn't. It's true."

"Still, I think I'll pass."

"Suit yourself. Your loss," Izzy concluded.

"Hello, gentlemen," interrupted a skinny waiter. "What are we eating today?"

Before they could respond, the waiter quickly continued — "Allow me to give you some advice," — and before they knew it, Izzy and Shel were held hostage to an animated diatribe about how unhealthy *this* food is, how dangerous *that* food could be, how it's best to avoid this, that, the other, and all of the above. The waiter even snatched the glass out of Shel's hand. "Even this water right here could have all sorts of nasty goobies in it. You never can be too careful."

Just then, a woman's voice chimed in. "Excuse me! Will you please moooooooove along?" Startled, the skinny man spun around to see a large cow standing behind him. "That'll be quite enough of that, thank you," scolded the cow.

Apparently, the man was not their server after all. He was simply a paranoid customer taking it upon himself to relieve restaurant patrons of their appetites by telling stories of food poisoning, germs, and the like. Shel reflected on his possibly premature condemnation of cantaloupe.

"Sorry about that nonsense," said the waitress. "Now, what can I get for yooouuu?" she mooed.

"Pssst! Best forget the steak!" said the skinny man as he drifted off to haunt someone else's table.

Shel nodded slowly, looking over the cow with wide eyes. "Right. Well, how about the chicken?"

Buh-kawk! came a loud cry from a nearby table. Shel craned his neck around the cow to see another animal server staring back at him. The chicken waiter gave a second loud *cluck!* in Shel's direction and then, without looking away, shouted, "Who ordered the broiled face with mashed potatoes?"

Frightened, Shel averted his gaze. "You know, I'm mostly a vegetarian anyway. How about just some steamed veggies?"

Izzy leaned over and whispered in Shel's ear, "What did the celery say to the carrot during their hike up the mountain?" Shel stared, unsure of where this was going. "It'd be pretty *radish* if you'd *lettuce* take a break, I sure am *beet*! Ha, ha, ha," he laughed.

Shel half-smiled, humoring the comedic pachyderm. "Very funny."

"Oh, come on. Don't be rude-I-beg-ya! Haha!" Then Izzy remembered and advised his compadre, "Oh, by the way, the chef is a cabbage head, like you. Hehe," he laughed some more. He was clearly in good spirits, likely feeling enlivened by their recent brush with death. "But seriously, I suggest you skip the veggie dish." Izzy motioned for Shel to take note of the waitress. She was not smiling, as if offended on behalf of her chef.

"No veggies then. Okaaay. How about... um... well, what do you recommend?" Shel asked the heifer waitress.

"The cantaloupe!" Izzy coughed, and Shel ignored him.

"May I recommend the seafood pasta?" said the cow.

Shel raised his eyebrows and nodded. "That sounds good." And then he ducked his head slightly. "Will that... offend anybody?"

"Not to worry," said the cow, "it's all the same to the clam."

"Well, okay," said Shel. "I'll have that then. Thank you!"

"You see," remarked Izzy, "A meal is quite different when you look at it from the meal's point of view."

Shel nodded enthusiastically.

Suddenly, their cow server began levitating. Shel had a flashback about falling up and landing in the flying shoe.

"Oh, heavens! Put me down, Geraldine! For the last time, this is *not* how you make a milkshake!"

Shel looked around the cow to see a girl, slight as the breeze, strong as Hercules, shaking the cow vigorously. His eyes widened and he looked at Izzy, who mirrored his expression.

"I can't believe it!" exclaimed Izzy. Geraldine stopped shaking the waitress and set her down, looking both apologetic and disappointed. "I didn't know you had milkshakes!" Izzy delighted.

Feeling vindicated, Geraldine beamed, snatched the cow back up right quick and resumed shaking. "One milkshake coming right up!" said the little woman.

"A-a-a-nd t-t-to e-e-eat, s-s-s-ir?" the shaky cow addressed Izzy. "Will you put me down, Geraldine?!" she demanded. Begrudgingly, the little woman set the cow down and walked away, feelings woefully bruised.

"Ah, yes. I'll have the cantaloupe, if you please, extra paprika," ordered Izzy, content beyond measure.

"Oh, um, I do apologize, sir, but we're fresh out of cantaloupe."

"Figures!" cried the elephant.

0 0 0 0 0 0

"How's your meal?" asked Izzy. "Food's pretty good here wouldn't you say? Despite the place being a total nuthouse!"

Izzy's comment rang a bell. "Izzy, you mentioned that the guy we're looking for is in a circus?"

"What guy?" Izzy replied, busy enjoying his non-cantalouped meal.

"The hunter in the circus. The man we're looking for in the Land of Happy."

"Ah, Ingonyama. Yes. What about him?"

"Well, I was just curious about the circus."

"Indeed! The great Falconovich Circus. Yes, yes. It's one of the wonders of the world... or at least it should be. A true spectacle to behold. Falconovich, the 'Falcon' as he's known, spent a lifetime collecting all sorts of rare talent from around the world. He recruited this amazing dancing bear from... Yukon I believe. He has a wash of witches from Eastern Europe whose specialty was cooking — maybe they weren't actually *in* the show, come to think of it... Anyway, he boasted a troupe of tumbling tamarins from South America, a union of unicorns from... well, around these parts, actually."

"Around here?" Shel's eyebrows went afloat in wonderment.

"I think so. I mean, maybe they came from a distant somewhere, but right here in eastern Champion Valley is the hot spot for Conductors.

"Conductors?"

"Unicorns, Shelby. Here we call 'em Conductors, on account uh the... whoooop." Izzy made a gesture as if pulling something from his forehead to indicate a horn. "It's certainly sayin' something that the

Falcon was able to corral a clique of Conductors. That was no easy feat, I'm sure. Must've been the mermaids' persuasion."

"Mermaids?"

"Yup! The Falcon had a few miscellaneous mermaids in his midst as well."

"Wow! And we get to see all these things?"

"Things?" Izzy scrutinized Shel's poor word choice. "I'd wager he used the mermaids to help him convince the unicorns to come onboard. Otherwise there's just no way. Unicorns are far too proud to join a circus of their own accord. Then again, the Falconovich show isn't just *any* circus. It's truly, truly magical. Or at least it was. Not sure what it's like these days. At one point the show boasted a swarm of sword-swallowing gypsies. Boy did they bring the heat. But that rabble proved to be too unruly and ran off with some wayward moonbeams, if memory serves."

"Moonbeams?" snorted Shel. "Oh, come on! Now you're just making stuff up."

"No, I'm not! Honest. The moonbeam romance didn't hold though, moonbeams being nigh ephemeral and whatnot. Er, maybe it's ethereal? Whatever. But get this: The Falcon even had a few giants in his back pocket... or maybe it was up his sleeve. Anyway, that was a long time ago, back in his prime when he could afford such larger-than-life attractions."

"He doesn't have giants anymore?" Shel felt a morsel disappointed, being a fan of the story of Jack Spriggins and his giant beanstalk.

"Actually, I think most of those attractions, most of that talent has moved on. The Falconovich Circus isn't what it used to be. But it's still amazing, I'm sure; so long as he's still got the one and only Ingonyama: the Falcon's golden ticket."

Chapter Seven

Stuck n' Stubborn

Back on the trail, Izzy and Shel walked much slower after having gorged on whatever dish they were able to order without someone getting their feathers in a fluster, skin in a scrunch, or hide in a heap.

"I'm stuffed." Shel rubbed his tummy and took a big gulp of the fresh breeze blowing past. "How was your cantaloupe?"

"Very funny," replied Izzy, still sore with disappointment. "That fig pudding was pretty phenomenal, actually. I dare say I might like figs better than cantaloupe now!"

"Whoa! Izzy!" exclaimed Shel excitedly.

"Oh, calm down. I was only kidding. Cantaloupe is still my favorite."

"No." Shel pointed at something in the distance, "I meant—"

"Seriously though, that pudding was superb." Izzy wasn't paying any mind to Shel's finger. "I've never heard of unicorn horn flour before. Have you? No, of course you haven't. You're from Chicago..."

Shel shook his head, but not in response to Izzy's rambling. He was trying to sort out what was going on up ahead.

"I mean, I had no idea that Conductors shed their horns every few years, and that you could grind 'em up and use 'em as a nutritional supplement. Makes sense when ya think about it though, unicorn horns being a healthy additive, what with the magic and all—"

"Izzy, will you be quiet?! Look over there." Shel pointed toward a grove of trees.

Sounding a smidge irritated at being interrupted, Izzy acquiesced. "Whaaat? Where?"

"Over there! There's a huge horse that looks to be— wait, what is that? That's not a horse. Oh my gosh! Is that a—"

"Speak of the devil!" whispered Izzy.

"Huh? Did you see Walter?" Shel straightened up and looked around excitedly, anxious to see his monster friends again.

Izzy's sarcasm bucket overflowed. "Yeah, kid. I just saw a werewolf ride by on a tricycle. No, you ninny! I was talking about the horse over there. But that ain't no horse. That's a Conductor if my eyesight is right... which it always is. But what in the world is she doing with her horn stuck through that tree?"

"I'm twelve."

"What?" replied Izzy, face crumpled in confusion.

"I'm twelve. I don't ride a tricycle. In fact I'll be thirteen soon."

"Is that so? A teen, eh? That's unfortunate."

"What do you mean by that?!"

"Nothing. Calm down. I just meant that kids are cool, that's all. All the curiosity and zest for life. It's refreshing. Teen town is where kids start turning into adults, and the imagination gets swapped out for dumb stuff. *'Gotta take care of business!'* — and all that," Izzy scoffed in a hoity accent.

"Well, I have no intention of doing any of that! I wouldn't trade my imagination in for the world! Besides, I'm actually looking forward to being a teenager. I think I've earned it."

"Oh! *Earned it*, have you?"

"Yeah, I have! I've put in my time as a kid, listening to people tell me what to do. I'm ready to make decisions for myself. I think I'd be—"

The elephant cut him short there. "Listen, Shelby, that all sounds good n' everything. Let's, uh, let's discuss this later shall we? I don't mean to be rude but it looks like we've got a situation here. You're going to have to mind your trap on this one, okay? All right?"

"Huh?" Shel coughed, taken aback.

"Well, I hate to be the one to break it to you, but you can be a bit of a chatterbox, and Conductors don't have much patience for jibber jab. If we're going to go over there, it'll be best if you just keep quiet."

"What?! *I'm* the chatterbox? Oh, come on! You're the one—"

Izzy gave Shel a forceful love tap in the ribs with his trunk to encourage the boy to zip it. Then, mostly out of the desire to protect the boy, lifted Shel onto his back. As he did, Shel got a better view of the thing which they were approaching. He couldn't help himself, too excited to keep quiet nor keep from stammering. "Izzy, I— I can't believe it! Tha— that's a… a unic—horn."

"Yes, Shel, a horn that long is quite unique. Appears to be a rare breed. Very perceptive of you. Now would you please keep quiet? I mean it, buddy. Conductors are very proud creatures that tend to keep to themselves. This one's obviously in a bind but she's not likely to admit it."

Slowly, they approached the magnificent creature.

"Ahem." Izzy pretended to clear his throat.

The unicorn pretended not to notice.

"Ummm, my name's Israel. And this is my friend Shelby." Izzy walked over his words in his softest shoes while the unicorn continued to ignore him.

"Looks like you—"

At that, the horned horse acknowledged their presence, but not in a good way. Her stare pinned Izzy and Shel down in crosshairs, and Izzy knew that he was now standing downrange of a very unpredictable, wild unicorn with a very sharp harpoon at its helm — a harpoon that happened to be stuck in a tree at that moment, but still dangerous none-the-less.

"Sooo, uh," Izzy pressed on. "Not sure if you were fighting with the tree or what... buuuut—"

Her stare intensified as he progressed. So Izzy opened his eyes as wide as he could, peered directly at the unicorn, and began making a strange humming noise.

"I seeeee youuuu. I seeeee that you neeeed—"

"Are you trying to hypnotize me?!?" The unicorn's eyes narrowed and her nostrils flared. "Really?? You dunder brain! Surely you know that Conductors can't be hypnotized! If anyone's going to be doing the hypnotizing, it's going to be me!"

Undeterred, Izzy kept humming. "I can seeeee that you neeeed sommmme—"

"You had better not say what you're thinking of saying!" scolded the unicorn.

Izzy decided to take his chances and slowly ventured dangerously out on a limb, despite the unicorn's warnings. "Sommme hellllllp," he gulped.

Instantly, the unicorn went raving mad and began thrashing around, trying with all her might to yank her horn from the trunk of the tree so she could stick it in the trunk of the elephant. She was snorting and grunting, jumping up and down and making all sorts of, "When I get out of this tree..." threats.

Izzy reeled back with an "Eek!", standing up on his hind legs — not an easy feat for an elephant of his size. But Izzy was no normal elephant. "I guess my hypnosis didn't work on her," he admitted.

"You think?" concurred Shel. "Is that what you did to me when you were up in that tree?"

"Not now Shelby. Now it's time for plan BEEEEE!" Izzy took a deep breath and wrapped his trunk around Shel for protection, waiting for just the right moment as the horned horse continued her stomping tantrum, which took some time until she nearly collapsed from exhaustion. When her snorts quieted and turned to sobs, Izzy seized the opportunity. Dropping down off his haunches, unleashing a blast of energy, he charged full speed, straight at the unicorn.

"AAAHHHHH!" the horse bellowed in terror as the immense tusker bounded toward her at a thunderous pace.

It was highly unusual for a Conductor to display such unbridled fear, but it was even *more* unusual for one of the supposedly dignified members of the animal kingdom to attack a unicorn (dignified compared to those unpredictable Gambrine creatures, the unrefined Banzakoot, or the entirely primitive Worst). An elephant ought to know better!

Izzy, who had reached full destructive velocity, bowed his head and tightened his grip on the boy. Shel, in turn, tightened his hold on the elephant, grasping for any scraps of hair he could find on the pachyderm's leathery back. (Why the elephant decided to haul his rider along on the rampage was anybody's guess. One could only surmise that Izzy had not thought his plan through. Par for the course, of course!)

The boy joined the unicorn in a chorus of anxious protest, but it was too late. Izzy's mass was in motion — a steaming locomotive of wrath and wreckage. With all his strength, he plunged a mighty tusk deep into the trunk of the tree, inches above where the Conductor's horn was stuck.

A resounding *CRACK!* echoed through the valley and Shel was instantly flung into the air, screeching a wail that would have sent the Worst beast fleeing in fear (probably not, actually, but it sounds more dramatic that way). Despite the elephant's tusk now impaling the tree right alongside the unicorn's horn, the formidable trunk held fast to the earth and refused to set the unicorn free. After all, how often does a lonely apple tree get the chance to brag about capturing one of the most rare and magical creatures in all the land?

But the descendent of mighty mammoths was not finished. He followed the stabbing of his titanic tusk with a ramming of his humongous head, throwing the full weight of his enormous body against the formidable tree. The small crack from the unicorn's horn merged with the substantial fracture from Izzy's tusk, like tributaries feeding a river.

Upon impact from the behemoth's head, a fatal fissure shot upward through the tree's core like a lightning bolt, shattering the trunk into splinters. The death blow had been struck.

This grand, old apple tree, who had witnessed the comings and goings of an age, standing like a sentinel over Champion Valley long before the time of Izzy, long before the Boot Brigade, possibly even before the reign of the Gambrine, finally came crashing down like the toppling of an empire. As it did, Izzy tumbled in a drunken ballet of summersaults and cartwheels, eventually skidding to a stop with a mouthful of sticks, leaves, dirt, and rocks.

The unicorn, having received a good portion of the energy from the pachyderm express, was sent hurtling, head-over-hooves down a hill blanketed in soft Augustine clover. Meanwhile, Shel's aerial foray was interrupted when he was caught, like a pop fly at Comiskey Park, by an adjacent tree, which, like his less fortunate neighbor, also happened to be filled with delicious apples.

It took a moment for the victims to shake off the dizziness and pain and inspect themselves for missing pieces.

"Wowzers! Everyone alive?" asked Izzy wearily, spitting out the debris and choking on the dust of chaos hanging in the air. There was no response. Perhaps he had knocked everyone unconscious… or worse!

Finally, a scratchy voice peeped up from beyond the hill. "No! We are *not* all right. And *that* was not okay!" The unicorn came limping back over the hill to face down her attacker. "Your reckless abandon and disregard for protocol is inexcusable, you— you big, bumbling buffoon! You violated a direct order from a superior quadruped to STAND DOWN! You are an embarrassment to the animal kingdom and a liability to all those around you. I will not stand for this treasonous imprudence! The Conductor order shall hear of this, and we'll have your tusks for—"

"For saving your life!" interjected a small voice from a nearby treetop.

The Conductor looked up to the crown of the apple tree where Shel sat, leaves and twigs sticking out of his hair and clothes. "He could have killed you too, little man, whoever you are. You should not associate with such a savage, such a brute, a barbaric, uncivilized—"

"Hero!" Shel cut her off again, officially declaring himself at odds with the beautiful, horned creature. Meanwhile, the elephant sat quietly in the dirt, wondering with wide eyes if he was going to be exalted, exiled, or... executed. "Izzy saved your life and you know it!" demanded Shel. "You'd still be stuck in that tree two weeks from now, with no food or water if it weren't for him. You'd just waste away if some creature didn't wander by first and snack you right up." Shel turned to Izzy for approval.

Izzy smiled in appreciation of Shel standing up for him, and then he suddenly became acutely aware of the darkness sneaking up on them. He quietly squeaked out the word "Worst" and sent it floating over to the

Conductor for her consideration. The unicorn locked eyes with the elephant, both understanding that the loud ruckus was likely to have caught the attention of some undesirable creature of the night, and they had better not linger any longer.

Izzy walked briskly over to the boy, plucked him from his perch, and set him in his proper place atop the elephant's back. "Come on, little Shelby, the deed is done. We'd best find ourselves a safe place to sleep for the night. Uni, you're welcome to join us if you like. Better than wandering out in the cold dark, all alone."

The unicorn scoffed, "I wouldn't be caught *dead* with such a motley crew. Besides, Conductors fare just fine on our own."

Izzy knew it was the pride talking. Conductors were rarely alone, preferring the safety of a herd, especially at night. "Suit yourself. But I ain't coming back to save your neck a second time. Good luck out there."

"I don't need your luck, thank you very much!" The unicorn stiffened her shoulders and held her head high. For an instant, Shel thought the magnificent creature looked to be nearly as big as Izzy. "Unicorns invented luck!" With that, she limped off, likely under the impression that it was her own luck that delivered Izzy and Shel to her aid. And who knows? Maybe it was. After all, unicorns are very powerful and mysterious creatures.

"Stubborn ol' girl," Izzy muttered with a hint of admiration sweetening his bitter tone. "All righty then. Come on Mr. Shelby, I know of a nice spot nearby where we can stay the night. I think you'll enjoy it."

"This apple tree forest is nice. Why don't we just stay here?"

"I s'pose we could. Trees are a bit far apart to string a hammock though," replied Izzy, taking rough measurements with his trunk.

"I didn't know you had a hammock," Shel queried, half sarcastic.

"Well I don't, that's the other problem."

Shel smirked at the silly elephant.

"Anyway, there's a rocky outcropping that overlooks the valley, just up ahead. Should be a decent spot. Looks like it could possibly rain again, too. I think I'll gather up some of the wood from this apple tree here, put the poor thing to good use, and set up a small fort to keep us dry. You'd better just sit back and rest up."

"I can help you," Shel offered as he slid off Izzy's back and began scrounging up some of the smaller branches.

"No, no, don't you worry 'bout it none. Save your strength, you're going to need it, for tomorrow we're going to build ourselves a boat!"

Interlude

Everything and Nothing

The misty morning rain hung in the air like dandelion tuft blown by too many kids making too many wishes. Sometimes it fell toward the ground. Sometimes it seemed to float up toward the sky (like Sheldon when he found the end of the sidewalk). Other times the moisture appeared to flow sideways or swirl in circles. It was a soft rain that cleansed and calmed everything it touched, as if casting a spell upon the valley.

Shel found himself staring out over the landscape, the bizarre reality of these strange days falling over him like the rain. Here in this wonderland, to most whom he encountered, he was a nameless boy with no history and no future. That thought brought him a feeling of freedom, and in that sense he was simply along for the ride, existing only for the sake of the experience: No agenda, no chores, no homework, no responsibilities, no expectations of him from anyone. Any identity that he had, now seemed to dissolve in the encircling precipitation. He was the adventurous young man on the back of a talking elephant, wandering through fields of broccoli, encountering all sorts of strange characters. At the same time, he was still the quiet, forgotten boy, lost in the noise of his apartment, lost in an anonymous classroom, lost in Chicago's sea of smog and indifference.

He was a wild child sitting in an apple tree, communing with a gentle rain that exuded empathy and defined contentedness. At the same time, he was a tame lad, sitting studiously in his bedroom, an emphatic spring downpour pelting his window like nervous fingers tapping on the desk of an expectant professor. He felt simultaneously to be nothing and everything, nowhere and everywhere.

His consciousness strolled beyond his mortal cage, becoming the mist floating in the air all around, washing over the landscape, touching every leaf, every blade of grass, squeezing the thin ribbon of life between his fingertips. Then, in a sweeping gust of warm, mid-spring morning breeze, the mist evaporated, taking his consciousness with it, and all went dark.

Chapter Eight

A Giving Tree

Shel gradually opened his eyes to a forested horizon, undulating steadily up and down as if he were on a lazy ship in a sheltered harbor...

His sleepy attention drifted like a sailboat on calm seas, from the far shores back to the gray, leathery hill on which he lay, anchoring a smile upon his waking cheeks in appreciation for his bed, his support, his caretaker, his big, foolhardy friend, Izzy the Elephant.

Looking around, Shel noticed that during the night while he slept, Izzy had made good use of the branches from the recently felled apple tree, constructing an impressive roof to keep them (mostly) dry from the drizzle that descended through the night. He lay back down on his hilly friend, slumbering peacefully, a slave to the sandman's profound rapture. Contented, he watched the sluggish sunrise taking its glorious time drying out the morning, spreading its colorful song to the otherwise silent and dark forest understory. As the light passed over pachyderm hill, the warmth brought an undeniable joy to Shel's heart. He smiled and embraced his friend, who was also slowly waking from the dawn splashing generously over his face.

"You're welcome, kid," Izzy mumbled with eyes closed. He permitted the boy's tender gesture to linger a moment before jumping up, sending Sheldon tumbling down his hilly sanctuary and sending the serenity of the misty morning swiftly into the past. With a scoop of his trunk, he saved the kid from disaster, placing Shel gently on the ground. Then, with a few well-timed trumpeting sneezes — spring pollen on the breeze — the elephant rang the morning work bell.

"Okay, Mr. Shelby, time to put on your boat-maker hat! I'll gather the wood for the raft and you assemble the pieces."

"Wha—? A raft? I don't know how to build a—"

"Not to worry, my man. It doesn't need to be fancy. It just needs to float."

Shel hesitated. When he saw Izzy was serious via a pair of raised eyebrows, Shel shuffled around to look busy, picking up random sticks and mumbling expressions of malcontent. Within a few short minutes, he ran out of arm space and dropped the sticks at Izzy's feet, unsure of what else to do with them.

Izzy sighed. "Look, just take the longer pieces and place them together... like this..." Izzy demonstrated, lining up boards like soldiers standing at attention. "And then lash them together with these..." Izzy tossed Shel some vines he'd gathered. He then lumbered off to finish the job of splitting the wood from the sacrificial apple tree. After bucking up the remnants of the tree trunk into logs, Izzy returned to find the boy sitting by the water's edge, eating an apple and skipping stones, and not even remotely building a raft.

"What's this?! Ol' Mister Moody throwin' rocks at the poor lake, not doin' his work?!" Izzy reached his trunk out to grab the boy, intending to lift Shel up into the air and turn him upside down — his new favorite pastime. "I wonder what that gloomy frown would look like if we flipped it on its head."

Shel gave Izzy a sour look and pushed the elephant's intruding trunk away before it got hold of him, then resumed his sullen rock skipping. "I don't know how to build a boat, Izzy. Besides, why do we even need a boat? Why don't we just walk? I enjoy our hikes."

"Ha! I'll bet you do!" Izzy scoffed loudly. "Nice, big 'ol elephant to ride on! Not much walking for you on our walks, is there? Who wouldn't like that?"

Shel frowned and skipped rocks harder in a minor tantrum.

"Regardless," Izzy chuckled, "there's no direct path to the Land of Happy. It would take ages to get there on foot. You'd have to scale those high peaks over there." He pointed his trunk toward a distant mountain range. "We'll get there *much* quicker by boat. Trust me."

Shel continued mumbling under his breath, uneasy about the idea of traversing an impressively large body of water on what was surely going to be an unimpressively small raft.

Ignoring the kid's display of the morning grumpies, Izzy commenced splintering the logs into smaller boards more manageable and better suited for a raft. After giving the kid some time and space to cool off, he thought he might attempt a little pep talk.

"I had a cousin who figured, since people are starting to do their laundry at wash-a-teria laundromats, leaving their clothes unattended for the day and such, that she might as well toss herself in too and get a free bath. Fair to say that she was a few sandwiches short of a picnic. Anyway, you can imagine that didn't... *turn*... out well for her."

Shel squinted at the elephant, who was looking sideways back at him, waiting for a laugh that never came.

"Point is, Shelby, there's no such thing as a free lunch — or in her case, a free bath. We all need to put in some effort, pay our dues for the things we take away from the world."

Being familiar with *this* lecture, having heard it a hundred times before from his old man, Shel looked down at the apple he was eating and did his best to tune out.

Izzy noted Shel's disinterest and changed his tack. "Good stuff, eh? Why don't we gather up some more of the fresh-looking ones before they rot on the ground? They'll make a nice snack on our voyage."

"Voyage, Izzy? How long will we be sailing on our little *raft* anyway?"

"Not sailing, kid. Just floating. We're going to simply float along with the current, going wherever life takes us."

"Wherever life takes us?! Wherever life—? I thought you said we're headed to find your friend who can help us find Manny."

Izzy laughed. "Relaaax. I did. Ol' Yammy-pants lives on a peninsula at the other end of the lake. The current should float us right to him."

"Yammy pants?"

"Yup! Though *you'd* better just call him Ingo. He can be a bit sensitive about his pants. Now, how about we engage in a little less jibber-jabber and a little more raft-building, shall we?"

"Wha? *You're* the chatterbox this morning!" Shel smirked, feeling a wave of sarcasm slowly pulling him out of his grumpy state. "In fact, you've been talkin' my ears off!"

Izzy lifted an eyebrow as if to say, "Is that so?"

"And walkin' my feet off. Now you're workin' my tail off! You're whittling me away to nothin', bossman."

"Hmm. I see. Well, I suppose there's nothing else to say except you're welcome!"

Shel had been jesting but the conversation suddenly took a more serious turn.

"You're welcome?! For what?"

"For helping you, little lizard, shed your old skin so you can grow into something new."

"I'm not a lizard." Shel picked up some lashings and got to work tying together the branches, sticks, and logs that were being tossed his way. He thought back to the blizzard lizard who snuck off into the light of the school doorway. "And what new thing am I growing into?" he continued.

"You said it yourself, mister wise guy: imagination helps us evolve."

"Imagination. Mmm hmm. I've got some of that." As Sheldon worked, the tender, bluish-grey berries on the vines popped like miniature grenades, covering his hands in a thick, crimson goo. The juice looked a bit like blood and he couldn't help but make fun of the mess. "I'm no lizard. I'm a zombie!" He held his palms up. "Oh, the horror!"

Izzy chuckled. "By the way, don't lick that stuff or you'll be seeing flying, rainbow-colored zebras in tutus."

"Wait. What? Are these Champion berries?"

"Nah, I'm just kidding," Izzy laughed.

"How about flying shoes and talking elephants? Would I see any of those?"

"Ha! You just might!"

They both laughed, cueing Shel to resume his charade.

"Arrrgh!" He gestured like a drooling madman, slowly advancing on Izzy.

The elephant just ignored him, focusing instead on his work.

"Oh, don't be such a Banzakoot!" chided Shel, but Izzy didn't take the bait. He just smirked without looking up, so Shel got back to his own bloody work. As he worked, he considered the possibility that maybe he'd eaten some Champion berries back at the farmhouse in Chicago. That would certainly explain a lot! Since the Thompson family never invited him to supper, he must've found a berry patch and helped himself. Shel figured he was probably still there, passed out on the lonely sidewalk, dreaming up this whole Arcania adventure, Izzy and all!

With a sigh, he conceded that, dream or not, here he was, so he'd better make the best of it. "You know," he broke the silence of efficient productivity again, "this tree has sacrificed a lot for us."

"Oh? How's that?" replied the elephant with a tinge of impatience.

"Well, first, it basically gave its life to free that unicorn. Then you used its branches to keep us dry overnight. Now it's providing the wood for our boat and apples to feed us. I'd say it's a pretty good friend, wouldn't you?"

"I'd say you're quite the sentimental type. That's what I'd say. It's just a tree, Shelby."

"Just a tree?! You're the one who can speak the language of the trees. Why don't you ask the tree how it feels about giving away everything and getting nothing in return?"

Sounding like a monk on the top of a mountain a thousand miles away, the elephant replied in quiet solemnity, "Nothing. Everything. It's all the same."

Izzy's words reminded Shel of his dream, the soft rain evaporating his identity. "You sound like Manny's cat."

Izzy's head bobbled up and down. "Fair enough." He descended from his imaginary mountain to engage in some real-world discourse. "But, nothing in return? Let's examine that, shall we? I'd say this tree has received the gift of wisdom in return for its sacrifice."

"Wisdom?" Shel queried.

"Precisely. Honor, gratitude, and contentment as a result of unconditional giving — giving of the whole self — such that others may thrive. That sacrifice, my friend, is a unique gift that can only be gained from experience, not given by any other thing, living or dead. *That* is wisdom."

"I thought wisdom came from going to school, studying and stuff."

"It can, *if* one goes on to live what they learn. Knowledge is the learning part. Wisdom is the doing. Wisdom cannot be passed from one to another like a blanket, or handed out like a bowl of soup. Wisdom is a gift that cannot be given but instead must be earned."

Shel remained silent, watching the elephant ascend back up his mountain then curl up in lotus position (metaphorically, of course).

"Many things in life never get such an opportunity, are never asked to give of themselves, are never challenged to put their talents to trial and really test what they have to offer. That is a special sort of soul-freeing assignment. Indeed, you should count yourself lucky if you are someday called by fate to place your unique piece into the grand puzzle, to prove your worth, and in doing so, ultimately realize your true identity."

Shel retrieved the puzzle piece from his pocket and held it out to show Izzy.

"Ah! There it is. The incompleteness of the whole illuminates the significance of the part. Am I right?"

"I guess so." Shel rubbed the piece like a magic lamp, secretly hoping a genie would appear.

"As far as the tree goes, this one is not sad over losing her apples, her limbs, or even her trunk. On the contrary, she is happy, very happy, and eternally content — as content as anyone who has realized their life purpose would be. For she has become a true tree of life, making the ultimate sacrifice so that others may live on."

Although the words resonated somewhere deep within, Shel found it difficult to follow the path of Izzy's philosophical meanderings. He was an odd bird, this elephant. Sometimes it seemed his head was filled with little more than peanuts and rocks. While other times he seemed to have all the answers to the most profound questions. Shel thought he seemed a bit like Winnie-the-Pooh: stuffed with fluff and philosophy, empty and full at the same time. Everything and nothing all at once.

Shel placed the puzzle piece back in his pocket and picked up a large chunk of wood formerly belonging to the apple tree. He held it close to his chest and said a quiet and sincere, "Thank you."

Izzy shook with laughter. "Sentimental to the core." He allowed Shel a moment then it was time to get back to the task at hand. "Now then, place all of that gratitude into your craft and we'll have one sea-worthy, possibly magical vessel indeed! By the by, you'll want to also use some of the reeds down by the water for added strength and security."

"Added security?" Shel had been enjoying this opportunity to test his skill at sailing knots. But Izzy's lack of confidence somewhat doused his fire.

"Always good to have insurance, especially when you're out at sea. Those berry vines are tough, but I'm not entirely sure how well they'll hold up underwater."

"Great," Shel sighed and rolled his eyes.

After what seemed like hours attempting endless variations of nautical nooses, the boy was ready to concede that perhaps his maritime skills rivaled Izzy's tree-climbing skills: both left something to be desired. Yet, when Izzy finished splitting wood and came to inspect Shel's progress, he seemed awfully impressed by what looked daringly close to a finished product.

"Hey, nice work, Sheldon! Looks like you have a talent for tying stuff together!"

"Well, I'm not sure it's ready."

"Which is a good skill to have in a land where everything's always falling apart," the elephant added under his breath. "Come on! Let's give it a go!" Izzy barked and pushed the raft — which looked more like a giant bird's nest — down to the bank of Champion Lake.

A pleasant shoreline composed of lush grasses speckled with reeds and rushes corralled a small beach of white pebbles, rounded and polished by years of being pushed around by a bully of a lake. Izzy let go of the raft-nest and let it slip halfway into the water, which was mostly calm with ankle-high waves lapping the rocky shore. Shel noticed that the loch was fed by a large, wide river emerging from a marsh of monstrously tall broccoli plants.

"Strange..." Shel remarked.

"What's that?" Izzy replied from the corner of his mouth without looking up from his work.

"I didn't notice this huge lake during our trek out from Manny's place."

"Champion Lake, my boy, is the pride of the Valley. It's kept full by the year-round flow of the great Champion River, which is fed by the glorious snowfields of the Champion Mountains." As he pointed his trunk up toward the clouds, he added, "The mountains are always resting above the clouds and—"

"Champion Clouds?" Shel quipped.

"What? No. Don't be ridiculous."

Shel chuckled until he saw the elephant was trying to be serious. "Sorry. Go on."

"Ahem. As I was saying, the mountain tops," Izzy looked at Shel to make sure the boy was paying attention, "are always shrouded in cloud cover and stay frozen pretty much year-round."

"Well, that all sounds terrific, Mr. tour guide, sir. Sign me up!" The boy was really tugging the elephant's tail now.

"The river, Mr. Shelby," Izzy continued with a scowl, "provides water to everything you see, including our world-famous broccoli. It is the source of all life and commerce in Champion Valley."

"It's amazing, Izzy. Truly. I'm just confused as to how in the world I didn't notice this huge lake or that big river before now."

"You need to *open your eyes*, my young friend." Izzy stuck his face in front of Shel and opened his eyes wide.

Brushing Izzy's face aside, Shel complained, "What's the deal with that stare of yours?!"

Izzy just laughed.

Although Shel liked to poke fun at the pachyderm, he was beginning to care deeply for him and enjoy his silliness. He reminded Shel of his mother's crazy brother, Uncle Marty, who had spent a good deal of time in central Asia and India and had adopted a somewhat yogic demeanor. He too had a larger-than-life presence, an intense stare, and could expound for hours on whatever topic seemed least relevant at the time. Shel giggled and added, "Well, you should know that your wide-eyed stare is awfully creepy... Mr. Face-That-Didn't-Launch-a-Thousand-Ships."

"Is that right? Well, my face can launch *this* ship!"

Shel felt a sudden *whap* on his back, sending him flying onto the raft. He stumbled and dropped to his knees, quickly grabbing hold of some of the rope keeping the raft together, barely preventing himself from falling overboard. "Gee whiz!" cried Shel, looking back at Izzy disapprovingly.

After knocking his first mate aboard and laughing uncontrollably at the process, Izzy clambered onto the raft with his usual coordination and grace, nearly falling overboard several times. In response to the elephant's mass, the raft ducked beneath the water's surface, trying to hide. The other side of the raft, where Sheldon was kneeling, shot high into the air.

"Ahhhh!" Shel let out a cry of protest while Izzy quickly shuffled toward the center.

Finding some stability, the elephant turned back to the shore. First, with a kick of his leg, then with a shove of his trunk, Izzy sent the raft adrift, committing it to the sea. As the small craft drifted away from shore, it ensnared a modest current complimented by a slight breeze, sending the unlikely sailors on their way, slowly but quite surely.

Chapter Nine

Big Love

As they sailed away from the shoreline, the blue-green water of Champion Lake faded to a dull gray. The raft, meanwhile, settled into a steady see-saw rhythm with the wind over the open water creating longer, undulating waves. The constant rocking might have caused Shel to lose his lunch except that he hadn't had any yet.

"Did we happen to pack anything besides apples?" he asked.

"We? What do you mean, _we?_" Izzy retorted without looking at Shel, his gaze fixed upon the water. "I didn't pack anything. _You_ were the one in charge of lunch, remember?"

"Well, how long is this trip going to take?"

Izzy shrugged his big, baggy shoulders and stared off into the endless watery horizon that was now their destination. "It will take all the time it needs."

Shel's face contracted, "Aren't we in a hurry?"

"Well, yes, and no. Of course we'd like to find Manny as soon as possible. But some things in life just can't be rushed no matter how rushed you try to go."

Shel sighed. He was concerned. Izzy had been doing a fair bit of sitting in silence and staring out at the water since they left the shore. It was clear he was preoccupied with something other than the horizon, like a detective trying to solve a mystery. Shel scanned the sea and sky but couldn't see anything that might hold the elephant's attention, save for a solitary cloud and the silvery surface of what may as well have been the ocean. "Is there something out there, big guy?"

Izzy replied only with a deep inhale and long exhale that wheezed like a deflating balloon as it wound its way through his long trunk. They continued sitting in silence for a while, the raft drifting further out to sea until the last sliver of land eventually faded away, taking with it any lingering sense of security. Neither of them felt tremendously confident in the meager raft. But Sheldon was also no longer feeling terrifically confident in Izzy's master plan for this expedition. _Just drift on the current? Wherever it takes us? As long as it takes?_ Shel repeated Izzy's troublesome words, shaking his head. It didn't help that instead of being his chatty, carefree self, the elephant was stoic. He seemed frozen with the anticipation of the next critical development, as if his plan depended on something and that something wasn't happening. The boy glanced nervously back and forth between Izzy and the gap between the sea and the sky, wondering what was out there. What was he missing?

Eventually, with a grand sigh, Izzy cracked open the vault of quietude and released the contents, much to the boy's relief. "I've always wondered what it would be like."

Shel paused, trying to guess what Izzy was talking about. "What *what* would be like?"

"That!" Izzy said, pointing his trunk toward a stretch of blue sky just above the horizon. Shel's squinting eyes traced the elephant's trunk but could not see anything. He put his hand to his forehead and shielded his eyes from the bright sunlight but it didn't help. He figured Izzy had finally crossed over to the other side of Bonkers Hill. That, or the elephant possessed supernatural powers of sight, which actually seemed possible, Shel thought, given those abnormally oversized peepers. "They're so beautiful and graceful," continued Izzy.

Shel was utterly perplexed, and so he gave up, shrugging to himself. *Oh well. Who cares if he can see ten thousand miles or if he's nutty as a Cuckoo? I'm starving!* Maybe Shel couldn't see anything out over the water, but he sure could see those big red apples and they were calling his name. He grabbed one from the sack and sat contentedly at the far end of the raft, away from his partner who was obviously suffering from scurvy or mutiny or seasickness or sea legs — some sort of sailing-induced affliction. Munching on the delicious apple from that generous old tree, he imagined curious shapes and creatures in an odd cloud that seemed to have been following them for the past hour or so.

"Woah. That cloud looks just like a gigantic—" Suddenly, a massive, pterodactyl-sized pelican swooped down from behind the cloud and, with laser precision, snatched the apple right out from Shel's hand. "AAAAHHH!" Shel screamed and launched himself backward in fear of losing his whole hand... or arm... or head!

"Wowww!" exclaimed Izzy in a calm, awestruck tone.

"DID YOU SEE THAT?!" Shel howled. He expected Izzy to batten down the hatches, man the battle stations, load the forward cannons… hoist the jib, come about, trim the sheets... at least swab the deck! Something. Anything! Instead, Izzy just sat there, cool as a sea cucumber, not preparing for battle in any shape or form but instead looking more prepared for a piña colada. He was reclining on stumpy arms stretched out behind him, trunk slung casually over his shoulder like a scarf. He looked intoxicated, mouth agape and a twinkle in his eyes.

"Izzy!" prodded Shel. "Did you not see that huge bird just steal my— *WHOA!*" he yelled as the giant pelican returned for more, grabbing the entire bag of apples in one fell swoop.

Izzy cheered a resounding "Woo-hoo!" — raising one arm high in triumphant celebration.

Shel was dumbfounded. "What's up with you?! That flying dinosaur just stole all our food! And you're cheering?!"

"Yeah. Wasn't that awesome?"

"WHAT?! No, that was *not* awesome!" Shel cried.

"They're masters of flight, you know — and stealth. Very cunning. And they perform their magic with the utmost grace." Izzy was almost drooling. "Pure beauty on wings."

Shel's suspicion that his friend had gone bananas was confirmed. He figured now would be a good time to formulate an escape plan. *Is there a life raft on this life raft?* he thought to himself. "Izzy, that thing is a terror! Beauty on wings?! More like a shark with wings! If we're not careful, that thing is going to come back for *me* next." Izzy frowned disapprovingly then looked back toward the sky. "Izzy! We have to do something! We're under attack! What's the matter with you?"

"Oh, would you calm down? We're not under attack." Izzy stood up, again nearly tipping over the raft, raised his trunk to the sky, and let out a high-pitched sound unlike any elephant noise Shel had ever heard. It was as if he were trying to mimic a bird. Within a few short moments, Shel could make out the silhouette of the giant pelican against the bright sky. He shrieked as the shark with wings came diving back at them. A flurry of wind and chaos descended over Izzy and Shel's miniature island as the massive creature flew down and perched right on the edge of the raft.

"AAAAHHH! He's going to eat us!" cried Shel.

"Reeelaaaax," Izzy shushed the boy. "*He* is a *she.* ...And *she* is not going to eat us." He placed his heavy trunk atop Shel's head to squash the boy's agitation.

"Well, *SHE*… is going to sink our ship!"

"Sheldon, please. Despite their size, Champion Pelicans (of course!) weigh almost nothing on account of their hollow bone structure, which is why they're able to stay aloft for hours on end, riding the slightest coastal thermal. Or in this case, the open sea breeze."

Hollow bone structure? Shel scowled, curious about the elephant suddenly being a bird expert. He glanced over at the pelican and his scowl evaporated to astonishment. She was blushing and fluttering her eyelashes, apparently in response to Izzy's 'compliment'. The elephant must have noticed, for he had adopted his own awkward, sideways grin and a dizzy expression as if he'd just been hit over the head (by a bag full of apples).

Shel couldn't believe what was happening. He did have to admit that the raft hardly responded to the presence of the overstuffed bird. But just as he was about to concede that he may have overreacted and that they appeared to be safe, the raft suddenly began folding up like a taco, finally succumbing to the undeniable mass of the giant pachyderm. Being at opposite ends of the vessel, Shel and the bird were lifted out of the water. Izzy, meanwhile, being squarely in the middle, began to sink — and in sinking, began to panic.

"Izzy!" cried Shel as the water crept over the elephant's waist, causing him to thrash about. With an expression of concern, the pelican noted that this was her cue to scoot along. A few flaps of her gigantic wings and she levitated safely beyond the ensuing catastrophe.

Izzy hastily responded to the pelican's departure, crying out, "Wuh — Wait!" The pelican froze in midair like a hummingbird. "Wait! Please! Please don't leave us!" Izzy stared at the bird with desperation in his eyes. "I'm not a good swimmer. If this raft sinks, I'm a goner for sure."

Concerned for the safety of the two wayward sailors, the bird swooped down, grabbed hold of one end of the raft, and yanked on it, grunting mightily. She was unable to move the vessel more than a few feet, however. With the elephant on board, she would not be able to haul them to shore, especially now that both Izzy and the raft were halfway underwater. Defeated, she released her grip and floated back into the air. There she hovered, catching her breath and looking at the crew apologetically.

Shel was suddenly struck with the notion that this was his fault. *If I had only done a better job with the lashings!* "Izzy," he yelled over the sounds of splashing water, "if the bird can at least carry you, if she can drag you off the raft, it probably won't sink anymore."

Izzy shot back, "Are you nuts?! But then I'll be *in* the water! I can't swim all the way back to—"

"She can't pull you, me, and the raft," Shel stopped him. "But maybe she can just drag *you*." The water was up to the elephant's neck. Izzy braced himself as best he could, trying to stay on the raft. "Don't worry," continued Shel. "I'll stay with the raft. You get back to land where you belong!" There was a brief pause — an exchange of frightened expressions — then Shel reassured, "I'll be okay, Izzy. You go!" Izzy looked at the boy with dread. "Go, Izzy! But come back for me!" Shel, Izzy, and the bird looked back and forth at one another, considering the difficult choice in front of them. "Izzy, you need to go! Now!"

The sinking seemed to slow in a time-warp interlude, as if the universe were pausing to make room for the possibility of a miracle. Izzy looked at the bird with desperation. "Please, don't leave me here." The bird hesitated, shaking her head at the impossible task. Then, unexpectedly, but with tenderness and sincerity, Izzy let slip the words, "Please, Charlotte... I love you."

Shel, who had been watching the pelican, shot a look of utter surprise at Izzy, while the bird's mouth dropped open from shock, revealing a half-eaten apple.

"Hey!" Shel whined, forgetting that his friend was both drowning and confessing his love at the same time. "Sorry!" He clapped both hands over his mouth. The elephant and the bird looked away from the hungry boy and back to one another.

"Izzy," said the bird in quiet despair, "I don't—"

"I'm sorry." Izzy hung his head in equal measures of shyness and shame. "I should've told you a long time ago. I've been in love with you since the ninth grade when I snuck into Mrs. Redhawk's Flyers-Ed class. I have no idea why she let a big, goofy elephant stay in a class for birds, but that year changed everything for me."

Shel managed another untimely interjection. "Is that why you wanted to be a pilot?" Charlotte tilted her head with piqued curiosity while Izzy stayed fixated on the pelican, ignoring Shel altogether.

"It's not drowning here that scares me, Charlotte," confessed Izzy. "Well, actually it does a bit. But what really scares me, is the thought of not getting the chance to spend just one day with you by my side... as more than my friend. Just once I'd—" was all that Izzy was able to get out before the sea breached his mouth, covering his head. His trunk broke the surface like a snorkel as he took in his last breaths, muttering the inaudible conclusion to his confession.

"IZZY!" Shel screamed.

Just then, the giant bird swooped down and grabbed hold of the elephant's submerged ears with her oversized, webbed talons, and with tremendous effort, lifted Izzy up just enough so that at least his head was barely above water, enough so he could breathe. The force of the air moving under the bird's massive wings, together with the shifting of the raft, was enough to knock Shel clean overboard.

"HALLELUJAH!" cried the soggy elephant as he grabbed hold of his savior and friend in any way that he could — clinging to life… and love!

"Come on, you big nut. Let's get you back to dry land where you belong." Charlotte the pelican began dragging Izzy through the water by his ears, his head bobbing just above the surface, legs kicking wildly in his best attempt at swimming. "I can't let the love of my life die the day he finally gets the nerve to confess, now can I?"

Izzy looked up in surprise. "Love of your life? You... you love me too?" Charlotte just smiled back. The answer was clear. Relieved beyond words, Izzy turned his attention to the boy in the water struggling to climb back onto the raft. "SHEL! I'll come back! We'll get a boat and come back for you! I promise!" As Charlotte made haste toward land, fearful of not being able to ferry the tremendous weight for long, Izzy added, "Don't worry, Shel! The current will carry you to the Land of Happy. Trust the current, Shel! Truusst the currrennnt!" And with that, he was gone.

"Izzy!" Shel called, climbing back onto the raft, which had largely returned to the correct side of the water's surface. "IZZY!" he yelled again in despair. Quietly, he said his friend's name once more before the silence of total solitude closed in all around him.

Chapter Ten

The Storm Dragon

Alone and adrift on an unknown sea, Shel was overcome with loneliness and an increased sense of remorse at having ventured so far from home. The raft, on the other hand, was apparently feeling much better, bobbing up and down like a kid with a lollipop. The lone pair were floating in a distinct direction, propelled by some invisible yet perceptible current. While the uncontrolled drifting gave Shel a feeling of dread, hope of Izzy's return, like his raft, remained afloat. He knew his friend would not abandon him, nor would the elephant abandon their quest to find Manny—

…Right?

He couldn't help but feel that he was putting himself through a lot of trouble to help out someone he had just met. After all, he didn't ask to be taken to Arcania in a flying shoe. He didn't ask for Izzy to hoist him up on his back and make him join the search for the dentist. A feeling of resentment crept into his heart, an uninvited guest.

"I didn't ask to be—" he started to say out loud as if placing an order for some pity pie with the invisible waiter of fate. But he stopped, suddenly realizing that perhaps he *did* ask for all of this to happen. Maybe his malcontent for life as an awkward boy growing up in the roughs of Chicago, son to a disapproving father, few friends to speak of… Maybe he *had* manifested this dramatic change. After all, he *did* wish feverishly for a life of adventure. Like it or not, he had exactly what he'd wished for: heaping mounds of adventure spiced with adventure; adventure trimmings and adventure garnishes; even some adventure dipping sauce on the side.

There ya go. Eat up!

How about some adventure for dessert?

Cue the thunder…

BOOOM!

As if conjured by his gloomy disposition, a sudden, tremendous thunderclap rang out across the sky, echoing over the endless water.

Oh, great! Here comes more adventure, he thought to himself as ominous storm clouds gathered like an angry mob in the skies above, obscuring the sun.

Flashes of lightning in the distance threw warning signs of things to come, while more explosions of thunder — terrifying exclamation points from the heavens — punctuated the warning.

The sky grew dark and the sea started to roll in a fury reminiscent of his boiling lake dream. A steady spit of rain began to fall on his head and almost instantly his eyes answered the call, letting loose a stream of tears. The fear that descended with each deluge of rain, each thunderclap was utterly overwhelming, like an anchor dragging his spirit to the depths.

He wiped the wetness from his face, attempting to rally his courage, and through the mist and moisture, scanned the horizon in all directions for any hint of land. But there was none, just as in his dream. He suddenly heard the prophetic screech of an eagle somewhere high above the storm clouds and decided his imagination was back to playing tricks. *Always at the worst time!* he thought, feeling perfectly miserable.

He looked up at the darkening sky. There, right in the middle of the mob of clouds was a break in the darkness, a spot of light shining through, a clear calm above the fray. That's where the eagle was, flying peacefully in its glory, safe from the gathering chaos, immune to heaven's wrath. Shel envied the eagle, longing to fly high, to rise above this dark storm pushing the waves ever higher from the sea, pulling the rain ever harder from the sky. The water was everywhere now, coming from all directions. The sea was a wild animal breaking out of its cage, a dragon full of fiery rage.

Shel looked upward again, searching for the bright spot in the sky, a ray of hope, but it was gone. Amassing reinforcements, the sinister clouds snuffed out the light once and for all. Shel gripped the raft tightly in whatever way he could as the vessel pitched and crashed against the pounding squall, waves getting bigger by the minute. The towering walls of water were growing large enough to resemble the towering buildings Shel encountered on his walk through Chicago. The dark of the water blended with the fog surrounding the raft, while rain and seawater continued to mix, pounding him from all sides until he could no longer tell sky from sea.

As if orchestrated by a mad conductor, the lightning, thunder, rain, wind, and waves performed a terrifying symphony, an awesome display of nature's power, her undeniable might. Soaked, hammered, and terrified, clinging desperately to his ragged raft, tumbling uncontrollably down and back up the shadowed sea giants, Sheldon cried out, convinced that he would not survive the seething tempest.

"IZZY! FICKLES! MOM! DAAAAD!"

His cries for help were drowned the instant they left his mouth. No sound could be heard above the crashing thunder and howling wind. There was no one around to hear them anyway. He was all alone, riding an angry dragon, this respectable squall in which any sailor would be honored to go down with their ship. His raft, however, without an enormous elephant on board, was turning out to be difficult for the dragon to subdue. Instead, the vessel just flipped and rolled and danced madly through the fight. Shel could do nothing but hold on with all his strength. Even that became an impossible effort as the waves crashed down over and over.

Unable to maintain a grip, he wedged his limbs between cracks in the boards and wrapped loose lashings around his torso like a belt, entangling himself in the raft, becoming part of it, just another log given up by the generous apple tree. Like it or not, he would remain with the raft now whether it stayed afloat or sank to the rocky bottom.

At first, our hero was holding out hope for the former. Eventually, exhaustion and fear became so overwhelming that either option would have sufficed so long as it meant an end to this terror. The storm dragon tuned into the boy's surrender. Now was the time to strike the final blow.

Shel, who had been keeping his eyes closed in a futile attempt to make it all go away, sensed a sudden change in the air. He opened his eyes just in time to see an enormous monster rise out of the sea — a dark giant with raging whitewater eyes that scraped the bottoms of the clouds, releasing jolts of lightning as if freeing wild animals from their cages.

This immeasurable wave towering over the boy in the raft — this black devil of a dragon the likes of which he had never dreamed in his worst nightmares — appeared to pause at its peak as if taking a moment to consider its victim and display its full might. There it stood, supreme, unchallenged by anything in the world — fear permeating through the very sky, across the expanse of sea. The air trembled. The rain stalled. The sea writhed. The dragon was everywhere, all around him, smothering his thoughts, beneath his skin, in his very breath. Even time seemed to succumb to its terrifying glory, afraid to move forward.

Shel knew that now was the moment to say a final prayer, to reflect on his relatively brief and insignificant existence. If ever there had been a way out of Arcania, a time to quit and go home, to abandon this adventure-seeking folly, this nonsense of chasing dreams, now was the time, his last chance. It wasn't too late. His father would be overwhelmed with relief at his son returning in one piece. And Shel would be eternally grateful to be back safe with his family. A life at the bakery wouldn't be so bad. He reasoned that he could, after all, give away his life desire, extinguish his destiny fire, in exchange for safety, stability, and the approval of his family.

...Or could he?

Running from the law; standing alone on the sidewalk at the farmhouse, night fast approaching; wrestling strangers in a flying shoe en route to a mysterious land; being chased by a beast with forty thousand claws; confronting werewolves and vampires... those were all frightening trials, no doubt.

But this, this was different. This was fear so thick he could taste the bitterness of it; he could feel the sting of it coursing through his blood, numbing his flesh, choking the life from his lungs. It was all he could see, for the great mass pressing on his eyes, smothering his vision. There was no room for courage in the dragon's lair, a desolate place where even hope dared not tread.

Unlike any other frightening situation he'd experienced, monsters and beasts included, this was the utter draining of his mortality. He could feel life slipping through his clenched fists, pouring from his tears, steaming from the top of his head, a deadly fever burning from his core, leaving nothing behind. Even his desperate screams were silent in the void. This was his life emptying all breath in preparation for one last goodbye.

In that final moment, a curious thing happened. There was no decision that could possibly be made, no answer to give. Yet, deep in his heart, in the soul of his soul, somehow, from within the extinguishing grip of the dragon draining his last drip of energy, Shel could feel a resolution emanating from his heart: a powerful emotion, clear as the calm, blue sky he once knew to exist somewhere above the madness. It was a wish. His last wish.

With all his being, through his body, down to his bones; with all his senses, through his spirit and his soul, he made his wish.

He did not wish to go home, back to the comfort of his apartment and the safety of his kin. Here in this place, in the darkest hour imaginable, he stayed resolute, resolved to face his destiny, resigned to this terrifying fate. For here was life on his own terms, and it would either be that or nothing at all.

He reached down to his innermost depths, and with his last evaporating puddle of consciousness, placed a wager with eternity, incurring a life debt. Facing the demon wave, he cried out with borrowed breath — for his was all but spent — "Come on then! Come get me! I'm right here! I am not afraid!"

A lie. He was very much afraid.

But all he could do was tempt the dragon to do its worst. This was his gauntlet thrown down at the feet of fate, posing the question: How far would God allow him to go as he drifted away from all he knew; away from his parents, from his old life, from his father's plan for him? How far would Asherah go to stop him from pursuing his own dreams, from living on his own terms? Here now was his answer.

With a menacing bow — a terrifying cresting of the monolithic wave — the dragon acknowledged the boy's resolve, honored his courage, and accepted his surrender. Then, in a great empyrean exhale, the wave toppled, crashing down upon the tiny raft with thunderous ferocity.

Under the tremendous force of water thrashing all around him, spinning him beyond control, Shel could feel the words, "Do not worry, young soul, I will make it quick," vibrate through his failing body and snuff out the last flicker of flame.

As the raging torrent of water finally receded, blending back to the sea, gone was the storm and gone was the dragon, gone was the little raft,

...and gone was the boy.

Chapter Eleven

The Joy of Life

The sea was an eerie calm, as if all the life within her had been utterly spent. An absence of even the slightest breeze indicated that the dragon had retreated to her watery cave, resting peacefully somewhere below the surface until her next trial. The sun was missing from the sky, a temporary casualty of the torrent, obscured by an early morning fog hanging low in the air. The only sound was that of a light lapping of water against the edge of what remained of the raft: little more than a tangled mess of broken sticks and vines, a ravaged rat's nest after a hurricane.

Somewhere woven into the fray, like soggy noodles strained through a sieve, hung the battered and bruised body of a young man, an unfortunate fly caught in a long-abandoned cobweb, leftovers of a life almost lived. The jean pants that clung to the limp torso were shredded almost into shorts. Remnants of a cotton shirt hung loosely around his still chest. Arms and legs, overexposed to the elements, were covered in cuts and bruises, tanned and burned after what must have been many hours, if not days, adrift. His hair was a thick tangle, not unlike the raft itself, twigs and twine poking out here and there as if a family of seagulls had taken up residence. Except, there was no sign of birds or any other life around his head, nor anywhere else on his body.

Meanwhile, the raft, which itself looked thoroughly inanimate, like driftwood washed up on a long-forgotten coast, was no longer a slave to the Champion current. It had reached its terminus, run aground on an anonymous shore. Finally, it and its passenger — dead or alive — had found land, and on that land there *were* signs of life. A specific life.

A girl.

The girl, who had watched the vessel slowly drift to shore, drew closer to investigate. She climbed aboard the rickety boat; poked and prodded at the curious body attached to it; tangled her fingers in his tangled hair; traced the outline of his face and eyes, the slope of his nose, the curve of his cheeks and chin; gripped his hands and studied the light freckles that ran from his fingers, up his forearms to his lean shoulders; finding no obvious signs that he was alive.

Yet, somewhere deep within and all around, the sacred gong of life rang out inaudibly, invisible vibrations on the breeze. Like a latent fire covered in layers of soil and wet leaves, the life inside the tangled body smoldered, weak and fragile, yet stronger than ever.

So when the girl tugged harder at his sinewy limbs, attempting to free the unconscious prisoner trapped behind wooden bars; when she caressed his brow and cradled his head in her healing palms; when she spoke softly to him, some strange language born in the depths of the sea; when she pressed her lips to his and breathed new air into his drowned lungs, the limp body began to choke and sputter and jerk until finally eyes cracked slowly open. Slightly at first, then wide to catch the dancing light as the survivor saw the truth of it: all had not gone black; life was still there, waiting for him, expecting him.

Life waited, but not the girl.

As Sheldon's consciousness trickled back like the first hint of rain after a long, dry summer, the apprehensive femme darted off to watch from a safe distance as her patient crawled his way back to the land of the living.

Sheldon took a deep breath and instantly began coughing uncontrollably, hacking up heaps of water. The violent jolts finished the job of loosening the sticks around his limbs and body until he was finally freed from his raft tomb. More water flowed from his lungs as he rolled onto his stomach and pulled himself onto all fours. He dragged himself off the raft and collapsed on the sand. Eventually his coughing subsided and he rolled onto his back to catch his breath. Looking up at the grey fog slowly clearing to blue skies, he saw a silhouette of a head suddenly appear above him.

"Hi!"

"Aaaahhh!" Sheldon managed a yell, sat up with a start, and immediately began coughing again.

"Oh, goodness! Are you all right?"

Tossing sand into the air, Sheldon stumbled to get to his feet before spinning around to face the intruder. He raised a hand to block the daylight and waited for his eyes to adjust, like a newborn seeing the world for the first time.

As she came into view, Sheldon noted that the stranger did not appear threatening in the least. She looked awfully friendly, in fact — comely even — a sweet face with a gentle smile. He was stunned to be seeing anything again after saying goodbye to the world. To be seeing a pretty girl on an otherwise deserted beach, he was at a total loss for words. And so, she proceeded in his silence.

"Bonjour! ¡Hola! Hi! Hellooooo!" The girl prodded in an exceptionally friendly voice, fishing for some response. "Parlez-vous français? Italiano? A lo mejor español? How about English?"

At the last option, Shel raised a hand to acknowledge her greeting, which made her giggle. He tried to speak, to answer, but instead of being dumbstruck, this time he found his throat was bone dry and only a dusty squeak came out, like the creak of an old barn door.

The girl, who looked to be maybe a year or two older than he, laughed. "My name's Joythea. You can call me Joy. Are you feeling all right?"

"Uh," he finally said, gulping down a tiny trickle of moisture in his mouth. "I... think so."

"Here." Joy held out a cup made of seashells, apparently containing fresh water. Shel jerked back without meaning to, a response fueled by the residual fear lingering in his bones. When he saw that she persisted, undeterred, he snatched the cup from her hands and eagerly gulped down the liquid like a ravenous barbarian, choking and coughing in a fit.

"You're thirsty!" She pointed out the obvious. "What's your name?"

Shel doubled over and got back to coughing up more water.

"You're not from around here. I can tell. I like your boat. It's very creative. I saw you drifting on your boat and I was so happy. I wished that you would drift all the way to my shore and you did! I watched you float near the beach for a whole hour, maybe more. I think your boat wasn't sure it wanted to land. But then it did! Right over there!" She pointed to his raft. "Isn't it great? It's so great. Where did you come from? Boy, you sure are quiet. So, what do they call you? Or should I just call you Thirsty?"

"Um. *Cough, cough.* My name is *cough* Shel." He tried to straighten up, his sore muscles providing plenty of resistance.

"Oh... my... gosh! I LOVE that name! It's like seashells. I looove seashells!" Joy did a little dance at the thought of seashells and her new friend. "I'm sooo happy! Aren't you?" She reached down, grabbed two handfuls of sand and tossed it into the air while spinning in circles, sea-bleached hair flying in a carefree dervish. Noticing Shel's arduous movements, she sprung at him and grabbed hold of his torso to help him stand upright. "Are you okay?"

As their eyes met, Shel saw a kindness in her smile and felt a tenderness in her touch such that he knew he'd never known before.

Embarrassed at the way he was looking at her, she steadied him and turned away quickly.

"And where did you sail from, dear Shel? Where do you hail from? Where do you send mail from?" She sang her inquiries in angelic tones.

He was already beginning to like this barefoot beach girl with salty hair, tan skin, and pleasant song. Unsure of what to say to her many questions, however, he thought he would simply try some (not very original) wit. "You sure are joyful, aren't you, Joy?"

"Yes! That's my name! I *am* joyful!" She spun in more circles. "That's who I am. It's who we *all* are. Everyone is happy here. It is our way of life."

"That sounds nice," he replied. His words, though soft on the outside, were gritty on the inside, like sandpaper against his emotions. He desperately wanted to feel the sort of joy this girl clearly felt, but it was impossible. He was still shaken to his core by the encounter with the dragon. Beyond this, he felt an overwhelming loneliness from Izzy's absence, and he was beginning to think once again about his family back home. "Where I'm from, happiness is not many people's way of life, that's for sure."

"Oh, that's sad." Joy stopped dancing, giving Shel a moment of sympathetic eyes. Her empathy was formidable. Shel couldn't help but feel it enhanced her beauty. "But now you're here!" (Sympathetic moment gone.) "And you can be happy!" She danced again for a turn then stopped and squinted. "But why have you come?"

Shel hesitated, pondering his unique situation and how best to divulge the details. Then he realized he didn't really know the details. Izzy had devised this elaborate plan to save Manny by finding some hunter in some circus named after some kind of bird or something. "Well, I'm not entirely sure, to be honest," he admitted. "I'm looking for— that is, I'm trying to find—" He started putting two and two together. "Wait a minute! Did you say everyone here is happy? What is this place called?"

"Oh!" Joy stopped gyrating and with arms open wide, presented the surroundings. "This, my friend, is Isla de Sonrisas, the Island of—" She stopped when she saw the look of disappointment fall across Shel's face. "What is it?" she asked. "Did I say something wrong?"

Shel sighed. "No. Nothing. It's just that, I thought, since you said everyone is happy here— never mind." He began to entertain the possibility that there was no Land of Happy, that Izzy was indeed a nutcase, or that he'd just made it all up so that he could get out to sea and find his Charlotte. After all, Izzy never did come back for him.

Despite that thought causing him near-crippling sadness, despite being thoroughly exhausted and feeling weaker than he'd ever felt in his life, he still, on some level, felt strong. He felt that he was no longer responding to the whims of the world, like following the farmhouse light or taking orders from others as he was accustomed to doing back home. A small fire ignited inside of him as he realized he would be making decisions for himself from here on. He straightened his posture and looked at Joy squarely. "I'm looking for someone to help me find a friend. I think he may have been kidnapped— or worse." Shel's eyes shifted away. *So, I guess we're calling Manny our friend now?*

Joy gasped, "That's terrible! Oh, I'm afraid, Mr. Shel, sir, that you have come to the wrong place." Shel's shoulders slumped. "There are no kidnappers or any such troublemakers here in the Land of Happy."

Shel's head drooped at first until he realized what she'd just said. Forgetting about his pain, he perked up and sprung at her, grabbing her by the shoulders and shaking her. "What did you say?! Did you just say this is the Land of Happy?!"

"Yes!" Joy yelled in fright. "Please let me go!" she demanded.

Shel realized he was terrorizing the poor girl. "Oh, gosh! I'm so sorry!" He quickly released her and forced an awkward smile, trying to reassure her that he was not a threat. As soon as she was free, she turned and began walking away down the beach.

Calming himself, Shel followed. "I'm truly sorry about that," he offered. She didn't respond. He wasn't entirely sure it was his actions causing her silence, however. After all, it was a minor incident. *Wasn't it?* She seemed to have something more weighing on her. Shel caught up and began walking next to her. After a moment, he decided to repeat his query, albeit more tactfully.

"So, this is the Land of Happy, then?"

She was hoping he might ask about her, whether she was ok, but he seemed focused on the location — which didn't make her feel amazing but piqued her curiosity all the same. She wondered about this strange, emotional boy in ragged clothes and messy hair, full of myopic enthusiasm for his mission, despite having only narrowly escaped death not so long ago. She stopped walking and looked at him, and in a softened tone, answered, "Yes, darling, Isla de Sonrisas is the Island of Smiles, a province in the Land of Happy."

On impulse, Shel hugged her and exhaled, "I made it!" He wasn't prone to emotional outbursts, certainly not spontaneous hugs, having been raised in a household where displays of affection were rare. Perhaps his recent near-death experience had awakened something inside. Perhaps he was already beginning to change.

Joy was still a bit shaken and remained unsure of the boy's intent, so she did not return his embrace. Instead, she patted his head as if to say, 'I accept your apology, but you'd better not scare me like that again, or else!'

Shel backed away and gave her a nod of understanding and the two continued walking. They walked for a stretch in silence until Shel's stomach reminded him that he hadn't eaten anything in a rather long while, only a few bites of an apple at most. His fatigue had all but evaporated in the warm sunshine, but the hunger remained like salt on a dried-up seabed. He wondered if there might be a market or an eatery nearby until he recalled that he didn't have any money.

Maybe I could hock my medal? he wondered as he clutched for his neck.

"No!" he gasped.

"What is it?!" Joy asked, startled.

"My medallion! It's gone! It must have fallen off in the storm!"

"Oh, that's terrible!" replied Joy sympathetically. "Was it important?"

Shel thought about the question and realized that, although he liked the medal, he was more distraught by the notion of misplacing the memory of the monsters than the medallion itself. He shook his head. "I suppose not. It was just something that some friends gave me to remember them. But I won't forget them. I'm sure I won't."

His thoughts returned to the present and he looked around, seeing no buildings, roads, boats, or any other sign of civilization. He asked with a curious squint, "Where'd you come from, anyway?"

She squinted right back and he realized his question wasn't entirely polite.

"I mean, where are *you* from, Joy?" He smiled.

She half-grinned. "Well, I asked you first."

Shel looked away and sighed. "I'm not from anywhere around here, as you already guessed. I'm from Chicago." He looked back at her. "Know where that is?"

She shook her head. "No. I don't. But I think I've heard of it."

"Yeah, it's a long way from here… I think." He looked out over the water, then turned back. "What about you? Where are you from?"

Joy smiled. "Well, I live here. My family has lived here for generations."

Shel looked around again. There was still nothing anywhere. "Here? In the Land of Happy?"

"Well, sort of. Most people live inland, across the desert." She pointed. "But my people live by the coast. We prefer to stay close to the water."

"Sooo, you were just walking along the beach and you saw me on my raft?"

"Something like that."

Her vague, semi-evasive response made Shel feel a tad suspicious, but he dismissed it for the time being. "Well, I'm glad you were here." He smiled. His words were sincere. He was relieved that someone had found him, especially someone who knew the area. That way he would not have to wander around, lost in a strange land, doomed to perish of starvation or get captured by pirates…

"You okay?"

His mind had started to wander. "Oh, yeah. I'm okay, just a little hungry." In truth he was starving. Hunger aside, Shel he was much luckier than he realized. He was completely unaware that Joy had saved him, that she had breathed divine spark back into his lifeless body. He was just happy not to be alone.

But he was also feeling something else, something rather unfamiliar. Sure, he had noticed girls at his school or around his neighborhood. He had even thought some of them to be cute or pretty.

But never before had he felt whatever it was he was feeling when he looked at Joy. There were no words for it. It felt prickly, like being prodded with a cactus. At the same time, however, it felt wonderfully soft, like a pillow. It was like being slugged in the gut and gently hugged at the same time, or being struck by a lightning bolt of cotton candy. He even felt sick to his stomach as if he had *eaten* a cotton candy lightning bolt. Whatever it was, the feeling tickled and made him want to laugh out loud. So he did.

Joy looked at the giggling youth and smiled.

He quickly looked away and swallowed his giggles.

Sensing his discomfort, she pushed the conversation down the beach. "What is it you're looking for again?"

"Um, well, I— I need to find a man who, I guess, lives somewhere around here. He's supposed to be the world's greatest hunter or something."

"Ingo," she said matter-of-factly.

"Bingo? Did I get it right?"

"Haha. No. I said Ingo. You're looking for Mr. Ingonyama. He's world-famous for his tracking skills and marksmanship with a rifle."

"Yes! Ingo. That's him! That's the name. Where do I find this Mr. Ingo... nammm... uh... Where do I find this man?"

"He's not a man," replied Joy.

Shel didn't know if she was offering her opinion, perhaps commentary... "Okaaay. Is he a boy? That would be weird because—"

"He's a lion."

"What?! A lion?!"

Joy laughed, as she tended to do, and nodded.

"Hmm. Well, I guess that shouldn't come as a surprise in this place. So, uh, do you know this Ingo the lion? Or do you know where I can find him?"

"Well, I do know him, sort of, but I don't know where he is, unfortunately. But the Falcon might."

"The Falcon? Oh, that's right! The circus!" Shel recalled Izzy's instructions.

"Yes! The circus. How do you know about—"

"Where do we find the Falcon?" he interrupted.

"I don't know," Joy admitted, with a slight scowl at Shel's lack of manners. "But the king will definitely know."

"The king? Oh! Is that King Skippy?"

"Ssshhhhh! Don't call him that!" chided Joy.

Shel looked around as though someone might be listening and he might be in trouble, but still, there was no one around. "Sorry. Well, how do we find the king?"

"No idea. But the magic flying hippopotamus will know."

"Oh, you've got to be kidding me."

"Yes, I am kidding," she laughed. "I can take you to the king, if he'll see you." She offered an outstretched hand. Shel hesitated. "What's wrong?" she asked.

"Um, nothing. It's just that— if I leave the beach, Izzy might not be able to find me."

"Izzy? As in, Izzy the elephant?"

Shel looked at her in surprise. "You know Izzy?"

"Yes, of course!" She cheered with a celebratory cartwheel, accidentally kicking sand into Shel's face. He shook his head to avoid the mess but didn't so much mind. Her exuberance was delightful, refreshing, contagious even. "Izzy was in the Falconovich Circus too. Until a few years ago when he just up and disappeared."

"He was?!? He didn't tell me that!" exclaimed Shel. "What do you mean he disappeared?"

"Not literally disappeared." Joy grinned at Shel's humorous look of puzzlement. "But he was in the circus, yes. People said he left shortly after he heard about a young elephant from another circus far away, an elephant who could fly."

"An elephant that could fly?! Really?"

"That was the story. They say it had something to do with oversized ears like wings. That, and a magic feather. Anyway, rumor has it Izzy left in search of that elephant, to see if the little flyer could teach him his secret."

"Whoa." Shel sat down and stared out at the water, thinking about his friend and how they first met. *Silly elephant-in-a-tree, longing to fly like a bird.* It all made sense now, Izzy crashing the flyer's-ed class and falling for the shark with wings. It seemed that Izzy and Charlotte were meant to be together. *And now that they are together*, Shel reasoned, *they might not be coming back for me.* Despite being sad about that possibility, Shel decided it was okay. Izzy had said that the lake current would send the raft straight on to the Land of Happy eventually, and that Shel would surely be met by some happy person who would be willing to show him the way to Ingo, or Falconovich, or the king... or at the very least, the magic hippo. Shel laughed. He didn't feel angry anymore. He felt happy for his friend. In fact, he felt overjoyed.

Joy sat down next to him. "Everything good?"

He sighed. "Izzy was supposed to come with me, on this adventure. We set out from Champion Valley together, the two of us on that tiny raft over there." He nodded in the direction of the disheveled pile of logs. "It looked a lot more like a proper boat in the beginning. But we had an accident along the way and he had to turn back. Now I'm not sure if he's coming back for me."

Joy reached over and took Shel's hand and that made him smile (it also made him a bit nauseous). Izzy or no, Shel knew that his mission now was to find Ingonyama, to not give up on Manny. After the showdown with the dragon, he knew he needed to see the mission through to the end, despite not really knowing the dentist at all. He knew the dentist's friends and that was enough. He reasoned that Izzy would be continuing his own search for Manny from wherever he was now, and that the flying shoe crew were also still out there looking.

I'm part of the team now, he thought to himself. *Even if I am alone, I can't give up on the team.*

Thinking of all these different players working toward the same goal reminded him of the puzzle piece. He reached into his damp pocket and was surprised to find it still there. The water hadn't done much to keep the piece in good shape, but it was still intact, and cleaner now. The brackish lake water had succeeded in removing a good bit of the dirt that his saliva could not.

"What's that?" asked Joy.

He looked at her and realized he was wrong. He wasn't alone. He had a wonderful new friend who was willing to take him to see a king. A king! How exciting! He held out the piece to show her.

She nodded. "We're all just puzzle pieces in the grand painting of life." Then she stood up and danced away down the beach.

Is everyone in Arcania a philosopher-poet? he thought to himself with a chuckle. Looking down at the puzzle piece in his hand he noticed that the 'e' at the end of the word 'image' was actually an 'i', that the word was not 'image' after all; the word was 'imagine.' The label which he had thought was simple and obvious was not so obvious, and it was not so simple.

Holding the piece up in front of his face, he followed its instructions: he imagined. He imagined a picture taking shape in front of him, a puzzle fitting together the pieces of his world. He imagined his parents and his sister back home in Chicago. Next to that he fit his school. Around that, formed his neighborhood with, of course, Hector's wonderful hot dog stand. Expanding the image, he envisioned the farm fields with the mysterious farmhouse and the dark woods at the end of the long sidewalk.

A large swath of indigo and starlight painted a transition from Chicago's woodlands to the brilliant green fields of Champion Valley. There in the dark, he saw the festoon Delilah and her crew. Manny's house, surrounded by the oak-rose forest appeared and he could see that crazy pachyderm perched in the tree, which made him laugh out loud.

The forest expanded and he saw the Worst beast staring at him with glowing eyes. He shook his head and the fear creeping up on him fell away like dead leaves from a tree. He saw the bushes below the forest and delighted when his monster friends appeared, sitting around a glowing campfire, laughing and telling stories. He reached up to feel for the medallion no longer hanging around his neck and his heart dropped a beat before he recovered, rejoicing for friendship, real or imaginary.

The crazy restaurant then materialized, along with the stubborn unicorn and the generous apple tree; then the beautiful Champion River leading to Champion Lake. There he saw Charlotte and Izzy, and he reveled, choking back tears.

Another dark swath materialized and spread like ink spilling over parchment. He knew right away... this was the storm dragon. He tried hard to refrain from crying but the trauma was too fresh, still living somewhere deep within, thriving in his bones or nerves or flesh. Overwhelmed, he broke down.

When it had happened — the attack of the dragon — he'd felt almost numb from the shock of the experience, adrenaline shielding his senses. Now, recalling the incident, he was flooded by a wave of emotion he hadn't seen coming and could not hold back. He had been certain, beyond any doubt, that he was not going to survive. Indeed, he had not. Though he'd been revived, a part of him died that day. Which part, however, he did not know.

When he found life again — or when life found him — the excitement and intrigue of meeting Joythea helped to shelter him from recalling the full near-death experience. Now that the ordeal was over, there was nothing standing between him and the awareness of his own demise. He buried his head between his knees, broke down, and wept uncontrollably, shaking, nearly becoming physically ill. Exploring the full gamut of feelings brought on by the encounter with the dragon led to a toppling of the walls barricading his emotions and soon he was weeping for Izzy's absence, then weeping harder at the memory of the Worst fright. He wept for his home and for his poor mother, always doing her best to buffer her children against her husband's temper. He even wept for his father, the grumpy old Banzakoot, and for all the things he would never be for his dad.

As he shed the tears of a child growing up — growing up and away from his parents — he felt sympathetic drops of rain begin to fall. Relief washed over him with each drop and he felt cleansed by the rinsing. He looked up and the rain fell harder, masking his tears. Though he did not feel ashamed of his emotions, he was relieved to know that he would not have to explain anything to his new friend as she would not be able to tell he had been crying.

He looked down the beach and watched Joy dancing like a mad woman, reveling in the heavenly downpour, that wonderful warm spring shower.

"She just doesn't care," he laughed to himself, feeling his mood lift. "And why should she? She's waterproof." His emotions subsided and his tears ceased. Only the rain remained. His cries turned to laughter as he marveled at the carefree girl dancing through the storm.

Looking again at the puzzle piece and the imaginary picture that had formed around it, he could see the raging squall over Champion Lake. The storm was still there but he was no longer in it. Instead, on a nearby sandy shore, there sat a young man, and next to him was another figure, one with flax-golden hair flowing in the breeze.

He looked back toward Joy. The rain had come and gone, much like his emotions, and the sun was now breaking through. And Joy was still there, dancing and spinning in the shore break, singing a song of words altogether foreign.

When she saw him watching her, she ran over. "Shel!" she said, smiling and out of breath. He looked up and smiled, then placed the puzzle piece back in his pocket. "I'm glad you're here," she said.

He pulled his soggy shoes and socks off and dug his toes into the warm, wet sand. "Me too," he replied quietly.

Joy jumped down next to him and caught her breath, burying her toes next to his. "Coastal rain is so amazing, don't you think? How it comes and goes so fast, like life."

They sat in silence for a moment, taking everything in.

"See?" She pointed out over the water. "The sun is coming out again already."

Shel smiled at her and nodded, then looked back at the water.

"It's a lovely thought, isn't it?" she continued, staring straight ahead, adding, "He did it, didn't he? I just know he did." She picked up the hand of this sweet young man with honey-colored eyes, taking him by surprise. He glanced down to find their hands intertwined. Looking back into her eyes, he let slip an accidental laugh, feeling terribly awkward yet terrifically natural at the same time.

"I like your laugh," She giggled, fingers of her free hand coursing through her hair.

Shel let loose a wide smile, impossible to keep in. "Who did what?" he asked.

"What's that?" she replied.

"You said that he did it. Who? Did what?"

"Oh! Izzy. He discovered the elephant's secret. He learned to fly, didn't he?"

Shel thought a moment about the events that led him to where he was, sitting next to this amazing girl full of light and wonder. He looked down the beach and admired the sublime landscape: the golden grass shining in the sun, bowing to the cool breeze keeping the youngsters' hair flowing wildly, giving them a playful and exotic allure. He delighted in the shifting sand, soft and warm under his skin. He gazed longingly over the water to wherever Izzy might be, eyes glistening from the blinding sunlight sparkling off the infinite horizon.

Joy squeezed his hand. "Is that a yes?"

He closed his eyes and reveled in the feeling of her soft, slender hand in his. Never had his heart felt so alive and full, and he could now imagine — or so he believed — the immense joy that Izzy must have felt at seeing Charlotte again — a fraction of it anyway — at reuniting with his love.

Shel sighed and wiped the remaining wetness from his eyes.

"Did he learn to fly?" he repeated, staring at the sea before turning to face the girl. As his eyes met hers, he knew the answer beyond any doubt.

"Yes. Yes, he most certainly did."

Book Three
All the Colors I Am Inside

Book Three is for all the characters and spirits behind the curtain.
Thank you for the magic and the gifts.

Introduction

Me and Him, Still Here

Me: *Ah, it's you again!*

Him: Yup, it's me!

Me: No, not *you*. *I'm* Me, you're *Him*, and I was talking to *them*.

Him: Ohhh. Got it. Hey, them!

Me: Well, Him, it looks like them's back for more. You up for narratin'
part three in the saga of young Sheldon?

Him: Oh boy, am I! Except... I don't entirely recall where we left off.

Me: Ah, well in part two, Sheldon and Izzy developed a close
friendship by persevering through all sorts of trials and
tribulations. You recall their encounter with the Worst beast?

Him: Oh, don't remind me.

Me: But then Shel got to meet Walter and Karl and Drac.

Him: That's right! And Walter rode off with his bike!

Me: Ha. Yup! And the incident with the unicorn stuck in the tree
following lunch at the Nuthouse?

Him: Well, I think it was supper. But, yeah, the Nuthouse, what a nutty
place! Then they built that raft!

Me: That ridiculous raft! Which sunk.

Him: Which sunk! Good grief. Those guys!

Me: But then Izzy and Charlotte reunited and finally confessed their
love for each other.

Him: Yeah. Ain't love grand?

Me: Except that left poor Sheldon all alone on the raft.

Him: Which didn't sink after all!

Me: Right. Despite the storm dragon trying her best to drown him.

Him: Boy, did she! How frightening was that?!

Me: Super.

Him: Super. But Sheldon made it through the storm!

Me: He did indeed, barely, with a little help from—

Him: Joythea!

Me: Correct-a-mundo! That's when he and Joy met, and he finally
found—

Him: The Land of Happy!

Me: That he did, yes. But no, what I was going to say was he found that
he was strong on his own. In his darkest hour he did not cry for
his parents but faced his fear and his fate, and he emerged
renewed and reborn on the other side of the storm.

Him: He's becoming his own man. Our little Sheldon is growing up.

Me: Indeed he is. He's finding that he is his own person. But he still
    has a way to go yet before he discovers his own path in the
    world.

Him: His calling. His destiny!

Me: Perhaps. But at the very least, his individual identity, apart from all
    the other things that have defined him up to this point in his life.

Him: Exactly. Okay, Me. I think I've got it from here! We left off with
    Joy and Shel on the beach at Isla de Sonrisas.

Me: Yup. And she was...

Him: Dancing!

Me: Haha. Good guess. She does that a lot, doesn't she? But I was
    going to say—

Him: Laughing!

Me: Also a good guess. She tends to do that, too. She's a happy one,
    that Joythea Costeros.

Him: Yes, indeed. She likes to enjoy life, and good on her for it! ...Oh!
    I know! She was taking Sheldon to see the king.

Me: Yes! That's exactly right. Okay, so you got it from here?

Him: Yup!

Me: Okay then. Take 'er away!

Prologue

New Flavor

Sometimes change comes like an avalanche: all at once, an overwhelming circumstance.

Other times it's like tipping a cup of tea into a lake: subtle and imperceptible, easy to mistake.

Sometimes it's like a new ingredient in an old, familiar dish. You notice something's different but you just can't place the switch.

You're not quite sure if you like it, or whether it's good for you. Will it help you grow taller or just wider? By ten feet, or just an inch or two?

You may decide the change is bitter and toss the dish in the trash. Still, the flavor will linger somewhere 'neath the surface, like wildfire ash.

Somewhere in your memory, deep or shallow, therein lies the seed. And in that way, change has been planted, whose fruit is guaranteed.

On the other hand, you may embrace the flavor, despite your reservations. (Did you make a reservation — at life's table — for just such a fated occasion?)

You may take a second bite, on second thought, and then a third in case you forgot. And still one more, making four, because you've never tasted such a taste before.

With a fifth bite you're all in, and a new beginning is beginning to begin.

By the sixth bite, a change has taken hold, and the dish you used to enjoy now tastes stale and old.

A seventh and then straight to the ninth bite. (The eighth needn't be had. We haven't got all night!)

By the tenth taste the transformation is complete; your empty, shining bowl reflecting a face you've been dying to meet.

Whether or not you knew it, you were craving more flavor in your stew. And so you sat down and devoured the old to fuel the magnificent new you.

o o o o o o

Young Sheldon's flavor of change came in the form of a playful light, calling to him, enticing him out into the world. Little did he know that the simple act of skipping school and following a meandering sidewalk to its end would lead to the end of reality as he knew it.

The familiar dish of daily life for Shel, within his small apartment, within the halls of Darwin Elementary, was now spiced with a flavor of which he had only previously dreamed: sweet adventure! And that is one ingredient which, once sprinkled on, cannot be sifted back out.

Although the new ingredient in Shel's stew of life produced a flavor impossible to ignore, the change taking place inside of him was more subtle. The experience of being in new places, making new friends, and being challenged in myriad ways was helping him grow from a boy into a young man. Spending time away from home was allowing him to discover his individual identity beyond simply being his parent's son. His interactions with Izzy, Joy, the Festoon Brigade, and many others were not only igniting new feelings inside of him, they were helping him form important bonds of trust and respect, along with virtues such as empathy... and even love. Sheldon was slowly but surely becoming someone entirely, magnificently new.

But the question remained: who?

Chapter One

Wild Ones

The intrepid young woman led the timid young man by the hand, as the two explorers climbed up and down, over and around, endless hills of calescent sand...

The sun grew oppressively hot as they strayed farther from the sea, ever inland, and it wasn't long before they were darting, fast as they could, between grassy tufts of spinifex and marram, or seeking refuge in the shade of small groves of birch and poplar trees. As the foliage grew increasingly sparse, the barefoot kids had to find other means of cooling their soles. They tried burrowing under the hot surface of the sand, which worked sometimes, somewhat. At one point, Shel removed his shirt and tossed it on the ground for both of them to stand on while they identified their next landing point. He kicked himself for leaving his wet sneakers back at the raft. *How glorious those soggy leathers would feel right about now!* Without shoes, the youngsters had to be very strategic, as the temperature of the sand became blisteringly unbearable.

"There!" Shel spotted a nearby patch of greenery and ran as fast as he could toward the little bit of shade, assuming Joy was following right behind. She wasn't.

"Wait!" she yelled, but Shel was so focused on getting to the bush that he ignored her altogether. He crashed into the branches and dug his feet into the cool sand below, reveling in the sound of hissing steam, like a hot pan plunged into cold water.

"My feet are *burning*!" he yelled at Joy. "They're literally steaming! I can hear it!" He looked back to see Joy kneeling on his shirt, digging like mad, trying to get down to cooler sand. "Joy, come on! There's room for—"

"That's not steam, you skoob!" she interjected without looking up from her project, which was moving along swiftly now that she had recruited a nearby stick for a shovel.

Shel scoffed with a *pshhh!* — suddenly distracted by the large berries growing all over the bush. The fruit looked like strawberries, deep red with small white seeds. Only, these berries were enormous compared to any strawberries Shel had ever seen, bigger than grapefruits even! And they looked irresistibly delicious with juices dripping from clefts in their surface like salivating mouths — not unlike Shel at that moment.

Joy looked up just in time to see Shel reach for one of the berries.

"Shel, no! Don't! Those are—"

"YEEEOOOWWW!" Shel screamed and bolted away from the bush toward Joy and her sand pit. She leaped out of the way as he flew into the hole, desperately trying to escape both the scorching sand and whatever it was that had just attacked him.

"Oh, my goodness! Are you okay?" Joy stepped carefully into the hole alongside her injured friend, who was crouching down, doubled over in pain.

"Ouch, ouch, OUCH! No, I am NOT okay! What was that thing?" Joy began to answer but the frustrated Shel cut her short. "Burning sand! Strawberries that bite back! How is this the Land of *Happy*? Sure doesn't seem very happy to me!"

Joy waited, letting Shel cool off a bit. "Nothing is ever as it seems, is it?" Joy's gentle expression helped calm his nerves, but only a little. "Come on, I imagine we'll have to get that treated." She extended a hand, intending to help him up. Shel reached with his left, his right hand clenched tightly, tucked into his body like the busted wing of an injured bird.

"That's the wrong direction anyway," Joy added. "We need to be going east. See that over there? The patch of green and white just beyond the next hill?" Shel barely nodded. "That's a birch grove. Plenty of shade there. We can rest a while and take a look at that bite. You'll likely need proper medicine, which means getting you to town sooner than later. I'll try to fashion something to ease the pain a smidge in the meantime."

Together they looked down at his hand. It was swelling up red and round and beginning to look a lot like... a strawberry.

"Let's go!" she exclaimed, and they made a dash for the trees, Joy dragging Shel's tattered shirt and Shel dragging his tattered hand.

By the time they made it to shelter, Shel couldn't decide what hurt worse, his chewed-up hand or his charred-up soles. Overwhelmed with pain, he began to feel sorry for himself, which made him think, not of home and his parents, but of Izzy. He longed for his friend, whom he had admittedly only known a very short time. But sometimes, even very new friendships run deep from the very beginning, especially those that overcome the sort of disagreements Izzy and Shel experienced at their introduction, and most especially those that endure such trauma as they encountered with the Worst beast and the sinking of their raft in Champion Lake.

Shel looked up with watery eyes to see Joy climbing one of the birch trees just like Izzy might, having fun and making the best of the situation.

"How do you do it?" he choked.

"Do what?"

"Stay so happy and positive all the time?"

Joy laughed. "I don't, silly. Sometimes I get sad. But I prefer being happy. Happy is more fun than sad. Don't you think?"

"Well, yeah, but—"

"But nothing," she snapped. Her scowl — though much friendlier than your typical scowl — reminded him of his parents or perhaps Ms. Kelsyan. Her expression softened and she smiled down from her perch. He couldn't help but smile back. She blushed and looked away. "Look, sooner or later we have to choose a path—"

"I can't!" He interrupted and shrugged. "I can't simply pick a path and go for it. I'm not free to go wherever I like, do whatever pleases me. Not like *you*. My family has expectations..."

Joy stopped him there. "You think I'm free to do whatever I want?"

"Well yeah, look at you, wandering around all by yourself, free to go on grand adventures to see kings and stuff."

"I'm not as free as you might think, Shelby. Besides, look at *you*. You're on your *own* adventure, right now, all by yourself, traveling across the great Champion Lake and now the Sonrisa Desert in search of the great Ingonyama, trying to save your dentist friend."

Shel looked around at the foreign landscape. She was right of course. He was, at that very moment, precisely as he accused her, out on his own, on a grand adventure.

Joy laughed at Shel trying to yank his foot from his mouth. "Anyway, I just meant that we need to pick a path to our next shade spot."

"Oh." Shel felt embarrassed at his overreaction.

Joy chuckled again, clambering around in the canopy of the birch trees, picking leaves here and there. "I don't think we need to know what we want to be when we grow up. *I* think we ought to just be thankful for being here. Feeling the ups," — she reached her arm high to grab some fresh sprouts at the top of the tree — "...and the downs," she concluded, leaping out of the tree to attend to her friend. "After all, things could be worse. *You*, my little injured bird, ought to be grateful." She laid the leaves onto a strip of bark and began mashing up them into a pulp using a short, thick branch.

"Grateful?! This hurts!" he whined. "Why should I be grateful for this?"

"Oh Shel, have you never thought that pain and sadness are just ways life reminds us to be grateful for the good times? People tend to forget how good they have it, tend to take life for granted. Pain and sadness help put things into perspective. ...*I believe anyway.*" Gently, with soft fingers, She began applying the poultice to his wound.

"I guess I never..." He paused. "What was that strawberry thing anyway?" Shel changed the subject, trying to stay calm and not whine as she meddled with his injury.

"Stop messin' with it!" she ordered. Shel withdrew his curiously intrusive fingers. "What was *what*?" She resumed tending to his hand with swift efficiency. "The thing that bit you? I told you, it was a wild strawberry. They're not tame. You shouldn't have tried to pet it."

"Pet it? I wasn't trying to *pet* it!"

Joy glared disapprovingly at his inference.

"Whaaat? What's the big deal? Where I'm from, strawberries are food."

She looked down and began wrapping larger leaves over the poultice.

"At least they were anyway, until the recession," he added quietly.

"We have strawberries for food here too, Shel. I'm just saying that here you need to be more cautious about what you can and cannot eat, more careful about what you assume is yours for the taking. That's all."

"Yeah, I know what you mean. Izzy and I learned that lesson back at the Nuthouse in Champion Valley."

"Oh? Learned your lesson did you? Doesn't look like it." She squeezed the wrapping tight around his hand, making him wince. "What's the matter? Is that uncomfortable?" She smiled. He did not. "This isn't Chicago, Shel. Here, a lot of things have feelings that you wouldn't think would feel anything. Like the wind, for example."

"The wind?!"

"Sometimes."

"Woah. Arcania really is a magical place, isn't it?" Shel looked around, wondering if he might catch a face floating by in the breeze.

"Well, Arcania is a special place, yes. Here, things tend to take on a life of their own, existing for themselves, not to serve others."

Shel felt like he could relate to that! He'd certainly been learning how to exist for himself ever since coming to Arcania.

"In truth, all the world is magical, Shel," Joy continued. "You just need the right mindset, the right eyes to perceive it. People are always talking about magic as if it comes from a wand or a bottle, but it can come from anywhere. A tree, a rock, a river... Everyone wants to find a magic genie who'll grant them their greatest wish, forgetting that's how they got here in the first place."

Shel didn't quite follow. "What do you mean?"

"Just what I said, all the world is magic, all of life a miracle. It's the deepest desire of the spirit to be granted a turn here, to get a ticket to ride this rollercoaster called life. It's the greatest blessing there is, the greatest privilege just to be here to experience it; all of it, the good and the bad. So hold still and stop complaining, you big baby," she concluded with a grin.

Her laughter set him at ease and made him smile. "I'm sorry I tried to eat the strawberry. Okay? I'm just—"

"I know, you think everything exists to serve you. I'm not surprised. Solipsism: it's the modern-day epidemic."

"What's saw lips...whatever? No, I was going to say that I'm really hungry."

"Oh."

"Aren't you?! I haven't eaten anything for ages!"

Joy looked at him and smiled. So far, Shel was turning out to be very different from the boys she knew back home, and she was reveling in playing nurse, having someone for whom to care. Yes, she was quite content with her curious, complicated, complainy... and awfully cute, companion.

"Joy?" He interrupted her thoughts.

"Yes, Shel?"

"What's saw lips siz... that word you said?"

She just laughed.

A dry wind rattled the tree branches, wringing the last bit of moisture from the leaves like a Nottingham Sheriff. The youngsters took advantage of the refuge, resting in the shade of the birch grove while the heat descended like a thick, uncomfortable blanket, lulling everything in the desert into a lazy calm. There they sat, imagining shapes in the clouds and branches, laughing and sharing stories, contemplating gratitude for pain, wishing desperately for rain.

Eventually, Shel began noticing odd shapes in the surrounding dunes, shapes that looked curiously like human figures and appendages. He pointed and giggled, "Look at that! It looks just like a nose."

Joy looked up, raised a few eyebrows, nodded, "Mm-hmm," and then returned to her project of ripping small sections of tree bark into fibrous strips, intending to wrap them around the leaves she'd placed over Shel's hand. "Did you know birch sap has been used as medicine for centuries?"

Not paying much attention, Shel scrunched his eyes and shook his head. His focus was on the curious shapes in the sand. "That looks like an ear! And over there, that looks like a mouth... and a chin!" He pointed in various directions, excited at the strange land formations. "And there's a hill that looks like half a head. Huh. Weird." His amusement was devolving toward concern. "And that one looks... exactly like... a hand. Wait a minute... What's going on?"

"I should tell you," Joy interjected, "the bite from a wild strawberry can make you see funny things sometimes."

"What?! Oh, no thank you! I already had *that* adventure back in the Valley. I'm not going through *that* again!"

"I'm only kidding!" Joy laughed.

He was not amused and Joy could tell. "Okay, I'm sorry." She stilled her laughter. "You had *what* adventure back in the Valley?"

Shel glared but nonetheless recounted an abridged version of his encounter with the monsters after having eaten the Champion berries.

"Wow. That's incredible," Joy replied. "Sounds like so much fun! You obviously didn't imagine that, Shel."

"No? What makes you so sure?"

"Champion berries need to be dried, crushed to a powder, and brewed into a tea along with a few other herbs for them to have that effect."

Shel squinted. "But, Izzy said—"

"Really? You're going to believe that goofball?"

Shel shrugged.

"I *will* tell you though, it's a good thing you didn't eat any of those wild strawberries, otherwise you'd be sleeping just like the Snoozants." She pointed toward some of the odd shapes in the sand. "They've been buried under there, sleeping for many, many years, and they only had one strawberry jam sandwich each — though, to be fair, they *were* rather large sandwiches."

Shel looked around, taking a moment to digest what she'd just said. "Snoozants? What in the world are Snoozants?" he asked, concerned that the shapes in the sand might actually be more than mere dunes.

"The Snoozants are what people call the sleeping giants buried beneath the sand."

"Wait! WHAT?!" Shel shrieked.

Joy couldn't help but laugh.

Her laughter made Shel conclude that she was just pulling his leg. "Ohhh, I see. You're full of jokes today, aren't you?" he smiled. "I thought you were serious. Giants sleeping under the sand. That's hilarious!"

"Yeah, it is," she laughed more. "Or at least it *was*. They were pretty hilarious... when they were in a good mood, anyway. They can be so temperamental."

"Who? What are you talking about, Joy?" Shel asked, back to feeling confused.

"The giants," Joy confirmed. "There's nothing worse than a giant in a foul mood."

Shel frowned, hoping she was joking again.

Joy laughed even harder at his expression. "Come on, silly goose. We need to get your hand wrapped in this bark." You'll be fine, I'm sure, so long as you don't go climbing up any of the giant's noses. That would certainly wake 'em up, and we don't want that!"

Shel looked at her in surprise and coughed, "WHAT?!?"

"And that's a wrap!" Finishing off the bandage then tying his shirt around his arm like a sling, she instructed, "Hold this in place until we get to town. Once finished with his hand, she got on to constructing two pairs of make-shift shoes out of birch bark. She fastened them to her and Shel's feet using stalks of spinifex woven together with strands of her own hair, which proved to be considerably stout. "There. This ought to give us some protection from the burning sand," she boasted with pride. Seeing the look on Shel's face, she smiled. "Whaaat? I know they're not fancy, but they'll save your feet... I think."

As she laced up his caveman sandals, Shel inquired, "How did you end up at that beach? I mean, at just the right time to save me?" She looked up at him and cocked her head sideways. "Where were you coming from?" he continued. "And where were you going? And where are *your* shoes?"

"Well... first of all, I never wear shoes," she laughed. "So, wherever they are and wherever they go, I do not know. They wander alone, without feet to guide them. Poor souls." She giggled some more and finished tying his laces. Playful as always, she jumped into the air, grabbed hold of a low-hanging branch from which to swing, then tucked her legs up between her arms and the branch. Folding her knees over the branch and letting her arms fall freely, she swung blissfully upside-down. "Now let's see. Not that-a-way. Hmmm." She pointed and plotted and pontificated.

"What are you looking for?" Shel asked, squinting at the sandy horizon.

"Fresh perspective. And maybe a hand to show me the way."

Shel looked around anxiously for a giant hand sticking out of the sand.

"Where I came from and where I was headed isn't important now, to answer your questions. What *is* important, my dear Shel, is why *you're* here."

Shel smirked. "Well, I asked you first. Besides, I already told you. I need to find—"

"No, no." She shook her head and smiled. "I know why you have come to the Land of Happy. But why have you come to Arcania? Why leave Chicago in the first place?"

It had been some time since Shel reflected on the myriad vicissitudes leading him to that moment. It was too difficult to explain everything, he felt, and the honest truth was that he himself was still trying to sort it all out. So instead, he just rattled off the first thing that popped into his head. "Well, I've always wanted to travel, to see new places. Plus, I've never really felt like I fit in there."

Sensing this was not a time for levity, Joy swung her arms forward, arched her back, and released her legs from the tree branch, sending her torso flying through the air like an acrobat. She landed solidly on the hot sand and quickly leaped back into the shade next to her friend, letting him know that she was listening.

It wasn't typical for people to take him seriously, thus it wasn't typical for Shel to open up. But for her, he did.

"It's just that I see all these other kids doing regular kid stuff, you know? Like playing ball games or chasing each other. I mean, I like games too... and having fun," he quickly added, remembering that his audience was most definitely a fun-seeker. "It's just that, I don't know, I like other things too."

Not feeling that he was making much sense, he tried a different approach. "It's as if all the other kids are listening to some music that I just can't hear, like they all got a ticket to see this show, and they're all living this life, moving along in this great big line toward some great big event. But I didn't get a ticket. I never even got an invitation. So I don't get in line. Instead, I just kinda wander around, feeling lost." Joy nodded and so he continued. "Some days I feel like I can almost hear the music, like I *almost* get what's going on. But, I... I don't know. I never quite get the rhythm or something."

"I think I get it," she reassured. "I like to pretend I hear my own music sometimes, a special music no one else can hear; accompaniments to the wind passing through the trees or waves crashing on the shore; the chirping of crickets at night or songbirds at dawn." She smiled and he smiled back. "I call it the magical music of the world. That's my favorite music to dance to."

"You really like to dance, don't you?" Shel asked.

"No. I don't like it. ...I LOVE to dance!" She stood up, did a twirl and danced around for a few seconds before the heat of the sand chased her back into the shade. She sat down, slightly out of breath, and added, "It's my way of showing gratitude for this incredible gift of life we've all been given."

Shel grinned at her refreshing positivity. He felt relieved that she understood what he was trying to say, that she didn't make fun of him or say that he was weird. On impulse, he leaned in and hugged her. She hesitated for a moment, and then squeezed him tightly, reassuring him that she accepted him: this goofy boy who didn't fit in.

"I'm still confused though... *ahem*," he cleared the tickle of embarrassment from his throat. "If you don't wear shoes, how did you—"

"Get to the beach through the treacherously hot Smile Desert?" She replied, guessing his intent.

"Yeah, and at just the right time to find me? Wait, Smile Desert?"

"Sonrisa means smile in español. I do love that name for it. And it's appropriate too, because, well, isn't it obvious why I showed up at just the right time, Shel?" She grabbed hold of his good hand and held it in hers. "We were *meant* to meet." She batted her eyelashes and giggled.

A tidal wave of nervousness washed over him and he froze, looking at their hands intertwined. When he looked up and realized by her expression that she was toying with him, the wave subsided and he caught his breath. They both laughed. Then Joy turned sharply around the corner of sincerity.

"Seriously though, I don't really have an explanation for that right now, Shel, other than kismet."

Shel looked down at their hands once more and resisted an introvert's tendency to withdraw. He had known this silly-hearted girl for less than a day but already really liked her.

"I didn't come this way, from the desert, I mean. And I didn't plan on walking inland, especially *through* the desert. We Costeroses avoid this route. And now you know why."

"Yeah, it's HOT! ...Costeroses?"

"Costeros is the name of my people. We come from a coastal region of the Champion Sea."

"Ah. So why are we—"

"Going through the desert now?" she forecasted. Shel nodded. "Because, you said you need to find Ingonyama. And the only one who knows where to find Ingo, is the Falcon. And to find *that* bird we need the king. And the king lives in a town at the other side of this terrible desert. We *could* go the long way around, along the coast, but that would take twice as long. Plus, that route has its own dangers, pirates and gryos and what-not."

Shel perked up. "Pirates?! Like, real pirates?" Joy smiled at him. "Huh. I wonder, do you think they might have some food? Because I'm starving!"

"Yes, you mentioned that just a bit ago."

"Well, I am! What's a gryo? Can you eat it?"

"A gryo? No! It's a fish monster thing. Actually, they have them in the Valley too, but those are land-dwelling gryos. Those're called glowing gryos. Out here we have the glimmering gryo, just as dangerous but they stick to the intertidal regions, mostly."

"Hmmm. So not food then?" Shel was thinking only of his empty stomach.

"No, you definitely wouldn't want to eat them," Joy laughed lightly, then jabbed, "How about some strawberries?"

"Not funny, Joy." Shel bent down to adjust his makeshift sandals.

Joy giggled and scanned the desert for their next destination. Suddenly she spotted an unexpected yet unmistakable shape in the distance, slithering across the horizon like an enormous black snake. "Or... perhaps a sword!"

"A sword? Come on, Joy," Shel snarked. "Who eats swords?!"

"That guy!" she yelled and dashed off across the burning sand.

Chapter Two

The Sword-swallower and the Boa

"*Waaaaait!*" Shel yelled, chasing after her as she took off prancing across the fiery dunes toward their next place of solace, which wasn't so much a place but a person, and it wasn't so much a person but a whole group of people...

A caravan of caballers — mystics, misfits, heathens, heretics, wanderers, wind-chasers, and gypsies — all lined up in a row, marching across the desert to sounds of deep grooves — drums, horns, strings, and chimes — all the while cutting a deep groove in the sand. With the cantankerous hooting, hollering, and sword-swinging, their presentation clearly conveyed that one was either with them as family or against them as an enemy, no room for anything in between.

"Hey! Hello! Please help!" Joy yelled at the rag-tag gang of ruffians. A few outlying members of the hoard paused and turned in surprise at seeing a young woman running wild and alone in that harsh land. Looking beyond the distressed girl, they noticed she was, in fact, not alone. There appeared to be some scrawny whelp chasing after her. No matter. Someone so pitiful would be all too easily dispatched.

A short, hirsute brute emerged from the rabble and gave a signal to two of the ruffians on horseback who immediately pivoted their steeds toward the girl's pursuer. With unflinching obedience, they drew their swords and rode off to defend the damsel in distress. The squat man who gave the order then turned his attention to the energetic girl now jumping up and down before him, trying not to fry her feet, makeshift shoes helping only minimally against the fierce heat. The man waved a hand at two feminine figures dressed in head-to-toe black robes and sitting on a nearby camel. The figures, working in unison as if one, instantly produced a thick carpet from the back of the camel and tossed it to the ground. Joy quickly jumped onto the rug as the man mumbled something in a gurgle language impossible to decipher. Joy squinted and shook her head slightly, indicating that she was unable to understand what the man was trying to say. Placing a finger in the air to pause introductions, the man carefully pulled an impressively long sword from his gullet, and with an, "Ahem," cleared his throat thoroughly. "Excuse me!" he coughed lightly. "I ought to know better than to talk with my mouth full." He smiled cunningly. "My name," he paused for effect, free hand gesturing in small, forward circles as he bowed low, "is Sandovar Sandovecchio, the great sword-swallower of Sandeen, at your service. And these good people," he stretched his arms to present his caravan, "my comrades in arms, are the fearsome Boogies! Of whom I am proud to be called chief."

"Yes! Of course, Mr. Sandovecchio, sir. I have heard of you and your famous Boogie caravan of nomad warriors," Joy replied with a modest curtsy.

"Warriors! Ha!" Sandovar laughed. "Warriors of love perhaps. We haven't fought a proper battle in ages." Joy smiled. "That said," he continued, "we do appreciate you bringing us a morsel for our sport, something to dull our blades and sharpen our skills!"

Joy stopped smiling. "Wait, are you talking about...? You think he's after me...? Good heavens!" She quickly turned to assess her companion's progress. Unfortunately, Shel was not getting on so comfortably as she. His path had been intercepted by scoundrels with scimitars and he was now hopping up and down in place, doing his best to keep his feet from catching fire while keeping his head atop his shoulders.

As one of the riders raised a long, shiny blade, intending to put the offender out of his misery, Joy let out a deafening siren call capable of parting the seas. The swordsmen swung around on their steeds so fast they nearly fell to the ground, looks on their faces suggesting that they expected to see either a sand giant waking up or the mythical Kraken rising from the deep.

"He's with me!" she demanded.

Despite their distance, they had no trouble hearing her. The executioner, robed like a buccaneer straight off a 17th-century pirate ship, hastily sheathed his blade, and with an, "Arrrrr! Ye be comin' with me," reached down and curled a large hand around the young man's trousers. Shel, who was at once both frozen from fear and melting from the heat, was instantly yanked into the air then draped over the back of the pirate's stallion like a chest of gold doubloons. With the treasure secured, the two horsemen bolted back to the caravan, which had formed a semi-circle around the young woman and their sword-swallowing chief.

"My deepest apologies, madame," Sandovar offered with another bow, outstretched hand presenting the horsemen, who skidded to a halt just in front of them. "We thought you were fleeing from this one." On cue, the henchman tossed 'this one' to the ground at the girl's feet. Shel crashed onto the sand with a solid thud, letting out a loud groan upon impact.

"Good gracious!" Joy cried as she knelt to comfort her abused friend, who was dizzy and out of sorts from the fall. "Shel! Shel, are you okay?" She called out to him, but there was no answer.

As Shel lay suffering on the ground, he could hear Joy's voice trailing off as if he were falling down a tunnel. His eyes locked closed, a safe for which he'd lost the key, and he could sense himself sailing swiftly into a dream state. Within a few short moments the scorching sand dunes had all but disappeared, along with the caravan and his lovely, happy friend. The last thing he heard as his vision faded entirely was the distant screech of an eagle. Then, just like in his dream of the pirates and the mermaid, the jungle cannibal and the boiling lake, he melted into darkness.

For what could've been seconds, minutes, or even days, he lay there in a void, until a spark from somewhere flashed like a struck matchstick failing to ignite. A moment later, the darkness yielded to a faint glow in the distance, a single star in a midnight sky. It was his old friend: that beautiful, implacable, omnipresent guiding light, the recrudescent celestial beam that he saw so long ago at the farmhouse.

Like a gracious host, the light expanded to welcome him. As he drifted through the tunnel, he began to feel a tingling in his body like blood returning to a limb gone numb. From somewhere in the nothingness came a sound, filtered mumbling, reverberating through a hollow chamber. Shel thought it could have been a song he once knew but it was too faint to place, the eerie noise echoing stubbornly just out of reach, tiptoeing on the fringe of recognition.

Gradually, both light and sound intensified around him until, in a flash, he was fully awake. Frightened and confused, Shel found himself lying in a strange bed, inside a strange room. *Could be... Mongolia...* His mind trolled random thoughts, fishing for answers. His body, meanwhile, fought to recover from the numbness. He could hardly move and his head ached terribly from being tossed to the ground by the pirate, like an empty bottle of rum. The pain in his head felt as though a tree were growing right out of the top of his brain, and his right hand throbbed from the strawberry gash in his flesh, around which a rash with small purple bumps had developed. *Could be the measles... or the mumps,* he thought, still fishing for answers. Looking down to inspect the damaged paw, he could see blood seeping through the bandage, a bandage which oddly was not his shirt — nor was there any bark nor leaves on the dressing. *Who changed my bandages?* he wondered. *And when?!* A deep sense of unease about this memory loss kept miserable company with his pain. He tuned into the music and was distracted momentarily from his worries and discomfort. The sound had been there in the background all along but he was only now fully aware of it, wonderful melodies spilling over from a nearby room, music which greatly eased his woes. Like he had done for so many others, the great Satchmo, with his joyful trumpeting, was raising the young man's spirits. For a moment, Shel's pain melted away as he reveled in that unique, scratchy, calming voice that only Louis Armstrong can conjure. That was, until the sound of oversized boots on old floorboards announced the arrival of a large man carrying a tray with a glass of milk and what looked like... *Could it be? A sandwich?! Oh food, wonderful food!* Shel thought. *But, who are you?*

Relative to the characters he'd been encountering lately: pirates, upright crocodiles, talking elephants, talking unicorns, talking pelicans... this man was rather plain-looking. Just the same, he was entirely unknown to Shel, who therefore found the situation decidedly unnerving. Yet, something about the man felt familiar, and his appearance was altogether nonthreatening, easing Shel's concern a smidge, if only momentarily.

The bespectacled gentleman wore a grey-blue flannel shirt rolled up at the sleeves and tattered jean overalls that covered the bulk of him. A red handkerchief sat contently in his side pocket like a little joey kangaroo in mama's pouch. The man bore the most outstanding features on his face. His eyes, nose, and ears were all much larger than Shel figured they should've been. He had never seen eyes so large on a person nor a nose that drooped down over his upper lip as if it were reaching, trying to smell the man's own chin. Still even larger were his ears. Goodness, the man must've been able to hear aliens in outer space whispering their cosmic secrets!

A moment passed and Shel realized he was staring. Not wanting to be rude, he blinked rapidly to break the spell and his attention slowly returned to the center of the man's face. There he locked eyes with his host. *Those peepers! Like searchlights staring into my soul*, Shel thought. The only time he'd seen a larger set of eyeballs was on his friend Izzy, and Izzy was, as we know, an elephant. Perhaps it was an illusion caused by the man's thick glasses magnifying his face, making his eyes look twice their actual size.

Shel tried to sit up, to get a better look at the man, to assert himself in the presence of the stranger, to accept the gifts of sustenance the man presented. But no sooner had he exerted the slightest effort than the pain in his skull exploded, radiating down his spine, a wildfire ripping through his torso. He clenched his eyes in response. An instant later when he opened them again, the room was spinning in circles and at the same time growing brighter then dimming as if the light in the room were breathing. Blackness took over and the room turned dark and silent once more. As his vision failed, his other senses followed like exhausted soldiers giving up the fight, laying down their weapons, bowing their heads in defeat and marching into oblivion. He could feel his body stiffen, tingles of pins and needles spread through his limbs as numbness and reverberation replaced comely light and Armstrong jazz.

Back in the hollow tunnel, the pain in his head subsided, along with all other feeling and sound, until all that remained was the tragedy of that uneaten sandwich. Shel was starving... *to death!* he agonized dramatically. But it wasn't the reaper's bony hand that reached out to claim the famished youth. No, death would have to wait for this one. Instead, someone else grabbed hold of him and shook away the darkness as if brushing the soil off a buried treasure chest.

"Welcome back to the land of the living," said a scratchy voice.

"No. Not you, foul pirate!" Shel mumbled in a stupor of confusion, not yet awake, dangling in purgatory between dream and reality. His eyesight struggling to transition from pitch dark to blazing desert brightness, he became convinced he was being eaten by a boa constrictor. "Ahhh! It's up to my neck!" he cried. "Get it off!"

"Calm down, Shelby. Everything's going to be okay. I've got you," someone said. The sound of a familiar voice was enough to entice the drifter further out of his dream state and Shel came rushing back like a wild river after the bursting of a dam. He opened his eyes to find himself in the familiar embrace of a moist trunk.

Chapter Three

Architects of Smile

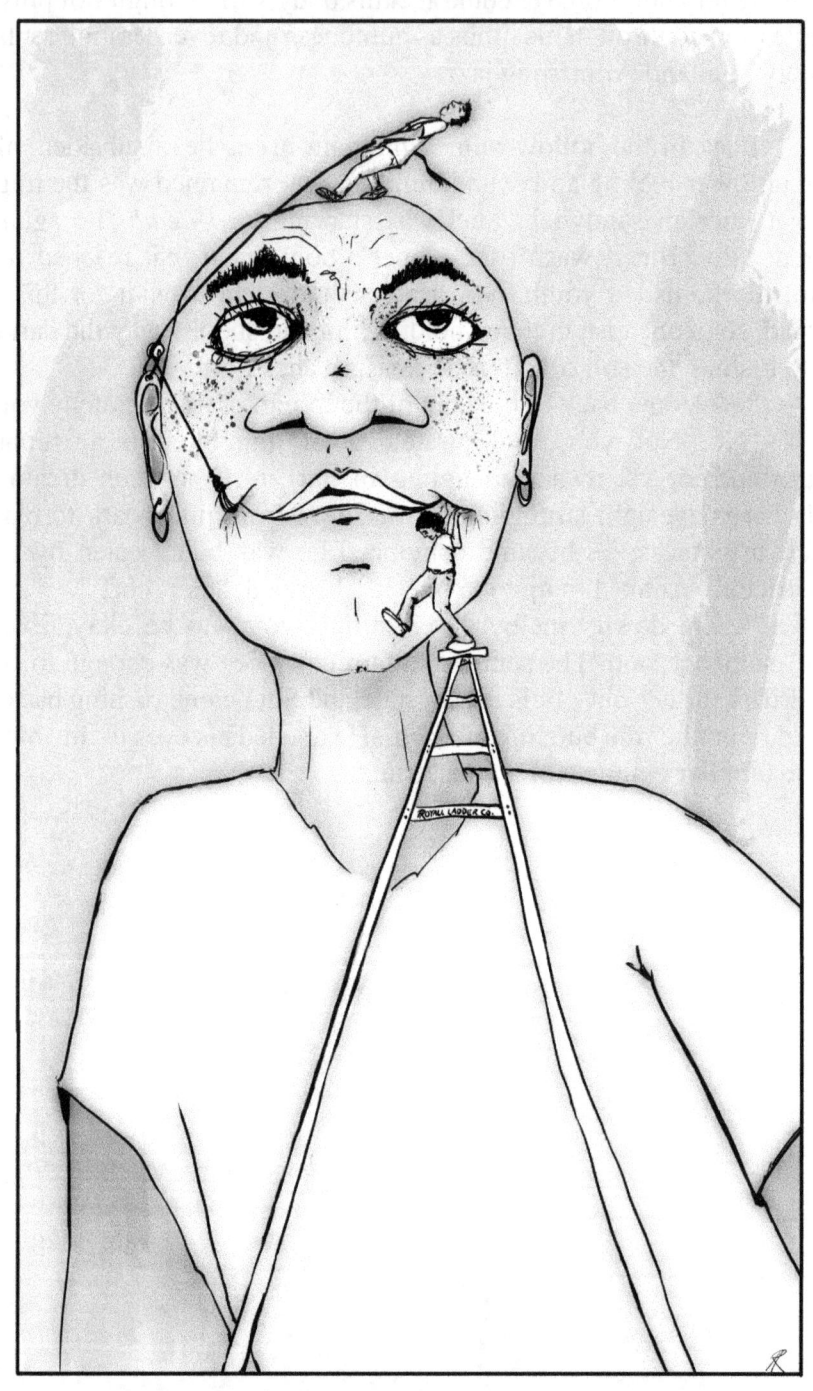

"*IZZY!*" Shel cried in astonishment.

"Hey kid," replied the tusker affectionately. "Falling asleep on the job, I see? Typical." He gave Shel a kind smile and wrapped his trunk tighter around his friend. "It's good to see you, buddy."

"You came back!" Shel exclaimed with equal helpings of surprise and relief.

Izzy laughed lightly, uneasily. "Of course I did, you knucklehead. I said I would, didn't I?"

"Well, yeah, but I thought—"

They looked at one another. Nothing more need be said. Shel hugged Izzy's trunk and sighed, "I'm happy to see you again, Izzy!"

At that very moment, a surly voice interrupted. "I'm sorry to break up this reunion, but we're on a tight schedule. It's not common for the Boogies to travel in the heat of day, but the king is expecting us, so we must be on our way." The chieftain stood up to address all who had gathered to get a look at the commotion, which was essentially his entire caravan. He took a deep breath and opened wide his impressively large mouth, intending a fiery command to bring order to the brouhaha and finally get his band of Boogies back on the desert trail. His flame was quickly snuffed, however, by a mighty wind by the name of Joythea Aquarius Costeros.

"Stay your halters, horsemen!" the young woman demanded, shooting daring glances all around, especially at Sandovar. "We have a wounded soldier in the ranks, and we'll not take one more step until he is properly tended."

The pirate and his ruffian brothers looked at their chief in stunned surprise, anticipating orders that they should restrain the insubordinate girl, perhaps bury her in the sand, at least up to her neck. But no such command was given. The stout sword-eater stood statuesque, marveling at the powerful beauty; not intimidated, not in the least, but impressed by her fearless fierceness. She commanded respect. A natural leader this one was.

After a moment of locking eyes with the girl in a silent power struggle, then coming to amenable terms without saying a word, Sandovar raised his hand, proclaiming loudly for all to hear, "The young woman is right. We are to blame for this man's injury. It won't take but a moment to tend his ailments." The chief then lowered his voice, speaking directly to those closest to him. "He'll need to be well-prepped for the journey anyway if he has any hope of making it — alive, that is."

Then he turned and looked at Joy, bushy brows swaying over dark eyes like sun-scorched willow branches drooping over abandoned railway tunnels. The murky depth in his face suggested he'd been everywhere and experienced everything in the world thrice over (which was perhaps twice too many). "We will see to it that he is well cared for, my lady." And with a low bow to the maiden and a wave to his Boogie caravan, he both conciliated his guests and dispatched his servants.

Swift as the wind, the two mysterious figures in thick, black gowns embroidered with colorful designs, dismounted their camel and approached the elephant, still holding the boy in his trunk. The figures moved with such fluidity and grace that one might easily mistake the people inside the robes for naught but smoke and water. As they moved, gold, silver, copper, and tin metal pieces woven into their gowns chimed lightly. It was impossible to observe them and not become entranced by their natural mystic, mesmerized and captivated by their mysterious allure.

Without words, one of the figures held out a hand to Shel, requesting his attendance, while the other, with a gentle touch, reassured the elephant that his friend would be safe and well cared for. Only the hands and eyes of the figures remained unclothed but not unadorned. The exposed hands were sable and soft, feminine, with dainty gold chains connecting rings on every finger to bracelets hidden up loose sleeves. Their fingernails were long and decorated like the rest of their hands, various tiny gems framing geometric designs drawn over the skin in earth-red ink.

Izzy and Shel instantly became lost in the enchantment of the human shadows, a common conclusion for those who gazed too deeply upon their beauty or lingered too long in their presence. At the touch from one of them, the elephant unfurled his trunk as if under a spell, releasing his captive, letting the boy slide slowly toward the ground while the other caretaker slipped thick shoes on Shel's feet, insulating his tender toes from the scalding sand. (Izzy wore his own thick-hided shoes. For him, the desert was uncomfortable but not unbearable.)

As the lovely figures led their patient toward a tent, Joy intercepted them to embrace her friend. She then shoved him to arm's length to look him squarely in the eye, demanding, "Don't *ever* do that again! You hear me? You scared me half to death!"

Shel smiled guiltily then followed Joy's eyes as she looked down. There, in her hands, sat a thick slice of bread smothered with glistening, red jelly. His eyes lit up and he quickly snatched the snack, forgetting his manners. With a mouthful of dough, he choked out the words, "Oh... my... goodness! Thank you! This is so delicious."

Pushing him gently but firmly, Shel's adumbral chaperones directed him onward. He stopped just shy of the entrance and turned back to Joy. "Do they have any peanut butter?" Joy laughed and shook her head as he was yanked inside.

The two figures sat their patient in the center of the tent. One handed him a cup of some curiously scented tea while the other gestured emphatically for him to drink. Then, quietly and swiftly, the two gypsy nurses got to work tending his wounds, one soothing his head with a poultice of ground-up eucalyptus leaves and elderberries while the other soaked his swollen hand in a warm broth of who-knows-what that smelled of mint. Though strange, the broth felt wonderful and took the swelling in his hand down almost immediately.

With his free hand, Shel continued to blissfully munch away on the jammed toast and sip the aromatic brew. "Normally I'd — *munch munch* — rather play —*munch* — soccer, or do *anything* else — *munch munch munch* — than go to the doctor. But I must say," he swallowed his last bite and commenced a loud sucking of the sticky crumbs from his fingertips, "this attention is quite nice."

The robed caretakers did not acknowledge Shel's food-filtered comment but continued their tasks in rote silence. "Say, you two didn't used to work at an elementary school in Chicago, did you?" Shel's rambling was interrupted by the canvas flaps flying open with violent authority, filling the darkened sanctuary with blinding light, and filling Shel with suffocating dread.

There in the entryway stood the massive silhouette of the wretched pirate who had thrown him to the ground so destructively. The pirate drew his sword and held it high, a menacing shadow extracting a respectable scream from the boy, precisely the response for which the buccaneer was hoping. The silhouette spontaneously doubled over and exploded with laughter that sounded as if a cannon had been fired, a great booming laugh born on the high seas, a guttural howl that echoed deep in the pirate's seemingly hollow core. The sound was like nothing Shel had ever encountered; something wild and terrible and yet wonderfully exhilarating, as if this pirate had perfected the precise melody for scaring off all formidable threats from any seafaring vessel. Whether mutiny, scurvy, or the deadly doldrums, none stood a chance — for his was a mighty wind to fill even the largest of sails and instantly hearten the weariest of sailors.

In the midst of his heart song, the pirate dropped his sword to the ground and held out two empty — but not harmless, make no mistake — very large hands, palms up; his way of waving a flag of peace. Though honorable indeed, the gesture did little to reassure Shel that the brute had not come for his head.

"At ease, matey. I be here to apologize, nothin' more." The pirate removed his large, black hat, dragged over a small medicine box and sat himself down squarely in front of Shel. "Took a mighty fall, ye did." The pirate leaned back, eyes looking down his long nose at Shel, as if assessing the infirmed youth. Then, leaning forward, much too close for Shel's comfort, he winked and added quietly, "And ye took it like a hearty old sea dog, too."

Shel almost heard what the pirate was saying. He was mostly distracted by the man's stench — a salty blend of seaweed and adventure. And then there was his curious appearance. Shel had never seen a real pirate before, being from Illinois. That, and from the 20th century.

"What be the matter, laddie? Ain't ye never seen a real pirate before?" The ruffian roared with laughter and rocked back and forth. Shel realized he was gawking rudely at the disheveled swashbuckler.

"I… I'm sorry, mister. It's just—"

"No misters here! Me name be Taudello, ma boy." He patted Shel roughly on the shoulder. "But ye can just call me Taud. Or Dells if yer feelin' like it's a good day to die. Ha, ha, ha!" Taud let his mighty laugh loose once more and it dashed about the tent like a parrot freed from a cage. Then, calming himself, he placed both hands on his lapels and puffed out his chest. "I be known to most me enemies, however, as Tauder the Marauder!" He raised an eyebrow and waited for a reaction that didn't come. "Has a nice ring to it, dontcha think?" The pirate looked at Shel sideways as if to say, 'Ye best be careful on how ye answer that!'

Shel's mouth dropped but no response volunteered to come out and parley with the pirate.

"No matter," spat Taud. "I's just seekin' amends fer roughing ye up's all. Ya see, I used to be rotten and mean, and ol' habits die hard, they do. Plus, there's me reputation to respect. Wouldn't want people thinkin' I'd gone soft. Savvy?" Shel sat silent, attentive … afraid. "But, this bein' the Land o' Happy and all… Well, I be tryin' tuh turn over a new leaf, I be. Or in me own case, since I be comin' from the sea, I s'pose I be turnin' over a new shell. After all, they say this be the place for those tired o' hanging the jib all the time. That there means frownin' somethin' awful, 'case ya didn't know. Anyway, they says this be the place fer those seekin' to recall what it means to smile and n'joy life agin. And why that be me to a T!" Tauder opened his mouth wide and, *BOOM,* roared the cannon!

"Well… you certainly turned over a Shel all right," muttered Sheldon under his breath. If the pirate heard it he ignored it.

"Any old ways, I fig'r that's why ye be here too, little landlubber. And I don't mean to be impedin' any other sailor's wind with me own sails."

Shel looked inquisitively at the buccaneer.

"He means you've come here to forget your sorrows and find happiness," said a voice entering the tent. "And he doesn't wish to interfere with your journey."

Shel whipped around and squinted at a figure standing in the half-opened doorway, silhouetted by the bright light outside. "He's referring to the legend of the giants and how the Land of Happy came to be." As the dark figure spoke, he lit a long wooden pipe. The smell from the meerschaum reminded Shel of his synagogue for some reason. The figure sat down cross-legged next to the pirate, the dim light of the tent barely identifying him as Chief Sandovar. "How are you feeling, my boy?" A puff of smoke billowed from the chief's mouth as he tried to contain a cough.

"Better, thank you," answered Shel hesitantly.

"Excellent! My lovely ladies in midnight madraga are renowned for their healing skills. Their kindness of spirit is unparalleled," Sandovar respectfully nodded at his companions. "Ladies, thank you for taking such good care of Master Shel here." He turned to the boy and whispered, "Joy told me your name. I hope that is all right." Looking back at the healers, he added, "Do you have any advice for your patient or is he free to go?" The ladies bowed in unison and one of them stepped forward.

"We have," came a voice of silk and honey from behind dark cloth. "Please be more careful about what you consume. Namasté." Both ladies bowed once more and receded into a dark corner.

Sandovar bowed back, then turned to Shel. "They're referring to your attempt to eat the wild strawberries I presume?" Shel nodded abashedly. "Well, all's well that ends well I s'pose," Sandovar asserted, laying a gentle hand on Shel's shoulder.

Shel smiled, thankful for Sandovar's kindness and for offering a bit of unspoken forgiveness for trying to eat the *strawbehhh... uh, fruited animal*, Shel corrected his thoughts.

"Right then. I see you've met my first mate." Sandovar extended a hand toward the pirate. "I hope he hasn't been boring you with too many tales of men he's hanged or had walk the plank!"

"No!" Shel's voice cracked. "*Ahem.* No, not at all." The undersized chief slapped his pirate friend across the back and the two of them laughed mightily at Shel's unease. Taud accepted the pipe from his friend and took a long draw. Smoke seemed to leak from everywhere on the pirate: mouth, nose, ears, even his eye sockets.

Sandovar nodded at Shel and smiled. "My apologies. We haven't been properly introduced. My name is—"

But Taud held up a hand, halting the introduction. He finished his puff, coughed lightly, cleared his throat, and stood up tall with arms gesticulating wide. "This here salty dog, be the infamous Sandman, the great sword-swallower, Sandovar Sandovecchio of Sandeen, chief of the gruesome, grievous, grungy, restless, rambling, raucous desert Boogies." Then, sounding like an advertisement, he added in his best hoity-toity accent, "And connoisseur of fine jams and jellies." Taud and the Sandman instantly broke into boisterous laughter as Sandovar stood to lock arms with his first mate.

"Thank you! Thank you, my good man! Although, most who know me just call me Sando — efficiency and all that. Do feel free, feel free. Yes. Yes, 'tis true. I love jams... and jellies too. Did you enjoy your bred and jam, by the way?"

For the first time in hours, Shel was beginning to feel that he actually might survive this terrible desert ordeal. "Yes, actually I did, very much. It was delicious. Thank you!"

They all smiled.

"But—" Shel coughed.

They stopped smiling.

"Yeeesss? Is something wrong?" asked Chief Sando.

"Well, I was just curious if you might have any... peanut butter?"

Sando gasped, "Woah!" and fell backward dramatically off his stool. "Did he just say... peanut butter?!"

"Arrr! That he did!" affirmed Taud, scrambling to his feet and reaching for his scimitar. He stood quickly and pointed the blade at the boy. "Time tuh meet yer maker, y'ungrateful toad!"

Shel jumped backward to avoid the advancing pirate and immediately fell over, tripping over the extended legs of one of the servant ladies crouching in the dark. She let out a howl that was not of silk and honey.

"Oh! I'm so sorry!" Shel apologized, then hurriedly looked up to see if he was still being hunted. On the contrary, Taud and Sando were both doubled over in laughter.

"This scallywag be more fun than a barrel uh monkeys! *Ah, ha, ha, ha!*" Taud hooted.

Sandovar wiped tears from his eyes, calmed himself and apologized for scaring the boy. "You'll need to lighten up if you expect to survive this place, my friend."

Shel collected himself and managed a slight smile, albeit a cautious one, relieved that he got to keep his head — for now. "So, does that mean," he ventured a sheepish query, "you *do* have, um, some peanut butter? Because I'd sure love—"

"No, no," Sando interjected with a raised hand. "I'm afraid not, young sir." He noted the look of disappointment on the kid's face. "It is unfortunate indeed, I agree. But, all the peanut butter, I'm afraid, is reserved exclusively for the king." Shel's squinting eyes and cocked head begged for further explanation. Chief Sando obliged. "Mmm. You see, it is by royal decree, my dear tourist, that any peanut butter made, imported, or otherwise discovered in the Land of Happy must be sent immediately to His Majesty, on account of His Majesty's insatiable appetite for the sticky sauce. Unlike the elephants of Happy, our king just can't seem to get enough peanuts — at least the butter o' them anyway. I fear it will be his untimely end."

Saddened by this news (about the lack of peanut butter, not Sando's forecast of the king's demise), Shel decided to change the subject entirely.

"Chief Sandovecchio, sir?"

"Please, Shel, call me Sando. And not to worry, kid, we're on our way to meet with the king." He tapped the side of his head with a pointed finger, looking thoughtful. "Perhaps, if you like, when we get there you can ask him to share some of his peanut butter with you. Although," he continued in quiet footnote with a slanted smile, "that is not particularly advisable if you prefer your head to stay where it is." The chief punctuated his warning with a dark chuckle and a slow dragging of his finger across his throat.

"No! No, that's okay," Shel replied with alarm. "Actually, I was going to ask about the giants. You said that Taud was saying something about how the Land of Happy was... um, well, that is... are there really giants sleeping under the sand, sir? Joy and I saw—" Just then came a rustling from the tent opening. A slender figure slipped in quietly and sat down alongside Taud.

"Speak uh the devil," remarked the chief. Joy had come to check in on her injured bird. Shel couldn't help but let loose a big smile. He was about to continue his question when Sando piped up.

"Sarah Karynthia, Sylvia Kats," he addressed the two caretakers in dark robes. "Would you please brew some of your herbal tea for everyone? And do join us on the carpet pretty please. Thank you, my dearies!" Then Sando turned back to Shel. "I'm sorry, my friend. You were saying?"

"Uh, well, I was saying that back there in the desert Joy and I saw—"

"Ah, yes! The Snoozants! Well, you see, it all began a long time ago, when our king was still a child. Back then, the Land of Happy was not a very happy place. In fact, the name of the kingdom was something altogether disturbing. They called it the Land of Hollerandwhine, if you can believe that, on account of all the whining and hollering in the place, as you might've guessed. You see, our present king's father and mother were not cruel, per se, but they were rather strict, especially Her Majesty, the queen. She demanded exacting formalities and uncompromising orderliness throughout the land. What's worse, she forbade any sort of child's play, celebration, or merriment."

Pausing to make sure his audience was sufficiently captivated — which they were — Sando continued. "Hollerandwhine was a productive land, efficient and well-organized. Problem was, the people weren't happy, not in the least. As a youth, the prince defied his mother's stale regime with outlandish games and childish shenanigans... as might be expected of an adolescent. Am I right?"

Shel nodded in full agreement.

"At any rate, over the years, much to the Queen's dismay, the prince sharpened his skillset for silliness and nonsensicalities. He even vowed that one day, when he became ruler of the land, he would bring happiness and joy back to the people. 'When I am king,' he would say, 'people will be rewarded for being silly and lazy!' To which his mother would reply," — Sandovar cleared his throat and put on his best 'Queen Mother' accent — "...'In that case, you will only ever be king if the world goes crazy!' *Ha, ha, ha*!" Sando laughed at himself. "He was a foolhardy child, no doubt. And the people rightly believed that his carefree ways would yield to prudence and solemnity as he matured. But that didn't happen. Wouldn't you know, the prince made good on his promise. When he eventually became king, still a rather young man in fact, everything changed. Word spread far and wide of a place where happiness and fun were paramount. There was only one problem — a very serious problem."

"And what was that?" asked Shel.

"People began coming down with an affliction called the liketobutnahs."

"Huh?!" Shel snarked.

"The liketobutnahs. It's a debilitating disease that prevents almost anything from getting done. Anyone who has it, if asked to do anything, they simply reply, 'Well, I'd like to, but nah.' And so, as one might expect, the Land of Hollerandwhine eventually came to be known as the Land of Everythingfallsapart. That's when the king sent for the giants. Known for their skill at crafting and building just about anything, and in record time no less, and maintaining everything they construct in tip-top condition, the giants were the obvious answer — or so the king thought."

Captivated, Shel urged, "And then? What happened next?"

"Well," Sando chuckled at the young man's enthusiasm, "unfortunately, building and maintaining is not the only thing for which giants are known. They're also known for being hugely temperamental. It's not uncommon for them to cultivate colossal melancholy. And that's when the wailin' starts. Oh, their incessant wailing! It's a terrible noise which can be heard for miles and miles!"

"Is that true?" Shel asked Joy, who nodded emphatically.

"Anyway, the king made a deal with the giants," continued the Sandman. "The giants would be the laborers of the land, building things and growing crops and whatnot, while everyone else played and messed about, just having fun and acting silly. In exchange for their labor, the king and his people would entertain the giants, put an end to their wailing, their monumental misery. Well, as you can imagine, it wasn't long before the giants came in droves to this place, seeking a remedy for their sorrows — Oh, thank you, my dearies!" Sandovar politely acknowledged his attendants as they served dandelion and nettle tea before slinking back into the shadows. "Now, where was I? Ah, yes, the giant immigration. Well, the problem was that the giants, after a while, just couldn't be consoled by the jokes and silly gestures any longer."

"Or perhaps the kingdom's supply of funny couldn't keep up with demand," offered Joy, nonchalantly tugging at a rogue thread in her skirt.

"Quite right!" agreed Sando. "You see, the fun-making methods were becoming rather repetitive and predictable. They continued to do the work of the people—"

"The giants?" Shel interrupted, doing his best to follow.

"The giants, yes. They continued working for the kingdom, but the entertainment had become old hat. It had lost its charm. And as a result, the giants receded to a state of chronic depression. So, the king devised a plan to build huge scaffolds on which the giants could rest their weary heads. The genius behind the design was that the scaffolds held the giants up by their mouths, but only at the very corners of the mouth. Thus, when a giant laid his head—" Sando paused when he felt Joy rap him over the head with a feather as a gentle reminder. "Right! Excuse me. The scaffolds held the giants by his or *her* mouth..." The chief looked at Joy for approval. She nodded, so he continued. "Anyway, the scaffolds would press up at the corners of the giants' mouths, like this—" Sando put his thumb and index finger to the corners of his mouth and pressed into his face, forcing an awkward grin. "And the giants would experience a smile whenever they rested their head on the contraptions."

"And that made them happy?" asked Shel.

"Well, yes, it worked, for a time anyway. You see, sometimes changes on the outside can bring change on the inside. For the giants, the delight of feeling a grin on their weary faces while being able to rest their weary heads, well that both lightened their burdens and lifted their spirits. And that's how the Land of Happy got its name: weary travelers coming from all over to lay their burdens down and be cheered up by the 'Silly King' and his unorthodox smile-making antics.

"But, I'm afraid that was ages ago. Since then, the king has grown old and weary. The years of making other people happy have taken a toll on his own happiness. Now, tired to his core after all the entertaining... not to mention his other tireless tasks like taste-testing apples for proper sweetness and lying in fields, holding the grass in place... Now the king's only solace seems to be eating peanut butter sandwiches — really sticky peanut butter sandwiches." Sando twirled the ends of his mustache in wonderment and reflection.

"But what happened to the giants?" Shel asked eagerly.

"Oh, right. Well, you see, not so long ago, the king— Hey! What is—?" Sando felt a large, wet noodle pushing on the side of his face. The noodle laid itself across the chief's balding head before sliding down his back and tickling his ribs. *"He, he, he.* Hey! Stop that! *Ha, ha, ha!"* He turned to see Izzy poking half his face into the tent.

"Excuse me, Chief Sandovar? I hate to interrupt, but I think you'd better come see this."

The chief pushed Izzy's noodling trunk away from his sides, "In a minute, Izzy. I'm in the middle of a story. So anyway, the king—"

"But sir," interrupted the elephant in an urgent whisper, "it's the fuzz!" Instantly, Taud snatched his blade and made to stand. Sando placed his hand on Taud's fencing arm, staying the pirate's angst.

"I'll take care of this!" the chief reassured his protector, and he sailed out of the tent like a desert sandstorm into the blinding daylight.

Chapter Four

The Nap Thief

"Ah. Captain Marcus of the please force. I might've known. How may I be of service?" Sandovar Sandovecchio of Sandeen greeted the constable.

"Yes! Well met. Please and thank you, my good man. Well then, I'm terribly sorry to have to put you in this position, Mr. Sandovar, sir, but it seems a crime has been committed... amongst *your* caravan no less. I am here to investigate, naturally, and to apprehend the perpetrator if necessary."

"I seeeee," replied Sandovar coolly, fingers noodling through his substantial beard as if searching for leftover baklava crumbs. "May I ask what crime has been purported? Perhaps I may be of assistance in tracking down the alleged criminal."

"Right. There'll be no need for that, Signor Sandovecchio. Please, if you would be so kind as to simply step aside and allow me to do my job. I'll be out of your hair in a jiff." With that, the bobby advanced toward the tent, intending to have a look around. He stopped just short of the opening, however, when the tip of a sharp object came out to greet him. The pleaseman (as the Happy Land police officers were known) backed up a step and a quarter as the object emerged from the canvas, identifying itself as the dangerous end of a dangerous outlaw's scimitar. Attached to the relatively safe end was none other than Tauder the Marauder.

"You remember my mate, Taudello, don't you, constable?" Sandovar grinned at the officer. "Maybe next time you'll think twice before cracking a comment about hair whilst in the company of so many baldos." Chief Sandovar rubbed his smooth head as if polishing a pot.

"Good sir, when I said I'd be out of your hair I didn't mean literally. You must understand—"

"No! *You* understand," interrupted Taudello and his advancing sword, "please department or no, I shan't be goin' quietly, ya hear? Knew the law'd catch up tuh me someday, I did; all me foul deeds come back like the bloomin' tide! By Kraken's beard, it'll be the plank fer me or nothin'!" The pirate opted for a thrill of theatrics, noticing the crowd of onlookers gathering. "I been destined fer Davy Jones' Locker since me birth, I has. Ain't no hangin' rope nor yardarm what can hold this ol' crustacean. And I sure ain't gonna rot away in no rotten brig!" Intent on making his last stand a performance to be remembered, the pirate readied himself for a grand duel. "I'll be takin' no quarter from the likes of ye. En guarde!"

"Now just a minute, Monsieur Taudello!" exclaimed the constable, leaping back to put some distance between himself and the pirate's blade. "There's no need for such histrionics, even if you *are* French. I'm not here for you. Besides, I've brought my own — *ahem* — hearties." He turned and signaled to his cavalry-in-waiting, stationed a ways off so as not to appear too aggressive. The Land of Happy law enforcement did, after all, have a reputation to uphold, lest they forfeit the honorary title of 'please force'.

"Jarbison! Mortimer!" Marcus the pleaseman called for his backup. From behind the crowd advanced two scruffy men in baggy black pants and dingy white shirts that opened in the front to reveal chests, not of gold, but covered in coarse, jet-black hair. Red scarfs hung from their belts and tri-cornered hats sheltered their faces from the sun, which was beginning to shuffle off to the west as if sneaking away to avoid the impending conflict. Tall, black boots kept the men's feet from frying on the hot sand.

Taud squinted, trying to get a look at the men and size up his odds. "Is that…?" he muttered to the wind. "Naaahhh! Couldn't be." The men approached. "Well, blow me down! It is! Pirate Morty and Captain Jarby! I'll be buggered!"

"Avast ye scallywag!" warned the pleaseman's enforcer, Captain Jarbison. "Scabbard yer blade, pirate, else we'll run ye through!"

The smaller of the two henchmen gasped, "Sink me to the deep!" as he stabbed his sword into the sand and extended his arms out wide. It was clear he had no intention of brawling with his pirate brethren. Walking briskly toward Taud, clearly anticipating a momentous reunion, the pirate named Mortimer roared, "Why, if it ain't me old mate, Tauder the Marauder!"

"Cleave 'im to the brisket, Mort!" commanded the apparently senile pirate captain, still unaware of who they were facing off against.

"Oh, go dip yer fuse in rum ye old, blind dog," replied pirate Morty to his superior. "Can't ye see who this be? Why, it be none other than Taudello, yer ol' quartermaster."

"What's this?" replied the pirate captain. "Could it be?" The old man squinted. "Well shiver me timbers!"

The three pirates lowered their defenses to sea level and embraced in a mighty hug that would have squeezed the breath from even the likes of Izzy (probably not, actually).

Suddenly, the three of them found themselves being hugged by a fourth.

"Arrrr! Ye were not invited to the huddle, Mark," Grumbled Captain Jarby to the pleaseman.

Marcus jerked backward. "Well, fine then. It's just hard to resist a good cuddle!"

"You bilge suckin' barnacle! This ain't no cuddle! I said *huddle*! With an 'aych'! Now git, before I slice ye into shark bait!"

"Okay fellas, calm down. If that's how it's going to be... I hate to break up your huddle-with-an-aych, but there's a crime here that requires solving. Monsieur Taudello, as I said, I'm not here for you. So, pretty please, just relax and step aside." The pleaseman turned toward Sandovar and exclaimed bluntly, "I'm here for the boy."

While the pirates were celebrating their reunion outside in the desert heat, inside the tent, Shel, Joy, and Izzy — teacups in hand (and trunk) — were enjoying a restful round of rooibos and reminiscing. Joy had all sorts of questions for Izzy about what happened to him after he left the circus and departed the Land of Happy. She was just a young lass when he left but she remembered him well. After all, such a big elephant with such a big personality is not so easily forgotten. While Izzy summarized the gist of what had transpired over the years, he insisted the details wait for when they had more time.

"Izzy, where's Charlotte? She didn't come with you?" Shel asked, a half-tone of empathy, the other half bitter. He was admittedly curious about why they never came back to collect him from the raft, but he wasn't about to put his friend in the hot seat straight off the bat. Besides, he figured it really didn't matter now anyway. All of that was in the past.

"I dunno," replied Izzy, thoughts drifting a mile away. "She said she was hungry and was going to wait back at her place on Fallshugger Ridge. Said she'd rather spend all day trying to scoop up tiny, stinging ants for supper than come back to the Land of Happy. Not sure exactly what she meant by *that*. Guess I'll just bring her back a souvenir, maybe a t-shirt, or a postcard saying something nice like, 'Without you, the Land of Happy just isn't'... or something. I figure that'll make her smile. What do you think?"

"Is she angry with you?" asked Shel, concerned.

"What did you do, Izzy?" Joy pressed, reading between the lines of guilt all over the elephant's face.

"Nothing!" Izzy shot back. "I mean, I may have let slip that she's been looking a little fluffier around the midsection lately." He looked at Shel with an innocent 'oops' and Shel looked back with a 'yikes'.

"Izzy!" scolded Joy.

"I didn't mean anything by it! I *like* her on the fluffy side. I mean look at *me* for Pete's sake! I'm as 'fluffy' as they come!"

Joy laughed and choked on her tea. A bit of it went up her nose.

"Thanks, Joy," Izzy scoffed with an overt eye roll. "Anyway, she said something like, 'love is grand and all... but lunch is lunch,' and stormed off to go drown her sorrows at the local fishpond. Sheesh, Pelicans. You never know what they're going to do next. Hey, look! A shiny object!"

In a flash, Izzy jumped up and bolted out of the tent, dashing off into the barren desert. Shel and Joy looked at each other in surprise and laughed, just as the pleaseman entered.

"Was that Izzy the elephant I just saw bolting out of here?"

Their laughter sputtered out as Shel and Joy composed themselves for their new guest.

"Hello," greeted Joy, friendly as always. "And who might you be?" There was an undertone of authority in her otherwise innocent inquiry. Shel glanced at her, thinking she even sounded a tad royal just then, but he figured she was just putting on airs.

"Ah, yes. Well received, miss. Please forgive the intrusion, if you please."

"Uh, oh. That's two 'pleases' in one sentence," Joy whispered to Shel. "That usually means either someone's in trouble or they have a favor to ask."

Although Marcus could hear what she was saying, he pretended not to notice. With a bow, he began, "My name is Sir Marcus O'Rillynice Gladface McGee, captain of the Happy Land please force, at your service."

"Please force?" inquired Shel.

"Gladface McGee?" added Joy.

"*Sir*... Gladface McGee, if you please. And yes, of the please force. Rest assured, we are still police officers, just officers with manners. Speaking of," Marcus glanced at Joy, "I wonder if you would be so kind as to permit me a word in private with the young lad?"

"Well, Sir Gladface-at-our-service, while it is a pleasure to make your acquaintance, I'm sure, now's just not a good time, I'm afraid. Oh, I know! How about we ledger a raincheck shall we? Say, same time, same place tomorrow?" She jested, knowing full well they'd be long gone by then. "Or next year perhaps?" She smiled wryly.

The young woman's cheek lit the officer's fuse. Still, though smoldering from within, Marcus maintained unphased composure. "I do apologize, my lady. I did not mean to imply that I am *literally* at your service for whatever you wish. It's just a polite thing to say, you see, when one first meets another."

"Ohhh-kaayyy. Your mother never taught you that it's bad manners to make false promises?"

After that comment, Marcus was a degree or two beyond smoldering. He took a deep breath, trying to remain calm. "And... who might you be, young miss?" Before Joy had a chance to answer, the pleaseman — whose patience (like his hair) was running thin — had thought better of entertaining her at all. He quickly waved his hands. "Never mind. It matters not. You're not a person of interest in my investigation and it's no business of mine who you are. You're free to be whomever you wish. It does, however, matter who this boy claims to be."

Joy frowned something serious. "Oh? And why, pray tell, might that be?"

"Begging your pardon, my lady, but it really is no business of yours. However, since I, Marcus O'Rillynice, am, as my name suggests, really nice, I shall tell you. It matters who *he* is because if *he* is the one responsible for the crime, then *he* shall be the one whom *I* shall be escorting back to His Majesty the king."

"Crime?!" Shel choked, spitting out a good bit of tea.

"What crime!?" demanded Joy.

The pleaseman squinted at the irksome girl then looked back at Shel. "I'll thank you to remain calm if you please. Now then, it has come to my attention that you may have taken a nap unbelonging to you. I am here to collect your person and transport you to the king so that he may judge for himself the charges against you, those being of theft... and possibly treason."

"Treason!" Joy exclaimed. "That's ridiculous!"

The pleaseman rounded on Joy, ready to scold her for continuing to interfere, when something suddenly burst into the tent, spinning Marcus around in surprise.

"Utterly preposterous!" demanded Izzy, storming right up to the pleaseman, an oversized silver spoon in his trunk. The thing was all bent out of shape and weathered from years of being exposed to the elements (the spoon, not Izzy).

"Absolutely absurd!" proclaimed Chief Sandovar, tossing back the canvas doorway, once more flooding the tent with the deep orange light of a sun rushing to descend before things escalated further.

"Yellow Jack Mutiny!" bellowed the three pirates, raising swords high, shoving their way into the tent, doing their darndest to insert themselves into the commotion.

"Booo," hissed the two servant ladies quietly from their dark corner. For a moment the entire group froze and looked at the women in surprise, for no one knew they had been sitting there the whole time, watching and listening yet minding their own affairs. It was also unlike them to offer unsolicited opinions.

Jarbison, the pirate captain, and his first mate, Mortimer, were the first to move on the officer, bringing all eyes back on Marcus. They approached their commander with harsh intent carved into their faces.

Y'otta be ashamed, ya squiffy biscuit-eater," scolded Jarby. "Had we been apprised of yer commission, we'd've never agreed to the mission!"

"Arrrr!" agreed Morty.

"Yarrr!" added Taud in pirate solidarity.

"Blarrr!" chimed Izzy, and everyone looked his way.

"Blar?" said someone.

"Sorry, I got excited."

Marcus, who had heard enough, raised his hands in the air and stepped onto a small ottoman, attempting to rise above the hullabaloo and make himself look authoritative. "Now see here! It is apparent that you're all upset, though I'm not entirely sure why. From what I hear, this boy is a newcomer, a tourist. It's not as though he is a friend of any of yours."

Various arguments rang out from the crowd. Izzy and Joy protested the notion that Shel wasn't a friend, while Sando, Taud, and others protested on the grounds that he was just a kid. And still others protested just to protest, given the anti-authoritarian bent of the Boogies at large.

Mark tried to listen to the noise for a moment so as to appear sympathetic, but an anarchist he most certainly was not; and to be a fugitive sympathizer, in Mark's eyes, was to be a traitor to the crown. He held up his hands and hollered loudly above the harangue, "Be all of that as it may, I have my orders. If I do not return with the boy, I should not bother returning at all… and I do not intend *not* to return to my king."

Izzy's eyes narrowed. "What is it to us if you don't return?!"

Disapproving of Izzy's inference that no one would care if the pleaseman simply wandered off into the desert and disappeared, Mark continued through gritted teeth. "If neither the boy nor I return, and soon, rest assured the king shall dispatch more troops. The Boogies will be tracked down and arrested — every… last… one." He looked around to make sure everyone was paying attention, keeping calm, and staying put. "As of right now we only have one alleged criminal who has yet to be formally charged with a crime. Defy the king's orders on this, however, and I assure you, you *all* will face real charges. I beseech you, please be rational and let's not—"

"That's enough!" Izzy cut him off. The elephant wrapped the pleaseman in his trunk and lifted him off the ground (as was his tendency). "No one is going to be charged with anything except defending the innocent, and those are charges, I'm willing to wager, we'd all gladly accept." The crowd rumbled in agreement. "This kid, as you yourself pointed out, is a tourist, a passerby, a visitor on holiday. He did not steal anyone's nap for goodness' sake! He was inadvertently knocked unconscious by one of Sandovar's guards. It was entirely *not* his fault."

"Be that as it may—"

"And 'twas entirely accidental too!" added Taudello enthusiastically, still seeking absolution.

"Hmmm…" Mark's stare let the pirate know he felt the interruption to be awfully rude. "Be… that… as it mmm—" Mark tried to continue but Izzy flexed his trunk, squeezing the breath right out of the bobby.

"Careful Izzy," cautioned Sandovar.

"Hold 'im steady," commanded Taud, raising his sword and digging the tip of the blade into one of the large buttons on the pleaseman's petticoat. "T'was always confounding how ye *please* officers don such heavy duds in the swelter o' the desert. But now I see it's on account uh ye bein' cold-blooded throughout."

Mark could feel the pressure of Taud's blade against his belly. He inhaled deeply, sucking his gut away from the sword, trying to create some breathing room within the grip of the constrictive trunk. "If you would just—" he began but was cut off again by the pirate.

"Hold yer tongue, landlubber; I ain't finished. This here caravan of Boogies be headed to see the king, regardless. So _we'll_ be the ones what be bringin' the boy 'fore the crown. Savvy? Yer welcome to tag along, so long's ye steer clear o' me blade. How them boots fit ye?" The pleaseman attempted to speak but Izzy tightened his snout further, taking up the remaining slack. To compliment, Taud extended his sword tip such that Mark felt a little prick each time he drew a breath.

"A simple nod will suffice," Sandovar suggested.

As Mark nodded cautiously, Izzy slowly relaxed his grip and began lowering his captive.

"Hang on just a minute, Izzy," called a fiery voice. Izzy paused while Joy pushed her way to the forefront, confronting the cop face-to-face. She stared at Marcus intensely for a moment, letting him know she meant business. "Your false accusations are far from polite. They are downright offensive and an affront to our otherwise peaceful holiday here in the Land of Happy. The king shall hear of my displeasure." She raised a glove, intending to punctuate her statement with a slap across the pleaseman's smug face (where she got a glove is anyone's guess), but her arm was caught mid-swing by Sandovar. She looked back to see who dared interrupt her reprisal.

Sando said nothing. He just shook his head as if to say, 'he's not worth it,' or, 'you're better than this,' or, 'we only slap police officers on Thorsdays and today is only Windsday' — it was hard to tell which.

The look on Shel's face was much less ambiguous. He was clearly dumbfounded by the entire incident. But even more incredible than a cop trying to arrest him for being knocked unconscious by a careless pirate, was the response by this unlikely group of, dare he say, friends. Shel never really had someone willing to stick up for him before, other than Allison Tamaroa — the bully-fighter at Darwin Elementary — but her work wasn't personal, it was just business. This was different.

Here was not just one person, but a whole gang coming to his defense, because he apparently meant something to them. Exactly what he did to deserve such royal treatment he did not know. He _was_ certain, however, that if the tables were turned, he would do the same for this rag-tag group of misfits. After all, what are friends for?!

Chapter Five

Despite the day having moved out, the night securely in, the caravan pushed onward through the dark. Across peaks of dunes as high as mountains, they marched, the Boogies and their new companions, led by Chief Sandovar and his belly full of swords.

Sandovar the Sandman was joined at the helm by Jarbison the pirate captain, and his two mates, Taudello and Mortimer. At the rear of the group were the mysterious beauties in their long gowns, Sarah Karynthia and Sylvia Kats, both sitting atop a slow and steady camel, leading Mark the pleaseman by a length of rope tied snugly around his waist. Marcus, who was made to walk while carrying a juvenile goat as punishment for his offenses against the Boogies' guest, would later recall the experience with fondness: "The walk itself was rather pleasant, good exercise for the legs... But the goat! Oh, she was disarmingly adorable. We really bonded during that trip." Sandovar would eventually gift the goat to Marcus as a symbol of peace and friendship, but not until much later in the saga of Marcus and Sandovar. For now, Mr. Gladface was a prisoner not to be trusted!

The radiant orange crescent moon hanging low in the twilight gave the band of nomads a magical, mysterious silhouette as they moved like dancing shadow puppets against the sky. As they walked, Sando and Izzy reminisced about days long gone in the Land of Happy, and of the unforgettable circus shows and parties hosted by the infamous Romanov Falconovich. Shel listened with great curiosity at his usual post atop the elephant's back, while Joy was treated to the second level of the pachyderm hotel, a human crown for Izzy's head. As a river inevitably flows to the sea, the topic of discussion eventually arrived at the legendary Ingonyama.

"What a lion!" exclaimed Izzy. "No other animal in history has ever completed such a metamorphosis; not even the Champion butterfly, who turns from caterpillar into butterfly then into a parrot-like bird with brilliant colors and an even more impressive song."

"True indeed!" chorused Sando. "It was incredible enough that society should come to accept him as a man, but the real miracle was that people no longer recognized him as an animal in the least, let alone a lion of Africa!

"Hold up!" exclaimed Shel, nearly bringing the mid-section of the caravan to a stop. "People thought the lion was a man? What? No way!"

"Yup!" answered Izzy. "But even *more* astonishing was that Ingo himself eventually *forgot* he was a lion!"

"Oh, come on!" scoffed Shel, giving Izzy a nice back scratch where he knew the elephant liked it. He was sure they were just having some fun, razing the new guy.

"Oh yeah! That's the spot!" relished Izzy.

"I never knew that. Are you sure about that, Izzy?" Joy asked in astonishment.

"Strange but true," replied the elephant. "Ask Sando."

"Yes, it's true indeed," confirmed the Sandman. "Ingo was welcomed into all the high-society establishments as a refined gentleman, and he looked every bit the part — fancy suit 'n tie, coat 'n hat, trimmed beard and oiled mustache... the works!"

"You've got to be kidding." Shel wasn't buying any of it.

"Oh, ye of little faith," rallied Sandovar. They even wrote a song about him. Izzy? Shall we?"

"We shall!" replied the elephant jovially, and the two broke into song.

Oh, he sipped English tea
And nibbled biscuits of sav-ory.
He relished French cabernet
And dined on mignon of filet.
He spun his silver fork
On Asian noodles steeped in pork,
And he never passed up
A German pie or cake-in-a-cup!
Though, his favorite treat,
As everyone knows,
Was the sticky, sweet,
Mushy marsh-mallows.

Sando and Izzy roared with a laughter that proved contagious to all who heard it.

As the ruckus quieted, Sandovar continued. "He was groomed and coached by his distinguished employer, the—" he paused and glanced at Izzy, "misunderstood? Misguided? Mischievous? How shall we categorize him, Izzy?"

Izzy attempted to sound indifferent, "Call him what he was: shady."

"Who was shady? Ingonyama?" Shel asked.

"No, Ingo's benefactor, Romanov Falconovich," explained Sandovar.

Izzy continued with a sigh. "Falconovich was shady for a number of reasons, one of them being that he captured Ingo while on Safari in Africa, when Ingo was still young, not yet in his prime."

Shel was still a bit skeptical. "How in the world did he capture a wild lion?"

"Not by force, I can tell you that," rang Sandovar.

"Indeed not," agreed Izzy. "You see, Shel, the Falcon was also quite young at the time, full of vinegar and... something else... what was it? Doesn't matter. Anyway, the two youths ended up striking up a conversation, and they discovered they had, surprisingly, a lot in common."

Shel laughed. "Oh really? Like what? They both liked collecting comic books?"

Izzy smirked but no one saw. "No. Smart aleck. For starters, they both loved the savannah. It also came to light that Falconovich didn't enjoy killing animals. He only went on hunting safaris because it was the activity of choice for his circle of high-society friends and family. Ingo appreciated the Falcon for his consideration, and vice versa — that is, Yams didn't much like eating hunters, the way his kin did."

"Yams? Another nickname for Ingonyama" Shel clarified.

"Yeah. Anyway," continued Izzy, "Falconovich saw something in Yams, something refined and sophisticated, but also something lucrative. Eventually, the Falcon was able to talk the lion into accompanying him back to America by enticing Ingo with the promise of fame — that, and an endless supply of marshmallows."

"Marshmallows?" Shel asked.

"That's right. Marshmallows were Ingo's favorite. Who knows why?"

"What does that mean, 'lucrative,' Izzy?" asked Joy. Though she knew a fair bit about Ingonyama, she'd never heard the details of how he came to Arcania.

"Well, Falconovich wanted to make Ingo the star of his circus," explained Izzy. "Because Ingo, unlike any other lion, any other *animal*, was a self-taught sharpshooter of the western hunting rifle."

"Oh, for Pete's sake!" cried Shel. Clearly this elephant had raided the pirates' rum when they weren't looking. This tale was too tall, even for Arcania.

"I know! It sounds crazy. But it's true!" Izzy contended.

Shel looked up at Joy, who nodded. "That part I do know to be true."

"Izzy is many things, Mr. Shelby," chimed the Sandman, "a silly goof, an eccentric philosopher, even a hypnotherapist when the occasion presents itself — but never a liar."

"Thanks, Sando," Izzy replied, humbled by the compliment. "As the story goes, the lion picked up a rifle from a safari hunter after dispatching the hunter, out of necessity of course. He spent some time investigating the contraption and after a good bit of trial-and-error, eventually learned to manipulate it, and to fire it."

"Get out of town!" exclaimed Shel.

"Eh? What town? We're in the middle of the desert, Shel."

"It's a figure of speech, Izzy," Joy clarified. "Shel's saying he thinks you're pulling his leg."

"What?! Don't be ridiculous! Why would I pull on his leg?! Why would I pull your leg, Shelby? And why would I have to leave town if I did? I don't understand."

"Izzy! Not literally!" laughed Joy.

"Come on, Izzy," poked Shel, "Get with the program!"

"Huh? What program?!" whined the elephant.

"Oh, now you're just being mean," piped Sandovar.

"Sorry, Izzy. I'm just having a bit of fun, that's all." Shel patted Izzy on the back.

"Well I'm not!"

"Ohhhh!" Joy and Shel gave Izzy a hug, letting him know they were sorry. Then Joy picked up the tale of the sharpshooting lion. "I actually got to see Ingo shoot once. It was incredible. He was a dead-perfect shot, never missed his target; hardly ever anyway. I didn't know the part about him coming to Arcania and transforming into a gentleman though. That's news to me."

"You actually saw him shoot?" asked Shel, still skeptical.

"I did! Once, when I was very young. I don't remember it well. But seeing a lion shoot balloons above a crowd at a circus is not something you easily forget."

Mostly recovered from Shel's teasing, Izzy decided to rejoin the storytelling. "So, yeah, Ingo was obsessed with the Western rifle and over the course of several years, he developed into a master marksman. By the time Falconovich finished grooming him, Yams was easily the most talented marksman in all of North America, possibly the entire world. Excepting, of course, that he wasn't a man. He was still very much a lion. But the Falcon figured he could fix that too."

"So, what happened then?" asked Shel. He was hooked, so Izzy proceeded to reel him in.

"Well, Ingo did indeed become the star of the circus, just as Falconovich planned. In fact, it was the talented rifleman show that gave the Falconovich circus its fame. And, as I said, he eventually transformed from a wild lion to a refined gentleman. But—" the elephant grew somber, "and here's another thing that made Falconovich shady as all get out... One day, the Falcon and a bunch of his buddies decided to take Ingo on holiday back to Africa... to go on another hunting safari."

"To hunt *lions*, of all things!" interjected Sando, eliciting looks of disbelief and cries of shock from nearby listeners.

"Exactly!" exclaimed Izzy. "Whose genius idea it was to take Ingonyama on a *lion* hunting safari, and in his homeland no less, I have no idea! I guess it just proves that people saw Yams as a fellow man through and through and not at all as an animal, not in the slightest. Well, suffice it to say that things didn't go so well. Nature is a force not to be underestimated, you know. When it comes to nature versus nurture, nature always has the final say."

A short pause allowed the story to sink in and for Izzy to take a drink of water from a large pouch affixed to his side, courtesy of Sandovar. Once quenched, the elephant continued his tall tale.

"In spite of the Falcon's best attempts to nurture Ingonyama, to mold him into a perfect gentleman, Ingo's animal nature remained alive and well somewhere inside; and it was there to greet him with open arms when he finally returned home."

Shel's eyes were focused, his attention fixed. With all the drama and adventure, this story was right up his alley.

"Their reunion was bittersweet, however — Ingonyama and his inner nature," continued Izzy. "The new, refined Ingo had no interest in returning to life in the bush. He refused to join the other lions who fully intended to eat the hunters. But he also refused to join the hunters, who fully intended to shoot the lions. So, feeling profoundly conflicted at being stuck in the middle, he simply laid down his rifle and walked away — rejecting both sides. In doing so, he left behind his pride — in all senses of the word — and just disappeared into the bush. For years no one heard from him. People didn't know if he was alive, if he went back to being a lion, if he joined the French Foreign Legion, or moved to New Zealand to herd sheep and live in a Hobbit hut, or what."

"Hobbit hut?" someone asked but Izzy ignored it.

"That is, until a number of years ago," Izzy pressed on, "when a regiment of the king's guard from right here in the Land of Happy, went on yet another hunting safari in southern Africa. As they approached a pride of lions, expecting to bag a few prize specimens to hang on the king's wall, a storm of bullets began flying over their heads. The men took cover behind an outcropping of rocks when they heard a man's voice coming from some nearby bushes." Izzy recounted the next part in his best lion accent.

"The voice said: *'Those are warning shots, gentlemen — And I use that term very loosely! These lions are protected by order of Ingonyama. You would do well to leave them alone and return to whatever forsaken place it is you call home. The animals here are not for your shooting pleasure. They have lives of their own; families and children. They exist by the grace of God and the will of Mother Nature. They do not exist as targets, nor trophies for your ill-advised sport.'* ...more or less."

"How 'bout them apples? Pretty cool, eh?" Sandovar appended, seeing Shel's expression of wonder, jaw nearly to the ground.

"Yeah!" Shel agreed enthusiastically, recalling his drawing of a lion holding a shotgun. "What did the hunters do then?"

"Well," continued Izzy, "as you might imagine, members of a king's guard are not generally inclined to back down from an aggressor, nor do they tend to tolerate being given orders by anyone other than the king. So, not knowing where the voice was coming from exactly, they began firing their rifles recklessly into the bushes. Not very smart I'd say."

At that point Izzy took a breath, reflecting solemnly on what came next in the story. He looked down at his feet, steadily shuffling across the now comfortable, temperate sand. He always wondered why anyone would attempt to cross the desert in the heat of the day.

The Sandman happened to agree. And because Sando believed it to be best, so it was that his caravan rested during the hottest and coldest times (many do not realize that the desert can get dangerously cold at night), traveling only in the more moderate morning and evening hours — unless a kingly need forced an exception.

"And? What happened then?" urged Shel, eager for more adventure.

Izzy did not respond. He was lost in thought; the hypnotizer had become hypnotized by the rhythm of his own feet — not unlike Shel during his walk along the sidewalk of fate. Izzy noted to himself that it would be midnight soon and therefore soon it would be time to—

"Stop!" yelled Joy.

"Izzy, watch out!" called Sandovar.

"*Oof!*" While he was looking down, losing all concentration, his train of thought chugging wearily toward the next chapter in the tale of Ingonyama, Izzy failed to hear Sando's order to halt the caravan, and he failed to see the halting. Thus he failed to halt. The result was a ramming of his head, smack into the rear end of the camel he'd been following for the last few hours.

"AAAHH! Camel butt!" Izzy yelled on impulse.

The camel instantly turned and gave him a wicked stare.

"Oooh, careful Izzy," warned Joy. "She's giving you Moogley eyes."

Izzy laughed but then noticed the camel's hind leg twitch, a warning to zip his trap and back off, lest he get a camel's foot-long, knuckle sandwich for a midnight snack.

Joy laughed. "I think she likes you, Izzy. You must've made an impression... in the end."

"Ha, ha. Very funny, Joy. How do you know it's a she?"

"Well, I just assume. She is, after all, wearing a brasserie on her... er, humps," Joy noted.

The camel stuck her nose in the air and trotted off toward where the caravan was already setting up camp.

"What's Moogley eyes?" asked Shel.

Joy replied in a spooky voice, "You mean you've never heard the tale of Moogley the Seer? The man with a tiny, little body and one massive eye on his oversized head? Looked like nothing but a floating eyeball, an eye that could see everything. And if you looked directly into it, you would instantly dieeeee."

"Stop, Joy," Izzy demanded.

"Why? You *scaaared*?" Joy pushed Izzy's buttons again.

"Don't be ridiculous!" Izzy scoffed. "Of course not! I just don't want Shelby here to get scared, that's all." He bent his head low to the ground, indicating that it was time to disembark the pachyderm express.

Joy slid off his head and down his trunk with a, "Yeah, right," while Shel jumped from his shoulders onto the soft desert sand, unsure what to think.

Unable to see where he was jumping, Shel landed on the side of a steep dune, scrambled for a few steps, then slipped over the edge and tumbled a dozen feet or so down the sand slope before catching himself and skidding to a halt. He immediately tried climbing back up but kept slipping in the loose sand.

Meanwhile, seeing that the campfire had already been sparked by Sando's efficient crew, and without thinking to wait for his friends, Izzy trotted after the camel and the rest of the caravan over to the camp. He knew that wherever there was fire, there was usually food. And since he was starving — and admittedly still a little sore over Shel's teasing — he decided to ignore the kid in the background yelling about this, that, or whatever, who cares!

Probably just making fun of me again with his fancy 'figures of speech!' ...Pulling my leg! Pssshhh! I'll pull YOUR leg, smart guy! Hmpf!

Also eager to sit down to a warm meal, Joy yelled something back at Shel that sounded like, 'quit messing around,' before she too ran off to join Izzy and the rest of the Boogies.

Shel called out some more, yelling at his friends to wait but no one was listening. (Food before friends, as the saying goes... right?)

The caravan formed a circle of tents around the campfire, preparing for some well-earned rest and relaxation before the morning push to their destination of Kantcomplainistan, in the province of Doinallrightsville. Kantcomplainistan, or Kantytown as the locals called it — Kanty for short — was the capital of the Land of Happy and home to the great Peanut Butter King in his grand Peanut Butter Palace (named for the king's insatiable appetite — addiction really — for, you guessed it, potato chips — just kidding — peanut butter, of course).

Between the noise of setting up camp and the darkness of night, no one could hear nor see the lost boy on the other side of his sand hill. He attempted once more to scale the steep precipice but the loose sand giving way beneath his feet proved an impossible obstacle to surmount as there was nothing for him to grab onto. Climbing to freedom was proving futile. So, he took a different approach and proceeded to walk around the escarpment.

After struggling, slipping, and scrambling mid-slope for what seemed a good fifteen, twenty minutes, doing his darndest to traverse the dune in the direction the caravan had been heading, he found that the steepness had not diminished. Indeed, it had worsened, with sections of the dune entirely inverted.

> *Cornices of sand defying gravity itself,*
> *towering over my head like a wave,*
> *readying to collapse and bury me forever.*
> *The silent desert becomes my eternal grave!*

Sheldon the poet turned his thoughts to the Snoozants, imagining them buried under the sand beneath his very feet. The feeling of fear brought back memories of the storm dragon and the night he nearly drowned in Champion Lake. A chill ran up his spine and he considered retracing his steps in the opposite direction.

But then I'd have twice as far to walk, he reasoned.

Twice as far to where? We don't even know where we're going! he argued.

If going back ends in the same result — no way out —then we'll be behind the caravan! If they decide to leave without us we'll never catch up!

Would they do that?!? Would they leave without us??

I don't know! I don't think so. But at least here we're out in front where someone might find us if they pass by.

But what if they don't?!

Don't what? Pass by? Or find us?

Either one! Both!!

I don't know! Don't ask me!!! I just work here!

He sighed, exasperated with his internal dialogue and the situation. He was thoroughly unsure of what to do next. So, frightened and out of options, he did the only thing he could think to do: he dug himself into the slope as best he could, leaned into the hill, and closed his eyes.

Chapter Six

The Mermaid's Tale

"Where's Shel?" Izzy asked Joy when she arrived at the campfire. The alluring aroma from the steaming bowl of chili in her lap ensnared the attention of her neighbors and several left the fire in a rush toward the chow line. She took a heaping spoonful and shoved it in her mouth with a shrug, indicating that she didn't know and didn't care...

It wasn't that she didn't care about Shel. Of course she did, that went without saying. She just figured he must be somewhere nearby, enjoying some alone time. She assumed he'd be along any minute with his own bowl of chili. Izzy caught her drift, agreed with a nod, and commenced eating various vegetables that had been dropped at his feet.

"Where'd you get those?" asked Joy.

"Sarah Karynthia," answered Izzy. "Or was it Sylvia Kats? It's impossible to tell when they're covered head-to-toe in those gowns. Especially at night."

"I believe the dress is called a thawb," Joy ventured.

"Right. That does ring a bell. Still doesn't help me tell them apart though."

o o o o o o

Shel was awakened by the sound of thunder from a storm brewing in the distance. He was surprised that he'd been able to fall asleep at all, given that he was standing nearly upright. He must have been beyond exhausted. And he still was. Even after just waking up, he felt he could easily continue sleeping. He called for help a few more times, but with no response — as expected — he slumped in despair and closed his eyes again. This time, however, he was unable to fall asleep, for his mind was restless, thinking about his predicament.

What if no one ever finds me? he worried. Then, feeling melodramatic and woefully poetic, he began riffing and what-if-ing out loud to the night.

> *Oh, this sad boy of the desert nowhere...*
> *What if the wrong people found him?*
> *And they put him in the ground in...*
> *A six-foot square box-bin...*
> *Or stuffed his ashes in a cigar tin?*
> *What if the incoming storm found him,*
> *and drenched him and drowned him?*
> *And struck him with lightning*
> *that toasted and... browned him?*
> *Now that would be frightening,*
> *and give him a...*

...frowny chin?

He giggled at his creative rhyme, making light of an otherwise uncomfortable, if not altogether scary, situation. A sudden thought about the Eye of Moogley set him on edge again. He didn't know what Moogley was — beyond Joy's description — but it sounded terrifying. At that very moment, a light shined on him and he screamed, "AAAAAAAHHHH!"

"Aye. Found 'im!" said a pirate voice.

"Ha! So we have. Not to worry, my boy, the Boogies are coming to getcha!" It was Sando and Taud to the rescue. They lowered a rope and Shel climbed to freedom, finally. "All right then?" asked Sandovar.

"I guess so. How did you know where to find me?"

Taud laughed. "Ya think you be the first landlubber to fall down a dune?" barked Taud with a smile.

Sando added, "This place is a regular stopover for the caravan. We know it well. Noticed Izzy and Joy sittin' at the fire without you. Naturally, we inquired as to your whereabouts. Said they hadn't seen ya since the caravan stopped. When Joy admitted to seein' you jumpin' off some dunes, we knew exactly where to start lookin'."

"Well, thanks again. At least *someone* bothered to come looking for me!" Shel growled. He was grateful to Sandovar and Taud but perturbed by the others' apparent lack of concern. He retreated into his head.

What if I had been gobbled up by a Worst beast?

No, Izzy said there weren't any in Happy Land.

Okay, fine. What if I'd been hauled off by a giant?

No, Joy said the giants have been sleeping for ages and wouldn't be waking anytime soon.

Well then, what if Moogley had gotten me? Huh?? What then?? Huh?!?

I have to find out what this Moogley Eye thing is...

Shel eventually joined the rest of the caravan around the campfire with his own, much-anticipated steaming bowl of chili. He had slept on his sand hill right on through suppertime and was therefore eating alone. Many of the Boogies had already gone to bed. But Joy and Izzy were still awake, waiting for him after Sandovar advised them, "Wait here. I think I know where the boy is. Fear not, I shall go collect him."

At first, Shel didn't say a word to either of his friends. He just sat in silence, eating his stew and stewing in self-pity. Eventually, Izzy slid over and nudged his old pal with a nosy trunk.

"You okay?"

Shel paused a beat then asked quietly, "Why didn't you come back for me? Or at least look for me?" He stared intensely at the fire which seemed to burn all the hotter for it.

Izzy looked at Joy, then back. "I just... Well, I thought you were right behind me... or with Joy. I kinda figured that the two of you might want to be alone..." There was another pause as they watched the hypnotic smoke emanate from the embers.

"I mean when you left me on the raft. Why didn't you ever come back?" Shel felt as if he were the very fire in the pit, crackling and burning from the inside, slowly desiccating to naught but ash. (Time to grab the cigar tin.)

Izzy was caught speechless. For what felt like an eternity, the only sound to be heard in that desert was the foreboding snap and pop of something going up in flames — but whether it was the fire or the sound of friendship being tested, only time would tell.

"Shel, I'm so sorry. I thought—"

"I nearly died out there, Iz. I thought I did die!" Shel interrupted. "You have no idea what it was like, all alone on that flimsy raft..." The night fell quiet again, everyone staring blankly into the only light around, likely for many miles, each avoiding eye contact with one another, each one light years apart from the next, it seemed.

"Shel—" Joy started.

"It's not your fault, Joy. You didn't do anything. I'm not mad at you."

Joy sputtered, "Are you... mad at Izzy?"

Shel didn't respond. He just sighed and chewed his chili, shaking his head. A moment later he confessed, "I don't know. I guess not. I'm just hurt that he left me out there." He started to shake a little. Either the cold air was getting to him or his nerves were acting up, recalling the terror of the experience. "That storm was... You don't understand ...*I* don't understand, Izzy. Just tell me why; why didn't you come back?"

Izzy struggled, "I... I didn't—" He didn't know what to say at that very moment, and he paused long enough for Shel to reconsider his approach.

Shel sighed. "...No, I'm sorry, Izzy. It's not fair for me to put you in the hot seat like this. I know you and Charlotte were... that you needed... Well, I'm happy for you, that's all. Really, I am. I know it's not your fault. You didn't know about the storm. For all you knew, I could've had smooth sailing all the way to Isla de Sonrisas. Besides, it doesn't matter now. Tomorrow I'm going to some dumb jail for some dumb king." Shel stood up and walked away, wooden spoon clanking restlessly in his empty bowl.

"Shel! Wait!" Joy called out and then quickly turned to the elephant. "Izzy! Aren't you going to go after him?"

Izzy's eyes followed his friend as Shel walked into the darkness. Choking back tears, he said, "He's right. I left him out there. He's just a boy, and I left him out there all alone..."

"He's not though, Izzy, not after what he's gone through."

Izzy nodded and sighed. "You're right. As usual. But boy or not, I shouldn't have left him alone."

Joy took a long, deep breath and, with much hesitation, reluctantly confessed, "He wasn't alone."

"But he was, Joy! You heard him!" Izzy snapped. "I was supposed to be there with him. I was supposed to be there to keep him safe! But I left... with Charlotte. I left him, Joy. And he went through that terrible storm all by himself! I shouldn't've—"

"No, Izzy. He didn't," she interrupted.

"Yes, he did!" Izzy blew up, fuse torched by self-loathing. "You don't know what you're talking about, Joy."

Joy took another breath as if trying to stomach some bitter medicine. "But I do, Izzy. You *had* to leave the raft or you would've drowned. Everyone knows that. It's common sense. No one blames you for leaving. You need to stop beating yourself up about that."

Izzy hung his head. He appreciated her words but felt no less guilt and shame. "But I should've been the one to go back and look for him. Same goes for tonight!"

"Izzy, you can't be so hard on yourself. You're not his dad. And he's not entirely helpless you know."

"Well, I know that, but still..."

"I also know that Charlotte went back to look for him," Joy continued. "That she spent hours flying around looking, risking her own life."

Izzy looked curiously at her. "How do you know that?"

"I know, Izzy… because I was there."

"What?!" he glared at the fire, avoiding eye contact with her, frustration clinging to him like a scar. "What does that mean, you were there?!"

"Well, remember when you first met Sheldon, he had just parted ways with the flying shoe crew?"

"Yeah," Izzy answered, tossing small twigs into the fire with his trunk.

"Well, they went off to look for Manny but they didn't find him, nor did they find the brocosmile he worked on just before he disappeared."

"Oh-kaaaay." The elephant wondered where this was going.

"So, when they didn't find any clues about Manny, what happened to him or where he may have gone, they returned to get Shel. But by the time they got back, Shel was gone. He had left — with you."

"Joy, how do you—?"

"Just… listen. The Boot Brigade knew you had been to Manny's house because, well, your tracks are kind of hard to miss. …Oh, yeah," she added with the sarcastic air of someone recalling something obvious, "that, and because his house was completely destroyed!" She glared at him.

"Oh… right. That."

"Yeah, you'll have to explain that one to me sometime."

Izzy grinned like a guilty fool full of regret.

"So, anyway, they began asking around and discovered you'd been spotted wandering around with a young kid, who they easily figured out was Shel since he wasn't there waiting for them at what remained of Manny's place when they returned." She frowned again at the elephant and he smiled sheepishly back at her. "They followed your trail all the way to the bank of Champion Lake. How exactly, you'd have to ask them, but they figured out— Oh, by the way, you'll have to tell me about the unicorn too sometime."

"How do you know about *that*?!"

Joy laughed a little. "Never mind that now. Anyway, suffice it to say that the Boot Brigade aren't the simpletons they let on to be. Case in point, they knew that you were looking for Manny, and they knew you were close with Ingo, so they figured there was a good chance you would go looking for the lion; to get his help. After discovering the leftovers of your little raft-building project, wood and vine debris discarded by the bank of the lake, they reasoned that you had attempted to *float* to Isla de Sonrisas, given that the land route is near suicide."

Izzy squinted at Joy, unconvinced that the Boot Brigade could deduce all of that from otherwise random clues.

"I know it's a little hard to swallow," admitted Joy, reading his gaze perfectly. "But you have to admit, it's not much of a stretch to guess your logic of seeking out Ingonyama. It's the obvious move for anyone on a first-name basis with the world's greatest tracker. The only thing that threw them off was the raft. They didn't think you'd be that… bold. But they were wrong. Turns out you *are* that bold!"

"Hmpf!" Izzy scoffed. "That was nothing! You should see me on ice skates when Champion Lake freezes over!"

Joy laughed uncontrollably, imagining the elephant skating in tights. "You'll *definitely* have to show me *that* sometime." She collected herself. "So, anyway, from there the boot crew set off in Delilah to find you, figured it wouldn't take much to find an elephant floating on the lake. But that's where they were wrong. Fortunately, they found me instead."

"I see," nodded Izzy, finally beginning to grasp the big picture for the puzzle pieces.

"They told me the story of the boy that crash-landed in Delilah and of what happened to Manny. And they asked for my help to find the two of you. But I wasn't having any luck either. That is until I saw Charlotte flying overhead. I'm no detective, but I do know the sea, and pelicans don't typically fly in a search pattern for hours on end without stopping to eat. I knew she was looking for something or someone. But as that huge storm set in, she of course had no choice but to retreat to land. So, she gave up her search, for the time being anyway. And Izzy, no one could blame her either. She wouldn't have been able to continue flying even if she wanted to."

"No. Definitely not," he interjected. "She gave everything she could that night."

"She certainly did. You have a good woman there, Izzy. Whatever you did to upset her, you'd better make it right."

Izzy nodded shamefully. "I know. I know. I will"

Joy continued. "Anyway, it was a stretch, but I had to start somewhere. So, I started from where she'd been circling and I followed the Champion current, exactly as the raft would have done. And sure enough, I eventually found Shel and the raft just as the storm was going from bad to worse. I did my best to keep the raft steady for as long as I could, but the storm was too strong. So, I did what I could; I stayed nearby, close enough to keep an eye on things. Until..."

She paused, seeing that Izzy was shaking his head and his eyes were beginning to well up, obviously thinking of Shel alone in the storm.

"Joy, I don't understand what you're saying exactly," he choked. "Why didn't you just pull him into your boat? Why try to save the raft? I don't… What am I missing here?" He shook his head.

She wasn't sure how to answer, but she could see that he needed comforting and *that* she could do. Her gentle embrace opened his faucet. She let him cry for a good few minutes before continuing her story, her gaze studying the flames of the campfire all the while.

"I stayed near the raft, making sure Shel was able to stay on it, until that monster wave hit him, capsizing the raft." She locked eyes with Izzy, who was staring at her. "Shel was thrown into the sea and nearly drowned. He lost consciousness for a time, but I was able to pull him back to the raft. And thank goodness too, because I would not have been able to hold him above water for long, and—" she stopped, noting Izzy's look of profound confusion.

The elephant wiped away his tears. His attention was shifting from Shel's trial on the high seas to Joy's curious work apparently *in* the sea.

"Are you telling me," he sniffled, "that you were swimming?"

She hesitated and looked back at the fire. "Yeah, but that's kind of what I do."

"What do you mean by that, Joy? You're a swimmer? Like, professionally? Olympic? What? What are we talking about here?"

She could see that she was going to have to just come out and say it. "No, Izzy. I'm... a mermaid, actually. But I—"

"WHAT?!" the elephant nearly fell off the boulder on which he was sitting. His shock evaporated to disbelief, however, when he realized she must be joking. "Haha. Oh man, I thought you were serious there for a second. You got me good. That was a good one." When she didn't share in his laughter, he looked up to witness the stoic look on her face. "Wait. You're serious?!"

Joy nodded without smiling.

"Woah! No kidding?! Whodda thought? Joythea, a mermaid?! I never knew. How cool!"

"Shhh! Izzy, please. I don't want Shel to find out."

"Wha...? Why not?!" Izzy protested in bewilderment. "It's incredible! You shouldn't be ashamed to—"

"I'm not ashamed!" Joy shot back. Then she looked away. "I'm just not sure he'll... I'm not sure he's ready. Or, maybe I'm not ready to tell him. I don't know. It just doesn't feel like the right time."

"But, Joy, he deserves to know the truth... about you, but also he deserves to know that he was not out there all by himself: that there were people — his friends — who were out there looking for him... That there were people... that *you* were out there, risking your own life trying to keep him safe."

"I don't know, Izzy. I mean, I *want* to tell him, but I'm afraid that—"

"What? That he won't like you? He adores you, Joy!"

She blushed. "It's not that."

"Are you worried he won't accept you for who you are if he finds out you're a fish?" he asked with a slight chuckle.

"Part fish, Izzy. Part, fish. No, it's not that either."

"Then what? What is it?"

"I'm not exactly sure. It's just... right now Shel believes he was out there all alone. And yes, in a way, that's terrible. But it's also empowering to know that you can endure something so terrifying and turn out okay in the end, that you didn't need anyone else's help. Do you know what I mean?"

Izzy sort of half-nodded.

"I know he deserves to know the truth, and I intend to tell him. But I think in some way he's benefitting from the confidence he gained that night, from having had that experience alone, at least *thinking* he was alone. I'm worried that if he discovers the truth, he will become flushed with doubt, maybe no longer believing that he has what it takes to face life's dragons alone and persevere. If that happens, I'm terrified that... You know about his relationship with his dad, right? How his dad doesn't support him, doesn't believe in his dream of being a writer? Berates and belittles him for it?"

"Yesss," Izzy replied softly, feeling even more sorry for his friend.

"Well, I'm worried that if he knows he had help during the storm, the dispiriting words of his father will endure, and he will lack the confidence to follow his heart, his passion, where it's leading him. He has a bright future, *if* he can just believe in himself."

"But Joy, *you're* his heart. Anyone can see that. He'll follow *you* if you lead him. Show him the way, Joy."

"No, Izzy. I can't. This is something he has to do on his own. But thank you, you're sweet. No, his heart is filled with adventure, imagination, art. Those things are the stones on the path laid out before him. If he doesn't believe in himself, if he believes what his father says about him, I fear he may never find the courage to walk that path, difficult as it may be. Instead, he'll end up taking the easy path his father has already paved for him."

Izzy breathed long and slow through his trunk. This was a lot to take in. He was still in shock about Joy being a mermaid. But more than that, he was beyond impressed by her insight about Shel. *How could a girl of her age — she can't be more than fourteen — be so in tune with the world, so wise about people?*

"Izzy, I... don't know if you ever found that flying elephant from the story." Izzy's eyes locked on the girl as she shifted from talking about Shel to bringing up a painful topic for him. "But, you know in that story how the elephant had a feather, and he thought the feather was the reason he could fly, but in the end it turned out to be his own abilities, not the feather?"

Izzy nodded slowly, feeling uneasy that this wise girl was about to shine a spotlight on him, bringing to light an issue he would prefer to keep hidden in the dark.

"That feather was a bridge from fear to flight, right? Well, for Shel, I was... I am... kind of like that feather in a sense, only maybe the opposite, I suppose. That is, I'm trying to *build* a bridge. It's a falsehood, I know. But it's a falsehood that is serving an important purpose right now. When the time is right, I will tell him the truth. I just think it's too soon."

Izzy stayed silent for a time, long enough for a Boogie to walk up, toss another log on the campfire, and walk back to *their* sitting spot, likely engaged in their *own* deep conversation, learning deep secrets about *their* friend, how their friend has *also* been living a double life and is now confessing that they're the Easter Bunny or something! (His mind was racing.) Suddenly he burst out, "Well... then why did you tell *me*?! I'm no good at keeping secrets!"

"Izzy, please," she said softly. "Do it for Shel. You've done a good job of keeping the secret of your father hidden for many years."

"That's different!" he whisper-shouted. "How do you even know about that?!"

"Izzy, you need to go find Shel and tell him what happened with Charlotte, about how she searched for him until she could barely fly and had to swim back to shore. And tell him that the festoon brigade was out looking for him too."

The elephant stared at her.

"I told you all of this so that you no longer have to feel you abandoned him. Izzy, you are part of a community that helps each other, even when we don't ask for help or know that help is available to us. You're part of this community because of who you are: a kind and caring soul. If you had not been who you are, Charlotte would not have gone back for Shel and neither would the shoe crew have bothered to go looking for *you*. But they did. Don't you see? Because *you* cared for Shel, so did they, and so did I."

Izzy looked as if he were going to start crying again. For such a big guy he sure was awfully sensitive.

"If *you* care for something, Israel," Joy poked Izzy's side, "...then that something must be important, and we will care too."

He managed a smile at this incredible woman sitting by his side. What a lucky guy Shel was to have such an admirer.

"And you must know," she continued, "to abandon Shel would have meant to turn your back on him completely and choose not to care, or if you had decided that he could finish the journey on his own — that he would be just fine without you. You did neither of those things. In the end, he was not alone. I was there. And you are here now. Tell him the truth about Charlotte and the Bootaneers. Tell him how sorry you are. Apologies *do* matter. He will understand and it *will* make a difference. I promise you."

Izzy sighed, "I suppose you're right." Joy raised her eyebrows, challenging him to do better. "No, no, you're right," he admitted. "I need to tell him."

"Tell him what?" said Shel, walking into the firelight from the dark nowhere, holding a second helping of chili. Izzy and Joy were startled silent. When nobody answered, Shel decided to push the discussion in a new direction. "So, what's this Eye of Moogley nonsense?" As he scooped a heaping spoonful into his mouth, Joy gave the elephant her own Moogley Eye stare.

Getting the message, Izzy started spilling the beans.

Chapter Seven

The caravan pulled into Kantcomplainistan just as the sun was warming up for its main heat and the sand was once again climbing beyond scorching temperatures...

Thankfully, the province of Doinallrightsville had palm tree-lined, cobblestone pathways throughout, so residents and visitors could travel the region in shaded comfort without worry of frying their feet off...

Being known across the Land of Happy for their generosity — deviant ways notwithstanding — Sandovar and his Boogie rabble were greeted with handshakes and hugs and plenty of good cheer from Peanut Butter Palace guards to street beggars and everyone in between. As was customary, the Sandman distributed spoils from his recent expeditions as his caravan snaked its way through the streets en route to the palace, exciting the good folk of Kantytown to no end. He had craftsman swords and weaponry for the royal guards; musical instruments, colorful oils, and paper with fancy quills for the artisans; and spices, chocolates, and liqueurs from the farthest corners of the world for those who indulged in the more refined vices.

As the caravan proceeded, Boogies peeled off in all directions to visit old friends, family members, barbers, beauticians... find baths to sleep in and beds to bathe in... (or some variation thereof). Mark, the pleaseman, now back on familiar turf, with home-field advantage bolstering his ego, joined Sandovar at the front of the caravan as they approached the palace doors. Izzy, meanwhile, marched casually with Joy on his head and Shel on his back.

Several men and women guarded the palace doors, many of whom looked more like jesters than knights.

"Ah, Sir Marcus O'Rillynice," spoke one of the guards to the approaching caravan. "You've returned, at long last! And with the perpetrator, I see. Come, boy, climb down off your elephant. I will take you to see the king."

Boy? Shel thought to himself but said nothing.

Your elephant? Izzy scoffed in his head. Being referred to as someone's elephant, as if he were a common beast of burden, added unwelcomed bitterness to his cup of tea. But he, like Shel, decided against challenging a Peanut Butter Palace guard right off the bat. Thus, he quietly lowered himself in a bow, allowing Shel and Joy to climb down. Sandovar, meanwhile, commenced greeting the guards with gifts.

Marcus decided this was his opportunity to resume command, speaking up as if he were the leader of the caravan. "Yes, 'tis I, Sir Marcus Gladface, captain of the please force. I have returned with my prisoner, as promised. And I shall—"

"Oh, can it, y'ol' windbag!" scolded Sandovar, home turf be damned. He placed a gentle hand on the shoulder of one of the guards and smiled. "It's nice to see you again, Alice." The guard returned his smile and raised him a nod and a blush as she opened the large doors leading to the great hall of the Peanut Butter Palace. Alice the guard walked through first. Sandovar followed. Taud, Jim, and Morgan entered behind him, with Sarah and Sylvia at the pirates' heels. Next came Mark, clutching his prisoner's left arm, Joy occupying the right. Izzy brought up the rear.

"Ho! Welcome friends!" boomed a voice loud enough to echo through the dimly lit hall not less than three-and-a-half times (yet not more than five). Torches in copper sconces tossed warm splashes of light upon the walls, while a grand, circular wood-burning fireplace illuminated the center of the room. The far ends of the hall remained dark such that the visitors could not tell from where exactly the voice was coming, though it was clear to whom it belonged.

"Welcome, welcome! Chief Sandovar, my old friend, wonderful as always to see you! What did you bring your favorite king this time?" Before Sandovar could respond, the voice continued, "Wait a turn! ... Hold your holy horses on high! Is that? Nooo! Izzy the elephant?"

A large figure emerged into the firelight. Long robes of red and gold hung lazily off his torso as if the man were melting. Down to his feet the gown sagged, sweeping the floor as he walked — much to the delight of the royal housekeeper. White fur lined the insides and borders of the gown. A smallish crown studded with rubies, sapphires, emeralds, and so on, replaced a terrific mane long since retired from the man's head. What remained of the legendary afro — which had, once upon a time, radiated out from his dome at least half the length of a regulation Wimbledon tennis racquet — had migrated to other parts of the landscape, taking up residence over his eyes and around his mouth. Despite his mostly kingsome appearance, underneath his robes the man wore rather plain-looking pajamas: A one-piece suit of long underwear that matched his robe. Beyond all of that, the man was completely barefoot! Still, what he lacked in formal style he made up for in color coordination, assuaging some concerns about the king's sanity — some, not all.

Occasionally, various members of Sando's caravan attempted to speak in response to the king's welcome, but His Highness just kept right on talking. "Please, do come in and make yourselves at home." The remnants of the caravan obeyed. "I understand we are also welcoming a purported thief whose reservation is nigh upon the scales of justice? How exciting this day is shaping up to be!" Mark attempted to rise with his prisoner. "But first," the king continued — Mark sat down — "let's address the elephant in the room, shall we?" The king approached Izzy. "How have you been, old friend? I wasn't sure that you were still... around. I was relieved to get news that you are alive and well... and... that you and Charlotte have reunited! How delightful! Where is she? I would ever so much like to see her."

Izzy bowed. "Your Majesty." Standing up to his full height, he continued. "You are correct, as usual. Charlotte and I reunited recently. She wanted to accompany me to Kantcom— ...to visit *you*, sire. But she couldn't leave Fallshugger Ridge, I'm afraid."

"Ah, that's too bad. I've always wondered what a pelican egg tastes like. Was hoping you might bring one for a scramble." The king's comment elicited a hushed hiss from the crowd but, oblivious as he could be at times, he took no notice. Neither did he notice Izzy's look of vexation rapidly deteriorate to disgust and then contempt.

"Oh... she'd be happy to lay something for you," cringed the elephant under his breath, "but it wouldn't be an egg."

"What was that?" asked the clueless king, wiggling a finger in his ear.

Izzy just shook his head and shrugged as if to say, "I didn't say anything."

Coming to his senses — at least one or two of them — the king realized his comment may have been a tad off-putting. Skippy cleared his throat and quickly changed the subject. "Ahem. So... Izzy, did you know there are others from Falconovich's circus in Kantytown?" King Solomon lifted his eyebrows and, without waiting for Izzy's reply, immediately turned to Sandovar. "So, Sandy, what do you have for your old friend, Skip? Eh? What'd ya bring me?"

Shel looked at Joy, standing by his side.

"Skip?" he whispered.

"Yeah, short for Skippy," she replied.

"Oh, right. Peanut butter!" Shel did his best to stifle a laugh. Joy nudged him, letting him know he'd better keep quiet. Mark, of course, noticed the commotion and hissed.

"Well, Your Excellency," started Sandovar, "we have brought for you—"

"Hold that thought, Sando. Everything all right over there, Marcus?" the king asked, a tinge irritated.

"Ah... yes, Your Highness! Sorry," replied the pleaseman.

King Skippy squinted at Mark, and Mark, in turn, squinted at the disruptive youths. "Sorry, Sandy," the king resumed, "You were saying?"

"Yes, Your Majesty, we brought you a very special—"

"Mark!" the king bellowed when he overheard more giggling.

"Deepest apologies, Your Majesty. I—"

"Bring the prisoner hither!" commanded the king. "Let's get this over with."

Instantly, the pleaseman tugged at Shel's arm, and the two stumbled forward, with Joy walking just behind. When they reached the king, who had proceeded to sit down atop his oversized throne in preparation for Mark's presentation, Shel was struck with the distinct recollection of the jungle cannibal from his dream. Mark tugged again at Shel's arm, forcing him to bow before the king. Joy curtsied.

"Your Highness, I present mister Sheldon Silvers of Chicago. We received a report that young mister Silvers took a nap that did not belong to him. After speaking with some eyewitnesses, we've determined that he did indeed fall asleep unauthorizedly and at a wholly unscheduled time."

The king eyed the young man. "Chicago, eh? I knew someone else from this… Chicago. Seems to me to be a place that breeds moral delinquents." The king scrutinized Shel's appearance as if he could deduce the young man's guilt or innocence just by looking at him. "Get this troublemaker out of my sight." With a wave of his hand, Alice and another guard grabbed Shel by the arms and escorted him out of the hall. "And would somebody please get me a peanut butter sandwich?!"

Although shaken by the king's command — certainly concerned for Shel's well-being — Izzy and Joy and possibly Taud and Sandovar, too, were not overly worried. Having spent time in the presence of the Peanut Butter King, they knew not to take anything King Skippy said too seriously. Sure, he ordered Shel to be removed from the great hall, but his gruff performance was likely little more than posture, probably just putting on a show for his guests — that, and being polite to Marcus by helping the pleaseman feel somewhat vindicated. Alice was probably taking Shel to a nice room in the castle where he could get washed up, have a yummy snack, and maybe even catch a bit of shuteye before the evening festivities, planned in honor of the caravan's arrival, as was customary.

Joy stepped forward, curtsied a second time, and presented a gift-wrapped peanut butter sandwich, the bread of which was made with a light flour unique to the coastal region. "Your grace," she said as she lowered her head and raised the dish. (Apparently, she'd been holding out on Shel when he was starving in the desert. If one had confronted her about the secret sandwich, she would have said simply that this one was made for the king and the king alone. Sorry Shel. In truth, she didn't want to risk being caught giving a peanut butter sandwich to anyone but Skippy. That would be grounds for imprisonment, or worse.)

"Well, Miss Costeros, how nice to see you. Though it is unusual for you to travel so far east, away from your home breaks, is it not?" the king queried as he plucked the unwrapped sandwich from the plate held out by one of his servants. There was a bite missing, courtesy of the king's official poison-tester. (It wasn't that the king didn't trust Joythea; it was just that anyone could have gained access to that sandwich during her travels, possibly adding an extra, unwanted ingredient.) "Would I be correct, Miss Costeros, in assuming a certain young man has inspired this current *expansion* of your horizons?" He took a large bite of the sandwich.

"As usual, sire, your perception is keen," she answered politely.

"Mmm." The king made a few noises and facial expressions that conveyed his approval of Joy's motivations, her flattery, and, most especially, her sandwich. "And how are things under the sea? I trust all is well with the queen."

"Indeed, your grace. The mermaids are flourishing in peace and prosperity thanks to your friendship."

"Oh, nonsense," he laughed. "I do enjoy the compliment but it is unnecessary, my dear. On the contrary, I believe it is *your* unfailing positivity, neoteric vision, and empathetic leadership which has renewed that community so." Joy smiled and curtsied in gratitude. "Is this one of your famous sea-wheat sandwiches, by the way? It is beyond delicious!"

Joy nodded. "Thank you, your grace."

"Well, it will be great to have your jovial spirit around to lighten our halls, so dark and dreary as of late." Then he leaned in and whispered, "In truth, there hasn't been much laughter in Kantytown lately. Not sure why." The king looked away in thought.

"I'll do my best, sire," replied Joy with a nod. The king smiled at her and then turned his attention to the elephant, who clearly had something to say.

"Izzy, you look expectant. Something on your mind?"

The elephant approached the throne. As he did, he bowed his head.

"You know," Skippy continued, "now that I think about it, the last time I saw you, you were departing your father's circus, embarking on a grand adventure to spread your wings. Tell me, how did that work out for you?"

"Well, it's good to be home, Your Majesty. My travels were both frustrating and fulfilling. Which is to be expected, I suppose."

"Mmm. Yes, I s'pose so, if we're lucky," replied Skippy.

"Um, Your Excellency, if I may speak frankly…"

"Of course, my friend. What's on your mind?" The king tossed the remaining bit of sandwich to a nearby dog, also dressed in a red and gold robe.

"I understand the laws of the land, and I do not wish to contest your authority…" The king squinted, unsure if he liked where this was headed. "If I may say a word about the character of young mister Silvers?"

Longsmiles paused, trying to predict the elephant's next sentence. "Pro-seeeed," he said cautiously.

"I have known Mr. Silvers for a good amount of time now, relatively speaking; longer than anyone in Champion Valley, I wager, certainly longer than anyone in the Land of Happy. He and I have been on several adventures together and have found ourselves in a few precarious situations that would test any man's character." Izzy looked at the king for approval.

"Go on," encouraged the king, once again itching the inside of his ear with a restless pinky.

"Despite adversity and the threat of mortal harm, on more than one occasion, Shel has demonstrated courage, fortitude, and honor, such would rival anyone I know."

The king raised an eyebrow, impressed by Izzy's praise for his friend.

"As you know," Izzy continued, "my father also hailed from Chicago, just like this young man. And while I have no idea what Chicago and Arcania have in common, why we seem to get visitors from that place and no other... I don't know about any of you," the elephant looked around the room, "but I never got the opportunity to travel to Chicago…

and I have absolutely no idea how Shel came to be *here*... I mean obviously the flying shoe crew had something to do with it..."

"Izzy!" Joy hissed, attempting to get the pachyderm back on track.

Izzy looked at Joy. "Right. Where was I? Oh, yes. Well, we all know what a charlatan the Falcon turned out to be, but this kid is nothing like Falconovich. Shel is kind and sensitive and thoughtful and courageous... and he is full of curiosity, but not the sort of curiosity what drives men like the Falcon to questionable ambition. Shel's curiosity is genuine and raw and pure and sweet, like sugar straight from the cane. It's the kind of curiosity that bridges differences and forges friendships; the kind of curiosity that stokes the fires of imagination," he glanced back at Joy, "...and passion." Joy blushed. "In all honesty, Your Highness, he reminds me of a young prince who defied his king and queen to bring laughter and happiness back to the kingdom."

The king took a slow breath, inhaling the elephant's testimony, recalling his own youthful days of rebelling against the royal regiments that bound him to what he viewed as antiquated tradition and regulation. As a young man, the prince had an innate desire to dismantle old, rusted customs, to remake them, improve them. He wished to grease the wheels of imagination and restore genuine happiness as a core virtue. And for his silly heart and his dreaming head, they said he would never be a suitable king. But when he grew up, he fought — a passivist's fight of course — for what he believed. So came the silliness revolution. And lo and behold, he won! For, as it turns out, it is popular to be happy and have fun. Who'd've thought?!

Chapter Eight

Add Your Own Spice

Draw something here. ↓

yes, you!

yes, right here, in the book! ↖

King Solomon Skippingston Longsmiles III, known throughout the seven seas and nine realms simply as "Skippy" (though he liked to think only his close comrades were apprised of the moniker), decreed that his first order as king — correction: his *second* order. His first was to change his family surname from Longscowls to Longsmiles. His *second* order was to enact a law whereby every citizen in the Land of Happy was required to contribute something which no one had ever done before. (For those interested, the original royal mandate read:

> *By invitation of His Majesty's administration, the Happy population may satisfy qualification of Royal Decree Number II through: Demonstration of a ground-breaking creation what might save civilization thereby resulting in great celebration; an ingenious exploitation of divine inspiration; some simple adaptation or distillation of a previous application...*

...and so on. The order continues ad nauseum, becoming rather tedious to digest for all the 'ations'.)

The smile-making scaffold system employed to hold up the giants' faces was one of the more effective examples of the king's 'Something New' mandate, as it was officially titled. There were other, less impressive entries, such as an umbrella made of paper and a self-reading book, the latter of which, as one might deduce, read to itself whenever it felt like it, saving many would-be readers a great deal of time but often leaving them feeling as though they hadn't read a thing — mostly because they hadn't. The self-reading book barely beat out the self-chewing gum entry, but only barely.

Indeed, the king set the bar as low as possible so as to include absolutely anyone and everyone. In fact, to qualify, a creation could be something so simple as, to quote once more from the royal decree, doing "a looney-baboony dance" or singing "a mumble-jabumble song." The only real requirement was that the creation or idea pass a simple two-question test: 'Is it unique?' and, 'Is it authentic?' "Unique and authentic" was, of course, the king's litmus for determining if a thing had intrinsic value and therefore provided a benefit to society.

It was often said that the king's philosophy was heavily influenced by a prominent mathematician from Germany, who, much to the dismay of the global academic community, decried imagination to be more important than knowledge itself — a radical idea that no doubt led many would-be accountants, doctors, and lawyers to abandon their lofty pursuits in favor of arguably less practical vocations such as art or literature (much to the dismay of Banzakoots everywhere). Such a notion may sound irresponsible and naïve. However, the mathematician (who, incidentally, turned out to be more of a theoretical physicist) eventually gained worldwide recognition for his unparalleled genius and was considered by many to be the smartest person to have ever lived. So there's that.

Proof being in the pudding, as they say, the king's plan worked like a charm. The creative silliness was contagious, and soon the Land of Listentoemholler transformed entirely into the Land of Happy, all because a boy chose to care more about imagination and fun than formal education and hard work.

After some internal deliberation, the king picked up his dialogue with the elephant. "So, what you're suggesting, Ser Tuskinsky, is that perhaps this young instigator, Mr. Silvers, shares similar interests to the crown. Is that accurate?"

The elephant bobbed his head noddishly, indicating "more or less."

"Very good. But does he also share a reverence for raw imagination, wild creativity, and unbridled silliness?" challenged the king.

"In truth, my lord, the whole story of Shel has yet to be revealed. But I suspect he does."

"I see," said the king, tapping his index fingers together. Longsmiles then considered the accused's other benefactor, Joythea Aquarius. Although she'd refrained from delivering an impressive monologue favoring the offender, she had said enough. It spoke volumes that such a respectable — albeit young — woman had traveled so far out of her comfort zone, in more ways than one, to help a perfect stranger. This Mr. Silvers must be a special person indeed. Skippy tugged at the tuft of hair below his bottom lip (known in some circles as the soul patch), deep in thought and consideration. Eventually he gave a nod to Izzy, dismissing the elephant for the time being.

Knowing his words were doing their work and that no more need be said, Izzy shuffled off to one side.

Still reflecting on the testimony and considering the consequences of pardoning the newcomer — that is, whether his people would lose faith or feel that some favoritism was at play — the king motioned that he was finally ready to receive Sandovar and his gifts.

"Your Majesty, anyone can see that you have a lot on your mind already, that there are many important items requiring your attention, as usual," Sandovar asserted as he approached the throne. "So I will keep this brief. As always, it goes without saying that it gladdens my heart to see you again, and in such good health." The chief bowed and the king nodded in appreciation. "We have, of course, brought you the standard favors of spirits and spices..." Sandovar signaled to his servants to pass the more common gifts to the guards. "However, our friend Izzy happened upon this tasty treasure as we were passing through the far reaches of the desert."

Izzy pulled the giant silver spoon from a nearby case — brought into the castle earlier by some Boogie or another — grasped the utensil in his trunk and held it out for the king's consideration.

"It is a remnant from the days of the giants. Not only is it a relic of nostalgia, but, given that it's solid silver, its worth is no doubt considerable. May it bring you both joy and prosperity."

Sandovar concluded his presentation with his signature low bow: left arm outstretched in front of him, motioning in circles as if trying to get a whiff of something, right arm folded behind his back. His forehead dipped down, almost touching the toes on his left foot as he rested it on its heel. His right leg bent slightly behind him, serving as his anchor. It was an awkward-looking maneuver that must have taken some time to perfect, but Sandovar made it look effortless thanks to his many years of practicing Qigong — a cultural treasure collected from his travels in the Orient.

"A gift befitting of a king, indeed," replied Skippy. "Long gone are the days of the giants. And while we do not necessarily lament that this is so, fond memories of better days with our tall friends remain in our hearts. This souvenir will hang in the great hall as a treasured reminder of an era in the Land of Happy not likely to be seen again for an age, if not longer. I thank you for this gift, Sandovar Sandovecchio... and thank you too, Ser Tuskinsky. And in return, I have a gift for all of you."

The king looked toward a dark corner of the hall and, on cue, in walked a small figure in long robes.

"All freshened up?" Skippy addressed the figure who nodded in return. "Grand. Please, step forward." The figure obeyed, emerging into the light to stand in front of the throne. Immediately, Joy jumped up, ran over, and gave Shel a big hug before remembering her place. "My apologies, Your Grace," she said with a bow.

The king laughed, albeit only slightly. "And you too, Marcus, please join the accused upfront." The king motioned an invitation to the pleaseman. "I am ready to give my decision."

Mark had a bad feeling that his prisoner was going to be acquitted before a trial even took place, and he made no attempt to hide his anticipation of disappointment, walking with a pronounced slump as he approached the throne.

"Stand tall, captain!" barked Skippy in encouragement. "Take pride, young man."

Now, Mark the pleaseman was not young by any measure. Indeed, he might have been a good deal older than the king. But Skippy, despite his youthful spirit, was an old soul who naturally asserted eldership over his kinsman. Of that fact there was no dispute. However, unlike the dissentient king, Marcus had dedicated his entire life in service to the crown and rule of law, just like his father and grandfather before that, and so on as far back as his family history was recorded. He held fixedly to a strict code of order, which not only, as he saw it, held together the fabric of society, it defined his family heritage. To deviate from that code would mean, to him, the dissolution of society, not to mention the crumbling of his own identity. The shenanigans of the silly king, in Mark's estimation, were dangerously close to chopping society, and Mark's family tree, to the ground.

Despite Mark's apprehension, he had to admit the truth of it: society did not descend into chaos when Longsmiles ascended to the throne. Marcus reluctantly admitted, on the contrary, that general contentment actually improved under Skippy's lackadaisical rule. Furthermore, at the same time, criminal activity — Mark's sharpest metric for social health — declined. Thus, Marcus remained a staunch loyalist to the crown, giving not only his faith but his sword to Solomon Longsmiles III. Though the king's methods were unorthodox and almost always rubbed Mark the wrong way — such as when he turned the *police* force into the *please* force — Skippy's results were irrefutable.

"Mr. Silvers, Sir Marcus Gladface, are you both ready to receive my judgment?"

Marcus nodded. Shel, on the other hand, being thoroughly confused by recent developments, decided he'd like an explanation before any sort of judgment was laid upon him. So, as he would do in Ms. Kelsyan's class on (rare) occasion, he raised his hand.

"What is he doing?" asked someone from the peanut gallery (literally — the palace hall had a museum gallery showcasing the evolution of the peanut).

"Mr. Shelby, this is not a schoolroom. We do not do that here," explained Lady Alice, Skippy's head knight.

"But what if I have a question?" asked Shel.

A gasp was heard again from the peanut gallery. The king laughed, "Young man, I can understand if you are not accustomed to the protocols of royal court," spoke the king. "However, if you are so moved to make your voice heard, then speak up! If you are out of place or do not know your place, rest assured we will remind you of it. Fair enough?"

"Yes sir. I mean, yes your honor. Um, your royal-ness?"

"*Highness* will suffice, thank you," advised the king.

"Right. Sorry, my highness."

The peanut gallery gasped and scoffed. Marcus slapped his hand over his face for shame. Izzy and Joy giggled. The king shook his head and grinned. Joy leaned in and whispered something in Shel's ear, and he opened his mouth, presumably to correct his error, but the king raised a hand and shook his head, letting him know there was no need.

"Mr. Silvers, may I presume, given your less-than-refined— er, style, that you have yet to inherit a suffix of repute?"

"Um, excuse me, *Your*... Highness? I don't believe I follow."

"An honorific, my dear lad, a telltale of your status, both familial and societal. The title is often appended to one's surname, after having achieved some noteworthy accomplishment or having proven one's worth. I understand it may not be common practice in Chicago, but here in Arcania, nearly anyone who has achieved anything is endowed with a surname suffix to highlight their accomplishment, or accomplishments. Why even your supersized friend there, on account of his... ill-advised obsession with flight, has been dubbed Israel Tuskinsky von Isibhakabhaka, a rather fun word meaning 'sky' in his native tongue. You may have heard people refer to him as Von Baka or the more spicy version, Baka-baka?"

Shel stared blankly at the king.

"No?" the king grinned. "No matter. Most just call him Izzy, which is probably for the best. Efficiency and all..."

Shel looked back at the elephant, silently mouthing, "Baka-baka?" Izzy just shrugged with a silly half-smile.

"And Joythea," the king made to continue but was stopped short by a loud *"ahem!"* from the young woman, followed by a subtle shaking of her head, eyes closed, indicating that now was not the time to share her extended title.

"Never mind Joy," Longsmiles retracted.

Shel squinted at Joy, perplexed as ever. She smiled back innocently as if absolutely nothing had happened. Shel turned back to the king and shrugged, shaking his head slowly, no idea what to make of all of this.

"Still not following, I see. Well then, permit me to lead on. Marcus, standing just there to your left, is another great example. Although he enjoys the rights and privileges accompanying his esteemed status of knighthood, he also retains his ancestral suffix of esquire, yielding a respectable, albeit loquacious label of Sir Marcus O'Rillynice Gladface McGee, Esquire." King Solomon raised his brow as if to ask, 'follow me now?' "Another example," he continued, "your friend the Sandman has appropriately adorned his name with the standard 'senior' after having sired a — quite fortunate if I do say so — heir to his nomadic empire." Higher eyebrows from the king nudged, 'You follow? You follow?'

Still not seeing the sought-after recognition in Shel's eyes, the king proceeded. "I, myself, am permitted the use of 'the Third' at the finale to my appellation. ...A little secret, just between the two of us..."

Shel looked around, confused, given the many people listening in on the conversation.

"I am indeed *not* the third man born Solomon Skippingston Longsmiles. Instead, I have *earned* the charming suffix in recognition of my productivity as a singular monarch being equivalated to that of no less than *three* kings." Longsmiles concluded with eyebrows floating the length of three foreheads above his eyes.

"Okay. I think I get it," replied Shel. "You're asking about my name, if I'm a junior or something."

The king nodded long and slow, eyebrows still soaring in the stratosphere.

"Uh, no," admitted Shel. "I'm just Shel Silvers."

"Ah," spoke the king. "No shame in that, I suppose. Not everyone is destined for recognition. Or perhaps you have yet to make your contribution? Remind me your age if you'd be so kind."

"I'm twelve."

"I see. Yes, still plenty of time to—"

"Going to be thirteen soon," Shel added with pride.

The king paused, irked by the interruption and curious why the boy deemed it a necessary intrusion. "Mmm. By that... timely... comment, I presume you're looking forward to the auto-promotion?"

"Sir?"

"The age advancement, Mr. Silvers."

"Um, yes, I am actually."

"Right. Well, by the time *I* was your age... " The king laughed. "Only joking, my friend! I know youths hate it when adults use that expression."

Shel smirked.

"I will say, though," continued Skippy, "given that you appear to be, even at your spritely age, a veritable social magnet, attracting impressive entourage," the king waved his hand at Izzy, Sandovar, Joythea, and the pirates, "I will be keeping tabs on you whilst you're here in Arcania, curious to see if you might *earn* your coveted 'teen' status as opposed to simply aging into it — as I did in *my* youth, incidentally."

Shel fumbled his words, not entirely understanding the king's meaning. "Uh, how does one, um, *earn* their age? Don't we just automatically get older, no matter what?"

"Oh, indeed we do!" replied the king. "Everyone and everything ages, no avoiding that. But while some people sit back and let life happen *to* them, as it inevitably will, others refuse to wait for their title. Some brave souls rush out to meet their destiny head-on. Sadly, some people, as they grow older, grow further from the magic they inhabited as children. Some may advance in years yet diminish in integrity, forgetting the fundamentals... such as the golden rule. Do you know the golden rule, my son?"

Shel, for some reason, decided this was a golden opportunity to recite a joke he'd heard recently on the Darwin playground. "Um, he who has the gold makes the rules?"

King Solomon roared with laughter, an invitation for all to join him, and so they did. Once the echoes in the hall, like lizards, slithered back into the cracks between the stones, and a manageable quiet returned, the king corrected, "Not quite, my good man. But I do appreciate the levity. No, I am referring to the rule that we should do unto others as we would have others do unto us. In short: be kind."

Shel nodded. Of course he knew of *that* golden rule. What school kid didn't?

"It was in kindness — my dedication to bringing back silliness, entertainment, fun, joy to my kingdom — wherein I earned my title. And in my long years since, I have concluded the virtue of kindness to stand above all, the one aspect that makes us most worthy of this precious gift we call life. So, let us see if you might collect the years owed to you whilst at the same time being proactive in seeking out your destiny, whatever that might be."

Shel's mind felt like a knotted-up ball of string that would require ample time to untangle, let alone absorb and digest the king's words. He felt both stuffed with information and completely empty all at once, as did many in attendance that day. And yet, from somewhere in the pit of his stomach came a thought — a thought which bubbled up to his throat and popped out of his mouth before he could contain it.

"But," he popped, bursting the reverent silence that had settled over the great hall like a fog. The audience had gone quiet, preoccupied dogs busy gnawing on the rhetorical bones tossed out by the king.

"But?" replied the king as if tasting something bitter.

Feeling bold, Shel continued. "But, how do I seek out something when I don't know what I'm looking for? I mean, I *think* I know what I want, but how do I know what my destiny actually is?"

"Ah, yes. How does one find that which is invisible yet all around us at all times? It is a good question. ...You must *feel* it, my son. You must be willing to accept, in your heart, the signs presented to you; and you must walk the path designated by those signs. Your agreement on those two conditions is the key to unlocking the door leading to your destiny."

"But," (There was that word again, and again Skippy looked as if he'd just swallowed a raw Brussels sprout.) "What signs? What path?" Shel begged.

"Alas, I cannot give you that answer, Master Sheldon. No one can, for no one can recognize that which fate has created for you and you alone. What I *can* tell you is that if you succeed in recognizing the signs pointing you to your path, and if you succeed in staying true to your path, no matter how long the journey, you *will* eventually arrive at your destiny and earn your proper title."

While Shel ruminated, fidgeting with the puzzle piece still in his pocket, Skippy took the silence as an opportunity to move on.

"Now then, I believe we still need a judgment on the nap issue, do we not? Mr. Silvers, did you still have a question regarding the charges against you?"

"Oh! Yes, I did! Well, um, you see — it's just that... if I could just— what I'd like to say is... I forgot."

The king stroked his chin. "Silvers, my good man, if it's not too much trouble, would you mind enlightening the throne as to your purpose here in the Land of Happy, ultimate-destiny-and-all-that aside?"

Silence resumed momentarily as Shel recapitulated, corralling memories like wild horses. For the next few minutes *(or possibly much longer)* the palace guests sat in rapture, listening to the curious tale of Sheldon Silvers: where he was from; bits about Chicago in general and his neighborhood, school, and folks in particular; how he came to arrive in Arcania; meeting the Flying Boot Brigade and Manny the dentist; his adventures with Izzy; crossing the Sonrisa Desert with Joy and the Boogies; and finally, how he ended up standing there before the king.

It was an engaging tale, one that illuminated, along with all the captivating details, that this young man was an entertaining storyteller, deserving of a spotlight on stage. But just how bright a light and how big a stage remained to be seen. The tale, incidentally, was also the first Izzy had heard of Shel's trial on the high seas, from Shel's perspective. Though he was big and tough, to hear what his friend had to endure because of his desire to sail Champion Lake instead of taking the long way around (even though the long way around is, admittedly, nigh impassible), that brought the big guy to tears — and don't think Shel didn't notice. After the young man concluded his story, the crowd waited in silence for the king's response. Longsmiles' face twisted and wrinkled all sorts during the monologue as he sat massaging his miniature goatee and mumbling various thoughtish, reflectoral, pensiverous words like 'interesting' and 'curious' and 'indeed.'

At the conclusion of Shel's account, the king sat in silence, no doubt wondering at least in part, how much of the story was true, but likely more concerned with the young man's purpose for coming to the Land of Happy in the first place — that being, of course, to find Ingonyama.

Chapter Nine

The Falcon

"*So! You have come* seeking the great Ingonyama Nifumo in the service of the infamous Romanov Falconovich, have you?" As Shel nodded, the king leaned around him to peek at Izzy standing further back. "Ser Tuskinsky, according to this young man's account, he was sent via homemade raft across the vast and dangerous Champion Lake, to La Isla de Sonrisas, under your direction, in search of... your dad."

Shel spun around in a flash and shot a look of utter confusion at Izzy, wondering what the king meant by 'your dad' — if the reference was an inside joke or a figure of speech or what. Could it really be that the Falcon was Izzy's father? And if so, why had Izzy not told him? Izzy didn't look at Shel but instead locked eyes with the king, wondering why the king felt the need to divulge something Izzy considered to be private or unimportant, or both.

"Are we to conclude then," the king continued, "that you do not know where your own father is?"

Izzy walked around Shel — who didn't take his eyes off the elephant — and advanced toward the throne. "That is correct, my liege. I haven't spoken with my father since I left." At that point Izzy finally looked at Shel and they exchanged expressions of misunderstandings and apologies. Shel started to speak but Izzy shook his head, letting him know now was not the time. Then Izzy proceeded to address the king. "He did not approve of my leaving, as you may know. He felt that I was abandoning the circus family... abandoning him. But I... we... need his help. So, I have returned. I assume he's still in Kantytown? Still operating his... show."

The king was silent for a moment then spoke calmly. "Israel, it is not the place for anyone, not even a king, to presume the intimacies between a father and son." The king hesitated as if readying himself for something. "That said, any father — any parent, I wager — knows that children must one day spread their wings and fly. The Falcon knew there would come a day when he too would have to say goodbye, let you walk your own path, especially given your nature — that is, being from the wilds of the savannah. He may have raised you as his own, but he knew you never belonged to him. I suppose it's no different than any natural-born child never truly belonging to his or her parent." The king shot a wink at Shel, catching the kid by surprise. "Izzy, your father loved you. Any sentiment of betrayal that he may have expressed, I'm sure, came from a place of fear."

"Fear, sire?" questioned Izzy.

"Fear. Fear of losing his son. His *only* son." The king emphasized that Falconovich never had any children of his own. "Now, all of that said, it *is* my place as king to be forthright, especially when it comes to my friends." Izzy squinted, trying to see what was coming next. "Izzy, your father is not here." Izzy's head dropped, more from frustration over missing a key stepping stone in the mission than disappointment at missing his dad. "It is with great sorrow," the king added, eyes shifting slightly, expression drooping, "that I must inform you of your father's passing to the great beyond."

The visitors — Sandovar, Joy, the pirates... all but Izzy — gasped. Even Shel let out a, "What?" as he looked back at his friend.

Izzy, meanwhile, remained silent, glaring in disbelief at the king. "What do you mean, Your Highness? What are you saying exactly?"

The king shifted in his throne and awkwardly adjusted his robe as if he were sitting on nails. "I'm very sorry to be the bearer of bad news, my friend. I thought you would have known by now. Your father was laid to rest, here in the palace memorial field, but a few short months ago."

Izzy remained stoic, stiff as a statue, silent and cold as stone. True enough was that Izzy and his dad had a tumultuous relationship and that old Falconovich wasn't the most honorable of chaps — always treasure hunting, scheming on how to get rich. Still, it hurts to say goodbye, and Izzy was clearly stunned by the news. Being the empathetic and compassionate person she was, Joy rushed to console her friend. At her touch, he melted, stumbled slightly, then sat quickly so he wouldn't fall over.

The king continued, "I'm so sorry to give you this news, Izzy, and I offer my sympathies for your loss. I know that a group of your friends, friends from the circus, set out to find you as soon as it was clear his time was coming to an end. When you did not show up, I assumed they had found you but you decided, for your own reasons, not to return. But here you are now, and so the plot has shifted..." The king shifted in his throne and a hush fell over the hall.

Shel had been standing firm, mostly afraid of offending the king by moving or talking. He was also remaining still out of stubbornness, truth be told, unsure of how he felt about Izzy keeping secrets from him. Still, when he saw the devastation in his friend's face, he swallowed his pride and, risking retribution from the king, turned and gave Izzy a big hug. "I'm so sorry, Izzy," he said.

Izzy looked at Shel. Sadness muddled with regret welled in his eyes. "I'm sorry too," the elephant confessed as he pressed his head into Shel's chest. Shel, Izzy, and Joy shared a tender moment of empathy. Then Izzy looked at Longsmiles. "I… I don't understand... How?"

The king rose out of his throne, prompting his audience to also stand before he waved a hand allowing everyone to stay seated. He proceeded down the throne steps, across the palace floor to the elephant, reached up and placed his hand on the pachyderm. "I've known you nearly all your life, Israel. Please know that my heart is with you. If you need anything, the kingdom is at your disposal."

"But, I don't understand. What happened? How could he be gone?"

The king took a breath and spoke quietly, "It was simply his time. That is all."

Izzy knew that his father was growing old and had been in poor health for some time. Still, news of his passing was a heavy weight to shoulder, and so the elephant collapsed further to the floor. Shel, Joy, and now Sandovar too, encircled him with hugs. The king, Lady Alice, the pirates, and many of the Boogies joined the circle, hugging or placing consoling hands on the elephant. Izzy felt paralyzed with sorrow, but he also felt a tremendous outpouring of love at that moment.

Releasing the elephant, the king turned to accept something from one of his servants. "Izzy," the king spoke, "as you know, your dad loved baseball. Before he said goodbye, he asked me to give you these. He knew you would return one day and he wanted you to have his prized possessions from his life in Chicago." The king handed the elephant a wooden baseball bat and a worn-out leather glove with an old ball still in the pocket. Izzy took the gifts and noticed the bat had the initials 'J.J.' carved in it.

"Goodness!" cried Izzy, the crowd backing off to give him space. "This was Joe Jackson's bat!" Izzy wiped away his tears with his trunk. "My dad used to talk about how he and Joe were kid pals together. I never believed him though."

Shel just couldn't contain himself. "Izzy! Your dad was from Chicago?! Are you serious?!? Why...? Why didn't you...?! And he liked BASEBALL?!? And he knew SHOELESS JOE JACKSON?!?! WHY DIDN'T YOU SAY SO?!?!?!"

Caught between feeling betrayed, confused, and elated, Shel was absolutely beside himself in the presence of Joe Jackson's real-life baseball bat. He marveled at the artifact, mouth open to the floor. Izzy didn't have an explanation. He just smiled and handed Shel the bat. Shel was speechless, awestruck as he turned the stick over and over, reveling in the magic and history reverberating within its grain. He pressed it to his face, breathing in the sweet scents of aged pine and glory.

The king smiled and stepped back onto the throne stage. He turned to address the hall. "Ladies and gentlemen, please spread the good word far and wide that tonight we shall hold a grand feast and celebration in the great hall to commemorate the life of Romanov Tuskinsky Falconovich, and the return of his son, Izzy Baka-baka!" He then descended the steps to approach Shel and Marcus. He put one hand on each of Mark's shoulders and looked him square in the eyes. "Marcus, you have done your job, and well. Tonight, I invite you to dine at my table." He gave Mark a nod of camaraderie, which Mark returned. The king then turned to Shel. "Mr. Silvers." Shel looked up and, still holding the bat, wiped from his eyes the tears of sorrow he had shed for Izzy and the tears of joy at being in the tangential presence of one of America's greatest ball players. "It is clear that you are not the criminal we suspected you to be. I see no purpose in charging you with any crime, and I expect there will be no reason to do so in the foreseeable future. You are free to go."

Izzy perked his head up at the verdict and placed his trunk on Shel's shoulder. Shel turned and smiled at Izzy, and the two swapped congratulations and consolations. Joy repositioned herself to embrace both her friends, as did a few others from the caravan. It wasn't long before the group was feeling better and chatting more casually amongst each other.

"Arrr, matey," the pirate Taud put a hand on the elephant. "Stood like a stout hearty, ye did. Been true me whole life that there be no happy endings, on account uh there be no escapin' Davy Jones' Locker fer any o' us in the end! Best we can do is start 'er off with a roar o' the canons and make the most o' the voyage, through sun and squalls, wherever the current takes us. Ever'un knows the Falcon had a heck of a journey 'cause he had his son as his first mate. No pirate could ask fer more."

The other pirates agreed with a loud "Arrr!" and an up-raising of fists and swords.

Izzy smiled at Taud and the group and then called out, "Well, then, come on everyone, let us celebrate the Falcon — that greedy, old miser!"

And the hall broke out in cheer.

The remains of the day passed with people of Kantcomplainistan coming and going to visit and offer condolences to Izzy. Many people wanted to spend time with Sandovar and the pirates on account of their unrefined — that is, exciting — demeanor and endless stories of high adventure on the high seas, which made them wildly entertaining.

Joy and Shel, meanwhile, were able to escape for a private walk through the extensive palace gardens to talk and get to know one another better. After Shel's trial in the king's hall, the recount of his life in Chicago, and his misadventures in Arcania, Joy had endless questions. Eventually, their conversation settled on how the two of them met and Shel's original reason for making the voyage to the Land of Happy.

"We're going to need to talk with Izzy about confronting the king," advised Joy. "Longsmiles knows you're looking for the dentist, yet he didn't offer any help. I find that odd. Don't you?"

"I don't know, Joy" Shel replied. "It's not really his responsibility to—"

"And did you notice how he avoided talking about Ingonyama once he found out we're looking for him?" Joy interrupted. "Makes me wonder if he's hiding something."

Shel shrugged. "Maybe he was just trying to be sensitive about the news of Izzy's dad." Joy's eyes suggested she wasn't so sure. "But I agree, something seems off," Shel continued. "Maybe we can talk to the king tonight during dinner. I'm sure Izzy will want to discuss it also."

"Discuss what?" Izzy asked, shuffling up to the kids.

"Izzy!" said Joy.

"How are you holding up, buddy?" asked Shel casually, trying to maintain a light tone.

"I'm okay, guys. It's been amazing, really, being back here in Kanty. Honestly, I had mixed feelings about coming back. I mean, I had planned on seeing my dad, for sure. I'd prepared this big speech about living my own life and how he should be happy for me. I suppose I was so focused on confronting him that I didn't think about all my old friends. Turns out there are a lot of them still living here, people I used to run around with, many of whom used to be in the circus... The support has been nothing short of incredible. I only wish my dad could have been here, you know? I wish I could have said goodbye properly, let him know that I'm not mad and that I love him."

Joy looked at Izzy. "Oh, he knows. I'm certain of it."

Izzy smiled. "So, what were you guys talking about? I heard something about something... or something."

"Exactly!" said Shel facetiously, and they all chuckled.

"We were saying that we need to confront the king. I think he's hiding something about Ingonyama," reported Joy.

"And we definitely need to find Ingonyama so he can help us find Manny, right Izzy?" Shel wanted to make sure they absolutely needed to confront the king. He wasn't very keen on confrontation, especially if there were other options.

Izzy didn't reply directly, deciding instead to address a different issue. "You can ask me about my dad, Shel. It's ok. I'm sure you're wondering why I didn't tell you the Falcon was my father."

Shel looked at Izzy for a moment then looked away. "I know you have your reasons. You don't owe me any explanations, Iz."

Izzy reached out his trunk and spun his friend back to face him, hugging him gently. "Thank you, Shel. You're a good friend. Better than me, that's for sure."

"Oh, knock it off," Shel smiled. "What's up with you? You seem... I don't know. Is there something else you need to tell me?"

"Oh boy," Izzy sighed. "...I never finished telling you about what happened to Ingonyama and the king's men... in Africa." The three friends walked through the gardens and Izzy told Shel and Joy about the king's hunters who shot haphazardly into the bushes.

"Their intended target was Ingonyama. Well, actually they didn't know for certain who their target was because they couldn't see anyone. They were just shooting at whoever was shooting at them in the *name* of Ingonyama." Izzy sighed and his voice grew heavy. "Unfortunately, there happened to be a family of elephants in the distance beyond the bushes where Ingonyama was hiding."

"Then it *was* Ingonyama in the bushes," noted Shel.

Izzy nodded. "When the shooting stopped," he choked back tears, "two elephants lay mortally wounded on the ground." He couldn't go on. The memory was too painful. As Izzy turned away to cry for his fallen parents, Joy answered Shel's look of concern and confusion.

"Those guards made Izzy an orphan that day," whispered Joy, head hung low.

Shel stammered, "Wha...? Izzy, no!"

"It didn't take Ingonyama long to discover what had happened," Joy continued. "And when he did, he decided those guards were going to pay for what they did."

Izzy composed himself and picked up the story. "Eventually, when none of his men returned, Longsmiles discovered what had transpired. He was furious over the loss of his comrades, so he sent a small army to retrieve Ingonyama and bring him to justice. But, being the intelligent lion he was, Ingo knew the king would seek retribution. So, when the king's men arrived, Ingo was waiting for them with a rifle and a proposition. He agreed to lay down his weapon and surrender without a fight, *if* the king's men agreed to take responsibility for the orphaned elephant, whom Ingonyama had been caring for since the shootout, and who would surely die if left alone in the wild." Shel hugged Izzy, thinking of him as an orphaned baby. Izzy choked back more tears before continuing. "The king's men refused to take responsibility for the elephant... *ahem*, for me, so Ingo convinced them to bring me to the man known as the Falcon. Ingo knew that Falconovich would care for me and give me a home in his circus as he'd done for him. So, having been saved by Ingonyama, I was raised by Romanov Falconovich, in a house of circus tents."

"So that was how you came to Arcania," Shel asserted.

Izzy nodded. "That was many years ago. Unfortunately, Ingonyama disappeared shortly after they brought him back to the Land of Happy. No one knew what happened to him. For all anyone knew, the lion was executed for treason.

"What?!" exclaimed Shel. "You mean... we came all this way for nothing?! If Ingonyama is most likely dead...?"

"No! Shel," Izzy interjected, "I may have misspoken there. You see, it would be extremely out of character for the king to have executed Ingo. Skippy is not a violent man. Truth is, the king is dead set against killing anything... except for occasional sport hunting, I suppose. But even that he doesn't like. I think he just allows his men to do it out of tradition. Although, tradition, when you think about it—"

"Izzy! Focus!" scolded Joy.

"Right. Sorry. So, unless he died of natural causes or choked on a marshmallow or something, Ingonyama is likely still alive. I had assumed Falcono— um, my dad... before I knew he was... well, you know... I figured he would've struck a deal with Longsmiles and that Ingonyama would have been left in *his* care, which is why I came up with the plan to come here in the first place. But, with my dad no longer around, I now assume Longsmiles has Ingonyama locked up somewhere or possibly working for him in some slave-ish capacity."

"I knew it!" exclaimed Joy. "I knew he was hiding something."

Shel perked up. "So, all we have to do is explain to the king that we need Ingonyama for, what, maybe three, four days, and then when we find Manny he can have Ingo back. Right?"

"Oh, you're so cute, Shel," said Joy condescendingly. "It's as if someone opened up your head, took all of the bad stuff out, and just left all the good stuff. I love it!" Shel looked sideways at Joy, not sure what to make of that comment.

"Shel," said Izzy, "I know you like to see the best in people, and Longsmiles is a nice guy deep down. He's a good king, there's no doubt about any of that. But there's just no way he's going to simply let us walk out of here with his prisoner."

"Well, what if a few of the king's guards go with us and Ingonyama stays chained up the whole time?" Shel suggested.

Izzy shook his head. "It's too risky for the king. Once Ingonyama is back out in the world, escaping his bonds would be a cheap parlor trick for such a daft animal." Izzy looked down. "And I'll be honest: out there, away from the palace, I probably wouldn't be able to resist the urge to free the one who saved my life."

Feeling a tad frustrated, Shel blurted, "Well what do *you* suggest then?"

"I don't know. A jailbreak?" Izzy shrugged.

"Don't be absurd!" scoffed Joy. "That would just land us *all* in prison… or worse."

"Guys! I'll talk to Longsmiles tonight during dinner. I think I can reason with him," Shel offered optimistically.

Izzy was taken aback. "You? Reason with the king? Really?" Shel scowled. "Okay, okay. Take it easy," Izzy reeled. "But I get to say I told you so when he tells you to take a hike!"

Chapter Ten

The Sandwich of Doom

"Are you cacahuates!" yelled the king. "Get this clown out of my sight!" At once the young man was whisked away by Alice and her team of enforcers, and not all too gently.

A wave of the king's royal hand and the celebration resumed, with live music from Happy minstrels that delighted, festoon lanterns that mood lighted, mouth-watering dishes that excited, and guests from all walks of life who united.

Sandovar provided a troupe of belly dancers who, in their exotic accoutrements, hypnotized partygoers as they weaved their way in and out of the maze of tables placed seemingly randomly throughout the great hall — a wonderfully chaotic design. A giant bonfire raged in the center of the floor, providing an ambiance of red-orange mystery and magic as it sent shapes and shadows leaping around the room like mischievous children.

The king's mead — and grape juice for the young'uns — flowed from fountains embedded in the walls, while sweet chocolate fondue rolled down miniature granite aqueducts fastened to concrete pillars.

"It's like rainwater dripping down vines wrapping around trees in the forest," commented Shel.

There were people and creatures of every shape, size, and color coming and going, talking, laughing, dancing, eating. Some looked like typical animals one might find in a zoo or a jungle or savannah; while others resembled mythical characters like the Pegasus, centaur, and sphinx. One even looked suspiciously like a small Worst beast! (Thankfully, it did not smell like one.)

At the head of the great hall, opposite the massive entryway, stood a thick wooden table about eight feet in width and whose length stretched nearly from the east wall to the west. At this kingly table sat Longsmiles in the center, with his closest comrades flanking him on either side. As promised, Mark the pleaseman was seated at the same table as the king, but at the very end with the crudes and the nudes. Indeed, there at the butt of the table sat the king's second cousin, Davison, who always wore a nice coat and tie but never could remember to put on pants. Next to Davison sat the king's roommate from college, Argus, who, after a stretch of living in a nudist commune, had grown his beard down to his toes so that he could wrap it around him like a robe and not have to bother putting on clothes at all. Next to the human beard sat Joshua, the king's tailor, who wore in place of clothes, a head-to-toe tattoo of a fancy suit such that it looked as if he were dressed when in reality he was naked as the day he was born. Next at the table came Marcus and his pirate henchmen, Morgan and Captain Jim. Next to Jim sat Tauder the Marauder, and next to Taud sat Sandovar the Sandman of Sandeen. Sandovar's assistants, Sarah Karynthia and Sylvia Kats chose not to sit but instead stood in silence behind their chief. Next to Sandovar sat the massive elephant, Israel Tuskinsky, who took up the remaining four seats on the east wing of the table.

"Apologies for that outburst," spoke the king. "It's just so difficult to find quality jesters these days. I fear this one never even graduated funny school." His guests laughed (obediently). "Mr. Silvers," the king addressed his newest guest, who sat directly to his right, beginning the western faction of the royal plank. "Are you enjoying the festivities?"

"Oh yes, indeed. Thank you!" Shel replied with a cautious grin. He wanted to relax and enjoy the wonderful soiree but was finding it difficult to ignore the anxiety brought on by his hidden agenda. The king, being remarkably astute, sensed it too.

"Something on your mind, my friend?" the king probed, tossing grapes into the air and casually catching them in his mouth.

"Um, plenty, sire," replied the kid.

The king raised his eyebrows, showing interest and inviting Shel to share.

"It's just that I had no idea Izzy was Falconovich's son, and that Falconovich was gone."

The king nodded. More grapes went flying.

"Meeting Sandovar and the pirates has been quite an adventure, too," Shel added. "Everything I've seen and done since leaving Chicago... It's all a bit... overwhelming."

"I can imagine," replied Longsmiles, moving on to saucy chicken wings, loudly sucking his fingers in compliment to his chef, the cook witch.

Shel tried to ignore the distasteful gesture. "And... I would like to thank you for sparing me, Your Excellency. I thought perhaps Mark would like to see me hanging from a noose or nailed to a cross."

"Nonsense!" the king laughed. "Marcus Gladface is not a malicious man. He is a man of law and believes in the rule of the crown, even if he disagrees with my verdict. Not to worry, you'll have no more trouble from the please force, I promise you that. Even if he did wish you harm, which I am certain he does not, that is not the way of our kingdom.

We prefer to have hug o' wars than tug o' wars, if you know what I mean. That way, everyone wins."

"But you do take prisoners, isn't that right?" Shel asked boldly as he stumbled into the tender subject of Ingonyama.

The king squinted at the kid, sorting out his intention. "Of course we do. But we always give our prisoners the opportunity for redemption. Why, pray tell, do you ask such a question?"

That's it! That proves it. Right? Shel thought, almost out loud to Joy, sitting to his right. *Ingonyama must still be alive.* As if reading his mind, Joy nudged him, urging him to broach the subject.

As if he, too, could feel the tension in the air, Izzy leaned around the king to look at Shel, eyes querying, "Are you sure you want to do this?"

Shel mustered his reservoir of courage and cleared his throat, "Ahem." But as he opened his mouth to speak—

"No," the king said plainly, looking straight ahead out at the party, not at all acknowledging Shel, eating his dinner as if no one else were around.

There was a moment of silence as Shel, Joy, and Izzy tried to figure out to whom the king was talking. They looked at one another, confused.

"Um," said Shel timidly. "What was that, Your Highness?"

"The answer is no. You may not have him." Longsmiles continued to avoid eye contact.

It seemed Marcus was catching a drift of the conversation, too, when the pleaseman looked toward them with concern.

Izzy decided to jump in, seeing as how the negotiations appeared to be ending before they even began. "Your Majesty—"

"As you might know, Israel—" the king interceded, "…or perhaps you don't — it matters not — Ingonyama is my prisoner for high crimes against the crown." Longsmiles was not smiling, long or short. He slowly turned and stared at Izzy, then turned to face Shel. "I'm sorry, young man. That lion, though once as refined as a London scholar, turned savage and killed many good men of mine; indeed, some of my very best; close friends…" he paused to catch his breath, "…including my own brother!" The king cleared his throat, trying to rein in his emotions. "And so, *ahem*, he is not free to join you on your quest, I'm afraid. You'll have to find your friend without the lion. But seeing as how you've gotten this far without him, I've no doubt you'll continue to fair just fine on your own.

Not that you're on your own, of course. You have each other, Izzy and Joy and... the others, whomever else you have recruited."

Shel looked down at his plate and then over to Joy.

The king continued, "I realize you have traveled a long way and have endured a storm of tribulations to get here. But there's just no way I can let such a dangerous animal wander free. I hope you can understand."

Shel wasn't sure that he *did* understand. "But... wasn't he defending unarmed animals?"

The king glared at the boy, no longer displaying any trace of kindness but instead looking slightly unhinged.

Despite the warning signs, Shel persisted, undeterred. "Didn't your men kill Izzy's parents?"

"That was an accident!" howled the king, forgetting that Izzy was just on his other shoulder. He caught himself and quickly turned to face the pachyderm. "I... I'm sorry Izzy," he said in a calmer tone. "That was insensitive of me."

Izzy did not respond. He just stared at the king with burning eyes. Whether one is a straggler or a sultan, it's just not a smart move to antagonize a full-grown bull elephant. The king looked away in shame... and possibly fear.

"Sheldon," the king eked out, "you have been hardened by challenges in both Champion Valley and the Land of Happy, and I'm sure you've had your share of obstacles to overcome back in Chicago. I have every confidence that you will persevere, together with your capable friends. Why, you have a veritable army at your side. It would take a formidable obstacle indeed to resist such a regiment. You do not need my lion... and you shall not have him."

Joy decided that she might have some success where the two others did not. "Sire," she started.

"My decision is final!" the king bellowed, standing and slamming his fist on the table, toppling his cup of mead and making dishes jump.

The celebration halted like a candle suddenly blown out. The party guests turned to face the drama, waiting to see what was coming next. Alice, Marcus, and the king's guard stood up, throwing their food aside and assuming defensive poses. The three pirates placed hands on swords in preparation for a brawl, though not entirely clear which side they would be fighting for.

"Argh! Enough of this!" commanded the king. "Alice! Escort these three to their rooms. Their motives have been laid bare. They are no longer welcome in my home."

Longsmiles did not bother to look at any of them as Shel, Izzy, and Joy were ushered out of the great hall by the king's guards. As they departed, the king glanced at Sandovar and Sandovar glanced back, careful not to appear aggressive. He motioned for the pirates to stand down and keep their scabbards sheathed, and so they did. And as they did, Sandovar spoke carefully, "My king, your judgment is fair. Perhaps you might find the mercy to allow them to stay the night. At first light I will personally escort them out of Kantytown and see to it they are on their way."

The king silently considered the chief's proposal. Longsmiles knew that Sandovar was a man of his word and the king could sense that the chief was being sincere.

"Marcus!"

"My liege?"

"Tell Alice that the elephant and his companions may pass the night in the stables. Sandovar shall make certain they depart first thing in the morning."

"Yes, my liege," replied the pleaseman and he turned to follow Alice and the guards.

The king then commanded, in his most kingly, commanding voice, to the hall and everyone in the hall, "ON WITH THE PARTY!" And so the party went on. Then, the king turned to a nearby servant. "Boy, what is your name?"

"Kish, sire," the boy — who was actually a boyish-looking girl — replied in a shaky voice that cracked rhythmically as if rehearsed.

"Rhymes with fish, eh? Clever. I like it. And what is your family name, Master Kish?"

"I come from the family of Khet, Your Majesty."

"Yes, of course! The Khets! I know the family well! Top breeders of Guernseys, if I'm not mistaken."

"Um... no, 'fraid not, sire. The Khets have never raised cattle. Not that I am aware of."

"No?" Skippy challenged.

"No."

"No! Of course not! I was merely testing you! Everyone knows the Khets are winemakers! The finest cabernet in Kantytown!"

"Uh, I do apologize again, my liege. We don't do wine either. Not a grape within three leagues of our farm in any direction."

"Well, what is it you *do* do, Mr. Khet?!?" the king snapped. Kish opened her mouth to reply — or at least correct the 'mister' designation — which may have been the last thing she did. But, to her good fortune, she was shushed by a kingly hand. "Don't tell me! I've decided I don't care. Instead, why don't you tell me what it is you most desire in all the world? Eh, Khet?"

"Oh, goodness, that's easy! A television set, sire. I've always wanted a T.V.! Life on the farm can be so—"

"A T.V. set! Splendid! A television set for Mr. Khet it shall be… *IF*… you can do this one simple thing for me. Go to the royal kitchens and inform Katryna the cook witch that she is to open the—" he paused, "now this part is very important," the king slowed his speech, "...the 1922 Peter Pan, and make me the most stickiest peanut butter sandwich ever concocted."

"Katryna. Got it!" The girl immediately turned to leave but was halted by further kingly instructions.

"She also goes by Katya. ...The *stickiest* you hear! ...And I want it FIVE MINUTES AGO!"

Miss Khet started off again but again stopped dead, nearly shaking with fear when she heard the king riddle eerily, "Do this for me... do it right, and a new T.V. set you shall have tonight. NOW GO!"

Kish ran straight to the kitchen to fetch the witch named Katya. When she found her, she presented herself tall and announced loudly, "By order of the king, you are to make me a sandwich!"

Katya smiled mischievously and — *POOF!* — suddenly the girl was turned into a giant sandwich with legs!

"Aaargh!" she screamed. "Help!"

"Oh, calm down," said the witch. "I was just having a bit of fun. What is your name?"

The wide-eyed sandwich, scared out of her wits, with trembling voice (more so than usual) and choking on a slop of tomatoes and mayonnaise, spat out the words, "Khet, my name is Kish Khet."

"Ah! Kish Khet. I see. Well, this will not do! Sandwiches are not named Kish, nor Khet. Reggie, Paul, Mimo, even Fidel perhaps, but not Kish, and definitely not Khet."

Little Miss Khet felt relieved, sensing that she was about to be a girl again.

"Those names are strictly reserved for... hamburgers! *ZAP!* The witch turned Kish from a sandwich into a hamburger.

"Aaargh!" she screamed again. "Nooo!"

Katya doubled over in laughter. "Now, *that* is funny!"

"Turn me back! I was sent by the king, you hag! I'm on a king's errand! There's no time to waste. Stop messing about!"

"Okay, okay. Don't get your pickles in a pinch." She waved her hand and — *POOF!* — Kish was a girl again, albeit a soggy one, with remnants of relish and mayo dripping from her head and clothes.

"Oh, thank goodness!" she sighed, patting her human self all over.

"Now, what, pray tell, is it that you want... or that the king wants? What is so grievously urgent, eh Khet?" Katya busied herself with a task at the stove.

Kish caught her breath and made sure all her body parts were in the right places then scowled at the witch and recounted slowly, "The king wishes you to open the 1922 Peter Pan and make him your stickiest peanut butter sandwich you ever made."

Katya stared at the prawns searing in her wok, threatening to burn. She was a master chef by any measure, able to make a delicious dish out of any combination of ingredients: Self-chewing gum-bo; floppy, sloppy, drippy, droopy, lumpy, bumpy goo; boilin' vat of spoiled brat-wurst... You name it. But when she heard this request for the aged Peter Pan peanut butter, she froze.

"Young lady," she hissed like the seafood in her saucepan, "the 1922 varietal is a relic, a collector's item, a showpiece." She slowly turned each prawn one by one as she spoke. "It was never meant to be eaten! If I feed that to the king he will most certainly keel over and croak, dead as a dinosaur. Get it? I won't do it! I refuse."

Now, being monumentally desperate for a T.V. set, Kish Khet was not about to take no for an answer. She told Katya that the king promised to remove Kish's head if she did not return with that specific peanut butter sandwich. This, of course, was a lie, but Katya didn't know that. Kish pleaded and prayed and held her breath until she was blue in the face, but Katya flat-out refused.

"Fine. You win. But I can't believe you're going to pass up this opportunity," scoffed Kish.

"What do you mean?" asked Katya, annoyed that the girl was still there, considering turning her into a taco.

"Why, the challenge of course..." Kish casually reached into the hot wok, snatched one of the sizzling prawns, and tossed it in her mouth, trying to act cool, ignoring the searing pain. "*Cough*, to demonstrate your, *cough*, unmatched, *cough,* talent." Kish Khet had firmly put her best salesman hat on. "If this peanut butter is as dangerous as you say — *cough, cough* — then there's no one in the world who could prepare it, no one who could serve it as a proper meal, no one but Katya the witch."

Katya raised a skeptical brow.

"Riiiiight?" encouraged Kish Khet.

The witch circled around the girl and they stared at one another from a new angle while the master chef considered the pitch that had just been tossed at her. Then, without breaking eye contact, in one swift motion, Katya yanked the wok from the stove, dashed the prawns onto a serving plate — "Order up!" — and retrieved a set of keys from around her waist. Kish followed the witch into an enormous walk-in refrigerator, at the back of which, on a small shelf covered in thick dust, sat a little black box. She inserted a key and turned the latch. With a high-pitched squeak, the door opened to reveal a medium-sized tin jar filled with a dark brown substance.

For the next several long minutes, Kish Khet watched in awe as Katya set about creating the impossible sandwich, first using a table-mounted, industrial rolling pin to squeeze the substance from the jar, like asphalt under a steamroller. Then, with the spry vigor of a collegiate athlete — which she most certainly was not — the witch hopped onto the chopping block and began beating the blob into submission with a ten-pound sledgehammer. An assortment of incantations and charms seemed to help soften the slop a smidge, give it some signs of life — at one point the peanut butter stood up and danced what Kish decided must be an Irish jig. Finally, Katya set upon the goop with a relay of instruments, including a handheld grinding wheel, a motorized percussion drill, and a blow torch, apparently curing the concoction into something resembling... stiff mud.

As soon as her masterpiece was complete — as complete as it was ever going to get — Katya ran and hid in the horse stables while Kish Khet brought the sandwich hastily to the king. She arrived, out of breath and eager for her prize. Bowing extra, extra low, Kish averted her gaze and raised the silver platter upon which the sandwich sat, voice cracking, "Your Majesty!"

Without waiting for his poison-tester, the king snatched the sandwich and sunk his teeth in deep. Immediately, the king began humming a chorus of "*Mmmm! Mmmm hmmm! Grmm nmm luuurrrrrrr mmmmm!*" A melody of profound satisfaction. It was indeed the 1922 vintage he had so desired, and it was indeed made to Katya's impeccable standards. Of that the king had no doubt. But the king could not get out any actual words such as, "So good," and, "So delicious," and, "Thank you, Kish Khet," and, "Good job, Kish Khet," and most importantly, "Here's your T.V. set, Kish Khet." For soon, the king couldn't open his mouth at all. The stickiness of the infamous butter had stuck, exactly as Katya had predicted. The king's jaws were no match for the vintage butter. Once the magnificent flavor had subsided, Skippy's face twisted into an expression of concern which quickly turned to worry and then to horrified dread.

Kish Khet started to worry too (somewhat about the king but more so about her reward). She told the king to, "hang tight," and, turning on her heels, ran fast as fire to fetch Katya.

The chef-witch appeared at once, as if by magic — though slower those days given her... antiqueness. But what she lacked in sprightliness she made up for in authority. The witch sprang into action, immediately calling for the entire kitchen staff — along with the royal guards and the entire medical ward — to join her at the king's side, post haste. She knew what she was up against, knew that this was a matter of life and death, make no mistake. The witch had told Kish Khet that this was a bad idea. She just *knew* that this was going to happen!

She had warned Khet, "One does not simply open a can of 1922 Peter Pan peanut butter and start chowing down. If one is going to crack open such a vintage, it first needs to be given ample time to breathe — given time for the bouquet to blossom. Following that, it should be shaken vigorously and then allowed to settle. Donning the proper protective gear, one then tempers it in a special forge. Once cooled, it is turned and churned and massaged and kneaded, encouraging the butter to rise and fall like the Roman Empire. Finally, the chunky bits need to be scolded like misbehaving children before being thoroughly squashed (also like children). The whole blobby mess gets whipped into a velvety splish before the final curing stage which culminates by tossing the entire contents in the rubbish bin! Perhaps on occasion one could toss the mess onto a compost pile instead of the garbage or recycle it into a doormat, but under no circumstances should it ever, *ever* be eaten. EVER!"

Chapter Eleven

Polish the Stars

As a regiment of royal guards whisked the king away on a stretcher of fine Arabian linen, Alice ordered the medical staff to fetch the royal dentist and prepare the king for emergency surgery.

"But milady! There *is* no royal dentist! There are no dentists of any kind in the Land of Happy, remember? By order of the king himself!" one of the staff reminded.

"Riiight. Of course!" replied Alice. "Why do I keep forgetting that? Well... what do you think, Katryna?"

Katya stepped forward. "I expect we'll need to find a good oral surgeon if we hope to get the king's mouth open again."

"Can't you use magic? You are a witch, aren't you?" asked someone in the crowd, and the crowd replied, "Yeah!"

Katya spun around. "Unfortunately, no. ...I mean, yes, I am a witch, obviously, but I can't use magic on the king in the state he's in now."

"Why not?!" someone challenged.

"Becaaauuuuse..." Katya growled back, her wand finger twitching, eager to turn someone into a hamburger, "I used a spell to prepare the peanut butter sandwich in the first place, an incantation designed to make that cursed Peter Pan peanut butter even remotely palatable. The spell, like the butter, is designed to stick!" The people groaned in disapproval. "Believe it or not, if I hadn't used the spell, and if the spell hadn't stuck, the king would be in much worse shape, likely already dead! I told them! I said, 'This butter is not meant to be eaten!' But they wouldn't listen!" The reproachful groaning grew louder. "Oh, polliwogs! Would any of *you* have dared defy the king in his hour of vexation? I don't think so! You all know how volatile he can be!"

Mumbles of general agreement intermixed with grumbles of disagreement, putting the issue to rest at a firm stalemate.

"Right then. What's done is done." Alice asserted leadership. "Does anyone here know where we can find an oral surgeon?"

"What about Dentist Dan?" someone spoke up.

"You mean 'Nentis Nan' from Wallenpine?" someone replied.

"Isn't he still yanking on that poor kid's tooth, stretching the string from Baltimore to Maine while on a pogo stick or roller skates or some such nonsense?" asked Katya. "No! Certainly not that looney! We need a *real* dentist."

Meanwhile, to avoid public panic, the king's advisors, including the reclusive Archduke of Feelingroovyberg, got to work ensuring that the party guests continued to be entertained with lively music, tasty beverages, the telling of terrible jokes by the very unfunny jester, who, taking his job extra seriously, began immediately attempting to juggle five, now six, now seven raw eggs… *splat!… kerplop!… kaplish!* Oops. Never mind the juggling. At least there was still the music, mead, and meals. Except that, unfortunately, where Katya was literally magic in the kitchen, her replacement while she tended to the king, was none other than Wanda, the 'weird' and 'forgetful' witch.

o o o o o o

Once upon a time, Wanda used to be a real witching witch. But, as age piled on her years and moss grew 'round her ears, she became a bit of a crackpot. (If you see an old lady flying around on a vacuum instead of a broom, yeah, that's Wanda.) Although she studied under Katya almost constantly, Wanda couldn't remember what she'd learned from one day to the next, and would, consequently, do all sorts of inappropriate things with ingredients such as the time when Katya told Wanda to use more carrots because they were good for the eyes. Katya turned around to see Wanda with two large carrots sticking out of her eyes, complaining that she couldn't see how the carrots were helping her eyesight in the least because she couldn't see anything at all!

Now, the preferred food for a good majority of people in the Land of Happy was of the Italian variety, on account of the wonderful flavors of course, but also the pronunciations made people smile endlessly.

> *Cannelloni, rigatoni;*
> *Scaloppini, tortellini;*
> *Carbonara, puttanesca;*
> *Arrabbiata, fettuccine.*

(See? Isn't that fun?)

Katya tried to teach Wanda the magic of these incredible dishes, but it was no use. So, following Katya's advice, Wanda stuck to mastering just one simple dish: spaghetti. But even spaghetti with meatballs was beyond the old witch's capability. The best Katya could hope for from Wanda was overcooked noodles with a sauce that could maybe pass as marinara if one hadn't eaten in three weeks and was on the verge of consuming their own shoes.

At that description, one would be justified in asking: If Wanda was so inept in the kitchen, why did Katya keep her around? Good question. Well, first of all, the two witches were cousins, so Katya felt obligated to look after Wanda. But also, Katya had looked into her crystal ball and saw that Wanda was destined to contribute something important in the saga of the Land of Happy. What, exactly, remained clouded. Still, Katya believed her bonkers-of-a-cousin would prove invaluable one day. Perhaps this day was *the* day.

o o o o o o

With Katya busy assisting the king, the task of feeding the hundreds of still-celebrating guests fell to Katya's sous chef. Thus, Wanda got busy making the one dish she knew. Toiling (as witches do) over how to make enough spaghetti for so many people, Wanda had her staff recruit some peasant bystanders. Together, the rag-tag team of cooks built a great bonfire smack in the middle of the royal kitchen. On top of the fire they placed an enormous cauldron — a relic from the days of the giants. Into her cauldron the witch poured all the pasta she could find in and around the castle, along with a pinch of a multiplying potion she thought — she prayed — might help with the taste while boosting the quantity of the food. As anyone could have — and should have — predicted, the flavor of Wanda's cooking was beyond help. The potion, however, charmed the noodles in a way that no one, especially Wanda, could have foreseen.

The witch quickly realized she'd grossly underestimated the potion's potency as the cauldron began spewing heaps of noodles into the air and all over the floor like a bubbling, burping, blasting volcano. It didn't take long for the kitchen to fill with a flood of pasta, an endless wellspring of starchy rope, forcing the kitchen staff to abandon their pots, pans, spatulas, and spoons, and run for their lives!

"Quick! Pour on the marinara!" instructed Wanda to her kitchen staff, as if adding goopy red sauce would improve the situation. Still, the staff did as they were told. And so it came to pass that a red mountain of spaghetti pushed its way out of the kitchen and into the great hall. Over the royal carpet flowed the Mediterranean mess like a tsunami of snakes, gobbling up tables and chairs and anyone too slow to get out of the way. As more and more guests became entangled, a handful of the rowdier partygoers decided this was their cue to do what any rowdy partygoer would do in such a predicament: they began tossing the spaghetti at one another like confetti.

"FOOD FIGHT!" someone yelled, and finally the *real* party commenced!

o o o o o o

The next morning, the sun seemed to rise slower than usual, as if the man — or woman — upstairs knew that day was going to be difficult, and they were not the least bit anxious to get on with it. As promised, Sandovar and his Boogies arrived at the palace stables at dawn to collect the elephant, the boy, and the mermaid, and escort them out of town. The three were already set to go, eager to get back to the mission of finding Manny, especially after this fruitless and frustrating detour in Kantytown.

They had enjoyed a wonderful night's sleep, given that the palace stables were nicer than most of the inns in the village, certainly nicer than a tent in the desert or a raft in the sea, a cave in the forest or an old apple tree; definitely nicer than a blackberry briar or stinky laundry pile, nicer by ten city blocks or a dusty country mile. At some point during the night, Joy's unfailing optimism convinced Shel and Izzy that they didn't need Ingonyama, or anyone else for that matter. They had each other and that was enough. Somehow they'd find a way. As nice as that sentiment was — and it did help boost their morale — deep down they all knew the truth: there was little hope the three of them would be able to find Manny on their own. And if they did find him, and he happened to be deep in the company of the Gambrine, as they suspected, they were certainly not going to be able to win a fight if the Gambrine chose to fight. And fight they most certainly would, for there was but a flying hog's hope that the Gambrine would give up the dentist for naught but three pretty smiles and a year's supply of goodwill. Sure, they had Izzy, and Izzy was big and could do a lot of damage. But Izzy was (and still is) a lover, not so much a fighter. Besides, one must always keep in mind the old saying, 'There's only so much one can do against ten thousand crocodiles!' And that was precisely why the three were extremely relieved to hear that Sandovar, Taud, and the rest of the Boogies — which now included Captain Jim and his first mate, Morgan — would be joining Shel and the gang on their Manny-finding quest.

"Once we witnessed the dishonorable behavior of the king," Sandovar confessed, "we knew which side we'd be fighting for, should the milk turn sour… and, alas, it has."

"Praise Poseidon!" rattled Captain Jim. "I be gettin' right rusted as an ol' tin boot, I am, waitin' on some action, I be!"

"Since when y'ever seen a pair o' boots what be made uh tin, ya blubber-blabbin' blowhard?" challenged Morgan. "Stow yer billowed sails, cappy. We'll be at war soon enough, we be."

Izzy laughed at Morgan and Jim, then turned back to Sandovar. "So that's why you offered to escort us?"

Sando nodded. "Because my caravan would be leaving at first light too, yes. Our business here in Kantytown is done, and for a long time I'd venture to say, if this is the way the king runs his castle now."

Izzy nodded. "I must say I expected much more from Solomon, being famous for cheering up an entire country."

The crowd mumbled in agreement as they loaded belongings onto camels. Then Sandovar added, "But, it seems Skippy got his just desserts after all."

"What do you mean by that?" asked Joy.

"Well, apparently after you all were escorted out of the party, the king was so upset that he demanded an extra-extra-sticky peanut butter sandwich, one for the history books," Sandovar explained. "He took one bite and his mouth instantly became glued shut."

"Glued shut? You mean he can't open his mouth?!" asked Shel in alarm.

"That's precisely what I mean by glued shut, Shelby," retorted the Sandman. "Even his witch-chef, the one who made the sandwich, can't get it open with her magic. But that's not surprising. Ol' Katya and Wanda are more potion-brewing witches than spell-casters — except for turning people into food items. They're surprisingly adept at that particular talent; God knows why. But I wager that ol' parlor trick won't do the king much good with this problem. Unfortunately, they can't get any potions down Longsmiles' throat at the moment. They tried pouring something up his nose but that only made him spout a geyser of buggers

like a snotty Old Faithful. So, there you have it. The long and *snort* of it."
The group couldn't help but let loose a slight chuckle.

"It's not funny, you guys!" reprimanded Joy.

"No! It's not," replied Izzy, trying to contain himself. "You see, Shel? Cacahuates! Peanuts are deceptively dangerous! They're the bane of all existence!"

Sandovar laughed loudly. "The bane of... Ha! I don't know about the bane of all existence... But yeah, they're certainly the bane of Longsmiles' existence. Especially now."

"Why don't they just take him to the dentist?" Shel asked.

"They can't! There *aren't* any dentists in the Land of Happy, kid," replied the chief as if Shel ought to know.

"No dentists? That's absurd. For real though?" Asked Shel.

Joy nodded.

"But... why not?"

"Well, it wouldn't be the Land of Happy if there were, now would it?" snarked Sando. "But listen, we'd better get moving, guys. The king blames you three for what happened. So you're not exactly at the top of his favorites list at the moment. And considering what he's done to Ingonyama — who never did anything to him personally — there's no telling what he might do to you!"

"Blames us!" was the general cry from Izzy, Shel, and Joy at various intervals, in various forms.

Sandovar affirmed the king's judgment and the caravan shoved off down the road leading out of Kantcomplainistan (where there was now much to complain about).

The gang did not get far, however, for as soon as they reached the border of the village, where the lush green grass of the farmlands turned back into desert, a great and terrible bird appeared in the sky high above them. As the bird approached, it became clear that the caravan was the intended target of some impending attack, likely sent by Longsmiles (whose long smiles had now been replaced by very short frowns).

Thinking like a true commander, Sandovar gave the order to assume defensive positions and the caravan shuffled about quickly, gathering slingshots and whatnots while Izzy grabbed Shel and Joy and headed for safety.

The pirates excitedly drew their swords, with Captain Jim yelling, "Finally, some action on the high seas!"

"This ain't the high seas, ya daft ol' windbag," chided Morgan. "This be the low desert. Couldn't be farther from the high seas, ya slimy squid!"

Although the pirates doled out insults like candy on Halloween, they truly cared for one another something fierce, and Morgan wasn't about to let some giant bird eat his beloved captain. Not today anyway. Tomorrow maybe, but not today.

Suddenly, Sandovar cried out, sounding like a pirate himself, "Ho! That ain't no bird! Stand fast, my hearties!"

The caravan squinted at the light blue sky, still in dawn, as the bird-that-was-not-a-bird swooped down and landed ever so ungracefully, nearly right on top of Sandovar and the pirates.

Shel looked up from where he was being smothered by Izzy for his own protection. "Hey! I know that shoe!" he yelled. Startled, Izzy released his hold on the boy and Shel jumped up and ran over to the bird-thing that had now landed.

"Fickleface! Picklepots! Tickletoes!"

"Shelby!" called the three in unison.

"We heard yous was in a bit of a pickle, and pickles are Pickles's specialty. *Ha!*" laughed Fickles.

"Oh, boy, am I glad to see you guys!" Shel exclaimed as he gave them all a round of hugs. "Did you find Manny?!" he asked, bursting with excitement. "Is that why you're here?"

Immediately Shel noticed the excitement in Fickleface's face drop several octaves. "C'mere, son," the captain said as he put an arm around the boy. "Listen, there's somethin' I gotta tell ya, and it ain't gonna be easy to hear."

"You didn't find him, did you?" Shel lamented. Then, he looked up to see the expression on the shoe captain's face. "Oh, no!" Shel gasped, "You *did* find him… you found his fossils!"

Fickles glanced over at his mates with a smirk and a shrug and then looked back at Shel. "Um, no, we did not find his… fossils."

"Do you know how fossils are formed, Shel?" asked Sandovar with a healthy belly chuckle. Shel shrugged. "It takes thousands if not millions of years." Sando giggled.

"Okay, whatever," dismissed Shel. "Then, what? Is he alive? Is he dead? What?"

"Is he somewhere in between?" interjected Izzy. "Has he been ghostafied? Tell us!"

Fickles looked sideways at Izzy with a mixture of disbelief and surprise. "You two feelin' okay? Because it sounds like you've been drinkin' out of the camel's water trough and contracted a case of bacteria brain." Joy, Sandovar, and the rest of the Boogies laughed and waited uneasily for an answer from the shoe captain. Finally, Fickles gave Shel and everyone the news. "We indeed found Manny... and he's alive!"

The crowd broke out in a celebration of shouts and hollers, whistles and woo-hoos that could likely be heard all the way back at the castle. Everyone was smiling and yelling and exchanging high-fives and hugs.

Noticing that the shoe crew was not participating in the celebration, Izzy prodded, "Wait, what aren't you telling us?"

"Hi Izzy," said Fickleface. "How are you?"

"Cut the small talk, beardo," snapped the elephant. "I don't trust you any farther than—."

"You can throw me, yes, yes, I know. I've heard the spiel before," replied the captain.

"We *all* have!" chimed Sandovar, and everyone laughed; everyone except Izzy.

"Look," continued Captain Fickles, "Manny's alive. That's the good news."

"And the bad?" pressed the elephant with his signature wide-eyed stare.

"The bad news," Fickles looked back at his crew then back to Izzy and the caravan, "...is that he's been captured by the Gambrine." The crowd gasped and mumbled. "He's being held in Gambrinsluk Prison." Another collective gasp. "Literally every brocosmile in the Valley is within a two-mile radius at any given time. We're talking, I dunno, thousands, maybe tens of thousands of 'em. There's just no way we can break him out."

"Then he's as good as gone already," lamented Izzy. The crowd fell silent as people began mourning for Manny, still alive but likely not for long.

"Were you able to discover the nature of their plans for him?" asked Sandovar, playing the role of the concerned, albeit optimistic, leader. "It's commonly known that the Gambrine aren't evil or malicious creatures. Foul-tempered when it comes to their broccoli, sure. But they wouldn't torture him or anything, right?"

"No, not exactly," replied Fickles. "They take him out into the fields with the mornin' farmin' patrol, 'bout near every day at dawn, and work him from sunup to sundown, weedin' and prunin' and harvestin' broccoli. I'm afraid, at his age, Manny won't likely last the month."

"That's right!" exclaimed Joy as if realizing something important. Everyone looked at her. "The Gambrine are hyperactive farmers. They don't keep prisoners locked up in cages. They put them to work!"

"And if they can't work?" asked Shel.

"I don't know," admitted Joy.

"They dispose of 'em," answered Taudello.

"Arrr. Make 'em walk the plank, they do," agreed Morgan.

"Yes, yes. Maybe," interjected Joy, trying to get back at a point. "But Fickles, how confident are you that they take Manny out of the prison daily?"

"Fairly," answered Fickleface. "Why?"

"Well... how long did you observe them?" she pressed.

"Several days. Why??"

"Okay. So, walk us through everything you saw. Tell us every detail," said Izzy as he crept closer to the captain, catching on to what Joy was getting at. If they knew the Gambrine's routine, they could plan a rescue when Manny was out in the fields, increasing the odds of a successful escape.

"Well, in truth, we really didn't see too much. Once we found him an' saw he was alive, we decided we'd better go get help right quick. So we came looking for y'all," admitted Fickles.

"Yeah, but then we decided to stop along the way and polish the stars," interjected Tickletoes.

"Zip it, Tick!" scolded Fickles.

"No, you didn't!" gasped Joy in disbelief and disapproval.

"Wait. What?" said Shel. "Polish the stars? What does that mean? Is that some kind of code for when you're wasting time doing something ridiculous when you should've been out saving your friend?"

"Good guess!" said Tickles.

"Sounds about right!" blasted Izzy, leaning toward Fickles ominously.

"Close. But, no," said Joy. "It's not a euphemism. They're being literal. Because of their unique flying machine, Fickle and his crew have been put in charge of polishing the stars when the space nuggets become dull and tarnished. It helps keep our night sky shiny and sparkly."

"Come on. You're joking," said Shel. "Space nuggets?"

"No, I'm not joking," replied Joy. "Believe it or not, it's actually a very important job that requires a great deal of skill and responsibility. Yes, space nuggets is what we call—"

"You're serious?! But the stars are way up in the—" He stopped when he saw the blank expressions on everyone's faces. "Oh, never mind. So, why were you, uh, polishing… ugh, the stars?" asked Shel in disbelief at the words that had just come out of his mouth.

"Well, because somebody has to do it," replied Picklepots.

"What Pickles means," Izzy explained, "is that they do it to keep morale up in Arcania. A long time ago, our ancestors endured the most frightfully tarnished stars before we had anyone cleaning them. The dull sheen in the sky resulted in a depression that plagued the whole of society. I'm talking an epidemic of sadness that threatened Arcania's very existence. So—"

"Um, no." Shel cut him off, hands waving, feeling that he couldn't absorb another far-fetched tale at the moment. "What I meant was, why now? Couldn't it… whatever you felt you had to do with the stars," Shel waived his arms about, gesticulating 'whatever' — "Couldn't it've waited until, I don't know, maybe *after* we saved Manny?"

"Huh, that's a good point. I guess I hadn't thought of that," confessed Pickles. "Except, making the trip north seemed urgent given the quarrel between the moon and the sun."

"Pickles!" snapped Fickles, growing impatient with his chef's wandering mouth.

"What are you talking about, Pickles?" asked Izzy. The gang looked at Captain Fickleface with eyes warning that he'd better let his chef speak, or else! So, Pickles rambled on.

"Well, a few days ago the sun and moon accidentally came out at the same time in the same part of the sky. Sometimes that happens and it's no biggie. They share the glory and get along just fine. But this day they just started arguin' over who was brighter and more adored by the people. Ugh, you shoulda heard 'em: 'I make the daylight!'; 'Well I make the night shine!'; 'I'm brighter!'; 'Well I'm softer!'... Gimme a break! Anyway, we decided someone had to mediate..."

"Oh really?" Joy interjected. "And how did *that* go, your '*mediation*'?"

"Not great," chimed Pickles. "Those two knuckleheads argued all day long. Or was it all night? I couldn't tell."

"It was day," clarified Tickles. "And that night there was a terrible storm as a result."

"Truth!" replied Pickles. "We haven't seen anything *that* bad in a long time. And I fear we may have made things worse by buttin' in."

There was a quiet that settled over the group. Then Izzy, being the great deducer he was, inquired, "Um, when did this happen exactly? What day was it, this terrible storm of which you speak?"

"Dunno," replied Pickles. "Musta been, what, about three nights ago. Great big storm. Can't've missed it."

An uncomfortable silence settled in like fog until Shel sliced through it. "Oh, no, believe me, we didn't miss it." He looked around and noticed the group staring at him, many with looks of confusion, but not Izzy or Joy.

Izzy looked ashamed, apologetic, pathetically sympathetic. Joy wore the soft look of empathy. It was clear she cared deeply for this boy. The attention from the lot made Shel uncomfortable.

He looked down at his bare feet. "I left my shoes at the raft," he noted, mostly to himself.

"What's that?" Pickles asked.

"Nothing," he replied.

"So all that time you guys were just flying around doing nothing?" Izzy challenged, annoyed that the Boot Brigade might have spent their time looking for Shel instead of helping to create the storm that nearly killed him.

Captain Fickles caught the elephant's drift and turned to Shel. "I'm sorry, my boy. We were doing what we thought was right at the time. Bein' up there in the heavens helps us think." He then addressed the crowd. "We were tryin' to sort out the best course of action to get Manny back. I know it might sound silly — in hindsight, I agree, it sounds awfully irresponsible — but we were at a loss as to what to do. Our heads were right spinnin' like windmills seein' Manny all indentured like that... We were losin' our cool and felt on the verge of just wingin' a rescue all on our own. 'Course, that would've been suicide. But as I said, we weren't thinkin' straight. We needed to clear our heads. Sure, you might say the obvious decision woulda been to come straight back to get you all, but we didn't know where y'all were, did we?"

General nods of understanding settled over the group.

Fickles glanced back at Shel. "We looked for you, Shelby... and you too Izzy. For days we looked, but we failed, again, and eventually had no choice but tuh give up. And I'm sorry for that. Truly I am. Soon as we got word that y'all were travelin' with the Boogies, and that you'd gone tuh find Ingonyama at the Peanut Butter Palace, we knew you had the right plan for a rescue, so we headed straight here."

The group looked at one another, assessing Fickles' account.

"Listen," he continued, "with Ingonyama on our side, we might actually stand a chance against the Gambrine." At that suggestion, Fickles was met with nearly everyone in the caravan dropping their heads. "What? What is it? What's wrong?"

"Fickles, the king has taken Ingonyama prisoner," Izzy reported. "He refuses to let him go, even temporarily, even under close and constant guard. It's just no use."

"Unless…" Sandovar prompted.

"Unless, what?" pressed Izzy, plopping himself down on the sandy ground like a dog.

"Unless we break him out!" Sandovar looked over at Shel with a grin. "Now that we've got a flying shoe machine, we might just stand a chance at a slick getaway!"

Shel stared back with wide eyes. "Is that… possible?" he asked, half hopeful, half apprehensive. Joy scowled at him.

"I don't know," warned Izzy, scratching behind his ear with his hind leg, again like a dog. "Seems awfully risky to me. Longsmiles has a mighty big army."

"Risky? It's suicide!" chided Joy. "No. Absolutely not! Our only hope was to get the king's permission but he's made his position clear. We'll just have to find a way to get Manny back without Ingonyama."

"But, Joy, without Ingonyama we don't stand a chance," growled Izzy, now lying down, gnawing on some old scrap of something he'd unearthed from the dirt. "Even if we had the numbers, we need someone with experience. Ingo's the only one with the ability, resources, and know-how to organize a mission of this sort. We need someone who understands military strategy, someone who has experience with infiltration, hostage negotiation, extraction…"

"Sounds like you've been reading too many comic books and old war novels, my friend," asserted Sandovar with a hearty chuckle.

Izzy didn't look up from his ruminative snacking. "I suppose you're not far off," he sighed. "Romanov loved... and I mean *adored* the story of Alexander Nevsky. I think he projected Nevsky's character onto

Ingonyama. Maybe that's why I've always seen Ingo as a leader, unmatched by any other."

"No, you're right," conceded Sandovar. "I've been in charge of the Boogies long enough to know a good leader from a charlatan. There's no one in the world like Ingonyama. If we're going to even *begin* to plan a proper rescue mission, let alone pull it off, we're going to need that lion. There's no one else like 'im. He's our only hope of recovering Manny from the Gambrine. Period."

"Well," Shel murmured, "maybe there's a way we can get Ingo out of jail after all. I think I have an idea."

Chapter Twelve

The Boy in the Iron-Pail Mask

As members of the caravan got to building a campfire over which to roast some breakfast sausages and scramble some eggs, the wonder kid from afar began laying out his elaborate plan to retrieve the lion and rescue the dentist…

He placed sticks and rocks in various positions in the sand to symbolize troops and scratched out routes of attack and retreat while the team munched on toasted bread, fresh grapes, roasted sausage, and scrambled eggs — eggs which Chef Picklepots, behind a great big smile, took it upon himself to rate egg-stensively.

"Oh my! These eggs are egg-ceptional! I'm not egg-saggerating either. Cooked egg-zactly right, egg-stra fluffy... the perfect egg-sample of culinary egg-cellence..."

"Are you finished?" Shel truncated the 'eggregious' critique and moved on to detailing his fool-proof, tactical strategy with instructions of, "you go here," and, "you patrol over there," and, "you strum this guitar while I ring this bell exactly at three o'clock," and, "you act like you're talking to your shoes—"

"How about _tying_ shoes?" someone suggested.

"Yes! Act like you're _tying_ your shoes! Good idea!" Shel agreed. "Who talks to their shoes, right? So, you fake _tie_ your shoes while Izzy does his hypnotizing thing on the guards and then Joy'll do a series of cartwheels over here to signal—"

"By Jove, I think it might just work!" exclaimed Picklepots.

"Hang on, buddy. I'm not finished," said Shel. "Joy will do her thing over here and—"

"Hey, Shel," piped Izzy, "How do you know so much about the castle?"

Although not excited about being cut off, he was excited about being recognized as an authority on something Arcanian, at least having special, insider knowledge. "Remember when the king sent me away? Well Alice gave me the royal tour, showed me around the library, kitchen, conservatory, hallways, closets, lavatory... you name it!

"Anyway, as I was saying, Joy will do cartwheels to signal the flying hippopotamus and then we'll tie this lasso around the Worst beast and ride him straight through the king's defenses, right on out to Delilah and then up-up-and-away to freedom!" At that, Shel grabbed a nearby pail, threw it over his head, picked up a stick, and with a, "This is how we'll attack!" began jabbing the stick about like a sword in his best warrior-knight impression, making all sorts of warrior-knight grunts and growls.

The group stood around scratching their heads and beards — those who had them anyway (beards that is, not heads) — silently trying to sort out what, exactly, had just been presented and if Shel was maybe suffering some sort of mental breakdown, a complication from when he had been knocked out.

"Ah! It's brilliant!" cried Tickletoes. "A true masterpiece of military strategy. Um, just one question…"

"Yes, Tickles?" invited Shel, lifting the pail off his head.

"Am I riding in the stone airplane or the human balloon?"

Tickle's question opened the flood gates and the group began dismantling Shel's plan, piece by piece.

"Won't they ask what's in the sack?"

"Where do we get a magic carpet?"

"A Worst? Really?" asked Izzy. "How in the world are we supposed to catch… and then *contain* that stinky beast? Count me out on that one."

Sandovar followed suit. "Just how are we supposed to see what we're doing if we're all wearing iron pails on our heads?"

Then Joy spoke up above the crowd. "Shel, we don't even know if we can wake the giants, or if they'll be friendly to us if we do." The crowd quieted down and turned to the girl, mesmerized by her natural leadership energy. "Look, Sandovar said the king is in trouble and needs a dentist, right?" The crowd sort of agreed in mumbles and nods. "And we're going to try and rescue possibly the best dentist this world has ever known, right?" Shrugs and head bobs indicated general agreement. "But we need Ingonyama to make it work, agreed?"

"Yes!"

"Absolutely!"

"Without a doubt!" agreed the group.

"Okay then! So, the king holds the key to his own salvation. We just need to get *him* to see that."

"And just how do you propose we do that?" challenged Izzy.

"Simple," rallied Joy. "We go back to the palace and negotiate. We tell King Longsmiles the truth, that he has only two choices: He can either hand over Ingonyama so that we can rescue Manny and bring the dentist back to the palace. Or, he can starve to death."

"Well, I doubt he'll choose the latter," asserted Sandovar. "Though it is stubborn Skippy we're talkin' about, so, you never know."

"Exactly," replied Joy. "That's why we present it to him as a choice, so that *he* makes the decision, or so he believes. When there's really only one option."

Although the caravan was apprehensive about going back into Kantcomplainistan without a giant or a Worst or some other relatively indestructible monster on their side, Joy's plan was a whole lot more digestible than Shel's. That much was certain. It didn't help matters, however, that Sandovar kept warning that they were all going to be locked away for treason.

"What treason?" asked Izzy.

"Siding with you three. Your lot will no doubt be charged for assault with a deadly sandwich!" he half-joked, and his caravan half-laughed.

"Well, it's nice to see you're having fun with all of this," said Izzy to the Boogie chief.

"Indeed I am. For what else is there to do but enjoy life while it lasts? Take it too seriously and you've missed the point." Sando pointed to the tip of his sword before lowering the blade down his throat.

"Ugh!" remarked Shel.

"What's the matter? Ye can't stomach the sword-swallerin'?" scoffed Taud with a chuckle. "That there trick be not fer the faint o' heart. He does it to relax the nerves, he does."

Izzy shook his head in disapproval, then having been signaled by Joy — who had picked up a small sword from somewhere (...pirates!) — he lifted her up with his trunk and set her atop his head. Feeling right at home, she stood on the pachyderm's massive noggin, giving herself a nice, high stage from which to address the caravan.

"All right gang," she smiled, but with absolute authority. Shel admired this girl even more as she stood tall and confident in front of the intimidating crowd. She was a natural leader, attractive and intelligent and firm, yet kind and infallibly empathetic, ever willing to put herself in another's shoes, to understand their pain or frustration, fear or… joy. "We're either going to face prison or we're going to save the kingdom!"

"Here, here!" called the crowd.

"And while we're at it, save a very special lion and dentist too." The crowd cheered. Joy paused to take a breath, fully committing herself to the cause, then continued, "So, put your armor on but keep your swords sheathed. Let us be ready to defend ourselves, though we dare to hope for a peaceful resolution yet." The crowd stayed silent, squinted and scrutinized. It was clear the Boogies wanted action. A rescue mission without a tussle sounded terrifically boring. So, if nothing more than to boost their enthusiasm, Joy added, "But make no mistake, we are prepared to fight!"

"Arrr!" yelled the pirates, eager for battle.

"Here, here!" cheered the Boogies at large.

"Ok," added the shoe crew, much less eager for confrontation as they were for a nice, hot bath at the palace, some good ol' Katryna cooking, and a soft bed.

"Grglmmfff," said Sandovar, fist in the air and sword in the belly.

"We're with you, Joy!" yelled Shel, tossing his pail over his head and raising his sticksword-adorned fist in the air too.

"We're *all* with you," added Izzy, from below.

"Alright then!" exclaimed Joythea as she pointed her pirate scimitar toward the camp. "Strike that fire and get this rabble on the road."

"To the king!" Izzy hollered, and with a blast of his trumpet the caravan began to move.

The crowd whooped and cheered as Joythea Aquarius Costeros thrust her sword high in the air and called out, "To the king! And to destiny!"

Book Four

Somewhere From Some Far-off Place

Book Four is for Shel.

And for Matt.
Thank you for sharing your dad with us.

Introduction

Me & Him, Always

Me: *Well, this is it!*

Him: Yup! It sure is. … … … …Um, Me?

Me: Yes, Him?

Him: What's it?

Me: This! The last book!

Him: Ohhh! Riiight! I forgot. Huh. Wow. Bummer.

Me: Bummer?

Him: Well, yeah. The story's over. Means we're done. Finished. All washed up. Kaput. Old hat! Old shoes, old shirt, old news... Just plain old. A couple o' has-beens we be.

Me: Hmm. We might have to agree to disagree on that, Mr. Old Hat. I say we're just gettin' started.

Him: Just gettin'… just gettin'…? What do you mean, just gettin' started?! Gettin' started on gettin' finished maybe.

Me: What I mean is that the end of one story is often the beginning of another. And this story's no different. These books we've been narratin'? Well, they're all about how young Shelby got his start, aren't they?

Him: Ahhhh, I think I see what you mean.

Me: Yeah? You sayin' what I'm knowin'?

Him: Yeah! I'm gobblin' up what you're throwin' down, my brother. ...Or is it gobblin' down what you're throwin'—

Me: NO, no! You got it right the first time. This right here is just the end of the beginning, not the beginning of the end.

Him: Yes! I love it!

Me: Well, then, now *that's* settled, what's say we get on with it?

Him: Absolutely, Me. Let's do it. Why don't you start, for old time's sake. You know, since you're the old hat and all.

Me: Well, I don't know about that... but okay. Here goes... Salutations my good people, and welcome back to the story of Arcania. Welcome back for the final chapter in our adventure!

Him: So exciting! Yes, yes, welcome back for the final… Um… Hey, Me?

Me: Yesss?

Him: Well, I was just wondering if we could call it something other than the *final* chapter? That just sounds so... final.

Me: Uh, okay. What did you have in mind?

Him: Oh, I don't know. Somethin' softer maybe, like the *next* chapter or the—

Me: Are you feeling sentimental, Him?

Him: Of course! I don't want to say goodbye! It's been an incredible
      journey. Our little Sheldon has grown so much!
Me: True. He's certainly experienced a lot. Do you recall in the last
      book, his friendship with Joythea really developed?
Him: Yeah! And when Izzy, that silly elephant, finally came back! ...Or
      how about when he stood up to King Skippy?
Me: Yes, that was impressive. And making all those new friends,
      Sandovar and the Boogies.
Him: And the pirates!
Me: Right. And how all of them, at the end of the last book, decided
      they're going to rescue Ingonyama from the king's prison?
Him: Boy, do I! I can't wait to see what happens next!
Me: Well what's say we get to narratin', see how this thing turns out?
Him: Groovy.
Me: Groovy?
Him: Groooovy.
Me: Oh, just one more thing, Him.
Him: Yeah, what's that?
Me: Heads up 'cause there's no prologue in this final... er, I mean, *next*
      book.
Him: What?! No prologue?!?
Me: Nope. We just dive right in, straight to the meat and potatoes.
Him: Huh. Well, okay then. I guess meat and potatoes are okay. But I
      like ice cream more. Can we just skip to dessert? Just get right to
      the good stuff?
Me: Hmm. I suppose. Why not? Let's just get right to the good stuff.
      Let's have our cake and eat it too!
Him: Mmm. Caaaake. But... I thought that was like a law of physics or
      something: you can't have your cake and eat it too. Are you sure
      we can do that? You sure that's... legal?
Me: Him, you and I can do whatever we want. We're telling the story!
      We can defy even the laws of physics! Heck, you think ol'
      Shelby obeyed the laws of physics in his writings?
Him: Huh. No, I s'pose not. Hey! You're right! Stories are more
      interesting and fun the more creative you get! I say let's go for
      it! Let's dive right into the dessert. Let's have the cake, eat it,
      and— Heyyy, I have an idea! How about we make our cake so
      that each time you slice into it, more cake shows up?! A cake
      that multiplies the more you divide!

Me: Him, I've never been a big fan of math but that just might be the best idea I've ever heard! So what you're saying is, there's enough cake for everyone! I totally get it! In other words, there's enough creativity to go around, for the stories to never end! And everyone gets a slice! ...Or better yet, everyone can add their own ingredient!!

Him: Yes! Exactly!

Me: Him, you're a genius!

Him: Gee, thanks, Me! So... you ready to get this story going so we can generate infinite channels of potential creativity for our audience? Spark inspiration? Inspire imagination?

Me: Well, I think the answer to that is: what would Shel do?

Him: He'd inspire!

Me: Exactly. So let's do the same. For Shel.

Him: For Shel.

Me: Groovy... two times!

Him: Groovy. Two. Times!

Chapter One

The Farmer & the Queen

Riding atop the intimidating, inimitable, idiosyncratic, Izzy the elephant, the infamous band of Boogies at her back, was none other than Joythea the brave… and giggly. With an intense stare fixed on destiny, she led the lion-freeing mission through the streets of Kantytown, right up the royal steps of the Peanut Butter Palace to the entrance of the great hall, and, throwing open the doors, ran right smack into...

...a mountain of goopy, droopy spaghetti!

An avalanche of overcooked, day-old pasta poured from the castle like lava. A tsunami of sticky red sauce and icky noodles from the previous night's party washed over the Boogies, burying any and all who traveled in the caravan that day. All but one.

"Look out!" cried Joy as she leaped from her elephant-head platform onto a stone ledge supporting a small gargoyle that looked a bit like one of the flying shoe crew.

"We've been shanghaied!" Mortimer the pirate cried as he became entangled in the goop.

"I always knew I would go like this — death by spaghetti!" cried Tickletoes, dramatically slipping under the noodles and out of sight.

"Oh, cut it out, Tick!" Fickles yanked his partner out of the starchy tomb. "No one's dying today. Uh, except maybe little Sheldon. Shelby? Anyone seen Shel?"

A small arm popped up from under a mound of noodles. It appeared to be Shel's two fingers, pointing skyward in a peace sign, signaling that he was okay.

"There he is!" yelled Pickles. "And he's ordering two hamburgers! Somebody get that kid a pair of patties!"

Fickles slapped a hand over his face. "Is everything always about food with you?"

Pickles nodded with pride.

"I don't think he's ordering anything except a helping hand," remarked Izzy, reaching down with his trunk to retrieve the kid. "If he wants food, he need but open his mouth and this ridiculous mush will flow right in."

With his head covered in a mop of spaghetti and meatballs, and a bit of cheese on his nose, Shel looked like a real-life Aiken Drum. "Thanks!" he coughed, emptying his mouth and nose of noodles and sauce. Izzy chuckled and patted him on the back.

After clawing their way out of the slop, the caravan — covered head to toe in pungent marinara — reconvened in the courtyard at the base of the palace steps. Sandovar yanked his scimitar from his gullet and looked around to assess the chaos. "Just what in the blazes is going on here?!? There's no one around. Look!" He swung his sword in a wide arc, presenting an empty courtyard. "The place is deserted. What in the name of Hades' hairdo happened here?"

"Oh, why, haven't you heard?" A voice sprang out of nowhere. The spaghetti-covered Boogies turned to see a large polar bear dancing his way toward them. He was skipping and kicking his legs all over the place.

"Is that... the polka?" squinted Sandovar.

"I think it's the hokey pokey," guessed Pickles.

"That there jig be the ol' jitterbug," asserted Captain Jarbison.

"Actually," *tippity-tap, kick ball change,* "you're all correct." The bear sauntered up to the Boogies with a final spin and bow. "There's a bit of every dance in my walk. Can't help it. Been dancin' for years. Not *four* years. More like ten or twelve... Hard to keep track..."

"Arrr! What be thy name, furry man?" Captain Jarbison interrupted with an outstretched sword, making no attempt to hide his crotchetiness. "And where be the crew of this here shanty town? Tell me quick b'fore I shave ye bald!"

"Pardon me?" reeled the bear, showing off a set of impressive teeth and even more impressive claws.

"Ah, you'll be needin' to excuse me mate." Mortimer put his hands up and stepped between the blade and the bear. "Captain Jarby here graduated from nasty school he did."

"That be a bloomin' lie! ...I never graduated. I was kicked out!" yelled Jarbison, "...on account uh bein' too ding dang down-n-dirty," he added quietly. "Anyway, this man here—" he pointed with his sword back at the bear.

"Let me stop you right there." The bear held up a paw about the size of Jarbison's head. "I'm not a man at all, pirate! And you'll do well to lower your weapon and take a lesson from your more civilized friend here, thank you very much. I'm a bear if there ever was one, with the teeth and claws to match, mind you. The name's—"

"Tooky?" Izzy blurted out as he rejoined the group, shaking noodle remnants from his limbs.

The bear's eyes lit up. "Izzy?! Is that you? Ho, ho! So the rumors *are* true! You've returned! ...After all this time!"

"Donachtuk, you old dog. Where in the world did *you* come from?"

"Why, I've been here the whole time! Circus is all but disbanded, but some of us are still around. You know, doin' this and that." The bear did a little tap dance to illustrate 'this' and 'that'.

"Huh. I see." Izzy turned to face his Boogie friends. "Everyone, I'd like you to meet Donachtuk Nanook, the dancing bear from up north, in *cold* country."

"Hi everyone. Please, call me Don... or Tooky if you like." The group mumbled greetings. Sandovar, having known Donachtuk for some time, bowed his usual bow.

"Don," continued Izzy, "where is everyone? Right now I mean? This place looks like a deserted island."

"Everyone is with the king," replied Don, "saying prayers and last goodbyes, putting in final requests..."

"Requests?" Captain Fickleface balked, picking bits of noodles from his beard.

"Yeah, you know, for things like new shoes, ponies, and T.V. sets." Don shook his head. "It's as if people think he's Santa Claus."

Izzy nodded. "Because of the sandwich."

"Well, I imagine it's because of his big, jolly belly, and the beard," replied Don. "His red robes don't help any either..."

Izzy squinted.

"Oh! You mean why are people saying last goodbyes?! Yesss, the sandwich... which *you* all made him eat."

"Hang on just a minute!" called a voice from the crowd. "We didn't force him—"

"Ah, you must be the infamous Sheldon," asserted the bear. "The one who's given the king so much grief."

"Grief?! Are you kidding?!" Shel snapped. "We just—"

"Cool down, kid. I'm just messin' with ya. I'm not your enemy. Nor do I judge your actions. I'm a friend. Isn't that right, Izzy?"

Izzy nodded. "For certain. Tooky is a good guy, don't worry, Shelby. He didn't mean anything by it. And because he's such a good guy," he turned back to Don, "he's going to take us to see the king. Isn't that right, Don?"

"Oh, I'm not sure that's such a good idea, you guys." Don fumbled his paws. "I mean, the king blames you for his demise, and he'll likely want your heads on a plate if he catches you."

Feeling the time was right, Joy approached and curtsied. "Mr. Nanook, you may not know me but I know you. I used to watch you dance in the circus when I was a kid. My name is Joythea."

Don's eyes widened. "My goodness, aren't you adorable." A grin spread across his face and his feet began to jiggle. His legs soon joined in, doing a kind of funky chicken boogaloo and he bowed to her. With a wink of his eye and a twitch of his brow, he invited, "Would you care to dance, my dear?"

Joy was caught by surprise but recovered gracefully. "Oh, Tooky, you're so sweet. I'd love to. But only for a minute, okay? We have an important errand with the king." Don didn't hesitate. He swept Joy off her feet and waltzed her through the courtyard. As the swaying couple moved, the caravan followed like a puppy, having become rather fond, and therefore protective, of their darling Joy. Don twisted and bopped and tangoed with his skilled dancing partner, out of the courtyard, down a rose-lined lane, along a pathway encircling a pond, and through an archway of vines weaving in and out of cascading branches from an old willow tree. There, in the middle of a large, colorful garden, the couple concluded their dancing soiree with a spin, a dip, a bow, and a curtsey.

"Thank you, Don," Joy smiled, catching her breath. "May I ask where you have taken me and my caravan?"

"*Her* caravan?!" grumbled Sandovar under his breath.

Don started, "My lady, this is—"

"The queen's garden!" concluded Izzy, glancing around in awe.

"That's right. Been here before, Izzy?" asked Don.

"No. I never knew where it was. Nor was I ever invited. I only heard tales of how amazing it was... and still is apparently!"

"Indeed it is!" agreed Don. "This garden once belonged to a farmer named Simon. But that was long ago. The garden was much smaller back then."

"Oh, allow me!" Sandovar raised his sword, unable to resist a good storytelling. "When Simon was just a boy, he planted a jewel — a diamond — and from that diamond, he grew a whole garden of jewels."

Don nodded. "Right-o!"

Sando ran the dull edge of his sword over his beard as if brushing it. "...I always wondered where a peasant son of a farmer got hold of a diamond?"

"He found it," answered Izzy, "inside of a fish." Shel and the group turned their attention to the elephant, who was rummaging through the garden foliage as if looking for something. "As a boy, Simon spent his days playing and fishing in the Sonrisa River instead of working the fields with his dad. One day, he saw something shimmering in the water, like nothing he'd ever seen before."

"A diamond!" blurted Shel, eyes sparkling at the notion of treasure.

"Close," replied Izzy. "It was a fish; a fish that shined all sorts of brilliant colors: sapphire blue, emerald green, ruby red... gold... silver... Of course, Simon became obsessed right then and there with trying to catch the unique specimen. He fished every day, trying to catch that prize. Well, eventually he did, and to his great fortune, the fish turned out to be magical, for when he ate it—"

"Hang on!" Shel interjected. "He found a magic fish and he *ate* it? That's terrible!"

Izzy nodded, his eyebrows remaining aloft as his head descended to level. "He had his reasons. You see, inside that fish, the boy discovered treasure! Not just one diamond, but a whole mess of jewels filling the belly of that magic guppy." Shel's eyes grew wider. He was hooked.

Seeing the youth's exuberance, Sandovar flung his sword around for dramatic effect. "Simon knew his father would have wanted him to trade the treasure for a plow or a horse. But, being a dreamer like you, Master Sheldon," Sandovar pointed his sword at Shel and winked, "...Simon kept the jewels a secret. Instead, he buried them right back in the ground where jewels are born." Sandovar punctuated his animated tale by stabbing his sword deep into the soil.

"That's right!" chimed Don with a wiggle and a shuffle. Simon's magical story was coming to life. "Who knows why Simon did what he did? Maybe the fish told him to do it or gave him instructions..."

"The fish *told* Simon to eat him?" Shel shook his head.

"No!" Don laughed and twirled in a pirouette (not unlike Joy, which made her laugh too). "I don't know how," the bear continued, "but somehow Simon knew there was magic in the soil, right here in this very spot. That, or those jewels were magic."

"Like Jack Spriggins' enchanted beans!" squawked Shel excitedly.

Don smiled and nodded. "Exactly! And before long, that boy had sprouts of jewels popping up everywhere, sending colors in all directions: jade greens, garnet reds, purples and oranges of opals, flicks of gold speckled here and there..."

Shel was in wonderland, imagining the jeweled treasure, gemstone rainbows reflecting in his pupils. "Wow!" he said slowly, wiping a spot of drool from his mouth. "Then what happened?"

Izzy laughed in appreciation of Shel's exuberance. "Well, Simon spent all his time tending his garden and growing his wealth while his father tended to the family farm, wishing his boy was there to help him. When the boy's father eventually passed on and the farm fell into the hands of the commonwealth, the boy — by then a young man — realized he'd been so focused on growing his own *branch* of the family tree that he'd neglected his *roots*. Roots are very important you know. As any farmer will tell you, the roots need as much attention as the branches... perhaps more."

Don nodded. "Right! After his father's passing, Simon attempted to grow food here in this garden, his way of resurrecting the memory of his dad. He planted asparagus, tomatoes, rhubarb, potatoes... cherry and apple trees too. Didn't take long, however, for him to realize he didn't know the first thing about growing food. He had an unrivaled green thumb for growing pearls and platinum but couldn't grow a peach to save his life... literally. You see, as the years wore on, the once young man grew older and ever more desperate to produce food."

Shel cocked his head. "But... if he was so desperate for food, why not just go to the market and *buy* some with his treasure? He must've had plenty of money!"

"Of course he had money," answered Izzy. "He was the wealthiest man in the land. But it wasn't desperation for *food* so much as *sustenance*, soul sustenance. He was desperate to reclaim the legacy of his ancestors, to revive the memory of his father and recover the years he'd given to his lifeless rock garden... instead of to living things, things that grow and give life in return. He wanted more than anything to get back the years he'd missed with his family. He was perhaps the richest man in all the world, but he would've traded all the garnets in his garden, all the stars that heaven yields, for just one more day with his dad in the fields."

Sandovar smiled at the poetic pachyderm. "Very nice, Izzy. That's true. But!" The chief yanked his sword from the ground. "He didn't *have* all the stars to give, did he? He only had his entire fortune. And one day, a wheelin', dealin' salesman happened upon the jewel farmer and the two struck a deal. In the end, Simon gave up his garden, jewels, land, and all. And in return, the salesman, who was very resourceful and well-connected, was able to reclaim a good portion of Simon's family farm from the commonwealth. The salesman got Simon his farm back, along with a team of horses, a herd of cattle, a trough of pigs, a gaggle of geese, a coop of chickens, a flock of sheep... goats, rabbits, dogs, cats, birds, bees, owls, bats... even an emu or two. You name it, Simon got it. He even got a barn-full of machinery and a host of farmhands needed to run it. ...He couldn't grow it, so he *bought* back his ancestral lineage. And wouldn't ya know it, after years of digging in the dirt, he even developed a green thumb for growin' delicious food, to the extent that he became — with the help of his farm hands — the most prodigious farmer in all the land, rivaling even the Gambrine! That man and his farm grew the tastiest food that ever did come out of the earth."

"But he lost his treasure!" complained Shel "He became a poor farmer in the end!" The twinkle in Shel's eyes grew dull.

"Quite the opposite!" rallied Izzy. "He became wealthier than ever! True wealth, Shelby, isn't measured in riches of jewels or money, but in family... good friends, good food, and good, rich soil if you're lucky to have that too, which Simon was. He even met a nice woman, and together they had a son, who eventually took over the farm. It's fair to say they didn't have a whole lot of money, but they had peace and love and everything they needed. And they were surrounded by beauty and the solace of a life rooted in nature."

"Indeed," added Don the bear. "Sadly, Simon was only able to enjoy so much of that life before his years caught up with him and he passed on."

"Oh, no! That's terrible," noted the tender-hearted Joythea.

"Yeah... terrible. ...Er, so, what happened to the salesman? The one who got the jewel garden?" asked Shel, the reflection of rubies and emeralds still glinting somewhere in his mind's eye. Joy frowned at him.

"Ah, that man, my young friend, became the first king of the land," answered Don, stretching tall to look as royal as he could.

"What?! That was Skippy?" Shel asked.

Don laughed, "No, that was Skippy's dad. He enjoyed many years of growing his wealth, which helped secure his reign. Eventually, however, time caught up with him too and he too passed on, but not before marrying and having a son of his own, an heir to his throne. Solomon Skippingston they named the child."

"So what happened to all of the jewels? Where'd they all go? How come they're not still here," pressed Sheldon, his mind desperately clinging to treasure.

"Haha!" Laughed Taudello, nudging his mate, Mortimer. "That there be a true pirate in the makin'!"

"Well, if you must know, the jewel plants eventually all withered away," Don replied.

"What?!" Shel lamented. "Why?!"

"That's just what plants do sometimes, in the absence of a caretaker. You see, through the chaos of losing her husband and trying to raise her son on her own, the queen neglected her garden. And so the jewel plants eventually died off. What treasure remained was picked through over the years by... well you name it, whoever was lucky enough to stumble upon this place. Even your Boogie chief, Sandovar of Sandeen, found a few morsels here and there as I understand, before the place turned mostly to dust." Donachtuk's ascended brows begged a courtesy from Sandovar and the chief obliged.

"At your service!"

Don continued after the chuckles died down. "Though the jewels were all harvested, the magic in the soil remained, for those with the magic touch that is. When the Peanut Butter Prince became king, retiring the queen mother of her duties to the commonwealth, the queen rediscovered her love of plants, and eventually reclaimed this garden as her private sanctuary — though, sadly, she was not able to grow more jewels."

"But, if you can believe it, she ended up marrying the jewel farmer's son! ...In an odd twist," exclaimed Sandovar.

"Is that so?" asked Joy. "How romantic!"

"Yup!" replied Don, taking Joy by the hand and spinning her around while continuing the story. "She used to come here every day. And one day, the son of the jewel farmer — Simonson was his name — he came back to the secret garden to discover the legacy of his father, and that's when he met the widowed queen. They became instant friends, spending a lot of time together; and they ended up falling in love."

"Awwww," hummed Joy.

"Magic indeed," agreed Izzy. "And Shel, for a time the queen's cousin, who had studied language arts, used to hold classes in this garden, teaching children the Language of the Flowers. ...Or reminding them, I suppose... You recall the language I was telling you about?" Shel nodded. "This place was perfect for teaching Artilan, on account of the essence of life being so readily available and abundant in the soil."

Shel looked around at the magnificent scenery. "I can see why." He turned in circles, mesmerized by the rainbow cornucopia of flowers and plants.

"It is a lovely place, isn't it?" offered Don. "I come dancing here every Friday. It is Friday, is it not? Friendsday as you Westerners like to call it."

Shel was suddenly struck with the realization that he'd been in Arcania — that he'd been gone — for over a week! What must his parents be thinking?!? Would he be presumed dead??? Would they even welcome him home when he returned?? His return! He hadn't thought about that in a long time.

"Yes! I believe it is Friendsday," remarked Sandovar, jolting Shel out of his ruminations. "And I'm sorry to say, but speaking of, I feel compelled to remind everyone of our purpose. May I ask, Mr. Nanook, why is it that we are here in the queen's garden when we wish an audience with the king?"

"Right!" Don replied. "We are here, Chief Sandovar, because… Oh! here she comes now!"

o o o o o o

The queen's garden was adorned with an abundance of lilies from around the world: yellow African Queen Trumpets as big as footballs, spotted purple Arabian Knights, Black Spiders, Manitoba Mornings... all adding an air of mystique to the courtyard. Fire Kings and Stargazers splashed deep orange here and there; and snow-white Casablancas, which were Don's favorite because they reminded him of the Arctic. If the visual array wasn't sufficient to overwhelm the senses, there were plenty of aromatics to do the job. Tucked between the lilies were every type of sage imaginable, from azure and scarlet salvia to the anise and horminum varieties which looked like blue and purple butterflies fluttering hither and thither. The scents dancing in the air (like Donachtuk the bear) were enough to lead visitors on imaginary trips to woodland forests, desert lowlands, and tropical paradises, all in one sitting.

o o o o o o

"May I present," Don began with an outstretched paw and a dancer's bow, "Her Royal Highness, the queen mother."

An elderly woman in casual yet elegant robes and a jeweled crown on her head acknowledged the bear's invitation with a gracious nod before addressing the group. "So, this is the company that is going to save my son." The 'company' remained quiet, wondering who would speak as their representative, but also distracted by the kangaroo, monkey, and zebra following the queen.

"Queen Ruth," Don filled the silence, "may I present our esteemed guest, also from Falconovich's hometown, Mr. Sheldon Silvers." Shel's ears perked up and his eyebrows followed, the introduction catching him by surprise.

"Pleasure to meet you, Mr. Silvers. I trust your time in Arcania has been enjoyable?" Other than a nod and slight grin, Shel stood stoic like a garden statue, feeling rather speechless in the presence of the queen mother. No matter. Don moved on, relieving Shel of the spotlight.

"Speaking of Falconovich, look who's returned from his globe-trotting adventures! It's Izzy the— well, you know. It's Izzy. Everyone knows Izzy."

"It is wonderful to see you again, Mr. Tuskinsky. You look well," the queen passed a smile and a nod in the elephant's direction. Izzy nodded in awkward silence in return, following Shel's lead.

Don continued. "Okay then. You know Sandovar, chief of the Boogies."

"Indeed. The famous Sandeen sword swallower."

"*Infamous*, if you please," corrected Sandovar with a grin and a bow.

"Infamous indeed," replied Ruth with an acknowledging nod. She turned back to the bear. "Did I see you dancing with a pretty young lady, Mr. Nanook?"

"*Ahem*." Don cleared his throat. "Yes, Your Majesty. May I also present Lady Joythea... um—"

Joy stepped forward and bowed. "Joythea Aquarius Costeros, at your service, Your Majesty."

"Ah! Costeros." The queen pondered something as she tapped her pointer fingers together. "Your mother and I were close friends, if I have the correct family. As children we used to play by the shore. Tell me, how is Queen Theia?"

"Queen?" Shel whisper-coughed in surprise. Joy pretended not to notice.

"She is well, milady, though her age restricts her, and so she too spends her days in her *own* garden under the sss—" Joy caught herself, "Under the... care of her... um, caretakers."

The queen looked at Joy curiously. "I see. If you're insinuating that I spend most of my days here in my garden, my dear, then you... are correct. It is the place I find most peaceful and relaxing in all the world." The queen noticed some commotion behind the crowd. "But do be careful, Mr. Sheldon, that plant there might have a bite out of your knee should you get any closer. It's quite attractive, I know, but it does especially like the taste of youth." Shel jumped backward, getting some distance from the kid-eating plant. The queen chuckled. "Please do come here, young man." Shel stumbled forward and knelt in front of the queen. "Hmmm," she murmured. "Proper... but unnecessary. Please stand up so that I may speak with you directly."

Shel stood and was immediately interrogated. Queen Ruth had all sorts of questions about who he was, where he was from, and why he'd come to the Land of Happy. While the queen was brought up-to-speed on Shel's adventures in Arcania and the mission to save the dentist, the rest of the caravan found comfortable places to sit, sip tea, and chit-chat with the queen's zebra, monkey, and kangaroo. Meanwhile, Izzy caught up with Don on the whereabouts of the other circus actors, while Joy slipped away for a much-needed dip in the nearby pond to refresh her... sea legs.

"Miles, you should not eat any more of those green bananas; you'll make yourself ill," said the queen to her monkey before turning to Shel. "So, Mr. Shelby, your plan is to convince my son to release the sharpshooting lion in your care so that you may rescue your dentist friend and bring him back here to save my son. Is that accurate?"

"Yes, Your Majesty. All of that is right. Except, it's not *my* plan. We all sort of put it together. Joy actually came up with the idea I think."

"Is that right? Well, it's a nice plan; logical, reasonable, and commendable. Good work everyone. I'm afraid, however, there is one flaw."

Shel's smile flipped upside down. "Oh. Um, what's the... flaw?"

"It won't work," the queen replied, nonchalantly snipping dead blooms off a climbing rose bush.

"Ah. I see." Shel dug his foot into the dirt, a little annoyed at being shot down.

But the queen wasn't finished. "It won't succeed as it stands anyway. You see, my son can be extremely stubborn, and he happens to blame *you* for his predicament. So, he's not going to be inclined to release the lion into your care. Nor is he going to trust that you will bring Ingo back once you've rescued your friend. Nor is he going to believe that you will bring the dentist back to save him. So, you see, that is three strikes against you. You do know about the game of baseball, being from Chicago, I presume?"

Shel nodded then dropped his head in frustration at not being trusted. "But we're telling the truth. We *will* bring Ingo and Manny back! The king *needs* Manny!"

"Indeed he does," agreed the queen. "But he may not be able to see that if he is blinded by spite. Or he may not wish to admit it even if he does see the truth of it. Regardless, your plan won't work, not without someone he trusts forcing him to listen. I think I may be able to convince him. Come, gather your party; we will go see my son together, and together we will get you the army you need to free your friend and save the king."

The queen then leaned over and picked a most unusual flower, one which looked very much like a human nose. As she sniffed it, reveling in its intoxicating aroma, the flower sniffed her right back as if to requite her affection. It was a tender moment, quickly dismantled by a disturbing commotion from the corner of the garden ensnaring the queen's attention.

"Donachtuk Nanook!" scolded the queen. "If I've told you once, I've told you a thousand times, that is *not* how we water the plants in my garden! Use the bathhouse by the pond, you wildebeest!"

Chapter Two

The Silver Fish

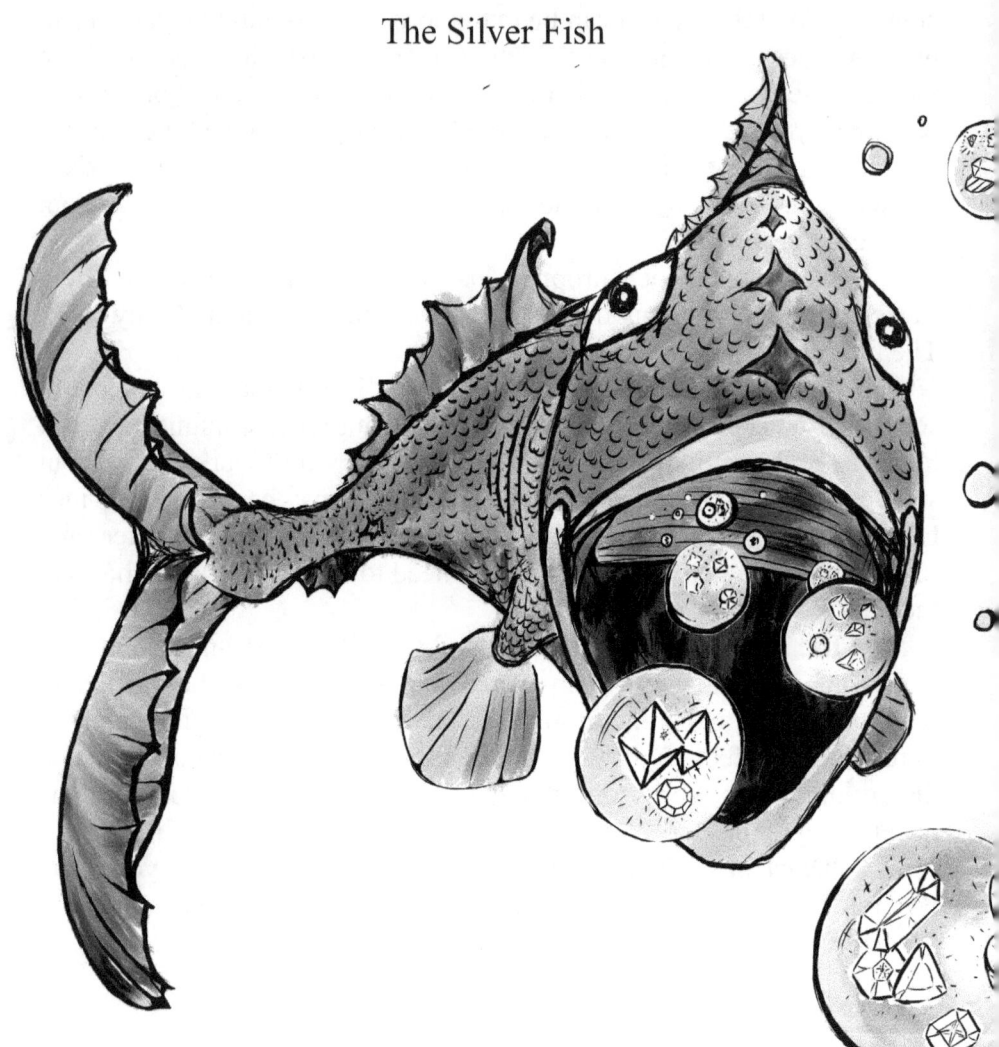

As the caravan approached the infirmary where the king had taken up residence, the royal guards swarmed the Boogies, encircling them with shields raised and spears lowered...

The caravan, however, did not respond. No swords were drawn (much to the dismay of the pirates) and no words were exchanged. Nothing needed to be said as the guards knew they were to escort the so-called 'traitors' directly to the king, while the traitors — er, the Boogies — needed an audience with His Majesty.

"Well, if it isn't the rotten convention!" blasted Katya the witch, with a sideways grin.

"Takes one to know one!" countered Izzy with a slanted smile of his own, eliciting a chuckle from the crowd.

Upon seeing the caravan approach, Longsmiles struggled, making all sorts of noises of castigation and reprimand, doing his best to scold and threaten. "Mmfrrlurghurklummm!" he murmured, but no actual words escaped his stuck jaws. He tried to stand and draw a sword (which incidentally would have been just for show since the king hadn't a violent bone in his body) but he was too weak. He had not eaten anything in more than a day and was depleted from trying to overcome the adhesion of the Peter Pan sauce. So, he simply sat back down and wept.

His audience waited.

When he'd calmed down, he signaled for his royal paper and royal crayon and began to write a royal message. Once finished, he held the paper up for all to see, pointing directly at Sheldon.

"*YOU* did this to me!" Shel read the message aloud. It was precisely as the queen had predicted.

Longsmiles turned the paper back and wrote another message. Again, as the queen predicted, this one — which he directed toward Alice and the royal guard — read, "Seize the boy!" But just as Alice made her move, a commanding voice rang out from the crowd.

"If you please!" exclaimed the voice, with resolute authority. As the crowd turned toward the voice, a pathway opened between the king and the interrupter, who happened to be his mommy.

Shel was jolted by the recollection of his dream about the jungle chief and almost being dinner were it not for the girl calling out, "Me first!" He looked at the king, half expecting to see a cannibal sitting on a throne of bones. But no, Skippy was still there and he looked terrified. His eyes were wide in surprise at the queen mother approaching his makeshift gurney-throne. The medical trolley had been adorned with strings of pearls and necklaces of fine jewels as a way to simulate a 'throne away from throne' for His Majesty.

"Wellllll, I see you're putting to good use your father's spoils from my garden," scoffed the queen. Her son grumbled the best he could. "Bit of a sticky situation you've gotten yourself into, my son. I told you one day that habit of yours would be your undoing. I told you so, right along with every other person in this kingdom. You're the only one who refused to acknowledge the destructive habit."

Nobody nodded their head in agreement more than Katya the cook witch. And don't think the king didn't notice! Skippy was growing furious. He tossed his paper and crayons to the floor like a toddler. The queen mother's eyes rolled disapprovingly and she sighed before continuing. "You've already had the pleasure of meeting Mr. Silvers." She paused and stared at her son quietly. "And I believe you also already know his companion, Miss Joythea Costeros." Another dramatic pause. "Well, Miss Joy and Mr. Sheldon have a proposition for you. You will hear them out if you've any notion at all of what's good for you." The king tried to protest but the queen mother ignored him. "Splendid! Mr. Sheldon, Miss Joy, if you please."

Shel knew that out of the two of them, Joy was the natural leader and should be the one to do the talking. But when he looked at her she just smiled and nodded, encouraging him to proceed. So, Shel took a deep breath and mustered his courage. "Mr. King, Sir Highness, Your Royal... um, ness..."

The king closed his eyes and shook his head. He would have gritted his teeth had they not already been fully gritted. Shel looked at Joy and she gave him sweet eyes and an encouraging smile.

"Sir, I think it's plain to see, and I think everyone here, all of these good people who care so much about you, they all will agree, you need a dentist... badly. And not just any dentist. You need the best! Well, sir, my friends Fickleface, Picklepots, and Tickletoes—" Shel pointed toward the back of the crowd where the boot crew stood, "They've found Manny the dentist. You all know Manny. He's the best there is. Isn't that right?" Shel looked around and was greeted with nods and affirming mumbles. Shel nodded in return and looked back at King Skippy. "We're going to go get him and bring him back here, to help you." The king's expression softened as the words 'help you' came to him. Shel continued. "But, Your Highness, Manny is being held prisoner by the Gambrine." The crowd gasped. "Sir, there are just too many of them." Shel paused, knowing his next statement was going to be difficult. "We need your help in order to save him. We need your help in order to save *you*!" The king's eyes lifted and met with Shel's. "We need the lion."

Shel could see the fire instantly reignite in the king's eyes. Clearly, his answer was still no. Then, the crowd, expecting the boy to do something like plead or pray, was caught by surprise when Shel — for he had expected this response — calmly asked the king, "Sire, have you heard the story of Lester the Wish Collector?" The king's reply was little more than a squint. "Well, it's about a boy named Lester, obviously, who encounters a genie. The genie grants Lester three wishes. But, thinking he's clever, Lester just wishes for more and more wishes in an attempt to ensure that he will never run out, so that he will always have enough wishes to wish for things for the rest of his life. Each time he has a wish to spend, instead of wishing for things like a new bike or an ice cream sundae, he just wishes for more wishes. Eventually he grows old and dies, having never gotten to use any of his thousands of wishes for anything meaningful."

King Skippy was appalled. How could a stranger, from Chicago of all places, think he could come here, to the king's own Land of Happy, and presume to teach the king himself a lesson about life?! Yet here he was. And Longsmiles had to admit that he wasn't quite sure what this young man was getting at.

"Don't you see? You're the king! Your wish is the command for thousands of people. You have everything at your very fingertips. But so long as you refuse our help, you're just sitting on your wishes as your own demise comes closer every day, every hour!" The king continued to stare and squint at Shel, contemplating the young man's argument, but remaining unconvinced. "Are you really willing to give up all of this?" The youth spread his arms wide. "Your friends, your family, your kingdom, just so you can cling to your obsession, hold fast to your ego?" The king pursed his stuck lips, displaying his impressive stubbornness. "You're going to deprive the kingdom of her king just so that you can keep someone in prison for defending an innocent family?"

The king's defenses were clearly still up but his eyes began to lower. Shel noticed that he was gaining the advantage. It was time to close out the inning. "Or," he added, "will you use your power as king to save a life, so *that* life may go on to save another, and then *that* life may go on to save a king? A king who is beloved by his people and who is needed by his country." With each breath (through his nose), Skippy considered the words of this young man who had apparently found his courage and his voice.

The crowd stood silent, admiring the speech. Those who were old enough to remember thought this young Sheldon reminded them of a once-young Skipingston. The king stared at Shel. Eventually, he signaled for paper and crayon and began scribbling. He turned the paper around to reveal the question, "Have YOU heard the story of the silver fish?"

"Ummm," Shel hummed. "Is that the story of Simon and his sparkly diamond fish?" The king's eyebrows lifted. He was surprised that this stranger would know about the story of his father's jewel garden. Longsmiles looked at Alice and nodded for her to continue on his behalf.

"It is the same, Mr. Silvers, but few know the full account. You see, Simon, the fisherman who caught the magic fish, was promised by the fish all sorts of riches if only Simon would release him. So, of course Simon let him go, only to have the fish swim away and not fulfill his promise. Well, one day, Simon happened to catch that very same fish again. And just as before, the fish made many promises if only Simon would let him go. This time, Simon built a fire and cooked that fish for dinner. And it's a good thing he did, otherwise he would not have found the jewels inside of the fish and our king would not be king."

Shel turned to look at Izzy and Joy. Joy knew where this was going and stared fixedly at Longsmiles while Izzy shrugged. During Alice's recount of the story, the king had been scribbling on several paper boards. He handed the boards to Alice who turned them, one at a time, so that Shel could read the words for himself.

"If you do not come back," Shel read the words aloud slowly, "…my little silver fish full of promises…" Shel pointed at his own chest and looked at the king with an inquisitive expression. "Am I the silver fish?" The king nodded prophetically. Shel gulped and read the third board. "I will catch you again..." Shel looked up from his reading with alarm as the king scribbled on yet another piece of paper then spun it around. "...and I will fry you up and eat you...? What?!" Shel's eyes looked as wide as Izzy's and he took a half step backward, nearly falling over. Suddenly, a reservoir of memory hit him like a tidal wave as he recalled being chased on his horse by the cowboy outlaws from his dream, how one of them shot him, and how that felt awfully familiar to when he and Izzy were being chased by the Worst and he got scored by the monster's claw. He then recalled his first encounter with the pirates in the Sonrisa desert and how they gave him the same sensation as the pirates in his dream, the ones who tied him to a pole. Then there was Skippy, reminiscent of the jungle cannibal chief. And then... *Oh my!* He gasped, putting his hands over his mouth and spinning around in sudden realization. He glanced at Joy just as a loud screech jolted the crowd. Everyone looked up to see a magnificent eagle soaring overhead.

Could Joy be... the mermaid? Shel thought almost out loud. The answer to that question would have to wait, however, as Queen Ruth snatched Shel's arm and pulled him through the crowd. He kept his eyes locked on Joy the whole time. As he stared at her, she saw something telling in his expression and sensed that he'd figured out her secret.

"Come along, my boy," Ruth whispered. "Mustn't dawdle. The king has conditionally granted your request. Best take him up on it before he changes his mind." Izzy, Joy, Sando, and the rest of the caravan quickly followed Shel and the queen as they headed straight for the palace dungeon.

Chapter Three

The Missing Piece

A lonely lion sat in his cold, dark prison cell made of stone and cement and iron bars, playing a game of rummy with a small mouse. Over the years the cat had grown accustomed to the dark, and to being alone. The mouse, who had wandered in obviously by mistake, hardly counted as a proper companion on account of the rodents' modest size, her timidness, her flightiness... her inability to make a proper toasted marshmallow sandwich — which everyone knows is a favorite of lions. However, when one is lonely enough, a mouse can be the best friend in all the world, for a mouse will not yammer on and on about their own troubles. Instead, they just sit quietly, judgment suspended, twitching their little nose, staring with those beady, black eyes, patiently listening to your tales of woe, waiting for you to share a crumb of bread or cheese or strawberry, please. So it was that when a horde of clamoring rabble came wandering into the dungeon, the lion quickly picked up his little friend, placed the rodent in his mouth for safekeeping, and withdrew into the corner of his cell to wait silently in the shadows for the ruckus to pass. But pass it did not. Instead, the disturbing clamor paused in front of the lion's (and the mouse's, thank you very little) cell door and eventually quieted, waiting for the lion to emerge from his hiding place. The lion, however, stubborn as a splinter, refused to come out into the light.

Wasting no time, an ominous figure emerged from the crowd and advanced with purpose, identifying themselves as the leader of the intruders; in other words, the lion's first target! Clearly, these uninvited guests had come to take the big cat away and deal with him properly, once and for all. Unbeknownst to them, however, this lion had plans other than dying that day. He would not be going quietly, without a fight!

As the advancing creature moved into the light cast by the mobster's torches, from his shadowy corner, the lion squinted through a distant fog of recognition. Could it be?? He stepped from the shadows, face screwed up in confusion and disbelief. "Do I know you?"

"Been a long time, old friend," said the visitor as he took another step forward, fully illuminating his face.

"Iz... Izzy? Is that you?"

"Yes, it's me, and Sandovar and Donachtuk the bear... and the queen mother herself. It's good to see you again, Ingonyama. Now, pack your things. We've come to get you out of here."

Upon Izzy's modest, and therefore unorthodox, introduction of Her Royall Highness, the queen mother stepped forward. "Hello, Ingonyama. I trust my son hasn't been mistreating you?"

"Your majesty!" Surprised, Ingo stood and approached the bars of his cell, throwing a nod in for good measure.

"My son has agreed to release you into the care of Izzy and the Boogies," the queen continued. "You are to accompany them on a quest to recover Manfred Pfaffen Jr., the renowned dentist from Champion Valley. He has been captured and enslaved by the Gambrine colony. Once he is retrieved from captivity, you are to bring him back here. The king is in dire need of him."

Ingo stayed silent for a time, contemplating the queen's news. "Probably safe to assume I am to be re-imprisoned upon my return?" the lion asked astutely.

"That remains to be seen," answered Ruth. "Men have been known to find it in their heart to pardon those responsible for saving their life."

"His life? The king is in mortal danger?" asked Ingonyama, thoughts rushing through his mind, not least of which involved the possibility of refusing the offer and instead gaining his freedom by simply waiting for the king to die. He quickly realized, however, that by refusing to help, he could be charged with further crimes against the crown, securing his place in that cell for the remainder of his days.

"I'm afraid the king's days may soon come to an end if he does not soon receive medical attention," explained the queen. "Which is why we must insist on prompt action. So, let us not delay. Are you ready to accept the king's terms and get out of this wretched confinement?"

Ingo hesitated still. "May I ask how he has come to mortal danger? What happened?"

Izzy stepped forward and pushed his face against the cell bars at the height of the lion, looking the cat right in the eyes. "Ingo, we don't have time to explain all the details right now. We can fill you in on our way back to camp."

The lion looked into Izzy's eyes and could almost read his thoughts. "He is in need of a dentist, you say? Would it be too bold to assume it has something to do with a peanut butter sandwich?" A giggle was heard from the crowd, presumably one of the flying shoe crew. The untimely disturbance ensnared Ingo's attention and he examined the rabble standing behind Izzy. "I'll take that as a yes." The lion looked back at the elephant. "I see you have a small army with you, my old friend. Why do you need me?"

Izzy nodded. "We sought you out because we needed an expert tracker to discover Manny's whereabouts. But, it turned out the Festoon Brigade was able to locate him on their own. You remember the Boot Brigade... and their dentist friend, Manny, right?" The shoe crew popped their heads out from the crowd and smiled. The lion did not smile back. He simply looked at them, one eye in a scrutinizing squint, the other wide with skepticism. Satisfied enough, he looked back at Izzy.

"No," he said plainly.

Izzy was taken aback. "What? You don't remember—"

"Of course I know the Boot Brigade. Of course I know Manny, Israel. My answer is no. You've wasted your time coming to get me."

"But... Ingo, I don't..." Izzy looked back at the group then back at Ingo. "Don't you want to get out of here?!"

"If you don't need a tracker but you've come here anyway, I must assume it's because you need a warrior, that you are planning some sort of rescue mission and you need fighters. Well, my fighting days are over, Izzy. You, most of all, ought to understand why."

The elephant lifted his head in astonishment. "You can't mean you'd rather stay in this cell than help rescue Manny and save the king!"

The lion took a deep breath and replied slowly. "When I was captured by the king, I made a vow never to harm another creature again so long as I live." He paused for another breath. "After witnessing the tragedy of what happened to your family, Israel, I just went blind with rage. The king's men shouldn't have been there, hunting innocent animals. There's no excuse for that. But they didn't deserve the fate I gave them. I deserve to be where I am, right here in this cell, alone." The mouse protested, squeakily reminding Ingo he wasn't alone, but no one took notice.

Everyone stood silent, feeling at a loss from this development. They needed Ingo and his battle expertise, his leadership. Beyond this, they didn't want to see the great Ingonyama waste away in solitude. Izzy's attempts to convince Ingo were as if the elephant were tightrope walking on an unraveling string, a string that Ingo was attempting to light on fire.

Just then, amidst the grave silence, Shel stepped forward, confidence fueled by his recent victory with the king. "Mr. Ingonyama, sir, my name is Sheldon. I came to Arcania from Chicago, like your dad."

Ingo cocked his head and squinted. This was certainly unexpected. He watched with great curiosity as the youth pulled the blue puzzle piece from his pocket and held it out. "I found this on the sidewalk in Chicago, after I ran away from home. It's... er, this *was* me." The lion looked utterly confused. "I just mean that I used to be one lonely puzzle piece, part of a big picture but left out... I was out of place in the world. But being here with Izzy and Joy, and Fickles and Pickles and Tickles, and Sandovar and Morty and Taud, and everyone... I feel I'm not a missing piece anymore." Shel took a breath, acknowledging the changes that had taken place within him. "I know right now you probably feel all alone down here in this dark jail cell, far away from everyone and everything..." Shel looked down and noticed the mouse looking up at him, nose twitching. "Not completely alone I see," he said with a smile and the mouse smiled back, finally someone acknowledged her. "But, maybe you could use this, like I did... to help you find your own picture, rediscover where you fit." He shrugged. "After all, the big picture is incomplete without each and every piece, no matter how small. Right?" He looked back at the mouse who smiled and nodded. Ingo followed Shel's gaze to the mouse. He bent down and picked up his tiny friend and she blinked at him, encouraging her friend to consider the newcomer's insight.

"I know that you still have an important role to play, Ingo," Shel continued. "This picture..." he spread his arms to indicate the whole group, "just doesn't make sense without you." Nods and mumbles of agreement filled the dungeon. "Can you see the picture? The story of Manny and the king? It's the story of all of us. Your story. If you can't yet see it, all you have to do is... imagine." Shel handed the lion the puzzle piece and Ingo held it in his paw, considering the gesture from this young stranger. He was struck rather speechless, as were Izzy and Joy and the rest of the group.

Queen Ruth, however, was not. "Here here. Well put, young man. Seems we'll make a prince of you yet."

Shel replied sheepishly, "Um, if it's all the same, Your Majesty, I've always preferred the idea of... of a knight."

"I see. Well, if a knight you are to become, then under a knight you must apprentice. Isn't that right, Sir Ingonyama?"

The lion perked his droopy head up and looked at the queen sideways.

The queen nodded to the jailer who swiftly sprang at the cell, fumbled with a ring of keys, then unlocked the door. Ruth stepped inside the cell then turned toward Sandovar. "Mr. Sandovar," she said.

"My lady?"

"Your sword, if you please."

Without hesitation, the chief unsheathed his scimitar (from his side, not his belly) and bowed his head as he held the sword out to the queen with both hands, one on the blade and one on the hilt. The queen took the sword with both hands wrapped around the thick handle. Though it was heavy for an old woman, especially a dainty queen, she handled the sword gracefully, for this queen had spent her twilight years turning soil, weeding and pruning and harvesting, milking cows, shearing sheep, and so on. She was not as dainty as she appeared. She turned the tip of the sword toward Ingo. "Kneel, Ingonyama Nifumo."

The lion vacillated. After all, going from spending days on end in a cold, dark prison cell to suddenly having so much attention from old and new friends alike, especially royalty, and then to be surprised with such reverence and honor... well it was all a bit overwhelming to say the least. Still, the lion knew better than to refuse his queen and what was likely to be a once-in-a-lifetime offer. He dropped his head and bent down on one knee. The queen placed the sword atop his shoulders thrice, one shoulder then the other, and then a final light tap atop his head. "Rise, Sir Ingonyama, knight of the Land of Happy and protector of her people... and of her king," she added with lofty brows.

Before he stood, his head still lowered, Ingo opened his paw and considered the little blue bit of puzzle that Shel had given him. Though overwhelmed by the turn of events, the simple piece somehow made sense, made him feel like he might have some purpose left after all. Izzy and the queen and everyone who had come to collect him were there now because of an unfolding story. Whether the story was about Manny the dentist, King Longsmiles, or neither of them, it seemed these folks considered the story incomplete without the missing piece called Ingonyama. That much was clear. Just one question remained: who was this curious young man bringing life lessons all the way from Chicago?

o o o o o o

With Ingonyama freshly knighted and freed from prison, it was time to get on with the mission. The queen led the caravan out of the dungeon and back to her garden. As soon as they'd settled in, Ingo got down to the business of discussing strategy. He was a natural leader given his status as an elder and his years of experience in battle. Under different circumstances and no better option, leadership might have fallen to Sandovar or one of the pirates. But the truth was that none of those free-spirited warriors desired to be burdened with such responsibility. That, and they weren't as adept at planning a military offensive as they were at, say, pilfering and burying treasure.

With leadership firmly established, the lion commenced commanding the 'new' Boogies, which now included — in addition to Sandovar and the original Boogies — Shel, Joy, Izzy, the flying boot gang, Taudello and the pirates, and Alice with a smattering of her loyal, royal guards.

"As capable as you all are I'm sure, we can't just show up on the Gambrine doorstep without a plan. We need to be strategic and coordinated. Whoever is expecting to be part of the mission will need to be at least somewhat trained and fit for duty. There will be no room for mistakes and no room for anyone not assigned to a specific task. All that aside, there is something I need to make clear before we go any further." The lion began to pace back and forth like a true general addressing his troops. "I will fight alongside you. I will fight to save Manny and I will fight to save the king. They both are worth fighting for. But let's get something straight right now, I will never fire another gun so long as I live. My shooting days are over."

"What!?" cried Sandovar. "But that's why…" *we sought to get you out of prison in the first place*, the chief was going to say but caught himself, realizing that would have been terribly callous. Plus, that sentiment was not entirely true.

Izzy approached the lion. "Yams, if I may. I understand why you feel the way you do. After everything you've seen and been through, I don't think anyone can blame you for wanting to retire the gun. But I can't see how we're going to wage war against the Gambrine without weapons. I mean, do we just expect them to roll over and let us pat them on their bellies?" Those within earshot chuckled.

Ingo also let a slight smile slip across his face momentarily. "No, Izzy. I do not think that is realistic, unfortunately. As much as I would like to simply show up with gift-wrapped concessions and reason with our scaly neighbors, I don't see a diplomatic resolution here. Being stubborn and short-tempered as they are, making them all the more dangerous, I doubt they're likely to give up their prisoner without a fight. Still, I must believe there is another way than bloodshed. If violence is the answer you can count me out. Just put me right back in the cell where you found me."

Grumbles and mumbles of disappointment and disapproval emanated from the crowd. But there were also those who felt relieved at the lion's admission and his insistence on a peaceful resolution. Namely, Joy and Shel.

Izzy rallied. "Okay. So how do you propose we fight without violence?"

"I don't have that answer just yet, Izzy. But if you'll permit me some time, I would like to consult with the queen, and with Alice and Joy too. All three of them are leaders, respected by their people for their level-headedness and compassion, and for their ability to find peace and cooperation where others see conflict and competition. As a warrior, I tend toward the latter and could use some counsel on seeking alternative solutions."

Izzy nodded, turned, and walked away, perhaps disappointed in the lack of a concrete plan; perhaps relieved that Ingo was adamant about a nonviolent solution. Perhaps he was contemplating what Manny must be going through after so many days in captivity. Perhaps he was going to speak privately with the Flying Boot Brigade. Perhaps he was just going to look for something to eat.

At his departure, others followed, catching on that it was time to give Ingo some space to plan the mission. Thus, the crowd dispersed, leaving only three in the company of the lion. Ingo and the queen mother looked at one another and, with a nod, locked arms and strolled off to discuss the sort of important things that queens and military leaders discuss, leaving Joy and Shel alone in the garden of life.

It had been some time since those two had a moment to themselves, and a lot had changed for both of them.

Shel had made all sorts of new friends and had experienced many challenges, injuries, threats on his life and freedom, opportunities to demonstrate his worth... He did not feel like the same naive kid who hopped on that ridiculous raft and set off across Champion Lake, let alone the shy youth from Chicago who ran away from home only a week ago.

As for Joy, since meeting Sheldon, she too had made many new friends and spent more time away from home than usual. Like Shel, she had never crossed the desert with a caravan of gypsies, never spoken directly to the Peanut Butter King and negotiated for the release of a famous prisoner; and she had never plotted an attack on a neighboring community. She too felt distant from the Joy she knew only a few days ago. She felt less sure of the world and less sure of her own inner joy.

"Um, hi," she spoke shyly to her friend.

"Hi. You okay?" he replied. He desperately wanted to ask about her mom, another queen. Did that mean Joy was a princess? But he'd learned enough about Joy to know she'd prefer he ask about her, that she'd bring it up when she was good and ready to discuss it.

"I guess so. Thanks for asking." She sighed. "It's hard to believe all that's happened since we left the beach."

Ah, the beach. Both were reminded of their brief time together at the edge of the sea, before life became complicated with the plotting of jailbreaks and the planning of war. Thinking of the sea, Joy knew she needed to return soon, her presence at the Costeros Palace long overdue.

"And you? How are you holding up?" she asked. It seemed small talk was all they could manage.

"I'm okay..." He wanted to tell her that he missed her company. With so much going on, the two of them hadn't had any time to just relax together, to sit and talk, or just walk like they did together on the beach and through the desert. Although he'd found the courage to stand up to a king, he still lacked the courage to tell this girl how he felt about her.

She tried to fill the awkward silence. "Well, it appears we have our army. So that's good."

"Yeah... So..." He began his inquiry of her family just in time for her to cut him off, possibly sensing what was coming.

"You know, Shel, I'm happy for you. You really seem to have found your voice."

Shel shrugged. "I guess." *If only she knew. If only I could find the words to tell her how I feel.*

"And your flock," she added.

"My flock?"

"Yeah, you know, the group of friends who take you in and care for you. Like the family you pick... or that picks you, instead of the one you're born into."

"Huh. Yeah." He paused and then bravely asked, "Are you... part of my flock?"

She hesitated. She was nervous, like him. But she also wasn't sure if there might be some ulterior motive behind his question. "Would you... like me to be?" she asked.

Shel opened his mouth to answer but was interrupted by Alice and the king's guard storming into the garden. For a moment he thought maybe they'd been tricked by the king and that they all were going to be arrested and hauled off to prison. Thus, he and Joy sighed in relief when Alice took off her helmet.

"We've gathered reinforcements for your mission," Lady Alice spoke with a bow.

Shel's eyes went wide. He didn't intend to be a leader of the mission. Why was Alice bowing to them?

Seeing that Alice was waiting for a response and Shel was hesitating, Joy stepped forward. "Thank you very much, Lady Alice. Your support is much needed and much appreciated. Have you yet spoken with Ingo? He is the commander of this mission."

"Not yet. As this is a mortal matter for the king, we are both obliged and honored to join the fight. You can expect our full support in whatever capacity you require."

"Splendid!" A voice blustered from the far end of the garden. Ingo was looking renewed, Queen Ruth still on his arm. "I'm sure we can use all the help we can get."

"Ingo! I—"

"Nothing need be said, Alice. You're loyal to the king and I do not hold that against you. You were following orders as any knight should."

"Well, I thank you for that kindness, Ingo, but... king's orders or not, your imprisonment was wrong, and I am so very sorry for my part. If we make it back from this mission and the dentist is able to save the king, we intend to make a few changes around here."

"We?" asked the lion, just as a loud cackling roared across the sky. A gang of witches flew overhead on brooms; one of them on a vacuum.

"Head's up!" yelled Don the bear, joining the group in the garden. "It's the witching hour!"

"They've come to join the fight," explained Alice. "Katya feels considerable guilt, being the chef who concocted the sandwich."

Shel scoffed in Don's direction, not forgetting the bear's comment about Shel being responsible for the king's predicament. Don grinned back sheepishly.

"And... she too is tired of being ordered to do things she knows in her heart aren't right," Alice concluded.

"I see," said Ingo. "Well, they are most welcome."

"Speaking of," Don interjected, "are you certain this invasion of Gambrinsville is the right thing?"

"I don't believe we have any other choice, Don," answered Ingo, "especially now that the king is in dire need of the dentist."

"But the Gambrine are many! Not well trained for war, but they have the numbers to put up quite the resistance, I'm sure." Don grabbed Joy's hand and spun her in a pirouette.

"The numbers aren't what worry me. I have a few tricks to even those odds. My concern is their leader, Supreme Chancellor Hume. From what I hear, *she* is a formidable adversary if there ever was one!"

"Indeed she is!" agreed the queen mother. "Underestimate the chancellor at your peril. Not likely to negotiate, is Hume. She has brought prosperity to the Gambrine, there's no denying that, but at the steep price of freedom. For Hume, it's her way or nothing; a dictator through and through. Good luck dealing with that one!"

"Plus, she's terrifying!" added Don. "Bigger than the two of us if you were on my shoulders, Ingo!"

Ingo laughed, though he knew it to be true: Chancellor Hume was, according to legend, one of the largest brocosmiles to have ever walked the land of Arcania. "I believe you, Donatchtuk. I haven't seen her in person but I know the stories. I haven't yet decided how I'm going to deal with Hume. They say she has only one weakness and I'm no good with flour and sugar."

"Banana tarts," spoke the queen.

"Exactly. And how a banana tart is supposed to help us win a fight, you got me," Ingo sighed.

Shel was suddenly hopping with ideas. He didn't feel it was his place to say anything, being amongst such experienced and wise leaders, but he couldn't ignore the obvious. He just had to ask, "What if we just baked a wagonload of tarts, gathered up some of the king's gold — he's got gold, right? I mean, he's got to, he's a king! ...Wait! No! His jewels! All the riches from the jewel farm. We could load up a heap of jewels and whatever else the Gambrine like, and take it to them to bargain. Couldn't we just *trade* for the dentist?"

"That would be the best option, Master Sheldon," answered Ingo. "Problem is, the Gambrine don't barter. They contend that they already have everything they could ever want or need."

Shel balked. "Wha? How could they not trade? Everyone trades!"

"Not in Arcania," Ingo replied.

"What does that mean?" Shel challenged.

"Think of it this way, Shel," chimed Izzy, who had sauntered into the garden somehow undetected. "Sandovar's Boogies live a nomadic life, right? Everything they do appears to revolve around their interacting and trading with other communities, cultures, creatures... yeah? Well, the Gambrine — and certain other tribes in Arcania — are pretty much the opposite. They pride themselves on being self-sufficient if not wholly self-contained. The Gambrine are one of the more extreme examples. Not only do they refuse to engage in trade, but they've essentially developed a culture of isolation. As you've heard many times before, they're only really dangerous when you—"

"Bother their crop. I know," Interrupted Shel. "And?"

"And, well, just because they're not dangerous much beyond that, doesn't mean they're friendly. They're not."

"So... what you're saying is—"

"You show up on their doorstep with a bunch of gifts, no matter how amazing you think your gifts are — and believe me, many, *many* have tried — the answer is always, will always be no."

"But, what about the tarts? If they're really the chancellor's weakness, she won't be able to say no, right?"

"Well, that's possibly true," answered Ingo. "In that case the chancellor would simply take the tarts then slam the door in our face, because, as Izzy pointed out, the Gambrine don't barter." The lion turned to address the group at large. "Please, everyone," the group quieted down and looked at Ingo. "As Nanook announced, it is indeed the witching hour and that means we all need to be getting ready for bed."

"Wha?" said a voice. "Bed?" said another. "What are you, our dad?!" said a third.

"Calm down! I know I'm not your dad and you're not my kids. But I am your commanding officer so long as this rescue mission is in play. As such, I must insist that you all get a good night's rest, for tomorrow we start our training."

Well accustomed to receiving orders, the Boogies got to work, scrambling in various directions, quickly erecting a camp just outside the queen's garden. Soon a massive cauldron was set over a roaring fire, emanating an intoxicating aroma of lentil puttanesca gumbo. A team of chefs, including Picklepots from the shoe crew, Katya from the king's kitchen, and Sarah Karynthia and Sylvia Kats from the Boogie caravan, worked diligently, chopping, mixing, sauteing, and serving.

Wanda was saved from the culinary burdens because she was, by all accounts, a right terrible cook; but also because Ingo had pulled her aside to ask about the spaghetti debacle at the palace. While she was ashamed at having created the mess, she was also an honest witch, and thus she told the lion everything.

"Thank you, Wanda. This information is very helpful," stated Ingo. "It gives me an idea for the battle which might help avoid any real injury. At this point, until we depart for Champion Valley, I feel you and Katya, and any other witches you may know, ought to return to the palace and help the king in any way you can. Try to get any sustenance into the king's belly lest he perish before we're able to return with the dentist."

"But, how?" Wanda asked.

"Try prying open a small section of his lips at the back of his mouth. If you can just open it a little, perhaps you can slip a straw through to get some water or juice in." Wanda nodded and turned to depart. "One more thing before you go," Ingo added. "After you've finished tending to the king, I have a special onion dish I need you to cook up."

o o o o o o

"Goodness me!" exclaimed Shel, dipping a finger into the concoction brewing over the fire then sucking the glop off his finger. "This soup is even better than your flying shoe stew! Pickles, what's your secret?"

"Aha! You noticed!" Pickles rejoiced. He retrieved a small vial from his pocket and handed it to Shel, proud as a president. "Clearly you've a taste for the finer ingredients in life. That little darlin' right there's what I call sky seasonin'. Scooped a bit o' the sunset into a canning jar one evening as we were settin' off to polish some stars. It doesn't look like much, on account of bein' so airy. But, a pinch of sky goes a long way, especially in the compliment of lentils."

"Ah, polishing stars... That fiasco," scoffed Shel. "Don't remind me." Shel twirled the canister in his fingers and nearly dropped it.

"Careful! That there morsel ain't easy to come by. Took some skill retrievin' that, it did!"

Tickles laughed at her brother and commenced to ramble on about the Boot Brigade's myriad celestial errands. Meanwhile, the aroma from the cauldron began attracting a real crowd, and soon the queue wrapped around the campground twice over. There they all stood, a rag-tag gang of misfits, waiting, mostly patiently, in the periphery of the magical firelight for both their dinner... and their destiny.

Chapter Four

The Big Sleep

"All right you Dungries, dish up your chow. After you've had your fill, it's lights out. Training starts at dawn," directed General Ingonyama before shuffling off to attend some errand.

"Dungries?" Shel asked Joy as they fell in line.

"Mmhmm," she nodded. "There's a legend in the Land of Happy about a giant who was called Hungry Dungry because he ate absolutely everything he saw."

"Everything? Really?" asked Shel, skeptical but intrigued.

"Everything. Food, rocks, houses… people."

"Ugh! Is that true?" he asked, looking around at the others, hoping Joy was just kidding.

"Of course!" butted-in Sandovar as he handed the two youngsters each a bowl of chow. "I knew him."

"Really?" questioned Joy. "Nooo. This is just one of your silly Sandy stories, isn't it? Hey, what's this?" she asked as Picklepots handed her a pair of chopsticks.

The chef laughed, "We ran out of spoons. Good luck eating your soup with these!"

Sandovar booed at Pickles then resumed his story. "Well, I didn't know him *personally*. We had a mutual acquaintance."

"Is that so?" pressed Joy.

"'Tis so indeed!" replied the chief. "When I was a kid I had a pet giant and he knew Dungry pretty well."

"A pet giant?!" challenged Izzy, carrying his own bowl of gumbo. He didn't need any chopsticks… or a spoon. He had a built-in vacuum hose. "That's preposterous!" he punctuated with a sonorous slurp of stew.

"Preposterous rhinoceros!" defended Sandovar, awkwardly scooping gumbo with his chopsticks. "It's true! I was young and King Longsmiles had just started putting the giants to sleep. I happened upon one slumbering down near Frenchman's Crick. I didn't know any better so I slung a rope 'round his neck and woke that big guy right up." He leaned aside to Shel and with an elbow jab, added, "I wasn't the brightest kid, you know." Then, sitting up he turned back to the group. "Anyhoo, not realizing the danger, I yelled at that giant; 'up-n-at-'em,' I said, 'You're mine now!' Haha!" Sandovar laughed.

"Really?" Izzy questioned skeptically. "And how did *that* work out for you?"

Still smiling, Sandovar scratched the back of his head and lifted his brow. "Well, lucky for me he turned out to be quite docile and sweet. He wasn't terribly happy that I woke him up but he was endlessly grateful that I woke him in time to save him from being put to sleep... if that makes any sense." Laughter bubbled up from the crowd. "I mean, I wasn't necessarily trying to save the poor guy. I just thought it would be fun to have a giant companion."

"I know the feeling," Shel smirked at Izzy.

"Hey! I'm not *that* big!" Izzy choked on his stew, eliciting more laughs from the audience.

"Anyway," Sando yawned, retrieving his story. "We steered clear of Longsmiles and most everyone else for months... as long as we could anyway. I kept that giant hidden under the Corcutt-Malley Bridge by day—"

"The Corcutt Bridge?!" Izzy interrupted. "That's just down the clearing, on the other side of the woods."

"Yup, that's right. I adhered to the old adage, keep it close to the king and they'll never suspect a thing. Anyway, we'd stay out of sight during the day and at night we'd go mischievate all over the countryside." Sandovar sighed and paused in memory. "Yup, he was my best friend... that summer anyway." There was another moment of silence then Sandovar began to laugh. "Ha, ha, ha! It was funny, when he was standing up I could never understand what he was saying because he was so tall, so far away... that and he talked so darned quiet." A wave of silent nods made its way around the campfire. "And my tiny words were too quiet for him to hear. So—"

"How did you talk to each other then, if you couldn't hear each other?" asked Shel.

"Yeah, I was just getting to that. We worked out a way of 'talking' where I would scratch on his toes to tell him things and he would tap his toes on the ground to tell me stuff in return."

Joy chimed in, "But, he was a giant. Eventually someone had to see him."

"Better believe it. One day, a couple of Longsmiles' guards found Charlie sleeping in his spot, down in the marshy sands of Frenchman's Crick," Sandovar pointed toward a forested area. As he did, he purposefully avoided making eye contact with Alice and the guards. "Charlie. That was his name, I think. It was either that, or Chattanooga or Chili Beans or Cha-cha Cherote. It was hard to tell in taps. Anyway, eventually he was discovered and they put him to sleep, just like Dungry and all the other giants in this *happy* place." Sandovar sarcastically emphasized the word 'happy', obviously upset about losing his friend.

Joy leaned over and put her arm around the chief. "Actually, that's not entirely true." Sandovar squinted at the girl. "Dungry was never put to sleep." A few chuckles, scoffs, and gasps came from the group, some thinking Joy was jesting, others thinking she didn't know what she was talking about, and still others believing her through and through.

"What are you talking about?" replied Sando. "Of course he was put to sleep, just like all the others who refused to leave."

"Not all were put to sleep," Alice chimed in. Sandovar spun around and glared at the royal guard with a squinty pucker. "In fact, Joy's right. We tried to capture the beast but Dungry was one giant who seemed unaffected by the onions."

"What? Why?!" asked Sandovar.

"The onions had no effect on him," replied Alice. "They say it was because he ate absolutely everything. So the king's guard had to find a different way of dealing with that troublemaker."

"So, what did they do?" asked Sando.

"They sunk him, like an old boat," Joy answered, before placing her own inquiry — "Wait, onions?" But her question was buried beneath a timely interruption from Shel.

"Sunk him? You mean they drowned him?" he asked uneasily.

"No, Shel. Giants can breathe underwater. Not great, but they can when they need to." Joy explained. "So drowning wasn't an option. They anchored Dungry to the bottom of the sea."

"Like, permanently?" he added in disbelief. Joy shrugged.

Shel looked shocked, as did others hearing the story for the first time. After a chill jolted through the camp, Izzy chimed in. "They call it Hungry Kid Island. But Hungry Kid Island isn't an island, it's the top of Dungry's head."

"What?!" coughed Shel.

"Yeah, normally just the top of his scalp sits above the water line, looking like a deserted island. He's been there long enough that some grass, bushes, and even trees have taken root on his head. Sea-goers will stop there from time to time to rest and what-not, seeing as how he's in the middle of the lake. Most never make it off the island. Sometimes when the lake is low, Dungry's face becomes exposed, even his mouth. When that happens, from a distance it looks like a cave. That's when you *definitely* want to steer clear."

"Is that why they put the giants to sleep?" asked Shel. "Because they were eating people?!"

Sandovar was nodding slowly but shook his head when he realized what Shel was asking. "No, no. Giants are generally not so dangerous. But there were a few who caused some problems for the kingdom. Dungry was probably the worst of 'em. You know the saying, 'one bad apple spoils the bunch'? The king decided he couldn't take the chance of the bad behavior spreading and decreed all giants leave the Land of Happy. Some left. Others refused to go. So, he ordered the ones who stayed to be put to sleep."

"Wow!" sighed Shel.

"But, they put them to sleep using onions?" Joy asked again.

"That's right. Onions cooked up by the witches!" the Sandman answered. "Onions steeped in a potion with an aroma altogether irresistible to the giants. So incredibly strong were these onions that one bite made the giants weep uncontrollably for days on end, exhausting the poor creatures to the point that all they could do was sit down and go to sleep. Once asleep, the potion prevented the giants from waking."

"I thought it was the wild strawberry jam?!" replied Joy, astonished and confused.

"Ha!" Sando laughed. "No. That's a myth, just something they tell people so they'll steer clear of those wretched berries. The jam from a wild strawberry isn't dangerous, it's phenomenally delicious. The bite, on the other hand, can be fatal if not treated. So, Longsmiles devised a plan to keep the people of Happy safely away from wild strawberries."

"Safe?" Joy queried, glancing at Shel.

"Well, could you imagine if everyone was out there trying to get at those delicious berries? We'd have a massacre on our hands! Just look at your Sheldon there. He barely survived and he only had a scratch."

"Barely survived?!" Joy choked on her stew and looked at Shel who was staring intensely at Sandovar.

"No sense in getting you all worked up at the time, so we didn't say anything. Why do you think he passed out so easily on the sand? Taud didn't drop him *that* hard. Yup, poor kid was knocking on death's door pretty loudly. It's a good thing death was out fishing, or whatever death does in his spare time."

Joy interjected, "But, I thought I did a good job treating—"

"Oh, you did! You did indeed," reassured Sandovar. "If you hadn't wrapped his hand in that salve of yours my dear, he would've likely been taken by fever, incapacitated in some way or another. And losing your faculties in the Sonrisa Desert is a sure path to disaster." Joy reached over and grabbed hold of Shel's hand. The two of them locked eyes. Sando continued, "Most likely he would've perished were it not for your attentive care; the talented and resourceful Joythea Costeros!" Joy stared at Sandovar, concern swirling in her eyes. "They're not to be trifled with, those berries," the chief added. "And now you understand why Longsmiles spread that little white lie."

Joy nodded slowly as she looked again at Shel, who'd obviously been considering his close call, evidenced by his pale face. Joy smiled reassuringly then turned to Sandovar. "I still don't agree with putting the giants to sleep."

Sando sighed. "Many people don't. I'm not certain I'll ever understand it entirely. I mean, I understand the need to do something about the bad apples, and I know Longsmiles gave them the option to leave and some refused. But I'm not convinced forced hibernation was the right solution."

Shel inquired, "You couldn't have gotten Charlie and his giant friends to resist? To rally against the king?"

Sandovar shrugged. "Charlie wasn't violent. Not at all. Plus, most of the other giants had already been tranquilized by the time I found him. He would've been knocked out too but he hadn't yet been discovered, probably because he took so many naps under the bridge, out of sight. And he always slept during the day… and I mean *all* day long."

"But why?!" Shel blurted.

Sando looked crossways at Shel and hollered back, "I don't know! I assume he was really tired!"

Shel looked away and smiled. "No. I mean, why did the king have to put the giants to sleep? It just seems… I don't know… cruel."

Sandovar's eyebrows stood up in ovation as he nodded his head. "Couldn't agree more, kid! Ohp! Look what the cat dragged in!" coughed the chief as Ingo walked briskly back into camp. With a loud clap, the commander interrupted everyone's conversations. "All right, team. It's time for lights out!"

"But Ingo," cried Tickles, "it's taking forever to finish this soup with these darned chopsticks!"

"It's not soup," corrected her brother with a smile. "It's gumbo!"

Tickles smirked at the unwelcomed correction.

"Well do your best to wrap it up as quickly as possible," replied the lion. "We need to stay focused on saving Manny and the king. There'll be plenty of time for soup, gumbo, bonfires, and chit-chat after we get back. Fair enough?"

As people began to clean up and prepare for lights out, Sandovar stood to confront his commander. "Ingo, I'm not so sure about Alice. I mean, after what she and her team did to the giants... and to you. Do you really think we can trust her when push comes to shove? Do you really think she has what it takes to—"

The lion halted Sandovar with a raised paw, stroking his beard like a true man of thought. "Sando, I know you to be a gentleman. I see the way you care for Miss Karynthia and Miss Kats, how you treat them with the utmost respect. Let us not now abandon our sensibilities under the pressure that precedes a great battle. You and I both know she was acting on the orders of her king, trying to save her people. One cannot hold judgment over her for that. Her motives were valiant and honorable."

Sando pursed his lips. The pain of loss that he felt for his giant friend made his heart resistant to Ingo's words. "Honorable? Valiant? Putting the giants to sleep was not—"

"No. You misunderstand me. We're not in a position, due to a lack of time and lack of information, to debate the validity of that particular decision, which was a decision made by the king, not Alice nor any of the guards, mind you. Those guards are sworn to carry out the king's commands. The charge of a knight, sacrificing one's own liberty, sometimes life, for the good of the kingdom... that is what I deem honorable and valiant. Right now, Sandovar, you are as a knight of the realm. And right now your Boogies need your leadership. And I need your friendship. As for Alice, she is like the wind: lovely yet unpredictable, glorious yet dangerous; very hard to pin down. She's been an adventurous soul all her life, always up for trying new things and adapting gracefully with change. Yet, she is dedicated to her king and that is why we can trust her to serve the mission. As for her capability, she could likely best any man in this rabble, including you and me... and she could probably do it blindfolded. I assure you, Alice is as capable as they come. Now, if that is settled, I have a favor to ask regarding Sarah and Sylvia. If it is amenable to you, I would like to borrow your lovely attendants for a few hours tomorrow, if I may. I have a special errand for them, which I think you will find most rewarding."

Sandovar replied as the gentleman he was. "How can I refuse?" With complimentary nods, the two bid one another goodnight and parted ways.

Ingo didn't get far before he was interrupted once more. (Being the commander came with the responsibility of listening to the concerns of his troops, regardless of the hour.) This particular distraction, however, was one that Ingo himself was anticipating. If he'd not been approached by her, he would have done the approaching. And so it was that Ingo and Joy took a walk in the late evening to discuss Joy's role in the impending conflict.

"I believe you know my family," Joy began as they walked. "And you know that our people are peaceful folk." The lion nodded. "I certainly hope for the safe return of the dentist and a healthy recovery for the king, but I cannot participate in an attack on the sovereign Gambrine colony. I know there are those in your company who believe that might makes right, that the best way to achieve peace is through a strong show of force — what they would call 'a good, old-fashioned fight' to decide a winner. But I feel differently." Her lofty brows punctuated her point. "I realize I may have sounded a bit militant when I was leading the charge to confront the king on your behalf, but—"

"Is that so?" Ingo interrupted and stopped walking. "I was not aware."

Joy looked down. Her assertive tone shifted to a softer key. "I may have gotten a little carried away," she smiled guiltily. "I suppose I was boasting in the moment. I would not have condoned violence against the king, but it did work to rally the cause." She smiled, and so did the lion.

"Well, I'm flattered. Thank you for rescuing me."

Joy smiled then got back to the matter at hand as they continued walking in the warm evening. "My point is that you and I both know that so-called losers of a conflict never just go away and disappear. When the loss suffered is sufficiently humiliating or devastating, conflict always has the potential to provide fertile soil for sowing the seeds of revenge. My mother taught me that."

"The Mermaid Queen is very wise."

"She used to tell me the story of General Cray and General Korr, about how they had the option for peace but insisted on war; and how their war raged on for years and years, long after the two Generals had perished, all because of the pendulum of revenge." Ingo stopped walking so Joy stopped too, though she did not look at him, preferring instead to marvel at the stars. "She used to say, 'revenge is a seed planted by the victor' in her lessons on diplomacy." Joy looked Ingonyama in the eye. "Ingo, if conflict is necessary, as you seem to believe, and if you should prove victorious, I would caution you to be careful how you treat the Gambrine when the dust settles. Yes, it is they who captured the dentist, but that is not an invitation to war. I believe you would do well to ascertain their motives for detaining Manny in the first place and be prepared to offer concessions for any past transgressions. For, while the seed of revenge may never germinate, the threat is always there. It can take years, sometimes even generations to grow. Meanwhile, the possibility of retribution will loom like a cloud over the Land of Happy, darkening her otherwise clear, glorious skies. I know I don't have to tell you, living in a state of constant paranoia does not make for a peaceful life, even for those who are mighty and victorious on the battlefield."

The lion looked at Joy. *How wise she is!* he thought, slowly resuming his walk. He pulled a stalk of grass that was soft and white, and chewed on it while strolling at a pace measured and slow. Of course he knew she was absolutely right. But what was the solution? They had to retrieve Manny; and knowing the Gambrine would not negotiate, he knew they were going to have to use force. The lion already had a plan in motion that would, fingers crossed, minimize any violence, but Joy's words were true: he had to consider reconciliation; he had to consider this campaign from the perspective of the Gambrine, and he had to consider the kingdom's long-term relationship with the Gambrine nation. "Heavens, I wish I had your wisdom when I was your age, young lady. Your mother will be proud when she hears of how you saved the life of a stranded boy, then went on to rescue an old lion from a life of incarceration, and then protected an entire colony of Gambrine while quite possibly saving the life of the king himself!"

"Well, that's all a bit of an exaggeration," Joy replied modestly. "That last bit will be up to you, Ingo. When your army departs for Champion Valley I will not be going with you. I must return home, at least for now. I fear my time here in the Land of Happy has taken a toll on me... and on my heart, in more ways than I can recount here."

"I think I understand," said the lion. And he did.

Chapter Five

Runners

The morning came much too early when Ingonyama woke everyone with a series of loud roars, knowing there was a good deal of training and planning to ready the troops for the mission...

The king, with his jaw stuck closed, would not have many days left before he starved and withered away. With any hope, the witches would ensure that didn't happen. As for the dentist, it was anybody's guess how long he would hold up in the 'care' of the Gambrine. Time was very much against them.

Ingo had, with help, spent a good portion of the night building a crude obstacle course, complete with rope swings, tree climbs, and treacherous pitfalls. As it turned out, spending months on end in a small prison cell gave Ingonyama an abundance of pent-up energy and he was going to make the most of every second of his new-found freedom. Unfortunately, many of his recruits weren't so keen on running that morning. So, he found a way to motivate the troops, which included Izzy, the shoe crew, Sandovar and his Boogies, Taud and the pirates, Alice and a few members of the king's guard... nearly everyone but Shel. With Ingo's permission, Sheldon left that morning to confer with Katryna, the cook witch. He did not divulge specifics, only that he had, "an idea how to help with the king's situation." Since it involved the king, Ingo let him go, to assist Katya in whatever way he could.

Everyone else, meanwhile, stood at attention as Ingo, with a wide grin full of sharp teeth, warned, "All right. Listen up you duffers. You'd better start running or I'm going to take a bite out of your butt! I may look sophisticated in my pressed shirt and trousers, but I'm still a lion. If you forget that, I'll be happy to jog your memory!" The group stood and stared at their commander, not sure if he was serious or trying to be funny or—

"Yeowww! You just bit me!" cried one of Alice's knights as the lion sunk his teeth into the warrior's leathers.

Ingo roared, reaffirming that he meant business. His ferocious growl sent the group scrambling through the obstacle course at breakneck speed, the lion giving chase. If anyone slowed down or tripped and fell, he was quick to remind them why they were running in the first place. By the end of the day, Queen Ruth and her monkey, Joy, Sarah, and Sylvia, all had their hands full bandaging wounds and passing out bags of ice for the warriors to place on injuries sustained in the obstacle course, many of which came from Ingo himself. The lion drove his disciples hard. As a result, it only took two days to toughen up the motley crew and make them work and move together like cogs in a greased wheel.

"They look like real soldiers!" Shel observed upon return, channeling his fascination with the military. He'd spent one day in the kitchen with Katya and therefore got one day to train in the field with Ingo, which was plenty of time for him to feel like a warrior. Ingo smiled at the kid before looking over his regiments with an approving nod. His fighters were ready. It was time to go get Manny back!

Ingo had planned to set sail that very night. "There's no time to spare. We'll sail through the night and attack at first light," instructed the lion.

"But we have no ship!" Taud the pirate asserted as they sat around the bonfire eating supper that evening.

"Taud's right. How are we supposed to reach Champion Valley without a boat?" challenged Izzy.

"Let me worry about that." Ingo stared off into the night as if the answer were hidden somewhere in the darkness. Seeing nothing, he turned back to the campfire and his troops. "The Boot Brigade will take as many as Delilah can carry. Shel, you will accompany the air attack. If they're able, the witches will cover your flank on their brooms."

Enthusiastic as he was about the idea of soldiering, Shel was suddenly frozen by the word 'attack', struck with the realization that they were really headed into combat. This was no drill, nor dream. Was he ready to fight? He wanted to save Manny but he was not a violent person, and he had nothing against the Gambrine. He didn't even know the Gambrine.

"Ingonyama, sir?"

"What is it, Sheldon?"

"I don't want to hurt anyone."

"Well it's a little late for that, don't you think?" replied the lion. "You've traveled a long way and accomplished much, including freeing me from prison, all for the mission to recover the dentist. Correct?"

"Well, yeah, but, it's just—" Shel found it hard to put his feelings into words.

"Change of plans," Ingo spoke to the group. "Alice, if you would, I'd like you to take my place leading the ground attack. I'll ride with the Boot Brigade. We'll cover the air." The lion winked at Shel and the kid immediately felt relieved. But he still didn't want to see anyone harmed.

"Ingo," pressed the elephant, "there's still the problem of how the rest of us are going to get there."

Ingo looked at Captain Fickleface. "Can Delilah carry all of us," he waved his paw over the group slated for the boot, "all of the weaponry and ammunition, and the elephant too?"

Looking less than calm, Fickles slowly shook his head side-to-side.

"Okay, that's a no-go," Ingo concluded. "Looks like you're sailing with the pirates, big guy."

Taudello was fast to reply. "Oh? And just how might ye be plannin' this grand sea voyage without a ship?"

Suddenly, a salty voice bubbled up from the deep, from somewhere in the darkness behind them. "Arrr! Who says ye got no ship?" The entire group spun around to see a black figure lumbering toward the firelight. A wooden peg under his left leg and a hook in place of his right hand immediately gave away the identity of the scurvy barnacle.

"Well bless me beard and call me captain!" cried Taud.

"You're no captain!" scolded the crotchety Captain Jarby, unaware of what was afoot.

"No, I ain't! But he is!" replied Taud, pointing toward the large silhouette clomping closer and closer.

The figure raised a rusty hook into the air and with a growl, stepped into the red glow of the fire, eerily illuminating naught but his face beneath his oversized black hat.

"Did me old ears hear someone call for a black-capped buccaneer with a black heart, a mighty sail, and even mightier cannons?" The figure scratched out a terrifying laugh and a cough that sounded like death.

Ingo stood to greet his old friend but Taud and Morty stood faster and with an "Aye!" and an "Arrr!" and a "Yo, ho, ho!" The pirates embraced in a roasting Jolly Roger reunion that threatened to steal the flame from the fire itself.

"Who be there?" gruffed Captain Jarby. "Don't ye know to greet the captain first? I'll have ye strapped to the mizzen for this mutiny!"

Taud and Mort laughed at the old man's whining. Then, out from the pirate huddle emerged a large hook and a long face with a curved mustache.

"Be good to see ye too, captain! If ye don't recognize the hook, perhaps ye recognize the leg!" He stuck his wooden leg right in Captain Jarby's face, as if he were attacking with a sword.

"Arrr! Back ye beast!" Jarby yelled, stabbing at the peg leg with his fork. The entire group burst into laughter.

"Hold the spyglass!" barked Morty. "Who be that youngster ye got with ya, Hook? Did ye finally land a proper first mate? A young buck who ye be groomin' to take yer place when ye finally meet ol' Davy Jones?"

Captain Jarbison interjected, "That ain't no sparky young lad! That there be a pretty lass if I ever saw one. Hook, ye old dog, ye finally settled down! And who be the lucky lady there?"

"Them's be fightin' words!" cried out Hook's companion. "I'll have yer head fer that!"

Suddenly the evening air was filled with the clanging of metal as swords and scimitars were drawn and flung about in a frenzy. The pirates and the Boogies had suddenly all turned on each other and no one was certain why.

"Hold it!" cried Ingo. "Calm down, everyone! Please! Save your fighting energy for the Gambrine."

As the ruckus quieted, the hook-handed captain reached behind him and ensnared his companion-in-question by the collar, dragging him into the light. "This here be no woman o' mine nor anyone else! Best be careful with yer blabberin' ol' Jarby! This here be none other than Blackbeard himself! The most dangerous of 'em all!" The crowd gasped and everyone stood frozen with jaws dropped nearly to the ground.

"Blackbeard?!? Where is his black... beard?" scoffed Jarby, poking fun at his fellow captain. Instantly swords were raised again, and again Ingo called for calm.

Hook thought the exchange was rather amusing and tried to contain his laughter. "Blackbeard lost a bet, he did. Had to shave his chin clean, else it would've been his throat what been cut 'stead o' his whiskers!"

The crowd began to unravel in laughter and side chit-chat, prompting Ingo to impose order so as to keep the group focused. He roared loudly and the crowd fell silent. Eyes shifting through the lot, the lion bent down in the sand beside the campfire and began drawing with a stick. "Friends, please! Let's settle down. Captain Hook and Captain Blackbeard have come to help us in our crusade to retrieve the dentist. They've offered to let us use their ships."

A brief moment of celebration and embracing, now that swords had been thoroughly sheathed, threatened to disrupt Ingo's order once more. "All right! Settle it and gather 'round. We need to go over our plan of attack." The lion began talking through his plan as he drew a map in the sand that identified the location of the Gambrine village in relation to Champion Lake and the Land of Happy. "The wind is in our favor tonight, so we ought to make good time crossing the lake. Captain Hook and Captain Blackbeard, we'll look to you to lead the marine attack. Your ships will sail through the night and travel up the Champion River in the early morning, arriving at the southeast end of the Gambrine village with the sunrise. Captain Jarbison and Mortimer will travel with Hook, along with Alice and the king's guard. Taud, you'll be on board Blackbeard's vessel with Sandovar and the Boogies. I'd like the pirate captains to stay with the ships, along with anyone else wishing to stay out of the trenches. The ship's cannons will come in handy during the fight and we'll need both ships ready to launch for a swift departure when the time comes. At dawn, when you see my signal, the ships will fire all cannons on my target, while Alice and her troops, together with the Boogies, will attack on foot from the west." Ingo looked around to see silent nods affirming that everyone was following along closely.

"Blackbeard, you'll drop Sandovar and his companion at the mouth of the Champion River, here," the lion pointed to the battle model he'd constructed from sticks and rocks. "From there, they'll make their way through the mountains and forest to cover the eastern front. His Boogies will stay on board the ship with you until you make port."

"My companion?" squawked Sando. "Are you talking about Taud or—?"

"Chief, I have a special task for you," Ingo replied. "You are to guide your companion, a secret weapon if you will, up Champion Ridge and approach the village from the east. At dawn, on my signal, you will descend from the ridge and meet up with the rest of us. Blackbeard's ship will carry you to your destination. He has by far the largest ship in the seven seas—" Just then, the ground shook and the group could hear the snapping of branches in the distance. "...And you're going to need every inch of it!"

On cue, the booming of something very large stomping across the countryside made the group fall silent and everyone stiffened, unsure of what was happening. Sandovar stood, then Ingo, then the rest of the group. The pirates drew their swords and the king's guard followed suit.

"There'll be no need for that," exclaimed Ingo with an upcast paw. "This one's a friendly."

Shel squinted. "Is that?! No! Ingo, is that…"

"A giant!" Sandovar finished Shel's sentence.

"Not just any giant, my friend," replied the lion, as the enormous man came into view. Everyone stared in utter disbelief as Sandovar's caretakers Sarah Karynthia and Sylvia Kats stepped into the distant glow of the fire, carefully leading a giant by a soft rope tied around his index finger. Joythea, Katya the witch, and Queen Ruth accompanied the giant as well. Sarah and Sylvia bowed as they reached their chief. Joy nodded, indicating that all was well.

Ruth stepped forward. "May I present, Chester the giant." It was Sandovar's childhood friend, only the giant's name was not Charlie or Cha-cha Cherote; it was Chester.

"But… how?" was all that Sando could get out.

"I had some help," replied Ingo as he stretched a paw in the direction of the group of women.

"But... how did you find him?" pressed the Chief. "How did you wake him up? How did you get him to follow you? How—"

The queen raised a hand to halt Sando's questions. "Charmed onions put them to sleep. It was charmed *garlic* to wake this one. We had help from the witches, naturally. Turned out, waking him was the easy part."

"Let me guess," said Sandovar, "the hard part was keeping him calm after you woke him. I'll bet he was in a right fit—"

"Actually, he's been very decent, a real sweetheart. Aren't you, Chester?" The queen looked up at the giant and scratched out a rhythm on his toes. A low grumble and giggle came from high above. "The difficult part was getting him moving. As you might imagine, muscles and bones grow rather tired after resting for so many years. Thankfully, a giant's metabolism is extraordinarily slow, being built for long periods of hibernation... though usually not forty years of it. You may be aware, it wasn't unheard of for the giants of old to hibernate for decades at a time... which, incidentally, was why Longsmiles approved the proposition of long-term slumber in the first place. Not that I condone the act... Anyhoo, after Miss Karynthia and Miss Kats told us where to find him, I conscripted a modest regiment of the king's guard to help excavate him from the cave. With Katya's spellbinding, we were able to resuscitate him and walk him back to the castle for rehabilitation."

"But… all of that would have taken *days* to accomplish!"

"Indeed, Sandovar," replied Ingo. "Which is why we began the process a couple of days ago, only hours after I was released from prison. Addressing the plight of the giants was my first objective as a free man." Izzy raised eyebrows, asking Ingo to clarify. "What happened to the giants has been on my mind for some time. I've given the issue a lot of thought while sitting alone in my cell. When you all charged me with commanding the invasion of Gambrinsville, I knew we were going to need a proper miracle. As soon as you mentioned your old giant friend," Ingo spoke to Sandovar, "and how he was somewhere nearby, I knew Chester could be that miracle."

"Do you intend to wake the others? Or... you already have?!?" asked Izzy, looking around nervously for more giants.

"No. Well, yes. That's, the plan: to wake them eventually. For now, we've only raised Chester. If this resurrection proves successful, we'll proceed with the others, *after* we return from Gambrinstown. Now listen, I need you to—"

Ingo had been prepared to launch into his plan for the giant, but Sandovar burst into hoots and cheers like a kid at Christmas, running to Chester and embracing the giant's ankle. Chester wasn't as happy to see Sandovar, however, given the grogginess still clinging to him after his forty-year nap. Plus, although Chester recognized something familiar about the Boogie chief, on the outside this Sandovar looked very different from the boy Chester knew so long ago. As Sandovar hugged Chester's leg, the chief could sense the tangible rift that time had opened between the two pals. They were just kids when they knew each other last. Now, they were both grown. But unlike Sando, Chester didn't know how he'd come to be so old, and a fair bit larger. He did not have the memories of an experiential life as Sandovar did. All he had were fast-fading memories of random dreams.

"He needs time," the queen said to the chief as she picked up on both Sandovar's disappointment and the giant's confusion, which was turning to sadness as Chester slowly became aware of just how many years had passed him by.

"Unfortunately, we don't have time," Ingo replied quietly to the queen but loud enough so Sandovar could hear. "Sandy, I can only imagine what this moment means to you. But we must stay focused on the mission to save the king in time." Sandovar looked at Ingo disapprovingly. Despite what the chief might have been thinking at that moment, the lion did not have a heart of stone. "I know what you must be thinking, Sando. The decision to wake him was not just for your benefit, nor was it solely for the benefit of the mission." Sandovar's expression relaxed a bit. "Longsmiles was wrong to put them to sleep in the first place. Certainly the dangerous ones, namely Dungry, needed to be dealt with. But the peaceful ones, like Chester here, ought to have been left to live in peace. Upon our return, we intend to initiate a great awakening, raise the giants from their slumber — those that can be awakened anyway. We will need Chester's help to make sure his kinfolk do not seek retribution against the kingdom. This means that between now and then, we need to do all we can to show Chester we mean him no harm, that we are friends, and that we are very sorry for what we did to him and his kind."

"You mean what *Longsmiles* did!" Sandovar replied coldly.

Ingo looked at the queen mother then back to the chief. "*We* are the kingdom, as one or not at all. We all must take responsibility for this injustice and work together to correct it. It is hardly sufficient to put the blame on one person alone. Because, then what? We have the king exiled, or worse? That would not serve justice for the giants. That would not assuage the pain and anger they no doubt will feel... that Chester must feel now. No, we must show them that the entire kingdom understands their plight and that we are full of remorse and regret; all of us. We must demonstrate that we wish to live alongside them and work alongside them once again. We must show them, one day at a time, that we intend to correct our mistake and heal the wounds of the past."

Sandovar took a breath and looked at Chester. He felt he could see, even at the giant's great height, the sadness in his friend's face. After a moment of thought and reflection, he replied, "All right. What do you need me to do."

"Sandovar, you and I are men of the sword and of the gun," replied Ingo. "We have known battle and conflict all our lives. This moment requires deep skill in the healing arts. For that we need kindness and empathy, but we also need inspiration and creativity, as we are, in a sense, giving new life to the giants." Sandovar nodded, giving Ingo his endorsement, so the lion proceeded while motioning to a young lady in the crowd. "If you'll permit, I would ask that you let Joythea guide you through your reunion with Chester and the healing process." Sandovar's eyes widened in surprise, begging for an explanation. Ingo placed a gentle paw on Joy's shoulder. "I was very surprised to see Joythea Costeros among you when you came to collect me from prison, given that she is royalty herself."

Shel looked over at Joy in surprise. Their eyes connected. He couldn't help but feel let down in learning such important things about her from public discussions. But, he had to remind himself, she did not belong to him, not in the least. *What did you expect?* he challenged himself. Joy could see Shel struggling with difficult emotions, whether frustration or confusion or disappointment, she wasn't entirely sure. But she knew the time to have an honest talk was now overdue. And yet, it could not be now, on the eve of battle. Especially now that she'd been charged with the important task of helping Chester reunite with his old friend and with the world. She looked away and Shel could feel the distance between them expand.

"But since we're lucky enough to have such a kind-hearted and creative resource in our midst," Ingo continued, "I have asked her to help and she has agreed. I have also asked Sarah Karynthia and Sylvia Kats to accompany her, as their healing skills are unmatched. Also, their kindness and compassion will go a long way to help Chester feel at ease. I suggest the five of you spend some time away from the group working on basic communication and getting the giant re-acquainted with his new reality. When you're ready, connect with Captain Blackbeard and see what you can do to help prepare the ship. I would like both marine regiments to be loaded and ready to set sail in two hours."

Joy stood up and walked over to where Sandovar was standing with Chester. Sarah Karynthia and Sylvia Kats rallied to their chief and the five of them walked into the night.

"Okay Yams, you have the troops," noted Izzy. "Now what? You said your fighting days are over and I don't see any weapons except a few swords. I heard you mention the cannons on the ships... Where's all the ammunition? Where are all the guns?"

"Not to worry, old friend. I have a plan to get Manny back. It's not ideal but it's the best I could do on such short notice. If all goes according to plan, we won't need guns or swords. If this works, no one will get hurt... much." The lion spoke up to address the crowd. "Wanda informs me that... You all know Wanda, right? The witch who flies on a vacuum and studies under Katya?" There were nods in the group and glances around the circle as people looked for the witches but didn't find them. "Well, anyway, Wanda has told me—"

"Where did the witches go?" interrupted Don the bear. "They were just here."

"I'm getting to that, Don," replied Ingo patiently. "Wanda tells me that right now, a good bit of the king's palace is still overflowing with spaghetti."

Some eyes in the group widened, others squinted, recalling the pasta avalanche.

"Did you know," the lion continued, "there are many good uses for spaghetti other than eating?" Looks of confusion were had by all. Ingo expected nothing less. "I have asked Wanda to re-create the mess she made in the palace… albeit in a more controlled manner. Soon we'll have enough pasta to feed a good portion of the people of Kantytown for a month."

"Are the people hungry?" asked Donachtuk, in surprise. "That would be weird because—"

"No, no," replied the lion. "The spaghetti is not for the people. It's not for eating. Sorry for the confusion. I just meant that we'll have a lot of it. Anyway, speaking of the people of Kantytown, I have asked the good citizens to collect as many fruits and vegetables as they can spare and we now have a considerable stockpile of watermelons, grapes, cherries, cantaloupes—"

"Yuck!" coughed Shel without meaning to.

The lion stopped and looked at him. "You okay, Shelby?" Shel nodded in embarrassment. "Right then. Where was I? Right. Food. So, you'll all have plenty of snacks for the trip… But most of it will be ammunition for the battle."

"Ammunition?!" barked Izzy.

"Ammunition," replied the lion coolly. "We have installed catapults on the ships, and the king's armory has prepared various sizes and sorts of slingshots as personal weapons for you all."

There were both outbursts of protest and cheers of excitement from the group. Others remained quiet in contemplation or confusion as they tried to wrap their heads around what Ingo was indicating.

As usual, Izzy was the first to raise his trunk and ask, "Sooo, we're going to throw tomatoes at them? Do I have that right?"

"That's precisely right, Izzy," replied the lion. "You've heard of a food fight? Well, this is a food war! A few of you experienced just how debilitating it was to be stuck in that mush of spaghetti greeting you at the palace steps. Well, once we locate Manny in the fields, we'll overwhelm the Gambrine with enough pasta to create a veritable marshland. They'll be like flies in a spider's web. We'll hold them off long enough to extract the dentist and then get out of there before they have a chance to retaliate."

The cries of protest diminished to mumbles of consideration as the group slowly conceded that this crazy idea might just be crazy enough to work.

"My friends, I told you that my shooting days are over. I've had my fill of guns and bullets, swords and sorrow." Ingonyama hung his head for the destruction and sadness he'd seen during his lifetime, then added quietly, "Violence only begets violence. I know that now." He lifted his head, took a breath, and continued, recalling his role as the group's leader and thus the need to stay strong. "The plan is to debilitate, not to harm. Everyone got that?" He looked around and locked eyes with as many in the group as he could. "In the end, we do not want to make an enemy of the Gambrine. They are not our enemy. Let me repeat that. The Gambrine are not our enemy. They are simply in the way of something we want. So, we only need to get them out of the way, temporarily. That's all."

"But Ingo, watermelons and cantaloupe thrown hard enough could still really do some harm. No?" Donachtuk pointed out.

"Indeed. That's why I need to ask you all to be cognizant of the fruit you throw. There will be plenty of over-ripe options. Those are okay to toss in the air. Rotten stuff will only cause discomfort... and maybe some nausea. That's exactly the sort of debilitation and distraction we want. But if you come across something hard, even something small like an apple, either mush it up before you launch it or set it aside... or maybe eat it. Because don't forget, it'll be important to keep your strength up, right?" Ingo smiled and people smiled back.

"Or, I don't know..." he continued, "let's say you have a hard watermelon. Instead of tossing it up in the air, try tossing it at ground level, rolling it like a bowling ball." He shrugged. "I don't have all the answers. You'll have to judge for yourself, so long as you keep in mind that ultimately the Gambrine are not our enemy. Historically, we've enjoyed a peaceful relationship with our scaly neighbors to the west. That peace has held because we keep our distance and do not disturb their way of life, especially their crop — a crop that has fed the people of Champion Valley for as long as any of us can remember. Right?"

Nods and mumbles affirmed his sentiment.

"Right. We won't be leaving without the dentist, that's a given. But we also don't want to leave behind insult and injury to inspire retribution. We don't want to return to save the king only to bring conflict and war to his doorstep in the future," the commander concluded.

A great murmur rumbled from the crowd, followed by a cloud of silence as everyone weighed the lion's words and his unorthodox proposition. In that moment, the only sound that could be heard was the crackling of the bonfire. This was the moment of truth when the group would accept Ingo's crazy plan or not.

Sheldon was so excited at this nonviolent solution — which actually sounded rather fun — that he burst into laughter. "Haha! Yes! I love it! Let's do it!" He stood up, walked over to Izzy, and gave his friend a hug. His enthusiasm ignited a fire in the group and others began to cry out in celebration.

"Okay. I'm in!" bellowed Izzy. "Let's give those Gambrine a taste of what we're serving up. Something *other* than broccoli!"

"Well, I'm glad you're on board!" exclaimed the lion. "Now, get on board! *Haha*," he laughed. "Delilah is being outfitted with catapults as we speak. I'll finish giving orders to the rest of the group and meet up with you all in one hour." He then turned to address Captain Blackbeard and the Boogies. "Captain, Sandovar and Chester should be back soon. Go ahead and prepare your ship if you would, please. We launch in one hour."

"Aye!" was all that Blackbeard said and he and the Boogies set off for the clean-shaven-pirate's ship.

That left Captain Hook, with Alice and her king's guard.

"Hook, you know what to do!" said Ingo. "As for you, Alice, I'm counting on you to keep the peace."

"Sir? The peace? I thought this was war."

"Indeed it is, Alice. And war must always end in peace, else, by definition, it does not end. Correct?"

Alice nodded, slowly. Impossible to deny, that logic was.

"And for all our sakes, we need peace to hold. To that end, this battle needs to be fought with good humor and result in as few injuries as possible. And once the battle is over, we'll need to mend relations with the Gambrine. That is, the Gambrine will need to be compensated for the trespass we are about to endeavor against them."

"I see your point," Alice said with a slight bow of her head.

"This campaign — the attack itself and the retrieval of the dentist — is going to put us in considerable debt to the Gambrine, not to mention the mess we're about to make with the food. The mess will need to be cleaned up and the debt repaid. I intend to set things right with the Gambrine, and this is how…"

Ingonyama proceeded to explain his post-operations plan to bury the hatchet between the Gambrine and the kingdom of Happy. One hour later, Ingo's troops were packed and ready to set course for Champion Valley.

Chapter Six

Storm

The fiery sunrise brought more than just a new day to Champion Valley, it brought a new world.

Aboard the Flying Festoon, soaring above the landscape, Sheldon looked eastward in the direction they'd come, watching the evening blues blend into a rich blood orange.

"With any luck, that will be the only blood spilled today," Ingo nodded at the sunrise.

Shel smiled hopefully.

As if thrown by Apollo before his grand entrance, thin spears of gold shot from the horizon, piercing the remaining stars still clinging to life in the highest corners of the sky. The brilliant green of the valley could already be seen glowing through the dense morning fog blanketing the basin. The scene unfolding was so magical Shel felt as if he'd leaped right onto the pages of a storybook.

"What a magnificent place," he whispered to himself. Turning north to look where they were headed, he spotted small figures bustling in the landscape. They looked like small lizards with miniature picks and hoes, rakes and shovels. "Brocosmiles?" he asked aloud to no one in particular, without taking his eyes off the land.

"Mmm hmm," someone replied, and at once Shel became nervous, for he knew the battle for Manny was about to begin.

The Gambrine were already out in the fields tending their crops in the twilight when Delilah came sailing slowly over the horizon, flying low in the dawn sky, concealing their arrival behind the blinding light of Apollo's sheen.

"Eyes up! Stay alert!" commanded Ingonyama, who had dressed the part in an old military uniform Falconovich had given him for circus performances. It was an outfit from the Eastern Europe of old, every button, every stitch as authentic as the blood stains on the collar and sleeves. Ingo's otherwise wild mane was tucked as neatly as possible under a large, metal helmet whose brim sunk just above his intense eyes. His suit was pressed neatly, shoes polished, gloves starched. Every bit of this commander looked as a man, tall and broad and stoic. If Shel didn't know there was a lion under the uniform, he would've guessed Ingo was just another one of the king's men. In fact, in this particular suit, Shel thought Ingo looked nearly identical to the soldier he'd run into on the streets of Chicago.

Noticing Shel's examination and reading his mind, Ingo smiled. "Good! That's exactly the response I'm going for. The fewer who know Ingonyama is here, the better. Today I am just another military man."

Shel smiled and nodded.

"What about you? What's that thing slung around your chest?" Ingo asked.

"You mean my pack?" Shel replied. "It's a satchel I borrowed from Sandovar. It's got a few things I thought might be useful for the battle. I brought a gift... for Chancellor Hume."

Ingo raised a brow in curiosity but did not inquire, sheer surprise at the youth's boldness scraping the words from his tongue. Instead, he just smiled and turned to Captain Fickleface, making ready to signal the first attack. "Ready cap-i-tan? Hold her slow and steady now..."

Somewhere below Delilah, the pirate ships sailed silently up the Champion River. Meanwhile, Katya and her cousin, Wanda, having completed both the lion's tasks, recruiting three more of their Wiccan sisters in the process, bringing the flying broom (and vacuum) contingent of Ingo's army to an even five, flew on ahead of Sandovar and Chester, escorting the Boogie chief and his giant through the Gambrine forest to their battle station at the top of Fallshugger Ridge.

With his chessboard set, all pieces in place, the Nifumo storm was nigh upon the valley.

o o o o o o

A flying boot is a hard thing to miss. So, as the Festoon crested the hills encircling the valley, the brocosmiles in the fields began to perch on hind legs and stretch their necks, giving them the look of curious meerkats on the savannah. One by one, the crocodile-like creatures stood up, forgetting their tilling and weeding and planting, as if they could sense something wasn't right about the incoming vessel. When they heard the warning calls from their kin working in the swamps down by the river, alerting them of more foreign vessels approaching, this time from the sea, their hunch was confirmed: This was not a friendly visit. This was not Grandma Gambrine bringing fresh-baked broccoli calzones in her antique pirate ship. No, this was an invasion!

Shel turned with a nervous smile to his comrades, his anxiety now joined by excitement, heart pounding out of his chest. As Delilah sailed over the fields, Shel marveled at the brocosmiles crawling around, scrambling about, fleeing and hiding. A few of the bolder ones stood and stared, while others pointed up at them with various things in their hands. *Could be just farm tools*, Shel hoped.

The battle stage was set. All that was needed was for Fickleface, who was frantically scanning the countryside with his trusty Evil Eye spyglass, to locate Manny so the lion commander would have his target. Suddenly, a premature war cry from Chester let the cat out of the bag, a giant warning echoing through the valley like thunder.

The brocosmiles jolted, turning away from the flying shoe to confront the invisible monster howling at them from somewhere in the forest. The grip of fear clenched its fist and brocosmiles scattered like flies, buzzing this way and that, bumping into each other, tripping over anything and everything. They now knew beyond doubt that they were under attack. Many of the brocos began throwing things like spades and pitchforks into the sky at the passing airship, signaling to Ingonyama that it was time to strike.

"Where's Manny?!" yelled Ingo. "Did we arrive on the wrong day? Is he still locked away in Gambrinsluk?"

Fickles shrugged nervously from behind his telescope.

Just then, Pickles cried out, "There! I see 'im! It's Manny! I can't believe it! There he is!!"

Shel leaned over the side of the ship, straining in the direction where Pickles was pointing, and immediately had to duck to avoid a head of broccoli sailing over the bow.

"Lookout!" cried Tickles. "They're onto us!"

Although he was still far away, the dentist was rather easy to spot since he was of considerably different shape than any of the gangly reptiles. His white dentist coat stood out like a sore molar against the green of the brocosmiles and the valley.

Satisfied with his target, Ingo turned and nodded to Chef Picklepots, who instantly brought down a mighty cleaver, cutting through the rope restraining a catapult full of pasta. As the catapult spun with a force that shook the ship from bow to stern, a massive tangle of goopy spaghetti flew high into the dawn, blocking out the rising sun.

WHOOSH!

Thick strands of noodles, twenty feet long and tangled together in a bramble only a witch could weave, swirled through the sky like earthworm storm clouds, raining down drops of marinara as they flew. Meanwhile, waiting in their mighty ships, the pirates saw the starchy signal and scrambled to their battle stations.

"Spark the cannons!" wailed Captain Blackbeard, and a wild ruckus roared to life.

BOOM! BOOM BOOM! The cannons hollered one by one, sending mushy watermelons, cantaloupes, and grapefruit sailing like a flock of wingless birds over the fields of Gambrinstown. As the fruit landed with echoing splats and splishes, the Gambrine scattered, running for shelter wherever shelter could be found.

The witches also saw the writing on the wall once the spaghetti was in the air and began flying around like gnats, encircling Chester's head, calling out instructions. In response, the giant reached into a large satchel at his side, laughing with glee as he pulled out handfuls of omelet mush and began tossing bunches of breakfast over the treetops, down into the farmland below.

Before any brocosmiles had time to grab their forks, tuck in their napkins, and give thanks for the meal they were about to receive, the skies became overcast in food fireworks of green onions, red carrots, yellow peppers, and purple cabbage. Not knowing what to make of this bizarre, never-before-seen onslaught, the brocosmiles' response was anything but unified — exactly the sort of chaos and confusion Ingonyama had hoped to create.

Some brocos stood still, bewildered by the colorful fare, "ooh-ing" and "aah-ing" as it flew through the air, until the mess descended *smack!* onto their spellbound stare.

Some laughed and danced in the rain of cuisine, mad as hatters, rejoicing in the splatters (if you know what I mean).

"What is this ridiculousness?!" they yelled in fright. "Who knows?! But sure is marvelousness!" they echoed in delight.

Others scattered and scurried to avoid being buried.

"Look out!" they cried.

"The sky is falling!!" they lied.

And still others took the flying grub as a welcomed invitation, eager for a good, old-fashioned, healthy altercation.

"Bring it on, you food-tossin' floobies!" they taunted, growing ever more sick, as more and more brocos became schtuck in the schtick; smothered in sludgy, rotten, slickity-ick.

At the water's edge, Alice and her knights sprang from the pirate ships to commence the ground assault along the western front, fighting not with their usual swords and staffs but with oversized stale bread sticks and sourdough baguettes.

"Ahooo! Look! The salt from the pretzel bombs... it's irritating their skin," called out one of the guards.

"More salt!" yelled Alice. "Pass the message to all the troops! Salt is the key!"

At the same time, from the north came a great crashing of trees and bushes. With the Boogie chief clinging fast to his shoulder, Chester the giant came bounding down from Fallshugger Ridge, smashing everything in his path. As he reached the valley floor, howling with delight, he found enormous blooms of broccoli sitting like teed-up golf balls on top of their long stalks. The jolly giant rejoiced in booting the vegetables across the fields and into the heart of Gambrinstown. In this way he'd found a cathartic outlet for his pent-up frustration at having been put to sleep for so many years. After such a considerable nap, once he got moving, he discovered that he was overflowing with energy!

The riotous onslaught coming at the Gambrine from all directions was absolutely overwhelming. Never before in Arcania had an invasion like this been conceived, let alone carried out. Champion Valley was, after all, a mostly peaceful place. Accordingly, the Gambrine's military regiments were ill-prepared and out-of-sorts, especially during the season of sowing, which was historically very peaceful, what with communities coming together to help in the planting of seeds and all. On the morning of the great battle, the Gambrine's weapons were stowed and their armaments unmanned, and so Ingonyama's invasion went almost entirely uncontested as the food piled up, around, and on top of the flailing brocosmiles.

On any given day, the Gambrine might experience the odd crop raid by wandering scoundrels. Some brocosmiles working in far-away fields late at night might stay a hair more vigilant against possible rogue Worst beasts lurking in the bushes. Sure, they had to remember not to accidentally start reciting poetry while pulling weeds, lest they attract a hungry Banzakoot. Other than all that, Gambrinstown was quite safe —

that is, if you happened to be a Gambrine. Visitors were not so welcomed. Then how did a dentist end up in the Gambrine village, one might ask? Indeed, that was the question on the mind of everyone fighting for Manny that day.

The lion's strategy was first to create utter chaos by throwing everything they had at the Gambrine: fruits, vegetables, grains, fungi… Even old, moldy cheeses and chunks of curdled pudding were hurled into the fray to add an extra element of yuck.

The pirates, meanwhile, ever seaward-thinking, tossed some fish they'd caught during the voyage over. The seafood, unlike much of the other stuff being thrown, was perfectly fresh, and brocosmiles love fresh fish, perhaps above all other food, including broccoli! With sardines, salmon, and sea bass now on the menu, holy mackerel was there ever a feeding frenzy!

The 'shock and awe' campaign was unfolding like clockwork. Once the Gambrine were sufficiently confused and distracted, the boot brigade worked to surround Manny with a moat of mushy macaroni while Chester made his way to snatch the dentist from captivity. Easy as pie.

(Heads up! Flying pie comin' through!)

But, just as the giant was closing in on Manny's position, something unexpected ensnared Chester's attention. He stopped, turned ninety degrees to the right, and began walking briskly away from the farm fields in the direction of Gambrinstown, sniffing the air as he went, like a bloodhound suddenly catching a scent.

"Chester!" yelled Sandovar, still fixed to the giant's shoulder. "What are you doing?!" The giant didn't answer; he just kept sniffing the air and twitching his nose like Ingonyama's little mouse. "Chester! We have to get down there to save Manny! Chester!!" Even the witches, still flying in formation around the giant, tried getting through to him, but Chester wasn't listening to anyone. Like a rat called by the Pied Piper, Chester the giant stumbled from the battlefield and marched right into the beating heart of Gambrinstown. A speck on the giant's shoulder, Sandovar considered abandoning his ride, but there was no safe way to get down from such a height. So, the chief just held on and watched the witches in the air and his fighting comrades on the ground, fade into the distance, unsure of what would be waiting for him in the Gambrine capital, other than a city full of irate brocosmiles.

As the fight closed in on Manny's position, Delilah's crew feverishly tossed fistfuls of fettuccini, bucketfuls of bucatini, and tankfuls of tagliatelle over her bow, doing whatever they could to create a barrier around the dentist. Meanwhile, two brazen brocos, seeing where the conflict was headed — literally and figuratively — ran directly into the fray, braving the milieu of marinara, and swiftly snatched the dentist from where he was eagerly awaiting his rescue.

Manny looked up at the flying shoe passing overhead, locked eyes with Captain Fickleface, and cried out, "Fickles! Hellllp meeee!" as the two Gambrine goons dragged him away.

Fickles' eyes grew red with rage, and he tore at the Festoon's laces, desperately trying to position Delilah for another bombing run, barking at his crew to, "Put everything we have in front of those brocosmiles! Cut them off!! Stop them from escaping!!!"

The crew responded without delay. Like the chiming bells of Notre Dame, the wooden catapults of the Flying Festoon rang out a blitzkrieg of feed, fodder, lunch, and larder. And as the airborne smörgåsbord choked the skies, scavenger sea birds began flocking to the mess, adding to the chaos. Gulls, petrels, and terns swarmed the air, followed closely by their larger cousin, the giant albatross. Fickles had to swerve evasively to avoid colliding with the birds and keep the Festoon afloat.

Jolted by something other than a bird — and other than Fickles' mad zig-zag steering, making everyone aboard feel ill — Delilah rocked and churned uncontrollably, tossing her crew like corn kernels popping in a pan. *BANG! BOOM!* Delilah was hit again and again, over and over. Stumbling, Ingo snatched one side of the ship and looked overboard to see what was attacking them. Catapults lining the forest's edge were flinging huge broccoli crowns into the air as fast as the Gambrine could load them.

"They're firing back!" he yelled, as if his mates weren't already aware.

"We need to set 'er down!" Picklepots yelled. "We'll be blasted out of the sky!"

"Fickles! Pots is right!" cried Tickletoes. "The Festoon ain't no fightin' bird. She's not built to withstand a proper broccoli beatin'!"

When a dark shadow passed over the ship, blocking out the light filtering through the fog, food, fowl, and fray, the Festoon crew looked up, afraid to discover what was descending upon them. Did the Gambrine possess their own fleet of flying machines? Were they prepared for an air assault after all?? Could this be the end for Delilah and her crew???

"Look, look!" cried Shel, pointing at the massive shadow. "It's Charlotte!"

The pelican winked at Shel and his shipmates before snatching a few broccoli bombs out of midair before they smashed into the boot. Two other pelicans joined in and together, their large mouths served as safety nets protecting the ship from incoming projectiles. Charlotte and her fellow pelicans flew in tight formation, encircling Delilah, catching broccoli crowns then dropping them over the catapults, giving the brocosmiles a taste of their own medicine. "You'd better get out of here before you're knocked out of the sky," she warned Fickleface before cutting sharply starboard to intercept another round of ordinance coming in hot.

"Phew! We're saved!" cried Pickles.

"Yeah, I thought we were in deep trouble! Figured we'd be grounded for sure! But ol' Jezebel flies again!" yelled a triumphant Tickletoes — who, it turned out, spoke too soon as a massive broccoli ball blasted right through the floorboards of Delilah, leaving a gaping hole in her sole. Stunned, the bootaneers peered through the opening with wide eyes. Below, the Gambrine waved and smiled up at them, celebrating.

"Uh oh!" Picklepots assessed the hole pessimistically.

"That's not good!" Tickletoes agreed. Clearly Delilah concurred, swaying back and forth as if knocked silly.

"Nope. Not good at all!" concluded Fickleface with a final prognosis. He glanced at the lion with distress. "Sorry, Yams, looks like we're going to have to set 'er down... and fast... 'for she loses all her beautiful buoyancy."

Charlotte and her pelican regiment continued to circle the shoe, doing what they could to help, but it was clear they would be out of work soon and so they readied to retire. "She's asking to be set on solid ground!" called Charlotte to the crew, assessing the ship while snagging more incoming projectiles as she passed, doing what she could to make their impending disaster less disastrous.

The lion grumbled, "Hmmm, all right then," and scratched his beard, trying to keep a cool head despite the mounting chaos. "Where's Manny now?"

Pickles quickly picked up the spyglass while Shel rushed to the bow to have a look around. Meanwhile, Tickles posted up on the deck of the ship, lying flat on her belly, sticking her head out of the gaping hole.

"Careful, Ticks," warned the captain. "Wouldn't want ya fallin' through. Might be the last we ever see of ya." Tickles backed away from the opening and grinned sheepishly at her brother.

"I don't see nothin'!" cried Pickles, squinting through the Evil Eye.

Fickles looked over, rolled his eyes, and wiped a glob of marinara from the lens. "There. Give that a try."

"Oh! Much better!" said Pickles, staring through the spyglass right at Fickles' face. "Have you always had that mole on your cheek?"

"PICKLES!" yelled Fickles and Tickles in unison.

"Manny's gone!" called Shel. "There's just a huge pile of noodles and glop down there."

"Oh no! We buried 'im alive!" yelled Tickletoes.

"Hey! There's Izzy and Alice and the king's guard!" Shel spotted friendly troops heading to where the Gambrine had set up the bulk of their defenses. The sheer number of brocosmiles was frightening. Despite the pelicans' best efforts, Delilah was slowly but surely being blasted out of the sky.

"See if you can land the ship as close as possible to those catapults," Ingo called to the captain. "Shel and I will join forces with Alice and Izzy while you three try and find Manny." Fickles nodded, maneuvering Delilah into position using the control ropes.

Ingo located Charlotte zigging and zagging through the obstacles filling the sky, and, with a nod, thanked her and her friends for their valiant effort and acknowledged that the birds would be of little help now that the air attack was coming to an end. And so, Charlotte and her companions turned sharply back toward Champion Lake, their fight in the battle now over.

"We'll have to finish this fight on foot!" Ingonyama roared. Seeing the look of fear in Shel's eyes, he comforted his young friend. "Do not be afraid, Shelby. Stay close to me. I will protect you!"

"Delilah, get us down there!" Fickles called to his ship. The captain was in a mad fit at seeing how close they were to getting his friend back. He yanked on the laces and, just like when Shel first landed in the Festoon back in Chicago, the ship pitched hard and began to roll upside-down.

"Ficks! We're going to crash!" yelled Ingo.

"Trust me!" Captain Fickleface called to his crew as they flipped through the air. Clearly he knew something they did not. A contingency escape plan for just such a catastrophe is, after all, the province of any good captain. Fickles reached into his coat and pulled out what looked like a bottle rocket. Holding it out toward his chef, he instructed, "Pickles, if you please?"

The chef knew just what to do. With the book of matches he always carried in his pocket (a good chef is always prepared to light a cooking fire) he ignited the rocket's fuse then quickly plugged his ears and clenched his eyes.

Captain Fickles, hands full of ropes and rockets, had no fingers left to spare. So, Tickletoes made the sacrifice and stuck her fingers in her captain's ears. The valiant gesture was unnecessary, however, for when the rocket exploded into the air, it released but a gentle whistle — loud, sure, but melodiously attractive. That was, after all, precisely its purpose. The lovely sound, together with the brilliant red and green flashes from the explosion, worked their magic. Everyone in the vicinity stopped for a moment to gawk at the fireworks, oooo-ing and ahhhh-ing as if rehearsed.

"Now when I say jump, everyone let go uh the ship n' jump! Got it?!"

The boot was heading straight for the Gambrine catapults, forcing brocosmiles to scatter lest they be crushed like the Wicked Witch of the West (who, according to legend, was Wanda's third cousin). And speaking of Wanda... like genies from a bottle, a gaggle of witches suddenly appeared, having been signaled by Fickles' bottle rocket. The broomed bedlam encircled the descending boot, prompting Fickleface to yell, "JUUMMMP!!!"

As his comrades leapt from the careening Festoon, the witches, like spiders catching flies in midair, snagged the falling sailors, securing them atop their brooms. One-by-one, Ingo, Shel, Fickles, Pickles, and Tickles found themselves saved from disaster. Sadly, the same could not be said for their ship.

CRASH! CLANG! BANG! BOOM!

Delilah came down right atop the Gambrine catapults, smashing the ramparts into splinters. The great flying shoe didn't fare much better. When Delilah finally came to rest, she took one last breath, her massive hull expanding then contracting, before going still and silent.

"DELILAH!! No!!!" cried Captain Fickleface, hovering just above the wreckage on the back of Wanda's upright vacuum — no brooms for that batty, old hag.

"Oh, no!" sobbed Picklepots, tears in his eyes as he flew by in what seemed like slow motion. The witches dropped him and Fickleface in a swamp of squash before flying off to engage in the escalating battle. Shel and Tickletoes, meanwhile, were set down in a nearby nest of noodles. Shel immediately had to restrain Tickletoes as she struggled to get back to Delilah to comfort her dying friend.

"There's no use," reasoned Shel. "She's gone!" But Tickles wasn't listening. "Tickletoes!" cried Shel. "Don't waste Delilah's sacrifice! We need to get to Manny. Stick to the mission, Tick! We came here to save your friend, remember?! Delilah can be rebuilt but Manny can't. Tickles!" Heeding his words, Tickletoes crumpled in Shel's arms and wept.

Meanwhile, Izzy, together with Alice and the king's guard, fought their way toward the wreckage, to make sure everyone was alive and okay. But as the rescue mission surrounded the crash site, an army of brocosmiles surrounded the rescuers. The enemy was closing in.

Chapter Seven

The Search

"*Hold 'em off!*" cried a voice from above. "We need time to find Manny! He's buried somewhere under that mound of pasta!" Ingo was still leading the offensive from his new battle station, zooming above the fray on the back of Katya's willow-branch broom...

A rusty voice rang out in response. "Arrr! If ye need be findin' buried treasure, a pirate be the right bloke fer the job!"

Ingo looked down from his perch. "Taud! Morty! ...And... Blackbeard?! Jarbison?! What are you doing here? I thought the captains were going to stay with the ships!?"

"Aye, that they were, but ships be damned!" replied Blackbeard. "Our hearties be in trouble, they be. And a pirate never leaves his mates tuh hang."

"Even if they be dry landlubbers! *Har, har, har*!" added Taudello, letting loose his indomitable laugh for all to hear; a deep rumble echoing through the valley, lightening the hearts of Ingo's army, dispiriting the enemy.

"Buhsides," snarled Jarbison, "the ships' cannons already clobbered the western flank. Ain't no targets left within range."

Ingo grinned. "Well, all right then! You pirates get to digging. Find that dentist! I'll help Alice hold off the Gambrine as long as we can. Set me down just there!" Ingo called to Katya, and so she did.

Once on the ground, Ingo grabbed all the fruit and vegetables he could carry and began lobbing them like grenades at the incoming brocos, before bolting like a hurricane to where Alice and her troops were fighting at the front. Jumping into the chaos of battle, the lion immediately began wrestling with the crocs, tumbling and flipping and rolling about in the slop, setting the example for others to follow.

The food was still flying in a frenzy but no longer from high in the air. The ground assault was in full swing. Ripe, red tomatoes were a favorite given the magnificent *splish* that resulted when exploding over the face of one's opponent, the gooey red juice giving the fight a more authentic feel.

In contrast to the rotten vegetables being thrown by the invaders, the raw broccoli being tossed by the Gambrine didn't feel so soft. But that was the only projectile they had. Luckily for the invaders, the Gambrine didn't use advanced weaponry like guns and bombs. Instead, they preferred catapults and spears. They also had, however, a whole lot of sharp teeth and claws at their disposal. *YOUCH!*

Who knows why, but the Gambrine have always been naturally talented in the martial arts. Hand-to-hand combat against a brocosmile is almost always a losing proposition. For veteran warriors like Alice, however — who was handy with almost any weapon, even a stale loaf of bread — dispatching one broco after the other was only slightly more taxing than a brisk hike up the Champion Mountain range.

And then there was Izzy, a full-grown elephant with a nearly impenetrable hide (though the Gambrine were certainly trying to penetrate it). Izzy couldn't really grasp a weapon, having no fingers, but he didn't have to; he had tusks for moving things aside, other animals included. Though he preferred to use it for pondering life's curiosities, his thick head was pretty useful for ramming things. It was his massive body that proved the handiest, however, as he shoved (as gently as possible) his adversaries left and right, like a bowling ball knocking down pins, one after the other. If the Gambrine didn't leap out of the way of the pachyderm express, they were launched out of the way.

"Wahoo!" some would yell as they sailed through the air, enjoying the free ride.

The battle was proving a rather welcome change of pace for some of the Gambrine. It was more excitement than most had seen in ages. And since a good deal of the fighters were only getting entangled, buried, or otherwise overwhelmed by food scraps, as opposed to the more serious injuries commonly sustained on a battlefield, there was very little grief or sorrow involved. The biggest casualty that day was the Gambrine ego, and that's not necessarily a bad thing. This was, after all, war in Arcania, and war in Arcania need not be violent. Indeed, it ought not to be. In fact, a passage commemorating the battle would later be added to the Harvest Hymn, the anthem sung at the opening of each Champion Valley harvest season.

T'was some good, ol-fashioned food-tossin',
Swamp-shakin', double-crossin',
Slop-wrestlin', fruit-fineselin',
Get-down on the farm!

Do-si-do atop ol' spaghetti,
Toss a peach, it's compost confetti!
Cut loose, go wild, n' have no fear!
Smush a banana in yer partner's ear!

It smelled so wrong but felt so right;
Sure had-a-lotta fun at the ol' food fight!

"How's it coming?" the lion called to the pirates, who'd been joined by Shel and the boot crew, all digging like mad, trying to find Manny under the pile of pasta.

"Arrr! Does yer dentist friend be havin' a long, fluffy backside?" asked pirate Mortimer, holding up what appeared to be a large, furry tail.

Speechless, Ingo squinted at Morty while keeping a large paw wrapped around a brocosmile's mouth. (One thing's for sure, you don't want to let a broco's massive mouth clamp down on you if you can avoid it.) The lion shook his head in disbelief as Morty yanked on the tail, pulling what was attached to it out from the tangle of noodles. Sadly, it wasn't the dentist. But happily, it was the dentist's philosophy-loving friend: that big, fat cat; old mister Buddha Baggs!

Izzy did a double take, skidding to a halt and jaw dropping to the ground when he saw Baggs dangling from Morty's hand. As soon as he stopped, a gang of brocosmiles jumped on his back, trying to bring the great pachyderm down. But Izzy simply shook like a wet dog, sending the brocos, like drops of water, flying in all directions.

It was at that moment when a great commotion erupted in the distance, followed by a harangue of shrieks, wails, and cries. Izzy, Shel, Fickles, and everyone else, turned to see a mass of brocosmiles and Ingo's troops alike, scattering, fleeing something. A figure, impossible to make out, was moving through the crowd. Izzy knew straight away it must be a Worst beast. It must've been alerted by the ruckus of battle, which, no doubt, could be heard in every corner of the valley. It made perfect sense! Of course a Worst would show up to take advantage of the chaos. Whether rotten fruit, animal, or human, finding a meal in this mess would be like shooting fish in a barrel for a Worst. There was no time to lose!

"RUUUNNN!" cried Izzy. "Save yourself!"

Shel started to follow his friend but stopped when something familiar in his periphery ensnared his attention. "Hang on." Shel squinted at the approaching terror. "Can it be??" He squinted harder until the thing became clear. "Oh my gosh, it is! It's them! Izzy! It's them!"

Izzy froze mid-bolt. "What?? Them? Them who?!?" Izzy looked back at where the Worst would've been, but the beast wasn't there. In its place were three, mostly regular-sized folks, small compared to an adult Worst... or an elephant. Thus, Izzy's fear diminished. "That's not a Worst!" he announced to the crowd around him, quelling the fear he'd just incited. "Are those your friends, Shelby? The ones you told me about?"

"Izzy, those are my friends! The ones I told you about!" Shel repeated, paying scant attention to the elephant, let alone his rolling eyes.

Walking casually — one might even say strolling —through the crowd, scattering creatures left and right with naught but their looks, came Karl the ghoul, Dracula the vampire, and Walter the werewolf... pushing a red bicycle.

"Hey! Shelby!" Walter waved from a distance. "We brought your bike back! Heard you were in the neighborhood, so we thought we'd swing on by." Walter spoke as if there wasn't a war going on, not a care in the world. And why should they care? The three of them together were the most fearsome gang in Arcania. To be fair, a gang of a Worst, a Banzakoot, and a storm dragon would be far more dangerous and terrifying, but those monsters worked alone. These three on the other hand could paralyze a victim with a bite from poisonous fangs, then eat the poor soul alive, bones and all, and then haunt them in the afterlife... if they wanted, which they most certainly did not!

"Heya, Shel! How's it?!" greeted a friendly Karl. "Everything good with you?" It was as if they couldn't even *see* the battle raging on around them.

"Uh, hi guys!" said Shel, doing his best to pretend he wasn't amidst a heap of swirling chaos. "Yeah, I'm okay. Just, you know, fighting a war with the Gambrine. No big deal." Shel smiled smartly.

Izzy chuckled, till a succession of grapes pelted the side of his head like rapid fire from a fully-automatic machinegun — *zap zap zap zap zap!* — prompting him to bolt in the direction of the assailant. "I'll get you for that!" he yelled, stampeding through a mess of noodles and smiling brocosmiles.

"Soooo, you guys come to help us fight? Orrrr..." Shel queried, holding out an abandoned rake he'd found lying on the ground.

"Oh, no, probably not," replied Dracula. "We don't really go in for that aggressive stuff so much these days; had our fair share of battles over the years; the many, many years... eternal souls and all. Besides, you may've noticed, we don't exactly have to fight. Our mere presence typically does the job. Sometimes a stereotype works in your favor. Haha!"

"Hey Drac!" called Walter. "Looks like you may have been a bit hasty. Check it out!" Walter pointed to a gang of brocosmiles heading their way, clearly intending to confront the paranormal pack, likely concluding — after witnessing their relatively docile attitude — that the monsters weren't as threatening as they looked. It didn't take long, however, for the brocos to realize their mistake. One loud roar from each monster was sufficient to send the Gambrine fleeing for their lives.

Farther away, another Gambrine platoon pushed their way to the center of the fight. Unlike most of the brocos fighting in the fields that day, however, this group was well-organized, well-armed, and led by what looked to be an armored tank.

Without warning, the tank stopped and stood on its back legs, revealing itself to be not a tank at all but a massive brocosmile, larger than any other, indeed larger than any animal Shel had ever seen in his life, save for the storm dragon. The dragon, by contrast, was bolstered by the power of the tumultuous sea, able to grow big as tidal waves. This beast came from the land and stood entirely on its own, for her own might was enough.

The broco tank paused when she reached the top of a hill of noodles, turning in a slow circle, surveying with a scowl the wreckage spreading over her land. Then, growing even bigger, she raised her arms, displaying a fearsome set of claws, and bellowed, "STAAAAAAWP!"

Upon hearing her voice ringing across the land like an air raid siren, vibrating through the air and the ground in subsonic tremors — as was the Gambrine method of communicating over long distances — nearly all fighting came to immediate arrest. Food fighters everywhere froze in battle poses like wax figurines, daring not to move.

Surrounded by her royal guards, the Gambrine High Chancellor stood on her hill of noodles rising above the landscape, sizing up Ingo's army. She was darker and bore far more scars than any of her kinfolk, looking as if she'd clawed her way, tooth and nail, to the top. This monster struck fear into the heart of every one of the invaders, save maybe for Alice (whose absolute lack of fear incited many a rumor that she was actually a cyborg with literal nerves of steel — an absolutely ridiculous notion, of course).

The Gambrine leader, whose family name was Hume (a shortened version of Humungor, the original Gambrine clan who settled the Valley a thousand years prior, give or take) bellowed like the horn of a cargo tanker on the ocean, "WHO IS RESPONSIBLE FOR THIS TRANSGRESSION?! This OFFENSIVE invasion! Show yourself! I demand RECONCILLIATION! I demand JUSTICE!"

Her ability to stop the war on command was beyond impressive. Even Ingo thought so. Everyone did. A deafening grave silence settled over the fields, so absolute that when a flea on the western front sneezed, a caterpillar way over on the eastern flank replied, "Gesundheit!" In that moment of quiet, Shel sensed something, an inaudible buzzing in his bones, a whisper on the wind, nudging him to look down to his left.

No, your other left!... Behind you!... Down here!

There in the food wasteland, looking like Sheldon when he was buried on the steps of the Kantytown palace, sticking out from under a pile of noodles and nectarines, broccoli and beans, was a hand.

As the moment of silence passed and Chancellor Hume resumed her demands of this, that, and the other, Shel's eyes widened, watching the hand twitch. He dared not move, however, lest he attract the attention of the reptilian tank, not more than twenty yards away. *She's as big as a house*, Shel thought. *Like the Worst beast... but bigger!*

Without taking his peripheral sight off the buried hand, Shel reached to his right and snatched Captain Fickles' shirt sleeve. Like everyone else, Fickles' attention was glued to the enormous brocosmile belting out a harangue of insults and ultimatums from her high post. Shel's incessant tugging was as a tenacious mosquito, irritating and unwelcome.

"What?!" Fickles whisper-yelled, annoyed that Shel would risk drawing attention to them both. "What is it?" He bent his head only slightly, frowning sideways at his friend. Shel gestured with his head, pointing with his eyes to a spot on the ground behind them. Fickleface glanced backward but didn't see anything right off. Shel persisted so Fickles looked once more. Upon closer inspection, he recognized the familiar-looking hand sticking out of the spaghetti. The boot captain couldn't help but let a squeak slip out before he caught himself, two hands clapped over his mouth, eyes shifting rapidly to see who may have heard. The coast was clear. Fickles collected himself, reached over, and began tugging on Picklepots' shirt.

Pickles had the same, annoyed reaction. Obviously they should all be still and silent like obedient students at a classroom lecture. "Knock it off, Fick!" But then he too caught a glimpse of the hand, and also squealed with delight. His reaction not only caught the attention of Tickletoes who scowled at her brothers, goofing off when they most certainly ought not to be, it also caught the attention of some nearby brocosmiles.

"Will you guys pipe dowwww..." Tickletoes stuttered as she caught sight of the hand. "Oh my goodne—urmph!" A pile of hands from her brothers smothered her mouth as several nearby brocosmiles crept toward them, intent on squelching what appeared to be a rebellion in the making.

The commotion also caught the attention of Ingonyama, however, who quickly deduced that a distraction was in order. Fine timing too, since he, as the leader of the invasion, was being called out by the Gambrine High Chancellor.

"WHO IS IN COMMAND OF THIS ASININE ASSAULT? THIS EGREGIOUS ERROR? This... This DERANGED and DEPLORABLE directive?? This unthinkable, ugly, utterly... Ugh! WHO IS IN CHARGE HERE?!"

"I AM!" Ingonyama boomed like a fifty-ton gong on a mountaintop, swiftly untangling himself from a pack of brocosmiles and standing tall. All creatures within earshot looked his way, including the gang of brocos approaching the boot crew. Adjusting his helmet snugly over his eyes and tucking his mane into the base of the cap — once again assuming the look of a military man, disguising his feline identity — he casually made his way through the tangle of noodles toward the chancellor, flicking food scraps from his suit as he went.

With the crowd enraptured by the impending confrontation between their respective military leaders, Shel and the boot brigade proceeded with their task in anonymity, albeit slowly, carefully, quietly. After a great deal of digging and scraping away food slop, they finally extracted, at long last, their old friend, Manny the missing dentist!

Chapter Eight

War and Peace

"*I am the one you want!*" With a final shoving aside of a few stray brocosmiles, Ingonyama approached the hill on which Chancellor Hume stood. At least a dozen brocos were working diligently, lining the tall mush mound with meatballs and mash, shoring up the chancellor's makeshift command post. Upon Ingo's declaration, four guards leapt from their construction tasks and slithered up to the lion, quickly binding his limbs with noodles. With two brocosmiles on each arm, Ingo the prisoner was escorted up Spaghetti Hill — the name given to the mound from where the high chancellor (as would be recorded in the Gambrine history books), "defended the Realm during the Great Battle of Champion Valley."

"Kneel, you scoundrel!" The guards tugged at Ingo's arms, pulling him toward the ground. "Bow before the high chancellor!"

Ingo's army erupted in protest, shouting and tossing food at the hill. It looked as though the tenuous peace would not hold. In response, Ingo twisted and spun like a martial arts master, effortlessly lowering his captors to the ground. He took a few long strides toward the colossal Hume, who looked large enough to eat Ingo in one bite. Her guards readied their spears, intending to perforate the aggressor, when he quickly turned to the crowd.

"Boogies! Stay your fighting! Alice, still your guards! Pirates, at ease my hearties!" The lion turned to the chancellor and with a bow of his head, dropped to one knee. "Your chancellorship. I take it the Gambrine are not in the mood for a good-humored, old-fashioned, friendly food fight?"

"Guards!" commanded the chancellor, and instantly Ingo was recaptured — though this time his hands were bound with more than mere pasta. Some dark green twine reinforced the noodles, twine that looked and smelled of broccoli (of course).

"Friendly? Food fight?!? GOOD HUMOR?!?! Is that your idea of a JOKE?! I am *NOT* laughing! How dare you attack our sovereign land! Who do you think you are?!" The chancellor paused long enough to give the rebel commander the idea it was his turn to speak.

"Your Highness, we have come—"

It wasn't.

"I don't care *why* you have come. It makes no difference *why* you have chosen to attack us. You think just because you've chosen, in place of cannons and swords, to use— What is this nonsense?" The chancellor bent down, picked up a handful of food scraps, "...Rotten vegetables?! You think that makes it—"

"Beg your pardon, Your Highness, but I think it does matter. If you would hear me out—"

"I WILL NOT! You can't erase what you've done here with mere words! The only thing that matters now is that we have you! All of you! You work for the Gambrine now! Every last one of you! You will clean up this disgraceful, repugnant mess; you will regrow the crops you've destroyed; and then you will work in our fields as our prisoners... for the remainder of your days! I hope it was worth it!" With that, the chancellor motioned to her guards to, 'take him away,' and — confident she'd successfully squelched the invasion — turned to depart.

In defiance, Ingonyama lifted himself off the ground, refusing help from his captors, cleared his throat, "Ahem," and announced, "I'm not finished."

The chancellor whipped around. "Oh, you are most certainly finished!"

Ingo nonchalantly ignored the lashing out of Hume's ego — "We *will* help clean up the mess..." — once again effortlessly ripping apart his bonds, eliciting cheers from his audience. The Gambrine guards assumed fighting stances and the chancellor squared off, readying for an attack that never came. Instead, Ingo stayed calm, casually brushing invisible dirt from his clothes. "...And we will help replant your crops. But we will not be staying beyond that. In fact, some of us will be leaving immediately." He winked subtly at Shel standing just in front of the boot crew, a drooping dentist clinging to the shoulders of Fickles and Tickles. This was their cue. Shel turned and nodded to Fickles, who nodded at his compadres, and they very slowly began shuffling their way through the soggy noodles, dragging Manny, who looked like a soggy noodle himself. Unfortunately, they did not get far.

"Leaving?! I don't think so!" Retorted the chancellor. "Perhaps you weren't listening; this is your new home! You all work for the Gambrine now. No one is leaving."

Upon hearing those words, brocosmiles everywhere adopted aggressive stances, doing their best to look like barricades against any possible retreat. Manny and the boot crew found themselves surrounded by brocos brandishing farming tools, blocking their escape. Of course Ingo noticed the blockade, as did Izzy and Alice. *But did Hume see?* Ingo wondered. *Does she know about the dentist?*

It was clear the lion and the crocodile were at a standoff. Ingo knew he had to be more persuasive or, at the very least, create another distraction so Shel and the Boot Brigade could press on. Thinking quickly, he snatched a spear from a nearby brocosmile, twirled it in a circle, snapped it across his thigh, and tossed the broken shards at the feet of the shocked and offended chancellor. He intended the gesture to be symbolic of breaking the Gambrine stronghold, breaking Chancellor Hume's illusion of control. Most everyone watching, however — eager for any excuse to resume the epic food fight — took it as a sign that the battle was back on. And so the food went flying once more, both Hume and Ingo ducking to avoid being splattered.

"THAT'S ENOUGH!" The chancellor roared, resuming control. She raised an enormous claw, halting a good majority of her troops. "Enough of this *nonsense*! Everyone!" Once again the fighters froze. She took a few steps toward the lion, looming over the defiant brute, baring a mouthful of giant, pointed teeth. "I know your type, commander. You're the sort of malefactor that throws a stone at a window just to see if it's open!"

Ingo risked a quick glance in the direction of the boot crew and was immediately relieved to see the gang able to continue their retreat with Izzy clearing a path. Returning his attention to the chancellor, Ingo shrugged and bobbed his head. "I've been known to throw a few stones in my day. Strike first and ask questions later, I always say."

Somewhere in the crowd Walter nodded at Karl bitterly. "He's clearly been spending too much time with humans."

Karl rolled his 'eyes'.

"I figure," Ingo continued, "It's better to ask for forgiveness than to ask for permission. Isn't that right my friends?!" Ingo addressed Alice and his fighters and they responded with cheers.

The chancellor's belly grumbled in distaste for the commander's audacity. "Hmmm. I, myself, have a slightly different version. *EAT* them first and ask questions later." She growled with a sinister smile and took a step toward the lion.

Ingo gulped. Though he knew the Gambrine weren't the sort to go around eating other creatures, they certainly could if they wished; this one especially. Hume had the most dangerous reputation of all, one that matched her intimidating size.

"Well, go on then," she challenged, "ask for forgiveness," adding in a slow growl, "see how that goes for you!"

Ingonyama straightened his back. "I think perhaps we'll skip that bit and get to the part where we negotiate peace terms. Shall we?"

"Peace?! You speak of peace, you war-mongering miscreant?! We *were* at peace before you INVADED!" Her farmers cheered in agreement.

"Ah, but that's not entirely true, is it?" Ingo roared above the crowd and the cheers calmed. "For how can you rest peacefully when the feathers that fill your bed have been plucked from stolen geese?"

The chancellor squinted.

"Three geese to be exact," Ingo clarified.

Hume scowled at the cheeky military man spouting riddles, wasting her time. Meanwhile, more Gambrine poured into the fields from the village as word spread that an invasion had been thwarted by the chancellor herself. Noting the engorged crowd, the chancellor rallied. "I don't know what you're playing at with your goose-feather gibberish, but as you can see, you're vastly outnumbered. Give up without any more of this food-fighting ridiculousness and we'll make sure you and your friends have a comfortable stay at the Gambrinsluk bed and breakfast."

(Of course, Gambrinsluk was no bed and breakfast. It was quite the opposite, known as the worst prison in Arcania: cold, dark, wet, stone cells, buried deep under the broccoli fields at the edge of Gambrinstown.)

Unafraid of the chancellor's threats, Ingo laughed. "You really have no idea who *we* are, do you?" With an outstretched, gloved finger, he pointed. "That there is Lady Alice, the most formidable knight in King Longsmiles' army. Were she here alone she could vanquish fifty of your fearsome brocos."

"Ah, but there aren't fifty of us!" roared the chancellor. "There are five hundred! And more on the way."

Ingo nodded, "Indeed," though he knew the chancellor was exaggerating her numbers. "And just the same, Alice is not alone, she has her king's army at her side, with more standing by at our ships just over the hill, down at the harbor… and a thousand more who could be here tomorrow."

"Tomorrow! Ha! By then we'll have—"

"And she has Ingonyama!" the soldier interrupted with a blast. "The famous rifleman… who never misses his target. Perhaps you've heard of him?"

"Ingonyama?! The sharpshooting lion?" the chancellor replied, visibly shaken but trying to keep calm. Everyone in Arcania knew of

Ingo's reputation as the most formidable warrior in the land. "That lion died a long time ago. That or he's long since departed these lands. Either way, no one's seen hide nor hair of that cat in years." Hume was distracted but doing her best to hide it, to believe her own words.

"He's here," replied Ingo. "I assure you. And closer than you think."

"Where then?! You're bluffing! He's hiding somewhere... In the bushes, perhaps?!" The chancellor looked around uneasily. "Show yourself you cowardly lion!" She shouted at the surroundings.

Ingonyama laughed from behind his uniform disguise. "Cowardly? Ha! Sounds like you have him confused with that stuttering dandy lion from our neighbor town, the merry old land of Oz. Arcania's version, I assure you, is no coward. In fact, he's standing right before you!"

Ingo swiftly removed his helmet and shook out his mane with a menacing growl. A tremendous gasp shot through the crowd. Several nearby brocosmiles jumped. Some even turned and ran. The chancellor herself nearly fell over backward. The Gambrine were up against the ropes, if only momentarily.

"Now that I have your attention... Hume!" Ingo proceeded, knowing full well that no one ever dared use the chancellor's given name. But Ingo also knew that his best option was to unsettle the formidable brocosmile, get under her skin, force her to make a mistake. Seeing her falter at the sight of him, then shutter at hearing her name, Ingo pressed his advantage. "That's right. I know who you are, Francis Pretmore Hume." The chancellor writhed, digging her claws into the surrounding food. "I know all about you and your insatiable pursuit of perfection. Nothing's ever good enough for Hume, is it? But, what I'm about to tell you is the best offer you're going to get. So, will you hear me out? Will you consider my proposal? Or will you choose all-out war and the destruction of Gambrinsville?"

The chancellor stared with daggers in her eyes. "The destruction of... hmpf! Is that your proposition, lion? Tell me, do you know what happened to the last visitor who arrived unannounced and uninvited, laden with his own proposal? He even dared to call himself a caretaker of the Gambrine. A caretaker! How precious! Well... I ate him! Pipe and all! Poor mister Fredrick; tasty young chap with a fancy derby cap." The chancellor took a few measured steps toward the lion. "And do you know what happened to the next fellow who stopped by, demanding his lost cat, if you can believe that?"

Ingo risked another peek at the escaping boot crew, now a good distance away, Manny still clinging to the bootaneers like a soggy cape. The dentist was worn down but still very much alive. Still very much *not* eaten.

"As a matter of fact, I do," Ingo replied defiantly. "He's over yonder, in the care of my good friends. I believe you know the Flying Boot Brigade."

"WHAT?!" The chancellor spun around, following Ingo's eyes, aghast at seeing her prisoner in the hands of the enemy.

Now, the Boot Brigade was not an actual enemy of the Gambrine, nor anyone else for that matter, at least not before the Battle of Champion Valley. The flying shoe crew had always been respectful of the Gambrine, at least their crop. If brocosmiles had friends — which they did not — the shoe fliers might have been considered among them. But after this little stunt, they would be lucky to ever be invited to the annual broccoli harvest festival again. Not that guests were ever really *invited* per se. During the festival, the Gambrine would just sort of scuttle off and disappear back to their huts or caves or wherever they called home, making way for the greater Champion Valley community to trespass in the fields for a few days, harvest whatever broccoli they so desired, and leave handsome payments in honor buckets hanging throughout the farm. If no payment was left, the Gambrine would surely find out. Somehow they always found out if anyone failed to pay. But the Boot Brigade always left full payment, plus tip. And so they were always welcomed back, year after year; given priority notice in fact. But that was before the war.

As for Buddha Baggs, Manny's cat, it was a rare exception indeed for anyone to have been tolerated as long as he was — what with his aimless wandering through the fields without care; reclining on the grass, puffing smoke rings in the air; waxing philosophically till the day was well done; all while watching brocos slave away in the hot sun...

The Gambrine were known to be highly communal creatures, but only with their own kind. Baggs being allowed such liberty was a testament to the fact that he was so calm and peaceful, so curious and personable, so darned cute and fluffy!

"STOP THEM!" Hume hollered, pointing at her escaping prisoner in the clutches of the boot crew. Her army, however, had no idea to whom she was referring, and so they just scrambled about, doing their darndest to stop someone from doing something. As a result — and because the onlookers were bored listening to the two commanders swapping insults — the food fight resumed, much to the delight of nearly everyone; everyone except Hume.

Ingonyama knew he had Hume unhinged. His plan had always been to create chaos, and here was more chaos erupting. Now was not the time to let up.

"And in case you hadn't noticed the others in our party, chancellor," the lion continued, "we've brought with us the most feared pirate fleet in all the seven seas! Now, I concede that, like Ingonyama," he placed a paw over his own chest, "this man is hard to recognize, what with being clean shaven and all..." He stroked his own fluffy beard then pointed to the crowd, identifying a figure standing tall and menacing in all-black robes and bottomless black eyes. "But that man there is none other than the ruthless Blackbeard!" Gasps rang out, exactly the reaction Ingo was hoping for, expecting even. "And somewhere near Blackbeard... where is my good man?" Ingo squinted into the crowd. "Somewhere... is another black-hearted sea devil... Blackbeard, where's Hook?"

Blackbeard shrugged.

"Hook?!" The chancellor stammered. "As in *Captain* Hook??"

"The very same!" replied Ingo with a smile, confident that this news would further unsettle the chancellor. And it did... at first.

Hume stumbled and fell back into her makeshift 'throne' of broccoli, meatballs, melon, and celery. There she sat, looking around intensely, searching for the one called Hook, her fated nemesis. (Somewhere in the distance a ticking clock could be heard echoing on the wind.)

"I... haven't heard that name in...," she sputtered. The momentary shock dissipated and Ingo watched, to his dismay, as a sinister grin swept across Hume's enormous mouth. She collected herself, diminishing Ingo's advantage.

"Hoooook... Yes, I think I recall him..." the chancellor growled, shifting in her throne to get comfortable. "Where is he then? Show yourself, Hook!" she spat at the crowd. "Is he also wearing a disguise? I might not recognize your face... it has been many years indeed. But I'd never forget that stench; the stink of worn-out, salt-soaked leather and fear! ...And there's something else," she feigned confusion. "Something else about you I'd never forget... What was it?? Oh, yes! Your TASTE!" Hume snarled, licking her chops! "I think I still have bits of your hand stuck in my molars... Someone bring me that dentist!" she blasted furiously. But Manny was well on his way to the pirate ships, unbeknownst to Hume. "Where are you, Hook?! Come out and face me!" she challenged. "I'm going to have my teeth cleaned and polished, ready to devour the rest of you, you pitiful pirate!"

Ingonyama was caught entirely sideways by this development, no notion that Hume and Hook had history. "Blackbeard," Ingo whispered as discretely as he could then shrugged his shoulders, silently asking, 'Where is Hook?'

Looking as dangerous as ever, mouth twisted in a snarl, baguette swords clenched in fists ready for more brawling, Blackbeard whisper-yelled back, "Arrr! Stayed with the ships he did. Said he's against crocs uh any kind. Can't abide 'em, won't go near 'em. Said he'd man the cannons fer when things need blastin', an' the sails fer when folks need escapin'."

Ingo was stunned. He could sense a sudden, unexpected shift of power, could almost see his advantage slipping through his fingertips. The Chancellor sensed it too. She scratched her way out of her throne and stood tall to receive the dentist. Except Manny didn't reach Spaghetti Hill because the boot crew, thanks in large part to their elephant escort, never found their way back into the clutches of the Gambrine. Even if they had, Ingo was ready to defend Manny at any cost. Seeing that another distraction was in order but running low on options, he resigned to his fate as commander of the mission. "A captain must be prepared to go down with the ship," he muttered to himself, helping to gather his courage. Though he knew he could not win in a one-on-one fight against the chancellor — she was just too big — he leapt anyway.

With a mighty roar, Ingo launched himself through the air, landing squarely atop Chancellor Hume's shoulders. Instantly a frenzied wrestling match ensued, food scraps flying as the two commanders tumbled and thrashed about. The bold act reignited the food fight across the battlefield and the war was back on!

It didn't take long for Hume to subdue her attacker, however. Though he was fierce, her sheer size was impossible to overcome, especially in the slop where stable footing proved elusive.

"Such a shame," the chancellor snarled, pinning Ingo in the mire. "You've come back from the dead only to die again." She pushed him down into the noodle slop, a food-scrap sarcophagus, expiring the light of day as his head sunk below the surface. Each time he tried to take a breath his mouth filled with some rotten sauce or chunks of moldy mush. "This time I'm going to make sure you don't return. You should've never come here, lion. You should've known that I cannot be beaten. My Gambrine are too powerful! Now I'm going to teach you a lesson. I'm going to drown you in this filth of your own making." Hume rolled her body over Ingo, pressing her full weight into him. He would suffocate for sure, if he didn't drown first.

Izzy, Shel, and the boot crew, who were by then a considerable distance from their commander, crested the last hill at the edge of the battlefield, ground no longer covered in food waste. Once Shel saw the pirate ships down at the harbor, he breathed a sigh of relief, a sentiment shared by the rest of the party. They'd persevered! They'd gotten Manny out! Mission accomplished!

Shel turned with a smile back toward where Ingo was still wrestling with Hume. His smile faded.

What if Ingo lost the fight? Will Chancellor Hume, like the jungle king, make Ingo her dinner? No way! That couldn't happen! Shel couldn't let that happen. After all, he'd gotten Ingo, and everyone else, into this mess in the first place.

Well, to be fair, Manny had a lot to do with it, he argued to himself.

Okay, sure, but the mission to recover Manny was my idea!

Eh, that was the Boot Crew... and Izzy.

Right. Fine. But who pressed the mission forward, across the sea and sand, all the way to Kantcomplainistan? I did! And who insisted on freeing Ingo and—

Well, that was Joy, really.

Okay. You're right. But who came up with the plan to invade the Gambrine village?

Ingo. Remember?

Argh! So, what have I done then? What have I even contributed since coming to Arcania?

Time on the battlefield seemed to stop as Shel quarreled with himself, pondering his significance, or lack thereof. He realized there were many characters sharing the spotlight on the Arcania stage, a plethora of protagonists in this play; a tale woven by many lives, many adventures all crossing paths at this point in history.

We've contributed quite a bit, actually. But we don't have time to get into all of that. Right here, right now is a great opportunity for us to contribute.

But... how?

Ingo. He needs our help.

He does? Are you sure?

Have a look.

Shel squinted until Spaghetti Hill came into view. There he could see Chancellor Hume attacking something, clutching a body, burying it into the noodled earth beneath her.

"Ingo!" Shel cried aloud.

Exactly! He needs help, his inner voice encouraged. *Come on!*

But... Hume is... HUGE! We won't stand a chance! She's too powerful!

All the more reason to help. If we don't, then why are we even here? Why have we come to Arcania?

I don't know! I've been trying to figure that out since—

Oh, don't give me that nonsense. You know exactly why we're here!

He immediately thought of his parents, of his father.

Dad.

Yup. We already decided we're not going to let fear rule our fate, decided we're going to make our own destiny. Now it's time to prove it!

"Shel! What are you doing? Let's go!" Fickles yelled, shaking Shel out of his head.

Shel looked at the boot crew one by one. "We can't just leave him!"

"Who?! Ingo? He'll be fine," contended Picklepots. "That lion's a fighter like no other. Besides, he's just creatin' a distraction, givin' us a fightin' chance at gettin' Manny out! He knows eh'zactly what he's doin'."

"Yeah," agreed Tickletoes. "If we go back n'try'n help 'im, we'll only make things worse."

Fickles added, "He wouldn't uh exposed himself, puttin' 'imself in harm's way like that if it weren't part uh his master plan."

"I don't know." Shel hesitated. With his shirt being tugged by Fickles and his back being shoved by Pickles, they started to move. "No! I can't!" Shel snapped. "He needs help!" And without another word, he sprinted off in the direction of Ingo and the chancellor.

"Shel, no! Don't!" cried Izzy, but it was too late. He was off, lost to the maze of tangled-up noodle warriors.

"Come on, Tick. There's nothing we can do. We gotta get Manny to the boats," commanded Captain Fickles, and the four dwarves retreated. "Izzy? You coming?"

o o o o o o

"Hey!" a small voice cried out in the distance. "Hey, YOU!" The small voice was getting bigger, and though it had been far away, it was approaching fast, faster than any human or crocodile could go, and it was bouncing up and down furiously. "YOU LEAVE HIM ALONE!"

Suddenly, out from in front of the voice came a large round thing, flying through the air like a Hail Mary soaring over a football field. As the overripe fruit splattered across Chancellor Hume's head, Sheldon — the small, faraway voice that was no longer small and faraway — cried out, "ME FIRRRSSST!" with tremendous satisfaction, reveling in his tomato-tossing triumph.

"Steee-riiiike! Right down the pipe!" announced Izzy, delighting in the terrific tomato mess all over Hume's face.

Though she was blinded temporarily in one eye, it was hardly enough to incapacitate her. It was, however, enough to shift her attention from Ingonyama to the elephant and the boy, galloping toward her at breakneck speed. The chancellor raised her massive torso using Ingonyama's limp body to steady her footing. Rising to her full height, she let out a ferocious growl, her razor-tooth-filled mouth screwed up in a menacing snarl. She wiped the tomato from her eye and roared from her bottomless soul, shaking the ground, making all within earshot halt their fighting and look her way. She was, at that moment, the most horrifying thing Shel had ever seen — worse than the Worst beast, worse even than the storm dragon. The Worst beast was wild, out of control, driven by hunger. Hume, on the other hand, was lethally calculating and driven by revenge. While the storm dragon was deadly — make no mistake — it was also indifferent, unconcerned with the plight of its victims. The chancellor was deadly for the opposite reason. For her, this was personal. She sought not only to dominate her enemies, she wanted them to suffer. There she stood atop Spaghetti Hill, triumphantly poised over her motionless victim, a demon-like savage enshrouded in fury, fiery wrath ablaze in her volcanic, beady eyes. She stared with malice like a missile, locked onto a young man riding atop an elephant. A new adversary approached, and she was ready.

As Shel and Izzy drew near, both at once rapt with horror and empowered by an unexpected resolve to destroy the evil staring them down. Without giving it much thought (which was how Izzy made most all his decisions) the elephant reached his trunk to the ground and scooped up an apple. He tossed it up to Shel, "Shelby! Catch!" then reached down once more to snag himself a cantaloupe. "On three! Ready? One, two, THREE!!" They fired the fruit at the massive brocosmile with as much force as they could, hoping for... well, they didn't really know what hitting Hume with more rotten food would accomplish, but they had to do something. They had to try, for Ingo's sake.

Hume had no trouble dealing with the onslaught, however, for she was laser-focused and quick to react. She opened her enormous mouth, easily catching the projectiles. Then, with no regard for ripeness, she swallowed the mess whole, worms, mold, and all.

The last assault of Izzy and Shel wasn't a total loss, however, as it gave Shel an idea. He reached down and pulled something from his satchel just as Hume leaped from her high post, mouth agape, intending to chomp down on Izzy or Shel or whatever got in her way. It didn't matter to Hume. She was in a mood to eat the world if it came to it. The world would have to wait, however, for first came the pie!

Shel cried out, "Bangarang!" invoking the spirit of Peter Pan as he tossed a homemade banana cream tart at the descending crocodile. (He'd baked the dessert because he'd heard it was her favorite and he wanted to do something nice to thank her for everything she'd done for everyone and... No, not really. The tart had a special ingredient. This was Shel's secret weapon!)

Despite sailing through the air, Hume could, with her heightened senses, detect the ripe, creamy banana filling and sugary sweet crust coming her way. Sheldon's aim — thanks to years of tossing a baseball — was spot on, and the pastry flew right into the brocosmile's mouth. Even if it weren't aligned perfectly, she still would've snatched it easily, unable to resist the banana cream, her one weakness. Her jaws clamped down and that, as the saying goes, was all she wrote.

The 1922 Peter Pan peanut butter — the special pie-filling additive — went to work straight away. By the time she hit the ground (Izzy had taken one step to his right and Hume landed *SPLAT!* just to his left), her jaw was locked tight. The chancellor would not be chomping down on anything for a very long time. It wasn't all bad for Hume, however. Despite being disappointed at missing her mark, distraught at failing to conquer her enemies, and dizzy from the impact, Hume couldn't help but feel overwhelming satisfaction at her tastebuds bursting with delight. As she lay on the ground, writhing in both frustration and ecstasy simultaneously, Shel's delectable treat worked its magic, literally. In addition to the dreaded peanut butter, Katya the witch had added a pinch of her own special ingredient: a potion designed to incapacitate — not by rendering the victim unconscious, but by inhibiting their motor functions, immobilizing them.

"What in the world?" Izzy stared at the zombified chancellor. "Did she just knock herself silly?"

"Fruit tarts," Shel replied with a grin. "It's the one thing I learned to make in my father's bakery. They're quite tasty, if you like that sort of thing. Turns out they're great for hiding secret potions and stuff." Shel kind of chuckled at the twitching brocosmile lying helpless on the ground. "I suppose once Manny's finished working on the king, they'll need him to come back to fix this one. That oughta be interesting." His thoughts quickly turned to Ingonyama. He leapt down off Izzy's back and scrambled up Spaghetti Hill, as fast as he could go. Izzy wasn't far behind, followed by Alice, Blackbeard, Taudello, and a smattering of Boogies and king's guards.

"Ingo!" cried Shel, rushing to where the lion lay buried beneath the mush. He began digging, doing his best to expose Ingonyama's face, to get air to him, give him room to breathe. As he cleared away the waste, he lifted Ingo's head, cradling it in his arms. But there was no response. Members of Ingo's army began to congregate. Meanwhile, a regiment of brocosmiles also gathered. With both leaders immobilized, the fighting had diminished to minor pushing, shoving, and name-calling. The ultimate outcome of the war had yet to be decided.

Though distraught over her fallen leader, Alice, who was second in command, knew the battle was not over. There were still important matters to conclude such as getting her troops safely out of

Gambrinsville, getting the dentist back to the king, and orchestrating the cleanup effort. Now was not the time to delay or show weakness. Ingo would've demanded the same were it anyone else who'd fallen in his stead. She needed to stay focused on the mission. There was one problem, however: the Gambrine High Chancellor, despite consuming the wretched tart, was still stirring up trouble.

It took eight brocosmiles to drag her body back up Spaghetti Hill and place her once again atop her command post. Though her torso was flaccid as a child's stuffed toy and her jaws were stuck, she was far from harmless, for her wit remained intact, conjuring wicked notions that her lips were still able to convey, albeit in little more than growls, grunts, and hisses. The chancellor squeaked slowly through involuntarily gritted teeth, "I don't know who you are or where you come from, Mr. Silvers..." — the chancellor had sorted out Shel's identity. The Gambrine were, after all, resourceful, sharp-witted, not ignorant by any means. "...But you and I will have plenty of time to get to know one another now that the lion can't protect you. ...And now that your little, bearded friends have crashed their flying shoe in my backyard... and you have no way out!" Two brocosmiles clutched Sheldon's arms. "A fair trade for the dentist, I suppose."

Shel was speechless. Was he to spend the rest of his days in Arcania, in Gambrinstown of all places? He'd always assumed he'd be going home, back to Chicago, eventually. Getting time away, finding his own path, that was one thing. He hadn't planned on never seeing his family again.

Satisfied, the chancellor's eyes drifted from Shel, falling on Alice. "I see you're in charge now that the lion has... retired. You have recovered your prize for your king. Now leave this place! I keep this one," — she indicated Ingo's body with the slightest nod — "as my trophy. ...The boy's mine too, along with a handful of your troops... to clean up and replant." More brocosmiles captured some of the Boogies and the king's guard. "The rest of you may go," she concluded, but no one moved a muscle. They could sense something wasn't settled. There was a strange vibration on the air, a methodical, subsonic thumping. Each who felt it believed it to be their own heart, nervously pulsating as if anticipating some unknown event. No one dared move.

"I suggest you get going before I change my mind and keep the lot!" growled Hume. "What are you all waiting for? The other shoe to drop? Ha! The Festoon was the only flying shoe in Arcania. There's no one else coming to save you!"

The vibration was not just in the air now, it seemed to shake the very ground, ever so subtly. Out of nowhere, a soft yet deep, weak yet powerful voice crept up behind the chancellor, making her eyes triple in size. "I wonder... where might one... acquire... a giant shoe... in which to fly?"

If Hume could've moved, she would've jumped ten feet in the air, for that is the appropriate response when seeing someone rise from the dead. He clutched her cloak with a giant paw and pulled himself from Sheldon's arms, sitting upright in his coffin of noodles.

"INGO!" Shel cried out, embracing his friend tightly.

"Now that's what I call a resurrection!" noted Dracula to Karl and Walter, both of whom nodded enthusiastically.

Ingonyama ignored Shel and the others, for now. He had unfinished business with the chancellor. Staring with vengeful eyes, the great lion growled, "I ask again: Where would one get a giant shoe?" Hume was stunned silent. "Why, from a *GIANT* of course!" Thunderous sounds of trees being crushed punctuated Ingo's conclusion, the booming vibrations in the earth rising to a crescendo, heralding the advance of not one, but two skyscraping creatures!

"Chester!" hollered Alice, delighting in the arrival of Ingo's pièce de resistance.

"And I believe you already know Chester's sister, Charlie. Isn't that right, Hume?" growled Ingo.

"Chester? Charlie?" The chancellor choked, and that was all she was able to get out before collapsing unconscious at Alice's feet. The return of Ingonyama was shock enough. The appearance of the giants, signaling the end of her military counterattack, was beyond her ability to stomach.

By the time she awoke from her 'nap' (an unauthorized slumber that would, no doubt, be investigated by Sir Marcus at some future date) a good deal of her farm fields had been cleared and her brocosmiles were back to their usual tasks of raking, weeding, hoeing, mulching... Only a handful of Ingo's army remained, assisting Hume's kinfolk with the task of replanting the broccoli — along with several other, new crops.

"So, they took my giant after all, did they?" Hume spoke aloud through stuck jaws, mostly to herself. Utterly defeated — physically, morally, and strategically — she sat, resigned, resting under a small broccoli tree where she'd been placed like a commemorative statue, until the time when she would be able to walk again. Keeping her company, making sure she remained captive, was the infirmed Ingonyama, also resting and recovering.

"You gave her a home when she had nowhere else to turn, saved her from the king's Nightshade campaign. She would be asleep, ten feet under the sand if it weren't for the Gambrine. But, her debt has been repaid many times over. She is free now... and reunited with her kin. Lady Alice is escorting Charlie and her brother back to the Land of Happy, for they are needed in the service of the king." Hume growled in protest. It was just the two of them now, no reason to fight. Instead, it was a time for words, to reflect and make sense of the war, if any sense could be made. "We're going to stay," Ingo coughed, choking on remnants of noodles stuck in the depths of his lungs. "...Some of us anyway, for as long as it takes, working side-by-side with the Gambrine. We'll help clean up the mess—"

"Your mess!" Hume hissed but Ingo ignored the invitation to another argument.

"We'll help clean the mess, help rebuild and replant... and implement Mr. Silver's plan for expanding your farming enterprise, leaving the Gambrine better off than when we encountered you just this morning."

"Expansion?! What expansion?!" Hume whined.

"The Gambrine's ability to grow the best-tasting broccoli is unparalleled," Ingo explained. "With the right resources, there's no reason you shouldn't also be able to grow other vegetables; food that will be just as sought-after to the entire community as your beloved broccoli has been; ultimately bringing you even greater prosperity. The kingdom of Happy is prepared to provide said resources for this expansion."

"And what if we don't want it?!"

"Don't be foolish, chancellor. More crops? More revenue? More land? Don't pretend the Gambrine wouldn't like more land."

"More land?" Hume was unable to hide her curiosity.

"More land," Ingo nodded, "and the resources to cultivate the land: tools and labor. Then, after the Gambrine are sufficiently established in their new enterprise, we shall part ways... as friends, having given the Gambrine much in return for what we've taken today."

"What a lovely sentiment," Hume scoffed. "But the fact remains, you can't just invade a sovereign nation, take things that don't belong to you, and change their way of life!"

Ingo remained calm. "Hume…"

"Don't call me that!"

Ingo sighed. "Chancellor, you and I both know that Charlie, Manny, and Buddha the cat — the three feathers of which I spoke, if you recall — do not _belong_ to anyone, least of all you. They are free souls who deserve to live in peace. Beyond them, slavery has no place in Arcania. Not that it ever did, but those old ways are long gone. You must renounce your practice of imprisoning people into slavery."

"Oh, I suppose you think your methods are better? Stash prisoners away in windowless cells, let them wither and die in the damp dark? At least my prisoners get to breathe fresh air and feel the sun on their skin. And they eat what they harvest, wholesome, nutritious, fresh—"

"Chancellor," Ingo interrupted, "I am not in a position to give you alternative policies. I am only delivering the message of the nations of Arcania: slavery is over. Ignore this message at your peril. Conform, and King Longsmiles will honor the long history of friendship between the Land of Happy and the Gambrine. That is the promise of the king... and the word of Ingonyama."

"Your word? Your word is no better than the garbage you've left all across our valley. Someday we'll repay you properly for this transgression; you and the _Happy_ King!"

"And what would that prove, chancellor?"

"It would prove that we're better than you!"

"No. More violent perhaps. Not better. Winning doesn't _prove_ the victor better, chancellor, you know this. There are simply too many variables, too much chance at play. Winning is not only ephemeral — victor one day, loser the next — it is also relative. Sometimes when you think you win, you lose; and sometimes when you think you've lost, you've really won."

"You think of yourself as quite the philosopher, don't you? Tell me, what sort of enlightened being goes around stealing other's honor?!"

"Enlightened?" Ingo laughed. "No. Experienced. And I can honestly tell you, I did not take away your honor. So long as you choose to respond with honor, you retain yours. If you decide you've only lost three prisoners — not your dignity, not your honor, not your sovereignty — then peace is already within your grasp." The chancellor squinted defiantly. "You must realize, chancellor, we could have come with *real* weapons, started a *real* war. We knew you wouldn't give up your 'prisoners' without a fight... right?"

"Of course not! Charlie came to us for protection... from *your* king! The cat came uninvited, meddling in our affairs..."

"Yes. I'm aware of all of that. But as I said, the practice of indentured servitude, for any reason, will no longer be tolerated by the other nations of Arcania. You're lucky we only brought rotten food. There are others who, no doubt, would've brought cannons and razed Gambrinsville to the ground. You're lucky I understand that violence breeds violence. No one needs to suffer for your stubbornness, chancellor. You're lucky my directive was to free your prisoners without anyone actually getting hurt."

"I got hurt!" a distant brocosmile voice whimpered.

"Mind your business, Jerry!" chided Hume, and the brocosmile got back to raking. "Lucky!?" Hume growled. "Hmpf!"

"Lucky," answered Ingo conclusively. "We all are."

Chapter Nine

The Whale-eater and the Dreams of Tomorrow

"Where is my lion?!" read the king's sign in red crayon, his mouth still stuck of course. After days of not being able to eat anything solid — water infused with soluble nutrients keeping him alive via a straw at the back of his mouth — Skippy was in no mood to see Shel standing before him empty-handed…

It wasn't that Shel was literally empty-handed. He was, after all, carrying a small, ornately carved wooden staff, a remnant shard of a Gambrine rake — a souvenir from battle. He just didn't have with him the king's prisoner whom he'd promised to bring back.

"Do you not recall the king's story of the silver fish?" asked the king's official spokesperson. With mouth sealed tight, the king thought it prudent to appoint a royal speaker to give commands on his behalf. For this task, the king chose none other than Marcus the pleaseman, on account of his unfailing, though oft overbearing, loyalty.

"And what of Alice? And the king's royal guards?" Marcus continued. He looked at the king and the king nodded in approval.

"Your Highness," Shel bowed, "Ingo and Alice have elected to stay behind to help clean up after the battle, in order to ensure the peace between the Gambrine and your kingdom holds into the future." Shel had rehearsed precisely what Ingo had instructed him to tell the king upon return. Ingo knew the king would not be happy, but the argument in favor of keeping the peace could not be refuted, even by Longsmiles — especially by Longsmiles.

Shel, Izzy, and the Boot Brigade, along with pirates Taud and Hook, had returned from the battle exhausted, hungry, and stained from head to toe in the remnants of every sort of food imaginable. The last thing any of them wanted was to stand in front of the king and be interrogated by his royal mouthpiece. But, there was no avoiding King Skippy or the pleaseman. The king was the first stop after docking Hook's ship, for more reasons than ceremony.

As Izzy approached Shel and the king, Marcus noted with great interest the package balancing uneasily atop the elephant's back. There sat a disheveled-looking old man with dark eyes suggesting he hadn't slept in days, and he too was covered in the stench of rotting food.

"Your Majesty," Izzy began, "may I present Doctor Manfred Faffen Jr., the world's premier dentist." Izzy bowed his head, allowing Manny a path to ground. The dentist jumped onto the elephant's trunk, tripped, and tumbled down what had intended to be a slide, flopping to the ground with a thud and a moan. "Oops!" coughed Izzy. "Sorry, Manny. You okay?"

Manny jumped up, tossed an 'all good' wink at Izzy, then turned his attention to the king.

"Your Royal Sovereign! Sure is a pleasure to meet ya... finally. Heard a great deal 'bout the famous King Longsmiles and his wonderful

Land uh Happy." Then Manny the bold decided to test the king's patience. "Always wanted tuh visit, but, 'dentists not allowed' an all."

At that point, the king would have interrupted if he could have, put the dentist in his place, or in a place of the king's choosing rather (someplace like the dungeon). Longsmiles' fidgeting, which indicated he wished to speak, went entirely unnoticed by his spokesperson who was distracted by the energetic dentist. Marcus scrutinized the little man, trying to predict his intentions.

Thus, Manny continued his rant uninterrupted. "It is lovely here, sire. I can certainly understand yer obsession with sandwiches, given all the sand an' all the witches in the place... Buuut, I advise against the extra sticky peanut butter varietals." He widened his eyes and pointed two index fingers at the king's mouth. "Case in point... with all due respect... Your Highness."

The king did not look pleased. He grabbed another piece of paper and began scribbling something. As he did, the dentist leaned back and whispered to Izzy that he was going to need something large and flat with which to pry the king's mouth open.

Manny looked back at Longsmiles just as the king presented his sign, but Manny wasn't interested. He swatted that piece of paper right out of the king's hands. "Oh, there's no need for any uh that! You just sit back 'n relax. I'll have ya fixed up right quick! ...Aaand while we wait for Izzy to return with ma tools... how 'bout a little story, eh?" The dentist stared at the king then glanced around at his audience, nodding as he scanned their faces.

Turning back to the king, Manny began, "Have y'ever heard the story of Bindala Bale? The little girl who ate a whole whale?" Longsmiles scowled at Manfred and Manfred happily ignored him. "That lil' miss sat at her table for eighty-nine years. Eighty-nine years! Can you buh-leeve that?! Never even left thuh house!"

Some people in the audience gasped, some chuckled, others mumbled or grumbled, and the rest either quietly reveled in astonishment or scowled in solidarity with the king.

"Yup! I used to visit Bindala, work on her teeth while she sat right there at her dinin' table. I'd be fillin' in cavities in between her bites, I would! She was the most food-obsessed person I'd ever met. That is, till I heard tell uh the great Peanut Butter King!"

The king pounded his fists on his chair furiously and began sweating. He couldn't recall the last time someone talked to him in such a manner.

Sympathetically stunned, Marcus looked around for something to pound *his* fist on. A thin branch protruding from a willow bush was leaning toward him, teasing for trouble. So, Marcus slapped that branch in a show of royal support. Marcus felt rather pleased with himself for a half-second until the bendy branch came swinging back, slapping Mark across the face. Touché!

Frustrated beyond words, Marcus hastily drew his sword, intending to cut the branch down to size. His frustration was only fertilized, however, when his fencing arm was stayed mid-swing by the royal gardener, who, with a slow, silent shake of his head, reminded the pleaseman it was not yet pruning season. Discomposed, Marcus fumbled to sheath his blade then bit his lip to blood as he waited in desperate anticipation for the order to haul the defiant, disrespectful dentist to the dungeon; teach him some good old-fashioned manners. But Manny wasn't going anywhere, least of all to any dungeon. He had other plans.

"Relaaaax, Longsmiley," (the king nearly exploded at the abuse of his name), "Ever'un knows yer obsessed with peanut butter. But you took it too far this time, didn't ya? Just like Bindala. Gave up her life for her obsession, she did." He paused for effect and then pointed two fingers at the king again. "And you almost did too!"

Longsmiles' scowls grew in marked intensity. But what else could he do besides scowl? Manny let the king have his contempt, which was, eventually — as Manny knew it would be — followed by a moment of reflection, at which point Manfred continued.

"But, no! This king's not gonna perish. No sir indeedy! We're gunna git you squared away right quick, we are!" Seeing a lumbering pachyderm heading his way, Manny called to the elephant at the far side of the crowd. "You bring what I asked fer?"

"Um, well, I know you said you needed some sort of dental spoon extractor thingy, but this is the only spoon I could think to grab." The elephant held his trunk high above the crowd to present the giant silver spoon which Sandovar had gifted to the king only recently.

Manny was a tad stunned. "Uh... huh. Well, I s'pose that'll have to do. I was hopin' to go about the job a little more... sensitive like, with a finer tool to chip away at the clay-like nutcrete. But, I s'pose you're right. Why beat around the butter? Let's just jab that spoon in there and pry on it until his face cracks wide open, shall we?"

The king's eyes nearly popped out of his head. Mark saw the look on Longsmile's face and eagerly stepped in front of Manny. "Now just a minute you—"

"Oh, I don't have time for this." The dentist stopped Mark short. "Izzy, do something about this party pooper will ya?" Manny ordered as he snatched the large spoon from the elephant.

With his trunk now empty, Izzy needed something to fill it. So, he grabbed hold of the pleaseman and tossed him aside without delay.

Meanwhile, Manny, being of small stature, was struggling with the oversized spoon. "Goodness! This thing weighs a ton!" Eventually, he was able to lift the spoon up onto his shoulder. With a shuffle of his little feet he approached the king, who was squirming in his throne. "Now just hold still Yer Royallness," (Manny winked at Shel), "Just imagine this spoon is filled with peanut butter. Open them lips wide as ya can an' show me them chompers. Come on now, smile fer papa!"

The king was not the least bit sweet on the dentist's instructions — Manny's bedside manner lacking manners, as it were, and he refused to comply. So, Manny did what any good dentist would do: he had his assistants, the shoe crew (and Sheldon too), hold Longsmiles' arms while he shoved that spoon right into the king's mouth despite all the fidgeting and groans of protest. Being a skilled tooth doctor, Manny quickly found a proper spot to wedge the utensil.

The dentist glanced back to see if Izzy had managed to subdue the pleaseman. Mark appeared to be resting comfortably on the lawn about fifteen feet away. No one needed to worry about interruptions from *that* man anytime soon. So, Manny got on with his work. Using the king's overbite as leverage, the dentist pressed the spoon as best he could in between the king's maxillary and mandibular incisors — that is, between his upper and lower teeth.

"Izzy, would you be so kind as to press up on the end of this spoon, ever so gently, with your most capable proboscis?" Izzy did as Manny requested. "Okay, now hold it right there for a moment." The dentist employed a pressurized bottle to spray a jet of tonic into the king's mouth, attempting to loosen the peanut butter cement. The tonic, concocted on the boat ride back from Champion Valley, consisted of salt water mixed with various spoiled foodstuffs, plus some herbs they'd collected from various inlets along the way, topped off with a good helping of Katya's dismembering potion. And with that, the king's head popped clean off...

(Only kidding. The potion was a *dissolving* potion, not dismembering. Bit of a thesaurical slip there!)

As Manny generously sprayed a waterfall of the *dissolving* elixir into the king's mouth, Izzy pried on the spoon. Katya, meanwhile, got on with waving her hands about, mumbling incantations to help grease the wheels of the crazy charade.

At first nothing seemed to be happening, except for the king shedding a deluge of tears, presumably from pain but could've been humiliation. For that matter, he could've been crying at the prospect of these nutty people trying to remove his tasty peanut butter mortar. Manny, for one, got a kick out of seeing the king so despondent. The dentist had been less than pleased about being banned from the Land of Happy simply because his chosen profession was considered a primer for anxiety and stress (which, as everyone knows, is!)

"If this doesn't work I'm going to need a hammer and chisel. We'll just knock his teeth out one by one until there's nothing for the butter to cling to," Manny jested with a chuckle. He wasn't serious, of course, but after the interrogation of the brocosmile, there was no telling of what this dentist was capable. The king, for one, had no idea Manny was joking, so he began moaning and crying even harder, providing even more moisture to the mortar. As his tears flooded his mouth, threatening to drown him, suddenly, a very faint *crack* could be heard.

"Hold it!" Manny commanded, a skosh concerned they may be starting to crack the king's jaw... or extract his teeth. "Just hold it right there, Izzy." Manny stretched his palm in Izzy's direction while inspecting all around the king's mouth. He looked back at Izzy with a rascally grin and a wink. "Well," he said, feigning resignation, "looks like there's no hope for *this* king. Anyone else want to try on the crown?"

Boy, did that send the king and crowd into a frenzy! Manny couldn't help it. He burst into a fit of laughter. Instantly, Longsmiles tried to wave his arms and stand up but the Boot Brigade kept the king solidly in check. With a twitch of his fingers as if signaling someone to come hither, Manny directed Izzy to press up just a hair more on the spoon.

While the dentist flushed the king's mouth with more elixir and the king's tears flowed like the great Zambezi over Victoria Falls, Katya intensified her chanting and waving into a stomping dance — at which point Wanda attempted to join in but Katya waived her off, fearing that the batty, old hag might accidentally turn the king into a newt.

Seeing bits of peanut butter begin to dislodge from the king's gums, Manny knew right then that he was going to prevail. He motioned for Izzy to press up just a bit harder and *creeeaaak!* went the king's jaw ever so slightly, ever so slowly. "Checkmate! I've got your king now!" he derided the peanut butter spirits. Like an excited grasshopper, Manny leaped up onto the handle of the spoon. "Let's go, Izzy! Elevator up!"

The elephant pulled up on the handle, lifting the dentist and prying on the king's mouth with elephantine force. And then, with a final *KE-RACK!* that could be heard all the way across Champion Lake, over in Gambrinstown (incidentally, waking up Marcus the pleaseman — who would now have to prosecute *himself* for taking an unauthorized nap), the peanut butter finally gave up its herculean stick and surrendered once and for all. The king's jaws were free!

Instantly, the crowd erupted, cheering and clapping for the dentist, and for their king (of course). Meanwhile, Longsmiles, exhausted and overwhelmed with pain, slumped in his throne and passed right out... but not before uttering one, last command in the slightest of whispers. The poor, starving, delusional king, in a labored ghost of a breath, requested… another peanut butter sandwich.

"Let's get this poor guy to bed." Manny looked at Katya. "He can sleep it off. That'll be best for everyone, I'm sure." Katya nodded at some nearby servants and they got straight to task.

"Wow! That was really something, Manny," said Izzy.

"Couldn't've done it without you, big guy," replied the dentist. "And thanks to yous guys toos!" he motioned in the direction of the boot crew.

"Manny, I can't tell you how good it is to have you back! I really thought you were a goner," Izzy confessed. The boot crew agreed with various expressions of "Yeah!" and "For certain!" and "Tally ho!"

(Tally ho?)

"Me too!" confessed Manny. "Let's hope Longsmiles is in good spirits when he wakes up, else all the trouble I put him and his kingdom through will come back at me like a fifty-ton boomerang."

"Trouble?!" reeled Fickleface. "What trouble? You just saved the king's life for goodness' sake!"

Manny chuckled. "Maybe. I just meant that if I hadn't run off to Gambrinstown in the first place, like a darned fool, y'all wouldn't've had tuh come rescue me, wastin' all that time, not to mention all that good food!"

"Oh, pish tosh! Put a cork in that bottle!" Fickles retorted.

"Busides, the food was all rotten tuh begin with!" added Pickles.

Izzy laughed. "Yeah. Searching for you, traveling all over, and fighting to get you back... that's been the adventure of a lifetime! Isn't that right, Sheldon?" While the bootaneers nodded in agreement, Shel stared blankly as if he'd been hit over the head.

"What is it, kid?" asked Izzy. "What's wrong?"

Shel shrugged. "I dunno. I guess... I just hadn't really thought about it before."

"'Bout what?" asked Tickles.

Sheldon sort of shuffled his feet. "Well, the end of the adventure, I suppose."

"Hmm. Right," remarked Izzy pensively.

"You're walkin' on a cloud, kid. Don't look down! Just keep on goin'!" Shel looked up and met the old eyes of the dentist, eyes which had seen a thing or two. Manny was holding Buddha Baggs in his arms, looking content, though he was clearly straining under the weight of the big cat. He looked at Baggs and added, "When one adventure ends, another always begins... so long as you're open to it. Just don't look down or you'll fall right back to the ground. And that's when you grow roots! Before ya know it, you're an old tree like me."

Shel smiled and nodded. There was a brief pause and then he said to no one in particular, "I need to see Joy."

On their voyage to Gambrinstown, on the eve of battle, Ingo had sat Shel down in the boot and gave him the news that Joy had gone home, that she was not going to be joining the fight to free Manny because she did not wish to fight; even if it *was* a food fight. Not only was she a peaceful soul, the Gambrine were neighbors, allies to the Costeros clan. It would not be right for Joy to involve her family in the dispute since it was not their quarrel.

Ingo didn't have an answer for Shel when the kid asked when Joy would be returning. The lion didn't know if Joy would be coming back at all. "But she wanted me to tell you that you are with her, in her heart, Sheldon. And she wanted me to give you this." Ingo handed Shel a small book, the pages of which were blank. Poor Shelby looked perplexed, and so the lion explained. "She said you're a storyteller, Sheldon, and that you have an incredible story that needs telling: the story of Arcania."

Shel wasn't sure what to say. He didn't think he and Joy would part ways like that, without words, without goodbyes, nothing to show for their friendship but a book of empty pages. He hadn't even considered the possibility that they *would* part ways. Something inside of him was sure she would always be with him. Now that they were back from battle, back in the Land of Happy where he'd met her, Shel knew he needed to tell her how he felt.

"I have to see her, but… I don't know where she is," he confessed.

Izzy and the boot crew remained silent, unsure of what to say. Then, with an audible inhale and sigh, Izzy relented. "I'll take you." The elephant knew the journey back through the Sonrisa desert would be long and dangerous, especially if the giants were being woken up, as was the plan according to Ingonyama. Regardless, he figured helping his friend was the least he could do after Shel saved his life. To him, helping Sheldon was worth all the trouble in the world. Izzy was adrift in thought when a gruff voice butted in.

"Arrr, there'll be no need of that!"

Shel and the group jerked around to see a dark figure standing behind them.

"Blackbeard!" Shel blurted. "Where'd you come from?"

"Ah! I be comin' in from the sea, as pirates tend to do now and again." The pirate — whose beard stubble was growing in nicely now, reuniting him with his namesake... and his villainous appearance — exchanged hugs and handshakes with Shel, Izzy, the boot crew, Manny, even Katya.

"Where's everyone else?" asked Shel. "Where's Ingonyama? And Sandovar, and the giants?"

"Alice and the king's guard?" added Katya.

The black pirate stared blankly back at the group for a moment, taking a deep breath before looking down at the ground. His drooping head shook back and forth as he spoke slowly and softly, well out of character for such a bawdy pirate. "I be afraid not everythin' went 'cordin' tuh plan."

"What?! What do you mean?!" exclaimed Shel. "What happened? Where is everyone?!"

"There were Glunks in the trunks and Zawfees in our coffee! There were Snitchens in the kitchen and Vaths in the bath!"

"What?!" Izzy tried to make sense of the black pirate's babble, but Blackbeard just kept babbling.

"We tried to hide behind doors, under dressers... Even hid under a pile of clothes..."

"Yeah, I tried that. It doesn't work," mumbled Shel.

"...We hid in garbage pails..."

"Ewww. Gross," commented Pickles.

"What in the monkey's rump are you blabbering about?" Izzy pressed, growing impatient.

"*I've* found," chimed Manny, stroking the mane of Buddha Baggs and staring into oblivion, "that the only place to hide is in the dreams of tomorrow." The group, including Blackbeard, squinted at the dentist, everyone trying to sort out what was just said.

Finally, Izzy blurted, "What... is... happening?! Has everyone gone mad?! Blackbeard, you'd better stop riddling nonsense and tell us what happened or I'm going to plant you like a rutabaga, headfirst, right here in the sand."

"Alrighty then," replied the pirate, hands up in surrender. "Calm yerself ya big bludder wuffer." Blackbeard's salty demeanor was back. "Ye friends be slow to disembark's all. So I figured I'd make sure the coast be clear 'fore we all got into a mess of boilin' oil with the king. But looks as though things be settled right proper if the dentist be wanderin' 'round free as a polly in paradise." Another wave of silence washed over everyone as they translated the pirate speak.

"Black, just tell us where Ingo is." The elephant cut straight to it.

"There! Look!" cried Fickleface, pointing in the direction of the seaport.

Marching over the horizon came a silhouette of various colors, shapes, and sizes, preceded by the pungent stench of decaying food.

"Arrr, my apologies." Blackbeard fumbled his soiled fingers through his coal-black hair. "Hadn't much time for pleasantries like bathing or scrubbin' rags, we didn't."

"Scrubbing rags? Oh, you mean washing clothes?" Shel interpreted.

"Aye, that too," replied Blackbeard.

It wasn't long before the silhouettes became distinct. A wild mane whipped pridefully like a triumphant flag in the wind.

"Ingonyama," whispered Izzy in relief.

Next to the mane moved a figure walking with grace and purpose, as if on a mission.

"Alice!" announced Katya.

On the other side of Ingo walked a smaller figure whose mane danced on the wind like Ingonyama's only not as bushy; longer and more playful. The figure moved across the sand with a flowy elegance, like Alice only without the unyielding determination and drive. This one, although walking with the group, appeared to be marching to the beat of a different drummer. Or, not marching at all, rather, but sort of sashaying with some intermittent skipping. And then... a twirl.

Shel's heart skipped. He felt for a moment that he was imaging everything. The sensation that he was in a dream washed over him like a rainstorm and he shivered. When the faceless silhouettes were close enough to come alive, identities slowly appearing on faces like a welcomed sunrise over a dark valley, all was confirmed. There next to the lion stood the strong and beautiful and whimsical mermaid princess, Joythea Aquarius Costeros.

Shel was instantly jolted by an invisible bolt of lightning affixing his feet to the ground. He felt immobile, bronzed to the earth, a statue for all of eternity to marvel at. (Goodness, how dramatic he was!) After a moment, he decided this was not a dream, this was real, as real as it gets, anyway. She was not a mirage and he was not a statue. He broke free of the shock and ran to her, engulfing her in a tremendous embrace.

This time she was not afraid. He picked her up and swung her around and around, and she laughed and laughed... as she does. For a moment they were back on the shore of Isla de Sonrisas, just the two of them, cool sea breeze in their hair and warm sunshine on their skin.

Joy looked down at Shel and began singing something in French as she flew in the air. He looked up at her with adoring eyes, eyes of longing, and fondness; eyes that had no idea what she was saying... and that did not go unnoticed by the perceptive and wide-eyed Izzy.

"Don't tell me you don't speak Spanish, Artilan, *OR* French!" the elephant teased, and everyone laughed, especially Shel.

Chapter Ten

Namesake

"*Ingo, where's Sandovar?* Where are Chester and Charlie?" Izzy asked after the initial excitement died down, embraces were had, and the laughter quieted...

"Yeah, where's Sandovar?" asked Pickles.

"And Alice?" asked Tickles.

"And the giants?" asked Fickles.

"Friends! Friends," Ingo held up a paw, invoking calm. "Sandovar and his Boogies are leading Chester and Charlie along a different road. They're passing through the desert, waking the Snoozants as they go. And they have plenty of help, including some of Katya's witch friends, who, as I understand, have recruited a few more of their paranormal brethren. I believe Shel knows 'em: Walter, Karl, and Dracula."

"Really?!" erupted Shel excitedly.

"Yup. They said they weren't so interested in the food fighting party, but that they wanted to do something to help nonetheless. I figured their experience with resurrecting things could come in handy. Drac certainly thought so." Ingo and Shel laughed together.

"So it's really happening then; the giants are returning to the Land of Happy?" Joy sounded positively enthusiastic. (But when did she not?)

"Yup!" answered Ingo. "Our friends are assisting Chester and Charlie in making sure the giants are reoriented properly, slowly, and with plenty of compassion. A new day is dawning in the Land of Happy, my friends. Things are about to change in a big, big way!"

Izzy nodded slowly, taking it all in. "Okay! Wow! Well, Ingo, in your estimation, do you foresee peace for the Land of Happy? Did Hume finally relent? Will the giants seek retribution?" He was really grilling his commander.

"Slow down there, buddy. First off, as for the giants, we'll have to wait and see if they have any demands, see where they want to live, what they want—"

"Well, yes, of course, all of that," Izzy cut him off. "But what about the Gambrine?"

"Well, Izzy," Ingo replied slowly, "I suppose only time holds that answer. But for now it seems we will have peace, yes. The giants made quick work cleaning up the food mess and replanting what crops were destroyed... Incidentally, the food scraps proved to be good compost—"

"Soil amendment!" whispered an astonished Pickles, snatching a handful of sand and letting the dry granules trickle through his fingers. "Makes perfect sense!"

"Exactly," Ingo replied. "And we contributed, best we could, to the acquisition of more land for the Gambrine, per our agreement. By the time we left, Hume seemed at least a little accepting of the changes. Of course she's never completely satisfied. But, short of perfection, I think we did a good job of getting the Gambrine back on track, ahead of schedule, even, according to the farmer's almanac."

Still holding big 'ol Buddha, Manny poked his head into the conversation. "Well, in that case, I believe there's cause enough for celebration, eh?!"

The revelry celebrating the reunion of friends and recovery of the king was unparalleled, made all the more fun by the return of the king's silly disposition and general good nature — an unexpected but welcomed bonus. He almost instantly forgave all past transgressions, realizing everyone had made tremendous efforts on his behalf. Rather than accusing anyone of any crimes, he attributed his ill-temper to his own ego, an ego sorely in need of a good humbling, which he received in spades thanks to the Peter Pan sandwich. Now on the mend, the king threw a grand picnic on the palace lawns, complete with a buffet, a band, several bonfires, and, of course, some badminton.

King Longsmiles loved the game of badminton. Unfortunately, he was still too frail to participate. Instead, Skippy sat in his wheelchair near one of the bonfires, munching on a sandwich (of ham and cheese, mind you), and cheering a team of his guards as they challenged various members of the extended Boogies.

Despite his jovial attitude and newfound appreciation for life, the king's passion for peanut butter had not subsided. Not one bit. He was still demanding sticky peanut butter sandwiches. His requests were, thankfully, thus far being carefully dodged using a combination of logic rooted in sound health practices, a smidge of manipulative psychology, and a pinch of pagan hypnosis administered by Izzy and the witches. Still, all were fast coming to their wit's end with the king's ridiculous obsession.

"Why doesn't he just add some jelly?" Shel casually suggested as they stood around a campfire, the witches complaining to no end about their stubborn king.

"What's that?" Katya challenged. "Jelly? On his peanut butter sandwich? Yuck!"

"What do you mean 'yuck'?" Shel defended. "You've never heard of a PB and J?"

"Pee-bee and what?" the witch asked.

"A peanut butter and jelly sandwich," Shel replied in the key of *duh* major.

"Never heard of such a ridiculous thing," concluded Katya. She looked at Picklepots and raised her brows, silently asking the flying shoe chef if he'd ever heard of this P B and J nonsense. Pickles shook his head.

Shel noted defenses being fortified. "Look, don't knock it till you try it. For all you know, the pee-bee-jay could be the best thing you've ever tried. Aaaand, it might just be the answer to your problem."

Katya squinted. "Ugh! Fine. How does it work then?"

"How does it…? What do you mean, how does it work? You put some jelly on the sandwich, along with the peanut butter. Done." Katya stared back at him. One could see Shel beginning to drift, dreaming about his glorious peanut butter and jelly sandwiches back home. Wanda snapped her bony fingers in front of his face and he came back to the bonfire, recalling that they were working on a solution for the king. "Well, anyway, I think it'll help."

"How's that again?" the witches asked in unison.

Shel shrugged and gave Katya 'obvious' eyes. "Becaaaause, it makes the peanut butter less sticky." Realizing it would just be easier to show them, he sought out Joythea. "Hang on. Where's... Ah!" He found her playing nearby and yelled to her. "Uh, Joy, I'm pretty sure cartwheels aren't allowed in badminton." Joy smiled back. "Hey, so that toast you gave me when we were in the desert... where'd you get the jelly?"

"What's that? Jelly?" She called back, swinging her racquet, smacking the shuttlecock and sending it zooming through the air. "I don't know…" *Swing! Swoosh! Twirl! Jump! Smash! Point for team Joy!* "Oh! The jelly on toast! I don't know. It was something Sandovar had."

The Boogie chief was of course away on his giant mission. His first mate, however, was keeping company with some Kantytown locals, just nearby.

"Hey, Taud," interrupted Shel, "got any more of the Sandman's special jelly stashed somewhere? I need to make a sandwich."

Taudello looked up curiously from his iced, wild-strawberry lemonade. "Arrr, whatever fer? There be plenty uh rations 'round here. Don't need a sandwich you nubbin chucker." Taud's audience chuckled at the mockery.

Shel paid no mind. "Nubbin chucker... That's a new one... Uh, no, I need it for the king. I want to try something." Taud squinted, paused, then hopped up, walked to a nearby tent, retrieved a jar, and handed it to Shel. "Thanks!" Shel then turned to Katya. "Lead the way."

The witch adopted a skeptical expression while slowly reaching for her broom. "Okaaay. Hop on, I guess."

Shel's previous and less-than-pleasant experience on a flying broom, zooming over the battlefield, was enough to make him hesitate. Katya was not feeling very patient.

"Look, either get on and let's get this done or give it up. I don't have all day. I'm next in line for badminton and I've been waiting all morning." Shel hopped on the back of the broom. "Now, hold on tight, young man, I like to fly fast!"

They arrived at the palace kitchens in no time. Katya collected Skippy's favorite peanut butter along with his favorite sprouted grain sourdough bread and Shel made quick work of assembling the sandwich. (The convenience and glorious flavor, coupled with the nutrition of the fruit and the protein of the peanut, is precisely why a PB&J is arguably the greatest invention since, well, sliced bread. Shel knew this. Indeed, all great adventurers know this. But King Longsmiles did not know it. Not yet.)

Katya flew Shel and his sandwiches (he took the liberty of making himself one too) back to the picnic party, right up to the king. The royal audience included Ingonyama, Donachtuk the bear, the queen mother with her husband Simonson and their kangaroo and monkey, Lady Alice, Mark the pleaseman, and a heaping handful of Kantytown villagers. They were all listening to the king's stories — he was very talkative after having his mouth glued shut for several days. They were also entertained by a lively dialogue between the king and the lion, the two of them having come from very different lives, both of which were extremely fascinating. Since Ingonyama's return, the king had made sure to keep the lion within sight at all times, for he had not yet made up his mind about Ingo's imprisonment. The lion had certainly proven his worth securing the dentist's return, and he had proven his loyalty by returning despite the uncertainty of a pardon for his 'crimes'. The king, however, still grieved the loss of his friends and brother, and still felt betrayed. And so, Ingo's future still hung tenuously in the air like the smoke from the campfires that warmed the faces and the hearts of the many friends on the palace lawns that day.

Longsmiles looked up as Katryna advanced with Shel in tow. "Ah, the hero approacheth," announced the king, locking eyes with Shel. It was clear to everyone that Ingonyama was a hero for leading his troops to victory and saving Manny. It was also clear that Manny was a hero for working his dental magic and saving the king. But many others contributed in essential ways and Shel was no exception. Katya stepped out of the way, and with a bow, Shel presented the sandwich.

"What's this?" asked Longsmiles with kingly kindness and curiosity. Before Shel could answer, however, the king's disposition shifted to almost uncontrollable excitement. "A peanut butter sandwich?!" He then tried to stand but fell into the arms of Donachtuk, who had to resist the urge to swing his feeble partner round and round (which would have been a royal mistake). Longsmiles was thrilled to see a peanut butter sandwich again, and he had intended to say, 'Thank you.' But, haunted by the trauma of his near-death experience, he instead shouted, "Are you trying to kill me?!"

All was well, however, for Shel, now battle-hardened, was unphased by Longsmiles' theatrics. After all, it was common knowledge that the king could be a bit of a drama queen.

"It's a peanut butter *and jelly* sandwich, Your Highness. Back home we call it a PB&J." Don sat the king in his throne-on-wheels, allowing the king to catch his breath and compose himself. "Katya provided me with your favorite peanut butter and bread, and Taudello provided me with Sandovar's prized jelly. I put them all together and now you have possibly the best sandwich the world has ever known! ...I can't believe no one here has ever heard of a PB&J!" The king squinted skeptically, as Katya had. "Sire, come on! Don't you trust me? Haven't I proven myself? If I wanted to harm you, would I do it with another sandwich? And in front of all these people? Would I have risked my life to find Manny and help bring him back to save you?" Shel let the king come to his senses. "Just calm down and try a bite!"

The king pursed his lips and examined the sandwich. "A pee-bee and jay, eh?" he finally said, then looked over at Mark the pleaseman. "Here!" he held out the sandwich. "You go first!" Mark jerked his head back in defiance. It wasn't so much that the combination of peanut butter and jam sounded terrible. It was just something new, and people can be funny about trying new things. Mark, who thrived on routine, was just such a person.

"Oh, for Heaven's sake!" exclaimed Alice, snatching the sandwich and biting in. Mark and the king stared wide-eyed at the brave knight who was famous for her adventurous spirit. She was, beyond a doubt, the boldest and most daring soul in the kingdom. But being bold and daring can come with its share of risk. Unfortunately, her impetuous act spelled disaster for the brave knight, for Shel was indeed trying to poison the king! As Alice fell to her knees, succumbing to the toxic snack, she struggled to pull her sword from its sheath in one last valiant act of upholding her sovereign duty to protect her king. But it was too late!

Just kidding.

What really happened was that Alice loved the sandwich and, being a bold woman of action, after taking her bite, she shoved that sandwich right in the king's mouth! After getting over the initial shock of the unorthodox force-feeding, Longsmiles could not ignore the amazing flavors invading his tastebuds. Within seconds, his expression shifted from utter surprise to ultimate satisfaction. Right then Shel knew he had a winner.

Following a moment of not-so-silent chewing, the king making all sorts of "mmm" and "ohhh" and "ahhh" sounds, Longsmiles finally swallowed... then opened his not-stuck mouth. "Peee beee and jayyy," he said slowly.

Shel smiled. "Not bad, eh?"

Longsmiles nodded and beheld the remaining sandwich that rested comfortably in his hands. "Not bad, indeed. All the flavors of my beloved peanut butter... and more!" He looked at Katya with big eyes. "And no danger of stuck mouth syndrome!" The witch nodded, satisfied with the result: a happy, and safe, king.

(Let us now recall the royal dog to whom the king fed a nugget of Joy's peanut butter sandwich in book three, for this dog — whose name also happened to be Skippy — nearly brought the picnic party to a grinding halt, almost losing his life in the process.) As the king brought that glorious sandwich to his lips for a second bite — this one of his *own* feeding — Skippy the dog jumped up and snatched that PB&J right out of the king's hands! Forgetting that it was he who'd trained the dog to also love peanut butter, the king barked furiously at the foul-mannered canine. "You come back here with that! Else I'm going to make myself a PB&D!!"

"PB&D, sire?" Katya squinted.

"Peanut butter and DOG!"

The crowd broke into an uproar.

Longsmiles, however, was livid. "'Man's best friend', my eye! Skippy, if I've told you once I've told you a thousand times: the only way you and I are going to get along is if I tell you what to do and you do it!" he derided the canine but Skippy the dog wasn't paying any attention.

More laughter erupted from the crowd, the contagiousness of which eventually got to Longsmiles too as he realized he was only getting angry at a dog for simply doing what dogs do. His fledgling smile grew a thousand times bigger when Shel pulled the second sandwich from Katya's satchel and handed it to Skippy (the king, not the dog). As he did, the king yanked Shel's arm and pulled him in for a hug.

The laughter and commotion caught the attention of the other partygoers and, seeing that their king was engaging in something momentous (he wasn't a big hugger), they began to migrate. Soon, a large crowd gathered. With a mouthful of food (he continued to feed himself with his left hand while hugging Shel with his right), the king stood up and placed a hand on Shel's shoulder to steady himself. From there he began delivering a speech to the enlarged crowd.

"It took me some time to see it. Perhaps I was blinded by grief, perhaps by fear. But I see clearly now that I am surrounded by friends who not only care about me…" He made eye contact with one friend after another, "You all care deeply about one another as well." The crowd nodded and smiled. "What's more is you care about the Land of Happy... and the whole of Arcania... and even unknown lands beyond our borders." He looked at Shel and then at Izzy. "I recall that the virtues of kindness and empathy do not have borders, are free of judgment, do not discriminate; things I knew long ago but had forgotten. Thanks to old friendships reignited," the king found Joy in the crowd, "I am recalling just how important it is to maintain good relations with our neighbors; not just for keeping the peace in our communities but also for keeping peace in our hearts. And, thanks to all of you, I recall the importance of keeping our bodies healthy." The king took a few steps, a little wobbly but entirely without help. "...And strong," he added, taking two more steps toward Ingonyama and placing a hand on the lion's shoulder, a gesture of kindness... and balance. Although he continued to address the crowd at large, he spoke softer, leaning in toward the lion, yet staring directly at Shel. "Isn't it incredible how a visit from a perfect stranger can bring about so much change?" The king paused in reflection. His eyes shifted from Shel to the ground, then over the crowd, finally coming to rest right next door on Ingonyama. "That young man over there fought for your freedom, against a *king* no less! And he didn't even know you." Then the king looked at Joy. "And this young woman here fought for your freedom too. As did Izzy and Sandovar and the Boogies…" He looked straight at the lion. "Who am I to deny the will of the people?"

"You are the king, Sire! That's who," replied Ingonyama with conviction.

Longsmiles shook his head. "No. A king does not hide behind his throne, using his crown to enforce his will. A king does not use his might to push his people toward some grandiose ideal, no matter how noble the cause. A true king walks alongside his people, through the muck and mire, using his power to clear pathways through the most challenging terrain, the fiercest storms, and always in the direction his people wish to go." He paused and looked around, inhaling deeply the cool, spring air. Then he looked squarely at the lion. "The people wish you to be free, Ingo, and so you are."

"Sire?" the lion sputtered.

"I should have been there to fight the Gambrine alongside you. Instead, you had to fight on my behalf. It is finally clear to me that you are good, that you fight on the side of good, and that you will continue to do good in this world. So, go. Be free. Go and do good things."

There was a moment of reverent silence while the crowd waited to see what would happen next. But nothing happened. The lion stared at the king, likely making sure this wasn't some game, a cruel joke. But the king said nothing more, just stared back at the lion. Finally, with nothing left to do, Ingonyama bowed and turned away. He took a couple of steps from the king — Alice quickly stepping up to take his place as Longsmiles' crutch — but then he paused and turned back to Shel.

"It wasn't so long ago that I had given up hope of ever roaming the free world again… until you and your friends came for me." The lion looked at Izzy and winked, then back at Shel. "But even then I wasn't sure I had anything left to offer." He reached in his pocket and pulled out the puzzle piece. "But you helped me imagine life beyond my jail cell, and finally I saw that I *did* have more to give. And for that, I can't thank you enough. For that, I honor you." He handed the piece back to Shel. "This belongs to you. I won't have need of it where I am going."

Shel looked down at Ingonyama's open paw and took the puzzle piece slowly, noting that it had once again become dirty while in the care of the lion, with the ending of the word 'imagine' smudged somewhat. As Shel was distracted trying to clean the bit of wood, the lion pulled something else from one of his other pockets. It was a large Gambrine tooth he'd presumably picked up during the battle. He had wound copper wire tightly around the base of the tooth to make a pendant, which he'd then affixed to a chain. He held it up.

"My pendant!" Shel blurted out.

"Yes. This also belongs to you," said Ingonyama. "A knight should always carry a reminder of the deed that won him his honor." The lion placed the necklace over Shel's head as he bowed in gratitude.

"But how did you—"

The lion cut him off with a raised paw and a shake of his head. "That is a question you will have to answer for yourself. Now, you are not yet a knight, officially... only the king... or queen mother — he winked at Ruth — can remedy that. ...But there is more to being a knight than holding title. You have shown your quality as a courageous and honorable man, one who is willing to put the well-being of others before his own. Those are the core qualities of any good knight."

Still uneasy about how the necklace came back to him, Shel protested. "But, Yams, I don't need anything to help me remember you and everyone, and I—"

"No," Ingo interrupted again. "This is not for you to remember any of us, Sheldon. I'm confident you won't forget your friends here. This is for you to remember who *you* are, who you *really* are, deep down, and the deeds of which you are capable. Don't forget the man you have become here in Arcania."

Shel was humblestunned. "But... what about you? You should be wearing this. You're the one who—"

Ingo shook his head. "The reminder of my deeds I carry with me in my heart, and in my heart alone. Those memories are too painful to wear on the outside." He looked down at his clothes and fidgeted with the shirt buttons. "Not unlike these clothes, actually." He looked up at Shel and smiled, turned to Izzy and nodded, then bowed slightly to the king. And then, Ingonyama the lion turned and walked away. Everyone stood and watched as the lion made his way across the palace lawns, removing his pressed shirt and pleated pants in stride, letting the clothes fall to the ground, then letting himself fall to the ground, landing on all fours. Without looking back, the lion ran into the fields beyond the groomed lawns and disappeared into the tall grass.

o o o o o o

Staring into the distance, pondering the wake of Ingonyama, the king held out a hand toward Mark the pleaseman. Mark was startled by the gesture as he knew what it meant but wasn't sure why the king would need a sword at that moment. Still, not being one to ever refuse a Longsmiles command (unless he wasn't paying attention), Mark pulled his sword from its sheath and placed the hilt into the palm of the king.

"Ingonyama is right. Any man or woman who has endured what you have who has certainly earned a place in the service of a king. And while my company would be honored to have you, I suspect the day is fast approaching when you will make your journey home, back to Chicago." On instinct, Shel glanced at Joy. She smiled sweetly then looked down. "But before you go, as a gesture of gratitude for saving this king's life..." Longsmiles paused and stiffened himself up. "Kneel, Master Sheldon."

Shel looked at Izzy, who smiled and nodded as if to say, 'Do as the king commands, you knucklehead!' And so, Shel did. As he bent on one knee, King Longsmiles placed the sword atop his shoulders and spoke some faint words in the language of the flowers. Shel of course didn't know what was being said until the king spoke once again in English.

"It is against our customs to knight children, as that would place undue burden upon the child's head. However, I think we can all agree with Ingo's assertion that you are no longer a child, not after what you've been through. Still, you are not yet a man. Close, but not quite. Thus, until you are of age to receive your well-deserved knighthood, rise, Sheldon Silvers, royal *teen* of the realm, protector of the king, and protector of the lands of both Happy and of Champion Valley, and of all the good people and creatures that live under these skies, forever and ever."

And with that, Shel stood up to a great roar of the crowd, cheering, "Shel Silvers, teen of the realm! Shel Silvers, teen of the realm!" Izzy plucked Shel from the crowd and held him up high and Shel felt on top of the world.

Longsmiles looked up at the young man. "Now then, what gift would you ask of your king? If it is mine to give, I shall give it... But please do not ask for a television set. That I do not have." (Somewhere in the background Kish Khet could be seen kicking rocks.)

Shel tried to think of something but his mind was blank, overwhelmed by all the attention. Since his mind was quiet, his mouth decided to blurt out, "Falconovich's bat!" Longsmiles squinted, as did

Izzy. "I mean… No, Izzy, what I meant was… I don't *want* it. I don't want your bat. I just meant that we could use it… we *should* use it, and the ball… and the glove too, I suppose."

Longsmiles interjected, "Sir Sheldon, what are you going on about?"

Shel collected himself. "I'm sorry, Your Highness. What I'm trying to say is that I would really love to play a game of baseball… with all of you. I mean, we have more than enough players… and we have Shoeless Joe's bat for goodness' sake! Are you kidding me?! We should get a game going!" Then he added more quietly, "Don't you think?" The crowd looked around at one another, not sure what to think.

"I love it!" Joy exclaimed as she jumped up and threw her arms high in the air. "But I don't know how to play," she added as she came back down to the ground.

"Does *anyone* know how to play?" asked Izzy. They looked around at each other a second time, shrugging and shaking their heads.

"That's okay!" interjected Shel. "I can teach you. I can teach you all how to play!"

Joy saw the enthusiasm on Shel's face, a look she'd never seen before. In that moment he was visibly filled with the love of the world. And in that moment she knew, without a doubt, that she loved him too, wholly and completely.

Chapter Eleven

The Ball Game

Sketch by
S. Silvers, teen.

The next day, after breakfast, the baseball game was on! Shel had Izzy playing second base, on account of the long reach of his trunk being useful to cover the gap between second and first. On first base, Shel put Alice because of her keen reflexes and all-around natural abilities. Joy played shortstop as that position requires a lot of energy. Next to her, on third base, was Sandovar of Sandeen, recently returned from his journey through the desert.

o o o o o o

"The job of waking the giants has proved much easier than expected," Sandovar reported to the king and crowd. "Dracula and his lot have provided invaluable expertise on how to properly resurrect a soul. Once awakened, Sarah Karynthia and Sylvia Kats turn on their charm, keeping the giants calm while Chester and Charlie reorient their brethren. With this approach, the giants seem to be accepting their new reality with grace, or at the least, understanding. They are, of course, not pleased with having been put to sleep in the first place, but they seem happy to be awake again."

o o o o o o

"Now remember, no swords in the belly, Sandman," warned Shel, much to the chief's disappointment.

Fickles, Pickles, and Tickles took the outfield slots while Manny, despite his age, decided he wanted to play catcher — with a designated hitter to take his place when it came time to bat.

Shel, meanwhile, assumed the pitcher's mound (don't mind if I do!).

"Now, Izzy, you sure you got this?" Shel challenged his oversized pal at second. "Your dad being from Chicago and all, and being friends with Shoeless Joe, I figure you know what you're doing out there. I'm counting on you to manage the infield."

"Fuhgetabowdit!" Izzy replied, mistaking Chicago for Brooklyn. "I'm a natural! After all, who can kick a football from here to Afghanistan? I can!"

"Okaaay," Shel mused. "You do realize that football is *not* baseball, right?" He glared through his bushy brows at the elephant before turning back to his mound to toss a few practice pitches at Manny.

For the opposing team, the pirates were assigned to the outfield: Taudello in left, Mortimer in right, and Blackbeard — who now looked more passable as a pirate with three-and-a-half-days of coal-black stubble on his chin — playing centerfield. Katya and Wanda, the cook witches, took first and second bases, while Sarah Karynthia and Sylvia Kats took shortstop and third base. Don the bear dared to mount the pitcher's mound, and his queen's kangaroo sat in as catcher.

Others, such as pirate captain Jarby, on account of his age, and Hook, on account of his, well, hook, filled the important roles of base coaches — although all Jarby did was berate his runners with taunts like, "Arrr, ye run like a dried-up jellyfish!" and, "me ol' granny be runnin' faster than ye, and she be dead by a hundred years she be!"

The stands were filled with King Longsmiles, Ruth and Simonson, and all sorts of Kantytown citizens, some with spaghetti stains still on their shirts, and all with great big smiles on their faces. Most of the smiles were in anticipation of the game, but some were in anticipation of the lunch that Katya had planned. She'd permitted Wanda to use some of her eccentric cooking methods to whip up the world's biggest hot dog. Until that was ready, there was plenty of peanuts and popcorn to go around. And for those lucky enough to sit close to the king, Longsmiles had a picnic basket full of gourmet peanut butter (and jelly!) sandwiches, which he gladly shared.

The king cried out, "Play Ball!" in his best umpire voice, as Shel had instructed him to do upon the signal: a wink and a nod from the pitcher's mound. Shel performed a tidy wind up and tossed the ball toward Donachtuk at home plate, the lead-off batter for the home team.

"Strike one!" called the umpire, who happened to be none other than Mister Rulebook himself, Sir Marcus O'Rillynice Gladface McGee. Don looked back at Mark and growled. Shel laughed, as did many of the other players. Mark did not.

Shel decided he'd take a little walk to home plate to remind the temperamental bear of a few fundamentals. "Okay, Don, try to keep calm. You have a few more tries. Just remember, you don't have to swing if the pitch is bad. But, if you do swing and you miss, like that last one, that's an automatic strike. Three strikes and you're out. Okay?" Locking his eyes on the bear, Shel cocked his head high then let it fall slowly to drive his point home.

"Hey Tooky, why don't you take some practice swings?" came a voice from the dugout.

"You need to tighten your grip, Don!" came another.

"Yeah! And choke up on the bat!"

"Straighten your shoulders and swivel your hips!" cried yet another, at which point, Don had just about enough advice, and with a mighty roar he chucked that bat clear into left field.

"...And work on your sportsmanship, too!"

The crowd laughed. Don did not.

By the time Fickleface returned from the outfield with the bat, Donachtuk had cooled down thanks to an ice cream cone, courtesy of Joythea.

"Ice cream? Where'd you get ice cream?!" cried Izzy. "I want some."

"Me too! I'll take chocolate," barked the queen's kangaroo.

"Vanilla for me!" wailed her monkey.

As Joy departed the field, happy to oblige the sweet-toothed animals, the bear gripped the bat firmly, thanks to his ice cream-soaked — and thus sticky — hands. He took a couple exaggerated practice swings before stepping back into the batter's box with a carefree whistle and a ten-pound smile. "Bring it on, pitcher!" he yelled at Shel, acting the part. With his bat positioned atop his right shoulder, he ground the ball of his back foot into the dirt a good inch or two, ready for the showdown.

Not heeding the bear's temper, Manny decided, poorly, to give Don something to think about other than the ballgame: namely, the bear's sister. "You're sister looks like a racoon, and smells like an armadillo!"

Now *that* was not nice!

Donachtuk, standing squarely in the batter's box, looked down at the foul-mouthed jaw jockey and growled between smiling teeth. "If I weren't a vegetarian I would take a bite out of your—"

"Steee-rike two!" yelled Marcus as a heater of a fast pitch came zinging over the plate. Marcus threw his right arm out to the side and extended two fingers like he was flinging a yo-yo. Instantly, Don whipped around and leaped at Mark while Manny jumped out of the way, not wanting to get clobbered. Shel doubled over in laughter and Alice took off from third base to meet Sandovar at home plate in the nick of time to keep Don from doing any real harm to the pleaseman — who was doing his best to remain polite, asking, "Please do not chew on my arms. Pretty please!"

o o o o o o

Donachtuk wasn't normally malicious, but he already didn't like Mark on account of the pleaseman threatening to arrest the bear the previous summer for allegedly stealing the oversized refrigerator out of the palace storeroom. Now, did Don steal the reefer? No! Of course not! ...Well, maybe a little bit.

You see, Donachtuk was a polar bear, in case that wasn't already made clear. And boy did it get hot in the Land of Happy during the summertime. So, Tooky simply *borrowed* for a bit the only oversized ice box around, so that he would have a nice place to rest and get some relief from the heat. He was going to return it, honest he was. But since it wasn't even being used at the palace, it was just sitting in storage, he figured he'd just hang on to it for a while until someone asked for it back. That was three years ago.

But why would a polar bear move from the Arctic to the sweltering Land of Happy, you ask? Well, poor Don was afraid of the snow. Who ever heard of a polar bear being afraid of the snow?! Meet Donachtuk Nanook.

o o o o o o

Shel walked to home plate once more, Don sufficiently restrained. "Don," Shel was trying to keep from laughing, "you have to try and stay calm. Remember, this is only a game. We're just here to have fun. Yeah?"

Don nodded somewhat shamefully.

"Look, out of everyone here, *you* ought to be the most cool-headed, being from the land of ice and snow. No?"

Don nodded, somewhat shamefully... again.

"And don't worry, Manny isn't going to say anything else to distract you. Isn't that right, Manny?" Shel scowled at the dentist. This time Manny was the one who nodded shamefully — but only after sneaking in a sideways grin. "Just try to relax, Don. Think of something that makes you happy — like dancing!"

Don looked confused.

"Think of me as your dancing partner," Shel continued, "way out there on the mound. You and I need to connect, just like two people dancing. And the way we connect is through this little ball here." Shel tossed the ball up into the air and caught it again. "So, when I throw this ball to you, it's like I'm reaching out for you to swing me around. But instead of swinging me you're going to swing that bat. You want to give *that* a try?"

One of Don's eyebrows stood up to get a better look at where Shel was coming from. Satisfied, the bear shrugged and nodded, "Sure. Okay. It sounds kooky but I'll give it a shot."

"Okay! Good." Shel walked back to the pitcher's mound. "Just remember, you and I connect through the *ball*. So keep your eye on the ball. Okay?"

"Yeah, okay. I got it!" Don replied.

"You sure you got all that, Fred Astaire?" teased Manny.

Donachtuk whipped around to face the dentist, looking as if he were going to tackle him.

"Don, just focus on the ball," Shel called to him. "It's just you, me, and the ball. That's the dance: you, me, and the ball. Here it comes now. Ready? Watch it!" Shel wound up and tossed the ball at the bear. Once Don saw the ball coming, he spun in a circle, a pirouettish twirl, and *crack!* — he smacked that ball way out into centerfield where Fickles and Pickles fumbled around attempting to recover it. The bear rounded second base and made it all the way to third by the time the ball got to the infield.

Joy tossed the ball gleefully back to Shel, who snatched it out of the air with a wink to Don, who was now grinning like a jester and dancing in circles, having the time of his life. The half-ton lug was almost floating he was so happy. And so was Shel, because now he had himself a ball game!

"Next at bat," called Mark in his loud, authoritative announcer voice, "Tauder the Marauder!"

o o o o o o

The game continued as any amateur baseball game might, with errors, mishaps, players running the bases in the wrong order, arguments culminating in the kicking of dirt onto other players' shoes, bats being thrown in all directions, hats being turned upside-down for good luck, endless laughs, cheers, and of course plenty of cartwheels (mostly from the visiting team's shortstop)… until finally it was time for lunch.

"Yay! Halftime!" Joy yelled as she ran off the field toward the makeshift kitchen set up to serve everyone.

"Actually, it's called the seventh-inning stretch," corrected Shel. "But it looks like we're going to take a food break. So, sure, you can call it halftime if you like. Whatever."

The sound of rolling battle drums announced a regiment of the king's guard carrying something on their shoulders. It looked like the trunk of a large redwood tree that might be used as a battering ram to knock down a rival's castle gate. The regiment set the log atop a large picnic blanket laid over the grass and began pouring what looked like ketchup and mustard on top.

"Goodness! It IS the world's biggest hot dog!" salivated Picklepots.

"Yeah," replied one of the guards. "But apparently they forgot to make the bun to go with it. Plus," he added with overt chagrin, "it's not even a *real* hot dog. It's a veggie dog! Can you believe that?!"

Well, that was music to Shel's ears… and to Joy's and Izzy's, none of whom were fans of eating meat. And then there was the king, who was plenty content with his PB&J sandwiches. For the rest of the crowd, starting with Pickles, the communal feast of the largest (faux) hot dog in the world commenced with a frenzy! Sandovar was so impressed with both the cuisine and the enthusiasm of the crowd, he vowed to open a hot dog stand of his own someday.

After a good hour or so of epic feasting and dialoguing, the crowd grew tired and the celebratory atmosphere quieted to a midday lull. Small groups wandered off to collapse in the shade of sycamore and maple trees. Others snuck back to more comfortable caches in houses or barns, wherever a bed could be found, as the seventh-inning stretch stretched out into a full-blown, proper siesta. After all, as Manny put it: "Ain't nothin' so glorious as a good after-meal nap!"

"Quite right!" agreed the king (with Marcus in the background double-checking the royal nap ledger).

Later that day, when the nappers began slowly waking, enthusiasm for this new game Shel had introduced was thoroughly renewed. What a day! In fact, that was the best day many in the Land of Happy could recall in a very long time. Sure, the dinner party with the avalanche of spaghetti was a blast, but the clean-up afterward was a real drag.

The home team ran and jumped and skipped onto the field to take their positions while the visiting team lined up to bat. Leading off was the fabulous head knight of Kantytown, Lady Alice. Don the bear glared at Alice with a grizzly stare. He wound up like a top and tossed a fastball straight down the pipe. Alice didn't even flinch. She just let that pitch sail right on by without even looking at it, as if it were some lowly admirer and she were a famous star of the silver screen.

"Steee-riiiike one!" cried Marcus, grateful to be umpiring for someone other than Don.

Alice's aloofness rattled Donachtuk, who didn't understand why she wasn't engaging, why she didn't swing at such a perfect toss. But Alice had a secret, a secret Shel had shared with her. "Never swing at your first pitch. This will allow you to size up your pitcher's style and help soothe the jitters." But Alice didn't have jitters. She was unphased, cool as a cucumber. She had fought all sorts of foes and battles, and the only thing that rattled her was the thought of settling down to a quiet, peaceful, provincial life.

There she was, a beauty at bat. And there was Don, the beast atop his hill. The kangaroo catcher threw the ball back to the mound and Don did a little dance before winding up again, again throwing a fastball right down the pipe. But this time his dancing partner did her own little wind up and *WHAM!* Alice rang that bell so loud the ball didn't know what hit it. Everyone in the stands cheered as the old leather and twine sailed clean out of the field. Meanwhile, Alice casually jogged triumphantly through the infield. As she rounded third base, the entire visiting team cleared the bench and went out to greet her at home plate.

Mark waited until the celebration died down and the players returned to the bench before announcing, "Next at-bat: Sheldon Silvers."

"Ahem!" the king cleared his throat.

"Oh! Excuse me. Sheldon Silvers, teen," corrected the umpire.

"Silvers teen! Silvers teen!" came the cheers from the crowd, encouraging the young man to recreate Alice's magnificent performance.

"Silvers teen," Shel repeated softly as he picked Joe Jackson's bat up out of the dirt, reveling in the attention and the sound of his new extended surname. He stopped smiling after a couple of practice swings when it struck him that Alice's performance would be a tough act to follow. His legs stiffened and his heart began to race. Up to this point, he'd been enjoying the game, errors and all. Now, he suddenly felt pressure to perform, as if he would let his team down if he didn't pull off something spectacular. Worse, he felt as though everyone were now looking at him as the *inventor* of baseball, and as such, expected a performance *at least* as spectacular as Alice's. Out of nowhere, the old feeling of being a shy nobody on the school playground crept up on him — something he hadn't felt in a very long while. He looked around and instead of seeing Don and Katya, Sarah and Sylvia, the pirates in the outfield — all of whom were his friends — he saw school kids, bullies even, staring back at him, waiting for him to strike out so they could laugh and make fun.

As he approached home plate he could feel his arms grow weak and his palms sweaty (which didn't help for maintaining a grip on the bat). *What in the world is happening*, he thought. *I thought I was past all this!* He thought he had grown and matured after everything he'd experienced since running away from school. But here they were, his fears and insecurities coming back to haunt him. But why now? Why here at the baseball game? He was so distracted and distraught that he forgot his own rule of not swinging at the first pitch.

"Strike one!" Shel heard Marcus call from somewhere in the distance behind him.

His vision blurred. He felt dizzy and stumbled out of the batter's box, stalling the game. As he looked back to the crowd behind home plate, he could see King Longsmiles watching him, disappointment in his eyes. In truth, it was concern but Shel was unable to see or think clearly. A moment later he no longer even recognized the king. His father's eyes, full of disappointment and disapproval, stared back at him. Overwhelmed, he lowered his head and dropped to one knee. As he did, he inadvertently stumbled back into the batter's box, clearing the way for Donachtuk to proceed — and he did, that ruthless dancer!

"Strike two!" called the umpire.

"That's not very polite, Marcus!" called Joy from the bullpen. Marcus shrugged. Was he supposed to lie?

Although it should have been obvious that Shel was struggling, he had been in such good spirits the past few days that Marcus and Don and most everyone else in the crowd figured the kid was just being silly and putting on a show, albeit a strange one. Since most of the people both watching and playing knew almost nothing of the game, many figured this was just some oddball ritual, beholden to the second batter in the bottom of the seventh inning.

What an odd game this is!

Some, however, could see this was no act. The king understood that Shel wasn't himself. Izzy could see it too. Joy knew it also. Almost simultaneously, Joy and Izzy, who had been sitting next to one another, stood up and rushed onto the field.

Don started his theatrical wind-up to what would surely by his third and final pitch, as he'd been throwing solid strikes all day. Time seemed to slow for Shel as he steadied himself against Joe Jackson's bat. Still on one knee, he looked up once more at the king, but the king was not there. The crowd too was gone. There, alone in the bleachers, stood Shel's dad, shaking his head.

"It doesn't matter what you think you've accomplished here," chided Patterson in a piercing, cold voice. "These people are not your friends. You're nothing but a dreamer." Shel could feel his father's words, like stones thrown at his weakened body. "Stop playing games, boy. It's time to wake up and come home. You're going to finish school and then come work with me at the bakery. Now get up. We're leaving."

Shel squinted at the apparition. Suddenly, a figure appeared behind his dad. It looked to be a man but he couldn't make out who it was. The figure was blurry as if he were looking through a tank of water. As the image slowly came clearer, Shel sorted out that the man was wearing a military uniform. An instant later, he could see clear as day that it was the man who had stopped him on the sidewalk!

How could this be?!? Shel thought, as he focused on the man's face. Something about him was presently familiar, as if he'd just seen this man earlier that day. But that was impossible. He didn't know the soldier on the street. Yet, he knew *this* man for sure, and the two were unmistakably one and the same. Standing behind his dad, the soldier, with his big, bushy blonde beard was staring at Shel, smiling. Suddenly it struck him: Ingonyama!

With a wink of kindness from the lion-man, Shel instantly felt all the anxiety and fear and insecurity wash off him like dirt in a rainstorm. He watched in relief as the residual muck drained to his feet then, seeping into the ground at home plate, disappeared.

The warmth of sunlight beating down on his back, bare feet against the tan, rocky soil, reminded him of the beach, and of Joy. He looked up to see her running toward him in slow motion and was suddenly reminded of the game still going on, fans waiting for him to snap out of his episode.

Feeling rejuvenated and strong, he looked back to the bleachers to see his dad still standing there, arms crossed, glaring. And there behind him was Ingonyama.

Instantly, Shel stood up and pointed Shoeless Joe's bat at Patterson. With a resounding "No!" he swiftly spun around and smacked Don's pitch — which had been soaring toward him all the while — straight into centerfield, well over the reach of Blackbeard, who didn't even attempt to catch nor chase the ball. The pirate just stood there and watched it sail over his head like a cannonball gone astray.

Like Blackbeard, Shel stood still. He didn't even bother running the bases. And because he stayed put, he was tackled by Joy, who was intent on comforting her friend, aggressively. But that was okay. Shel still needed comforting despite his recovery.

Onlookers didn't know what to make of the scene, especially King Longsmiles who was thoroughly perplexed after watching Shel point a bat at him and yell, "No!"

"Good gracious! What did I do?" The king queried, glancing sideways at the queen mother.

Ruth just smiled. "Kids these days. They're so dramatic."

"You okay, Shelby?" Izzy asked as he picked Shel and Joy up off the ground. "You looked like you were having quite a moment there."

"Izzy! ...Hey! Where did you get that red handkerchief?" He pointed to Izzy's neck.

Izzy reached his trunk up to inspect the scarf. "What, this old thing? The Falcon gave it to me when I was a kid. Figured I looked a bit more sporty with it on. Plus, we're playing his game, so, you know, I thought I'd honor him by wearing it."

"Well, it looks pretty smart on you," Shel replied. "But, I swear I've seen it somewhere before. It looks familiar." Izzy shrugged. Shel shrugged. "Oh well. You're up to bat, big guy!" Shel handed the bat to Izzy.

"Oh, no. That's okay. I think we'd better call it quits after your little episode. Besides, it's getting late. I'm sure people are tired of watching us play."

"Are you kidding?!" Shel rallied. "We're not ending on *that* note. No way! Besides, I want to see three home runs in a row. Alice's hit was a surprise and mine was a miracle. But you, everyone knows you can hit. Come on, let's see you send it all the way into the pond!"

"I don't know, Shel. Maybe we should just take it easy."

"Izzy, I'm fine. Here." Shel pushed the bat at him. As the elephant lumbered hesitantly toward home plate, Shel added quietly, "Hit one for your dad, like I just did."

Watching Joy and Shel retreat to the bench, arms around one another, Izzy had the urge to follow after but instead dragged himself to home plate, taking a few practice swings as he walked. At the plate, he was greeted with a cheering crowd that made him feel right at home and he confidently faced Don the bear. The crowd was in a frenzy, anticipating something exciting, to be sure. After the back-to-back performances by Alice and Shel, the crowd was so excited they began chanting, "IZ-E, IZ-E!"

Izzy looked at the people standing and clapping and calling his name. He hadn't received such a welcome since his days in the circus. The attention made him forget about Shel. He stepped into the batter's box and with one eyebrow poised like a high diver on a cliff, he lowered his head and cocked his father's bat, ready for war.

Don was ready too. He twisted and twirled in his customary wind-up, and then... *ZOOM!...* he let the ball fly. Like Shel, Izzy also forgot about the rule not to swing at the first pitch. He zeroed in on the ball careening toward him, wound his trunk up like a spring, and let 'er rip! *BOOM!* That ball went flying like a rocket... straight UP! The ball flew so high, so fast, that it disappeared completely into the bright blue yonder.

"Where did it go?" asked Skippy. Everyone shrugged. Izzy just stood at home plate, wondering what he should do, until a voice cried out,

"Look!" and everyone squinted at the sky. The smallest dot way up in the clouds was slowly getting bigger as it returned from orbit.

"Wait a minute," barked Marcus from behind home plate. "That doesn't look like a—"

"It's a bomb!" another voice yelled as the thing descended. It wasn't a baseball at all. It was far too big. But it wasn't a bomb either. Whatever it was, it was falling fast, heading right toward Izzy.

"Izzy! Look out!" cried Manny from the dugout.

It appeared that Izzy's pop fly had sailed so high it knocked a bird right out of the sky — oh my! — and that bird was now falling, heading straight for Izzy's eye! (Good grief!)

But Izzy did not move. He was stunned, watching what was heading toward him. In a flash, the bird opened its wings and halted its freefall, pushing down a tremendous gust of wind that stirred up a considerable sandstorm, obscuring the elephant almost completely and forcing everyone to shield their eyes from the encircling dust cloud. Down came the enormous bird right on top of Izzy. The crowd wondered if he'd been crushed. Manny stood up and ran toward home plate. "Izzy!" he cried. "IZZY!"

A few moments later, as Manny — who did not run so fast on account of his short legs and long years — was just getting to his friend, the settling dust revealed a great surprise. Izzy had not been crushed... not his body anyway... perhaps his heart, but in a good way. For there, atop Izzy's back, stood a massive pelican.

"Hello, Charlotte."

Charlotte opened her mouth and dropped the baseball on Izzy's head with a *bonk!* "Lose something, my love?" she said with a dangerous smile, and the two love birds embraced.

"Wow, nonstop excitement!" King Longsmiles commented from the bleachers, stuffing his cheeks with popcorn and peanuts. "I've really been missing out on this baseball thing!"

With Izzy smiling up at Charlotte, Charlotte smiling down at him, and the entire crowd smiling at the two of them, no one noticed that the other two love birds had flown.

Chapter Twelve

Tell Me

Sketch by
S. Silvers, teen.

On the sandy shores of Champion Lake, west of Kantytown harbor, Shel and Joy strolled in the late afternoon light of an unforgettable spring day. Their time on that beach, however, was quite different from when they first met on Isla de Sonrisas. The sun on this particular day burned mildly, yawning as it prepared to say goodbye. From the chill in the air, one might think fall was around the corner, but spring wasn't even over yet, let alone summer. Something else, however, was...

Shel didn't know where to begin. He felt he wanted — needed — to say volumes. He'd never met anyone even remotely like this girl before, and no one had ever made him feel the things he'd felt when he was with her. She was stunning to watch; her radiant beauty, her charismatic charm, her passion for life. He felt honored just to be in her presence. *Oh, that sounds stupid!* he thought. He hadn't realized, but all the while he'd been thinking of all of these compliments, the two of them had been walking in silence. Joy's head, as a result, was reeling, wondering what he might be thinking.

"Will you tell me I'm cute?" she wondered aloud, breaking the serenity.

Shel looked at her, surprised. He'd heard what she'd said but wasn't sure she actually said what he thought he heard her say. Oh, his head was full of rocks!

"Sorry!" was his chosen response, regrettably.

"Sorry? For what?"

"What?" he said, obviously distracted and out of sorts.

"Are you feeling okay?" she asked.

"Huh? Yeah! Yeah, I'm okay. Why? You okay?"

"I think so," she replied. "I was just thinking it would be nice to hear a compliment from you."

Shel opened his mouth.

"But be honest!" She added quickly.

He stuttered, "Um... well..." He took a breath to collect his courage while his brows vaulted over his eyes, asking, 'Are we really going to do this?' He was both relieved and frightened to discover his answer was 'Absolutely!' "Um... I think you are very cute." He gulped and then jumped in with both feet. "Adorable in fact."

She smiled on the outside and the inside.

"You're amazing!"

She smiled bigger.

"... But everyone knows that," he added.

Her smile faded.

"No, that's not what I—" He tried to recover. "I just meant it's obvious." This wasn't helping. "I mean, I see more. Way more." He stopped walking and turned to face her. Taking her hand in his, he added, "Joy, you're incredibly beautiful." Her frown melted and she looked down and blushed. "And I don't just mean your pretty face or your fabulous hair..." she pulled her hair back on one side and tucked it behind her ear. "I mean everything: The way you laugh, the way you dance, the way you can cheer up anyone no matter what's going on... You are, without a doubt, the most wonderful thing I have ever known."

His sincerity, although moving, was almost too much. She felt the need to lighten the mood.

"Thing? You think I'm a thing?"

Of course he didn't mean she was a *thing*! He meant it as a compliment! But how can calling someone a *thing* be a compliment?! *Oh, what an idiot!* "No! Of course not! What I meant was—"

"Oh, I'm just kidding! Relax." She reassured him with a sweet smile. "But so long as we're being honest, you may as well know that I think you're moody and sloppy and—"

"What?!" he exclaimed.

"Oh! But it's okay!" she added in a playful, aloof tone. "You just be you. Don't change on my account... 'cause I don't really like you anyway."

Shel's eyes and mouth burst open. He was stunned! *Is she serious?* It took a moment for the obvious to navigate through all the sticks and rocks and mud inside his head. Eventually he sorted out that she was just messing with him. So he decided to play along, maintaining his expression of surprise, playing the part of the offended friend.

"Oh, did I say something wrong?" she giggled.

"Oh, no, no. It's fine!" He dropped her hand and put some distance between them, pretending not to care. She walked slowly behind, grinning silently. He turned back to face her and they resumed their walk together, side-by-side. "Did I say you were beautiful? What I meant was you're hideous!" Joy's face adopted the same expression he'd had only a moment ago, which was his goal. So, he continued. "I mean, you must be part Worst beast I think."

She opened her mouth even wider and then closed it tightly and squinted disapprovingly.

Getting carried away, Shel brought his hands up to his face. "I mean, that smell!"

She gasped! "You did NOT just say that I smell! That is *not* nice!"

Shel couldn't hold back a laugh as Joy punched him in the arm. She turned and walked briskly in front of him as he attempted to recover.

"I'm sorry." He tried to contain a laugh. "Joy! Wait. I'm sorry." He giggled a bit more, which didn't help. "That was too much. I was just kidding!" She knew that, but it still hurt for some reason. It wasn't the ridiculous (and rude) insult. There was something else. She was trying to pretend that everything was fine. But it wasn't. She walked on and he followed. "I actually like your smell."

"Please don't talk about my smell," she retaliated without looking back.

"Okay. I'm sorry. Your scent. Can I say your scent?"

"No!" she replied, again without looking back. Shel was confused. He thought they were having fun, joking around. He didn't mean to insult her. He opened his mouth to say something but decided against it, figuring he'd dug a deep enough hole already. He hurried to catch up and took her hand. She looked at him and grinned then placed her head on his shoulder and they walked on like that in silence for what seemed like forever.

"That was really fun, playing baseball. Thank you for introducing that game to everyone."

Shel nodded and smiled.

"So, are you feeling okay?" she asked. Shel's brows, like kids raising their hands in class, asked politely for her to clarify. So she did. "It was pretty scary when you collapsed back there."

"Oh. Yeah, I think I'm all right. I think it was just some weird breakdown. For old anxiety, as they say."

"Old Anxiety?" she asked.

"Yeah, you know, that song they sing on New Year's … put the old troubles behind you and move on and stuff."

Joy cocked her head and laughed. "Wait, are you talking about Auld Lang Syne? The song?"

Shel shrugged.

Joy began to sing softly, "We two ha' run a-bout the braes, an' pou'd the gowans fine, we wan'dred mon'a weary fit, sin' auld lang syne."

Shel stopped in his tracks, stunned by her incredible voice. She kept walking.

"Joy," he said.

She looked down and raised her hand to her face but did not stop walking. Shel ran to her and grabbed her arm, gently, very gently, to stop her. Turning her slowly he saw that she was crying. This surprised him and he didn't know what to say, so he just looked at her and she looked back at him with tears in her eyes. Without words he pulled her close and she buried her face in his chest. There he held her a while, as if he were embracing infinity, all the world and everything in the universe, right there in his arms, right there close to his heart.

Without looking up, deep sadness in her voice, she spoke, "That song is about saying farewell." She looked into his eyes and they shared a moment of silent understanding as the sun drowned into the sea, the world of fire and light blending with the world of water, spreading brilliant colors across the sky, extinguishing all time and task. There was nothing left for them to do, nowhere left to be but that very moment.

"This is the last sunset I ever want to see," he whispered. "I just want to hold onto this one — this one right here — never to be replaced by another."

She squeezed him tighter and spoke softly through her tears. "Tell me..."

He wiped his own eyes then wiped the tears from hers, and with a half-smile, said, "You're very cute, Joythea Aquarius Costeros."

And then she kissed him.

It was an innocent kiss, unplanned, sincere; an expression of deep caring, gratitude for dear friendship, and of sorrowful farewell. She pulled away slowly and they smiled at each other, remembering the past, trying to see into the future. She touched the side of his face gently and wiped a tear from his cheek.

"You're silly." She smiled softly. "I meant, tell me about your old anxiety."

Shel didn't expect that inquiry and withdrew, his warmth chilling unexpectedly. It was an automatic response. He turned and began walking.

Joy walked alongside, holding his arm. "Talk to me, Shel. Tell me what happened. Please."

Through challenging relationships at home, school, around his neighborhood, Shel had learned to keep to himself, keep his emotions tucked away. He did trust Joy, as much as he could trust anyone really. But maybe that wasn't enough. He wasn't sure the feelings she was asking him to share were even accessible for sharing.

She nodded reassuringly. "It's all right."

Her kindness was thoroughly disarming. He took a calming breath. "Well, um, as I was walking up to the plate, I started thinking of home, back in Chicago." He paused. She nodded to let him know she was listening and that he could proceed. "And I started thinking about school… and my dad…" Joy put her arm around his waist, pulling herself closer to him. "Anyway, I don't have any friends at school, really… and… my dad, he wants me to be someone I'm not. He wishes I were someone else entirely." Joy looked at him. He stared elsewhere. "Things are just… different back home. Here people accept me for who I am. They like me."

"Yeah," she said. "We do."

He smiled and continued with a sigh and a squint. "It was the weirdest thing. When I was standing there at home plate, I began to see everyone out there on the field as people from my life back in Chicago. Like the witches and Sarah and Sylvia and Don and Alice… even the queen. Everyone started to look like people from my school; people I don't really know that well… and that don't really know me…" He looked at Joy. She looked back with deep concern. "And then, I turned around and saw my dad up there in the bleachers."

"Really?" she asked, pausing.

Shel stopped walking too. "Yeah. The king and everyone else were gone. They just... disappeared. It was just my dad, standing there telling me to wake up. To stop dreaming." Joy looked away and Shel noticed a cloud of discomfort rush over her. "I know it doesn't sound all that terrible, my dad wanting a certain life for me…"

"It's not that," Joy tried to reassure him, but he wasn't finished.

"The reason why it bothers me so much, I guess, if I really think about it, which I try not to honestly, is that... our parents of all people are supposed to love us, unconditionally, right?"

"Of course!"

"Of course they are, right? Well I'm not sure mine do."

"Wha—?"

"If they do, they have a strange way of showing it."

"Shel, I'm sure they—"

"Because they make it pretty clear they wish I was someone else. At least my dad does. He doesn't like me, Joy. My own dad doesn't even like me."

She wasn't sure what to say. That was a deep sentiment. She knew it likely wasn't true, but what if it was? Shel *must* be exaggerating. Then again, what if he wasn't? She didn't know what his home life was like. Who was she to judge?

Shel knew what her silence meant, knew that last bit was hard to swallow. He'd been trying — unsuccessfully — to digest it all his life. "It's okay. My time here in Arcania has taught me that I'm actually worth liking, that I have something — though I'm not sure exactly what, haha..." He tried a little humor to lighten the mood. "...That I have something to offer; that there are things about me others appreciate... or enjoy... or whatever."

"You have *so* much to offer, Shel! Much more than you know."

He smiled and began walking again, Joy holding tight to his arm.

"But... I don't really care about that," she continued. "I'd like you even if you only had peanuts to offer."

"Oh, Joy, course you would. You *love* peanuts!" He punched her lightly on the arm and they both laughed. "It just feels good to think that I *am* worthy of being someone's friend, of being... loved. I don't know."

Joy stopped walking. "Yes! You are! Of course you are, Shel! I..." she hesitated. "I think you're wonderful."

This time she walked on without him. He watched her walk away for a minute then caught up to her, snatched her hand in his, and they strolled in silence, watching the waves roll in from the sea. The evening sky was growing darker and an early moon was rising in the east.

"It's strange..." Shel said after a while.

"What's that?"

"In the stands behind home plate, behind the image of my dad… I saw... Ingonyama."

Joy smiled. "Ingonyama? Are you sure?"

"Yeah. But, it wasn't him, obviously. I mean I know he's gone. And yet, it *was* him. I saw this man there, dressed just like a man I ran into back in Chicago. I didn't think anything of it at the time, but now, something tells me that Ingo and the man in Chicago are definitely the same person. Don't ask me how that's possible. I just know it. And all the friends playing the game, reminding me of people back home…" he paused. "I... never told you what happened, but when I passed out in the desert, after the fall from the horse…"

"You mean when Taudello threw you from his horse?"

"Yeah," he laughed slightly. "Anyway, I dreamed that I woke up in a strange house… and there was this guy there. I didn't know who he was, and I woke up before I could see him clearly or find out what house I was in. But in my vision I clearly saw that same red handkerchief that Izzy had around his neck during the baseball game."

Joy remained quiet a moment, then gently challenged, "A red handkerchief is pretty common, Shel..."

"Well, okay, sure. But this one was different. I can't really explain it."

"It's okay," she replied, meandering down to the water's edge, letting the waves crash upon her feet. (Contrary to popular myth, many mermaids do not automatically go from human legs to fish fin at the touch of water, salt or fresh. Many make the transition by intention. Joy was just such a mermaid.) She walked pensively through the waves lapping the beach. "I think I understand."

He sort of skip-ran to catch up with her. Any words that might've been floating around in his head evaporated. He began picking up interesting-looking pebbles in the shore break, turning them over in his fingers and tossing them back into the water. "What do you think that means, Joy?" he asked eventually.

She shrugged. The low, orange moonrise sparkling on the sea was mesmerizing. She felt herself drawn to the water and knew it was time to return home.

"Joy?"

"Hmm?"

"Is… this a dream?" He looked around slowly. The beach was magical: bloodfire moon dancing on a polished, royal blue floor. Anyone would've thought it was a dream. His gaze settled on his bare feet shuffling through the blonde sand. When he looked up, Joy was smiling gently. She took his hand in hers. There were no words for it. "Am I dreaming?" He asked again. "Has this… all of this… Arcania and everything… has it all been just a dream?"

Joy stopped walking.

Without thought, as if under a spell, Shel kept walking ever so slowly, dragging his toes through the wet sand. Their intertwined hands tugged at one another briefly before slipping apart, falling at their sides.

Shel's hand felt more empty, cold, and lonely than it had ever felt. He looked back at her but kept walking forward, compelled by some invisible force. He didn't feel sad. He suddenly couldn't feel anything. It was as if he were watching himself from a distance, detached and indifferent. Of course he wasn't indifferent to anything that was going on, yet some irresistible force was pulling him out of the moment. Even if he could fight it, he sensed it would be folly to try.

Knowing he needed this moment to process things, Joy did not follow but instead stood and watched her love walk away.

His mind was drifting, eyes staring ahead into the coming night, when suddenly he heard a faint splash behind him. He was instantly transported back to the present and a rush of nervousness flooded his heart. He turned quickly to see, staring coldly back at him, the puissant heart-wrenching expanse of nothingness. He was alone.

"Joy?" he spoke to the breeze. "Joy!" he yelled at the sea. He ran back to where she'd been standing but found only emptiness. He stood motionless as a numbing cold took hold of him. The feeling of shock was familiar, the same as when he fell into the lake of boiling water, or when he lost consciousness in the Sonrisa Desert, or when he sank into the sidewalk while in the clutches of the Chicago street cop. The desolation that surrounded him began to seep inside like an eerie song that one hums without realizing. It was heavy, this emptiness; too heavy to stand. And so he sat, weighed down by her absence, watching the earth spin as the deep dark of night fell upon his deserted island.

Chapter Thirteen

No Happy Endings

$\mathcal{Shel}$ awoke the next morning to a soft rain through light fog and the sound of small waves collapsing on the shore like shipwrecked survivors...

Somehow he'd fallen asleep despite the cold, despite being utterly despondent over Joy's sudden departure, beyond which he could recall nothing. He couldn't even remember having dreams. That almost never happened. It was as if he were simply placed there, like a freshly wound-up toy set down on the empty beach by some insidious puppet master.

He sat up and looked around to see if there were any witches or ghouls nearby who might've been manipulating him, putting him under a spell. Really, he was just looking for Joy. He called out once more, "Joy!" but there was no reply. Still alone.

Drenched from the rain and sea spray, sitting on the wet sand, he began to shiver. He curled into a ball, hugging his shins, head buried between his knees. In that desperate moment, he thought he heard someone call his name.

"Joy?! Is that you?" he lifted his head excitedly.

"Shel! Where are you?"

He stood up to get a better look but the veil of fog obscured the source of the voice. "Hello? Joy?"

"Shel?" the voice called out, and from behind a stand of bushes crashed an elephant followed by four dwarves. "Shel! We found you!"

"Izzy!" Shel ran to his friend and they embraced. "Fickles, Pickles, Tickles! Manny! You're here too!"

"Sure 'nough! We're on our way back tuh my place," Manny replied, placing his hand on Pick's shoulder. "Still got a missin' tooth tuh fill fer our friend here."

Shel shot a glance at Izzy, thinking about Manny's house, or what used to be a house but now looked more like the ruins of ancient Rome. Izzy guessed at Shel's thoughts and couldn't hold back a laugh.

"Relax, Shel. I told Manny all about what you did to his house. He's made arrangements to have it repaired by the time he gets back. Put the giants to task on it. Should be no sweat for them!"

"What *I* did?! WHAT I DID?!?" Shel yelled, shocked. They couldn't help it and all burst into laughter.

"He's just messin' with ya, Shelby." Fickles coughed. "Not to worry. It's aaallll good. I mean, it's not good that Manny's house was destroyed. But—"

Manny cut him off. "It's not Izzy's fault, Sheldon. It's mine. I shoulda told y'all where I was goin', what I was goin' tuh do."

"Bet your buckets you shoulda!" chided Izzy.

"But I didn't really have uh plan," Manny added. "Alls I knew was that I had tuh get Buddha back." There was a moment of looking at one another then Manny quickly changed the subject. "Buhsides, who hasn't ax-uh-dent-ly destroyed a house-r-two b'fer? Lord knows I have!"

The gang looked at Manny with expressions of surprise, confusion, and apprehension. So, Manny continued with a chuckle. "Haha! I wasn't always a dentist, ya know. 'Fore workin' on teeth I worked on bild'ns. Was a forem'n for a prom-y-nint 'struction firm. But, one day, I ordered the demolition uh the wrong house — aaannnd that was the end uh my foreman career — *and* the beginnin' of my life as a dentist!"

"Well, that explains the demolition of that poor brocosmile's mouth," Izzy muttered under his breath.

Shel stared at Manny, or more precisely, at his cat.

"Wuuuuht?! People can change. You yourself uh done changed a fair bit lately, so I hear." Manny smiled at Shel and Shel nodded.

"It's not that. It's just… I thought… Izzy, you told me that Buddha had been eaten by a brocosmile."

Izzy shrugged. "That's what I thought."

"It's what we all thought," admitted Tickles.

"'Cept deep down, I knew that couldn't be right," Manny added. "I mean, y'all saw it! The Gambrine can be mean for certain. And yeah, they can be dangerous…"

"If you mess with their crop," everyone spoke in concert.

Once the laughter died down, Manny continued. "But they're not malicious. Even when y'all attacked 'em with that mess uh food, they barely retaliated. They wouldn't uh just eaten a cat, like a Worst beast… or a Banzakoot, if the cat were a poet… which Buddha is! Huh. I never thought about that…" Manny the rambler was rambling. "Anyway, when that brocosmile came into my office tuh have that abscessed tooth pulled, well I knew right then, *that* was my opportunity to get to the bottom of it!"

Shel looked at Manny and then Izzy. Izzy could see the kid was a bit lost, so he explained. "The Gambrine share everything. There's nothing one brocosmile knows that every other brocosmile doesn't eventually figure out soon enough. It has something to do with chemistry, the scents they give off… or maybe it's their deep guttural growls, tummy vibrations bouncing off the surface of the ground. Who knows? But it's something like that."

"Aaaanyway," Manny snatched his story back. "So me, I strapped that brocosmile down real good like, an' stuck every dental jam I had in that big guy's mouth — keep 'im from chompin' down on me, see? Then, I crawled in that big, stinky mouth uh his and I just started yankin' teeth, one by one, till he told me the truth 'bout Buddha."

Shel's mouth fell open. He couldn't believe his ears. Manny the tooth man sounded more like a hitman!

"It's not as bad as it sounds, kid," interjected Izzy again. "Remember, brocosmiles are polyphyodonts, just like—"

"Ele-fonts! I know! You told me that joke already. It wasn't funny the first time," Shel chided.

"Oh, well, excuuuse me!" retorted Izzy. "Point is, their teeth grow back. Now, does that make it right? Course not. I'm just saying it's not as bad as—"

"Let's just skip to the part about Buddha, okay?" Shel wasn't in the mood to hear any justifications. "That brocosmile must have told you something, Manny, because you just up and disappeared."

"Indeed he did!" replied Manny. "He told me everythin'! Spilled the beans, the broccoli, *and* the bacon, he did! That reptile told me about how he stole a piece of cheese from the grocer when he was nine. He told me about the time he cheated on a math test in eighth grade. He told me about when—"

"MANNY!" the gang yelled in unison.

"Right. Sorry. Anyway, he told me that the Gambrine had taken Buddha and put him to work in the fields, forcing him to pay off his debt."

"Debt? What debt?" Shel asked.

"Well, apparently Baggs had been hangin' 'round in the broccoli fields for the past few months, makin' friends with the Gambrine, chattin' 'em up on his philosophications, action through nonaction 'n all that. 'Parently he'd inspired quite a followin' and was accident-ly… or maybe on purposefully, I don't know… either way, he was creatin' a culture uh indolence and passivity. Problem was, those partic-ly-er field hands used tuh be a very efficient and productive crew. The Gambrine authoritators calc-uh-lated that Buddha owed a great deal uh service to make up fer lost productivities. So, one day when he was out talkin' with his disciples," — Manny emphasized the word 'disciples' with animated gesticulations — "they arrested him for incitin' laziness. Fer many weeks they just played ignorant, lyin' straight tuh my face! Telling me they hadn't seen 'im, didn't know where he was…" Manny was starting to relive the traumatic experience, becoming visibly irate and red all over. "But I showed them! I got right down to the truth and I went and found my cat after all! Teeth never lie!"

"And you got captured in the process, Manfred! Some rescue!" Fickles reminded him.

Manny sighed. "Yeah. Lookin' back... I prolly shouldn't uh done it. But I was just so ding-dang-darn tootin' mad!"

Tickles gave him a pat on the shoulder.

Manny took a breath and continued. "What I shoulda did was tell all yous." He looked at the boot crew. "An' we coulda gone together, gathered a small army to get Buddha back like y'alls did in the end. But I wasn't thinkin' straight. I figured that if ya found out what shenanigans I'd got up to, you might try'n stop me, talk me out uh it. Or worse, y'alls might'uh tried to come with."

"You're darned right we woulda!" exclaimed Fickleface. "Together! We shoulda all gone together!"

"Yeah? Then what, eh?! What if somethin' uh happened to one uh yous? I'd never've forgiven myself!" cried Manny. Everyone grew quiet, nodding. "So, I slipped out the back wind-uh quick as an x-ray. Didn't stop tuh think about the broco in my office, or that y'all might uh thought I got eaten. Good heavens! I guess I thought y'all were smarter n' that!" Manny laughed... alone. "Yeah, well, I thought y'all would just figure I went for a walk or somethin', I don't know. Like I said, I didn't think it through. And I regret it, guys. Guys, I'm real sorry. I am!"

The boot crew did not hesitate. The three of them surrounded the dentist with reassuring hugs and murmurs of, "It's okay!" and, "Don't worry about it, old pal."

Shel just stood there shaking his head. Izzy gave him a little nudge and a smile as if to say, 'Pretty crazy, huh?' Then Izzy's gaze drifted and he began looking around at the beach. "Did you stay out here all night, by yourself? It must have been freezing!"

Shel looked back toward the water. "I guess so. I didn't mean to. Guess I just fell asleep." Sensing what might have taken place, Izzy looked at Shel with big, sympathetic eyes and gave his friend a tremendous hug. Shel looked up. "Joy's gone, Izzy." He choked back tears. Izzy nodded as if he already knew.

"I'm sorry, Sheldon," he heard Manny say. "I know she's a close friend. But if I may say, I have a feelin' you two'll be seein' each other again 'fore long." Shel wasn't so sure. "Well guys, it's time we're off too!" continued the dentist. "Put that tooth off far too long. Time tuh git to it!"

Pickles smiled, displaying the gap in his grin.

"What do you mean? You guys are leaving too?" Shel was starting to feel desperate.

Fickleface approached Shel. "We're sure gonna miss you, little man. Turned out to be a pretty great guy, laundry monster and all. Chicago's lucky to have ya."

"Ain't it?!" agreed Pots. "Be sure tuh look us up next time you're in town. Here, I wrote this down for ya. Enjoy it with some good friends!" Pickles handed Shel a scrap of paper with his broccoli gumbo recipe written on it.

Shel was reeling. He didn't know what was happening. "But—" he started to say but Pickles grabbed him in a fond embrace.

"You're a great friend, Shelby, even if ya did knock my tooth out!" The boot chef smiled. "Take good care uh yerself and don't let no one tell ya who y'are. You know who y'are now."

"Thanks, Pick. Really. But, I'm not so certain. I mean, I've done a lot recently, a lot more than I ever did back home. But as far as who I am…" He shrugged.

"Shel, don't forget, this is *your* story," Tickles offered with a tapping on the side of her head. "Ya got good tales to tell and a gift fer tellin' 'em. Go an' share yer gift with the world. And once ya done that, if ya still haven't figured it out, I'm sure the world will show ya just exactly who y'are."

With one last tickle from Tickletoes, and an embrace from the rest of the crew, they waved goodbye, turned and walked away.

"You're *walking* back to Champion Valley? Why not take Delilah?" Shel called out after them.

"She's in for repairs," the boot captain called back without looking. "Besides, Delilah doesn't belong to us anymore. She's got a new captain!"

"What?! Who??" yelled Shel, the boot crew barely within earshot.

"Ask the big guy!" was the last thing Shel heard before the triplets rounded a boulder and were gone. Curiously, Manfred had stopped walking. He was just standing there on the beach, staring back.

"I think he's got something to say to you, Shelby," remarked Izzy.

Shel looked up at the elephant then back to Manny. The dentist hadn't moved. He was still there, staring at them.

"Go on. I'll wait here for ya," Izzy nudged, and Shel started walking, reluctantly, unsure of what was in store.

"What's up, Manny?" Shel asked cautiously as he approached.

"Well, I got to thinkin' 'bout somethin'... I didn't mention it b'fore because, well, truth be told I didn't even think a lick of it there's just been so much goin' on... Anyhoo, when I first met ya, I didn't know a flea's fart aboutcha. Then when I finally learnt some of who ya'are, just yesterday n' fact, and where yer from...'"

Shel quinted.

"Well, anyway," Manny went on, "the Falcon and I usedta be pals. Not super close, mind you, but we usedta get together now and again, blow off steam, shoot the breeze 'n all that jazz... ya know?"

"'Kaaaayyy...'" Shel hung in there, waiting for Manny's rambling to go somewhere.

"So anyspit, this one time, he told me this story 'bout a friend uh his who lived nearby, in Chicago. Jewish fella, like you, good guy. I guess the two uh them went way back to when they was kids. Turns out their families were both from Eastern-ish Europe 'n so they had a buncha stuff in common. Anyway, when they got older, this friend of Romanov's had a son who really loved rocks and animals 'n all things related to nature, fossils 'n such... *specially* fossils."

"Romanov Falconovich... the Falcon," Shel clarified.

"Right!"

"The Falcon had a friend who likes fossils?"

"Had a friend whose *son* liked fossils," Manny corrected.

"Okay. And?"

"I'm getting' there, kid. Keep your pants on right-side-up. ...Problem was, Romanov's friend was pretty darn strict, stuck in old ways 'n what have ya. *You* know how that goes," Manny prodded Shel's chest.

"Boy don't I," Shel sighed.

"Yeah you do! Well, any-which-way, I guess the family business — butchery or bakery or whatever it was — didn't provide much income. See, Romanov's friend, he wanted his son to do something respectable-like, climb the ol' ladder, become a banker or lawyer or what-have-ya; do somethin' that made good money for the family."

Shel nodded. It wasn't always easy to follow Manny's unique vocabulary but Shel figured he was getting the gist.

"Yeah, so, as you can imagine, the father was in a right frazzled fit about the notion of his son becomin' a naturalist. Said there wasn't no money nor honor in it. Said that if the kid couldn't do somethin' to earn a decent livin', then by golly he'd work the family business, at least then he'd earn *somethin'*, at the very least he'd earn the respect of the family. So, in the end, the son gave up his dream of bein' a rockologist or whatever—"

"Geologist."

"Whatever. As I was sayin', in the end he gave it up. He took over the family business, gave away all his rocks and fossils and began learnin' to bake, just so's he could make his father proud."

"Okay." Shel was starting to recognize some familiar aspects to this story.

"So, a number uh years later, give er take, when Romanov and his friend were gettin' old, this friend got candid, he did, 'n shared that he'd stocked up a good pile uh regret 'bout how he raised his kid, regret about how intolerant he'd been of his son's curiosities, and how he'd forced the kid to follow in his footsteps 'stead uh followin' the kids' dream of bein' a fossiler or what have ya. See, he'd projected his own desires 'n fears onto his son. Said that was his greatest failure in life: failin' to help his son become his own man and achieve his own dreams. And uh course, as fate tends tuh do, by watchin' his son grow up with a hardened heart, full uh bitterness and regret, the man had manifested his own greatest fear."

Shel stared at Manny, trying to pick out what lesson would be best to take away from the story. "Sooo, I, uh..."

"Can I give ya some advice, kid? When ya get back home, if ya don't have any partic-ly-er plans for that there thing 'round your neck," Manny pointed at Shel's chest, "why not see if yer old man has any interest fer it?"

"Wha?" My pendant?" Shel wasn't sure he wanted to give that away to his not-so-sweet dad.

"I know Ingo gave it uh ya tuh remember yer valiant deeds 'n all. All's I'm sayin' is maybe consider doin' just this one more valiant deed." Seeing that the kid was stuck in his head, Manny clutched Shel's shoulders. "Don't forget, the kid in the story wanted to study *bones*." Manny winked. "You want your dad to accept you, right? Well, sometimes the best way to get somethin' is to give somethin'."

Izzy waited patiently as Shel made his way back.

"All good?" the elephant asked.

"I guess so." Shel was still contemplating the story, slowly putting the puzzle pieces together. "Do you think it's possible the Falcon might've known my grandfather?"

"What? Is that what Manny told you?"

"I'm not entirely sure *what* he just told me."

"Huh. Well, that'd be an odd twist, eh?"

Shel nodded.

"But, I suppose anything's possible."

"Yeah, I guess."

"Shel, for real, anything is possible! So long as you keep believing in the magic of the world, the world will be a magical place. Don't ever forget that." Shel smirked, which made Izzy laugh. "Yeah, you'll be all right, kid." The elephant nudged his companion. "Come on, time to be getting back."

"But, I don't know the way back to the castle," Shel sniffled as they began walking.

Izzy smiled. "You'll find your way. Don't worry."

Shel was jolted and stopped walking. "Don't tell me you're not coming back with me either."

"Shel, we're not... going back to Kantytown."

"What? Where are we going? What about the king and Alice and—" he paused, slowly realizing what was taking place. "What about Sandovar?!" he yelled. "What about Taud and the pirates? No, Izzy. Come on! I'm not ready to—" He stopped himself. *Was* he not ready to go home?

Izzy knew that despite his protests, Shel could see what was unfolding and that he knew it was time to say goodbye. Only, there weren't going to be any more goodbyes. The great goodbye for most had been the incredible baseball game. Shel stared at Izzy while everything sank in like a steel anchor.

Izzy started walking down the path again. "You ever realize that happy endings mostly come from sad times, Shel? And even then the ending isn't really happy... more just relief that it's over. But your time here has been pretty happy, no?"

Shel didn't answer. He wasn't sure that Izzy was entirely right about happy endings, but his time in Arcania *had* been pretty wonderful.

"Happy times often have *sad* endings, Shelby."

Shel figured that seemed about right, but it didn't make him feel any better. As he walked, he thought about King Skippy, about how the king's life was pretty much back to normal — actually, probably much better now that he had been introduced to the magnificent PB&J. He thought about Manny being rescued and Ingonyama being freed. He thought about the triumph of Izzy and Charlotte reuniting and the return of the giants to the Land of Happy. With all these accomplishments, Shel did indeed begin to feel an undeniable impulse to return home to his parents, as if a great many problems had been resolved and stories concluded.

Still, there were a thousand reasons for him to stay in Arcania, and if it weren't for his family back home, he almost certainly would. But a typical twelve-year-old is only *almost* grown and ready to leave the nest. *Almost.* Not quite. And Shel was no exception. Despite the difficulties back home, whenever he'd thought about his parents and sister, he felt a tremendous weight of grief. He knew that to continue trekking further into the world with such a weight on him would be next to impossible. If anything, he figured he needed to get home, disconnect the anchor, let it fall where it may, then head back out on his next adventure, unencumbered and free.

"Yes, it is time," Izzy said softly.

"Wait, you can read my thoughts?!" exclaimed Shel.

Izzy laughed harder than he had in a long time. "Nah, but I can hear you when you talk!" He smiled.

Shel joined Izzy in the great state of laughter as they walked down a path leading away from the beach toward a grassy field of wildflowers that seemed to go on forever. The coastal fog and morning chill burned away as they walked inland and soon the magical dance of a zillion orbs of insects, dust, pollen, and seeds was in full swing, floating all around them in the hazy sunlight of that warm spring day. The scent of flowers and chirping of songbirds soothed the sorrows of goodbyes and Shel was beginning to feel much better. He was settling in comfortably to the rhythm of being back on the trail, just the two of them. The path cutting through the meadow was well-worn such that little thought had to be given to where one was walking. Thus, the pair meandered in silence for a time, marveling at the surroundings and pondering all that had transpired.

"So! I assume you're the big guy Fickleface was referring to?" Shel noted cheerily, picking a dandelion and blowing the bloom into the breeze, watching it float away like miniature paratroopers off to battle.

"Could be," Izzy replied, doing the same with his own dandelion.

"What did he mean by that? Are you really the new captain of Delilah? For real?"

"Could be."

"Wha?! How?!"

"Well, after the Gambrine food fight, the Boot Brigade concluded, sadly, that Delilah was no longer fit for long-distance flights. They made the tough decision to retire her, put her out to pasture as it were. When I got wind of it I offered to restore her, for use as a local touring vessel, something to get me around the Valley, nice and slow like. No big trips, nothing too demanding."

"Woah. So that means..."

"Yup, I get my wings after all," Izzy smiled.

"Wooooaaah. Cool! ...Hey! Maybe you and I can go for a ride sometime!?"

"I'd love that, kid," Izzy sighed with a grin.

Shel noticed that Izzy seemed to be drifting a little, not unlike the dandelion tuft — floating in a daydream — because the elephant began straying from the path, slipping haphazardly further and further into the field of wildflowers.

"Izzy, be careful!" Shel warned. "The trail!"

Izzy stopped walking momentarily but didn't look at Shel. Instead, he stared into the distance, lost in thought. "Shel," he said slowly, "there's one more thing to say before..." He paused.

Still standing firmly on the trail, Shel squinted at him, prompting, "Beforrrre...?"

Izzy still didn't make eye contact. He just sighed deeply and bobbed his head uneasily. "You know how everyone in Arcania always says stick to the path?"

Shel's mind leapt, trying to get ahead of the conversation. "Yeeeaaah..."

"Yeah, well... don't," Izzy concluded and walked off through the weeds.

Shel stood motionless, dumbfounded, watching his friend walk away. He had no intention of letting Izzy leave without him... and yet, he'd been scolded enough to make him hesitant to abandon the safety of the worn trail. "Izzy, hold up!" he called after, but the pachyderm didn't stop. Shel was caught in a conundrum. His mind and heart wrestled for a moment until he settled on a simple bit of logic. *Izzy wouldn't leave me behind... He must just be heading into the forest for privacy's sake, to visit the little boy's room.* ...Still, watching him wander off like that made Shel awfully nervous.

"Izzy! Hey, IZZY!" Shel yelled at the familiar swaying elephant butt, getting smaller with each passing second.

At the edge of the field, where dense forest took over, obscuring anything and everything beyond it, Izzy stopped briefly. Turning his head to the side, he replied, "See ya on the other side, kid." Then he slipped into the understory and disappeared into darkness.

o o o o o o

It took some time for Izzy's words to register in Shel's brain, like the light of distant stars taking millions of years to reach the eyes. "Izzy?" he spoke softly, figuring the elephant would pop out of the forest any time now. But he didn't. "Izzy?!?" Shel grew more anxious. "IZZYYYY!!!" he yelled and bolted from the path, caution tumbling in the wind behind him, a kite cut loose from its tether.

As he ran toward the tree line, desperate to catch up to his friend, something curious happened: He became distracted by the shapes of the trees. Without thinking, he hesitated in his pursuit, marveling at the thick, twisting branches suddenly resembling the trunks of elephants.

He squinted in wonder when, a moment later, shapes of elephant heads appeared in the wood. From there, his gaze naturally drifted up to the green crowns of the trees tangled together like a heap of wrestling crocodiles. "Gambrine," he whispered aloud.

A wind descended, shaking the treetops, making the branches sway and cross, like clashing pirate swords. The breeze descended further, running invisible gossamer tendrils through his hair, and he felt the dry grass of the meadow brush against his legs. The blades were soft and golden, reminiscent of the mane of a well-groomed lion, or the salty, sun-dried locks of a mermaid.

He looked around and turned a half circle. The many colors of the wildflowers appeared as magnificent jewels in the crown of a king. He felt overwhelmed by the beauty surrounding him. It was impossible to feel sad; his heart couldn't possibly feel empty.

He looked up at the sky, squinting in the sunlight so bright he could barely see, and he laughed at the sight of a cloud in the shape of a boot. "The Brigade!" he sighed. And there was another cloud in the shape of a pirate ship. And there! He squinted harder. His heart raced. There was one in the shape of a giant bird. An eagle! An eagle that appeared to be getting closer, and closer, and closer...

Chapter Fourteen

The Return

Sounds of jazz filled the cool night air, gently rousing Shel from his slumber. When he finally opened his eyes, he found himself staring at a glass of milk and a peanut butter and jam sandwich sitting atop a tray being held out by a large man in faded jean overalls. The man was wearing a large smile and even larger eyes framed behind a pair of spectacles.

"Izzy? Is that you?" Shel asked groggily, slowly waking up, as confused as ever.

"You had quite a trip, young man. The name's Eli... Elijah Isbell. And yes, my friends call me Izzy. You're welcome to call me that, too."

Shel closed his eyes again, reeling from the pain in his head. "What happened? Where am I?"

"You're safe, in my house. I found you lying out on the sidewalk, out front." Eli gestured with a nod. "You were unconscious with a bloody head. Seems you fell trying to run away... after knocking rather loudly on my front door."

"Oh, I'm sorry! I—"

"Oh, psshhh. Don't be silly. I'm just glad you're all right. You had me worried; talkin' a heap while you were out, all sorts uh gibberish. Nearly woke up a couple times but you kept falling back into your slumber. Thought you might be going mad for a spell. I considered tossin' you in my truck and taking you into town to see a doctor, but given the hour, most all doctors'd be closed up for the night. Plus, I wasn't right sure it'd be safe to move you that far. Just getting you inside seemed to cause an awful lot of discomfort. So, here we are."

Shel touched his aching head and encountered the bandage wrapped around his skull. He was pretty sure, given the pain, that the bandage was the only thing keeping his head from falling off.

"Lucky for you, I was a doctor in another life." The man laughed. "No, not really. But out here on the farm I've had to fix a few broken things now and again... tractors, turkeys, gates, goats... I've seen this sort of thing a time or two. You'll be fine, I'm sure."

"How... long have I been asleep?"

"Oh, I reckon you've been out for a good few hours or so. But like I said, you kept waking up now and then so I figured you'd be right in time, just needed to sleep it off. How're you feelin' now?"

"My head hurts. It feels like it's full of spiders..."

"Spiders, eh?"

"Yeah, or webs, catching bits of memories here and there."

"Hmm. How about something to drink or eat? That might help you feel better." The farmer held out the tray.

Shel was definitely hungry but the pain was squashing his appetite. More than that, he was completely overwhelmed at waking up in a strange place, his friends no longer anywhere to be found, like the light of a candle suddenly blown out. *But a candle can be relit... can't it? How can this be?* he thought. "I know it was real," he mumbled and rolled over to face the wall, away from the man in overalls. Eli didn't catch what Shel said but figured it wasn't meant for him anyway. Now that Shel was awake, the man decided it was high time to get this kid back to his family, assuming he had one.

"Don't suppose you've any recollection of your house whereabouts?" Eli asked. "Figure it's about time we contact your parents. Don't you think?"

"Joy!" Shel called out, thinking only of his lost friends. When Eli did not reply, Shel thought maybe he'd up and disappeared too, like everyone else. But when he turned over, he saw Eli still sitting there by the bed. Something looked different about him, however. Shel looked into his eyes and instantly recognized the unmistakable likeness of his friend, Izzy the elephant. "Izzy!"

Eli smiled, and that too looked just like the elephant's smile. "Joy isn't far, Shelby, of that you can be sure. And I'm right here." Elijah pulled the fateful red handkerchief from his pocket and handed it to Shel. "Here, dry your eyes, kid. You'll be all right."

o o o o o o

The ride in Elijah's royal blue, 1931 Model-A pickup, back into inner city Chicago seemed to take a lifetime, which was just fine with Shel. Mr. Isbell didn't say much, he just listened to Sheldon talk about Arcania and all the friends he'd made along the way. "Boy, Izzy, I can't believe everything we did. I can't believe you destroyed Manny's house! And that ridiculous raft you made me build! I nearly killed myself on that stupid thing! Hey! Where's Charlotte?" Shel looked at Eli, eager for an answer.

All the man said was, "Charlotte is a long way from here now. But she's in a good place. Don't you worry about that."

"That's nice," Shel smiled, staring out the window at the passing landscape. "I can't believe we saved that stubborn unicorn! A unicorn, Izzy! Can you believe it? I never thought I'd ever see one of those! ...Oh, my goodness, I don't even want to think about the Worst! That was *the* worst! I wonder whatever happened to those monsters, Walter and... what was his name? Oh yeah. Karl! And that crazy restaurant where you couldn't order anything without offending someone. That was wild!"

Shel went quiet again and looked up at the stars. "I wonder if I'll ever see Fickleface and the Boot Brigade again. I really liked those guys. The pirates too. Tauder the Maurader... What a guy! I feel like Hector might somehow know Sandovar, like they're cousins or something. You think?" Elijah just nodded slowly. "He was a good friend, wouldn't you say?" Shel pressed.

"Who's that? Sandovar?"

Shel nodded enthusiastically, which made his head hurt.

"He sure was. Anyone who can swallow a sword is certainly a friend of mine!" Eli laughed and so did Shel.

"Longsmiles! What a nut! Huh?"

More slow nods and soft smiles from Mr. Isbell.

"I'm really going to miss Ingo. Aren't you, Izzy?"

"Mmm."

"Good, ol' Ingonyama. He was really someone I could look up to. A real leader, you know? Of course *you* know! He was kind of like your older brother in a way, both of you being raised by the Falcon and all." Shel paused, realizing the path he was walking down. "Izzy, I'm really sorry about everything that's happened to you; losing your family... and Falconovich..."

Eli sighed, reached behind the bench seat of the pickup, and retrieved a baseball bat with the initials J.J. carved into the stock. "Here. I think this actually belongs to you." He handed Shel the bat.

"Your bat! I can't take this."

Eli smiled, knowing that the kid definitely could take it, and that he would. Sheldon set the bat aside as his eyes grew moist and red. "I'd give anything to see Joy again."

o o o o o o

"We're here, Sheldon," Elijah said quietly as they pulled up to Shel's apartment.

There was no response. Shel was fast asleep, groggy from his injury. Injury or no, riding in vehicles for any length was a sure way to put the kid to sleep. The ride home took a good hour or so, plus the time needed to stop at a phone booth and ring Shel's folks since Eli did not have a phone at his farmhouse. He wanted to be sure and notify them that their son had been found and that he was on his way home. That, and Eli needed directions, because all Shel knew was that he lived on W. Palmer Street, which was just enough information for the operator to connect the call to the appropriate family.

When the Model-A pulled up outside the Silvers apartment and Elijah gave two light raps on the horn, Patterson and Alanna came rushing out to collect their son and to thank Mr. Isbell for retrieving him, tending to his wounds, and bringing him all the way home.

"It's my pleasure, Mr. and Mrs. Silvers. You have a very special boy there. Quite the imagination!"

"Wherever did he get such a dirty face?!" inquired Mrs. Silvers. "He looks as if he's been rooting for truffles and eating berries straight off the vine!"

Mr. Silvers reached into Elijah's pickup and struggled to lift the sleeping youth into his arms. Sheldon felt much heavier than Patty remembered, and Mr. Silvers felt foolish carrying what in the dark looked almost like a grown man. He paused momentarily, attempting to give Mr. Isbell payment for the farmer's time and troubles but Eli refused flat out.

"Oh, that won't be necessary. It was no trouble at all. Just doing what any decent person would do. After all, isn't that what community's all about?" He did not, however, refuse Mrs. Silvers' bag of homemade baked goods.

With a firm handshake from Mr. Silvers and a kiss on the cheek from the missus, Elijah turned to leave and make the long drive home. "Uhp, almost forgot." He turned around. "Your son's journal." He retrieved a small, leather-bound book from his coat pocket and handed it to Mr. Silvers. "I hope he doesn't mind, I took the liberty of writing down some of the things he mumbled while he was out. Couldn't help it, really," he chuckled. "Fascinating stuff! Must've been quite the journey!"

"What's this? No. That doesn't belong to Sheldon. I've never seen it before in my life," remarked Patterson gruffly, refusing to accept the book.

Mr. Isbell withdrew, stroking his beard. "Is that so? Hmm. Well, why not let him hold onto it just the same. I'm sure he'll enjoy reading through it when he wakes."

"I'd rather not," barked Patterson. "If you ask me, it's best to leave all the adventure nonsense behind... with you. He's got enough to think about without sticking his head in the clouds!" Shel's father wasn't warming up to Mr. Isbell one bit. He turned and walked away.

Elijah was stunned, unsure of where to go from there. Luckily, Sheldon's mother came to the rescue, gladly receiving the book. "Thank you, Mr. Isbell. That's very kind. We'll make sure it's at his bedside when he wakes up."

Patterson halted upon hearing his wife intervene. He spun back around only to face a stern look from his wife, a look that said, 'Leave it alone,' and he knew immediately that he'd overstepped some boundary. Mrs. Silvers softened her expression to appeal to a more gentle side, if a gentler side to Patterson existed. "What harm could it do? Really," she whispered and started into the house. She stopped just short of the front door and turned back to Patterson. Leaning into her husband's back as if to hug him from behind, she reached around and pressed the book into his chest, right over his heart, and whispered into his ear, "Let the boy dream."

Feeling woefully put in his place, Patterson looked with chagrin at the book now resting atop his son lying heavy in his tiring arms. He felt his ego flare and thought for a half-second about spitting some defensive nonsense at the night, at whoever might listen. But no one wanted to hear his rant and he knew it. Giving way to better judgment, he quietly turned and walked inside the house with his son in his arms. Mrs. Silvers turned to follow.

"Ah, one more thing, Mrs. Silvers, if it's all right with you." Elijah reached back into his truck once more and retrieved the baseball bat, giving Mrs. Silvers a fright, truth be told. "Apparently your son liked the notion of this old bat. He's welcome to it." Elijah handed Mrs. Silvers the bat then quickly jumped in his truck. "Yup, that's one fine kid you've got there. I expect this won't be the last I hear of young mister Sheldon Silversteen."

"Silvers... teen?" Alanna asked with narrowed brow.

"That's what he kept mumbling; assumed it was his surname," Eli replied with a wink. "And what a good name it is!" With that, Eli fired up his old Model-A and puttered off down the road, back to his farmhouse with the light in the attic shining brightly, calling him home.

The next morning, Shel woke up in his familiar bed, in his familiar bedroom, in his familiar, noisy apartment, with a splitting headache. A light rain tapped on his window, asking him to come out and play. For a while he stayed in bed, listening to the weather and staring out his window, his mind a rocket, racing through recent events, spinning in circles around his room in search of some place to land. Eventually he sat up, reacquainting himself with his room, feeling considerably out of place at not waking up in a flying boot or in some random cave, on a wandering raft or in a tent in the middle of a desert; not waking up on the back of an elephant…

The rain outside intensified to match his escalating emotions. He sighed and thought about his parents, about how he ought to get up and go see them. He missed them terribly, especially his mother. But he wasn't quite ready to rush back into his old life. Not yet. Looking around, he noticed the baseball bat leaning against the wall, just next to his bed. He grabbed it and held it a moment, recalling the epic baseball game where Alice hit that incredible home run and the ghost of Ingonyama helped him overcome his fear. He smiled, set the bat down, and immediately something else caught his eye. Atop his desk sat a book he recognized but couldn't quite place. He tossed back his covers and got up to retrieve it, his head throbbing from the sudden movement. As he walked toward the desk, he realized the book looked to be the same journal Joy had given him. He snatched it, hopped back into bed, and began idly thumbing through the pages. Inside were sketches of the characters and scenes he'd encountered in Arcania, alongside scribbled notes chronicling his adventure. The handwriting looked unfamiliar. And yet, Shel sensed it was his. He could almost recall writing the words and sketching the pictures. Almost, not quite. Noting the foul weather outside and taking advantage of the fact that no one would be bothering him to get up and go to school — not today anyway, what with his injury and all — Sheldon grabbed a nearby pencil and began adding to the stories and sketches. As the minutes, or hours, ticked on and his head nodded, succumbing to weariness and fatigue, the words of a certain flying shoe chef drifted through his mind like a biplane dragging a banner. "You have stories to tell. Go and tell them," echoed in his head, sending him to dreams.

"Honey? How are you feeling?"

Shel awoke to the sound of his mother's voice. Apparently he'd fallen back to sleep with his journal across his chest. He was now incredibly disoriented as he had just been dreaming about Joy, Izzy, brocosmiles, and all sorts of random things flying (in boots) through his mind.

"Hi Mom," he replied slowly. "My head hurts a little, but I feel okay. I'm just tired."

"Oh, darling, your poor head. The doctor said I should try to keep you awake, if possible. But you've already been sleeping so much... Maybe I ought to get you up to go see Dr. Hook. I'm sure his medicine will—"

"No!" Shel exclaimed. He was in no mood to go see a doctor, especially one by the name of Hook! "I mean, no thanks. I'm okay, really."

Mrs. Silvers pulled him close and hugged him tight. "I'm just so thankful you're all right. We were worried sick, calling everyone, driving around everywhere. You know you scared us half to death!"

"I'm sorry, mom. I didn't mean to—"

"What were you thinking, running away like that?!"

The tone in her voice was shifting from consolation to castigation. There was nothing to be done but apologize repeatedly and promise never to do it again. So that's what he did.

"Oh, Shelby, where in the world did you go?" she asked.

I went beyond where the sidewalk ends, to the edge of the world, and over to the other side!

He wanted to say it. He wanted to tell her everything. But he knew she wouldn't believe him. So, he just shrugged and apologized some more.

"Well, all right then. I have to run a few errands. I'll be gone for a little while. Your sister's at school, and of course Patterson's at the bakery. Your father wanted you to go to school today but the doctor suggested you stay calm."

Of course his dad wanted him to go. Never a moment's rest!

"Will you be okay here by yourself for a bit?"

Shel nodded and replied that he would likely just lie in bed and read books, which was a satisfactory answer for his mother.

"When I get back I want you to tell me all about what happened. All right?"

Sheldon nodded and, feigning indolence, cracked open an old book from his shelf, lending credence to his charade. As soon as his mom was out the door, however, Sheldon tossed the book and began preparing for the mission. This was no boring rainy afternoon with nothing to do but chase the cat and pour ketchup in one's shoe! No, Shel needed answers, and there was only one place to go for answers like this. He had to go see the Collector. Yanking off the bandages wrapped around his head, replacing them with a baseball cap — White Sox of course — Sheldon quickly got dressed, grabbed the journal, and headed out the door.

The morning rain had finally found someone who wanted to play, someone in Michigan or New York by the looks of the dark clouds to the east. Over Logan Square, the sun had come out to shine for a change, to shine down on him! He hadn't thought about the Gambrine tooth pendant in a while, but passing through his route toward Darwin Elementary he was reminded of it. He stopped and scratched at his neck, suddenly realizing it wasn't there.

"Wha…? Where is it?!" he cried aloud. For a moment he thought it might've fallen off when he was running out the door, as it had during the police chase. But then he recalled not being able to feel it when he changed his shirt a moment ago back at the house. Aha! His mother must have removed it while he slept. She did those sorts of things, as mothers do. It must be hanging on his bedpost or desk chair. *No time to go back for it now*, he thought and ran on. It didn't take long for him to reach Hector's stand. But when he did, he found it completely empty and locked up. In fact, it looked as if Hector hadn't been there in years. All the decorations and trinkets were gone. There wasn't even a residual scent of food. "No!" Shel repeated over and over. *How could this be?!* He flung his torso over the stand and buried his cracked head in his arms.

"Thought I'd take a little vacation, maybe boogie on down to the desert, someplace warmer and drier." Shel perked his head up and swung around to see Hector standing there, packed bags in hand. "Word is, there's loads of people there been eating too many swords; lack of decent food choices, I reckon. Figure they could use some o' them hot dogs with everything on 'em!" Hector laughed his hearty laugh.

"Hector!" Shel ran to his friend and gave him a big hug. "I thought maybe I dreamed you up too!"

Hector dropped his bags and returned the young man's embrace. "Funny thing about dreams, Shelby, they're very mysterious. We can never really know where they come from, never know what to expect while we're in 'em, and we're never sure where the dream goes — along with all the characters in it — when we wake."

Shel looked up at the hot dog man, understanding more than ever Hector's signature gibberish. "I need your help, Hector."

"Of course. Whatever you need, kid."

As they pulled up to the farmhouse, Shel could see the midday sun reflecting in the attic window. Other than that, there appeared to be no lights coming from within the house. That didn't deter him. After all, it was daytime. He jumped out of Hector's truck and ran toward the gate with the latch like a rifle.

"Shel, hang on a sec!" Hector called out but Shel wasn't listening. He wasn't looking either, for as he launched himself onto the farmhouse porch and rapped on the Marley knocker, expecting a reunion with his friend, Izzy, there stood in the yard a sign advertising the house for sale. Hector's heart dropped as a confused and disappointed kid stepped away from the front door and jumped down off the porch. He looked up at the windows to see nothing but emptiness. There was no life in this farmhouse.

"But Mr. Isbell lives here!" Shel yelled at the house as if it were alive. "Elijah Isbell!" Hector didn't say anything. He simply removed his hat and scratched his head. Shel turned and looked at Hector. "But IZZY lives here!" he cried.

Hector exhaled deeply. "Life's full of all sorts of things that don't make sense, Shelby."

Shel slinked his way back to Hector and the two of them sat on the lone sidewalk, feet hidden in tall blonde grass, Shel's mind trying unsuccessfully to pry open the mystery of the farmhouse. After being monumentally disappointed, Shel requested they take a little walk to the end of the sidewalk, just in case, before they headed back to town. But when they got to where the sidewalk stopped and the wild fields began, nothing happened. No one fell up into the sky and no boots zoomed overhead. Seeing the disparaged look in Sheldon's eyes, Hector put his arm around the kid. "The inexplicable magic and coincidence of life can be fascinating and wonderful. And it can be infuriating and disappointing when we can't figure it out, when we can't unscramble the puzzle to get the answers we seek."

Shel looked at Hector. The Collector was holding out his hand, palm up, displaying a wooden puzzle piece. "Where did you get that?" Shel asked, surprised and confused. Hector just nodded in the direction of the kid's pocket, so Shel retrieved his own puzzle piece — the one with the word imaginæ on it — now quite weathered from all the adventure it'd seen. Though it was warped and worn, it still matched perfectly with the one Hector was holding. Together, the two pieces completed one word: imagination.

"I don't understand, Hector. I found this piece on the sidewalk not far from here. How could you have—"

Hector smiled. "Just because we can't explain how things are possible doesn't mean they're impossible."

Looking at Hector, Shel distinctly recognized the essence of Sandovar of Sandeen and immediately felt a tremendous sense of relief. They both nodded and smiled at one another.

"Come on, kid. It's high time I get going on my journey. And it's time you get back home so you can get goin' on yours. Never a good idea to keep destiny waiting."

Chapter Fifteen

A Dreamer

When they arrived at Logan Square, Shel asked to be dropped near his father's bakery. He figured he could walk home from there. Plus, it was time, he decided, to confront his dad.

"What are you going to do?" Hector asked.

"Well, Hector, I think you already know… but I'm going to write." Hector's countenance begged for more details. Shel obliged. "I'm going to start by writing down the stories of Arcania, stories of all the folks I met there. I'm going to be a writer, Hector!"

Hector smiled and nodded in approval. As they said their goodbyes, good-lucks, and God-speeds, Shel knew this was the last time he would see Hector the Collector, at least for a good long while.

"One more thing, Shelby. I believe *this* belongs to *you*." Hector pulled from his pocket a rusted chain attached to a crocodile tooth pendant. Shel's jaw dropped as he reached for the necklace. "Some army guy dropped it off at my food stand a while back, said you ran off without it… when you were running from the *cops*!" Hector gave Shel a wide-eyed look of surprise and scrutiny.

"Oh, yeah, that." Shel felt ashamed but also shocked by the turn of events circling him like a hurricane.

"Hmm. Well, best not make a habit of *that*, I'd say."

Shel nodded, lowering the pendant around his neck. "No, definitely not. But Hector, how in the world did he know to give *you* the pendant? That you and I—"

Hector waved a hand. "Just listen, okay? He told me to tell you that this ought to remind you of the brave things you've done, that you're a man of action now, and that you're ready to stand up to Patterson, or anyone else; show everyone just who Sheldon Silvers is. Although he must've been confused 'cause he kept calling you Silversteen."

"What?! But how did he—?"

Hector just smiled, hopped into his truck, and fired up the motor. Then the Collector winked, adding, "I dunno, I think I might like it better than Silvers. Silversteen has a nice *ting* to it. Anyway, he said to tell you that Ingo sends his greetings, whatever that means." With that Hector's truck sped off, leaving Shel in a cloud of dust and confusion… and with a great big smile on his face.

o o o o o o

Patterson was sweeping the floor after a slow day at the bakery when his son walked through the front door.

"We've just closed for the day," said the old man without looking up. "We'll be open first thing tomorrow."

"You're a hard worker," said Sheldon softly.

Recognizing the voice, Patterson stopped sweeping and looked up to see his son standing in the doorway.

"I don't give you enough credit for what you've done for our family, what you do every day, the sacrifices you make to ensure we're taken care of."

Patterson was silent. He was unaccustomed to hearing such talk from his son, never received such recognition. He resisted the urge to lash out, thinking this could be some kind of rouge, his son playing a joke. But Patterson had never known his son to be cruel, insincere, or, for that matter, inclined to jest.

"I know I haven't turned out to be the son you hoped for, and I know you think I'm odd, that I waste my time with drawing and writing and things. I know you want me to be more like you, take advantage of my privilege, opportunities that you never had growing up. For that — for all you do for us — I thank you."

"Sheldon," Patterson finally spoke, but he didn't get far.

"With respect, sir, before you respond, I'd like to say one more thing."

"Sheldon," his dad started again, apprehensive and not accustomed to being put in his place by anyone, anyone except Mrs. Silvers that is. Nevertheless, Shel persisted.

"First of all, I want you to know that I love you, dad. I want you to know that you mean the world to me and that I will never forget what you've done to help me grow up healthy and strong. Next, I want you to know—"

"Sheldon, please. I don't know what you're up to—"

"Second, I want you to know that I am grateful for the opportunities you've worked so hard to give me; the opportunity to live in a nice neighborhood, attend a good school, and work a good job at your bakery." After that comment, Patterson felt pretty good about where this conversation was headed. His son was finally coming around to accept the plan he'd laid out for him. Thank heavens!

"*Our* bakery, son. It's *our* bakery. I built all of this for you. And when the time's right—"

"And I want you to know..." Shel cut him off again — which at any other time would have sent Patterson into a fit. But, given what was unfolding, Patty let it slide, barely. "...that I intend to take full advantage of my privilege and not waste the opportunities I've been given."

"Great! That's great, son! I—"

"Which is why," Shel pressed his luck and Patterson stifled a frown, "...I will not be working at the bakery." Patterson's broom fell to the floor with a deafening *crack*. Shel forged ahead, nevertheless. "I'm going to use the talents God has given me. I am going to be a writer."

Patterson was stunned, blindsided by the sharp turn in the conversation. He could instantly feel a geyser of fury bubbling up inside, ready to explode. He quickly bent down and picked up the broom, muscle memory telling him it was time to teach the boy a lesson. Yet, standing there, fists tightening around the handle as if wringing a wet towel, eyes burning till he could barely see straight, he felt something else growing inside. It was gratitude. He felt grateful for his son's recognition. And he could scarcely believe it, but he was feeling a tinge of pride seeing his son stand up for himself.

Without warning, like a snake bite in the desert, his gratitude turned to empathy, and for the first time he understood his son in a way he never had before. Oh, how confusion washed over him like a baptism, all of these new emotions stirring a storm inside his chest; terribly uncomfortable... and yet refreshing. But before he could act, his son approached, grabbed hold of his hand, and placed the crocodile tooth pendant in his palm. Then, without a word, Shel turned and walked out the door, leaving Patterson utterly beside himself, confused, and exhausted by the emotional rollercoaster, ready to drop to the floor were it not for the broom propping him up like a strawman.

Patterson stood, staring down at a fascinating archeological specimen, head spinning wildly with no way to stop it. This man of impeccable logic couldn't think his way out of this one, couldn't settle on a single word to respond. Since his mind was a muddy mess, he did the only thing he could. He dropped the broom and ran out the front door.

"Sheldon!" he yelled. "Wait!"

Shel didn't know what awaited him should he obey. Was his father calling him back for a beating? Did he decide right then and there to enroll his son in boarding school? Or worse, military academy? Would he pull him out of school entirely and force him to work at the bakery full-time?

"You think you're a man now, is that it? Gone and had yourself an adventure out in the world and now you know everything, do you?! Well, let me tell you something, you don't know nothin'. You hear me? You hear me, boy?!

Boy? No thanks.

"Don't you bother coming home tonight if you think you're goin' to refuse what I've built for you, all that I have planned for you, the life I've laid out for you!"

It was as he suspected. But this time Shel knew better. He'd learned the sound of empty threats. He recognized it from the bullies on the playground at Darwin. He'd heard it from Mark the Pleaseman, King Longsmiles, and Chancellor Hume: The language of the ego; loud barks from toothless dogs.

He had learned that when people are serious about doing something they'll often not say anything at all. Like when Joy left, or when Izzy left. Now *that* hurt. But his father, making all these threats as he always had — threats that used to terrify him — these hollow words now bounced off him like an echo. The only thing the words made him feel was sympathy. His poor dad, hollow on the inside, plastic on the outside; nothing but a shell of a man.

"A shell of a man," Shel whispered as he stood there watching his father's mouth move but hearing nothing. He shook his head at the pitiful Patterson tossing his arms about in a rage, swinging the broom handle back and forth through the air, the threat coming closer and closer and—

"Sheldon? You okay?"

It had been some time since Shel's mind ran off on him. In Arcania, land of wonder, his imagination had no need to go above and beyond its normal duties. Now back in Chicago, it was back to its old tricks, and he had drifted, indulging in a terrible fantasy induced by Patterson's signature temper.

Shel came back to reality to find himself standing on the sidewalk outside his father's bakery, yet in a place altogether foreign. He found himself in the arms of his father, in a firm embrace not the least threatening but full of gentleness, neither one of them entirely certain how they ended up like that nor where to go from there.

"Thank you, son," Patterson said, eyes watering, 'from the bright sun in my eyes,' it would be said if the story was ever retold. Which it wasn't.

It would later come to light that Shel's father had suffered an anxiety attack during his son's disappearance. Though he wasn't entirely sure what emotions were coursing through his body, Mr. Silvers was profoundly concerned that he might not see his son again. He didn't admit to it at the time but he'd feared the worst. So, when Mr. Isbell returned Sheldon safe and sound, assuaging Patterson's anxiety, Mr. Silvers had resolved right then and there to be a better father from that moment on. And he was.

o o o o o o

Along his walk home, Sheldon decided to take a detour to one of his favorite spots, to sit and ruminate in the soft afternoon light. After all, he'd made himself a nice PB&J, which he hadn't had the chance to sample yet. He wanted to take some time and look through his journal, especially since this day had turned out to be so pleasant, with enormous billowing clouds making all sorts of interesting shapes in the sky — just like on the day he departed Arcania. If there wasn't already a sketch of Joy in his book, he intended to draw one now while he could still recall every detail of her lovely face.

He found a cozy spot under his favorite tree, the shade of which was beyond comforting, as if it were tailor-made just for him. The shadow of this magnificent tree was just the right temperature and provided just the right amount of diffuse light by which to sketch. He looked up and said, "Thank you," quietly to the tree for providing this restful spot and realized for the first time that it happened to be an apple tree, not at all unlike the ones in Arcania — except this one didn't have a unicorn stuck in it. That thought made him chuckle while he unpacked his satchel, laying out his pencil and sketchbook methodically.

He sat in the generous shade of that apple tree, sketching the various characters he'd met during his adventure, bringing them back to life, one by one. Some of the images made him laugh, some made him cry, and some, like silly old Izzy, made him laugh and cry at the same time. Drawing an image of an elephant with a pelican on top gave him the idea to include a short love poem in honor of his friends. He soon discovered that writing humorous poems about the characters and events of Arcania helped to soothe the trauma he felt over his abrupt departure and the sudden loss of so many wonderful companions. Rhyming came to him with surprising ease, inspiring more and more silly poems, one after the other. (He had a sudden urge to look around and make sure he wasn't being stalked by a Banzakoot!)

He sketched Fickleface, Picklepots, and Tickletoes, and laughed out loud as he detailed the Boot Brigade in Delilah, their fantastic flying shoe. He described Manny, the ridiculous dentist-with-a-vengeance and his oversized, philosophizing cat. He wrote about the proud Peanut Butter King and his sticky situation. He scribbled about the pirates and the Boogies and the monsters. And he outlined a story about a magnificent lion, uniquely talented with a rifle, who could easily pass as a gentleman.

After taking a break from his journal to munch his delicious peanut butter and jelly sandwich, he decided it was finally time to draw his special friend, Joythea Aquarius. Smiling from ear to ear, he completed a rough sketch of a sun-kissed girl with flowing hair, dancing barefoot in the sand. As he did, he suddenly became flushed with an overwhelming sensation that he was most certainly destined to see this girl again.

Looking up, he greeted a friendly ray of sunlight streaking through the branches. Without thinking, he tore the page from his journal, folded it up, and placed it in his pocket, deciding that this picture was not for sharing. This one he was going to keep for himself.

To his astonishment, the torn-out page revealed something in the middle of his journal that he had not previously seen. A short passage written in soft, wispy penmanship read:

Although I'm not there to share your space,
as you sit and write and draw awhile,
somewhere from some far-off place
I think of you, and I smile.

He finished reading and closed his eyes tightly to keep the tears at bay. He wanted to feel happy at the memory of his friend, not sorrowful at the prospect of never seeing her again. He took a few long, deep breaths to calm himself and reveled in the late afternoon air filled with the scent of spring.

When he finally opened his eyes, his vision struggling to clear against the bright sunlight, a curious scene slowly came into view. He squinted, half in disbelief, half trying to see more clearly. As he realized what it was, his heart raced and his breath floated just out of reach. For a moment he thought he must be dreaming. He pressed the tip of his pencil into his leg to make sure, to be certain this wasn't his imagination playing tricks. The pain didn't bother him. On the contrary, it made him laugh out loud, for it proved this was real. It meant that the day was real, the clouds above him and ground beneath him were real, and what he was seeing, that was real too; and there was nothing he wanted more than that.

There he sat, under that sturdy, old apple tree, watching in wonder, marveling at the miracle of it all, and laughing from a heart overflowing. For there at the far end of the field was a girl with long, blonde hair, twirling in cartwheels and spinning in endless circles, dancing in the warm sunlight, dancing free to the magical music of the world.

The End.

www.ingramcontent.com/pod-product-compliance
Lightning Source LLC
Chambersburg PA
CBHW061505020726
47502CB00006B/1947